THE
BARROW

THE
BARROW

MARK SMYLIE

an Imprint of Prometheus Books
Amherst, NY

Published 2014 by Pyr®, an imprint of Prometheus Books

Based on a screenplay by
Mark Smylie, John Smylie, and Hidetoshi Oneda,
and on the setting and characters
created by Mark Smylie in the comic book Artesia.

Cover illustration © Gene Mollica
Cover design by Nicole Sommer-Lecht
Interior maps © Mark Smylie

Inquiries should be addressed to
Pyr
59 John Glenn Drive
Amherst, New York 14228
VOICE: 716–691–0133
FAX: 716–691–0137
WWW.PYRSF.COM

18 17 16 15 14   5 4 3 2 1

Library of Congress Cataloging-in-Publication Data

Smylie, Mark (Mark S.)
    The barrow / by Mark Smylie.
        pages cm
    ISBN 978-1-61614-891-1 (pbk.)
    ISBN 978-1-61614-892-8 (ebook)
    I. Title.

PS3619.M96B37 2014
813'.6—dc23

                                                                            2013037715

Printed in the United States of America

For Monika,
with my love.

For John and Hidetoshi,
with my thanks.

And for those who have been waiting patiently,
with my apologies.

THE KNOWN WORLD
IN THE YEAR 1471

THE GREAT MIDLANDS

THE THULAMIT CITADELS

THE SPINE OF THE WORLD

SEA OF SANDS

THE KESSITE KINGDOMS

TH R WAS

THE EM THESS

THE GREAT SOUTHERN SEA

THE SPICE ISLES

MERA VERTA

0   500   1000
MILES

PANOCH
SEA

THE
GOLDEN
SEA

PALATIA

DÉSKÉDRÉ

KHAEL

THE
SUN'S
ANVIL

THE MIDDLE
KINGDOMS

ILLIA

MERA
HELIA

HE
ED
STES

MERA ARGENTA

LEAGUE OF CITIES

MPIRE OF
ID-GOLA

AMORA

ULIK
DESERT

W E
S

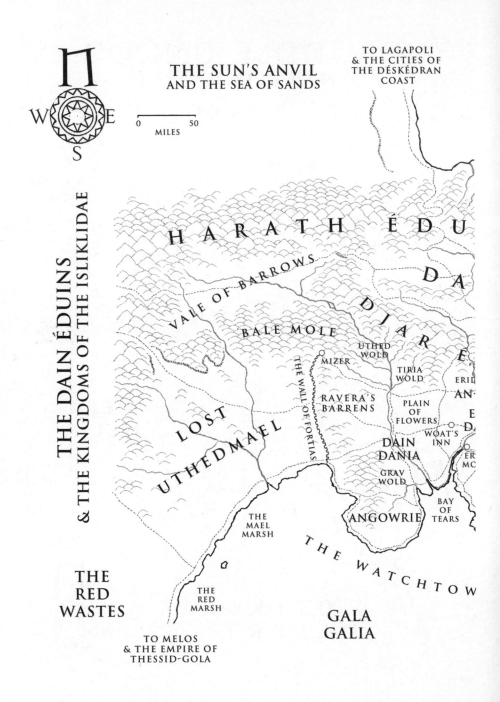

THE SUN'S ANVIL
AND THE SEA OF SANDS

TO LAGAPOLI
& THE CITIES OF
THE DÉSKÉDRAN
COAST

W E
S

0   50
MILES

THE DAIN ÉDUINS
& THE KINGDOMS OF THE ISLIKLIDAE

HARATH ÉDU

VALE OF BARROWS

BALE MOLE

DA

DJARE

UTHED WOLD

MIZER

TIRIA WOLD

ERIL

RAVERA'S BARRENS

PLAIN OF FLOWERS

AN

LOST
UTHEDMAEL

THE WALL OF FORTIAS

DAIN DANIA

WOAT'S INN

D

ER MC

GRAV WOLD

BAY OF TEARS

ANGOWRIE

THE MAEL MARSH

THE WATCHTOW

THE
RED
WASTES

THE RED MARSH

GALA GALIA

TO MELOS
& THE EMPIRE OF
THESSID-GOLA

THE MIDDLE KINGDOMS
WHEREIN OUR STORY LIES

COAST OF BLACK SAILS

GALA
DESKA

TO PALATIA

MAL IRAMA

MERA
AUDRA

I N S

R A D J A

UMAT

D U I N S

WOLD

HARAS
WOLD

ATHAIR

RID
ANIA

PLAIN
OF
STONES

ID
RE

SARE
WOLD

PLAIN
OF
HORNS

ARASWELL

VESSLOS

PLAIN
OF
GAVANT

DAINPHALIA

THE GIFT OF HETH

TO ILLIA
& THE SUN
COURT

AURIA

JURET
RAMA

ATALLICA

THERAPOLI

MANON MOLE

NERIS
WOLD

HADA
WOLD

HUELT

BAY
OF
GUIRANT

UMIS

DENTYN MOORS

CAPE OF FANGS

TO THE
LEAGUE
OF CITIES

ER COAST

WAEL

MERA
DÜRÉ

MERA
ARGENTA

TO YEFRAM
& GRAWTON
& POINTS WEST

THE OLD AQUEDUCTS

THE OLD KIN

THE HIGH

TO
PIERHAM
& THE
ABENBRAE

WEST
GATE

THE
MARKET
QUARTER

THE
OLD
QUARTER

THE
FOREIGN
QUARTER

SOUTH
GATE

SHIPYARDS

SOUTH
FISH
TOWN

TO
DURINHAM

1. THE MARKET HALL
2. MARKET PLAZA
3. FULLER CORT'S LAUNDRY
4. THE NEW BATHS
5. LOW PLAZA
6. THE GATE OF ELDYR
7. THE GATE OF ERGINUS
8. THE SLEIGHT OF HAND
9. SAYLES & GRIM
10. THE UNIVERSITY
    & ITS COLLEGES
11. THE FORUM
12. BAKER STREET
13. THE OLD BATHS
14. THE PUBLIC TEMPLE
    OF THE DIVINE KING
15. THE FUNERAL PLAZA
16. THE HIGH PLAZA
17. THE PLAZA OF ERGIST
18. THE HOUSE OF ORWAIN
19. THE CHAPTER HOUSE
    OF THE INQUISITION
20. THE GREAT TEMPLE
    OF THE DIVINE KING
21. THE HIGH KING'S HALL

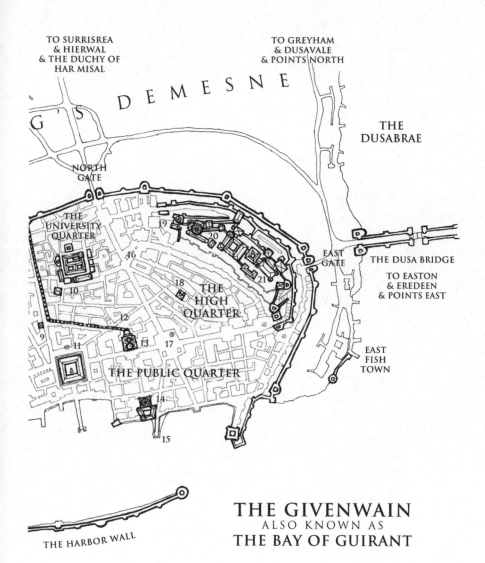

TO SURRISREA
& HIERWAL
& THE DUCHY OF
HAR MISAL

TO GREYHAM
& DUSAVALE
& POINTS NORTH

THE
DUSABRAE

G'S   DEMESNE

NORTH
GATE

THE
UNIVERSITY
QUARTER

9

20

16

18

THE
HIGH
QUARTER

10

12

9

11   13   17

THE PUBLIC QUARTER

14

15

21

EAST
GATE

THE DUSA BRIDGE

TO EASTON
& EREDEEN
& POINTS EAST

EAST
FISH
TOWN

THE HARBOR WALL

THE GIVENWAIN
ALSO KNOWN AS
THE BAY OF GUIRANT

THERAPOLI MAGNI
CAPITAL OF THE MIDDLE KINGDOMS

CONTENTS

CONTENTS

PART THREE: IN THE BARROW OF THE DEAD AND DYING

İN THE HİLLS OF THE ΠΑΝΟΝ ΠΟLE

İN THE YEAR 1471 iA

S omewhere in the dark, a woman whispered.

As was in the nature of the upper reaches of the Manon Mole, the hillside did not provide a great deal of cover for the men trying to hide upon it: dried chaparral, small gullies, and outcroppings of exposed and weathered stone. Further down in the lower hills the trees and thickets would be larger, closer together; not quite a wood, but easier for men and even horses to hide. But here, further up, where the wind was stronger, where the wind was weirder, the hillsides were not kind to those that did not wish to be seen. A set of sharp eyes would almost certainly have counted out eight of them, spread out a bit along the slope, huddled by rocks and small brush, clustered in two small groups of two, a group of three, and a last lone figure bringing up the rear: rough men—for they were all men save the woman in the rear, but she was dressed as a man, which in the Middle Kingdoms was essentially the same thing—not quite arrayed for ambush, but who nonetheless preferred that others did not spy them so quickly, and who made do as best they could with what skill they had and with the scant protections provided by the uncaring earth.

But even sharp eyes might have missed the three men the furthest up the hill, almost a hundred yards ahead of their fellows, firmly pressed against a hillock rise of gray-green moss and dark stone in the weird wind, and peering intently up the slope toward its summit. That summit bore a crown of upright stones, ancient *menhirs* marking a place of *fae* power, and a pathway of more *menhirs*, some of them fallen over or reduced to piles of rock, was visible up ahead of them. The man in the furthest lead didn't pay them attention, instead focusing his own sharp gaze on an outcropping of rock and stone just below the summit of the hill. From most angles the outcropping would have seemed solid and unbroken. But from the vantage point the trio had chosen, the thin vertical maw of an opening could be seen, an entrance through the rock into the hill's side.

The man in the lead studied the thin sliver of darkness in the rock for long minutes, not moving, pressed flatly against the side of a large block of mossy stone. He was dressed in a dark brown high-collared long coat of stiff leather, tight blue-black cloth breeches, and black leather boots, all splattered with mud and dirt. His clothes were finely crafted, and dull bronze buttons, corded trim, and faintly embossed patterns in the Athairi style on coat and breeches prevented them from being described as plain. But they were also worn and rough-used, the mark of a man who spent long days in travel. A point dagger and heavy-bladed falchion were strapped to his side by a broad black leather baldric, which doubled as an extra layer of protection across his chest.

He had a spyglass in one of the satchels strapped to his body, but they were close enough to their intended destination that he did not need to use it. His sharp eyes would occasionally flicker left or right, to scan along the hillsides and nearby ridge tops, or up to track a sparrow hawk wheeling in the distance against the clouds, only to return to stare at the door into the earth. He listened to the weird wind, hearing the faint jangling of small bells and the whisper of what could have been a song sung backwards. He sniffed the air, and inhaled wet earth and old stone, moss and scrub thickets and tree heath, and from somewhere near the hint of something dead and rotting.

The two men hidden in the rocks slightly behind and below the man in the lead did their best to imitate his stillness, but despite their patience and good sense, neither was a woodsman, either by training or by birth-right. They did not see what he saw, or hear what he heard, or smell what he smelt. The closer of the two had blond hair and fair skin, a golden youth of noble breed and bearing, though dressed down for the occasion. His fine travel coat and breeches were woven of good dark wool with silk trim, the sheen of the weave enough to tell that they were of quality. His sword brace held a dagger with a silver-wire-wrapped pommel and a matching rapier. He was obviously charming and just as obviously trouble. He bore a faintly bemused expression on his face as he waited for the man in the lead to move, but his eyes were nervous.

The third was older than his companions, perhaps almost forty years of age, but improbably he was also quite handsome despite the wear and tear: chiseled sun-burnt features, a hint of mischief about the weathered mouth, cunning in clear blue eyes, rough stubble and dirty blond hair dangling before his face, the air of surety and danger about him that came from being a veteran (though a veteran of what might have been less certain). He was dressed in a simple padded doublet of black cloth, opened to reveal an unbuttoned shirt and hairy chest, two long daggers strapped to his side and a scabbarded broadsword and round metal shield slung over one shoulder, along with several leather packs and satchels. Vambraces of dulled steel were strapped over each forearm.

It was this third man who finally stirred and spoke. "Black-Heart," he grunted. "Can we get on with it?" He spoke low but did not bother whis-pering; there was no one nearby to hear them.

The man in the lead stared at the hillside ahead of them a moment longer, then turned and looked back. His name wasn't Black-Heart—it was Stjepan, son of Byron and Argante—but enough people had called him Black-Heart over the years that it might as well as have been his name. His features were distinctly Athairi: sun-kissed copper skin, short-cropped dark hair, high cheekbones, and a sharp, prominent nose with a diamond-shaped bump in it. Stubble darkened his chin and jaw. His left ear was pierced twice, as was common amongst some Athairi men, and set with small silver loops. He would almost certainly have been considered handsome, at least at first glance, until perhaps the eyes. His eyes were piercing, even unsettling to many, and his sharp gaze was tinged with a hint of hate, or perhaps simply disgust, as though whatever he was looking at had been judged and found wanting. And that gaze fell on the third man, and for a moment the third man regretted speaking.

Stjepan stared at him a second, then looked past him to take in the rest of their group, a hard-looking lot of grim-faced murderers and thieves spread out in the brush and rock below them, all dressed in dark travel clothes, haphazardly armed and lightly armored, with an occasional cuirass or ringed brigandine amongst them. They had been told to stick in pairs, but Stjepan noted that one man had moved forward to join the group in front of him, leaving a slight figure alone in the rear. He squinted and frowned in annoyance, though as he was often frowning it would perhaps be better to say that his frown deepened. But he was not surprised; that last figure in the rear made many men uncomfortable, though they could not perhaps put their fingers on why.

He turned back to look up the hill.

"We're fucked," Stjepan said, low and calm. "No cover between here and the entrance worth talking about. Not for our lot. The old *fae* stones might help a bit, Erim and I could maybe make it there without anyone seeing us, but not the rest of us. Not in the day. So either we make a straight run for it and hope no one's watching, or we wait until dark."

"Shit," swore the third man, his sure expression wavering for a moment. "Shit," he repeated.

"It's all right, Guilford," said the second man. He glanced around at the nearby hills, the expanse of the range across the horizon, and made a short subtle gesture with his hand. "We haven't seen anyone for half a day. Not since that backwater village where we left the horses."

Guilford looked up at the second man. "You've never been up here, Harvald. Stjepan and me, we have," he hissed. "There's always someone watching up here. If it isn't one of the bandit knight descendants of the Wyvern King waiting to rob you blind, it's some of the fucking hill people, waiting to cut your throat and cook you for dinner. Those same fucking villagers watching our horses are probably following us, waiting to do us in. *If* they're not busy chopping up our horses for their cooking pots."

Harvald's bemused smile grew wider in response. "It's true I was not summoned to the campaign against the rebel Earl of Orliac, praise be to the Heavens, so I defer to your combined experience of these hills, of course," he said. "But is it possible, given the disastrous outcome of said campaign, that you're just shitting your pants at the memory?"

"Fuck you, Harvald," hissed Guilford, suddenly angry enough to make most men take a step back. "You weren't fucking there. Night battles, ambush and kidnappings, corpses strung up and flayed . . . the people of these hills do not fight fucking straight. They're vicious little shits worse than anything you've ever seen in the big city. And the Rebel Earl and his men are still out here somewhere, a thousand fucking strong."

"No doubt," said Harvald, nodding sagely. "No doubt."

Guilford was about to respond when Stjepan glanced back. "Shut it, both of you," Stjepan said in a quiet voice that brooked no argument. Guilford was a Marked Man with a crew and certainly thought of himself as tougher than Stjepan, but still he paused, and nodded.

Stjepan turned back and contemplated the hillside ahead of them. His stern gaze swept over the ring of *menhirs*, nearby hillsides and brush covered slopes, rocky crags and bleak summits, and in the distance the main high range of the Manon Mole, snow-capped against cloudy gray skies. It was a beautiful sight, he realized. *Almost as beautiful as home.*

He listened to the weird wind for a little bit longer.

"Ah, fuck it," he said finally. "Let's go."

Somewhere in the dark, a woman whispered. They had come creeping to her in the dark, her children and her lovers, her Nameless bringing word of brazen interlopers, cruel huntsmen from the cursed lowlands. Eleven men, one of them fae-born *and marked with wood-magics, and another a Servant of the Bright King walking*

in disguise. It was not the first time that men such as these had come, though the Servant of the Bright King surprised her. Did he come as an emissary? Or as an enemy? So she had rolled her bones—for of bones she had plenty—and she had been filled with despair.

Erim glanced about, mostly behind them back the way they had come, as was her job as the last in the line. She was supposed to be paired with Gap Tooth Tims, but the moment they'd stopped he'd slunk forward to hunker down with Porter and Smitt behind some thorny bushes. She didn't mind; in truth she was probably better off alone, so she could move quick and quiet, and without having to worry about what Gap Tooth thought of her. She counted off the others in the group ahead of her, looking at the backs of their heads: Gap Tooth and Porter and Smitt, then old Jon Pastle and Llew the Stew, then Colin of Loria and the tall thin man everyone called the Stick. A mix of Aurian and Danian commoners, united in their greed, amorality, and desperation. A hard lot, meant for hard things, and therefore perfect for the occasion.

Up beyond them she could make out the three men way up in the front. Three handsome men, clinging to a hillside. Some might have considered themselves quite lucky to stumble into those three, in a different place, say in a tavern or a revel or feast perhaps; except for the aura of danger that lurked about them, and that hard gaze of hate in the lead. But that gaze might just quicken some pulses all the more. She wondered at the fact that the three best-looking men in the group were the ones in the lead. Was it just coincidence, she wondered, or did men like that get together and plan it all out, the worldwide league of dashing rogues?

Her mind wandered unbidden, staring up at the three of them, back to a story she'd heard being loudly told in a tavern back in Therapoli by three sailors just returned from the decadent cities of the Déskédran coast. The sailors had been on a merchant cog that had stopped in Lagapoli, looking to trade for spices. Like all good sailors they had visited its infamous temples to Dieva, the Evening Star, and they regaled their eager audience with lurid stories of the priestess-prostitutes there. A particularly beautiful one, a raven-haired temple dancer with bronze skin dressed in nothing but golden chains, bracelets, and anklets, had invited them to experience a rare and special sacrament to her Goddess; and there on the altars of the temple they had lain with her all at once. They claimed she'd cast some spell over them, and anointed their cocks with a special oil so that they found themselves harder than usual, and that after furiously fucking her for what seemed an age they'd spent themselves the first time, only to find themselves still hard, and that they'd then switched places and rutted her again until they'd spent themselves a second time, and finding themselves still hard had switched places yet again; so that by the end of it they'd each spilled their seed one time in each of her wet, eager orifices. The sailors had claimed the Déskédrans even had a name for it, the *trephallas treferrai*, and they'd claimed it was the most intense sex they'd ever had.

Not everyone listening in the tavern had believed them. One old man said they'd been fooled by the priestesses there, who he said dosed their patrons with a potent of the poppy plant that made men have vivid waking dreams of impossible acts of pleasure.

But she had believed them. She had been surprised to discover how very, very much she had wanted to believe them.

She flushed at the memory of that story, and felt herself grow warm and wet between her legs, and she was briefly ashamed at being aroused while hiding behind a rock in the middle of some of the most dangerous country in the whole of the Middle Kingdoms. She took a deep breath, and dug a nail into her wrist to give her mind something sharp to focus on. If she had been a different woman, she would have quickly offered a prayer to some god and a warding sign to drive off Ligrid, the Queen of Perversion; but in her case she knew that was of no use, and she just gritted her teeth at the pain.

Erim looked up and saw the three men up in the lead rise. No more sneaking about, then. Guilford turned and signaled to his men to follow them up the hill. And they were indeed his men, the seven between him and her. If anyone had asked Gap Tooth or the Stick "Whose man are you?" they would have quickly answered: "I'm Guilford's man, Guilford of the Run Street in Vesslos." A meaningless answer, in most quarters, as Guilford wasn't a noble or a knight, just a rough man that other rough men followed; but in other quarters, it meant a great deal, as Guilford bore a brand from the Guild of Therapoli. Everyone knew that Stjepan and Harvald were true Kingsmen, with Harvald noble-born to boot, and so what their answer would be. But if someone had asked her "Whose man are you?" she wasn't sure how she would answer. Not just because she wasn't a man, but because she didn't belong to anybody. And in most of the Middle Kingdoms, that meant you were nobody.

As the group started up the hill she was glad to be moving again, stretching her long legs. She saw that a few of Guilford's crew mumbled curses and hobbled about, cramping after being immobile for so long, and she stifled a needless laugh. *No point in making this lot hate you even more*, she chided herself. But as everyone started to get stretched out they picked up speed, conscious now of moving up the hillside in the open, for anyone to see.

She moved quickly, her soft calf boots quiet against the mossy earth. She wore a black cloth doublet with dark bronze studs and brown leather cord trim, fitted tight against her boyish figure, and black flared breeches, puffed in the Eastern style. She was splattered with mud and dirt like everyone else. A pair of point daggers and a wire-hilt cut-and-thrust rapier hung at her side from a black leather baldric, the surface tooled with ornamental squares. Her dark hair was cut short and trim along the sides and back of her head by her ears, but then a bit longer on top and in front, so that wavy locks fell in front of her blue eyes. She wore a black silk neck scarf wrapped tight to hide the smoothness of her throat. Like several other members of Guilford's crew she wore a metal codpiece that poked through a flap in her breeches. Not as large as had become the fashion in the eastern Aurian lands of Dainphalia, where in imitation of their king, knights and courtiers wore steel metal codpieces sculpted into impressive (and in some cases very lifelike) erections. But her codpiece was of some size, nonetheless. As a woman, she would have been considered plain, perhaps even mannish; her eyes were small, and her jaw too square. But as a man, oh, yes; she made a very pretty and attractive young man in the eyes of most who saw her, even if in her case the codpiece turned out to be empty.

Her breathing was hard but measured by the time the group reached the rocky outcroppings near the top of the summit. She looked up at the stone circle above them and slowed, watching Guilford's crew disappear into the earth one by one. The entrance into the earth looked to her like it must have been a natural fissure in the rock at some point. But the carved narrow arch, eight feet in height, that became visible through the split in the rock was clearly made by men. She saw that Guilford's crew was about to leave her behind and sped up, sliding her rapier and one of her point daggers out of their sheaths as she did. She caught up with Gap Tooth and Porter just as they slipped through the entrance, and she barely had time to think before she was through the arch into the darkness.

It took a moment for her eyes to adjust. Gap Tooth had a torch out in one hand and a heavy axe in the other, and that helped a bit, but not much. She could see several torches appearing and disappearing ahead of them as they moved through the earth. In the flickering torchlight she could see that they were in a narrow shaft that appeared to have been carved out of the rock itself, and she felt more than saw the packed earth under her boots. Behind her the entrance was a bright vertical crack in the dark; the wind whistled past the opening, making it sound like someone was whispering behind her, and she suppressed a quick shudder. The group was moving forward and she followed. She saw the torches ahead of her lowering into darkness, and soon she was at the top of a narrow stone stair leading down into the earth. Gap Tooth went ahead and she had to be careful following, as his torch was right below her and it sputtered and coughed smoke and embers into her face if she was too close behind. The stairwell was steep and narrow, and it almost felt like it was more like a ladder made of stone; if there had been defenders below it would have been a tough fight. The ceiling of the stairwell was close enough that she could put her hand against it to help brace her way down.

They hit the bottom of the stairs and found themselves in a small room, a landing of sorts. Arches were set in the four walls, one being the arch they had descended into the room through, and the other three opening onto stone stairs leading downwards. Each arch was set with human skulls along its entire curved length, and each skull was marked on the forehead with an ugly black rune. She didn't know magic, not the way that Stjepan and Harvald did, but she instinctively knew the runes were bad runes. Her left hand, holding the dagger, went to her chest, and she felt for the amulet tucked under her doublet with a couple of spare fingers: a bit of amber with an insect trapped inside it, set in a gold chain and enchanted. It had been a gift from Stjepan, back when she'd first done a job with him. "To ward off black magic and the Evil Eye," he'd told her. And she'd believed him.

She watched and listened as Stjepan talked with Harvald and Guilford on the other side of the small (and now very packed) room. Everyone was crowded in on each other, trying to stay in the center, trying to stay away from the stairwell openings. *Too close*, she thought. *No room to fight swords here, daggers only.*

". . . No, the spirits here are long gone," Stjepan was saying as he consulted a map in his hands. "The account we found in the archives said that during the Wars of the Throne Thief an expedition mounted out of Truse had come here, and that a company of priests and magisters led by none other than the knight Sir Olsig had worked a great ritual and driven all the trapped guardian spirits out."

"The Ghost Killer himself. Trust us, if there were still ghost wardens present here, we'd already be in big trouble by now," said Harvald. He looked around at the arches, eyeing the skulls that decorated the arches with a kind of wary nonchalance. "Can you imagine the struggle to purify this place? All these skulls . . ."

Guilford shuddered. "Who were they, do you think?" he asked. "Victims of the Nameless Cults? Or adherents, letting themselves be bound here as guardians?"

"Doesn't really matter," said Harvald with a shrug. "The end result is the same."

Stjepan moved in front of the archway to the left of the one they had entered from and slipped the folded map back into his stiff square satchel. He pulled out a piece of chalk and marked the side of the arch with an arrow pointing down. "This one, according to the map in the archives," he said to the group. "I'll go first. Follow the downward arrows, then reverse them if you have to get out." He gave them all a wry half-grin, and Erim watched as he took a torch and started down the narrow, steep staircase.

Her whispers grew more urgent now. Once long ago this had been a place of great power, until the book-men had come from their tower on the Plain of Stones and rendered this sacred place silent with violence and the curses of their false Divine King. Long years it had taken the Faithful to restore the temples and shrines, and her chest swelled with pride to think of what had been accomplished; but with that pride came despair, as well. If only she'd had a few more years, or had known how to bind the guardian ghosts. The Nameless at Dyre Callum had promised to teach her the ritual, but always they delayed, and raised the price, and now it was too late. And so she whispered what she knew, and called for His help.

Downward they'd gone, hitting on three landing rooms like the first one above them, and on each landing Stjepan had picked out and marked an archway down; after the first one on the left, he picked out three on the right. Some of the landings had other stairs going up rather than just the one they entered through. Erim started to have an inkling that the whole hill must have been honeycombed with stairs and rooms going up and down. By the fourth landing, she could feel the weight of the earth around and above them, all those narrow steps winding back up through the dark, and she could feel the panic starting to eat in the back of her throat. The air here was totally still, *dead*. She could see it in the wide eyes and sweating brows of the other men as well. The descent had started to take its toll on them.

"Two hundred and six," she heard old Jon Pastle whisper.

"What?" hissed Porter.

"Two hundred and six steps, so far," old Jon whispered back. "I counted 'em."

"Aye, I was counting too," said Llew the Stew. "Thought it was two hundred and four, meself, but close enough."

"Fuck me," someone moaned, but she couldn't tell who it was.

Erim had never been good with numbers bigger than she could count on fingers and toes, thus ten times ten she could handle up to a hundred; so the idea of being two hundred and six steps below the earth was only slightly more scary than the idea of counting that high. Men who knew the lore of numbers, like Stjepan and Harvald, and could count and do additions in their heads, always impressed her; but then, Stjepan and Harvald were practically magicians. Llew the Stew used to be a steward, hence his name, so it made sense that he could do numbers; but she was a bit surprised that old Jon Pastle could count in his head like that. Then again, he probably didn't become *old* Jon Pastle without learning a few tricks. She wished she'd been smart enough to even think of counting the steps, though she wasn't sure what good it did them.

Luckily this landing seemed different than the others. Instead of opening onto more staircases up and down, the archways opened onto straight level passages lined with stone slabs. Stjepan picked one, marked it, and slipped through it, followed quickly by the rest of them. Erim found herself last again, though being rearguard had now taken on a different tenor. Behind her stretched the inky blackness of empty tunnels and stairs up and down through the earth, and the darkness was starting to fill her with fear. She hurried to keep up with Gap Tooth and his sputtering torch as their short column moved through into a wider antechamber, with pillars carved out of rock and black arches opening into who knew what, and then a turn and out into a short passageway again. She was starting to get worried that if she panicked she wouldn't know how to get out, that she'd forget to look for the markings and take a wrong turn. Or if the torches all went out; how would they even see the chalk marks?

Suddenly they slowed, and she almost ran right into Gap Tooth's back. She wasn't sure what was happening ahead, but the entire group was moving with caution, backs crouched, weapons and shields up. Instinctively she did the same, adopting a fighting crouch, dagger and rapier ready, side-stepping her way forward. The moment she did she found herself calming, the familiar pose triggering a steady breath. *Ah, right, that's what training's for*, she thought to herself. It was an odd feeling—fear and excitement coursing through her, preparing her body for a fight or for flight, and yet at the same time the calm of her training settling in, centering her, making her feel safe and certain. *I know what to do*, she thought. *I'll just kill whatever comes in front of me.*

And then she was moving in behind Gap Tooth into a large under-ground chamber, and she straightened and let out a long slow breath of relief and wonder as she walked forward. The torchlight from the others spread out with them throughout the room, lighting its high walls and ceiling with flickering hues of red and black and orange and illuminating other archways opening out in its walls to other dark chambers. Several great columns flanked the central aisle of the chamber, carved with obscene images and strange, barbaric letters that she couldn't read, and there were frescoes of some kind on the soot-darkened walls. But at that moment it wouldn't have mattered, because she couldn't take her eyes off the great bronze idol that grinned at them from the other side of the chamber.

Twenty feet tall it must have been, depicting the seated body of some demonic creature, the top of its head and horns almost reaching the ceiling. It cradled a massive brazier in its cross-legged lap with its hands, and there was a wide stone altar set before it. She brushed her hair out of her eyes so she could see it better, and wondered for a moment how they'd even gotten the massive idol into the chamber; perhaps the bronze had been poured and fired right there? Or perhaps some foul sorcery had moved it through the earth? She stared at its face, at a wide flat nose, a grinning mouth of ser-rated teeth, two great spiraling horns jutting out and up from its forehead.

Beneath heavy brows flickered two sources of reflected light: its eyes were great red gemstones easily the size of her head. Her eyes trailed down and she saw that the creature's nipples were two large spikes jutting out from its chest, and that behind the brazier its long thin phalli emerged from its lap like a thick curved spear. Given the broadness of the idol—it was probably twenty feet wide at its base—the thinness of the phalli struck her as almost comical; but the bronze phalli had to be almost eight feet long, curving upward at an angle over the brazier to a sharp, barbed head. She swallowed hard and blinked.

"What the fuck is it?" she finally asked. It was the first time she'd spoken in hours, and she forgot to pitch her voice low as she usually did. She glanced around quickly, mentally kicking herself, but she saw that the others were so busy that they must not have noticed. Harvald and Stjepan were already hauling themselves up the side of the great bronze idol, and about half of Guilford's crew were excitedly but quickly overturning urns and pots scattered along the walls and corners of the chamber, emptying the temple offerings into their bags and satchels, while the other half stood guard at dark entryways.

But Guilford heard her and responded, though if he noticed that she sounded more like a woman than usual he gave no sign. "One of the *Rahabi*, the evil spirits of the Underworld," he said as he walked over to watch Harvald and Stjepan's progress up the idol. He'd moved quick and one of his satchels was already heavy with coin and metal, poured out of one of the offering urns. "Might be a *Bharab Dzerek*, if I'm not mistaken. Spirits of iron and fire, amongst the guardians of the Six Hells, and often they are patrons to those in the Nameless Cults who worship Nymarga, the Mask of the Devil. For we are indeed in one of their temples." He made a sign to ward off Evil, and she followed suit.

Harvald paused midway up the statue, using one of its spiked nipples as a foothold, and turned back toward them. "I've read about how they use an idol like this," he said casually. "Some of their victims are slaughtered on the altar there. But for their special rituals, they impale their victims alive on this giant spear of a cock right here, and light the brazier up all nice and hot, and roast them over the fire." He grinned, waving up at a set of chains and ropes and pulleys that hung in the dark up by the ceiling. "Barbaric, don't you agree?" Something in his voice made her think that he didn't really find it all that barbaric.

It was not hard to remember what she'd heard as a little girl about the Six Hells, back when she listened to the old wise women whispering in the herb gardens, back when she still went to the Divine King's temples. The Old Religion of Yhera, the Queen of Heaven, did not agree on much with the younger cult of the Divine King, but they both agreed that there were Six Hells in the Underworld. They both agreed that Hathhalla, the lion-headed goddess of vengeance, had created and ruled the Six Hells, and that she had appointed Servant-Rulers for each of the Six Hells to act on her behalf.

On the first Five Hells there was common agreement about who ruled them and whom they were for. The Servant-Ruler of the First Hell was Amaymon, the Whisperer, the Prince of Intrigue and Secret Power. He was served in turn by the *Baalhazor*, great barbed and horned demons, and he ruled over a Hell reserved for the greedy and corrupted, such as thieves and grave robbers. The Servant-Ruler of the Second Hell was Geteema, who was once the beloved sister of Geniché, the Queen of the Earth and the Dead, before Geteema turned on the Queen of Heaven and waged war against the ancient people of Düréa. She was served by the *Golodriel*, winged demons with vulture heads, and ruled over a Hell reserved for the jealous, the covetous, and the ambitious. The Servant-Ruler of the Third Hell was Ishraha, the Rebel Angel, who had rebelled against the Divine King and been thrown down for his impudence. He was served by the *Nephilim*, great giants and hell-goblins, and ruled over a Hell reserved for betrayers, oath-breakers, and usurpers. The Servant-Ruler of the Fifth Hell was Irré, the Black Goat of the Wilderness, the Black Sun, the bow-bearer of plague and fire. He was served by the *Bharab Dzerek*, great demons of fire and iron (a statue of one of which she was apparently standing before), and ruled over a Hell reserved for the merciless, callous, and savage, such as murderers, pillagers, warmongers, and destroyers.

Most of the men she was with were destined for either the First or Fifth Hells, she would guess.

Both the Old Religion and the cult of the Divine King agreed that the Sixth Hell had no ruler, just an empty throne reserved for Nymarga the Devil for when his spirit finally passed into the Underworld. But after that they parted company a bit. In the folk lore of the Old Religion, Hathhalla had set a pack of the *Tiranhim* and *Iyyim*, wolf and jackal demons, to rule a Hell reserved for the eaters of unsanctified meat until Nymarga arrived to take his rightful place. But the temple priests of the Divine King rejected that interpretation of the Sixth Hell, as they rejected sacrificing meat to the old gods, and so they said instead that the Sixth Hell was for apostates, idolaters, and heretics who rejected the divinity of the King of Heaven and made sacrifices in the old way.

She'd eaten unsanctified meat in her time, so she sort of hoped the Divine King's priests were right, but in Erim's mind this argument was strictly for the temple priests and hidden priestesses; none of those Hells really mattered to her. The only Hell she cared about was the Fourth Hell, ruled by Ligrid, the Queen of Perversion. Ligrid was served by the *Gamezhiel*, demons of lust and sex that could seduce or rape the unwitting and unwilling, and Ligrid ruled over a Hell reserved for the depraved and lecherous, such as rapists and molesters. For the perverted, the licentious, and the wicked.

For people like her.

She stared at the phallic spear. She couldn't help but wonder what it would feel like to be suspended spread-eagled in the air and lowered onto that evil-looking tip. Which hole would they use as their entry point? Would it feel good at first, then turn to pain? And then the fire would come . . . *if only they didn't roast you in the fire* . . .

Erim shuddered, and almost sobbed, and she shook herself out of her fear and wonderment. *Do something*, she thought. *Set yourself a task*. She was about to go collect some loot—it was why she was there, after all—but then a glint of light off the altar top caught her eye. She stepped forward and inspected the altar before the huge idol; the surface of the altar was smeared and splattered with black ichors and dark dried liquid, but some of it looked fresh. She reached out with a finger to test some smears of liquid on the stone surface, and she experimentally tasted a drop off her finger. She spat to the side.

"Black-Heart. This altar's been used recently. Blood. Probably human. This temple's still active," she called out huskily. Old Jon and Smitt perked up their ears at that and walked over, nervously standing beside their captain as they looked over the altar.

"I thought you said this temple was desanctified and purified by the priests during their raid," said old Jon. "And that they'd left all the temple offerings behind, refusing to take the blood money."

Stjepan had managed to work himself up on top of the idol's head, and he was leaning over its brow, trying to get the gemstone out of its right eye with a small curved metal pry bar. He didn't look away from his work as he responded. "Aye, so it said in the archives. But that was two hundred years ago. Plenty of time for the Nameless Cults to rededicate it. And to add to the offerings in the meantime."

"Fuck me," said Smitt angrily. "Boys, hurry it up!" he called out, and the men ransacking the temple offerings started to move faster.

"Shit, Harvald," said Guilford. "I told you someone was watching us come in here." He looked around in disdain. "Fucking hill people. All sorts of forbidden shit hidden up here in their caves and chasms, where the sunlight of our Divine King does not shine so brightly. An active temple? Getting in here was too easy. Where are the fucking guards? Where are the priests? Why no new guardian spirits?"

Harvald grinned casually down at them, perched on the shoulder of the great idol. "Come now, Guilford," he called down. "The Nameless Cults might be forbidden but they can be found anywhere, even in the bright, prettily decayed streets of our beloved capital."

"Aye," agreed Stjepan, though he didn't bother looking up from his work. "Even amongst the priests of the Sun Court of your Divine King."

"You're a heathen fucking Athairi bastard, Black-Heart," Guilford replied, though there was no heat in his words and he grinned amiably. "You keep your Old Religion shit to yourself."

"Stjepan may be Athairi and a heathen, but he's our heathen," said Harvald. He was the only one amongst them to always call Stjepan by his real name, Erim had noted.

Guilford gave a short bow. "Aye, one of the High King's own fucking cartographers, at our service."

"Aye, as long as all this remains our little secret," Stjepan said. And with another grunt he succeeded in prying out the gemstone eye with a loud *pop*.

They moved in the dark with her now, her Nameless. Sharpened bone spears dipped in shit and poison, curved swords and wicked implements of pain and war, fierce masks of horn and brass, short horn bows pulled with fire-sharpened arrows; pride and despair filled her again. The roll of the bones had been bad, very bad, and so she whispered still, promising fresh blood and meat and spirits bound in chains, promising herself to her Liege for Him to do with as He pleased. She hoped that He heard her, hoped so very much that He did.

Harvald hefted the gem in his hand while Stjepan stuck his hand into the empty eye socket of the idol, searching.

"Look at the size of that gem," Guilford said quietly.

Harvald smiled down at him. "Here, catch," he said. He tossed the gemstone down to Guilford, and Erim's eyes went wide and her heart leapt into her throat as it caught the torchlight in its blood-red facets tumbling through the air. In a flash she pictured it shattering against the stone floor, but it landed smoothly (albeit heavily) in Guilford's hands. He grunted in surprise but didn't drop it. Guilford weighed it for a second with a grin, then wrapped it in a soft cloth and slipped it into his shoulder bag, already crammed with cooper, silver, and gold coins. "As per our agreement," Harvald called down.

"What, you're just giving it to him?" Erim said, her mind boggled.

Harvald laughed. "Ah, young impressionable Erim. Things are never what they seem. Never get distracted by the obvious bright bauble." Stjepan, having not found anything in the hollow space behind the right eye gem, scrambled across the top of the idol's head to its left gemstone eye and he began working to pry it out; Harvald followed across the idol's face as he spoke, using its nose and teeth and brow as hand and foot holds. "There's treasure, and then there's treasure. The real treasure here isn't these gems, but what we hope to find behind them."

Guilford leaned closer to Erim. "Don't listen to the University boys, kid," he said conspiratorially. "They'll just get you deep in the shit. Better to stick to the simple things in life. Gold, wine, women . . . and gems the size of your fucking head." He winked at her and she felt a little warm inside.

"Maybe the gems are fake?" she asked him. "You know, made of paste or something?" She'd heard of clever men who could do that back in Therapoli.

"No, I'm pretty sure they're real," Guilford said. "Red *topakh* crystals out of the mountains on the other side of the Red Wastes. They're not as valuable as you might think, but these two specimens will fetch a high enough price for me to be able to buy myself a house back in Vesslos' Free Quarter."

Stjepan pried out the second gemstone with another loud *pop*.

She could hear them now, in the great temple, defiling it. Rage built inside her, displacing the fear, the hopelessness, and she whispered fiercely, summoning Him up from the dark depths of Hell. Something was coming, she could feel it now, but would it be too late? Did He come himself, or send a blessed servant?

Stjepan handed the second gemstone to Harvald, who tossed it down to Guilford. Stjepan didn't mind giving up the crystals as part of the pay for Guilford and his crew, who were worth every penny amongst the dangers of the Manon Mole, but he still felt a pang of regret as the gem sailed through the air, and he silently wished that Harvald were not so cavalier about it. "Here, a matched set," Harvald called down as Guilford caught it. Harvald, coming from the landed Orwain family, holding the Barony of Araswell, could shrug off a thousand shillings or two with nonchalant ease, but that was several years' wages for Stjepan and most of the men.

"You two are fucking crazy," Guilford said, shaking his head as he wrapped the second gem in cloth and slid it into his satchel. He hefted the satchel over his shoulder, tying a spare strap across his chest to secure it. It was very heavy now, and he gave himself a small shake to try and settle all the weight he was carrying properly.

Harvald grinned down at them. "Maybe, but you're right here under the ground with us, yeah?"

"Too true, too true," Guilford laughed. *"A baseborn fool am I, am I,* sings the bard."

Stjepan tried to ignore them as he fished around in the second eye socket, biting his lower lip. This hollow was a little deeper than the first, and his fingertips brushed against something hidden far back within it. "Definitely something . . . ah, got it!" he said, and he slowly pulled out a long slender copper tube faintly inscribed in runes. Holding it carefully, he inspected it with narrow eyes.

He could see three different runes etched repeatedly in the copper surface, all from the *Labira Grammata*, sometimes called the Witch Runes of ancient Ürüne Düré, sometimes the Riven Runes. One was a *ward* rune useful against magic and divination; the second was a rune of *structure*, to give strength to the scroll tube; and the third a *hex* rune. The second and third runes were inscribed in touching pairs, so that in some way their magic was combined. The *hex* rune gave him pause; often they triggered at the mere sight of them. But he was protected by his own charms and amulets, and had not felt or heard any of the usual signs that his own wards had been challenged by an active and dangerous spell. So something else, then, tied to the structure of the tube.

"Runes of warding against detection," he said quietly to Harvald. "And against it being opened, I think. A hex of some kind on whoever does the deed."

Stjepan moved back from the edge of the idol's head so that Harvald could clamber up and look. The top of the idol's head wasn't perfectly flat, instead being slightly curved, but there was plenty of room for the two of them to settle in and spread out a bit. Harvald slipped a carefully wrapped torch from one of his satchels along with a small packet of powdered and enchanted *ajuga* flowers. He crushed the packet open in his palm and blew the contents onto the torch, and suddenly it bloomed with a heatless blue flame, lighting the top of the idol's head so they could see what they were doing. Stjepan pulled a soft cloth from one of his satchels and set the scroll tube on it so it wouldn't roll. The two of them looked at each other as they knelt and crouched over the scroll tube, Harvald with an irrepressible grin, Stjepan with a small smile finally tugging at the corner of his mouth.

Harvald reached into one of his satchels with his free hand and pulled out a small vial of clear elixir. Stjepan knew it would be a potent of the *wormwood* plant, prepared as a bane against enchantments. They started whispering the words of the cleansing rite together over the scroll tube, as Harvald poured a bit of the liquid in the vial onto it. "*Demes matta, illume matta, porte a matta. Grammata illuso resistrata libri. Grammata libri. Porti ouset matta. Grammata illuso resistrata libri. Grammata libri!*"

Stjepan could feel a bit of pressure building up behind his ears, as though he had climbed to a great height, and they both started repeating the words of the spell faster and faster as the pressure built. Stjepan started to feel dizzy, and fear gripped him that whoever had made the inscriptions had done so too well. But then the runes on the tube began to glow, faintly at first, then more strongly as though they were etched in liquid fire. The runes grew very bright, and for a moment Stjepan thought his head might burst, and then all of a sudden the runes fizzled and *popped* with smoke. They both froze in mid-syllable for a moment, and then relaxed as the runes dimmed.

Stjepan waved away the smoke as Harvald grinned and laughed.

"What's in the tube, then?" called up Erim.

"If we're lucky, a map," Stjepan said with a slight cough.

Erim peered up at them. "What? A map? A map is worth more than these gems?" she asked. Guilford chuckled.

"Well, that depends on what the map is to," Stjepan said. "How'd we get here, to this treasure, young Erim?"

Erim paused, thinking for a moment. "Well . . . a map, yeah?" she finally called up to him.

"Yes, copied from the cartographer's archives at the High King's Court," Stjepan said as he inspected the ends of the tube until he found the seam of the cap on one end. "And how do we get to the *next* treasure?" Stjepan slowly uncapped the tube, and paused, holding his breath. When nothing happened, he relaxed and let out a long sigh. He tilted the tube and carefully slid out a rolled piece of parchment.

Slowly, slowly, her Nameless slid forward, filtering through the outer chambers, bristling with death and vengeance. Firelight flickered ahead from the great temple, and glistened off barbed points and horns and chains. Her fevered whispering dropped low. If only the roll of bones had not been so bad, she would have been filled with joyful gladness at the slaughter that was about to commence.

Erim smiled brightly. "Another map," she said. "That map."

Stjepan unfurled the parchment paper on top of the bronze idol's head as gingerly as he could. He had spent a long time handling maps and papers that were centuries old and practically disintegrated in his hands, and he had no desire for their prize to be snatched away from them now that they were so close. But he was happily surprised that the parchment appeared to be soft and supple. As it opened, his tone became almost reverent. "For the likes of us, the map is always the thing," he said quietly. "It leads us to the next prize, the next journey, full of possibilities and promise." Stjepan spread the parchment out, slowly revealing a set of symbols, drawings, letters, and diagrams.

What a thing of beauty, he thought. His face relaxed into a smile for the first time in days, and he lost his train of thought staring at the map.

"Every map is a chance to remake ourselves and our fortunes, find a way out of the lives that imprison us," Harvald said, picking up where Stjepan had left off, his tone almost as reverent. Almost. "And this map . . . if it's what we think it is . . . this one could be a map to end all maps."

"They're fucking dreamers, kid, always looking for the treasure that will let them write their names in the history books," said Guilford. He clapped a hand onto Erim's shoulder. "Trust me, keep your eyes on the prize in your hands, the one you can actually touch, not the one in your mind's eye that you can only get in your dreams." She swallowed hard, looking up at his handsome face, feeling the warmth of his hand on her shoulder. Part of her wanted to melt inside. He didn't seem to notice, and he turned and looked up the idol. "What's this map supposed to be to, then, Black-Heart?"

"The Barrow of Azharad," said Stjepan in a whisper, staring at the map. Harvald opened his mouth as if to stop him, and then just winced when he realized it was too late, and hoped that no one had heard what Stjepan had said.

But if a pin had dropped in that chamber then, it would have been as loud as a clarion bell.

She froze, hearing the words spoken in the great temple, and her Nameless froze with her. She had heard the words in the tongue of the lowlanders, the Middle Tongue: the Barrow of Azharad, *one of them had said. She'd heard him as clear as day. And she was filled with rage and wonder and disbelief. Could it be true? Could such a Secret have been hidden inside her own temple all this time? She suddenly understood why the Servant of the Bright King was there. But in an instant she also knew she would have no part of the great endeavor, and she felt a hollow pit opening inside her, the rage and wonder turning to despair and giddy hope; she stifled a sob, and cursed the uncaring bones.*

"What'd he fucking say?" hissed the Stick, standing tall and straight and with a frown on his face. They were all standing and looking up at the top of the idol now, the urns and offering pots forgotten.

"The Barrow of Azharad," said Guilford quietly. His grip on Erim's shoulder had suddenly gone hard, his fingertips digging into her flesh even through the doublet, but he didn't realize what he was doing. She bit her lip against the pain, and against something else. Erim was a bit confused; she could sense the others in his crew coming closer, the sudden tension in the chamber.

"The Barrow of Azharad," Guilford said again, and laughed suddenly. He'd heard any number of men, in any number of taverns and street corners, claim they were going after that barrow. Hell, he'd had any number of peddlers offer to sell him a map to it. Or to the tomb of Palé Meffiré and her enchanted horn, to the Barrow of Githwaine the Last Worm King, to the secret hiding place of the Throne Thief, to any of dozens of legendary hoards and treasures. And he'd known better each time, had laughed and moved on. But Harvald and Stjepan were different. Stjepan was different.

Stjepan didn't bullshit.

Particularly there, in that place. Deep under the ground, standing before a great bronze idol of one of the *Bharab Dzerek*, with the blood of who

40

knew how many victims smeared on its altar and its great phallic sacrificial spear, Guilford could feel it in his bones. There was no way Stjepan would bullshit him. Not about this. And he knew that map was real. *He could feel it in his bones*, and he laughed the laughter of a man who suddenly realized he was going to be rich beyond his wildest dreams. "You're . . . you're going after *Gladringer*. You're going after fucking *Gladringer*," Guilford said, having to repeat it to himself in order to get his head around the idea.

"Well," said Harvald faintly, smiling and trying to make the best of a bad situation. "If the map is real."

"You fucking cheap bastards!" Guilford roared, suddenly very angry. Erim thought he was about to rip her arm right off. She hadn't felt him draw it but his broadsword was in his free hand, the tip pointed up toward Harvald and Stjepan up above them. She wasn't sure what to do. "You think to foist us off on these fucking coins and a pair of gems while you go after the *sword of the fucking High Kings*?"

Stjepan snapped out of his reverie and in an instant realized the mistake he had made. Cursing inwardly, he stood up on top of the idol, his head almost touching the ceiling, and looked down on Guilford and the others gathering on the other side of the great brazier below them. "Don't worry, Guilford," he said calmly. "You and your crew can be in on that job too. My word on it."

"Black-Heart, you better fucking believe—"

She could hear the dissension in the great temple before them, and she took a deep breath and a step forward. This was their moment. As she did, so did her Nameless, and one of them accidentally let the barbed metal tip of his spear catch on a low-hanging arch. She whirled on the Nameless responsible, fixing him with the Evil Eye, but the damage was done.

She cursed the bones. They were always right.

Guilford cut himself off before finishing his sentence; almost everyone on the temple floor turned to the left as one and raised their shields and weapons.

The sound they'd all heard from the dark of the outer chambers, despite their fixed attention on the sudden prospect of fame and fortune, had been unmistakable.

The sound of metal scraping against stone.

Everyone froze, poised as though prepared for war and listening, staring at the yawning black arches that were visible beyond the columns on the left flank of the chamber. Gap Tooth Tims was closest to the arch from whence the sound had seemed to come. He swallowed hard, then inched forward until he reached the line of columns. He paused there, one of the thick massive columns by his left shield side, almost using it as cover as he peered intently into the dark arches beyond. He raised his shield, an old steel heater that had kept him safe through many a fight, until the top was almost level with his eyes, and lay the tip of his broadsword to rest on top of the heater, pointing into the inky blackness beyond the arch.

Erim found herself holding her breath along with everyone else as they watched his progress. She felt a sudden pang. Gap Tooth was her line mate. She should be backing him up. But Guilford hadn't let go of her shoulder, in fact he had pulled her back until she was almost behind him and he had practically placed himself as a shield between her and the arches. It was an oddly chivalric gesture, and for a moment she wondered: *does he know?*

And then Gap Tooth was turning and yelling "We are discovered!" and she didn't have time to think about anything else but death. She had barely started to duck before a flurry of arrow shafts peppered the room, hissing out of the darkness. She heard screams as some of the men were hit even as they were diving for cover. The volley of arrows still seemed to be in the air when dark shapes began to swarm into the chamber, bristling with horns and barbed points, rushing amongst the now scattered men. For a split second she was afraid they were being attacked by a horde of demons up from the bowels of one of the Six Hells, but then it registered that they were men, men wearing masks made to resemble horned demons, men wearing black feathered hides and a hodge-podge of armor pieces about their bodies (when they were clothed at all), men wielding spiked clubs, archaic curved swords, and barbed spears.

She practically breathed a sigh of relief. *Devil-worshippers. Nameless Cultists. Followers of the Forbidden Gods.* Joy coursed through her. *I know what to do*, she thought as she plunged the tip of her rapier into the throat of a horn-masked man running straight at her. She felt his spiked club whistle past her head as she ducked under it and the cultist's momentum took him past her and she almost lost her rapier, but she managed to wrench it out of him, sending him spinning and blood arcing even as she sidestepped another horn-masked berserker and punched her dagger into his gut. *I know what to do. Thank you, gods*, she thought.

Atop the idol, Stjepan snarled a curse. At the first volley of arrows that had scattered Guilford's men, he immediately started to roll the map back up. Harvald crouched next to him, putting the heatless torch down onto a seam in the great idol's head and holding the waiting scroll tube for him, and together they carefully slipped the map into the tube.

The moment they were finished Stjepan turned and glanced over the chamber below them as Harvald dropped the scroll tube into one of his satchels. Black shapes swarmed throughout the room. *Too many of them*, he thought sadly. It looked like Llew and Porter were down already, and as he watched a gaunt, naked horn-masked man covered in blue-ink tattoos ran a barbed spear through old Jon Pastle. He could see Guilford laying about him with heavy blows of his broadsword, while Erim moved smoothly, surely, even gracefully through the battle. *But we might still have a chance*, he thought, and he crouched, preparing to start clambering back down the idol.

He felt a hand on his shoulder and looked behind him. Harvald shook his head and nodded up at the ceiling.

"There's always another way out," Harvald said quietly. Stjepan looked past him, and was surprised to see the outline of a trapdoor in the ceiling, now illuminated by the heatless torchlight. He didn't remember that on the maps.

Erim was almost in a trance. The fighting on the temple floor was chaotic, brutal, a real every-man-(and-woman)-for-himself melee. Which suited her just fine. She figured she was better at fighting this way anyway, where she didn't have to worry about anyone else, about keeping the line, about the shield wall or the pike hedgehog or the other things that soldiers trained to formations had to think about. She could just *flow*. So she did. She practically danced, and everywhere she danced a man with a horn-mask died. Somewhere she could hear a woman's voice chanting, singing, and she wondered if she was imagining it, or if some dark *fae* spirit was playing an accompaniment as she worked. She danced over the body of Colin of Loria, his ugly blond-haired head split open by a sharp blow, his brains leaking out under her boots, and the horn-masked swordsman who had killed him gurgled a scream and dropped to the ground, blood spurting from his missing sword hand and a perforated lung. She danced in next to the Stick, beset by two horn-masked warriors, and stabbed one horn-mask up through the throat into his brainpan, and then with the withdrawal she cut the other horn-mask's bloated belly open, splashing his guts all over the floor. She danced back-to-back with Gap Tooth Tims, glad he was still alive, and put one rapier point through a horn-masked spearman's eye even as she drove her point dagger into another's groin. The horn-mask screamed at her for his ruined manhood, and she kicked him full in the face, sending him flying back through the air.

Bodies were dropping left and right, and Guilford could hear that terrible chanting, but he could also hear a voice in the back of his head: *you're going to make it*. Smitt went down trying to hold his guts in somewhere on his left, but Guilford could see the Stick still fighting to his right, and he caught flashes of Erim and Gap Tooth fighting back to back, and he marveled for a moment. *We're going to make it.* He smashed the rim of his shield into one of the devil-worshipper's faces, feeling skull and flesh crumple underneath the blow, and brought his broadsword down in a long arc onto another man's shoulder, almost cutting him lengthwise in two.

Then he saw her. A woman emerging in the dark from behind the last of the swarm, a giant vulture-head mask on her face; she was topless, a black feathered cloak about her, a shimmering black metal dress around her legs as she swayed in a ritual trance, in a full-throated chant, and now Guilford could just about make out the words, though he didn't understand them: "*Sseniss huthadde, Bharabazzhi. Venai. Venai. Festa hus gobblin gaspa, Bharabazzhi. Venai. Venai!*"

Guilford smashed a horn-masked cultist aside, and dropped his broadsword. He reached down for a barbed spear lying on the floor, picked it up, and hefted it once. "King of Heaven, guide my throw!" he whispered, and then he hurled the barbed spear across the room at the priestess, catching her full in the chest. Her chant ended abruptly as she went flying backwards with a wet thud.

It was suddenly quiet again, except for the heavy breathing of tired men and the moans of the dying.

Guilford looked around. Gap Tooth and Erim were all that were left standing, and Gap Tooth was wobbling, blood soaking the breeches of his right leg; they looked at each other, then at the carnage around them, panting, weapons streaked in blood. Well, not *all* that were left standing; Guilford glanced over to where he'd last seen the Stick, and for a moment he was confused by what he saw until he realized that the tall man had been decapitated, his head nowhere to be seen, the body still standing upright and swaying.

And then the Stick's body fell over.

Guilford knelt down and picked up his broadsword. He picked his way through the bodies, some still and silent, others quivering and moaning, over to where the priestess of the Nameless Cults lay. Her body was shaking; she was still alive, despite the barbed spear springing upright from her chest. He looked down dispassionately and noted that her body was beautiful, with pale alabaster skin, a flat stomach, curved hips, and firm full breasts with pierced nipples; now ruined by the spear plunged through her center. He'd probably missed her heart by an inch or two, but there was no doubt she'd be dead soon. He could hear her trying to say something, whispering to herself in a strained gurgle. He used the point of his sword to tip her vulture-headed mask off and grimaced. Her body might have been beautiful, but it was a hideous, almost deformed face that looked up at him with hate-filled eyes, hate-filled eyes that had an oddly insane look of triumph about them. She grinned and bared her filed and sharpened teeth, and then coughed blood, still trying to say something. He thought for a second she was laughing at him, though he had no idea what she would have thought funny about a spear through the chest.

"Fucking hill people," he muttered to no one in particular, then raised his voice to a shout. "Black-Heart! What was she chanting?"

He looked up and was surprised to see Stjepan helping Harvald disappear into a hole in the ceiling above the great bronze idol.

"She was performing a summoning," Stjepan called down. "Something's coming. We should go."

Guilford turned and looked out the darkened arches that had spawned this horde. They yawned black in front of him. And where before the air had been still, now he could feel an ill wind, a weird wind, from beyond the arches.

Something was in the corridor beyond.

Guilford went very pale.

"Something's coming," he said weakly.

"Get up here!" Stjepan shouted as Harvald's boots disappeared into the ceiling. "Now. Climb, climb!"

In a sudden panic, Erim, Guilford, and Gap Tooth Tims all rushed for the great bronze idol and started to clamber up, Gap Tooth stumbling and almost falling as he tried to run. Erim reached it first and she swung up the sides of the idol quickly, barely sparing a glance at its long curved phalli as she passed it. Guilford was next, and then Gap Tooth slammed into the base of the idol last. Throwing away his heater he tried to haul himself up, but his wounded leg made climbing difficult. Guilford was surprised to find himself slowed a bit by the heavy bag of loot tied onto his back.

"Fucking help me, you bastards!" screamed Gap Tooth. Guilford looked down, and saw that Gap Tooth was having trouble, and wavered for a moment. He cursed, and looked up. Erim had stopped, almost at the top, and was looking back down at them.

"Keep going!" shouted Guilford, and he turned and dropped back down to the crook of the idol's arm. He reached down, grabbed Gap Tooth's hand and hauled him up into the idol's lap.

Erim watched this for a moment, helplessly, and then she heard Stjepan above her speaking calmly. "Erim," he said. "You have to keep climbing. Now." She turned back and locked eyes with him, meeting his sharp gaze, and suddenly she felt very calm and sure. She nodded, and in a short move she was the first to reach the top, and Stjepan helped pull her up and then in one smooth motion he lifted her so she could reach the trap door. She quickly pulled herself up and out.

The torches and braziers in the temple chamber started to flicker and go out as Guilford sensed rather than saw something big and dark with glistening spikes and horns slowly squeeze its way through the arches into the room. A smell hit them all then, the smell of a thousand rotting corpses, boiling sulfur, and buckets filled with fresh shit and stale semen. Guilford vomited into his mouth, the stench was so foul, and he abandoned any thoughts of trying to help Gap Tooth. He turned and tried to spring up the sides of the idol.

Stjepan could see the darkness spreading, the scattered dropped torches guttering and dimming. The darkness slowly swallowed up Gap Tooth as he scratched at the bronze idol's chest, trying to find purchase to reach the idol's shoulder with only one leg to stand on. Gap Tooth retched and started to scream, and then Stjepan couldn't see him anymore, couldn't see what was happening to him, and Stjepan was thankful for the darkness then.

Stjepan reached his hand down as Guilford reached the perch of the idol's shoulders and started to clamber up its face. The darkness in the room was almost complete, the single heatless torch atop the idol was all that was left, and it barely illuminated the two of them. Guilford looked up at Stjepan, and their hands finally locked. Stjepan could barely see his face in the waning light, and Guilford wore a look of desperation and terror, as though he knew he was spent, the fatigue of the fight and weight on his back was draining

47

him, and then suddenly his expression changed, his grasp went soft, and his eyes went slightly glassy. Guilford gasped softly.

And then there was a wet, chewing, rending sound that Stjepan thought was just about the worst thing he'd ever heard.

Guilford's eyes rolled, watering with tears, and then finally with a last bit of will he was able to focus them on Stjepan.

"Promise me, Black-Heart," he hissed, suddenly fierce. "Fucking swear it!"

Stjepan nodded grimly. "Seven days of prayer, to guide you to the Heavens," he said softly. "You and yours will have it, I swear it."

Guilford nodded, and as he looked into Stjepan's sharp eyes it occurred to him that for the first time he wasn't looking into Black-Heart's usual gaze of hate or stern judgment, but instead saw nothing but a look of love and compassion. He was surprised, and opened his mouth to say something, when he was pulled with a sudden yank right out of Stjepan's grasp and down into the darkness.

Stjepan turned and leapt, catching the edge of the trap door and pulling himself up into the ceiling just as the last torch guttered out.

When Erim finally stumbled out of the rock onto the high hillside, she gasped and sobbed and fell to her knees and crawled and rolled. She did not think she had ever been so happy to see the light of day. Her mind was mush, driven into fear and panic by the wild run through the dark, following a single torch held up by Harvald and Stjepan with his map. She didn't know how he'd found their way out, but somehow he'd managed to orient themselves on his map, and up and down stairs they'd scrambled and climbed, legs burning with the effort, and then up, and up, and up again, until finally she'd felt packed earth under her boots and she'd seen an upright sliver of bright light up ahead.

Her hands dug into dirt and peat moss, and somehow that steadied her, even though she knew that somewhere deep underneath the solid earth was hidden a chamber of horrors. She crawled to get away from the opening into the rock, seeing Stjepan and Harvald downhill a bit, also slumped to the ground, panting and heaving. Harvald was on all fours, his head buried in his chest, whispering in prayer, and she briefly wished she had a god or goddess to pray to. But there were none but the Damned that would take the likes of her, so the temple priests had assured her when she was young and they had played with her in the dark.

The sun had broken through the clouds while they were below the ground, and she leaned back on her haunches, reveling in the light and heat. She unstrapped her water bottle and brought it to her lips, the cool clean liquid tasting unbelievably sweet on her lips, in her mouth, in her throat. Harvald had slipped the copper scroll tube out of his satchel, and he was staring at it in wonder. She saw Stjepan stand and walk a few feet to face the sun, and he sank to his knees, his hands open as if in supplication.

Stjepan was Athairi, and like most of his people he was of the Old Religion, and worshipped the Queen of Heaven and her Court. He would never have uttered the Divine King prayer for the Dead. But most of the men who they'd just left behind had been brought up in the cult of the Divine King, as was the wont in most of the eastern Middle Kingdoms. And so it was a variant he uttered, the so-called Erid Prayer for the Dead, first worded by the Athairi to pray for Danian comrades who had died by their sides.

Dawn Maiden. Awaken!
Bright Star. Awaken!
Sun's Herald. Awaken!
And announce the death of
loyal servants to the Divine King!
Dread Guardians, light their way
on the Path of the Dead!
Seedré, Judge and Gatekeeper,
welcome them below, and know that they are claimed!
Islik, King in Heaven, once King on Earth!
Your servants fall to Death, your hated enemy!

> *King in Heaven, know their names:*
> *Jon Pastle; Colin, son of Corwin of Loria;*
> *Smitt, son of Heoret; Jack Porter of Vesslos;*
> *Tims Orwed; Llew, son of Duram Tain;*
> *Cole, son of Gable Gower;*
> *and Guilford, son of Guy of Vesslos.*
> *Send your bright messengers to the*
> *place of Judgment, to claim their spirits*
> *from the grasp of their accusers!*
> *Bring them from Darkness*
> *to your Heavenly Palace!*
> *Save them from Death!*

She knew without having to ask that Stjepan would utter that prayer each morning day and night for the next seven days, until either their spirits had found their way to peace in Heaven or judgment in the Underworld, or had been lost forever. She frowned.

"Cole, son of Gable?" she asked.

Stjepan looked over at her. He thought she looked exhausted, frightened, exhilarated. He smiled softly. "That was the Stick's real name," he said.

He looked at the ground for a moment, and then stood and surveyed the horizon with his sharp gaze. He listened to the wind, to the faint jangle of unseen bells, to a song that seemed to be sung backwards. He sniffed the air, smelt wet earth and old stone, moss and scrub thickets and tree heath, and from somewhere near the hint of something dead and rotting. The sadness in him grew deeper and was joined by . . . anger? Hate? His gaze grew piercing and unsettling, as though he was a man with murder on his mind.

"Let's get going," he said finally, and started off down the hillside. Harvald shook himself, and followed, rubbing his hands as though he was a child about to open a present.

Erim looked about, at the three of them on a sunny hillside, with ancient *menhirs* ringing the hilltop and the high range of the Manon Mole off in the distance, the blood of a dozen men splattered on her clothes to mix with dirt and mud. She suddenly thought to herself that if anyone asked her, she would say she was Stjepan's man. She shuddered in the weird, high wind, and looked back over her shoulder at the cleft in the rock.

"See you in Hell, boys," she whispered. It was the closest thing to a prayer that she could offer. And then she turned and was off down the hillside.

Somewhere in the dark, a woman whispered, and something huge and hungry feasted and fucked.

PART ONE

IN THE CITY OF MONEY AND FILTH

CHAPTER ONE
AT THE GATES OF THERAPOLI MAGNI, CAPITAL OF THE MIDDLE KINGDOMS
THE 10TH OF EMPERIUM, 1471 iA

The walls of Therapoli normally shone with a sandy, sienna color that could look like burnished gold in the right light. But in the hues of early morning before the rising of the sun, the city was just blue, as blue as the rest of the world. Erim could hear the quiet conversations of men and women in the morning gloom, waiting for the West Gates to open: farmers from the High King's Demesne, bringing fruits and grains to market; traders and tinkers, with wagons and carts piled high with barrels, sacks, and baskets; horse sellers and cattle men, pilgrims and weary travelers, all of them waiting patiently, bleary-eyed in the sleepy light of the pre-dawn hour. A donkey brayed nearby, and further away several roosters answered. From her vantage point atop her horse, a large part of the city was visible beyond the gate and walls: the crowning heights of the High King's Hall and the noble tower houses in the High Quarter, the University on its rise past the Gate of Eldyr, and then the lower parts of the city down by the docks below. She could see small, faint sparks of orange and red appearing amidst the blue where fires were being stoked. Bakeries and smithies would be the first to stir, to get their ovens and kilns hot for the workday. The Morning Star hung bright in the blue sky above the city to the east, and as these were Divine King lands the prayers she could hear to Ami the Dawn Maiden from amongst the more devout in the waiting line named the star as the Divine King's Herald.

PART ONE: IN THE CITY OF MONEY AND FILTH

Erim shifted in the saddle of her horse, a reasonably sedate Danian half-bred courser named Cúlain-mer that Stjepan had picked out for her, and her gaze fell on a similar line of wagons and people at the South Gate, then on the docks inside the city and the bay beyond, and the fish towns that stretched down the coast from the city south to Durinham. The fisher fleet was already starting to put out into the waters of the bay, and she could see small coasters sailing out between the larger ships that waited for the main docks to open. Erim had grown up in a port city, Berrina down in the Kingdom of Huelt, and so she could class her ships and sails. She could see dozens of merchant hulks and clinker-built cogs from around the Middle Kingdoms and from across the *Mera Argenta*, from Hemispia and its League of Cities; high-masted lateen-sailed caravels and square-sailed carracks from Palatia; even a few Déskédran *dhorrows* and decorative, lug-sailed *baferrils*. All of them were waiting for dock space so they could disgorge their cargo, their orange lanterns flashing messages back and forth to each other and the docks in the blue light of the morning.

The city waited, its breath held for the start of the day, and Erim waited with it.

While Stjepan and Harvald had found the map they were looking for, the expedition could hardly have been called a success; not simply because of the deaths of so many of their compatriots, but because they'd had to leave most of the immediately useful loot behind. Indeed, they would have actually been worse off than when they'd started, having spent their own coin for food and lodging along the way, had the dead men's horses and supplies not refilled their purses. Erim had been almost surprised that the horses were all still alive and accounted for upon their return to the small hill village where they'd stabled them before the rough march further into the hills, along with what they judged to be most if not all of the small pack items left behind. She had found herself regretting the suspicion with which she'd eyed the poor villagers.

They had decided not to leave the Manon Mole the way they entered it, even though it meant being in the hills longer, and so Stjepan had led them across the spine of its high, deserted range, sticking to old shepherd's trails. They had to hide several times when they saw mounted parties moving in the distance, but they made it down into the foothills after two hair-raising days, looking over their shoulders the whole way. Then it had taken them another day in the Hada Wold, sticking to the trails that skirted the Tilbrae River. She'd have probably preferred they skip the woods, but Stjepan had explained that the Hada Wold was the domain of the Court of the Stone Wood, and the *fae* of the Stone Court tended to leave mortals alone. And sure enough they were unmolested on their journey through the dark, leafy trees. Stjepan had found an old shrine made of stones piled about the hollow of a great, dead tree, and he prayed there for their lost companions on the Path of the Dead.

They'd made it safely all the way down to Tilfort, and they'd sold the eight riding horses and two spares and their tack and harnesses and extra supplies to some traders there. Erim thought the price they'd gotten was low, a hundred shillings a horse and another thirty shillings for the tack and harness, but the gear wasn't in great shape and the market at Tilfort wasn't a big one. The traders could probably sell the horses for closer to three times what they paid for them, even in a small market like Tilfort; the horses were good stock, sturdy Danian palfreys. But traders never gave full price anyway, she figured, otherwise they wouldn't be able to make any money selling them again. Stjepan had thought the price was fair. They could've gotten more perhaps in Vesslos, but Stjepan didn't want to walk into the city with Guilford's horses in tow, which made sense to her.

Still, it was enough of a sale that the traders had paid out twenty-seven gold crowns and two hundred and twenty in shillings, big sums for Erim to work her head around. Stjepan had paid a couple of shillings to have mourners at the temple of the Divine King in Tilfort say the prayers for Guilford's lost crew for the rest of their time on the Path of the Dead, and then he had insisted they return through Vesslos; from Tilfort they could've gone to Soros or Abenton and found a barge or a ship to take them across the bay to Therapoli, which Harvald argued they should do, but Stjepan had said it was the right and proper thing to return through Vesslos. Guilford had people there, a young Danian woman and a squalling baby that shared the rooms he let above the Dancing Stag on the Run Street. Erim and Harvald had waited in the tavern's common room as Stjepan visited with the young woman and the child upstairs, shifting uncomfortably as the locals gave them sour looks; they'd known instantly that Black-Heart had brought bad news. She found out later that Stjepan had given the woman a dozen gold crowns for her and the baby, easily enough for a year's room and board with some left over, and then when he came downstairs he bought a round of drinks in Guilford's memory for the house, and spent some time quietly recalling Guilford's life and death with some of the hard men there. The young woman and her baby had come down later, dressed in mourning black, and Tall Duram, who owned the Stag, and a bunch of the regulars went with her and Stjepan to the Divine King temple. Erim didn't go with them, and neither did Harvald, but she found out later that Stjepan had paid for the mourners there too, and for another priest to pray for Guilford and his crew in the last few days of their journey on the Path of the Dead.

Stjepan still hadn't finished; most of Guilford's crew had been young men, street men, except for Llew the Stew, but he had no known surviving family, and old Jon Pastle, who had been a widower and had two grown sons who were tenants of the Lord of Kielwell. Erim and Harvald had waited in town while Stjepan rode out west the ten miles to the farms there to deliver them eight gold crowns and the news of their father's death. Harvald had gone to find better accommodations at an inn across town, but she'd stayed in the common room at the Dancing Stag until Stjepan returned well after dusk. She had sat in a dark corner, eating her dinner, lamb meatballs in a mushroom sauce with onions and garlic over a bowl of herbed rice, and observed the locals as they drank to Guilford and told stories about him and the Stick and Gap Tooth Tims. She had tried not to weep into her food. Eventually a couple of them had worked up the courage to come and ask her about the details of Guilford's death.

Since Stjepan hadn't told her not to, she told them in a low voice about the harried fight in the temple, the swarms of cultists, Guilford killing their vulture-masked priestess with a thrown spear and then dying at the hands of a *Rahabi* demon while trying to save Gap Tooth Tims. She had tried not to embellish too much, but hoped that when they repeated the stories to his woman and child that they'd see him as a hero; judging from the awed expressions on the men's faces, she'd told the story right. The two men had thanked her quietly in serious tones, and then had rejoined their fellows, repeating what she'd told them. *And so legends are born*, she'd thought to herself as she had raised her glass to the ceiling in a silent toast.

She and Stjepan had slept in the common room on padded benches built into the back table booths, and it had been the best night of sleep she'd had since the disastrous fight in the temple. She'd watched Stjepan sleeping next to her for a while, his face peaceful, the anger and danger gone out of it, then drifted off with a warm sensation in her chest.

"Don't come back, Black-Heart," Tall Duram had said to Stjepan as they'd left in the morning to find Harvald. There hadn't been any heat in his words, though.

"Don't make me, Tall Duram," Stjepan had replied, fixing him with that gaze of his.

"Fallia and the baby will be well taken care of, my word on it," Tall Duram had said, and they'd nodded to each other and Tall Duram had gone back inside the Dancing Stag.

Having lost over a full day in Vesslos, they had tried to hurry the rest of the way back to Therapoli, aiming to cross the Abenbrae at the bridge at Tauria and then cut east across open country belonging to the Baron of Misal Ruth to cross the Harbrae at the bridge at Grawton, then down the West King's Road through the High King's Demesne to the capital. About fifty miles of road and country in total. But they'd had some trouble finding Harvald and got a late start, so they'd missed the closing of the gates at Grawton, and then the local inn on the west side of the river was so jammed even the common rooms were full, so they'd been forced to spend the night in the fields with other travelers who had been late to the bridge.

It hadn't been an unpleasant evening, trading gossip and news with tinkers and traders, banding around campfires for warmth and security from the Black Hunter in case the Wild Hunt was loose in the night. Of course, if the Black Hunter had come calling they'd have been fucked, except that some of the tinkers had discreetly set out folk charms around the campfire to ward off the Wild Hunt, and luckily no one minded.

The traders and tinkers had told them that the passes up into the Highlands of Daradja had opened up early that spring, and traders were already winding their way back and forth; that a man named Fearam, son of Ishal, had been outlawed for murder by Wallis Liefring, the Baron of Misal Ruth, and was being hunted as he fled north for those same fresh-opened passes, hoping to reach the safety of the mountains; that a black stag had been seen near the Darker Tower, and that was certainly an ill omen to the locals there, and huge flocks of carrion crows and vultures had been seen winging their way out of the Plain of Stones, so something terrible and tragic was on the horizon. Useful tidbits all, but getting caught on the west side of the river overnight meant they'd lost a bit of travel time, and the next day they'd wound up arriving too late to enter Therapoli as well, missing the closing of the gates by about an hour.

The inns just outside the capital city's walls at the North Gate were notorious for their high prices, so they'd moved down to the West Gate to see if the lodgings might be cheaper, but had found no room at the inns there. Not wanting to keep going to another gate, they had found a wagon train of farmers and traders from Pierham who'd also missed the gate closings and who let them hunker down with them for a few pennies. The farmers had shared a bottle of apple brandy and fine signing voices, so it had been another fine evening under the star sign of the Star-Child.

Erim had woken up in the back of a hay cart with the rise of the Dawn Maiden, the world around her turning from deepest black to pale blue. A single distant bell had tolled over the city to announce the coming of the Morning Star. As the wagon train had slowly stirred, and other farmers with carts and travelers from nearby inns had started to queue up for the gates, they'd finished off their dried figs and hard cheese and the potato-onion bread they'd gotten back in Yefram on the West King's Road, still surprisingly fresh, and Stjepan had counted out the last of their coins from the sale of the horses.

"We've got seven gold crowns and a hundred shillings left over, give or take," Stjepan had said. "So that's a little over a hundred shillings each." But when he'd counted out the coins he'd given her four gold crowns and twenty shillings, Harvald three gold crowns and twenty shillings, and then kept sixty shillings and change for himself. When she'd protested, he'd shrugged and said quietly, "You need it more than me." Which was true, so she hadn't argued much. Harvald had income both from his father's estates and his clerkship at the High King's Court, and so had the most money of any of them; he was also a stickler for his fair share, though Stjepan never seemed to begrudge him that. Stjepan had his income from the High King's Court as a cartographer, so he'd be all right. But she didn't have any regular means.

The temple bells in the city finally started ringing, announcing the coming of the sun and Divine King, and the call to morning prayers. "Islik, King of Heaven. Hail, King of Heaven!" shouted out some of the men up ahead of them as they greeted the sun and dropped to their knees to pray, and the line began to stir. *Pilgrims*, she thought. *Or at least devout men; but by their dress they're not locals.* Therapoli Magni was not merely the capital of the Middle Kingdoms, and the seat of the High King; it was a jewel of the ancient world, founded during the Golden Age by King Culainn of the Danians exactly four hundred years before the ascension of Islik to the throne of the King of Heaven, and now over eighteen hundred years old. Its most infamous king, Myrad the Mad, had actually imprisoned Islik in his fabled dungeons for a time, while Islik was in exile from his earthly throne, and it was there that Islik had met the other three Kings in Exile. That made the city a holy site, sacred to all that worshipped the Divine King, and devout pilgrims flocked to the city from all the lands around the *Mera Argenta* to pray in its great temple; though if they looked to visit the dungeons where Islik had been held they would be disappointed, as they had been buried and sealed below the city centuries ago.

Stjepan and Harvald sat on their horses and said nothing, and neither did she. They were all wrapped in an extra layer over their travel clothes to ward off the spring morning chill, Stjepan with a rough wool blanket drawn about him and an oiled leather hat with broad brims that curled up on the sides, Harvald with a brown hooded cloak, and her with an old sleeveless fur-lined half-coat. *A right band of ragamuffins, we are*, she thought.

A small sally port opened off to one side of the gate barbican and one of the Watch wardens appeared. He wore the colors of the High King, a gold wyvern embroidered on a red surcoat, and he started walking up the lines. "Two lines. Two lines!" he called out. "Wares on the left, simple travelers on the right. Two lines, two lines. Anyone headed to market or with something to sell, on the left!" They were already in the right line, having done this before. Their long weapons were already wrapped and stored with their saddlebags, even Harvald's; he might have been from a noble family, but he wasn't knighted, and so didn't have the privilege of carrying a sword openly within the city. The gates finally opened and the lines began to move forward.

Theirs was the faster line, as the guards were largely just counting heads and collecting the three-penny entry tolls. They'd pay an extra penny for their horses, and an extra penny for their swords and bows. She hadn't thought the three-penny toll worth bothering with—many other towns and cities would charge six pennies for entry—until she'd brought it up with Stjepan once when they'd been waiting in line.

"Well, three pennies might not seem like much to you or to most of us, though there's plenty for whom that's a hardship, but you have to look at the big picture when it comes to a city the size of Therapoli and how it generates tolls and taxes for the High King," Stjepan had said. "At least a few thousand people come into the city on a slow day from the surrounding countryside and from across the Middle Kingdoms and the Known World, or reenter having left. Each one of them pays three pennies, or more if they have a horse or are carrying a formal weapon of some kind, even if they can't legally use it in the city. If they're bringing goods for sale, then an extra penny for each wheel of a wagon or cart, pack animal, and teamster animal, and an extra penny for each animal for sale."

He had pointed down to the docks. "Each ship docking pays a fee to the dock masters, ten shillings a mast, as well as a fee for the weight and content of the cargo that it's delivering. So just from the coming and going of men and animals, the city probably generates, oh I don't know, I'd say maybe thirty thousand pennies on a slow day, many times that during one of the festivals. And that doesn't begin to account for the flow of money from tenant rents, business licenses, usage fees, and poll taxes that fill the city's coffers throughout the year."

She'd felt dizzy when she'd thought about it. *That much each day, and just from the gates and docks of this one city; no wonder the High King is the wealthiest man in the Middle Kingdoms*, she'd thought. *Though he's also got a lot of expenses.*

"Further, the fact that the toll is cheaper than other towns and cities acts as an encouragement for people to come here with their goods for sale rather than another market," Stjepan had added. "Plus, since the toll is only three pennies, the High King can raise it for a month or two and people will still think it's reasonably fair. He's done that six times in the last decade when he's needed to raise some extra funds quickly, though everyone starts to grumble after a bit."

They paid their pennies dutifully when they got to the head of the line, and received the usual warning about weapons in the city. "Swords may only be borne in the city by knights and the high nobility, unless by dispensation of the City Watch," said the bored guardsman. "But then you lot know that, eh, Black-Heart?"

"Aye, we know that," grunted Stjepan.

The gate captain appeared on a stone landing just inside the gates and called out to them, waving them over to the side. "Ho, Black-Heart!"

said the man, a tall, balding Aurian with pockmarked skin. He wore an infantry half-harness and the High King's colors, with a mail skirt, cuisses and poleyns, and light leather boots that laced in the front, his brace of sword and dagger hanging on his left. The landing was high enough that he had to lean over a wooden rail to shake Stjepan's hand, even with Stjepan mounted. "Welcome home."

"Sir Owen Lirewed, good to see you," said Stjepan. "You remember Harvald and young Erim?" Harvald barely looked over at him, his eyes intent on the city street before them, but Erim gave Owen a courteous half-bow from the saddle.

"Aye, that I do," grinned the gate captain. "Is your return to the city official?"

"I think perhaps it might be best if I were still somewhere afield," said Stjepan, casually slipping some coins into Owen's hand.

"I'll leave your names off the official reports, then," Sir Owen said. "Best of luck with the unofficial ones."

"Yeah, well, nothing we can do about that, really," said Stjepan sourly.

"I suppose not," laughed Sir Owen. "The city missed you, Black-Heart."

"You're a liar, Sir Owen. I'm sure it didn't notice I was gone at all," Stjepan said with a light touch of his fingers to the brim of his hat, and then they urged their horses forward into the growing morning traffic of the street ahead of them as the gate captain laughed at their receding backs, jangling the coins in his hand.

The West Gate opened up onto the start of the High Promenade, which ran straight out in front of them to the main plaza of the Market Quarter in the outer city, through the Gate of Eldyr, up to the great University of Therapoli and its Quarter, to High Plaza, and then angled down through High Quarter to the foot of the High King's Hall. The other great avenue that bisected the city, the Grand Promenade, stretched from the South Gate of the city to the lower plaza of the Foreign Quarter in the outer city, through the Gate of Erginus, split around both sides of the Forum, and then went all the way to the Plaza of Ergist abutting the High Quarter to meet the High Promenade where it descended in front of the High

King's Hall, and then angled around the Hall to the East Gate. The two broad avenues cut across the entire city, largely paralleling each other and the shore of the bay until the High Promenade curved down to meet the Grand Promenade.

Despite the early hour, with the sun barely up, the street was already bustling as merchants and shopkeepers began to unlock their doors and windows, and the market plaza's stands and kiosks were being occupied and opened. The quarter's Market Court was already open, the hall's great double doors already filled with merchants and sellers lining up their carts and wagons to have their goods weighed and measured for sale in the plaza or at auction. The trio paused by the side of the Promenade, the traffic flowing around them.

Erim noticed that Harvald had his hood pulled over his head, shielding his face. "Think you can escape notice?" she asked.

"One can only try," he said with a smile, but his eyes were nervous again, scanning the street traffic.

"There's no way to enter this city without being seen," Stjepan said quietly. "One of the guardsmen in Owen's command is in the pay of the Painted Prince, Owen knows that for certain. And another reports to Lord Rohan, which Owen may not know at all." He met Erim's gaze, and raised an eyebrow with a half-smile.

Ah, our little game, she thought. *Spot the thief, spot the spy.* They both turned and started looking discreetly about. "There's one of the Gilded Lady's rats," Erim said casually after a moment, nodding at a young street urchin begging at the nearest corner of the market plaza. "And that lot over there is with Jon Dhee's crew, and they'll be looking to cut a purse or two," she said, indicating another group of urchins scampering about at the entrance to an alleyway.

"Mm, there's a couple of others that report to Dhee here, this is his corner of the city. He'll sell what they see to the Guild Princes, and to Liam White-Eye, and to Petterwin Grim," Stjepan said. "And then Liam and Petterwin will sell to the Squire of Mud Street, Mardin Green down by the docks, Mina the Dagger, and Mother Silva. Though Petterwin Grim and the Fat Prince will have their own lookouts here somewhere." He squinted down the street. "And I'm going to guess the drunks in front of the Spiked Maul are Lord Hugh's men," he said. "They're a little too polished for this hour of the morning; the Inquisition never gets that right."

"Ah, the old broad over there," said Erim, indicating with her chin a muttering old woman in drabs pushing a cart into the market plaza. "That's the Fat Prince's chief lookout near this gate. There's another lot of urchins that she uses as runners. They'll be nearby somewhere."

"And the bravos up on that balcony over there, with a perfect view of the gatehouse; I've used that balcony myself," Stjepan said, indicating three slim, rough-looking men in tight black leathers with head scarves tied over their long blond hair and short swords and daggers on their sword belts, casually eating from a bread basket as they observed the passing traffic. "From the Bastards of Baker Street, but I'd lay odds they're on hire to another crew to be in this part of the city, and looking for someone in particular. Hopefully it's not us." One of the men caught that Stjepan was eyeing them, and they gave each other a slight nod; but the bravo went back to scanning the travelers entering the gates. "Nope, not us."

Erim scanned the rooftops. "Lots of birds," she said with a bit of apprehension. Sparrows, pigeons, and doves perched on the rooftops, occasionally diving into the street after some morsel. More waddled past them; gulls and terns circled lazily in the air up from the docks and the shore of the bay.

Stjepan glanced up, his eyes narrowing. Erim could hear him whispering under his breath. "Aye, some of them are rune-marked, and have the hint of a binding enchantment about them. Probably eyes and ears for the Brass Coven, and for Naeras Braewode, and the Sisters of the Scales," he said after a moment. "And so news of our arrival will be spread far and wide through the underground of the city amongst those that trade knowledge for coin, if any should happen to care about it."

"It's funny that someone will make a bit of coin or earn a bit of bread just to tell someone else that we're back in the city," said Erim. "I mean, I'd be happy to tell them myself if they paid us. That'd be a fine play, to walk up to Jon Dhee and say 'Hi, I'm back, now give me a penny.'"

"Do you think . . . do you think the Nameless Cults will have someone here looking for us?" Harvald asked, licking his lips, his voice a low whisper. "I mean we did just raid a temple of the *Rahabi*."

Erim hadn't thought of that, and she looked around with a bit more concern.

"Maybe," Stjepan said with a shrug. "Even if they don't have a lookout here, one of this lot will sell to them, maybe without even knowing it. Some of this lot could even be from the Nameless themselves, serving two masters at once. The eyes and ears of the Hell-Prince of Intrigue are everywhere, and Amaymon the Spider takes many guises as he spies for the rest of the Forbidden." All three of them spat to the side at the mention of the name of one of the Forbidden.

"And on that note, I guess it's time to split up," Stjepan said cheerfully. "If you get followed, run."

Erim barked a laugh. "Fuck you, Black-Heart," she said.

"We'll meet at Gilgwyr's tonight. Be there by midnight. Leigh should be there by then, assuming he manages to get into the city," said Harvald.

"Ah, Leigh doesn't need to walk through the gates," said Stjepan with a cold laugh. "And if he does, he won't look like himself. He'll be there."

"And we'll translate the map then, yes, once Leigh's here. I think it's important that he be there," Harvald said to Stjepan, his voice straining.

"It's fine, I already told you that I would wait," Stjepan said, holding up his hands, much to Erim's relief. "I'm even letting you hold onto the map, just so I don't get tempted." It had been the only real source of tension on the journey back to Therapoli; Stjepan had wanted to begin translating the map while they were still on the road, but Harvald warned they should only do so in the relative safety of the city, with its resources at their disposal, and with some exiled magus named Leigh that Erim had never met present to aid them in the deed. She'd seen a real fear in Harvald while she watched them argue, and so had Stjepan, who had finally relented with a puzzled look on his face.

PART ONE: IN THE CITY OF MONEY AND FILTH

So they split up, Harvald heading due east up the High Promenade, intent upon the city house of his father, while Stjepan and Erim headed south down toward the Foreign Quarter. Stjepan let rooms over near the University Quarter, but he always stopped at the baths of the Foreign Quarter upon returning to the city.

Stjepan paused at the Fountain of Ymaire, where he would continue down Sea Way toward Low Plaza and the baths, leaving Erim to turn onto Cobble Street to make her way toward her rooms above Fuller Cort's Laundries. His gaze scanned the morning crowd of laborers and artisans heading to work or the markets. He listened to the wind, heard the cries of shop clerks and heralds, the rattle and clang of industry, the call of gull and cormorant. He sniffed the air, smelt horse offal and human piss, baking bread and wafting perfume, hearth fires and the salty brine of the bay. *It's not home, but at least it smells clean*, he thought. He looked up and saw vultures circling in the air, high above the city.

"I wasn't kidding; if you're followed, run," called out Stjepan.

"I wasn't kidding either; fuck you, Black-Heart," Erim called back in response.

She watched him angle off down the narrow Way. She was always amazed at how Stjepan could look both completely at ease almost everywhere he went and yet not seem to be a part of the place he was in. He seemed at ease roughing it in the wilderness, with not a soul around for miles, and at ease moving through the busiest parts of the city, as though he was comfortable being in his own skin, and she was a bit envious of that. But at the same time there was always something different about him, and it wasn't just that he was an Athairi in the middle of an Aurian city, or that he was wood-born in the Erid Wold but had a University education. *It's the look in his eyes*, she decided. *That look of judgment, as though he's not one of you; half the world sees that look and wants to get away from him. The other half instantly wants his approval.* She watched him disappear down the street, then turned away.

68

Though she was city-born, Erim felt like she could hold her own in the country—at least Stjepan had felt she could, which was good enough for her. She might not have Stjepan's knack for sights and sounds, or know the name of the bird making a lovely song, or which leaves from what plant could make a poultice for an infected cut. But she didn't have to have a roof over her head, or a bed under her, to fall asleep at night, though admittedly she preferred it. She liked to look up and count the stars, and see if she could guess which one was a great hero and which wasn't. She didn't fall behind, or complain, or step on the wrong twig at the wrong moment like some city folk might.

But she always felt like she risked doing something wrong, of not seeing the danger signs when they were coming. The country often made her feel lonely, and small. The general lack of human contact, of human structure, of the *man-made*, left her at a loss. She didn't understand its rituals and behaviors, the languages and signs of animals and birds and trees, of hunters and farmers, its codes and rules. The deeper she went into the countryside, the more tenuous became the rule of the Middle Kingdoms; so tenuous, so risky, that deviance from its considered norms could bring ruin and disaster. Where Stjepan found freedom and open air to breathe, she found constriction and confusion. In the country, amongst either Danians or Aurians, a woman dressed as a man wouldn't want to be discovered, for in her experience country folk tended to be more fixed in their ways than city folk, and looked askance at anything different. Except the Athairi, perhaps, but they were different than just about everyone else anyway, thanks to their varied ancestries, their *fae* blood and Düréan blood, the touch of magic that sparked within them.

Or unless, as amongst the hill folk of the Manon Mole, or maybe the savage clans that filled the Highlands of Daradja and the Mael Kingdoms of the west, that a traveler was so far outside of civilization that the rules of culture no longer applied, and a descent into barbarism was the inevitable result. But someone like her could hardly think of such wild places, amongst outlaws and brigands and barbarians, as places of safety or refuge.

Cities were where the civilization of the Middle Kingdoms had its deepest roots, where Divine King culture felt at its strongest, and there-fore cities were where cracks could appear and be tolerated, where deviance and difference took an honored place beside and within the rush and roar of commerce. Back in a city, her adopted city, she started to feel the many layers of herself again. *I know this*, she thought. *I know what to do.* She knew how to read the street and ken where trouble was brewing, when to step to one side so the ashen-faced herald on his galloping horse missed her, where to buy the best fresh-baked bread in the city (the Date & Plum on Baker Street), how to avoid getting her purse cut on Upland Street. She knew the names of the Princes of the Guild, even if she didn't know their faces, and of many of the Marked. She knew where all the brothels were, and which dancing girls in the taverns on Wall Street and the Street of Furs were willing to give the customers a little extra for the right word and tip, and where the rent boys sold themselves over in the Old Quarter. She knew where, if she were running low on coin, she could earn her next meal, doing something that sent a little shiver of a thrill up her spine.

She felt a nervous excitement, her skin alive and tingling with the possibilities of a city, her city. The city made it so easy, dangled every vice and temptation in front of her, and promised to look the other way. It *rewarded* her when she gave in, when she said *yes, please.* She could see it in the moon-eyes that young serving girls were giving the knights prancing by on their finely caparisoned steeds, hear it in the wolf whistles that ne'er-do-wells hanging on the corner gave to a young strumpet strutting by, in the occasional long glance that a man or a woman would send her way. *The city is calling you: we're all going to Hell, you fit right in here, so come along with us for a fine fucking ride.* She swallowed and pressed ahead for home.

She found herself almost short of breath, flush with excitement, when she arrived in front of Fuller Cort's Laundries, and dismounted and led Cúlain-mer into the rear courtyard, greeted by the familiar sight of laundry lines hanging with sheets and shirts, the smell of soap and bleach and per-fumes, and the singing voices of the washerwomen. The mute young stable boy, Giles, came and took her horse with a grin and a short bow. His silent greeting was followed by a long *meow* from a large calico cat, one of the yard cats the house kept for ratting, and she bent down to scratch its head. She'd nicknamed it The Countess, after the notorious Countess Uthella, wife of the Earl of Uthmark, though she didn't dare use that name out loud. She slung her satchels and bags over her shoulder before stepping into the back halls. It didn't take long for the mistress of the house to spot her.

"Ah, Master Erim, you've returned!" the plump, shiny woman called out.

"Lady Cort, it's good to be back," Erim said with a slight bow. Everyone called her Lady Cort, even though she didn't have a drop of noble blood in her.

"Fuller's over on the other side of the laundries, he'll be so very glad to see you," Lady Cort said, and Erim blushed and nodded. She headed off through the laundry rooms, past the huge vats of steaming water, ignoring the giggles and glances of the women working. She found Fuller Cort paying out some coins to a deliveryman near the front doors of the laundry.

"Young Master Erim," said Fuller, glancing over at her.

"Your wife said you'd be here, Master Cort, and I am glad she was right as usual," replied Erim with a stiff bow. Fuller looked her over once with his beady eyes, long and slow, and smiled, dismissing the deliveryman with a nod.

"You owe me thirty shillings, Master Erim," said Fuller when they were more or less alone. "We held your rooms like you asked, while you were gone, with the promise of payment upon your return. That's two months of winter you owe us for, and now spring is upon us a full ten days."

"I have the money, Master Cort," she said huskily, looking up at him from under her dark bangs. She fished out one of the gold crowns that Stjepan had given her, and dropped it in Fuller's open palm; he looked surprised and almost disappointed. "The expedition didn't go as we thought, and a full return on our efforts might take a little while longer. But I'm told it will be considerable."

"Well done, Master Erim," said Fuller, with a smile that seemed forced. "I've been very patient, and have kept this a secret between you and me. I have had to deceive my wife, and tell her that you are up to date in your payments."

"For which I am eternally grateful, Master Cort," said Erim quietly. "I hope to be able to leave some small coin on deposit, should I have to leave again soon."

They looked at each other for a bit longer in awkward silence.

"Well then, I assume you'll want a bath, after your long journey," said Fuller finally. "I'll have some of the girls bring up hot water to your rooms. So you can get nice and clean."

"Thank you, Master Cort," said Erim, with a short bow. She felt his eyes on her backside as she left.

She was happy to wend her way up several flights of old wood stairs to the loft room she let up on the top floor of the laundry building, followed by the softly padding paws of The Countess. It had taken her a while to find the right place to live in the city; the building was old and made of plastered stone, and often the odors from the laundry downstairs were a bit overwhelming, but the Corts largely let her alone and didn't ask too many questions, though she was certain Fuller Cort very much wanted to. The loft was quiet, and isolated, and the building, being a laundry, had lots of pipes put in, and most importantly her space came with its own copper bathtub. Stjepan could head off to the public baths, but she couldn't. She opened the shutters to let in light and air, glancing about at the rooftops and balconies nearby, then unpacked and stowed her things and checked on the odds-and-ends she'd left behind while some of the washerwomen brought up buckets of hot, steaming water to fill the tub. Some of them would giggle and blush and smile, and she eyed a few speculatively, but most were plump, and plain, and looking for something she couldn't offer them.

She waited until they were done and gone, then slipped the latch on the door, and undressed as The Countess prowled about the loft, reclaiming her territory. She slid into the hot water with silent thanks, and brought soap and sponge nearby so she could begin her bath. Soon soapsuds covered the surface of the water and she was scrubbing the dirt and filth of the road from her body. Like her face, her body was lean, hard, almost boyish; sword work and fight training had given her strong shoulders and arms, a limber back, long muscular legs. She was the opposite of the soft, curvy ideal so prized by Danian and Aurian custom, which suited her just fine.

Her fingers slipped between her legs, and she started to clean herself, and as she did her mind wandered. She could feel pressure in her chest and the back of her throat, a slight shortness of breath. Her mind drifted to Stjepan, and poor handsome Guilford, and to a pretty young Danian woman who had smiled at her on the High Promenade. Her breath grew quicker, and her fingers were no longer engaged in cleaning.

She didn't allow herself to finish, but stood up after a bit, the water slicking off her warm skin. She dried off with a towel, and slipped a long, fresh, clean linen shirt over her head that came down to almost mid-thigh, and went and sat down on her bed. She could smell bleach and flowers from the fresh sheets.

There's so much to do today, she thought. *The whole city beckons, and I've got fresh coin in my pocket. And then Gilgwyr's tonight, and the start of our new adventure. Gladringer, the sword of the High Kings. One for the history books, indeed.* Despite her excitement, she could feel the lids of her eyes growing heavy, her breath slowing as she lay back against the goose down pillow. She didn't want to fall asleep; she was picturing herself wandering the Grand Promenade, and perhaps eating some fried fish down at the food stands at the Plaza of the Bay, thinking of all the ways she could get herself into a bit of trouble, but the soft bed felt very good beneath her. The Countess leapt up onto the bed, and curled up next to her and started purring and licking herself. Erim scratched her behind the ears, and stroked her soft fur.

And soon Erim was fast asleep, softly snoring as the temple bells rang the call for mid-morning prayers in the distance.

CHAPTER TWO

⊙Π THE WAY
TO THE FORUΠ

G ilgwyr walked down the street, his cock freshly sucked and the world his oyster. He didn't just walk, no; he *strode*, he *sauntered*, he *strutted*. He whistled a jaunty tune, a self-satisfied smirk playing across his long, narrow features. *Today is a great day*, he thought. *Truly, a blessed day*.

Having a freshly sucked cock was not the cause of such joy. Indeed, for Gilgwyr, being the owner of a brothel, a freshly sucked cock would hardly have been something to brag about. He took great pride, however, in not sampling the wares of his own shop needlessly. He considered it beneath him, the mark of a poor pimp, to demand services from the women in his employ—or for that matter from the handful of men, and those in between, that called his establishment, the Sleight of Hand, their home, for Gilgwyr was well known as a genuine libertine willing to cater to just about every predilection, despite the threat of the holy writ of the Inquisition of the Sun Court. Gilgwyr considered himself an expert in the many varieties of female flesh that crossed the city from the corners of the Known World, and at one point or another had sampled them all. The local women—dark-haired, fair-skinned Danians and blonde-haired, fair-skinned Aurians, or those who mixed both lineages—could certainly be beautiful enough, though they tended to be soft and perhaps a bit plump for his tastes and, given the teachings of the Divine King that most had been brought up with, given to more conservative sexual habits. Dark-haired Maecite girls from the Watchtower Coast and the cursed hills of the west tended to be short and scrawny and a bit underfed, but were usually wild in the sack. The Athairi were rare in an establishment like his; their *fae*-born looks and lithe bodies made them an exotic treat, but their culture, steeped in the Old Religion, was quite liberal, and the notion of charging money for sexual favors was somewhat alien to them. But every now and then he would luck out and an Athairi dancer from a traveling troupe would spend some pleasant hours entertaining his customers on her back just for the fun of it. Or even better an Athairi man, as the blood of satyrs often ran deep in their veins.

He had dusky, brown-skinned Sekereti in his stable, and curly-haired Galians, and showcased them to give the Sleight of Hand a decadent, imperial flavor. He had brown- and ebony-skinned Amorans amongst his girls, as the Amorans had for some years been establishing a presence in the Foreign Quarter of the city, though he had yet to score one of the dark southerners from the Mountains of Gold across the Ulik Desert. He had statuesque blondes and redheads with pale, freckled skin from the far north, bought from the Palatian slave trade. He had a woman from the Dawn Isles, and a woman from the far west who still smelled sweetly of the spices of Samarappa. He had Highlander courtesans from Daradja, down from the mountains; they were a mixed bag in terms of looks, a veritable melting pot of nations, but were usually strong and tall and lean, and well versed in the sexual arts. Women from the cities of Déskédré who had been trained in the great temples of Dieva there were, of course, the most prized by his customers: bronze-skinned beauties with long dark curly hair, wide, supple hips, and full breasts, who knew all the secrets of the Goddess of Pleasure; for Dieva the Evening Star had given the world fellatio and cunnilingus, copulation and buggery and much more in her twenty-two sacred positions and all their seemingly infinite orgiastic combinations. Though to his personal tastes copper-skinned Palatians and exotic Thulamites made the best dancers.

Generally speaking he was actually bored with all of them, and found it something of a recruitment aid that he treated the entertainers in his service with some measure of respect, and even kindness. Any brothel owner could be a thug, and beat his girls, and take them whenever he wanted, and plenty in the festering underbelly of this great city did just that; but Gilgwyr had no intention of being just *any* brothel owner. The Sleight of Hand might not have been a temple to Dieva, but it was the closest thing to one that could be found in this city. There was no doubt that one or two would occasionally catch his eye and his mood—there was that gorgeous young man from Umat with one of the most beautiful cocks Gilgwyr had ever seen, for example; and the brand new girl, Ariadesma, a Palatian acrobat and dancer who had spent several years in Dieva's temples in Lagapoli was the cream of the crop, a petite beauty with an innocent angelic face, long, supple legs, a tight firm ass, pert breasts, a saucy temperament, and a trick with a bottle that he found quite thrilling—but rarely would he ever seek the pleasure of their company.

No, when it came to getting his cock sucked, Gilgwyr played a different and more difficult game, for he much preferred his customers to be sucking his cock, rather than his employees. Their gender didn't have much to do with it, though obviously the bulk of his customers were men; Gilgwyr didn't care what was on the other end of his prick, as long as it was wet and ever so slightly unwilling. Not quite blackmail, no; given his business, he was the holder of many deep dark twisted secrets, and that would have been the easy route. But easy did not excite Gilgwyr. He considered simple outright blackmail not only beneath him, but ultimately bad for business in the long run, and there were uses aplenty for the kinds of things that Gilgwyr knew about the more sordid and perverse patrons of his brothel.

No, for Gilgwyr's little game, the idea had to come *from the customer* for it to play right in his head, and opportunities at least abounded. He let young noblemen run tabs until they were deep in debt and begging to do anything, *anything*, for him not to go to their wealthy fathers for payment. Sometimes one of the girls would forget to drink their *pennyroyal* potents, and some poor married slob would find himself an impending father by accident, and who would not offer to suck a cock to get out from that under that stroke of ill fortune? Customers never had enough money, never had enough friends, someone always needed that extra favor, and inevitably one of them would ask, "Look, what can I do to make this happen? I really, really need for this to happen," with just the right look of desperation in their eyes. And then they would wind up on their knees, doing their best to please him. And the moment he looked for, the moment that gave him the sharpest thrill, was the moment when some of them discovered they liked it.

This particular morning had been a special treat, for the lips wrapped around his cock had belonged to none other than a member of the afore-mentioned Inquisition, and a seemingly devout one at that. Young Alain had been dispatched by his superiors on a secret mission, to procure a beau-tiful young woman for a secret rite, but the young Templar had been chosen because of his devoutness, his loyalty, and his discretion, not because of any particular knowledge he had on where to find such a woman, and he had despaired at first. Finally Alain had quietly asked one of the older Templars, Sir Berrick of Édain, whom he considered a worldly man, about how to find a prostitute; and while Sir Berrick didn't really know about such things either, he was able to introduce Alain to his friend Under-Captain Gerard Torgis of the City Watch. Captain Gerard knew a few things about finding a prostitute but being something of a devout man himself this was only as a result of his duties and not from personal experience, so he was actually not much help; but he took pity on the devout young man—assuming that the Templar was seeking to lose his virginity—and referred Alain to one of his Watchmen, Baldwin Summers, whom the Captain knew to be a man of bad habits but good taste. Baldwin was true to his reputation and introduced Alain to Gilgwyr, much to Gilgwyr's good fortune and eternal thanks.

When Gilgwyr had heard the young man's request that morning, he had pretended to blanch; for the rite was one long forbidden and only whispered of in old books. Luckily Gilgwyr had read those old books. Some men might have spent their time at University studying the great elixirs of alchemy, or the wisdom of Acelsus' *Khodex di Aballah ibn Basillus et Basilla* (*The Book of Words for Lords and Ladies* in translation), but not Gilgwyr. Such things had bored him to tears, and he'd spent his time in the great Library tracking down every lurid and obscene legend and report ever written in the history of letters. And so he knew that Islik, the Divine King of Heaven, had been born of the union of the mortal woman, Herrata the Blessed, and Illiki the Bull, one of the gods of the sun. Everyone knew that, of course, that wasn't the lurid part, and Illiki

78

was depicted in most temple sculptures and art as a man with a bull's head and a sun's halo, but occasionally He was shown as just a bull. The Feast of Herrata, held during the next month of Ascensium, celebrated the Divine King's mother and His holy conception. Less well known was that in more ancient and less civilized times, the climax of the feast was a reenactment of that conception, with a priestess of the cult of Herrata standing in for the Sacred Mother, and a priest of the cult of Illiki wearing a golden bull mask and standing in for the Sun Bull and Sacred Father. Gilgwyr very much suspected that the rite had been copied from the ancient Athairi Spring Queen rites, when the priestesses would lay with men in the fields in order to ensure the earth's fertility. He'd thought about writing a paper to that effect, but did not think any of the Magisters would have accepted it for consideration.

But thanks to his lecherous researches, Gilgwyr knew that beginning in 970ia, the High Patriarch Hereclaus had instituted a different version of the reenactment in the celebrations at the Sun Court itself, and according to dark legend each year of his reign he had chosen the most beautiful amongst the priestesses of Herrata, and had her fornicate with an actual bull painted in gold.

Needless to say this was not a much talked-about period in the Sun Court's long and checkered past. After Hereclaus' brutal and difficult reign as Patriarch was over, ended by a trial in which he was convicted as an adherent to Ligrid and other Forbidden Gods and then tortured to death, the reenactment of the Divine King's conception was officially banned from the rites of the Feast of Herrata in any form. And so it had been in the five centuries since. But Alain's superiors knew someone of power and position that very much wanted to see such a thing during the upcoming Feast, a fanatic that felt the Sun Court had strayed from its true and ancient teachings. This someone had already reinstituted the reenactments of the Divine King's holy conception in his private temple, having a man with a golden bull mask copulate the local priestess of Herrata during their celebration of the Feast. But this someone didn't think that was a true enough reenactment of the divine act. This someone of power Alain's superiors very much wanted to impress, and this someone would be in Therapoli next month just for the occasion of the next Feast of Herrata, and bringing his favorite stud bull just for the act. An actual priestess of Herrata was presumably out of the question for so extreme a performance, and hence, Alain's path to Gilgwyr's esteemed company.

And so Gilgwyr had found himself faintly protesting: "King of Heaven above. Such a thing. It's . . . unimaginable. It's strictly forbidden, condemned by your own order. And besides, even if I could find someone beautiful enough to stand in for Herrata, and yet also willing enough to contemplate the doing of such a perverse act, the danger to the poor young woman alone would be enough to give me pause . . ."

He had demurred, and protested, wrung his hands and paced and worried, prayed for guidance, all the while watching as the desperation filled Alain's eyes. He finally relented to Alain's pleadings, but only after Alain had agreed to arrange a meeting with his superiors. Gilgwyr would have to play that one carefully. *I have to be there to protect my young charge*, he would explain to them. *I cannot allow one of my girls to come to harm.* Of course, even if she survived the depraved ordeal in one piece it'd be unlikely they'd let her live to talk about it, or him for that matter, and in his mind he already had her death-price fixed, and the possibility of a blood-bound patron in the Inquisition was worth his own weight in gold. But despite all the risks, more than just about anything he very much wanted to be in that room during the performance, to see whom it was that had commanded it. He had his suspicions—rumors of King Colin Corwin Phalia's private little rites had already reached his ear—but he had to know for certain.

And finally, with a bit of coaxing, a bit of prodding, Alain had sealed the deal. "How do I know this isn't some kind of trap, set for me by the Inquisition?" had asked Gilgwyr suspiciously. "What sign can you give me that you will be in as much danger as I, should I make this performance possible?" It didn't take long for them to come to an understanding, and Alain had reluctantly knelt before him.

"King of Heaven, forgive me, but I do this for you!" Alain had breathed right before his lips had slipped over Gilgwyr's erect cock, already stiff to bursting at the image in his mind: *the Feast of Herrata, the high arched halls of the Inquisition's innermost chambers, the spring sunlight falling from stained-glass windows, temple bells ringing in the distance, the assembled Inquisitors and Templars in their ranks, the king of Dainphalia and his knights their honored guests, Gilgwyr as Master of Ceremonies, and in the center of the ring, his beautiful Palatian acrobat getting the wildest, hardest ride of her short, sweet life from a rutting, bellowing golden bull.* And Gilgwyr had looked down, and been very happily surprised at the devout expression on Alain's face as he worshipped on his knees.

That particular bit of good fortune, however, was not the cause of Gilgwyr's great joy that morning, but rather had merely been the feather in the cap of a string of good news. That string had begun a week prior, when Sequintus, the aging household enchanter of the Sleight of Hand, had trudged up the steps to Gilgwyr's private chambers to report that a Sending had arrived from Harvald, written in their cipher upon the magic mirror in the enchanter's workshop: *The deed is done. We have it.* No more than that was needed for Gilgwyr to break into a merry jig. He had spent the days prior to that Sending in dark doubt, for he'd gone to three separate fortunetellers who plied their trade in the back alleys behind Murky Street and the omens had been mixed and grim. *Success, yes, but death, much death, and blood, much blood, and much trouble ahead*, they'd hissed at him. He'd even crossed over to the Foreign Quarter to the Street of Shrines and found a woman who claimed to be from Khael and had her perform a Reading of the Book of Dooms, but her report was no different.

Sequintus himself would normally have spent his time contentedly brewing potents of almond oil to make the entertainers their most alluring, or brewing *liveche* leaves, mandrake root, and *baalha* weed into an elixir to increase the lusts of entertainer and customer alike. But in the days that followed that happy message, instead (and much to his great annoyance) he found himself trudging his rusty bones up and down the steps to Gilgwyr's chambers to report more news. The first Sending was followed soon by others, indicating that Harvald and Stjepan were both safe and secure; that they were making with all due haste to return to the capital; and that they had the map and would attempt its translation upon their arrival in the city.

With each Sending, Gilgwyr grew more and more excited. Three days ago the Sending from Harvald had made him positively giddy: *I've convinced him. Summon Leigh for the expedition.* And finally the Sending of the night before: *We arrive tomorrow. Expect us at the Hand by midnight. Gather a crew.*

The night of the first Sending he'd had dreams, beautiful, wonderful dreams. And the dreams had only gotten stronger and more vivid with each passing night. He felt blest, star-touched, *fae*-kissed, so lucky to be alive. He was convinced they stood on the precipice of a great achievement that would change their lives, and possibly the world, forever. He arose that morning knowing that Harvald and Stjepan would soon be in the city, if they were not there already. He knew Harvald would have some duties to attend to at his father's city house, and that Stjepan would most likely hit the baths and then report to the High King's Hall. But then tonight they would all be together and he would see the map. *Today is going to be a blessed day*, he thought. That his night of beautiful dreams was followed in the morning by the surprise possibility of a bit of intrigue involving a mysterious man of power and a lewd, forbidden rite, and Gilgwyr felt like he was already in Heaven.

Of course, not all the news had been wholly good. He had expressed appropriate sadness over the deaths of poor Guilford of Vesslos and his entire crew, and though he had never met any of the poor sods he had paid some of the girls some extra coin to go down to the temples and offer daily prayers for their safe journey on the Path of the Dead, and drew a black tear below the corner of his left eye to indicate he was in mourning. And he was in mourning, of a sort, for their mass deaths had left him with a problem to fix, and so that morning after getting his cock freshly sucked by the desperate and eager Templar, he'd dressed in his best dark finery and strolled out for a solution. He'd picked a dark damask doublet with gold buttons, black silk breeches, black hose, and black leather shoes with gold buckles, and a dark purple half-coat with fur trim against the chill spring air. The ruffles of his silk shirt billowed out from the sleeves of his doublet and coat. He tucked soft leather calfskin gloves into his tooled leather belt, and dangled a jeweled dagger and plain money belt from one side. A black, wide-brimmed tricorn hat with gold lace trim and gold buttons adorned his head. His codpiece, in contrast, was bright red, and was shaped into quite an obscene bulge, as fit his current peacock mood.

He looked quite the mourning dandy, then, as he sauntered and strutted down the Street of Silks toward the Grand Promenade of the lower city. He tipped his hat to worthy ladies as he passed them, and laughed and sneered at their askance glances. He nodded resolutely to a pair of grim-faced country knights as they stared and frowned, their colors showing they were men of Enlos on the eastern shore. *Stuck between the sea and the hill lords of Umis, no wonder you're humorless bastards*, he thought. Every now and then someone from amongst the street vendors or shopkeepers would shout out "Ho, Master Gilgwyr. Good morrow to you!" since he and his house did a great deal of business amongst the silk merchants, and he would wave in response.

In excellent humor he hit the main thoroughfare of the lower city, the Grand Promenade, and blended into its teeming throngs. During the day the wide avenue was a constant stream of people, animals, and wagons, and Gilgwyr stopped looking at the faces of the passing crowds and simply concentrated on moving as quickly and safely as possible through the bustling masses. The Street of Silks deposited him onto the Promenade fairly close to the Forum, his current destination, so he did not have to suffer the jostling and shouting crowds for long before he'd slipped through the outer arches of the Forum and into the quieter inner arcade of the Market. Once inside he relaxed and strolled its shops, pretending to be interested in one stall selling glassware and copperware from Palatia, in another's fine selection of amethyst jewelry and *blancha* pearls from Amora and Meretia, and in the heap of furs that the seller swore were Daradjan wolf pelts but that

Gilgwyr was certain were the smaller Gray wolf variety dyed black, until he reached a quiet corner meeting house offering strong spiced drinks from the ends of the Known World (Sabuta, to be exact, beyond the Mountains of Gold).

He stepped inside and immediately spotted his quarry, no great feat considering that Guizo the Fat was indeed one of the fattest men in the city, and even seated took up the larger part of the back wall of the small meeting house. Guizo was also an Amoran, with dark brown skin that was almost black and wiry black hair trimmed close to his scalp, and therefore part of a distinct minority in the city. He had not set up shop in the Foreign Quarter of the city, where most of the other Amorans lived and worked, but had chosen this spot in the Forum as his domain, and Gilgwyr could not remember ever seeing him elsewhere. Gilgwyr had wondered before if they simply cut a hole in the seat beneath him so that the obese man could shit himself without having to move.

Some rough-looking Amoran and Danian toughs occupied the chairs and tables nearest the doorway. Gilgwyr nodded silent greetings to Guizo's obviously hostile crew as they eyed him over, but as usual none of them tried to stop him as he strode past them to the back, doffed his hat with a small bow, ran a hand through his slicked-back black hair, and slipped into the seat opposite Guizo, briefly upsetting the small flock of sparrows that hopped about the table pecking at the fat man's crumbs.

"Master Guizo," he said with a toothy grin. "I trust the Dawn Maiden has welcomed you into this day with open arms."

"Master Gilgwyr," Guizo said, barely looking up from the navel orange he was peeling, one of the first of the spring season. The effort involved in the simple task was enough to make him wheeze softly. "I am not used to seeing you so early in the day. Indeed, I am surprised you even know there is a Dawn Maiden."

"My profession keeps me mostly in the company of her more accommodating sister, I admit," Gilgwyr said cheerily. "But urgent matters have roused me from slumber and sped me to your noble presence."

"No," said Guizo.

"I beg your pardon?" asked Gilgwyr.

"I said *no*," said Guizo, before popping a slice of orange into his wide mouth. He chewed it for a long moment, then swallowed, and wheezed. "I cannot help you."

"You don't even know what I'm going to ask," Gilgwyr said, his smile frozen.

"Who do you think you are talking to?" breathed the fat man. "Do you think you are the only man in this city to deal in knowledge?" He leaned forward to rest his heavy elbows on the table, almost tipping it over, and sending several sparrows to flutter in the air before coming to rest again. "Rumor has already visited my table many times this morning, since before the first fishing boats set sail to ply the waters of the bay. She whispered to me that the spring thaw had come early, and that the first Daradj merchants were already being hosted in the halls of An-Andria, with a batch of wyvern eggs intended for market. She whispered to me that a fine pearl necklace had gone missing from the city house of the Baron of Chesterton during the night. She whispered to me that the King's Shadow had woken up on the wrong side of the bed this morning, and had already signed the secret death warrants of ten men before breakfast. She whispered to me that the Lady Freya of Caes Coryd had arrived at first light with an entourage, ostensibly to commission a set of fine new dresses in the latest style for use in the Tourney circuit this summer, but secretly in the hopes of cuckolding her husband, Lord Oslac. That last one I extend to you for free, as Rumor also says that Lady Freya is quite beautiful," he said with a weak smile. "And Rumor set down at my table this very morning and whispered to me that Stjepan Black-Heart had returned to the city not more than an hour ago, fresh from leading eight men to their deaths in a hidden temple to the Nameless Cults of the Damned, somewhere in the blasted heaths of the Manon Mole."

"Yes, well," said Gilgwyr with a shrug and a sigh. "*Rumor.* I mean, you can't believe everything she tells you. In fact I have it on good authority that the Lady Freya looks like a baboon."

Guizo laughed, his jowls and neck quivering. "Regardless, the answer to whatever Black-Heart wants will be *no*."

"My dear Guizo, I am at a loss," Gilgwyr said, genuinely puzzled. "I admit that I am indeed here on behalf of Stjepan Black-Heart, and I know things didn't work out entirely the way we expected the last time we all did business together, but due to unfortunate circumstance we find ourselves in need of a crew of hard men willing to take great risks for great reward with as few questions as possible. And I have never known you to not at least listen to the proposition."

"Did you not know?" Guizo asked. "Guilford of Vesslos was a Marked Man."

Gilgwyr went pale, and suddenly he heard the words of the fortunetellers in his head: *death, much death, and blood, much blood, and much trouble ahead.*

"But . . . Stjepan recruited Guilford from Vesslos; they knew each other from serving with the Grand Duke in last summer's campaign against the Earl of Orliac, when Guilford was serving as the levy proxy for some country lordling. They'd fought in the hills together . . ." Gilgwyr said faintly, trying to piece it together.

"Aye, Guilford was from Vesslos, but his father Guy was originally from this city and had gained his Mark before retiring to Vesslos to serve as the Guild's man there," Guizo said, smiling sweetly. "Ah, the infamous Gilgwyr does not know everything, then. But then Guy's time in Therapoli was long before you arrived in the city, and Guilford only spent a few years here to prove his worth in inheriting his father's Mark before returning home, so you shouldn't feel too bad."

"I'm afraid that Stjepan failed to mention this small set of details," Gilgwyr said, idly wondering if there was any way he could get the Inquisition to accept an Athairi man for use in their secret rite.

"That is the third Marked Man in whose death Black-Heart has had a hand," Guizo said quietly. "Siobras Faine was the first, who died in a brawl started during the War of the False Book, when he followed Black-Heart into battle against the men of Highwall College. The second was Mud Street Maris, who died on Black-Heart's sword after Black-Heart interrupted Maris raping a young boy. And now Guilford, son of Guy, dying at the hands of the Nameless. Black-Heart is still alive now only because the Princes of the Guild have found him useful in the past and expect to do so in the future; because two of those deaths were of men who willingly followed him; and because the third was richly deserved. Any other man not of the Guild responsible for the deaths of three of the Marked would be a dead man and cursed, bound for Limbo."

"Surely . . . surely Black-Heart will be allowed to speak in his defense to the entire Court of Princes," said Gilgwyr, thinking furiously.

"The Princes consider this a purely administrative matter," said Guizo. "It is not a matter of the Court's Judgment, requiring a hearing. Black-Heart had not been condemned; he has simply been . . . black-listed." A small smirk played over Guizo's fat lips, and Gilgwyr considered stabbing the fat man, but then thought better of it.

Gilgwyr licked his lips. "But . . . if you were to simply hear him out; there are riches beyond measure at stake, and I think you know I not a man to exaggerate . . ." Gilgwyr said, barely able to contain himself. He felt like screaming out *it's the Barrow of Azharad, you fat fool! It's fucking* Gladringer *that Black-Heart is after!* But the truth was that if the Guild were to turn its back on them then the fewer people that knew their intent, the better.

"It will not matter what the proposition is, my dear Gilgwyr," said Guizo with a sad sigh. "No man of the Guild will help you, or Black-Heart, in this matter." Guizo leaned forward even more. "Indeed, from me, you can tell Black-Heart to go to the Hell of his fucking choosing."

Gilgwyr heard the finality in Guizo's tone, and despite his desperation he knew that there was nothing he could say that would get him a different answer. Anger burned in him, that his fine mood of the morning was now so thoroughly and rudely spoiled, and he stood.

"My dear Guizo," said Gilgwyr with a dangerous smile as he slipped his tricorn back on his head. "Let me repay the sharing of your Rumor-hoard with some of mine own from last night. The men come down early from Daradja are not merchants, but brigands of the Bloody Hundred, their wyvern eggs the eggs of condors painted to fool those none the wiser.

87

Before the day is out they will have committed murder in An-Andria, avenging the death of their brethren at the hands of Baron Avant's knights last fall. The pearl necklace from the house of Chesterton can be found for sale in the back room of Ginty's Tavern on the Street of Sails; knock three times and say you're looking for Pellas the Quick. Lady Freya is indeed very beautiful, and quite eager to be laid, but Lord Oslac is well aware of her intentions. He slipped incognito into the city last night ahead of his wife, not to stop her, but to arrange to watch her debauchery in secret, and even now he conspires with the owners of the Gabled Inn to make his voyeurism possible." Finally he leaned in a bit more closely, his voice barely a whisper. "And my dear Guizo, the King's Shadow did not sign *ten* death warrants this morning, he signed *eleven*; but the reason your contact told you it was ten was because the eleventh warrant is for you. You'll be dead within the week."

At that he straightened, and saluted Guizo with a touch to the brim of his tricorn. "All that I have just told you is true, save for one thing. I'll let you guess which one was the lie," he said, and turned and walked out of the meeting house.

Behind him, Guizo wheezed and laughed.

Gilgwyr stood beneath the arches of the Forum's arcade, breathing heavily and watching the sea of people flow past. *By the gods we're fucked*, he thought. He thought of turning to another Prince of the Guild, perhaps to Bad Mowbray or the Gilded Lady, to see if there was a way he could appeal to the entire Court, but in his heart he knew there was no way around it. He wondered when the decision had been made, and why no one had told him directly, and he grew even angrier; *they've been watching and waiting, waiting for me to come to them, just to see me twist in the wind.* He toyed with the notion that Guizo might have just been spinning the tale out of spite because of that last botched job, but he knew that was just false hope, as no sane man would ever lie about the rulings of the Princes and expect to live, not even one of the Princes themselves. No, better to abandon any thought of a Guild crew on this barrow run, he knew, and instead start thinking of the independents that worked in the margins of the city, scratching their living out on the scraps and leavings of the Guild. *Better that way anyway*, he rationalized; *less quality, but more control.* He'd have to move fast, however. Now that he'd been told, word would start to trickle down that the Guild had blacklisted Black-Heart, and then everyone would want to say no.

And so Gilgwyr launched himself into the flowing crowds on the Promenade, trying in his mind to sort out whom to ask first. Their old friend Jonas the Grey and his crew would probably say yes, but Harvald didn't like Jonas very much, too much history there. Tyrius and his Hooded Men had broken up the month before, squabbling over the spoils of a minor robbery. The Temple Street Irregulars had just been jailed, the entire lot of them, for raping the daughter of a minor spice merchant; since the merchant was not particularly wealthy and had no noble patron, Gilgwyr wondered if perhaps a few coins in the right hands at the City Watch could get them sprung. There was that Amoran crew over in the Foreign Quarter that did good work, under Rafaelas Huelas, but they'd never been outside the city before. Pellas, perhaps, fresh from his robbery of the Baron of Chesterton? The gutter rats that belonged to Jon Deering down by Old South Road? Red Rob Asprin's men, themselves already blacklisted by the Guild?

As the honor roll of the city's worst ran through Gilgwyr's head, he pressed through the jostling throng, his mind divided between finding just the right name and gleefully devising ways to murder Stjepan Black-Heart. He thought of the beautiful dreams he'd been having, and the feeling of a young Templar's sweet lips on his cock. *Today is a great day, a blessed day*, he thought to himself, *and soon will come the best day of all.*

And he whistled jauntily while he walked, his codpiece bright red and bulging.

CHAPTER THREE
IN THE CITY HOUSE OF
THE BARON OF ARASWELL

*T*oday will be a day like any other, Annwyn thought. *A day in which I will pray to die, and yet will live.* She looked at the candle-lit reflection in her finely polished mirror and would have wept, had the last of her tears not left her years ago.

The beauty for which she'd once been famous had not been drained from her face with her tears; if anything, she might have been even more beautiful than when she was younger. Smooth, pale alabaster skin that had not seen direct sun in years; straight golden hair like silk, being pulled back and worked into a bun by her handmaidens; full pale lips, wet and glistening. She wore no rouge or powder. Her beauty was not marred by the overwrought efforts that other women took to improve upon what the gods had given them, and so perhaps for that reason the gods had rewarded her by making her beauty seemingly impossible to improve upon. Her clear blue eyes were the only things to tarnish her looks, being, as poets and bards had long ago declared, the so-called windows to the soul; for as her soul was dead, so too were her eyes.

Not that that mattered much in the minds of men when they had the now-rare opportunity to look upon her, for she had always found that most men looked at the surface of a woman and rarely looked inside. She was hardly the first to think that, and she knew she would not be the last. But the very predictability of their stares and banality of their pleasant compliments came down on her like a crushing weight, made her feel like she was drowning; and so even if she had been allowed to step outside the doors to her father's house on her own, she would not have done so willingly.

Had she been allowed to lie in bed all day, and simply wait to die, she would have gladly done so. But since her mother was herself long dead, Annwyn was now the Lady of the house, with a myriad of small duties to attend to and a household to run. And so that morning she allowed her handmaidens to rouse her from her bed before the coming of the Dawn Maiden, and dress her in her daily mourning clothes: first a silk shift and hose as her undergarments, then a plain black petticoat, and finally a long full-length dress of black brocade silk. For footwear, the more daring fashion of the moment in Therapoli was for thickly heeled shoes and boots, a style imported from decadent and censured Palatia, and once upon a time she might have enjoyed the sense of danger; but only once upon a time, and all she had were flat black shoes to choose from. The fashion for the upper garment was still either the square-cut or arched front bodice; amongst the younger and more fashionable, the cut would come quite low, exposing what cleavage was available to show. But Annwyn wore a black velvet brocaded bodice that buttoned clear up to her chin, with hanging half-sleeves over a black silk shirt, and was thus more in the style of the conservative women of the Hemapoline League of Cities across the *Mera Argenta*.

Her handmaidens dressed in imitation of her, when in her presence. She knew that when they went out on errands without her most of them changed into more fashionable bodices and higher heels, particularly the youngest of them, Henriette and Ilona, both unmarried and hopeful for husbands. Well, almost all of them except Malia Morwin, the oldest and closest of her handmaidens and the sole Danian girl in her personal service, who had seemingly chosen a life of spinsterhood. Malia always wore a high-buttoned bodice in the style of her mistress no matter whether she was in Annwyn's presence or not. *Lady Annwyn's Widows*, she knew that they were sometimes called, particularly when on the rare occasion she had to accompany her father or her brothers on some duty about the city, and brought her full entourage. She supposed they were quite the sight to the twittering mocking birds of the High King's Court.

When she was finally dressed and presentable as Annwyn Aliss Orwain, only daughter of Baron Leonas Orwain of Araswell, she and her hand-maidens descended in the dark to the first floor of the great tower house, to the household shrine to their ancestors and the Divine King. Once upon a time, when the household was in its full power, almost a hundred members of the household staff would have awaited her arrival; but now, with the family out of favor in the years after the scandal, just under forty were left. Her father and two of her older brothers, Conrad and Leon, were unexpectedly out in the field with the Grand Duke Owen Lis Red, Crown Prince Edrick, and King Colin of Dainphalia, somewhere on the Plain of Gavant, and were not expected back in the city for weeks, not until before the Feast of Herrata. Campaign season and tourney season were not yet upon them, but once the first of spring had come, they had lit out for the plains to shake off the winter doldrums and prepare for the duties of the coming summer, and brownnose with those who would still entertain their presence. When she had been younger, she would have accompanied them, for all sorts of girlish reasons, but she did not ever think upon those lovely days now.

Archpriest Oslac, the highest Divine King priest of their baronial canton, held his duties to be at their household temple in their country estates at Araswell, as was good and proper, and so remained there even when her father was in Therapoli. Instead he sent one of his assistants, Theodras the Learned, to serve as her father's personal priest and advisor when he was away from Araswell, and Theodras had left with him for the Plain of Gavant. Once upon a time they would have had more priests to go around, but the scandal had made it much harder to keep the posts filled. Her eldest brother, Arduin, was left in charge of the household and the family's affairs at the High King's Court, but she knew he would not appear for the morning prayers, while her second eldest brother, Albrecht, held the family's home castle at Araswell with his knights. And as for her younger brother, Harvald, well, she had not seen him for weeks, and she cared not at all to find out where he was hiding himself.

So that left it to her as lady of the house to lead the morning rites. There in the shrine she lit candles and made libations to Islik, the Divine King of Heaven, and to Ami the Morning Star, the Dawn Maiden who would soon herald the sun's arrival. She offered prayers for the health and safety of Awain Gauwes Urfortian, High King of the Middle Kingdoms, King of Atallica, Dragon King of Therapoli, Seated King of the Sun Court, True Vassal of the Divine King, and for his Court and household. She offered prayers for the health and safety of her father and brothers, and to the memory of her beloved mother. She offered prayers and libations to the noble ancestors of her family, a storied Aurian lineage that could be traced back to the very shield-thanes of the household of King Orfeydda himself, conqueror of this great city; a prouder lineage, in some ways, than even that of the High King, who was not descended of Orfeydda or his household, as her father was sometimes proud to point out. Over a thousand years ago her ancestors had been amongst the first to step foot on the Gift of Heth, the Aurian name for the eastern shore of the Middle Kingdoms, and bring fire and sword first to the eastern Danians and then to the Athairi. Things were gladly different in the present age, of course, and now Aurian, Danian, Athairi, and Maecite Kings and nobles and their subjects all lived peaceably, side by side, united under the High King.

If she wanted to add another name to her prayers, she gave no sign, but everyone in the shrine knew she wished to, and as all that still remained in their household all loved her, their hearts broke for her when hers could not.

And when her duties in the shrine were finally done, she dispatched the household to begin their own. The windows of the first floor were thrown open, and the slowly brightening light of dawn allowed to enter into the dark house. The kitchens on the ground floor began to hum and crackle with the preparations for the morning meal and the stoking of the cooking fires, and soon the smell of baking bread was wafting through the house. Groomsmen tended to the horses in the rear stables, and lit the fires and braziers in the first floor great hall. The floors were swept, and fresh rushes strewn about to freshen the scent. The squires were dispatched upstairs to prepare the clothes of her brother and the knights of the household that still remained. And then slowly one by one those same worthies arrived in the great hall to take their seats and break their nightly fasts, with those of the knights that were married joining their wives from amongst the household and her handmaidens at their tables. Finally her brother

arrived and set himself at the head table, and many of the rest of the household then sat down at their places, and though others still bustled about
the house on their duties the meal finally commenced: bread and pastries
with butter and olive oil for dipping, hard and soft cheeses, roasted chest-
nuts and hazelnuts with dried figs, fresh oranges and pears, Danian *tour-
tels* (herbed egg-and-spinach tarts that had become quite popular amongst
their Aurian overlords), and poached eggs in a savory mushroom sauce.

Had her father been present, she would have been expected to take
her place at the head table between him and her brother Arduin; but she
gave silent thanks whenever he was abroad in the field, as that allowed her
to claim her duties drew her elsewhere, and Arduin at least never pressed
her. She ate sparingly, and alone, as was her wont, in a small room off the
kitchens that served as her day chamber while the meal was being prepared
for everyone else.

And so that day began like every other that she could remember in a
long, long time. She spent that morning going over the household books
of account with Malia and the master of kitchens, Tomas, reading aloud as
she entered notes into the ledgers about the morning's deliveries from the
various merchants and vendors beholden to her father's house. Reading was
a rare skill amongst Aurian noblewomen, even for the lady of the house;
but after the scandal, her scandal, they had found it impossible to retain
a chief steward of any quality. And so she had taught herself to read and
write, with the help of Tomas and a tutor from the University that she had
discreetly hired. She still had to whisper the words aloud, even when by
herself, but reading was perhaps her only remaining pleasure in life.

She broke from her work only to wish her brother and his knights
a speedy return from their duties at Court and about the city. She felt
the cloying darkness lift off of her shoulders as they rode out through
the rear stable gates, and for the first time that morning she felt like she
could breathe. The house itself seemed lighter, and brighter, as though the
windows had suddenly grown larger. Sirs Lars and Colin Urwed and their
squires were the only ones to remain behind as the House Watch; she knew
their duty was as much to be her minders as it was to protect the house-

hold of her father, but she did not begrudge them their dual mission, for it was not due to any fault of theirs, and for the most part they left her to her own devices.

Annwyn returned to her day chamber and was working there with Malia when she heard the commotion at the rear gates and knew without having to ask that her brother Harvald had suddenly returned. She raised her head, listening to his voice in the rear courtyards talking to Sir Colin, and she took a deep breath, feeling that familiar oppressive darkness settle upon her once more, and she tried to calm the troubled knots in her stomach before standing and smoothing the folds and pleats of her dress and bodice. Malia barely looked at her, simply standing and falling in behind her as she walked out of the room and toward the great hall. Malia's face was a smooth mask, much like her own. *And so this house makes all of us such great actors and dissemblers*, Annwyn thought. *That is the inevitable price to be found, when you live in a prison of despair.*

She walked down the rear steps of the house into the rear courtyard, passing several porters carrying small bags and boxes, presumably intended for Harvald's chambers. Groomsmen were already stabling Harvald's horse, and her brother stood talking with Sir Colin and his squire, Herefort Hrum. She chose to stand and wait for him at the bottom of the steps, seeing no need to interrupt the warm welcome he was receiving, while Malia lingered several steps up behind her.

But finally Harvald spotted her waiting, and excused himself to come and greet her.

"Annwyn. Dearest sister," he said, clasping her hands and bringing them to his lips so he could kiss each in turn. He leaned in and kissed her once on each cheek. "My heart is gladdened to see you brightening the steps of our father's house." He looked past her to take in her chief hand-maiden. "And loyal Malia, my greetings to you as well."

"Dear brother," Annwyn said softly, as Malia gave a slight curtsey. *I did not know you had a heart.* She took in the dust and mud splattered across his boots and breeches, the state of his hair and the stubble on his chin, and the knot in her stomach grew tighter. She willed herself to blankness, and said nothing about his appearance. "Welcome home to our father's house, and to our fair city. I thank the King of Heaven that he watched over your safe return."

"I have traveled far, dearest and most beloved sister, and hopefully return with a prize that may help reinstate the fortunes of our great family," he said with a grin. "I gather that Father is in the field? I suppose that's well enough. My news should remain a secret for the moment, as he would think me a foolish dreamer, as he always does." He paused, contemplating her, and she waited for his game to begin. "You know, I was originally thinking there was too much to do, but seeing you here, so fresh and beautiful, has reminded me of how poorly the road has treated me. I think perhaps a bath is in order. I hope you do not mind the burden of my company?" he said as he placed a hand on her elbow and steered her back toward the house.

"Your company is never a burden, dear brother," she said quietly, as they walked up the stairs into the dark hall, Malia trailing in silence and sorrow behind them.

For what were once a sea-going people descended of Heth, God of the Sea and the Deep, Aurians had a decided aversion to water in large volumes. For where once they had sailed out of the Far North on their longships and spread terror to the shores of the *Mera Argenta*, they were now landlocked, cursed at sea by their own ancestor-god for their hubris and their crimes, and so they had abandoned his worship for that of the Divine King. Annwyn had never seen the curse take effect, though she had heard the stories in her youth, and the Bay of Guirant outside the city was supposedly littered across its bottom with hundreds of ships and the bodies of thousands of her countrymen, called down into the Deep by their ancestral god. And so they were now country lords, who turned their backs on the sea and instead only traveled where their feet or horses could take them.

Over the centuries that fear of the sea had permeated into their culture as a general distrust of water. The more ancient cities of the eastern Middle Kingdoms, Therapoli in particular, had been built in the age of Düréan expansion, and echoed the architecture and achievements of their Great Palace culture, which included aqueducts, underground cisterns, fountains, waterworks, and baths. Any house of quality in the city had pipes that brought water from the city cisterns; but whether they were actually used for household baths was a separate matter of taste and culture. Aurians tended to avoid the bathhouses of the city, or even the use of a filled bathtub in their own home; rather, they washed using a washbasin, towels or a sponge, and hand soap, and then anointed the body with perfumed oils.

And so the household servants had brought a basin of hot water for his bath up to his chamber from the kitchens, and set it on a table beside a polished, full-length mirror, and then mixed the water with rose petals. They arranged the soaps and towels and sponges by the basin, and then Annwyn dismissed them. Malia lingered, the last of them, and then stepped outside the chamber. Annwyn knew she would be there, listening, as did Harvald.

She turned away as her brother disrobed and stood in front of the mirror, looking at his reflection. She began to wet the bar of soap and the sponges, rubbing them in the water until foam started to appear.

"Things will be different soon, dearest Annwyn," said Harvald, as she started to wash his back. "I can't tell you the details yet, can't talk about it until the time is right, and you probably wouldn't understand anyway, but if what we've found is what we think it is, and we are successful in our next endeavors, then things will change for all of us very soon!" He seemed positively giddy.

"We?" she asked politely, running her hands and soapy sponge over his skin, rubbing away the dirt and grime of days of hard travel.

"Oh, yes, Black-Heart and me and some others we know," he said. "You know, Stjepan, son of Byron, a man of An-Athair. I think I've told you about him before, we went to the University together."

She nodded, as she knelt behind him so that she could wash his buttocks and his legs. "Yes, the one that Father doesn't like," she said.

98

Harvald laughed. "Well, you know Father," he said. "He hates the Athairi worse than he hates the Danians. Can't stand that I'm friends with one of them. And it doesn't help that he blames Stjepan for causing all that nonsense back in the War of the False Book. Quite unfair, really. I mean, Stjepan was hardly the worst offender back then, even if he became one of the most infamous. And we all know I was never going to get higher than a clerkship at the High Court anyway, so that can hardly be Stjepan's fault; I know Father was hoping for the Lord Chamberlain's office, but we'd fallen too far from favor for that, and whose fault is that?"

Harvald turned around. His penis was erect and swollen, jutting angrily toward her face. *My fault*, she thought. He paused, waiting to see if she would react, but as always her face remained an expressionless mask, and instead she soaped the front of his legs and then his erect member, as though it were just another part of him. "No, if this all works out, Father will have to be thankful for me being just a clerk in the Chancery," Harvald said, his eyes never leaving his sister's hands. "It's always about being . . . in the right place at the right time, if you know what I mean."

Yes, I know what you mean, thought Annwyn and she felt as if a dagger had been plunged into her womb. But she did not allow herself to show it. "I'm sure it will all make sense when you get the chance to explain it to me, dear brother," said Annwyn, rising to wash his chest.

"I'm sorry to be so mysterious, dear sister," said Harvald. "You know that normally I would confide in you utterly, as you once confided in me, in happier times." He smiled at her then, and she felt as if he had stabbed her again. She didn't allow her expression to change at all as he searched her face with his gaze. She knew the game was about to start in earnest. She broke eye contact with him so she could turn to the basin. There was a ladle there, and she started to pour water over his body, rinsing away the soapsuds.

"I so miss your singing from when we were all younger," Harvald said softly as she worked. "You never seem to sing anymore, and you had such a beautiful singing voice. Everyone thought so, even the High King. I think especially the High King. What was that Athairi song you used to sing? You know the one."

He waited as she finished rinsing his body. Finally, she said, "The *Chant Amora d'Afare y Argus*. The Love Song of Afare and Argus."

"Ah, yes, that's the one, such a lovely song, so tragic and yet so moving. The Athairi had a beautiful language in those days. It's always impressed me that you mastered the song so well," he said, handing her a bottle of scented body oil from the table, then pausing, looking for any sign of her misery. "Can you sing it for me now, dear sister? Please?"

She remained expressionless as she nodded, refusing to give him any satisfaction. "Of course, dear brother," she said.

And so she turned away a bit, and cast her eyes at the floor, and began to sing as her brother turned back to the mirror. Her voice was perhaps not what it once was, fallen ever so slightly out of tune by years of disuse, but that would be like saying that a rose was slightly less beautiful on the second day after it had freshly bloomed. She sang in old Athairi, which she was not sure her brother fully understood, but not knowing the meaning of the words would not have made the song any less beautiful to listen to. And as she sang, she anointed her brother's back and buttocks with the oil, her hands sliding and slipping over his skin. She sang of Afare, the beautiful young mortal princess of the Court of the Golden Wood, and her True Love, Argus, the Knight of the Green Star. She sang of the disapproval of Afare's father, the *fae* King of the Golden Wood, and his banishment of the knight beyond the Erid Wold of An-Athair.

Her brother turned around and faced her, and as she sang of the undying love of Afare and Argus, she anointed his chest with oil and then slowly sank to her knees before him. As she sang, she slid her oily hands over his erection and his scrotum until his member glistened in the light from the windows. As she sang, his hands closed firmly around hers, and he started moving her hands slowly back and forth along his turgid length. As she sang of the trials and tribulations of the separated lovers, she stroked his member under his guidance, the rhythmic wet sound of the oil under their fingers an accompaniment to her lovely voice, and one of his hands went to the top of her head, tilting her beautiful face up to look at him. Expressionless, she sang to her brother, looking up at his face, seeing it

100

flushed red with anger and seeing the hate in his eyes, the hate he bore her, the hate he bore their family, the hate he bore their father. His mouth open and jaw thrust forward, his nostrils flared as her hands worked faster and faster on the erection before her, and she sang of the star-crossed lovers finally reuniting, their passion and love bright enough to light the sky.

And as she sang of the final doom that overtook them, her brother started to moan, and she stroked him harder and harder until at last he grunted and strings of his seed shot from the head of his swollen, glistening member to splatter down upon her upturned face. She didn't blink or flinch as he ejaculated upon her, didn't miss a note or a word, but sang until he was finished and the song was over, and Afare and Argus were dead.

He left her in silence, afterwards, as he always did, saying nothing to her as he dressed and left, clutching one of his satchels tightly to him. Alone in his chambers, she washed her face in the basin, and dried her skin with a fresh soft towel of cotton. It was only when she looked down into the basin and saw his semen there, mixing in the water with the rose petals, that she allowed revulsion to roll like a wave over her, and she dropped to the floor, shaking and dry-heaving. She would have wept and screamed until her voice was hoarse, but the tears had left her years ago and she knew the screams would only make her brother smile. On her knees she offered up silent prayers to any god that would listen. *Let me die, today, and bring an end to it. Let me be with him again, even if it is in Hell*, she asked.

But no one answered.

Annwyn struggled for long minutes to regain control, and rose finally when she did. She went and opened the door, where Malia, expressionless and silent, stood waiting in the darkness of the hall. Without saying anything to each other, they gathered up the basin and the accouterments of her brother's bath, and then went back downstairs, slowly closing the door behind them on the shadows of the empty room.

CHAPTER FOUR
BAKER STREET

Leigh Myradim, son of Llew of Bainwell, had not been in the city of Therapoli for ten years. When he'd last left it, on his way into ignominious exile with his possessions piled high in an ox-drawn wagon, he had turned back to look at its sienna-colored walls and had screamed a curse down upon it, shaking his fist in the air. "Your bodies will be aged and bent. Your heads and brains will be crushed in iron vises. Your eyes will be put out with pokers burning white and your foreheads will be carved with my name. Your ears and noses will be filled with the shit straight from my bowels. Your fields and pastures will lie fallow and in ruin. Your mouths and throats will be filled with the jism of my loins, your chests and hearts with straw and needles, your stomachs with glass, your blood with urine and fire, your hands and feet and all of your members sawed from your bodies. You will be cursed going in and going out. You will be cursed in your city, in your towns, in your streets and your squares. You will be cursed when sleeping, where you will fall into nightmares from the Six Hells, and when awake, when you will see plague and ashes, boils and festers, fall upon your houses. Wrack and ruin will seize your ports and your markets, your temples and your courts. You will be cursed when eating and when drinking, when everything will taste of ash. You will speak nonsense to each other and hear screams when you are silent. You will pray for death, but the skies will be made of brass, so that the Divine King cannot receive you, and the earth will be made of iron, so that even the damned Underworld will be barred to you. You will be cursed in all places and at all times!"

Cursing an entire city was a tall order for one man, even for one as good a magician and enchanter as Leigh, and he had hardly expected the curse to take hold. Staring out across the broad city upon his return, he was nonetheless disappointed to note that none of those things had, in fact, yet come to pass, and that quite to the contrary, the city seemed to have thrived in his long absence. *Well, we'll just have to fix that*, he thought.

He'd spent the last ten years living, appropriately enough, in a tall haunted wizard's tower secreted in the Sare Wold along the western bank of the Dusabrae. It had been built six hundred years before by Ergedryd Eridaine, a magician from Therapoli who had fled north into the woods after he had been connected, rightly or wrongly, with the mysterious "Bacos Regis," the pseudonymous author of four of the key books of magic and alchemy written during the Bronze Age in the Middle Kingdoms: the *Speculum Alchimiae* (*The Mirror of Alchemy*), *De Alchemia Mirabli* (*The Wonders of Alchemy*), the *Speculum Lapidium* (*The Mirror of Stones*), and the *Speculum Astrologiae* (*The Mirror of Star Signs*). Copies of those books were considered mandatory on the shelves of any Middle Kingdoms practitioner of the hermetic arts, but magical writing invariably attracted all of the wrong attention. A pedigreed and historic home at its start, then, even if no one knew whether Ergedryd had really been the Bacos Regis or not, and even if over the centuries his tower had fallen into disuse and then eventually some dark notoriety. The necromancer Pafeyr the Black had used it for a while, summoning up foul creatures into its highest chamber, and then a century later Doral Galdore had been caught dissecting missing children in its cellars by knights from the Duchy of Har Misal and its reputation had been sealed. Bandits and ghosts and mad *fae* spirits that had seeped up all the way from the Court of the Drowned Wood had occasionally made it their home, and then eventually it had fallen to Leigh to claim its cold and crumbling halls.

He hadn't actually set out to find a haunted wizard's tower, of course, but when a disgraced and exiled Magister is asking around for a quiet place to live and work, it was only natural that the people he asked would look him up and down, shrug, and then direct him toward a place like Ergedryd's tower. When he'd first seen it he'd sighed and shaken his head; the top of the tower was festooned with stone gargoyles, its roof half missing and filled with nesting crows, the uneven steps up to its great door flanked by a series of carved stone statues, most of them defaced into grotesqueness. *Ah, yes, of course, this will surely help my claims of innocence, to take up residence here*, he had thought glumly, and he had sworn to himself that he would only take shelter there for the night before pressing on, perhaps north to Juvic Pass and into the Highlands, where an exiled enchanter could expect a warm welcome.

But he'd stayed the next night, and the night after, and the night after that, finding slowly that the dark, ruined halls suited him. He had kindled hearth fires in its great fireplaces, hung dried rushes in its rooms, and installed his books and laboratory and his precious store of alchemical and herbal ingredients, all the while listening to the whispered secrets of its ghosts and shadow spirits. He had started a small herb and vegetable garden amongst the stone statues that circled the tower, and soon the local woodsmen—deeply superstitious Danians, still secretly worshipping the Old Religion—had discovered his presence there, and they had brought the fruit of their hunts and the tidings of his old world and past life to trade for his potents and tinctures. Missives from that past life would sometimes arrive, either brought by messenger through the woods, or borne in on beating wing, or sometimes even just the wind, which would come and sit by his worktables and whisper words intended for his ears.

In time he found he had made himself a home of sorts, and his thoughts began to turn back toward his exile and then, in turn, toward revenge. He had spent long hours mulling the comeuppance of those that had brought his estate so low, naming each of his fellow Magisters that had spoken against him and enumerating the disasters and tortures that would befall them for their temerity. It became almost a daily litany, whispered as he lay waking in his bed in the evening, or falling asleep as the Dawn Maiden rose; shouted into the wind from the highest parapets of his tower, or down into the echoing well in the cellars; enunciated, reworked, and rephrased while he measured off his potents and elixirs, prepared his meals, made notes in his grimoires.

". . . Magister Fulric, holding the Chair of Argument; he shall be castrated with a dull spoon, then his skin shall be flayed from his body and he will be staked over a fire ant hill. Magister Clodarius, holding the Chair of Letters; he shall be locked naked into stocks, and force-fed the contents of his precious Library from both ends. Magister Harald Thorodor, holding the Chair of Arithmetic; he shall be broken upon the wheel, in the center of the Upper Quad, and there be left to feed the crows. Magister Arathon Lis Red, holding the Chair of Heraldry; he shall have his nose and ears cut off, his naked body shall be covered in pig shit and the ashes of the dead, and he shall be driven at spear point to wander the countryside, recounting the crimes of the noble rulers of each barony he travels through to any that will listen . . ."

He was terribly lonely, with none but mad shadows and hungry ghosts around him for long periods, for though they revealed many things in their whispers to him, they were terrible listeners. It was impossible to have a *conversation* with a shadow or ghost in their conditions; they had much to say, and sometimes quite urgently, but were incapable of having the slightest empathy or interest in his complaints. His occasional visitors, even from amongst his old friends from the city or his former students at the University, stayed only long enough to complete their business for the most part, and were ever eager to leave his presence as soon as possible. The only visitors who had seemed to enjoy his company and new home had been a few from amongst the Lords of Book and Street, the ferocious, angry young men who had burned so brightly in the years before his dismissal and had finally brought decades of University decorum and tradition crashing down around them in the process. That had been the first time he'd felt old, watching that lot rage against the rules that bound them.

But they came only infrequently, having grown a bit older, and a little less angry, with one or two exceptions. And so as the years had passed, he had found himself talking mostly to himself, reconstructing and constructing whole conversations from his past and his future, practicing the arguments that he would present upon his triumphant return from exile, the pronouncements of doom that he would recite to his enemies as they fell before him. He had realized he was quite mad one day when he found that he had been standing in front of a plaster-coated stone wall in the tower for some hours, lecturing it on the proper means of addressing him, egged on by the shadows of *fae* spirits from the Court of the Drowned Wood that clung to his back and made him feel like he was carrying a pack filled with stones. *Drown them all, they do not love you, they hate you, they deserve death, they deserve death*, went the thoughts that ran through his mind as he hectored the wall, but he had suddenly realized that it was the shadows that were saying that, not him. He had banished them from his presence with a word, and then had paused for a moment in the sudden silence, looking wild-eyed at the wall and ceiling above him; finally he had giggled. *If you're going to exile me, and brand me a madman, I will embrace it, and claim the birthright that comes with the name Myradim, as a descendant of one of the Hundred Sons of the Mad King, Myrad*, he had thought in that lucid moment.

And then he had started writing on the blank wall with black chalk: *drown them all, they do not love you, they hate you, they deserve death, they deserve death.*

The news that had arrived from Sequintus, the enchanter in the service of his old pupil, Gilgwyr, had made him the most excited he'd been in many years, though he was also possessed of many fears. He had not been back in Therapoli for a decade, and it was a city filled with his enemies. Would they know he had returned? Would they seize him, and imprison him, and condemn him to death for violating his exile? He had paced and worried for a long and sleepless day, shouting and screaming with the ghosts and spirits of his household; for naturally they hadn't wanted him to leave. And he had almost not made the journey, until he had remembered that he had in fact been working and planning for this moment every day for years. *If I don't go now, I will have failed myself and all those that matter in the end*, had been the thought that finally appeared in his mind, and that was an even bigger fear than getting caught. And so finally his certainty had returned to him, driven on a spear of fear, and he had drawn about his person his wards and protections, and armed himself against his enemies, and had left the dark, haunted tower that was his home with determined footsteps.

Overcoming his disappointment that Therapoli was still standing, he had intended to make straight for Gilgwyr's with all due haste once he was inside the city, to hide himself from the many enemies that might still remain vigilant for his return. His one-time pupil was now the owner of a brothel, apparently, and some small part of him remembered that once upon a time that would have been exciting news. But Leigh had lost any real interest in the actual act of sex long ago, and when his thoughts turned to sex now it was for purely academic reasons. He was too concerned with much graver matters and grander schemes to have the time, energy, or inclination to worry about his member. Indeed, if he'd been asked, he would have hard put upon to remember his last erection.

Once inside the city gates, however, his determination and purpose fled his mind and body and he faltered. The city streets were overwhelming at first, and he found it difficult to put one foot in front of another. The sights and sounds, the hustle and bustle, the tumult of the crowd, it all came rushing over him in a wave of confusion and bewilderment after a decade of near solitude. And he could see warden and watcher spirits bound into the forms of birds and hovering by the gates of the city. He was certain there were other magical wards and eyes that rested upon the city's entrances—set there by the Magisters at the University, or magicians from the Hermetic Guild, magi in the service of a cult or a great family, or any of a dozen wizards and warlocks that called the city home. He did not think the watchers saw him for who he was, but for long moments he was certain that at his very next step he would be seized and arrested. As each step passed unmolested, and finally the gate receded far behind him, his breathing started to relax, his heart's pounding grew less urgent, and his steps once again became confident and measured.

His haste to find Gilgwyr's brothel was entirely a matter of safety. But instead of making directly for the address he had been given, he found himself wandering the streets, drawn down once-familiar routes now made imperceptibly strange. A new storefront here, a different sign there, new paint on a building, sometimes a new building altogether; while the fundamental structure of the city and its streets remained the same, the small details had often altered enough to make him marvel at the speed of change. He supposed it had been silly to think that the city would be exactly the same as he remembered it, as though trapped in amber the moment he had left, only to reawaken as if from magical enchantment the moment he returned; but this was also a crushing blow to his ego, a disheartening disappointment to see the city changing and growing and even thriving without him, as though his absence had hardly been worth noting. This made him very angry, and very, very sad, and he wandered as if half in a dream, half in a stupor.

He found himself on Baker Street, the smells of bread and pastries and pies wafting through the air. *At least some things haven't changed*, he thought wistfully. He wandered past the open storefronts and raised wooden and linen awnings of bakery after bakery, looking over their offered wares, smelling the delights of their repast. For bread he'd usually gone to the Date & Plum, like so many others, but his special favorite had always been the *pastelle de nata*, a kind of puff pastry filled with an ever-so-slightly-burnt cream custard filling, a Palatian delicacy that had made its way into the city and was best made at the House of Gailbas. And soon he found himself in front of the great windows of the pastry shop, the quality and clarity of the glass in their timber frames a testament to the success and popularity of the shop's wares. There, laid out in neat rows and glistening in the morning sun behind the glass, were dozens of his favorite pastries, the long suppressed memory of their smell and taste suddenly hitting him with a force to make his belly moan and grumble as he stood in front of the window and stared and stared.

He didn't realize he was talking, even shouting, out loud until he was interrupted. He paused in mid-sentence, turning to peer at the old man who had dared to distract him from the objects of his affection. ". . . but if you don't leave we'll have to summon the City Watch," the man was saying to him. He was short and slightly round and ruddy-cheeked and white of hair and beard, the very picture of a successful baker. Leigh thought he looked vaguely familiar.

"What?" asked Leigh. "Are you speaking to me?" He looked around, and there didn't seem to be anyone else nearby.

"You're frightening our customers away, sir, with your speechifying, sir," the old man said firmly but with a hint of nervousness. Leigh could see several clerks, all women of varying ages, hiding within the shop, watching to see the outcome of the confrontation. "I do not know what language you are speaking, sir, so I gather you are a stranger here, but public speeches and proselytizing are only permitted in the public plazas of the city. I have no wish to make a scene, sir, but if you continue then I will have no choice but to summon the City Watch. Indeed they may already be on their way, as others on the street have noticed your behavior." Leigh looked around more closely, and he saw that the other people on the street were giving them a wide berth, staring and in some cases pointing and whispering as they hurried past. *Ah, that feels familiar*, he thought. He frowned, remembering his desire to be unnoticed in the city. *That is bad. I do not want people doing that.* He tried to remember how long he'd been in front of the shop, and couldn't recall. ". . . I really must insist, sir."

"Oh, you must, must you?" Leigh asked icily. He drew himself up to his full height, which was not very high, but nonetheless was taller than the shorter older man. *"Do you have any idea who I am?"* Leigh practically screamed.

The old man looked at him puzzled and a bit frightened. "No, sir, I do not," he said faintly.

Leigh was about to scream at him again, when he suddenly realized that this was a good thing. So he barked a laugh instead. "Of course you don't!" he said with a giggle. "No reason at all you would know me. I don't even look like me. In fact I'm not me at all." The old baker seemed to just get more confused. "Not to worry, however. I am in fact a customer, and I wish to buy some of your most excellent pastries. Two dozen, in fact!"

At first Leigh thought the old man might refuse him entry into the shop, but apparently the prospect of a fast sale of two dozen pastries was enough to sway him. Leigh followed him inside, and he *ooh'd* and *aah'd* as they picked out the best looking of the glistening *pastelles de nata* from the displays, and carefully wrapped them up in a small cloth-lined woven basket. For the whole presentation it cost five shillings, more than most people spent on food for an entire week, but to Leigh it was well worth it, particularly as the silver coins he paid them with had once been basest lead; the ritual application of a single dose of the *Alkahest* from the *Opus Magus* and a simple Incantation of Making to shape the once-lead in the imitation of coins had been enough to fill his coffers with a year's wages. He smiled and chatted politely and inconsequently with the shopkeepers as they worked, their relief palpable as they counted up their sale.

"I'm terribly sorry about earlier, what with the mention of the Watch and all, sir," the old man said apologetically as he placed the once-lead coins into his strong box. "You did give us a bit of a fright, I'm sorry to say."

"No need to apologize," Leigh said with a wave of his hand. "The fault is entirely mine. I've only just arrived in the city after a long journey from far away, and I am not myself this morn. Fatigued from all my travels. The pastries are for a party I am having to celebrate my return!"

As he left the shop, he smiled politely at the old man and his assistants, before reaching deep inside himself to pull up the hate, the bile, the anger that seethed within him and wrapping it up into a hex. "*May your bowels run free until you die*," he said to the old man with a sudden snarl. He slammed the door shut as he left, barely bothering to take satisfaction at the startled look on the face of the old man as the binding seized him, making him wince and double over in sudden cramps.

He sat on a low carved stone bench in a corner of White Horse Square, savoring the bites of his beloved *pastelles de nata*, and smiled in contentment at the world. The small, quiet plaza was tucked just off of Baker Street right where the street passed under the aqueduct arches that brought clean upland water all the way to the Old Baths. Several dogwoods planted in the plaza had begun their spring flowering; bees hummed in the air, and white petals skittered softly in the wind over the cobblestones and collected in the corners of the square. A small stone fountain with the bronze statue of a rearing horse adorned the square's center. It was a lovely part of the city.

As he savored each bite of flaky pastry and caramelized custard, he looked out over the pedestrians and other plaza-goers that shared the square with him. He chuckled and giggled in delight, his mind filled with the visions of the fates that awaited them in his plans of triumphant return. A pretty young Aurian couple, seated nearby on another stone bench, gazed chastely into each other's eyes, dressed in merchant class finery: *he shall be cut open and his intestines fed to ravenous dogs; she shall watch his disembowelment while being raped and disfigured by a line of vicious brutes.* An Aurian woman of middle years walked past him, flanked by two plump children and trailed by a servant girl, a serf who was a slave in all but name; *the matron shall be flogged to death by her slave, while her children shall be impaled on stakes, their blood and bile draining into a vat; and when the slave is done, her head shall be held down in that same vat until she has drowned.* A Danian man walking briskly across the plaza, a long loaf of bread sticking out of a leather bag slung over his shoulder; *he shall be hung upside down from meat hooks driven through his heels, and be beaten until all of his bones are broken.* Leigh could see these visions playing out in his mind's eye as though they were happening right in front of him, and he rejoiced in this glorious glimpse of his grand revenge upon the city completed.

He watched as City Watchmen hurried past the plaza, their whistles shrill in the air, undoubtedly summoned to the House of Gailbas to investigate a case of suspected witchcraft. *Let them come for me,* he thought. *They know not where even to look.* He caught himself in his hubris and chided himself. *No, no; careful, careful; there's too much at stake, far, far, far too much at stake.* He slapped himself in the face and laughed.

He looked out over the square, humming and chortling to himself as he ate every last pastry in the basket, licking his fingers until they were clean.

CHAPTER FÍVE
ÍN THE BATHS ⊙F THE FⲞREÍGⴖ QUARTER

The city of Therapoli had two bathhouses, the older and first being the Great Baths in the main part of the old city, right off the Grand Promenade. The newer and smaller could be found in the Foreign Quarter, also off the Grand Promenade but outside the Inner Walls in the new parts of the city, which had been built as an expansion of the original walls to accommodate the growing population of the most important urban metropolis in the Middle Kingdoms. The Great Baths were certainly historic, having been built soon after the city's founding, but that also meant they were in need of repair, and a bit dingy, and as the Aurian overlords of the capital did not much care for the baths, there was no serious effort in maintaining them.

Even though he usually stayed near the University Quarter in the old city, Stjepan much preferred the New Baths in the Foreign Quarter. Palatian engineers had built them, shipped in just for the purpose, and so the heat and steam in the building were much better handled than in the Great Baths, and the Bath Association, made up of local merchants from the Foreign Quarter, paid for its upkeep and maintenance. The Great Baths were usually filled with the Danian men of the old city, along with a few Aurians willing to brave the waters. A problem with prostitution and complaints about the improprieties of the sexes mingling together when naked had led to the banning of women from the Great Baths, except for one day a week when women were allowed and not men. At the New Baths women at least had their own section for daily use, though the sexes were separated in deference to the Divine King's modesty. Being an Athairi and of the Old Religion, Stjepan found such customs odd, but he at least found the New Baths close enough in culture and comfort to his own to enjoy their use. A wider variety of clientele used the New Baths, and Stjepan felt more at ease rubbing shoulders with the more worldly men and women of different nations from across the Known World that lived in the Foreign Quarter, listening to the babble of their different tongues and voices. It was almost enough to make him forget that he was in Therapoli, and not some other distant city.

After stabling his horse—a Danian half-bred courser named Cúlain-mal that was the brother to Erim's horse—he had left his weapons and clothes in the changing rooms under the watchful eyes of the Bath Association's attendants, who were well known for their honesty and vigilance and thus were yet another reason to patronize the New Baths, and not the Great Baths, where theft could occasionally be a problem. After washing the road dirt and sweat from his body in the main men's baths, and performing a discreet ritual of purification, whispering the words under his breath, he had slipped a long towel low slung around his hips and walked toward the rear steam rooms. Like many Athairi men, his lean, muscular chest was smooth and hairless, and his nipples were pierced with small silver rings, and he caught the eye of some of the other men that he passed, particularly when they saw where he was headed. But there was something in his gaze that stopped them from following him.

The three steam rooms that were the furthest back had a reputation, of course, as might be expected in a bathhouse. Sexual contact between members of the same sex was forbidden under the laws and customs of the Divine King, and considered one of the perversions of Ligrid, though amongst the Athairi and others of the Old Religion they were more properly placed as amongst Dieva's many pleasures. From Stjepan's perspective, it often seemed that the cult of the Divine King was intent on outlawing Dieva altogether, and making her and Ligrid into one and the same, and he found that odd and sad. And so in the old city, the pleasures of life were driven underground, and brothels and prostitutes thrived, and Forbidden Cults gained sway, and the Great Baths were well patrolled by Watchmen and even Templars; another good reason to avoid them, as far as Stjepan was concerned.

But in the New Baths, the Bath Association looked the other way, and paid the Watch to do so as well, and the three rooms in the back could gain a reputation.

At this hour, Stjepan knew they would mostly be quiet, though in the first room he passed he could see several pairs of naked men moving softly and wetly in the steam and the heat, watching and performing for each other. In the second, there were only three men, but one of them was young and slim, and bent over between the other two much larger, more muscular men, and they were vigorously using him to their mutual delight. He stopped and observed for a moment, watching the two large, erect cocks as they slipped in and out of each end of the slim young man. The Baths were a veritable cornucopia of cocks, and Stjepan had often idly noted the differences, or lack of differences, between men of various nations. The primary difference to note, at first glance, tended to be circumcision, which was practiced mostly by adherents to the Old Religion; though that was not universally true, as in recent centuries the practice had become more widespread for reasons of perceived cleanliness and hygiene. One of the muscular men was a tall Northman, blond and bearded, and probably a sailor fresh into port; they tended to be on the larger side, and Stjepan hazarded a guess that he was circumcised, based on what he saw sliding in and out of the youth's stretched lips. The young man clearly already had a great deal of experience, as he was taking the length of it into his throat, almost to the root. The other, behind the youth's spread and upraised ass, was a black-skinned Amoran, and clearly descended of the Sun Bull, with an impressive member made all the more swollen by an iron cock ring slipped over shaft and scrotum. A Divine King man, as most of the Amorans were, but many of them held the Old Religion in their hearts as well, and so they were often circumcised, as this man was. Stjepan couldn't really see the younger man's cock as he was bent over between the two larger men, but he'd guess he was Danian, and therefore likely uncircumcised.

If this is what he's into, and he certainly seems to be, then this is his lucky day, Stjepan thought. *Though he may be getting more than he bargained for, particularly with that cock ring.* Most Amorans seemed to be of average size, but the blood of the Bull ran strong amongst them, Stjepan knew, and also amongst the local Aurians, as Heth, in addition to being the God of the Sea, was also the god of the *aurochs*, the wide-horned northern bulls. Amongst most other cultures and nations it was the luck of the draw, depending on whatever the gifts of lineage had happened to provide. Though amongst his own *fae*-blooded people, the Athairi, many of them had the blood of satyrs or, even luckier still, centaurs in their lineage, and so would prove quite popular in bathhouses such as these.

The Amoran spotted Stjepan watching, and called out to him. "Black-Heart, join us," he grunted. "This one's tight and eager." The Amoran grinned. "Unless you'd rather take his place? We have eaten of the *lamba* root today, and are only getting started!" He gave a big laugh, his muscles shaking. *Lamba* root, imported from beyond the Ulik Desert, was highly sought after, but most of the potents sold in the city were almost certainly fakes.

"Perhaps later, Nannos," Stjepan smiled, and watched for a moment longer before walking on to the third room.

The third room was empty, and Stjepan took a seat on the first level of marble benches. He undid his towel, opening his knees, and leaned his elbows back on the next level of marble seats behind him, relaxing in the heat and steam.

He waited for a while, listening to the muffled sounds echoing from the other room, until Jonas walked in and settled down next to him. Jonas the Grey was a short, hawk-nosed Danian, with a goatee and long straggly black hair that came to his shoulders. He was wiry and well muscled, with black hair on his chests and arms. He did not remove the towel wrapped around his waist, either out of modesty and deference to the Divine King, or perhaps out of some sense of embarrassment about the size or shape of his member, Stjepan wasn't sure. He couldn't recall ever having seen Jonas naked. But Stjepan didn't pin him for a religious man. He sat down next to Stjepan and they were silent for a few moments before Jonas glanced at him.

"Black-Heart," he said with a half-smirk. Jonas was always smirking, or close to it. "Good to have you back in the city."

"Grey," said Stjepan. "Good to be back. And how has this fair city fared in my absence?"

"You might be surprised to know it's survived without you just fine," laughed Jonas. "Lord Orrigard still thinks you're out surveying the Dentyn Mire, so you probably have a few more weeks before he starts to wonder why he hasn't seen your face."

"Yeah, it's easy to get lost in the moors," said Stjepan with a shrug.

"Best assignment in the world," laughed Jonas. "No wonder we don't have any good maps of it, none of our cartographers ever actually go there." He paused, his face slightly more serious. "Half the knights in the city have lit out early with the Grand Duke, he's eager to stretch his legs, and they're all sporting it up on the Plain of Gavant. Coogan and Cynyr are up there, attached to the Grand Duke's headquarters company. Looks like he's going to try for Porloss again this summer, and it's going to be big. He's been steaming about it all winter, and by all reports the Erid King is champing at the bit for a second shot as well; the Duke of Enlos is joining in this time, same with the King of Huelt, even the eastern Watchtowers. Everyone with a grudge against the blood of the Wyvern King. They want to go in and burn them all out. The biggest army in decades. It's going to be an epic disaster. So word is you can expect to be summoned for that one at some point."

"Fantastic," said Stjepan, shaking his head. "Back into those fucking hills. Goddess, what a nightmare." He breathed deep for a moment. "Where's Duram, then, he's not with them?"

"Duram's been dispatched to Warwark, bearing letters and maps for King Derrek."

"Any word about Austin?" Stjepan asked.

"No, still no word about Austin," said Jonas, the smirk disappearing entirely for a moment. "Duram is supposed to look while he's over there at the Wall, but even the Readings are coming back vague. Never seen such puzzled looks on a fortuneteller's face before. It's like Lost Uthedmael just swallowed him up."

"So Austin may have joined Fionne in the Underworld," Stjepan said. "And another Lord of Book and Street is laid low."

"Maybe," said Jonas with a shrug. "Austin's a clever man, though, and at least the Readings aren't coming back filled with death and blood and disaster." Jonas paused a moment. "Speaking of which, I was sorry to hear about Guilford."

"Aye," said Stjepan softly. "He was a good man, for one of the Marked, and will be missed. He would have been a stalwart companion to have beside us again, if we're to go after the Earl once more this summer."

"I heard old Jon Pastle was amongst his crew?" asked Jonas.

"Aye," said Stjepan. "Took a spear right through the belly from a naked Nameless berserk."

"I didn't think anything would ever kill that man, not after the fight at Cael Maras," said Jonas, shaking his head. "Bad way to go."

"No, his was a clean death," said Stjepan. "He was one of the lucky ones." Jonas looked at him, but Stjepan was staring into space through narrowed eyes. "The priestess of the temple managed to summon a minor *Baalhazor* to aid her," he said finally. "If she'd managed to summon the *Bharab Dzerek* itself, I probably wouldn't be here right now."

"Islik's balls," cursed Jonas, a bit wide-eyed. "An actual fucking *Rahabi* demon?"

"Aye," said Stjepan. "Islik's giant bloated balls, indeed."

They sat in silence for a little while, soaking up the heat and the steam.

Finally Jonas stirred. "Word's out, you've been blacklisted by the Guild," he said.

"Aye; nothing that can be done about that now," Stjepan replied with a shrug. "That was a certainty the moment that Guilford, son of Guy, died in front of me."

"So what's the call now?" asked Jonas.

"I'll see what Gilgwyr comes up with," Stjepan said. "If he reaches out to you on this one, say no."

"No need to worry on that account, I have no interest in going where you're about to go," said Jonas with a smirk. Stjepan half-smirked back. "Some games are more dangerous than others, and I for one actually want to live to see my old age. Besides, I've already got my marching orders."

"May Yhera Fortuna and the Fates smile upon you, then, Jonas the Grey," said Stjepan.

"And on you, as well, Stjepan Black-Heart," said Jonas as he stood. "I'll tell everyone you said hello."

After Jonas left, Stjepan sat alone for a long while, soaking up the heat and steam. He listened to the muffled sounds of grunting and the slap of wet, slippery flesh from nearby. Slowly he stood up, exited the third room and walked back over to the second steam room in the rear of the New Baths, leaving his towel behind.

He watched for a moment from the doorway, and then, naked, stepped inside.

CHAPTER SIX
AT THE HIGH KING'S COURT

"**W**ho in the name of the King of Heaven is that ugly cow of a woman?" asked Arduin idly, looking across the assembled nobles and courtiers gathered in clusters in the outer galleries of the High King's Hall.

The High King's Hall anchored the eastern end of a great complex built upon the highest, easternmost crest of the city's rise. While imposing, it was perhaps not strictly speaking a castle, as it relied more upon the height of the hilltop for defense rather than the addition of outer walls and towers, its design either incomplete or betraying the hubris of its original architect, who had perhaps assumed that the city walls themselves would be sufficient. This hubris had been betrayed at least twice, once when the Aurians under King Orfeydda had conquered the city and the Hall, and then when an army sent by the Worm Kings had sacked the city during the Age of Legend and then briefly ruled it. Dauban Hess, the Golden Emperor, had not had to invest the city or the Hall when his armies had invaded and conquered the region, for he had defeated King Orfewain in the fields of Pyr's End, south of Abenton, and there had accepted his offer of tribute; otherwise most certainly that would have been a third time when the Hall had fallen.

The innermost parts of the High King's Hall were the great hall itself, one of the largest interior spaces in any building in the Middle Kingdoms where almost the entirety of the High King's Court could meet when summoned, and the king's private chambers and offices in the Tower of Myrad. Surrounding this core were several outer layers of halls, galleries, courtyards, and arcades built into the promontory, connecting a variety of towers and outbuildings into one seamless structure that stretched to the westernmost part of the rise, ending in the city's Great Temple of the Divine King.

Most of the courtiers filling the outer galleries were from the eastern Middle Kingdoms and therefore long familiar to Arduin, though with the Grand Duke already in the field there were fewer knights and high lords amongst the assembled worthies than usual for this time of year. He could see clusters of courtiers and noble Ladies from the Principality of Auria, left behind by the Crown Prince, eyeing with barely concealed hostility some young Danian lordlings down from Umat, probably sent to get their first experience of the High King's Court. Courtiers sent from the Baron of Collwyn mingled with magisters from the University of Truse, come to petition the High King about some matter related to their charter, and he recognized Sir Garin Theodrum, a knight in the service of the Baroness of Abenton whom he had jousted in the lists a long time ago, but Sir Garin appeared to be studiously avoiding eye contact with him.

There were also the first courtiers of the season from the two Danian kingdoms of the west, Dain Dania and Erid Dania, sent on some errand or another by their kings or earls, but none that he knew personally. The chief vassals of the Danian west would not likely see the High King until the Tourney circuit during the summer, which started in the Plain of Flowers between the two Danian kingdoms. His father always liked to say that was why he preferred the Court in winter, as usually there were very few Danians present, since most of them were from the west or the north shore and wintered at their estates.

A group of Hemispian exiles clustered around Belerin of the House Nisander, who had once been Prime Minister of the Hemapoline League of Cities across the *Mera Argenta*, and who had almost daily come to the High King's Hall for thirteen years in the vain hopes that Awain might supply him with money or knights to take back his position. Clerks, scribes, Divine King priests, Inquisitors, handmaidens, and heralds milled about and came and went, adding to the throng, but as far as Arduin was concerned they were mostly just filler, bodies of no importance that simply took up space.

They were all awaiting news of whether or not the High King would be holding an open session of his Court that afternoon, or hoping against the odds that the doors to the inner halls would open and a messenger would appear and summon some lucky aspirant into the presence of the High King (or at the very least to speak to some other member of the High King's inner circle). Arduin could remember the days when on occasion the doors would open and a herald would call out his name or his father's, and they would be swept inside past envious rivals for a private audience. But those days were long gone, and Arduin knew he would wait in vain for such a moment to occur again. If an open session of the High King's Court was called, however, then at least Arduin could go and be in the presence of the High King or his assembled councilors, and hope that by some chance their gaze would fall upon him, and perhaps be reminded of his value and his worth and not the scandal that had tarnished his family's name and position.

Arduin hoped he would stand out amongst the crowd, though not overly so; he had dressed in a grey silk arming doublet, with the shield and *auroch* horns that were the sigil of his house embroidered in gold over his left breast, along with the cadence mark that proclaimed him the first son of the house. He wore the leg pieces of his best harness over his hose: gold-chased cuisses, knee cops, and greaves, and finally stiff leather shoes. As a knight he could appear armed in the city and the High King's Hall, and his embroidered leather gauntlet gloves were tucked into the black sword belt decorated with gold ornaments that adorned his waist, and his sword and dagger hung from a pair of black scabbards also decorated in gold. They were a matched set, the belt and scabbards, a gift of the High King himself, no less, for one of his victories in the Tournaments, and he had worn them to remind others of what he had once been, and so he stood there and hoped and prayed for a miracle.

But that morning, the only time the doors had opened had been upon the arrival of an emissary of King Gavant Peliate of Huelt, who was apparently expected and immediately whisked inside.

And so eventually out of boredom his eyes had fallen upon one homely woman also fresh arrived, and speaking animatedly with several Ladies from the Crown Prince's contingent. Her face was long and somewhat horsey, with too much makeup to Arduin's tastes, and her blonde hair was frizzy and unkempt, threatening to come undone from under the bonnet and veil that was unfortunately not pulled over her visage. He had kept Sirs Helgi Vogelwain and Holgar Torgisbain with him as his retainers, having sent his knights Sirs Clodin Perwain, Theodras Clowain, and Theodore Lis Cawain off on other errands, and the two men scanned the crowd until they spotted the woman he was asking about.

"I'm not sure, my Lord," Sir Helgi finally said with a frown. "I do not recognize her. And for that I find myself thankful."

Sir Oswin Clodias, an older knight of the High King's own household, happened to be passing by, and hearing their conversation stopped for a moment. Arduin remembered him as a decent sort, and sure enough he squinted and chipped in. "Oh, that's the wife of one of Bessiter's vassals, usually stays at their country keep," he said. "I heard she decided to come to Court to see if her presence could gain some favor for her husband, but he'd have been better off if she'd just stayed at home." He shook his head and sighed. "That's the quality of the women we're getting in the Court these days. It's not like the old days, when your sister still made her appearances here," he said to Arduin, who in surprise looked for some hint of irony or mockery in the knight's face, but could see none. All he saw was pity and patronizing sympathy, which might in fact have been worse, but at the moment he'd take it. "Please give her my best, and greet her for me in the name of the King of Heaven," Sir Oswin said with a slight bow, and then he moved off into the crowd.

Arduin was so startled by the simple kindness that he forgot to say anything in response, and he chided himself in his head. *This is the whole reason you're here, you idiot*, he thought. He thought for a moment of running after Sir Oswin, but he knew instantly how stupid and foolish that would look, and instead shook his head. *Patience, patience. Don't be like Father, running around kissing everyone's ass. Look at it as a small building block, and build on it the next time you see him.*

124

"He's right, you know," said Sir Holgar. "I must say it seems as though someone's hidden all the jewels. Where's Lady Sigalla? Or Lady Ilona, Duke Tenreuth's daughter? Or the Baroness of Karsiris? She might be married, but at least she makes for something pretty to look at."

"They are all at the city house of the Baron of Djarfort," said a clerk standing right behind them that Arduin hadn't noticed. "The Baron's daughter, Lady Silga, has come of age and the Baron's wife, the Baroness Siglette, is throwing a small afternoon revel to celebrate, and prepare her for the coming season."

"Thank you . . ." said Arduin to the young clerk, a young man of Danian lineage but dressed in the colors of the High King, as he held out a silver coin, and trailed off, one eyebrow raised.

"Gerard, youngest son of Baron Jonas of Cermore," supplied the young man. "I have the pleasure of knowing your brother, Harvald, who works in the Chancery with me."

"Ah, well met, then, young Gerard, and my thanks once again," said Arduin, as Gerard pocketed the coin and moved off with a smart bow. *Such small victories*, he thought, and sighed. *And thanks to Harvald, of all people.* Lady Silga, then, would be one of the prospective Queens of the Tournaments this coming circuit. Arduin wondered briefly whether this news could be of any use to the fortunes of his family; he knew his father would be eager to find him a bride this coming season as he had been every recent season, but given the tarnished name of their family, there had simply been no suitable matches offered that his father would consider. Lady Silga came from a great family in the Kingdom of Dainphalia, however, and would certainly be of the proper breeding and background for a match. He suddenly wondered if that was why his father had hurried off with the Grand Duke, as King Colin was also reported on the Plain of Gavant. His face soured, imagining his father trying desperately to impress the King of Dainphalia, who despite his excellent pedigree had always struck Arduin as a stuck-up boor.

He tried to picture Lady Silga in his head, and remembered a pretty young thing at one of the dances at the Tournament of Gavant a year or two ago. *Pretty enough if I remember right*, he thought, *but once you've seen the sun, all other things in the sky do not seem quite so bright.* Still, a marriage to a Djarfort would do wonders for their position, and Arduin knew his duty.

This should have been good news, then, or at least something to potentially act on, but the more he thought about it, the more pained he became. And not only because he knew that there was probably no chance for a marriage. A time had been when no revel of such a sort in this city would have been considered complete without his sister's presence, and she would have been amongst the first to receive the gilded invitations that marked such an auspicious event for a young woman of breeding and position. But that was in the days when he and his family were amongst the High King's favorites, and had moved through a crowd such as this as men of power and influence, rather than standing as he did now on the periphery amongst the other beggars and hopefuls they had become. Because of the scandal. *Because of his sister.*

In his mind's eye there was a flash of memory: *a glorious pale body, a beautiful voice crying out in passion and then in surprise and fear.*

And then in a second it was gone, willed away by steely discipline.

Arduin stared up at the banners hanging above the massive doors to the inner halls, depicting the Royal Wyvern of the line of Urfortias in dazzling gold thread, and used the image to calm himself despite the bitter taste in his mouth. *Duty to the High King and the honor of my family above all else*, he thought. *He is a Vassal of the Divine King, and his words are the words of the Divine King.* He let his eyes wander about, falling on the unkind faces of leering sycophants, the desperate and the bored milling about the hall, for all the world like a pack of jackals out in the desert, waiting for the lion to finish with its meal. He watched the horse-faced woman married to one of the Baron of Bessiter's vassals talking and talking, braying like an ass, oblivious to the mocking looks of the Ladies about her. *Is this what our great line has been reduced to?* he wondered. *Is this what I have been reduced to? To wait all day, for a few words of a knight's pity, news of a party my sister wasn't invited to, and the name of some useless clerk who knows my useless brother, and therefore thinks he knows me?* It was enough to make a man weep, had he been the weeping sort.

He turned to Sirs Helgi and Holgar. "Right. I think it's time to go," he said to them quietly. "I have had my fill for the day."

The trio turned and headed for the nearest stairs, his household knights falling in silently behind him. As they did, Arduin could see a slight commotion as the nearby crowd parted for some nobles of higher station. He strained for a moment to see who it was, and saw that the courtiers were giving a very wide berth to Lord Rohan Brigadim and Duke Pergwyn Urfortias of Enlos, a distant cousin to the High King, and the entourage of armored knights from the Duke's personal household that trailed behind them.

He didn't blame the courtiers, for it was hard for Arduin to think of a more intimidating pair in the High King's Hall that day. Duke Pergwyn was one of the High King's most trusted battle lords, perhaps second only to the Grand Duke Owen Lis Red, and he had once taken a sword cut to his right brow and cheek that had left a deep white scar down across his visage and taken his right eye with it. A polished white stone now nestled in the empty socket, and it gave him a decidedly otherworldly quality that spooked the superstitious in particular, looking for all the world like the Evil Eye out of story and fable, and some whispered that he actually had that power. He clearly relished the effect it had, cutting a rakish and bold figure with slicked-back blond hair, lamb chop sideburns, and a thick mustache; his gold chain of office hung thick with power over a long sable coat and his embroidered red arming doublet. Lord Rohan, on the other hand, didn't *look* very intimidating—indeed, by outward appearance and dress he was virtually indistinguishable from any of the dozen or so clerks and under-secretaries in the Chancery that milled about the hall—and he had the generally unimpressive title of "Lord of the Keys" which he even shared with Lord Baldwin, but the tall, thin Danian was nicknamed the King's Shadow and widely known to be the High King's spymaster, a man who delved into the darkest and deadliest affairs in the realm.

Arduin often thought it ironic that a man who worked with secrets was so widely identified. "How can what you do be a secret, if everyone knows who you are?" he once asked Harvald at their evening supper, as he knew that Harvald sometimes saw Lord Rohan working about the Chancery and the High King's Hall.

"Smoke and mirrors, my dear brother," Harvald had laughed. "*Smoke and mirrors*. Everyone assumes it's true that Lord Rohan is the King's Shadow, but no one knows it for absolute certain, and uncertainty always breeds doubt, and makes men pause when they should act. Besides, say it's true; what would anyone do about it? I suppose an enemy of the High King could kill him, but he'd just get replaced, and then you'd have to figure out who the new spymaster was." Harvald had been quite tipsy that evening, and had leaned over to loudly whisper. "Some at the Chancery think it's really someone else that's the spymaster, and that Lord Rohan is just the man they point to as the distraction. But I'll tell you what I think; I think there is no spymaster at all, no mysterious order of royal assassins waiting in the shadows, just a few rumors that a clever man like Rohan has spread to give himself an air of importance that have taken on a life of their own. I mean, no one's going to actually ask the High King to confirm that Rohan is his Shadow, are they? No one's actually going to ask the High King if he has trained assassins that do his secret bidding, are they? *You are what people think you are*, brother. And a man who knows how to use smoke and mirrors can make himself look much larger than he actually is."

Arduin had disapproved of his brother's argument; after all, everyone thought they were a ruined family marred by scandal and dishonor, and while he had to admit there was some surface truth to it, Arduin most certainly did not agree with the notion that that was who they were. No, for Arduin there was a deep distinction between the current reputation of the Orwains of Araswell and their truth: theirs was a proud family, a great family of ancient lineage, and he had been an honorable King's Champion, and would be so again.

But perhaps not this day.

Arduin suddenly realized that Duke Pergwyn and Lord Rohan were heading to the same set of stairs as he was. On any other day, he would have been thrilled at an opportunity to quickly rush ahead to the top of the stair, to stop there and casually greet the Duke, and then bow and give way to the Peer, to show that he was not intimidated like the others. On any other day, but not this one; *is this what I have been reduced to?* was all he could think. He was sick to his heart of the Court and the little games he had to play, and so he simply stopped and stood respectfully off to the side to give them plenty of room to take the stairs ahead of him.

It seemed for a moment in fact that they would pass by without even seeing him, as Lord Rohan was busy saying something in hushed tones into the Duke's ear, and this would have suited his current mood just fine. But to his surprise Arduin thought he saw the slightest gesture from Lord Rohan that drew the gaze of the Duke's one good eye right to him. He barely had a moment to wonder if he had imagined the gesture when he found himself locking eye with the Duke, and he was so startled he forgot to bow.

"Ah, Lord Arduin. Were you leaving too? Come, walk with us," the Duke called out, and then Arduin suddenly found his feet carrying him forward to walk down the broad stairs next to the Duke and Lord Rohan, his knights falling in beside the Duke's trailing entourage. His heart leapt into his throat; any number of nearby courtiers in the hall had heard the Duke's invitation, and Arduin could not have been more astonished at this sudden good fortune.

"I think you may know I am a blunt man," Duke Pergwyn said as they walked down the stairs and out into the lower galleries, clerks and minor courtiers scattering out of their way with scraping bows and curious glances. "It's why my cousin listens to me, I suppose, and made me a member of his privy council. I've always meant to tell you that you have had my greatest sympathy during the troubles that have befallen your family, but I regret that I have not had a chance to do so. Sir Oswin mentioned that he'd spoken to you, and so you were on my mind when we passed you by. A happy coincidence."

"Please know, my Lord, that your dignity under duress has not gone unnoticed these many years, and that there are those of us who have watched from afar, hoping very strongly that some way back into the good graces of the High King might be found for you and your line," Lord Rohan said quietly. "Your father is, well, perhaps not pursuing the best path . . ."

129

"I suspect my father wishes to marry me to Lady Silga, if that is what you mean?" Arduin replied, suddenly thankful that the young clerk's news allowed him that guess.

"Yes, and that, alas, will not likely happen," said Lord Rohan, shaking his head. "Baron Guiton is very glad for the attention, but he will not be the one to rescue your family."

"Your father's wasting his time, is what Rohan's trying to say. After ten long years he's desperate for patrons, and he's thrown in his lot with the Crown Prince and the Iron Cock, and they've dangled Djarfort's daughter in front of him as a carrot, and they're going to string him along as long as they're enjoying the flattery and the money," the Duke spat. "A marriage makes perfect sense, but it won't come first. You'll have to do something to make a good marriage possible. And I mean *you*. Your father thinks that he can redeem the honor of the Orwain name, but he can't. It's got to be you."

"But how?" Arduin blurted, then immediately regretted. "Father . . . I must admit Father has also urged me to return to the Tournaments this summer, and aim for the Champion's crown again, and I have thought hard upon it."

"It would be good to see you back in the lists, I admit; we jousted a long time ago, didn't we?" the Duke asked.

"Yes, at the Tournament of Flowers, almost ten years ago, before . . ." Arduin trailed off. "Before . . ." *Before I killed him.*

"*Before*, yes," the Duke said, coming to a stop in the middle of the Lower Courtyards and turning to face Arduin, staring at him with his one good eye. "That won't do. That won't do at all. No one blames you for what happened; well, I guess some do, but we all know accidents happen. But returning to the jousts, seeing you take to the lists again? No, a decade may have passed, and luckily for your sister Uthella of Uthmark has remained the most conspicuously scandalous woman in the Kingdoms, but that will just trigger a lot of unpleasant memories, and give people a chance to retell old stories." Arduin flushed, and hung his head for a moment. He felt the Duke's one eye studying him. *But which eye?* he suddenly thought.

"My cousin Owen and the Erid King are planning a summer campaign, and they mean to have Porloss' head on a platter before the end of it," the Duke said finally. "This time I'll be joining them, and so will King Gavant of Huelt. We are to raise a force of three thousand knights and seven thousand footmen, the largest army we've gathered during Awain's reign as High King, and we're headed right into the Manon Mole. We're not just going after Porloss, but after all those hardscrabble hill knights that have called that place home since the dawn of time. I know Owen has passed you by for his recent rosters, I'm sure he had his reasons, but I decide the men who will travel with me. Come with me this summer, as part of my contingent, you and your household knights and a portion of the levy from your country estates. Action in the field, Lord Arduin, in defense of the High King; that's the way back into his good graces."

Arduin stood there, thunderstruck. "My . . . my Lord Duke, it would be an honor," he finally managed to get out. "I have seven personal knights and five squires at your disposal, and by right can raise a levy of fifty sergeants-at-arms from amongst the tenants of our estates."

"Good," Duke Pergwyn said with a soft smile. "The plan is to start right after the Feast of the Four Kings, probably the second or third day of Myradéum. So spend the spring preparing, and expect my summons and letters of commission sometime during the month of Sirenium." He clapped Arduin on the shoulder.

"Congratulations, my Lord Arduin," said Lord Rohan with a short bow, and then they were off, with the Duke's entourage loudly clattering by.

When they were gone, Arduin finally let out a long breath.

"Pardon me, Lord Arduin, but *Islik's balls*," said Sir Holgar, his mouth gaping. "Did that really just happen?"

The Duke of Enlos, cousin to the High King, just offered me his patronage, and a chance to redeem my family's honor, Arduin thought. He looked up at the bright spring sky. *After ten years, oh happy day. And all thanks to a stray question about some country lordling's horse-faced wife.* He had the sudden urge to run back up to the High King's Hall and give the woman a kiss. He wondered for a moment what his father would say when he told him, then decided with a sudden laugh that he didn't care. He felt like everyone in the Lower Courtyards was staring at him. *As well they should*, he thought.

"Gentlemen, to the Great Temple of our Divine King," he said, feeling himself in good humor for the first time in . . . well, in years. "For I believe offerings in His name are very much in order. Then let's find the others, and get home." He grinned. "We've got some swords to sharpen, and a rebel earl to kill."

CHAPTER SEVEN

AT THE LIBRARY OF THE UNIVERSITY OF THERAPOLI

Harvald crossed into the streets of the University Quarter of Therapoli in keen high spirits—feeling refreshed from his stop at the city house of his father—but with a stomach full of butterflies and a burning sensation in his ears; it was a feeling that he had been unable to shake since Stjepan had slid the map out of its scroll tube. *Someone is talking about me*, he thought with a laugh. At his father's house he had changed from the dirty, grubby travel clothes that he had felt like he had been wearing for three weeks into clean, fresh city garb: a black doublet with unobtrusive gold thread embroidery on the sleeves, black brocade knickerbockers and breeches over hose and a subtle codpiece, and pointed leather shoes. He had grabbed a plain brown sleeveless half-coat lined with fur to help ward off the spring chill, and he had affixed a small gold badge in the shape of a wyvern clutching a quill to his coat to show that he was a member of the Chancery. His leather satchel, with its precious cargo, was slung over one shoulder, and a dagger and coin purse were discreetly slung next to his left hip. To anyone glancing his way he would have appeared to be more or less what he was: a clerk from the High King's Court, perhaps from a moneyed family, on his way on some errand into the oldest and greatest University in the Middle Kingdoms.

Except, of course, that his business had absolutely nothing to do with the Court.

The University sat on a rise in the middle of its own Quarter of the city, north of the Forum and west of the High King's Hall and High Quarter.

The original buildings of the University had been built in the Golden Age in imitation of the Golan Great Schools, but none had lasted to the present day. The University had been damaged or destroyed twice, and rebuilt, most recently in the years following the Worm Kings' sack of the city. Its central core was a sprawling marble building that once wrapped around a grid of four square quads. The two lower quads were named the Lower Quad and the Library Quad. The wing that separated the two upper quads had been destroyed during the War of the Throne Thief, and rather than rebuild it the two quads had been allowed to connect into one large Upper Quad. Over the centuries the University had effectively expanded into the streets surrounding its original core and campus, and now many of its administrative offices and the residences for students and magisters were now found in adjacent or nearby buildings, including the student colleges that had been chartered as affiliate parts of the University: Highwall College, the oldest and most prestigious, and now largely a bastion of noble Aurian elitism; Drewson's College, which had been started as a counter to Highwall, and served as a haven and sponsor for students of low means; the College of the Globe, a haven for alchemists and natural philosophers who believed that the world was round; and the Mottist College of Therapoli, the youngest and most controversial college in the University. A Black College, dedicated to the occult and the Nameless Cults of the Forbidden Gods, was naturally also rumored to exist, but if it did, then it at least had no official building to call its own.

Outside and around those buildings had grown an entire Quarter, filled with merchants and vendors eager to serve the University and its students. Book binders and booksellers, paper shops and quill makers, scriptoriums, laundresses, boarding houses, cheap taverns and eateries, money lenders and brothels all clustered together in the narrow streets and alleys that sprawled, maze-like, out from the University itself. Harvald felt a pang of nostalgia as he passed amongst them: Mercer's Fine Books, where he had purchased his first copy of *The Secret Book of Azoth*, a grimoire on the use of magic mirrors by the pseudonymous "Mercury King"; the boarding house at the corner of Ink Street and what the locals called Backstab Alley, where he and Stjepan had rented rooms for several months; the Feathered Quill, the tavern on Gate Street where the Lords of Book and Street had first formed up for battle during the War of the False Book. *By the gods that was a silly name*, Harvald mused as he passed the Quill. *The Lords of Book and Street, who had come up with that? Had that been Fionne, the poor bastard?*

Upon arriving there as a young man, Harvald had been told by older students that the maze-like nature of the University Quarter was the mirror and manifestation of its "underground self" because, according to campus legend, it had been built not only upon the previous incarnations of the University but also upon the ancient dungeons of Myrad. Harvald knew that strictly speaking that was not likely to be true, as the University had been founded about forty years before the rule of the Mad King. But many students reported that they became lost while wandering in the streets of the Quarter at night, and the superstitious did not like to travel after dark. Harvald had never felt afraid there. The notion that a thing or a person might have an "underground self" that was different, in ways large or small, than their outer self had been very exciting to young Harvald, for he certainly found that to be true about himself. He, Stjepan, Gilgwyr, and some others had spent more than a few hours poking around in the basements and cellars of the University, looking for the entrance to the old buried dungeons, but while they delved deep and found many things to wonder at, including buried rooms and halls that belonged to the Golden Age University, they never found anything that seemed to fit the bill for the dungeons that had once imprisoned the Divine King.

The whole city, in fact, had a deep underground life: the layers of older parts of the city, now buried and built upon; the cisterns and sewer and waterworks, which fed the fountains of the city's plazas and its two Baths before emptying into the bay; and cellars, crypts, and ancient passages built by the inhabitants of the city over the course of almost two thousand years. All interconnected. Enough secrets to keep a man who enjoyed secrets busy for a lifetime.

And while Harvald enjoyed secrets, and had traversed parts of the city underground in pursuit of them, he was most interested in the kind that brought with their discovery the potential for some useful reward. The kind, he very much hoped, that he carried in his satchel.

Though no longer a member of the University, Harvald's position as a clerk in the Chancery of the High King's Hall allowed him access to the campus and, most importantly, its vast Library, the greatest in the Middle Kingdoms bar none. The Library had grown from a small scriptorium and scroll room at the University's founding, to now fill three of the four building wings of the Library Quad, effectively forming a single large U-shaped wing of the University. While most wings had multiple entrances—certainly many from the interior quads of the University, and usually one or two from the exterior streets surrounding the University campus—the Library had only a single entrance at one end of the U shape, located in the center wing in the middle of the quads. Most of the windows and doors on the lower floors were bricked up and walled over. The rest of the U-shaped wings were filled with chambers and halls filled with books and scrolls and study rooms, arranged in somewhat haphazard fashion and cared for by a small cadre of librarians under Magister Clodarius, master of the Chair of Letters. In general the chambers and halls were readily accessible by students, save for the chambers in the furthest part of the U shape, where the University housed the rare books in its collections too valuable to let students handle without supervision, and books the access to which had been restricted or even outright forbidden. Such books were kept behind locked and magically warded doors: grimoires of occult spells, books on necromancy, secret screeds on the Forbidden Gods of the Nameless Cults of the Damned.

Which, naturally, was exactly where Harvald was headed.

He passed under the main arched gateway to the University off the High Promenade, went up the stepped street to the heights of the Quarter, and approached the main doors at the South Wing. The few guards there spotted his Chancery badge and recognized him, and just waved him through. He glanced up at the statues that lined the main entry hall as he passed them, depicting some of the first and greatest magisters of the University, beginning with the flanking statues of Eldyr and Maderyd, two of the Hundred Sons of Mad Myrad. He wondered what they would think of an impostor walking so cavalierly through the front doors.

Crossing the Lower Quad felt a bit like a homecoming as it always did, and his mind was already beginning to anticipate the more difficult parts of his intended expedition. Ignoring the curious glances that his Chancery badge earned from some of the younger students that saw him, he passed into the doors of the Center Wing of the University and turned right into the long corridor that would take him to the doorway to the Library.

Getting into the University itself was never really a problem, even if the front gates were locked as they sometimes were at night; there was always a door or a window somewhere left unattended. Entry into the Library was a bit trickier, as he and Stjepan and Gilgwyr had discovered during their days as students. The only entrance was the one he now passed through, and it was attended at all times. He forced himself to look and more importantly *feel* casual. *You've done this a hundred times before, and this time is no different*, he repeated in his head as he approached the front desk of the Library.

Luckily he recognized the librarian behind it, a sour old Danian nick-named Grim Liam by the students, and relief washed over him. *By the gods, I can even try to make this easy*, he thought. Like most of the librarians, Grim Liam had been a student once himself; many remained as librarians out of love for the Library and the University; out of love for Magister Clodarius, who was one of the most popular teachers there; or, as was the case with Liam, because they were unable to find service with a lord's household or at the High King's Hall, and did not wish to risk the more unpredictable life of a scribe- or sage-for-hire. Most of the latter sort of librarian accepted their lot in life with equanimity; but not Grim Liam, who took his disappointment and anger out on the students that had to deal with him.

Harvald, however, had seen in Liam's anger an avenue to friendship and perhaps with it, opportunity, and so over the years he had gone out of his way to break down Liam's surly demeanor by buying him drinks when he saw him in the local taverns, and confiding in him some juicy but meaningless bits of gossip from the High King's Court. He'd even taken Grim

Liam to one of the less reputable dancing halls over on Penny Street to ogle several fine-looking temptresses. Of course, he had hardly singled Grim Liam out in some prescient fashion preparing for just this very moment; rather, he'd spent time and money like that with hundreds of men and women across the city over the years, all as a way of *tilting the odds*, as he liked to think of it.

And on this occasion, his gamble had paid off, for rather than looking up from the ledgers to observe his approach with the scowl with which he greeted most other visitors, Grim Liam's face broke out in a huge, friendly grin when he saw that it was Harvald walking toward him.

"My dear Harvald!" Grim Liam said, standing and offering a hand. "How is life at the Chancery? It's been a dog's age since I've seen you here in the Quarter."

"Aye, what was it, last Midéadad, I think?" Harvald replied, heartily shaking his hand. "Over at the Pig & Prince."

"I believe you are correct, right after the Feast of the Scales," said Liam, pleased that Harvald had remembered. "They must be keeping you busy over there. Just the other day I was thinking to myself that I hadn't seen you yet this year, nor this past winter either."

"Aye, haven't been in the Quarter much of late, spent most of the winter deep in the Records Hall at the Chancery, and only got back from a journey out of the city just recently," said Harvald. "Court business, and all."

"Ah, perhaps then a few tales over drinks might be in order?" said Liam hopefully.

"Indeed, I may be headed back out of the city in a few days, but perhaps we could try for the Pig & Prince again, say the evening of this Secondum?"

"Excellent!" cried Liam. "I look forward to it. Of course, if the Court takes you elsewhere, I would understand completely."

"If I am forced to leave the city beforehand, I promise I shall find you upon my return," Harvald said with an easy smile. "We are long overdue for a drink." He allowed a cloud to cross over his face. "This latest work has been most troubling, and I would not mind a chance to unburden myself. Indeed, I am glad it is you at the desk this day, as I have an unusual request. I've been asked to make a copy of some of the pages of the *Libra di historum Manonesian* for someone at the Chancery. They don't have a copy of it there, it's quite rare as you know, and the only copy I'm aware of in the city is the one in the rare books collection here. Some interesting stuff came up during the campaign against the Rebel Earl last year, some stuff about the old histories of the Manon Mole and the Wyvern King, and the only thing left to be done is to compare what was learned up in the hills with what's written in there."

"Nothing unusual about that. If it's one of the rare books rooms I'll just enter you into the ledgers with the name of the Chancery Lord requesting the copy to be made and fetch you the key," said Grim Liam, grabbing a brown leather ledger from beneath the desk, where it sat next to a rarely used black ledger.

"Ah, that's the unusual part," said Harvald, and leaning forward he dropped his voice to a conspiratorial tone, and let his eyes fill with meaning. "I can't tell you the name of the Chancery Lord."

"What?" said Liam, a puzzled expression on his face. "Well, that is un . . . oh!" Liam gave a start, as he unraveled the hint, and he also lowered his voice. "You mean; it's for *him*."

"Yes!" said Harvald. "I mean, it's just a bit of research, but still, it's very exciting. Apparently he very much liked the work I did for him copying the transcripts of the trial of Lord Wilhem last year. I think I told you about that, didn't I?"

"Oh yes, a terrible business, that!" said Liam. "Well, then; I suppose it might be best if this one was off the ledgers completely, wouldn't it?"

"I was afraid to ask, old friend, but that would be most excellent indeed," said Harvald.

"Then let's just put that particular ledger away," said Liam, slipping the brown ledger back under the desk. "I can just enter you as having entered into the general Library, then. Would that work, do you think?"

"Yes, I think that'd be fine," Harvald said; after all, some students and guards had seen him enter the Library doors so it might stand out later if for some reason his name was not recorded anywhere. He watched as Liam wrote his name into the main ledger of the Library, and then could barely stand it as Liam stood and consulted a massive bound ledger, the Catalog of the Rare Books Collection, that was on a separate desk behind him. After a few minutes that seemed like hours to Harvald, Liam finally reached down, rummaged a bit in a drawer beneath the desk, and fished out a brass key.

"Here we go," said Grim Liam. "The key to the Blue Room in the Rare Books Wing, where you can find the *Libra di historum Manonesian*. The password is *regismata*."

"Most excellent, old friend," said Harvald with a smile. "Most excellent!"

As he walked through the halls and galleries of the Library, Harvald discovered he'd been sweating into his shirt during his interaction with Grim Liam, the fear building in him that someone would come along and interrupt before he'd had a chance to make good his entry. But now relief that he had cleared the first hurdle flushed the fear away, making it difficult for him to keep a measured pace as he made his way deep into the wings.

He passed the scriptorium halls, where students and scribes diligently made their own copies of the books they were studying, or were employed in creating copies of some work at the request of a noble or member of the High King's Court. *Still the old-fashioned way*, he thought as he remembered the many hateful hours he'd spent there doing the same. Printed books had finally appeared in Therapoli, imported from Palatia and Hemispia beginning a hundred years ago, and were now increasingly available, being produced even within the city itself. But the University did not own a printing press—though Harvald knew of eleven in operation in other parts of the University Quarter and over in the Foreign Quarter—and neither did the High King's Court, a mark of the general conservatism of the city's most powerful institutions. Instead, students and clerks spent many hours laboriously hand-creating copies of ancient texts and important documents, and therefore duplicating in some cases the errors and editorial decisions of some previous generation of copyists.

During his time at the University, a great debate had raged about the appropriateness of the use of both printed editions of books and the use of Indices created to make their perusal easier, both of which were rejected as foreign concepts alien to the proper traditions of the University. Only the more cosmopolitan students of the Mottist College—named in honor of the Lord Mott, Vizier of Palatia and inventor of the first Indices—embraced the printed word with enthusiasm. *Hard to believe that those debates had come to bloodshed*, he mused. But now, only a few years later, the debate was muted if not largely over, the presence of printed books firmly established in the city and the University, and their ascent was almost certainly inevitable. *Try standing in the way of the future*, he thought, glancing at the rows of students diligently bent to their task, *and it will sweep you aside*.

After the scriptorium halls, he passed through the four great halls of the main Library wing. Each hall held copies of the books of the four Ages of History, going back chronologically. So the first hall was filled to bursting with the books of the current Age, the Age of Iron and Fire, which began when Akkalion, the Emperor of Thessid-Gola, fell into what came to be called the Gray Dream; the second with the books of the Bronze Age, which began after the Catastrophe that ended the Worm Kings and the darkness of the Winter Century; the third with the books of the Age of Legend, which began after the sinking of Ürüne Düré and the end of the War in Heaven with the ascension of Islik to the throne of the King of Heaven; and then finally, the last hall filled with the books of the Golden Age, that most ancient time when gods and men walked Geniché's earth together, stretching all the way back to the Age of Creation. Only one book had been created during the Age of Creation: the Great Book of Yhera, the Queen of Heaven, written with the blood and skin of the Great Dragon, and from which grew her Sacred Tree. And that book could only be found in the Otherworld, where the World Mountain and the Sacred

Tree met Yhera's palace in the Heavens. Only the greatest of magicians and heroes could ever hope to see that book, and get a chance to read it or, if they dared, inscribe their lives within it.

The scholar-magicians of the Golan Great Schools had been the first to outline the concept of the Ages of History, and their schema had been widely adopted throughout the cultures of the *Mera Argenta*. The end of the Age of Iron and Fire was already widely predicted; indeed, mendicant proselytizers and holy men were an increasingly common sight in the public areas of the city, and even out on the roads and trails of the countryside. They'd passed half a dozen different apocalyptic preachers by the side of the road or in small village squares on their way to and from the Manon Mole, each of them proclaiming a different way in which this Age would end, and the next Age would begin. *They're going to need to build a new wing when this Age is over*, he thought. *Though maybe they could just kick out all those useless copyists and turn that room into the Hall of the New Age.* But the idea that they were on the cusp of a great change in the world excited Harvald, particularly given his current self-appointed mission.

In the first hall, the Hall of the Age of Iron and Fire, he stopped and perused the shelves until he found a copy of *On the Language of the Mael Kings*, by Gammond of Wael, luckily a fairly common book, if one not in particularly high demand. The further back he went in the building, the quieter it became and the fewer students and clerks he saw, until by the time he turned into the central corridor of the Rare Books Wing it was practically deserted. He passed only a single open door, to the Green Room, and saw a single student therein, busy at work copying some ancient text; he did not recognize the young man, but whoever it was must have been a favorite of some Magister, to be allowed to work alone and unsupervised.

Harvald stopped in front of the Blue Room, and slid the key into the lock. "*Regismata*," he whispered as he turned the key, and then breathed a sigh of relief when he heard the lock click open. The warding enchantment was a simple one but strong, bound into the lock of the door by Magister Clodarius, and he changed the passwords for each room in the Rare Books Wing each day.

Harvald opened the door and slipped inside; against the customs and rules of the Library, he closed the door behind him. He walked quickly to one of the empty drafting desks that stood in the middle of the room. Selecting one he liked that faced the door, so that anyone that entered could not immediately see what was spread out upon the tilted surface of the desk, he set down *On the Language of the Mael Kings* and took off his half-coat and opened his satchel. There was a single window in the room, high set against the wall and barred with rune-inscribed iron, and though the midday light streamed through it the room was still dark and gloomy, so he lit an oil lamp over the desk. Fire was, of course, the greatest danger and worry in the Library, but it was simply too expensive to use the enchanted potents of the *ajuga* flower to spark the heatless flames of magic, and so care and discipline in the handling of fire was drilled into every student and clerk. He quickly pulled out from his satchel blank sheets of parchment of varying sizes, an inkbottle and quills, and a water bottle to quench his thirst, and arranged them on the desktop and in its special-built holders.

It took him almost a half hour to find the *Libra di historum Manonesian,* as there was no particular order to the books and scrolls that filled the room. The books were arranged on straight shelves, while the scrolls of papyrus and parchment were arranged in latticework cubbyholes. He had started in a hurry, and went through the room once without finding it, before he forced himself to breathe more steadily and start over, being more thorough the second time. He finally found it and with as much care as he could, hauled the large, three-century-old volume over to the desk. He slowly turned its pages until he found a nice page to set it open to, spotting the words *regis wyvernnis* on one side opposite an illumination of some horrible battle. *Suitably grim*, he thought, then slipped the key back into his coin purse and slung the satchel over his shoulder.

He had selected the *Libra* and the Blue Room for two reasons. One was that he actually might need the book, as appended to the fables of the ancient Wyvern King and his barbarous descendants was a later history of the bandit knights of the Manon Mole and, most importantly, of the beginnings of the Nameless Cults there in the centuries after the Worm

Kings, when worship of Nymarga the Devil and the Forbidden Gods took root amongst the most depraved of the hill peoples.

The second was because the Blue Room was located right across from the stairwell that led to the top floor of the Wing, and the warded Black Rooms of the Library: the collection of the forbidden.

He slipped two amulets out of his satchel, and then slipped them over his head. One was a small glass vial filled with a clear liquid, and hung from a gold chain. The other was a small copper square on a copper chain; inscribed into its surface was a circle of small runes from the *Daedeki Grammata*, the set of a dozen magical symbols created by the magician-god Daedekamani during the Golden Age and given to the men of the Gola. The small runes were a rune of *making*, a *ward* rune, a rune of *becoming*, a rune of *cleansing*, and a rune of *light*, making the amulet a fairly basic magician's aid. He rubbed the copper amulet with his fingers and concentrated on the rune of *making*, picturing it in his mind as he closed his eyes, and began to recite words combining the Incantations of Seeing and Making: "*Open my eyes and open my ears. Let me see the World. Let me see the North. Let me see the South. Let me see the East. Let me see the West. Close their eyes and close their ears. Make me invisible. Let me walk unseen amongst friend and foe. Let me walk unseen in the North. Let me walk unseen in the South. Let me walk unseen in the East. Let me walk unseen in the West.*" And then he took a deep breath and walked out the door.

He heard the locks slide back into place as he closed the door of the Blue Room behind him, and then he slipped as quietly as he could across the hall and into the spiral stairwell. One twist of the stairwell went down into the lowest levels of this wing of the Library, and he'd eagerly explored that with Stjepan and Gilgwyr back in the day, but he ignored it and headed up, listening in case there was anyone above him. Up to the Blue Room he was within his rights and could easily explain his presence; but now, moving up to the top floor, he started to sweat again even with the incantation, for he knew it wasn't foolproof. He paused at the landing, listening for noise in the corridors beyond. Hearing nothing, he slid out onto the top floor.

The windowless corridor was only dimly lit, the only light cast from a few haphazardly spaced oil lamps on sconces, but the incantation made the corridor shine a bit more brightly in Harvald's eyes. Deep, dark doorways flanked him on both sides of the hall as he moved toward the Black Rooms, and he came to a halt outside the outer door. It was large, made of blackened oak and bound in elaborate bronze fretwork which was shaped in its center into a *Daedeki Grammata ward* rune like the one he had on his amulet: a six-pointed star set within a circle.

Rituals had a way of leaving bits of energy and power behind in the places they were performed, so any place where men and women performed magical or sacred rituals on a regular basis could soon become a repository of latent power: temples and shrines, for example, or a wizard's tower. Natural parts of the landscape could also hold reservoirs of power for those who knew how to tap them: glens and groves, lakes, waterfalls, caves, hilltops and mountains could all become sacred places thanks to the whims of nature or the veneration of men, animals, or spirits. The *menhirs*, the old *fae* stones, were a way for the *fae* and other peoples of the ancient world to identify and access such spots. And the same was true for places of death and ruin, such as battlefields, gallows, and graveyards, where the spirits of the dead had congregated and passed out of the world.

The University itself was no different; not only was it a place where over its many centuries thousands of students had performed magic rites large and small, copied spells and rituals, and worshipped their gods with prayers or offerings, but it was also quite possibly built on top of an ancient maze and labyrinth which had been the scene of much death and suffering. And thanks to his incantation he could see an impressive enchantment worked upon the door, tapping into the magical and spiritual power of the building and the earth upon which it was built, and binding some of that power into the *ward* rune to prevent anyone from entering without the key. Unlike the keys to the Rare Books Rooms, which were held in the safekeeping of the librarians at the front desk, the keys to the Black Rooms were worn on a chain hung around the neck of Master Clodarius. Once upon a time other Magisters had been allowed to carry their own keys to the Black Rooms, but that had stopped after a recent scandal and now only Clodarius and Clodarius alone could open the door.

Harvald stood before the door, inspecting it. The fretwork *ward* rune was affixed into the center of the door, just about chest height, and the keyhole was dead center to the rune. He slipped the key to the Blue Room out of his satchel, and holding both of his amulets in one hand, he began to slide the key into the keyhole. Keeping the rune of *making* in his mind again, he began to whisper into the keyhole, his voice almost seductive: *"Make this the Key. Make this the Key to this Door. This* is *the Key. This* is *the Key to this Door. Open the Lock to this Door. Open this Door!"* He could feel the enchantment resisting his incantation, could feel its strength pushing back at him; but he wasn't trying to break the enchantment, just fool it. And against the tapped power bound into the enchantment, siphoned up from the bones of the ancient building, he'd brought a reservoir of his own: a vial of his sister's last tears, collected years ago as she wept in her sleep, with all her grief and despair trapped within each drop of True Love.

The lock never had a chance.

Harvald took a deep breath and then exhaled slowly as he turned the key. It turned perfectly, and he could hear a metal mechanism clicking away on the other side of the door. The door swung open, and he stepped inside quickly, and closed it behind him.

The space he was in was pitch black. He held onto his copper amulet, the rune of *light* in his mind, and whispered a quick Incantation of Making: *"Illumina mundi!"* The more ancient the language, the more powerful the incantation, but unlike Stjepan, who had an easy facility with many different tongues, Harvald had only memorized a handful of incantations in any language beyond the Middle Tongue. A cold blue light began to shine from his amulet, and as he began to make out his surroundings a figure loomed in front of him. He gave a start, his hackles rising, and then immediately felt foolish as he realized it was just a statue made of marble. The statue depicted one of the *Sharab Deceal*, the winged harpy guardian spirits of the Underworld which were often set as watchers over the treasure troves of magicians, glaring with a drawn and upraised short sword at whoever entered the room. But if the statue had once served as the locus for a binding enchantment for an actual spirit once, Harvald could see no evidence that there was one present now, and he breathed a sigh of relief.

Beyond the statue, he could see three doors; each identical to the door he had just passed through. The contents of each room were closely guarded secrets, and men had paid with their lives for trying to get a peek at the catalog ledgers for the Black Rooms kept in Master Clodarius' chambers. Stjepan, Gilgwyr, and Harvald had spent a small portion of their free time at the University trying to figure out ways to get a glimpse into the catalogs to see what was there, and could never find a suitable plan worth risking everything for. But Harvald had different ways through the world now, years later, and different friends, and he had asked a very special friend in which room he could find a translated copy of *De Malifir Magicis*, the very rare and quite forbidden *Book of Curse Magic* of Ymaire, the enchantress daughter of Eldyr. And luckily that friend knew which room it was in, and so Harvald went directly to the door on his right.

He repeated the steps that had gained him entry through the first warded door, and was rewarded with the opening of this second door. He stepped inside, and stifled a laugh of giddy awe.

Harvald stood in a fabled place, where few eyes had ever been allowed. He wondered, for a moment, if he was the first trespasser this Black Room had ever seen in the four centuries since it was created; there were stories amongst the students of cunning thieves and dastardly wizards who had stolen into the Black Rooms to make off with powerful grimoires, and while Harvald suspected that most of them were probably just campus folk tales, some instinct told him that he was not the first sneak-thief to stand where he was standing. Still, for a moment he luxuriated in the achievement, taking in the bookcases made of bronze, the dark cabinets and occasional tables and chairs. The shelves, he could see, held not just books, but an assortment of odds and ends; there appeared to be a collection of ceremonial sacrificial knives, several rune-marked skulls, chalices, wooden boxes chased in gold and jewels and filled with lead tablets inscribed with curses, hands made of wax, riveted brass heads . . . a veritable treasure trove of occult paraphernalia. Harvald gaped, and he had to fight the urge to stuff his satchel full of as many things as he could grab. Oddly he found the words of his own advice running through his head. "Don't get distracted by the obvious bright bauble," he'd told young Erim. *Sound thinking*, he thought. *Eyes on the prize, as Guilford might have said, the poor bastard. You're here for a reason.*

He set about finding his quarry, and it took him almost thirty nerve-wracking minutes to find the small black-bound copy of *De Malifir Magicis*, and miraculously right next to it, a translated copy in the Middle Tongue with the name *The Book of Curse Magic*. There was no seeming organization to the room, even worse so than in the Blue Room downstairs, though he also conceded that it was more understandable here, as these books were by definition *forbidden* and so it wasn't as though people were supposed to have an easy time finding them. He doubted what he held in his hands was the original *De Malifir Magicis;* Stjepan was better with books as well as languages, but Harvald guessed from the crumbling gold-stamped black bindings and the look of the parchment that it was made perhaps six centuries after Ymaire's time on earth, probably sometime during the Bronze Age. The Middle Tongue translation looked to have been made within the last century. He held them both reverently for a moment, and then slipped them into his satchel.

He stepped back out into the room with the statue, closing the door to the Black Room behind him. He checked to make sure that the enchantments on the door appeared as they did before, and to his relief they did. He raised his amulet to his mouth and doused its light with a quick exhalation through pursed lips, then slowly opened the outer door and stepped out into the hallway, closing it behind him.

He had to fight the urge to run as he walked down the corridor, his first mission there accomplished, his body alive with tension and relief and the sharp desire to be safely downstairs. He allowed himself to pick up the pace as he approached the stairwell down.

Until suddenly one of the doors between him and the stairwell opened, light and voices flooded into the hall, and several men started to step out into his path.

148

Almost without breaking stride he side-stepped into the nearest closed doorway and froze, dropping back into the shadows, for he knew instantly that there was no way to make it past the opening door to the stairwell, and he couldn't make it back to the door to the Black Rooms in time. *Gods, let the incantation work*, he prayed, clutching his copper amulet with one hand while the other slid to the hilt of his dagger. He paled as he recognized first the voices and then the faces of the men emerging into the corridor: no less than three of the University's Magisters.

". . . then it is settled. I will lead an expedition to Abenton, and attend upon the Baroness, though my mission may prove wholly fruitless," sighed the first man as he stepped out into the corridor. Harvald recognized the familiar face of Magister Arathon, who held the Chair of Heraldry; his gold chain of office was very elaborate, and his rich brown gown was adorned with extensive gold thread embroidery. The barrel-chested man wore a black felt skullcap, the mark of a full Magister, but unlike the others his skullcap was embroidered in gold to match his gowns.

"Your disappointment is phenomenally unconvincing," snorted Odrue following behind him. "You know full well she is the niece of the High King, and though her position is increasingly perilous, she is still one of his favorites." Odrue was tall, white-haired and white-bearded, hawk-nosed, and a foreigner, the only Palatian to have ever risen to the heights of a full Chair at the University, that of Geography.

"I assure you that the politics involved never crossed my mind," laughed Arathon.

Magister Clodarius, master librarian and holder of the Chair of Letters, was the last out the door, and he locked the room behind them. "You never think of anything *but* politics, Arathon," the gray-haired, gray-bearded librarian said wearily. "Indeed, it is the very nature of the Chair that you hold at this University."

Harvald licked his lips and started to slide his dagger out of its sheath, slowly revealing the Riven Runes etched upon its blade. To contemplate the attempted murder of a single Magister at the University was difficult enough, a horrible crime beyond reckoning; to contemplate killing three of them, swiftly and silently, was to contemplate an epic act worthy of history. Particularly since he had attended lectures of all three, and Arathon had been his patron in the study of Heraldry. Odrue and Clodarius were certainly quite old, even ancient (rumor had it that Odrue was one hundred and forty years old, almost as old as Duke Urech of Palatia and the Lord Mott, whose lives had been extended by magic and the blessings of their foreign gods), and the stocky Arathon was at least fifty, but they all held about them an unnatural air of vigor. Every Magister at the University was a skilled and practiced magician, even if they eschewed the term; with the Incantation of Seeing still effective upon him, Harvald could see they bore about their bodies amulets and talismans of power, wards to protect them from harm and danger, and in the case of Odrue, a bound *Dhuréleal* spirit that was manifesting the spirit form of a gray and white eagle perched upon his shoulders, its great wings stretching up to the high ceiling of the corridor.

Harvald knew well the limitations of magic; he knew that fables and stories of wizards calling down fire from the Heavens and bringing buildings down with a gust of wind were just that, fables and stories from fevered and superstitious imaginations; but might they know a word that once spoken could stop him in his tracks, make him forget who he was? Might they let the *Dhuréleal* spirit loose, or have time to summon something even worse, as the sorceress had done in the temple beneath the hills of the Manon Mole? Three Magisters of the University possessed knowledge far beyond Harvald's limited understanding.

But they've never faced the likes of me, he thought, licking his lips. In his mind's eye he could see it: *throw a binding hex at the spirit, a frenzied surprise attack so that they don't have time to figure out what's going on, fast dagger work, go for throats and lungs so they can't scream, then drag their bodies into the Black Rooms where they will be safely behind a door that few would dare unlock, even if they had the power to do so, and use their gowns to clean up the blood. This is doable.*

And then the *Dhuréleal* turned in his direction, its blank white eyes and sharp beak sweeping the corridor, and fear struck him deep and he pressed as far back into the arched doorway as he could, as though he was trying to become one with the wood of the door behind his back. *I'm a fool and my life is at an end*, he thought.

But the *Dhuréleal* did not see him. It eyed the corridor briefly, and then, seemingly satisfied, turned and looked in the other direction.

". . . In the meantime, may I suggest we use this reminder of the dangers of the Gray Dream to sharpen our own vigilance here on the campus," said Clodarius. "Six students in the past semester alone. That's the most in one semester since Alefric actually let the cult operate openly at the University. It's a wonder that we have managed to keep the problem discreet."

"I see no gain in summoning the Inquisition to prowl amongst us once again," said Odrue. "It took the University thirty years to remove them the last time. May I suggest that we call the Chairs to secret council and appoint one of the Under-Magisters to root out the cult that has clearly taken root amongst us?"

"And may I suggest we start with the Mottists?" asked Arathon with a touch of glee. He turned, and to Harvald's relief began leading the other two Magisters down the corridor away from him.

"By all means, let us waste our time," Odrue snorted. "There is no evidence to suggest that the students of the Mottist College are somehow more prone to the Cult of the Gray Dream than any other. The whole point of the college is that they look to the north, to Palatia and the Lord Mott, for their inspiration, not to the south and the Empire. Indeed I cannot help but point out that of the six students fallen into the Gray Dream last semester, none was from either the Mottist College or the College of the Globe."

"You bait too easily," Clodarius sighed. "But surely you do not mean to suggest that your former countrymen are impervious to the call of the Gray Dream?"

"Of course not; hidden Dreamers can be found anywhere. But I would certainly be willing to suggest that they have fallen into the cult with far less frequency than the men of the Hemispian cities, or this city, for that matter," Odrue said, as the trio faded down the corridor. "And we all know that in the Empire itself men fall to the Dream as though it were a plague . . ."

Finally Harvald was alone in the corridor. He let go his breath, and gave a quick prayer; he had been sure the *Dhuréleal* spirit was going to see him, if not one of the Magisters. *Thank the gods the incantation held*, he thought. He waited until his breathing had returned to normal and the corridor was completely quiet, then slipped back out to the stairwell door.

Harvald slipped back into the Blue Room and closed the door behind him. He let go of the incantations that he had been holding and he was shocked at the sweet relief and fatigue that the release washed over him. He hadn't realized how much of his energy and concentration had been bound up in maintaining the spells for so long. He leaned by the door shaking like a leaf until his nerves calmed and he was in control of himself once more.

He moved to the desk and set his satchel down. He guzzled from his water bottle, amazed at how thirsty he was. *Six Gray Dreamers in the last semester, that's a bit of news*, he thought, and then almost laughed out loud at how little he cared. A few weeks before and having a juicy tidbit like that would have been the highlight of his day. *But not now. Not with this.*

He opened his satchel and from it placed upon his desk first the freshly liberated *De Malifir Magicis* of Ymaire and its translation, his student copy of Magister Gwyrfyr's *On Ciphers and Cryptograms*, and then the copper scroll tube. He opened the tube and carefully slid the rolled parchment out, and then spread it open upon the desktop. He rummaged about the holding compartments of the desk and pulled out four small iron paperweights, which he placed at the four corners of the parchment to keep it flat and in place, and then stepped back to admire it.

A map to the Barrow of Azharad, if he could translate it.

Stjepan was better qualified to translate the map. They both knew it. Stjepan was the actual cartographer, versed in old maps and map ciphers, familiar with the Éduinan, Golan, and Maelite alphabets and a fluent reader of many of the languages that used them, including Old Éduinan,

Emmetic, Athairi, Danian, Aurian, Daedekine, Sekereti, the Eastern Tongue, and Maerberos. Harvald had always been jealous of Stjepan's skills with language and letters; but then it was also true that Stjepan had applied himself more diligently to their study than Harvald, who had often been distracted with other passions during their time as students, and Harvald had had no regrets. Up until now.

Getting Stjepan to wait until they were back in the city had been difficult. But Harvald knew he couldn't let Stjepan translate the map. Not without first lifting the curse on it. And how could he have explained to Stjepan that he knew the map was cursed? He'd only recognized the four ornamental marks at the corners of the map for what they were because he'd known to look for them, been warned that they might be there. Stjepan had always had a nose for when Harvald was hiding something, and though he had managed to keep secrets from him over the years, he was always nervous when that terrible, judgmental gaze of Stjepan's fell upon him. For all sorts of reasons, none of which he ever wanted to discuss with Stjepan.

No, this plan is the best, Harvald thought. *I shall remove the curse, and either translate the map myself, or failing that, make a faithful copy without the curse enchanted into it that Stjepan can work on.* He stared at the map a long time.

I wish I'd paid more attention in class, he thought faintly, and then reached for the translation of *The Book of Curse Magic*.

CHAPTER EIGHT

ROUND MIDNIGHT, WHEN IT ALL GOES EVEN MORE TERRIBLY WRONG

S omewhere in the dark, a woman whispered.

He moved across the attic by the dim light of his covered candle lantern, finding his way as much by memory as by vision, until he reached the proper spot, kneeling and as quietly as possible shuttering the lantern so that its small light was covered and the room plunged into black. He lay down flat on his stomach and felt for the small iron eye-ring in the floor, found it, and then pulled up on it slowly, opening the peephole cover. He pressed his face to the floor, his eyes blinking and squinting to focus on the woman in the room beneath him.

Annwyn was dressed in a simple but finely made robe, seated upon a plain hard bench in her private chambers. The room was austere, even cold, virtually bereft of any memento of sentiment or personality, any hint of softness. Two large armoires held her clothes, though long ago she had given away anything other than the habitual black ensembles that constituted her mourning armor. As the Lady of a proper Aurian noble family, she naturally had such ensembles in a variety of seasonal styles, though someone unversed in the minutiae of city fashion would undoubtedly have simply thought her armoires full of the same set of black clothes over and over again. But Annwyn's sense of style was so formidable that even when she wasn't thinking about it (which she had not, for over a decade), she instinctively chose well when it came to tailoring and stitching.

The candles in Annwyn's rooms burned brightly. She had a small leather-bound book in her hands, and she read slowly, whispering to herself as she constructed the words in her head. Where once she had found pleasure in so many things in life—in dances and revels, in hosting company at her father's castle, in long rides into the countryside, in singing and bards and poets, in the formalities and intricacies of the Court, in her friends and rivals in the great social order of the Middle Kingdoms and its capital—now the only thing that she looked forward to each day was a small bit of escape, when she could read words written or printed on paper and let her mind wander to other places, other times, other people, and forget who she was, and what she had done.

"My Lady," came Malia's voice from the doorway.

But even this simple pleasure must come to an end, Annwyn thought. She looked up, and smiled softly at the appearance of her most loyal hand-maiden. Malia forever wore a slight frown and look of consternation, as though worried that she had forgotten something very important. Which, Annwyn supposed, she probably had. Malia was so very good at forgetting. "Malia," said Annwyn. "Does it grow so late?"

"Yes, my Lady, the hour grows very late," said Malia. "The rest of the household is mostly asleep, but I had Henriette and Frallas fill a hot bath for you. If you will forgive the presumption, I thought you might want it after such a . . . long day."

"It has been a long day," Annwyn said, and closed her book. She ran her fingers over the cover, tracing the gold debossed letters in its surface. The cover read *The Romance of the Dragon King*, the name of a popular version of the *Adüra Draconum Fini*, the epic song cycle *Last of the Dragon Kings* by the bard Üsker that many considered the last great epic in the old Danian language, being printed and sold in the city from one of its new printing presses; popular, yes, but also a much simplified and glamorized version of the song cycle, taking considerable liberties with the history of Erlwulf, last of the Dragon Kings, and seemingly adding in a romantic lost love unmentioned in any other record of the period. Still, it sufficed for her purposes.

Annwyn stood up from the wood bench and stepped to one of her armoires. She opened the doors and then a small interior drawer, in which several other small leather books were placed, most with the word "romance" in their titles. She sighed, and then followed Malia through a curtained door in the rear of the chamber. As she stepped through it, her robe began to slip from her shoulders, and then she was gone from sight.

He cursed softly, nervous and excited. He carefully replaced the peephole cover, and sat up before cautiously feeling for the covered lantern. He opened up the shutters, allowing more light to spill through, and then stood. He forced himself to move quietly and slowly, knowing that the floors did occasionally squeak, but so, so eager not to miss anything.

Erim loved the city at night. She had never been to Palatia Archaia, or the city of Hemapoli in the League, or to the Imperial capital at Avellos, all of them reportedly cities where the markets never closed and even in the dead of night the streets were ablaze with light; but Therapoli had to come pretty close, she reckoned. Some of the food shops and eateries along the Grand Promenade were still going strong, and she knew the outer arcades of the Forum would still be filled with groups of men singing and drinking; she could hear them in the distance all the way from where she walked. She smelled lamps burning and pies baking, pigs roasting and the sweet, putrid mix of piss and vomit, and felt light with joy at the simple pleasures of a night filled with revelers.

PART ONE: IN THE CITY OF MONEY AND FILTH

She turned up Wall Street and headed up into the Old Quarter, nodding to the men from the City Watch that walked past her, the hilts of their broadswords and heads of their long-spiked billhooks glistening in the lamplight. Had she been dressed according to her gender, they might not have been so easy to walk past; a woman alone in most parts of the city at night would either immediately be offered an escort for protection, should she be deemed a lady or woman of repute, or questioned as to her intentions, should she be dressed too provocatively. And depending on her answers, that could lead to her arrest, or if she fell afoul of the wrong group of Watchmen, a more vigorous and far less desirable form of questioning. But as she was dressed as a man, they saw her as a man and paid her no mind.

Of course, turning up toward the Old Quarter might well have been a signal to them of a man's poor intentions, as the Old Quarter was where most of the city's brothels and streetwalkers could be found. But the Princes of the Guild who ran the Old Quarter had long ago made it worthwhile for the Watch to spend its energies elsewhere, and so soon she found herself walking past dancing halls and taverns, with drunken men and scantily clad dancers visible through the doors and windows, if not spilling out into the streets. Heavily inebriated men singing loudly walked past her, stumbling past couples discreetly heading to apartment doorways. A bit further up and painted women were actively trolling the street, greeting her with smiles that ranged from the genuine to the desperate, while street urchins begged for coin and eyed her purse, or offered themselves for sale. But she merely shook her head politely at each invitation and kept going.

She finally turned into a wide cobble-stoned alley off Wall Street and nodded her head nonchalantly to the two bravos leaning against the wall and warming their hands over a fire in a large metal bucket as she passed them. They gave her a quick once-over and she wasn't sure if they recognized her, but at least they didn't read her as a threat. She walked down to the unmarked metal gates built into a large arch in the north wall, and knocked on it twice. A spy hole in the gate slid open, and a pair of dull, heavy-lidded eyes stared down at her for a long moment. The plate slid shut, and then the gate creaked open. She nodded at the big burly men standing behind the gate, and let the growling Highland pit bulls that they had on leashes sniff the back of her hand, then walked through the short cobble-stoned entry passage and out into a large courtyard. Horses and even a couple of coaches were lined up to one side, either tied to hitching posts or held by squires or menservants. On the other side of the courtyard she passed into a covered arcade, and followed it until she reached the top of a dark, broad stairwell with a single silent sentinel. She nodded to him then followed the stairs down. At the landing she turned in through a doorway under the building. There were no lights here, so she had to feel her way along the passage, taking two turns, until she felt heavy brocade curtains in front of her. She pushed her way through, and blinked in the dim candlelight. She nodded at the two big burly men in the small chamber, and they nodded back. She could hear music and voices from beyond the next curtains, and she crossed the chamber in a few short steps and pushed her way through the velvet brocade curtains into the Sleight of Hand.

Gilgwyr is, if nothing else, a showman, she thought as she paused at the entrance to the long vaulted brothel hall decorated in imitation of a sumptuous harem. The hall was more brightly lit with candles and low braziers, but still managed to seem dark and dangerous. Drummers and musicians were putting out a sinuous, rhythmic music; raucous laughter and cries of passion punctuated the smoky air, while barely-clad dancers shimmied and shook on tabletops. A rough-trade crowd of wealthy johns and dandies from every part of the city, rival pimps and prostitutes, Marked Men and their crews with black teardrops drawn by the corners of their eyes in mourning, and other denizens of the night and the city's underworld filled the room almost to bursting, all of them come to lose themselves in the intoxicating bit of theater created by their host. There were far more of them than she could count. She could even see what she guessed were perhaps as many as thirty masked lords and ladies, slumming it amongst the other common customers and brave enough to rub elbows with men who would gladly rob them elsewhere: men like Petterwin Grim, still handsome despite his scars, and a half dozen of his Grimsmen, and old Potter Aelias and his crew, taking a night off from preying on foreign sailors on the docks. She spotted

Jon Dhee, master of the Market Quarter, his long stringy hair coming down in front of his mean, scrunched up face, and then she spotted the unmistakable profile of Long Nose Ludwyn, a notoriously cruel rapist. All four were Marked Men of the Guild, but still the blacklisted Red Rob Asprin was nonchalantly sitting a few tables over with several of his men, sipping a glass of wine while a pretty blonde Aurian dancer slobbered all over his erect cock; two masked Aurian noblewomen stood nearby, watching the casual show with excited eyes and parted lips. Mina the Dagger, called by some the most vicious and terrifying woman in the city, was over by a long wood bar with a tall thin pretty boy on each arm; Erim knew that despite their painted, bored faces and frilled doublets that her boy toys were expert duelists, with over a dozen kills apiece. Mina had several women from her stable with her and they looked like they were happy for the night off. A wild-eyed Helgi Ketildram drunkenly stumbled past her, shirtless, his massive muscles and the barbaric designs on his inked skin enough to part the startled crowd of johns and dandies. He was trailed by several of his girls, and they didn't look happy in the least.

She was already impressed with the evening's roll of deviants and delinquents when she spotted the Gilded Lady holding court in a corner, along with her ladies-in-waiting, and she almost let out a low whistle that Gilgwyr was getting Princes of the Guild into the Hand. The Gilded Lady was of course not a lady at all (and neither were her ladies), but a man whom Stjepan said had once gone by the name of Cole the Killer. Even with a Prince present in the room, there were plenty of grudges that out on the street could rapidly lead to drawn swords and daggers and bloodshed, even amongst the Marked, but Gilgwyr was a respected independent and she figured it would take a lot of alcohol to make any of them break the law of hospitality.

The crowd parted a bit on her left and Erim almost did a double take. A woman was passing through the johns and dandies toward her, topless, her shapely bronze body glistening in the firelight with oil and gold dust. She wore a jeweled black lace choker and a black-feathered raven half-mask, gold armbands and bracelets, and a loosely-woven fishnet dress tied low about her hips that did little to conceal her shaved pubic mound. A red velvet wrap that was chained to her bracelets trailed behind her. Long legs and black chunk-heeled ankle boots made her seem taller than she was. Her fingernails were long, almost like spikes, and were painted black. Between her full breasts and pierced nipples hung a long ivory unicorn horn, suspended from a gold chain around her neck. There was no mistaking her outfit, or lack thereof: she was dressed as a priestess of the Forbidden Cult of Ligrid, the Goddess of Perversion.

Oh, you go too far, Gilgwyr, Erim thought. *Is that unicorn horn real?* Gilgwyr had steadily built the Sleight of Hand into virtually hallowed ground for the city's underworld, not simply with the quality of his stock, but with a steady showman's hand and an eye toward lewd, obscene, and yet totally artful performance. Many in the crowd, for example, were watching in a mix of awe and lust as a nude dancer spun and contorted in midair using long silk scarves dangling from a chandelier, her aerial dancing a new kind of spectacle in the city. But to have a woman dressed as a priestess of the Nameless Cults was to be genuinely inviting the unwanted attention of the Inquisition and the City Watch. She shook her head.

"A most excellent costume," she said and bowed slightly as the priestess passed her by. She inhaled the woman's scent, and she smelled of gold and lavender and sex.

"This isn't a costume," the woman replied, looking at and startling Erim with piercing black eyes. Erim felt like she was nailed to the floor, unable to break the woman's gaze; she was almost overcome with a sense of age, and deep wisdom, and an unfathomable corruption. The priestess reached up and stroked Erim's face with a finger, and the sharp point of her long nail nicked Erim's lip. Erim started at the sharp pain, the spell broken, and she frowned and brought her hand to her mouth as the priestess licked the tip of her fingernail, smiled at her, and moved on into the crowd.

Holy shit, Erim thought. *What the fuck is Gilgwyr playing at?* She flushed and looked around as she checked her mouth to see if it was bleeding, wondering if anyone had seen the exchange; but no one nearby seemed to be paying her any attention. Deeply unsettled, she decided to find Stjepan and Harvald as quickly as possible.

She brushed her way through the crowd, glancing this way and that, until she found herself in the circle of men watching the suspended dancer. Erim paused for a moment, admiring the lithe, athletic body and long, copper-skinned limbs of the woman as she spun and twirled through the air. The way she used the silks to hold herself up and in the air made her seem like a magician who could fly, and Erim knew how strong and flexible the woman had to be to hold the poses she was taking for the crowd's delight. *Hair's too curly to be an Athairi, so maybe a Palatian*, Erim thought. *Another coup for Gilgwyr.* The Palatian dancer glanced over and caught her eye; there was a spark there, but a different one than with the pretend priestess. The dancer pivoted in the air slightly, reworking her limbs and her silks, and then suddenly she swiveled and her whole body reversed until she was dangling upside-down in front of Erim, her pelvis swinging gently before Erim's face and her head level with Erim's codpiece, her legs scissored wide and feet pointed at opposite walls and the winking lips of her vulva puckering in invitation.

"Go on, boy, have a taste!" someone in the raucous crowd yelled, and a cheer went up around her.

"Gold, wine, women . . . and gems the size of your fucking head," Erim whispered to herself. "Hope you found the Heavens, Guilford." She leaned in a bit, and took a heady whiff of the Palatian's sweet aroma.

Someone sidled up to her and slipped an arm over her shoulder, and joined her in eyeing the dancer's proffered pelvis. She knew it was Gilgwyr without having to look, but she did anyway. He was dressed in subtle and expensive finery, a golden-yellow silk doublet with gold thread embroidery on the long sleeves, black and gold puffed trunk knickerbockers, and black hose and boots. A black sash crossed his chest, pinned with a gold brooch in the shape of a curled dragon. He could be arrested for that outfit in the streets, as the city's sumptuary laws prohibited cloth-of-gold for anyone not of noble birth. *But then, I suppose this is the King and Knave of Coins in the flesh*, she mused.

"So, Erim, what do you think of Guilford's wake?" he asked her, nuzzling her ear.

"Ah, is that why so many of the Marked are here, and a Prince of the Guild as well?" she asked.

"Yes, I have some special treats in store for our friends to mark the occasion," he said. He had a pursed, wicked smile and one raised eyebrow as he contemplated the visual spread before him. "I see you have met her cunt, but have you had the pleasure of being introduced to Ariadesma, our newest import all the way from far Palatia Archaia?" he asked. "Tonight is her debut."

"I have not," said Erim. "A most impressive performance, Ariadesma."

"Ariadesma, this is Master Erim, one of my close friends," Gilgwyr said.

"Ana plaisant'a connaita. A pleasure to meet you, Master Erim," said upside-down Ariadesma, with a heavy Palatian accent that Erim found instantly endearing.

"Ariadesma was a dancer in the Palatian capital, but felt her true potential was not being reached, and so she made her way to Lagapoli and spent several years in training at the temples to Dieva there. The silks are just a taste of her skills; her performance is just getting started tonight. I've got to get her in training for something truly special," said Gilgwyr, then he leaned in closer. "I hear you are breaking the hearts of all of my dancers one by one," whispered Gilgwyr in her ear. "They pine for you, for your handsome beauty, and ever seem disappointed that they do not win your favor. Are you really so experienced as to be the master seducer?"

"Oh, you might be surprised," shrugged Erim.

"Careful, young Erim. Very little surprises me," said Gilgwyr, straightening a bit and speaking a bit louder. "And where is our dear friend Stjepan?"

Erim turned her head so she could whisper in his ear. "Right behind you," she said.

Gilgwyr turned, a bemused expression on his face, and Stjepan was standing right behind them, dressed in a tight high-collared black leather doublet, black breeches, and high black leather boots. He nodded casually at Gilgwyr, who grinned in response.

"Stjepan Black-Heart, old boy. Where have you been? You're late," said Gilgwyr as he disentangled himself from around Erim. The two men embraced, and Gilgwyr took the opportunity to whisper in his ear. "Leigh's waiting. But the Gilded Lady wishes a word."

"Can't keep Leigh waiting, can we? But then, when a Prince of the Guild calls, you best answer," Stjepan said, indicating that Gilgwyr should lead on. Erim stepped back from Ariadesma's suspended body, and gave a slight bow. She noticed that the woman dressed as the Ligrid priestess stepped in behind her to take her place before Ariadesma's opened and upside-down crotch, and would have stayed to see what happened next but Stjepan softly called her name.

She followed the two of them through the crowd over to the corner in which the Gilded Lady sat with her ladies-in-waiting. The Gilded Lady wore a black arched-front mourning bodice and silk damask dress over a cloth-of-gold petticoat with brocaded patterns. She wore jeweled bracelets and an ornamental gold girdle. A chain of office, made from a string of gold crowns, ducats, florins, and livres in imitation of the collars of the nobility, marked her as a Prince of the Guild. Her bodice came up to her chin, and under the high collar she wore a black lace choker over her apple. Her hair was black and swept up above her head in an elaborate coiffure, pinned in place with gold jewels. Her face was surprisingly untouched by makeup, unlike her ladies-in-waiting, who had faces painted pale and rouged cheeks. The Gilded Lady was content with heavy eyeliner and thick lashes, the gold eye shadow that inspired her name, and ruby red lips that she pursed in a pout. She looked fabulous. She and her ladies-in-waiting all bore a black tear, drawn in by the corner of their left eye. *My kith and kin*, thought Erim.

"My Lady," said Stjepan with a bow. He kissed the offered hand of the Gilded Lady and then he took an empty seat that was offered to him across from the Guild Prince. Gilgwyr remained standing off to one side, and Erim took his cue to do the same.

"Black-Heart," purred the Gilded Lady, her voice incongruously deep for her appearance. "It's been too long."

"It has, my Lady, but your beauty has only grown in the passing of the seasons," Stjepan said with a half-smile.

164

"Flattery will get you everywhere, most especially onto the tip of my cock," the Gilded Lady laughed, and her ladies-in-waiting laughed with her. Erim felt like they were sizing up both her and Stjepan like sides of meat. "Everywhere, of course, except off the blacklist."

"I would never dare to ask such a favor of the Guild," Stjepan said quietly. "The decision is a fair one, and I will stand by the Guild's judgment, and wait for a summons to make amends, should it ever come."

"You know the Fat Prince and the Red Wyrm will never want you back in the Guild's good graces, for their own selfish reasons," said the Gilded Lady. "But Mowbray and I shall do what we can, when we feel the time appropriate."

"Then I will be in your debt," Stjepan said, with a slight incline of his head.

The Gilded Lady paused, and Erim thought she saw the Lady's eyes go moist. "Did . . . did he say anything about me?" the Gilded Lady asked. "In the moments before he died? I did not dare hope that after all these years . . ."

Stjepan shook his head. "I'm afraid not, my Lady," he said quietly. "His last moments were spent in concern for the fate of his crew, and in fear of the *Baalhazor* that sought his doom. I wish it were otherwise." The Gilded Lady and her ladies-in-waiting blanched at the mention of the *Rahabi*, and they all made signs to ward off the Evil Eye. "But we did talk a bit about his days in Therapoli on our journey up into the hills, and he did remember you with fondness."

The Gilded Lady sobbed a bit, and then held her breath, as though fighting back a tear. She shook herself and gave an exasperated little cry. "What am I, some poor heartbroken damsel pining for the one that got away?" she exclaimed loudly. "Fuck that, I'm the Gilded Lady!" Her fist pounded down on the table and her ladies-in-waiting roared their approval lustily. "A toast to departed Guilford!" she cried as her ladies-in-waiting poured brandy into glasses that were scattered about the tabletop. One was handed to Stjepan and he raised the glass to the ceiling before joining the others in downing it.

Stjepan smiled and stood, giving her a short bow. "I'm afraid I must take my leave of you, my Lady," he said. "There is some urgent business that awaits us."

"Without introducing me to your companion?" the Gilded Lady asked expectantly, licking her lips.

Stjepan paused and considered the Lady for a moment. "My apologies," he said, and motioned to Erim. Erim stepped forward and gave a short bow. "This is Master Erim, a sure duelist if ever you need one."

"Duelists, assassins, and murderers I have aplenty, my dear Black-Heart, but pretty young things that would look good bouncing up and down on my great, big cock are in short supply," the Gilded Lady said with a dangerous-looking sneer, and Erim flushed a deep red. "Oh, and he even looks pretty when he blushes as well. Please do lend him to us when you're done with him, and we'll make sure he's well taken care of." Her ladies-in-waiting tittered.

Stjepan and Gilgwyr bowed and excused themselves, and Erim surprised herself by stepping forward and taking the offered hand of the Gilded Lady and giving it a kiss while looking into her eyes. "Oh, well done," whispered the Lady to her with a wink, and then Erim turned and hurried off after Stjepan, swallowing her heart back into her chest.

They passed through the back of the hall and up a broad set of stone stairs to the ground floor of the building. After purchasing the compound soon after his graduation from the University, Gilgwyr had bricked up all the entrances into the building on the ground floor so that entry could only be gained by going down into and through the great vaulted cellar, though Erim was sure that Gilgwyr probably had some secret means of egress. All the windows facing out onto public streets and alleys had been bricked off, as well, and the only windows unobstructed were up in the bedchambers of the first floor that faced the inner courtyard, where the women of the brothel would take their customers. At the top of the stairs was a large hall where Gilgwyr's customers would pick from amongst his girls, if they had not found one on the prowl in the main brothel hall below. A few scantily clad women lolled on padded benches and ornate couches, taking breaks

166

from their busy night. She spotted the house's enchanter slowly making his way toward the stairs carrying a small box, and Gilgwyr shouted out to him, "Better hurry, the show's about to start!" Sequintus grimaced and waved a hand in response but his pace didn't seem to change.

Gilgwyr grabbed up a lantern and led Stjepan and Erim back through dark corridors and empty halls into a chamber packed with casks and barrels and boxes under a low vaulted ceiling. This wing of the compound clearly wasn't used much, and the room was dark, lit only by the flickering light of several small braziers. Erim could barely make out an old man sitting behind a table by himself; he was solemnly preparing a Book of Dooms, shuffling the deck of cards ritualistically. His hair and bushy eyebrows and beard were still dark, almost the same blue-black as his robes, and Erim immediately thought that he must dye his hair, because the lines in his face seemed to mark him as a man whose hair should be gray or white, if he still had any hair at all. Deep lines were visible at the edges of his mouth, creased into his cheeks, under the bags of his crow-footed eyes. He was dressed in dark blue-black robes, the hood thrown back from his head, with flashes of gold jewelry and amulets at his wrists and around his collar, and gold rings were woven into his beard.

This, Erim thought, *must be the enchanter Leigh that I've heard so little about.*

Leigh placed a card down on the table in front of him; it was The Sphinx, the card numbered with an XV. It showed a winged sphinx—a chimera with the body of a lion, the upper torso and head of a beautiful woman, and the wings of a vulture—perched upon an anvil and holding the chains of a bound and naked couple. "The Sphinx . . . the catalyst of desire, the voice of deceit and influence. Hello, old friend," Leigh said quietly as if to himself, and then raised his voice to a bizarre loud singsong in greeting to them as they approached. "I . . . have . . . been . . . *wait* . . . ing!" Stjepan started to explain but Leigh held his hand up. "Spare me," the enchanter snorted. "I've had a long journey and, well, as you know I'm really not supposed to be in the city, so I shouldn't show my face, at least not where I might be recognized. Or so Gilgwyr keeps telling me. I'm quite convinced the city wouldn't care if I walked down the street naked. But as it is, I'm stuck hiding back here by myself."

"Then apologies, Magister," said Stjepan with a short bow. "I hope your journey will prove worth it. It is good to see you outside of your tower, if you do not mind me saying so."

"I do mind, but it was always kind of you to visit, so I won't hold it against you, Black-Heart," said Leigh with a smile, but for some reason Erim didn't believe him.

Stjepan gave a short bow. He turned to Gilgwyr. "So we have the map, and the enchanter. Now we need a new crew. Any word on someone to replace Guilford and his lot?"

"No," Gilgwyr sighed. "You say you're going after a wizard's barrow and that tends to dry up the available talent."

"I would imagine all but the greedy and the desperate," said Stjepan. "Or the insane."

"The *criminally* insane," corrected Leigh.

"Or just the flat-out stupid, who don't know any better," said Erim quietly. She felt a pang of guilt, remembering the sudden eagerness in Guilford when he had realized what Stjepan and Harvald were after. *And which was poor Guilford?* she wondered. *Which are we?*

"Yes, well . . . add to that the fact that news that you are on the Guild's blacklist has spread far and wide throughout the city, and replacing Guilford here in Therapoli has become, I'm afraid, an impossible task," said Gilgwyr.

"Did you ask Jonas and his boys?" Stjepan asked.

"I did, but they were already committed to another job. Or so they said," Gilgwyr replied with a rueful smile.

Stjepan shrugged. "Jonas's a smart man," he said. "How about Tyrius and his Hooded Men?"

"Broke up last month. You were out of town," Gilgwyr said apologetically.

"The Temple Street Irregulars?"

"In jail, the lot of them," said Gilgwyr. "Please believe me, I asked any independent crew of sufficient quality, and some of insufficient. Pellas the Quick, Mother Silva, Jon Deering, Rob Asprin, the Bastards

168

of Baker Street, Rafaelas Huelas, Jon Galbroke, Fulric Fingers, the East End Promenaders, Myrad's Mad Dogs, Corbin of Melos . . ." As Gilgwyr reeled off his names, Leigh flipped over several more cards, almost casually: the Knave of Swords, but reversed, depicting a dangerous looking man in armor wearing a mask and bearing a sword; the Knight of Swords, depicting a gallant knight in shining armor raising his sword; the Knave of Coins, depicting a masked man wielding a dagger and holding a coin in the palm of one hand; the Knave of Cups, reversed, depicting a masked priest holding a dagger in one hand and a chalice in the other. That last card he tried to hide before anyone could see it, but Erim saw it disappear up his sleeve, and she frowned, wondering what the card meant.

Finally Stjepan held up his hand and sourly waved off the recital

". . . yes, well, anyway, everyone's either said no or they're not available," Gilgwyr said, finishing with a sigh.

"Yeah," Stjepan said sourly.

"Knaves, knights, and more knaves . . . don't worry, we'll have a crew," Leigh breathed, looking at the cards dealt onto the table in front of him.

"The predictions of the Book of Dooms aside, I might have to come with you this time," Gilgwyr said. "We'll have to find a crew on the road somewhere."

"And leave this cozy place? That's a surprise, but I get it; this is a big one, if the map is real," Stjepan said with a sharp laugh.

"*If?* I came a long way because of this map. It's not translated yet?" Leigh asked.

Stjepan stared at him for a long moment. "Harvald specifically asked me not to translate the map until you were present. All I got was a glimpse of it in the shrine. Looked real enough. Harvald has it; I let him keep it," Stjepan said, his frown deepening.

Gilgwyr looked a bit surprised and worried. "He was supposed to be here two hours ago, Stjepan," said Gilgwyr. "He sent a message saying that he was going to try to get here early to talk to Leigh, but I hadn't really worried about it; I mean, you know Harvald, he's always late . . ."

They all looked at each other.

"What if he's ditching the lot of us? What if he's trying to translate it all by himself?" Erim finally asked.

Stjepan suddenly looked alarmed. "Shit. I think I know where he is," he said, and an instant later he was grabbing up a lantern and rushing out of the room, Erim following closely behind. Gilgwyr stood there for a moment, looking after them bemusedly.

Leigh returned to staring at his cards, tsking to himself. "So much for honor among thieves," he said.

Gilgwyr shouted after them: "Don't worry. Harvald won't let us down. We're partners. A veritable *band of brothers!*"

Leigh placed another card down; it was The Hanged Man, reversed, numbered XII. The card showed a man suspended by one foot by a rope from a crossbar, which rested upon two leafless trees. His free leg was crossed behind him, and he wore red and white clothes; a golden halo shown about his head, and from his coin purse came a shower of golden coins. Harvald looked at the card and did a double take. "Shit, I'm missing the show!" he groaned with a sudden start, and then he hurried from the room.

Leigh smiled to himself, alone again in the semi-dark. "A magician seeking answers . . ." he whispered, softly stroking the cards on the table before him.

Harvald muttered to himself, trying to voice the incomprehensible language of the old Mael Kings as his finger underlined an arcane symbol. He flipped through the pages of the *Libra di historum Manonesian* almost randomly, and then through *On the Languages of the Mael Kings*, and stopped on a cryptic reference. *Someone is breathing heavily*, he thought idly, and then he realized it was himself. He felt tired, so unbelievably tired, like the fatigue had set into his very bones, as he sat looking at pages of indecipherable text, his vision blurring, his eyes tearing up. The panic and fear was eating through him now, making it almost impossible to think. His hands traced the arcane symbols of the map spread out across the desktop before him. *So close. So close.*

A drop of blood fell onto the table, and then another, and then a piece of flesh dropped on a symbol on the map. Harvald stared at it blankly, wondering what it was.

His hand moved upon his erect member as he pressed his eye to the hole in the floor, hunching his hips, his teeth biting down on his lip to prevent himself from groaning. He did not think that she could be as beautiful as he remembered her in his dreams, and yet there she was, even more beautiful than ever.

Annwyn lay in a tub of steaming water, her body partly obscured by flower petals, as some of her handmaidens moved about the room, tidying and talking softly. She had never been as afraid of water as some of her kin, and she found that lying in the hot bath was often the only thing that could get her body to relax. Being in that house the whole day was like being trapped in amber, and her body would feel stiff and rusted by the end of the day, as though the slightest pressure would make her break. Without the bath to help her relax, sleep was almost impossible.

Annwyn appeared lost in thought but her eyes drifted up to the ceiling, and then almost deliberately toward a small hole that had been cut there, and then—

He pulled back from the peephole with a sudden start and slid the cover closed, wincing in the dark and praying that he hadn't made any noise. Had he imagined it? Did she know about the peephole? He could have sworn she had looked right at him . . .

A guttering lantern flickered in Stjepan's hand as he crossed the Lower Quad of the University, flanked by Erim on one side and a confused looking gate guard on the other.

". . . I understand that you're a member of the Chancery, Master Stjepan, with special privileges here, but this really is most unusual," said the guard, who held a lantern with one hand and a ceremonial spear with the other. He hurried to match his strides to theirs, but Stjepan and Erim were moving very quickly.

"I don't have a lot of time to explain," Stjepan said as they crossed into the center wing and turned toward the Library entrance. "You can call the City Watch to arrest me afterwards if you feel you have to."

The Library was often open throughout the night for the use of students and Magisters, and luckily they arrived at the entry hall to find the doors open and the front desk occupied by two librarians. Stjepan walked right up to the front desk and around it, to the protests of the librarians and the guard. He grabbed one of the two librarians and hauled the surprised man to his feet.

"Find Magister Clodarius, wake him up if you have to," Stjepan said to the man in a voice that did not brook an argument. "Tell him that Stjepan Black-Heart is here and insisting upon seeing him." The startled librarian paused for a second, saw the look in Stjepan's eyes, and immediately gulped and ran into the library. The second librarian scrambled out of the way as Stjepan pulled out the ledgers that recorded the names of the users of the Rare Books rooms. He scanned the pages, and cursed under his breath.

"His name's not on the lists. But he wouldn't just use one of the main halls, it's too open, he'd need some privacy. You!" he said, turning to the other librarian. "Are there any keys to the Rare Book rooms unaccounted for? Well, come on, man, are they all here?"

Harvald worked feverishly at his books and papers, his hands starting to shake. The sound of his pained breathing grew louder, and he tried to speak the words on the map in front of him. He was so tired, so confused, nothing made any sense.

He thought he heard something. Was someone calling his name? Harvald raised his head, his vision swimming, and listened, frozen for a moment and holding his breath, then turned back to the map. He stared blankly at the decaying flesh on his hands.

Leigh placed another card down on the table, The Hermit, numbered VII and depicting a cloaked and hooded man bearing a staff in one hand and a lantern held aloft in the other; he stood upon a mountaintop, and rather than looking up and out at the vista before him, his gaze was instead cast down, intent upon the long drop at his feet. But the card was reversed, upside down, and Leigh immediately frowned.

"The Hermit, reversed; the seeker after knowledge finding doubt . . ." Leigh said, his bushy eyebrows hunching over troubled eyes. *Not a card I would have looked for, with so much at stake. Far, far, far too much at stake for doubt to enter into it . . .* His hand lingered over the deck, as though trying to feel the direction the next card would take. He felt a sudden panic rising in his chest. *Not now, not now . . .*

Blacklist us, will you? Well, this is one wake none of you will forget, Gilgwyr thought in a black mood as the crowd pressed in to see the spectacle. Men were standing on chairs and tabletops to get a glimpse. He could see Petterwin Grim standing on a table with some of his crew, and Long Nose Ludwyn doing the same on another, his hand squeezing his crotch as he barked in anticipation; Jon Dhee pushing for space in the crowd, angry that he couldn't get a good angle; the

Gilded Lady with her ladies-in-waiting standing in the front row next to real lords and ladies from the High Quarter, fanning herself furiously with a black lace fan. Gilgwyr watched lasciviously as the priestess of Ligrid walked in a slow circle around the suspended body of Ariadesma, helping the dancer wrap her silks around her thighs and arms so that her body was horizontal to the ground, face and breasts up to the ceiling, and her legs were open in a wide split, exposing her wet vulva to the room. She looked like she was floating on a bed of air, waiting for her lover to take her.

But the Palatian dancer had a slight look of consternation on her face, her eyes tracking the priestess' rolling hips, and the unicorn horn that bounced and swayed in front of the masked woman. The priestess had removed the horn from around her neck, and had fastened the gold chain it hung from around her hips, and now she held it to her groin as though it were a long, stiff cock. The crowd was roaring its obscene approval, pressing in and around to see what was going to happen next.

Sequintus stepped forward and the aging enchanter poured an amber-colored oil into his gnarled, shaking hand, which he then proceeded to spread over Ariadesma's full breasts and flat stomach and smooth hips, rubbing it into her taut, firm flesh. It tingled a bit as it was absorbed into her skin. "Que'st'a?" she asked him, blinking up at him.

"Just something to help you, my dear," Sequintus said with a kindly smile. "To turn pain into pleasure." She gasped in surprise and the crowd roared when the old man pinched her clit and slid two fingers into her cunt, pressing some of the oil into her. She could feel her body becoming warmer, instantly aroused by a fire kindled deep within her loins, her nipples hardening and popping out from her breasts, and her hips undulated softly in the air of their own accord as she strained against the silks.

The priestess stepped between Ariadesma's spread legs and positioned herself in front of her blossoming cunt. The crowd roared as she started to line up the tip of the long unicorn horn with the dancer's puckered slit. Ariadesma couldn't really tell from her vantage point, straining her neck to look down her floating, spread-eagled body, but to her it almost looked as though the unicorn horn was now sprouting from the priestess' crotch as

174

though it were rooted there like a real cock. *She's real*, the Palatian thought in a sudden panic. *She's the real thing, a priestess of the Goddess of Perversion.* "Dieva, aidé'me!" she gasped.

"Dieva cannot help you now, little bird," the priestess purred in a voice of honey, fixing her with black eyes, and she reached forward to stroke the dancer's breasts and flanks with her long fingernails. "Only making me happy can save you." Wherever the long fingernails stroked her skin, bleeding razor-thin lines appeared, and Ariadesma gasped at the sensation of mixed pain and pleasure, writhing her pelvis up toward the priestess.

The priestess grasped Ariadesma's hips with strong hands, her nails clawing into the dancer's muscular flesh. The priestess opened her mouth and bared her teeth in a leering grin, her tongue flickering out like a snake's, and she pulled the dancer toward her as she thrust her hips forward, sending the tip of the unicorn horn deep into the cunt before her. Ariadesma's head snapped back and her body went rigid and she gasped, eyes wide, skewered helplessly in the air, as the crowd roared and roared.

He scrambled quietly in the dark, then calmed his breathing. That was too close, he thought. *But he couldn't resist another look. He covered the lantern and bent for the peephole cover.*

Annwyn returned to her armoire and retrieved the book she had been reading as Malia prepared her bedding.

"My Lady, it is already very late," Malia said disapprovingly.

"I know, but just a little more," Annwyn said with a small smile. "I am not yet ready for dreams. Go on to bed, I will be fine." Malia curtsied, and then departed quietly into the dark. Annwyn heard the door to the chamber close, and then sunk down onto her bed. She stared absently at the cover of the book, tracing the debossed letters with her fingers, then slowly opened it and found her place again. She started whispering as she read, the shadows growing deep in the candlelit gloom.

Stjepan led Erim, the gate guard, and the librarian down the central corridor of the Rare Books wing; both Stjepan and the librarian carried lanterns, casting long shadows against the closed doors of the hallway.

"Harvald?" Stjepan called out loudly as they approached the door of the Blue Room.

Through the door, muffled, they could hear words being chanted. *"Tedema dorus, tedema urus. Me curess tharass te me dorus. Nathrak arass tedema urus!"* They froze, Stjepan and Erim exchanging glances as they recognized Harvald's voice.

They ran to the door, and Stjepan tried to open it in vain. They could smell smoke. "Who has the spare key?" he cried angrily.

"Clodarius!" said the librarian. "I will see what's taking them!" he said without prompting, and he ran off back in the direction they'd come.

"No time to wait," Stjepan said quietly as he ran his hand over the lock, and then he started whispering to himself. His gaze fixed on the ward enchanted into the lock. He brought the Labiran rune of *making* into his mind's eye. *And no time for finesse*, he thought. *"Desundro grammata resistrata. Desundro il laboro de Daedeki. Desundro grammata propitio. Sunder this ward!"* he whispered. There was a sharp crack and a flash of flame from the lock.

Stjepan reared back and kicked the door right by the lock with full force. The door shuddered and there was a splintering sound, but it didn't give. He reared back and kicked again, and this time Erim kicked with him, and the door burst open, wood and metal fragments spinning through the air from the shattered lock. They leapt through the open doorway, followed by the gate guard, and froze.

The Library room flickered with light as papers and books and parchment burned in a makeshift brazier on a table, embers and ash dancing in the air in front of them. Harvald stood with his back to the door in a large magic circle drawn on the floor in blood, making gestures with his arms in the air of a ritual. He held a rolled parchment in one hand and a brightly burning torch in the other.

"King of Heaven, a fire in the Library!" gasped the guard.

"Harvald!" Stjepan cried out. Harvald turned and looked at Stjepan; his skin had turned bluish-white and was blackening rapidly. Pieces of his flesh were missing, his face and neck a patchwork of gaping holes and rot. Even his clothes seemed to be decaying before their eyes, flaking off into ash. His eyes were sad and desperate. "Harvald?" Stjepan asked, almost unable to recognize him.

"*Nathrak arass tedema urus. Nathrak arass urus!*" Harvald cried out, and he brought his hands together, igniting the parchment with the flame of the torch.

He was confused at first when he saw the small lights dropping toward her. At first he thought they were fireflies, though it was too early in the year for them to appear in number, or perhaps embers from a fireplace, though no fire was lit in her room. Then as he squinted he thought he could make them out as letters, but he knew that couldn't be.

He watched as one, then another came to rest first on her shoulder and then on her back. She didn't notice the first one; it glowed briefly, then seemed to dissolve into her nightgown, leaving a burn pattern. Then the second landed, and he grew worried.

Annwyn sat alone in her bed, reading and whispering by candlelight. Engrossed in her book, she did not notice the strange runes and symbols that were floating in the air above her, glowing softly, floating down from the ceiling like ash. She scratched as one landed on her, then another. They floated, circled aimlessly, and then with sudden purpose alit on Annwyn in her bed like a swarm of insects.

She gasped suddenly and rose, dropping her book. She swayed, clawing at the air, as the glowing fire-lit runes and symbols swirled about her. It sounded as though she were drowning.

Harvald spit blood and collapsed, trying to repeat the enchantment as the map and torch fell from his blackening fingers.

The gate guard rushed from the room. They could hear him crying "Alarm! Alarm! Fire! Fire!" as he rushed down the corridors in search of help. Erim leapt forward, horror on her face, but Stjepan held her back from crossing into the magic circle.

"Don't break the circle!" he hissed.

"What's happening to him?" she cried out, looking at the burning parchment by his writhing body. "The map. Is that the map?" Erim lunged forward again but Stjepan retained his hold on her.

Finally she tore away, but not toward the circle, instead running to the table and searching it frantically, tossing burning papers out of the brazier, finally spilling its contents across the tabletop.

Leigh waited, and waited, his hand hovering over the deck, his heart in his throat; and then finally he quickly took and flipped another card on the table.

And it was Death, numbered XIII, depicting a naked woman bearing a great scythe, and standing over a field of black earth sown with heads and body parts as the sun descended behind a mountain in the distance.

He leapt up and back from the table in alarm, a look of horror on

178

his face as the table rocked and shook. He made a warding sign and then reached his hands up to the ceiling. He cried out hoarsely in anguish, "What does this mean? What have you done? *What have you done?*"

Gilgwyr watched, his cock near to bursting in his codpiece, as the crowd roared in shock and lust and disbelief, wide-eyed at the debauchery being performed before them. *This is a triumph*, Gilgwyr thought. *And it will only get better from here on out. A great change is coming.* He surveyed the looks in the eyes of the crowd and gloated. But he did not notice that the Gilded Lady held up her black lace fan in front of her face to hide her expression, her eyes narrowed in disapproval and knowing calculation.

Ariadesma's heaving flanks and legs were crisscrossed with razor-thin cuts, her breasts shaking and her skin shining with a mix of sweat and oil and blood. The priestess was thrusting wildly now between her spread legs, laughing madly as she pistoned the unicorn horn deeper and deeper into the suspended dancer's gaping cunt, its spiraled ivory length flashing in and out her flesh, shining slick and bright in the firelight. Slowly the glistening ivory was becoming streaked with red, and droplets of blood splattered against the priestess' thrusting hips. But the moans and gasps being wrenched from Ariadesma's throat were nothing but pure passion and pleasure, her face wracked with ecstasy.

Careful, careful, don't break the merchandise, nothing permanent that Sequintus can't fix, Gilgwyr thought, laughing silently to himself. The enchanter stood nearby, his eyes clinically observing the proceedings, his box of salves and ointments and precious White Elixir at the ready. *If you like this, my dear sweet Palatian, then just wait until the Feast of Herrata.* Gilgwyr looked up at the ceiling, toward the Heavens, the rapture in his face mirroring that of the pinioned acrobat. *Today is a great day, a blessed day, and soon, very soon, will come the best day of all. A great change is coming!*

Annwyn fell onto the floor, gurgling and flailing as if in a seizure, her nightgown burning in dozens, perhaps hundreds of small spots, the cloth fraying as it burned. She tossed and turned trying to get free of the tormenting magic, her movements so sharp and sudden that she was in danger of hurting herself. The runes and symbols swirled in the air, landing on her disintegrating gown and her writhing body, crawling onto and into her skin.

He didn't know what to do, could not comprehend what was happening to her. Fear ran deep into his core. Finally with a great cry he tore himself from the peephole and slammed it shut. Grabbing up the lantern, he did the only thing he could do, and ran softly off into the dark.

As Erim tossed through burning papers and the smoldering remains of several books on the tabletop, Stjepan knelt and looked at the burning parchment lying within the magic circle next to the twitching body of Harvald. He could see inscriptions and symbols being devoured by flame as the last bits of the parchment folded into fire and then crumpled into ash.

"The map . . . oh, Harvald, what have you done?" he said quietly. He shook his head and sat back on his haunches, and started to pray.

> *Dawn Maiden. Awaken!*
> *Bright Star. Awaken!*
> *Sun's Herald. Awaken!*
> *And announce the death of*

a loyal servant to the Divine King!
Dread Guardians, light his way
on the Path of the Dead!
Seedré, Judge and Gatekeeper,
welcome him below,
and know that he is claimed!

Erim shouted at him. "Stjepan, the map's not here!" Harvald's body shuddered a last time as Stjepan bowed almost to the floor. He was vaguely aware of a general commotion, of other men rushing into the room finally, some bearing buckets of sand.

Islik, King in Heaven, once King on Earth!
Your servant falls to Death, your hated enemy!
King in Heaven, know his name:
Harvald Orwain, son of Leonas of Araswell.
Send your bright messengers to the
place of Judgment, to claim his spirit
from the grasp of his accusers!
Bring him from Darkness
to your Heavenly Palace!
Save him from Death!

"Damn it. The map's not here!" he could hear Erim's voice cry out, but she seemed far away.

The last parts of the map rose into the air as ash, and the heat carried the ash into the darkness above.

An ash-like dust fell in her chambers as Annwyn screamed. And at last, her prayers were finally answered.

CHAPTER NINE
THE PUBLIC
FUNERAL PLAZA OF
THE CITY OF THERAPOLI

THE 17ᵀᴴ OF EMPERIUM, 1471iA

The funeral of Harvald Orwain, son of Leonas, Baron of Araswell, was held on the last day of his spirit's seven day journey through the Otherworld to the Place of Judgment, where he would be stand before the Judge of the Dead. This was later in his journey than was customary, and the first unusual element of note in his funeral. As faithful worshippers of the Divine King, his family and their household had spent the last seven days in prayer for the intercession of their most holy God and His agents, in the hopes that an *Archat* of the Heavens would be sent to claim Harvald's spirit for its rightful place in the heavenly palace of the Divine King, there to spend eternity basking in His radiance. In accordance with Divine King custom, his body was to be cremated so that his ashes, in ascending to the skies, might draw the gaze of the King of Heaven.

His body, in as poor condition as it was, had been brought not to the Great Temple of the Divine King that sat astride the city as part of the sprawling hilltop complex of the High King's Hall, but rather to the Public Temple of the Divine King that sat at the water's edge by the docks of the Public Quarter; this was the second unusual element of note in his funeral, as by right and custom as the son of a loyal baronial vassal to the High King he should have been granted the honor of cremation on royal grounds. His body had been brought into chambers beneath the Public Temple and carefully washed and anointed with sacred oils by priests and undertakers, then wrapped in gauze. It had been brought out onto the public funeral plaza, a broad marble-paved and walled enclosure that stood on a small promontory into the bay behind the Public Temple, and there it was placed upon stacks of corded firewood on a low stone bier that would serve as his funeral pyre.

The plaza was quite crowded in anticipation of his cremation. The spring weather, thankfully, was clear, though slightly overcast, giving the proceedings an even grayer tone; the wind blew softly from the north and west, which was considered propitious, as his ashes would be carried off over the waters of the bay. Funerary urns were stacked against the walls of the plaza and steps that led to it, and filled the shallows by the sides of the promontory, as it was a custom amongst some Aurians of the lower classes that their remaining ashes would be gathered and then the urn dropped into the bay, as a gift to their ancient and estranged ancestor-god. Braziers were lit and filled with incense, torches neatly stacked nearby to light the eventual conflagration. Priests of the Divine King wandered amongst the mourners, and lined the broad walkway to the funerary plaza. Three priests in holy vestments stood at the head of the bier, intoning the cult's prayer for the dead, their words echoed by thirty paid professional mourners dressed all in black, who knelt to their right.

> *Islik, King of Heaven, King of Earth!*
> *Islik, O King, the funeral pyre is lit.*
> *We raise our hands to you in mourning,*
> *and your servant's ashes rise to find you.*
> *Here lies Harvald Orwain, son of Leonas!*
> *Save him from Death, your hated enemy!*
> *Save him from Darkness, your hated enemy!*
> *Arm him against the Underworld!*
> *Send your angels to ward his path!*
> *Send your angels to claim this spirit!*
>
> *Bring your vassal to the Heavens,*
> *to your Golden Palace high above.*
> *Order a throne of gold for him,*

and place upon his brow a crown.
Give him a scepter and an orb,
and set him as a King amongst Kings,
favored amongst your subjects.

Islik, King of Heaven, King of Earth!
Islik, O King, the funeral pyre is lit.
Save us from Death, your hated enemy!
Save us from Darkness, your hated enemy!
Great King, save your servants!

As was the custom amongst many Aurians, a veiled woman dressed in white stood in the far corner of the plaza and sang a mournful dirge, her voice mingling with that of the priests and their choir, and with the hushed conversations of hundreds of gathering mourners.

The third unusual element of his funeral manifested itself in the disposition of said mourners, for though his family seemed initially unaware of it, there were in effect two separate funerals occurring simultaneously, and mourners arriving at the plaza quickly divided themselves roughly into two major camps. The first camp was centered on Harvald's brother Arduin and sister Annwyn, who stood at the foot of the bier receiving a line of well-wishers. They were dressed in mourning finery and attended by squires, knights, handmaidens, other members of their household, and priests from the temple. Men and women from the Court and from the upper echelons of the city's social strata dutifully took their place in the line, and expressed their most heartfelt condolences to the family, then took their place amongst the nearby mingling crowds to whisper and gossip, craning their necks for a glimpse of Annwyn's fabled beauty under her mourning veil.

The second and less illustrious camp was centered on a more dangerous-looking crowd, also dressed in mourning black, if not as finely done. Stjepan and Gilgwyr stood amongst this camp, as did Jonas the Grey, and the three of them had been joined by two other surviving members of the Lords of Book and Street, ridden down with haste from the Plain of Gavant upon

185

hearing the news. Coogan was a stocky, solidly built Danian, with a chest and arms of solid muscle and a receding hairline; Cynyr was shorter and cheerier and his head was still full of short dark hair, but his pleasant expression was spoiled by the eyes of a mad-dog killer. All of them were dressed in black long-coats, black doublets of cloth or leather, black breeches and boots, and had a black tear drawn by the corner of their left eye, except for Stjepan, as this was apparently not an Athairi custom.

Around them extended a most peculiar entourage. Erim stood slightly behind Stjepan, craning her neck to scan the growing crowd. Sequintus stood doddering nearby, one arm held protectively around the beautiful young Palatian Ariadesma; she was attracting almost as many looks as Annwyn, being dressed in a Palatian style, a daring dropped shoulder corset with lace sleeves and a black netting collar, her black dress split to reveal a red brocade petticoat, her curly hair pulled up into a high coiffure behind her mourning veil. Three dozen other members of Gilgwyr's staff and household were there looking as presentable as possible, as Harvald had been a frequent customer. Petterwin Grim was there, with his entire crew, some thirty-odd men, and the Squire of Mud Street with his (and indeed their mourning clothes, despite their best efforts, still seemed to be half covered in mud). Jon Deering and Red Rob Asprin had brought their crews as well, and Mina the Dagger was there with her guardian pair and several weeping and wailing whores, but Tyrius arrived with only about a third of his Hooded Men, apparently still on the outs with the rest of them. Naeras Braewode was there as well, but the notorious back-alley warlock had masked himself with someone else's face, so only a few people knew. Barkeeps and tavern owners and booksellers who had dealt favorably with Harvald over the years wandered about as well, many of them bearing bottles of liquor or ale, and some drank from them either surreptitiously or openly. Mixing with both camps were the braver of the clerks of the High King's Court, and scribes and copyists who had been Harvald's classmates at the University, who would first pay their respects to Lord Arduin and then, spotting Stjepan and Gilgwyr, would wander over to have a word.

Stjepan received their condolences with grim thanks and quiet words, but

Gilgwyr appeared to be all out of sorts, often ignoring those who were trying to speak to him. He took frequent swigs from a small bottle. All week long his mood had been black, to see this potential path slammed shut in front of him; black and terribly confused, for to his deepening bewilderment his beautiful dreams were getting stronger and more beautiful, to the point where he would wake from sleep exhausted and covered in sweat, his member as hard as wood. His face was pale and drawn and haunted as he scanned the gathering crowd. *Why do I still dream of triumph?* he wondered. *Why do the gods torment me so?*

"His funeral is much delayed," Gilgwyr finally said with a sour look when they were just amongst themselves. "His Seven Days are almost up."

"I'm surprised they're letting him have a public funeral at all, given the nature of his death," said Stjepan. "Priests sent from the Inquisition by the Patriarch himself and Magisters and alchemists from the University have been squabbling and fighting over his body for most of the week. I don't think they'd ever seen a curse quite like the one that killed him."

"Aye, I suppose this is more mourners than I would have expected, given the nature of his death, but still, a poorly attended funeral when it comes to his own family and the high worthies of this city," said Gilgwyr, bitterness in his voice. "Not a single one of the University Chairs, not even Magister Arathon. Not a single senior member of the Chancery. Oh, he is ill used in death. Neither his father nor his eldest brothers have returned from the field and the Grand Duke's sport. Instead they send paid mourners in their place. Everyone is afraid to show their faces . . ."

"Aye, his father could have made it down here in time," said Coogan. "We did, with a bit of hard riding. So they should have no excuses."

"Instead the Baron's holed up in his tents, in council with his sons and advisors, trying to figure out the next play," said Cynyr, and he spat to one side. "Pathetic."

"Theirs is a family marred by tragedy," Stjepan said quietly. "And this death puts a cloud over anyone who has crossed paths with him, most particularly us." He looked at Coogan and Cynyr with a half-smile. "It's always good to see you, but you probably shouldn't have come back to the city. Everyone's going to have to tread carefully."

"Any excuse to see the Lords again," said Coogan, a twinkle in his eye. "Was Orrigard surprised to discover you were back in the city?"

"Yes, you could say that," said Stjepan sourly. "I might actually have to go map the Mire this time."

"You heard about the Grand Duke?" Coogan asked. "It's back into the hills for us this summer, as if the ass-kicking that Porloss handed us all last year wasn't bad enough. It's like the idiots never fucking learn to let well enough alone."

"Aye, I heard," said Stjepan. "They won't figure it out until we're carting the Grand Duke's dead body back from the Manon Mole."

"He's a good man, maybe the best of the sorry lot save King Derrek, but better his dead body than ours," said Cynyr. They all nodded in assent and made warding signs in the air to ward off the Evil Eye.

Jonas did a double-take. "Islik's balls. Heads up," he said, straightening up and unconsciously smoothing his clothes down. They all looked where he had indicated and started to do the same.

The crowd was parting as a small column of men and women in black approached them, led by no less than two Princes of the Guild. Bad Mowbray, a tall thin Danian man with pockmarked cheeks, thinning gray hair, hawk eyes, and a hooked nose, was dressed in a long fur-lined black damask coat over black silk doublets and breeches, a cloth-of-gold codpiece, and stiff black leather boots. And he had the Gilded Lady on his arm, dressed similarly to her ensemble in the Sleight of Hand the week before but with the addition of a mourning veil pulled down over her face. Like the Gilded Lady, Mowbray wore a chain of office made from a variety of gold coins linked together. Behind him came the members of his crew, each of them escorting one of the Gilded Lady's veiled ladies-in-waiting. *Ah, Harvald*, thought Gilgwyr. *I hope you are looking down on us now, because you would not believe the honor you are receiving.* The Lady did not normally sally forth during the day, as the harsh revealing light of the sun was not always her friend, but she had quite apparently chosen to make an exception.

The two Princes of the Guild came to a stop before them, and the five men bowed, joined by many others standing nearby, including Erim and the entire Sleight of Hand contingent.

"Almost all of the remaining Lords of Book and Street, then," said the Gilded Lady softly in her deep voice. "It is unfortunate that you are reunited under such terrible circumstances."

"My Lord. My Lady. Thank you for honoring our compatriot," said Stjepan.

"Your days of service may have passed, but we remain ever tied to you and yours by blood and history," said the Gilded Lady, her eyes twinkling. "We will not forget you, and hope very much that you will not forget us."

"Never, my Lady," the five said, practically in unison and with slight bows.

"Even you will undoubtedly be of service once again, Black-Heart," said Mowbray with a smile that seemed genuine. "Do not despair of the blacklist. All things change in time." Stjepan inclined his head and made a short bow.

"I understand that we too must offer you the sadness of our hearts," said Jonas smoothly. "We have heard this morning that the Fat Prince was taken by the hand of Death, poisoned during the night. It is a shock and horror to us all."

"Perhaps not all," said the Gilded Lady with a cunning smile. "For we were told that one amongst you threatened him with death to his very face not more than a week ago."

Gilgwyr paled. "My Lady. My Lord. I assure you, the words I spoke to the Fat Prince were made in warning, not as a threat. I shared my Rumor-hoard with him in fair exchange, and told him of the order given to the royal knives. If he failed to act on it, either to settle whatever debt or grievance had earned him the enmity of the King's Shadow, or to protect himself as best he could, then surely the fault is not mine . . ."

"No, dear Gilgwyr, I suppose it is not, despite your storied rivalry," said the Gilded Lady. Her eyes narrowed as her gaze fell on Ariadesma. "Ah, our exotic entertainer from poor Guilford's wake. Looking none the worse for wear and tear, I see."

Ariadesma stepped forward beside Gilgwyr and curtsied. "At'a vos servica, ma donna," she said with a smile. "*Magus* Sequintus is a . . . how do you say? . . . a miracle worker? So I am yours to command."

"The safety of the entertainers of the Sleight of Hand is always paramount in my concerns," Gilgwyr said, his hand going to the small of Ariadesma's back. "She was never in any real danger. Ariadesma brings with her many secrets from Palatia and Lagapoli, and is eager to demonstrate them to us all. We have great plans for her." He smiled.

Indeed, never one to let something like the death of a close friend interfere with a bit of potential business, Gilgwyr had met with several masked members of the Inquisition the day before at a safe house, and the meeting had gone splendidly. Even though they'd worn masks, he'd been able to identify them with ease. Heoras Clogoar, the Chief Inquisitor, had the unconscious habit of snorting in the back of his throat on occasion while he breathed; Oswin Urgoar, the High Priest of the Inquisition and one of the patriarchs of the priestly Urgoar family, had broken a finger when he was young and it had not set properly, and he had neglected to conceal the crooked digit; and the Templar Captain Sir Conrad Colewed wore a mask that did not cover his entire face, and so his ridiculous blond moustache was easily detectable. *Never send a boy to do a man's job*, he'd thought, shaking his head. *But no wonder young Alain is so eager to please them. It's the Inquisition's bloody royalty.*

". . . I believe I have the perfect young woman for your needs," Gilgwyr had said once they'd gotten past the initial negotiations. "A beautiful face and body, petite but very shapely, very graceful. A dancer from Palatia, with all the skills that entails. I trust the fact that she is a foreigner will not prove too much of a problem?"

The Inquisitors had all glanced at each other behind their masks. "No, that should be fine. Being foreign might be a plus, as it spares a fine Aurian woman from the ordeal," had said the Chief Inquisitor. "Indeed our patron has a particular dislike of the Palatians, and so I think it works on many levels."

"And all of the records would seem to show that blessed Herrata was in fact black of hair, so she could be considered somewhat accurate in duplicating Herrata's appearance," had said their High Priest.

"But what of Herrata's rapture?" had said the Templar Captain. "Will she display the proper passion? It would be most unfortunate if her response to the act being performed upon her was not sufficiently . . . ardent."

"This particular young woman is not only a consummate performer but she also has an insatiable fire within her. And there are ways to . . . enhance her experience. Leave that to Sequintus," Gilgwyr had said, indicating the aged enchanter of his house who sat in the chair next to him.

The enchanter had perked up, as though recognizing his cue. "Ah. Yes, our potents," he'd said. "Our house has a great deal of experience with medicinal and magical aids. The lady that Gilgwyr has selected will participate most vigorously, I assure you, and enjoy herself immensely without limits."

"Which brings us to a delicate point," had said Gilgwyr, licking his lips. "The stud in question . . . how can I put this? I am sure you've heard the expression you can lead a horse—or in this case bull—to water, but you can't make it drink." The Inquisitors had looked at each other. "It could be quite embarrassing for all involved if the star of the show were led in, done up in gold, only to have no interest in the mate presented to it. Wouldn't you agree?" The Inquisitors had shuffled nervously in their seats but other than a cough gave no response.

Gilgwyr had smiled. "I hope I do not assume too much when I suppose that no one wants our patron to be spending his time watching a crew of handlers maneuver a recalcitrant stud into a less-than-amorous coupling," he'd said. "That would hardly seem a suitable reenactment of the glorious conception of our Divine King, and I think that would quite ruin the mood of the celebration, yes? I don't suppose the stud in question has had any training or experience in this sort of thing?"

The Inquisitors had looked at each other again. "As far as we are aware, this particular stud has not," had said the Chief Inquisitor. Gilgwyr had been intrigued by his choice of words. *Patience, patience,* he'd thought. *Don't ask too many questions yet.*

Gilgwyr had leaned forward in his chair. "As a professional entertainer, this potential problem vexed me, and so I put it to Sequintus here to see if he could think of a potent that could be useful in this sort of thing, and he could not," Gilgwyr had said, turning toward Sequintus. "Could you, dear Sequintus?"

"Ah, no," had said Sequintus, nodding wisely if a bit absently. "No herbal concoction that I am aware of seems applicable. The only thing that occurred to me as a solution was to find a way to summon a *Rahabi* spirit to possess the stud bull, that could control its actions."

Gilgwyr had turned back and looked at the Inquisitors, the hairs on the back of his neck standing up. *This is the moment*, he'd thought. *Either this all comes crashing to a halt, or we've got them sewn up tight.* For what Sequintus had just then proposed was quite, quite forbidden.

"Summon a spirit," had said the High Priest in a flat tone. "One of the *Rahabi*."

"Ah, yes, one of the *Gamezhiel*, I would think," had said Sequintus matter-of-factly, as though he had been discussing a recipe for baked bread or a turn in the weather. "Should be a simple matter of discovering the name of one of them, summoning it at the appropriate time, striking a bargain and binding it into the stud, and then banishing it once its task is complete. An *incubus* spirit would do the job rather nicely, they are supposedly always looking for opportunities to fornicate with mortal women, no matter what their outer form."

The Inquisitors all looked at each other behind their masks.

"Would the spirit possession harm the stud in some way?" had asked the Templar Captain.

"No, it should be fine, as long as it doesn't come to any physical harm during the coupling," had said Sequintus. "And that is of course of far greater concern to the young woman involved."

The Chief Inquisitor had leaned forward. "And you can do such a thing?" he'd asked.

Gotcha, had thought Gilgwyr.

When they'd stepped back out onto the street once the meeting was over, Gilgwyr had adjusted the tricorn hat on his head and then had bounced on his heels merrily, smelling the breeze wafting through the city. No one would've been stupid enough to actually admit in front of three members of the Inquisition that they could do such a thing, oh no; but for the right price, inquiries could certainly be made. For the right price, perhaps including a one-time Inquisitional pardon, marked with the seal of the Chief Inquisitor of their Order? *Today is not a great day, not a blessed day. And the best day of all is not yet coming*, he'd thought. *But this ain't so bad.* "Just when I think this city holds no more surprises for me, it proves me wrong," he'd said, smiling to Sequintus. "I am giddy with shock at the level of corruption that surrounds us."

"Oh, please," said the old enchanter with a jaded sigh. "Just wait until you're my age, and by then you'll have seen much, much worse."

"It really was the most shocking performance," said the Gilded Lady, a scandalized leer on her face. "It absolutely would have been the talk of the town, had not poor Harvald met his death in such spectacular fashion on the same night."

"I'm sorry I missed it," Bad Mowbray mused, looking the Palatian over.

The Gilded Lady clapped her hands as though she'd just had an idea. "I know. A command performance, then!" she cried. "A repeat of the entertainments of that night, but this time at a different wake, that of the Fat Prince. Would you agree to host the Guild, then, and honor our fallen Prince? Can a repeat be arranged?"

Gilgwyr looked stunned at the offer. *A wake for a Guild Prince. At the Sleight of Hand. Oh, wouldn't Guizo have hated that. A bad week is definitely looking up*, he thought. "We will repeat it and top it, my Lady," Gilgwyr exclaimed, as Ariadesma blushed and looked as though she was about to faint. "You need but name the day!"

"This coming Priadum is the Festival of the Serpent, marking the last of the star-signs of the Celestial year," said the Gilded Lady with a knowing smile. "Perhaps that evening, then, on the 19th? Is two days enough time for you to prepare?"

"We will be ready, my Lady," Gilgwyr said with a deep bow.

"Fantastic," said Bad Mowbray, nodding his head and looking about. "Outstanding. Oh, well done." He and the Gilded Lady inclined their heads and those nearby bowed in response, and they stepped to the side to greet those amongst the Marked that awaited them, and allow the members of their crews to come forward and express their condolences. As they did, the pair of Princes paused by Erim.

"Oh, and this is the exquisite young thing I was telling you about," the Gilded Lady said to Mowbray. "Black-Heart's new friend."

"Ah, yes," said Bad Mowbray, looking Erim over. "I see what you mean. Delicious."

And then they moved on, and it was Erim's turn to blush again.

Arduin grew even angrier as the funeral progressed, if such a thing were possible. He had begun the day in a foul mood to begin with, for the week had brought an onslaught of bad tidings, one thing after another. After the celebratory high of Duke Pergwyn's offer had come the strange events during the night in their household, and the next morning had brought with it word of Harvald's death and the first hint of the unusual circumstances surrounding it. A fire in the great Library of the University; a maleficent and strange curse that had caused his brother's body to rot and decay from the inside out; the revelation of a theft and malfeasance at the Library, for which Harvald was seemingly responsible, and the destruction of the University's property; rumors of occult and forbidden magic. The tidings had grown dark indeed over that first day.

Then had come word the next day that the city fathers were refusing to relinquish Harvald's body for its rites, and instead were examining it to determine what kind of magic had been involved. The City Watch, the Magisters of the University, members of the High King's Court, Templars and Inquisitors from the Inquisition of the Sun Court, had all come to ask exhausting and perplexing questions. Then had come word that his father and brothers would not be returning for the funeral at all, leaving him to make the arrangements and plea for the release of his brother's body on his own. After several days of such humiliation, the City Watch had finally released Harvald's body, only to inform him that the Great Temple of the Divine King would not be available for the cremation, and that he would have to use the Public Temple. *Someone must have warned Father ahead of time of the slight*, Arduin had thought angrily when he learned of the Court's decision. *And so he leaves it to me, and poor Annwyn.* And all week long he had felt the sinking feeling in his stomach, the certainty that this scandal was going to bury their family, and his anger at Harvald and the whole world had grown ever more furious.

The growing turnout at the funeral only confirmed his worst fears. A small turnout would have been a blessed thing, to allow his family to grieve in private and send Harvald off in peace; or a large turnout with many notables at the Great Temple, as that would have signaled perhaps some embrace of the family in their time of trouble. But this was the worst of all possible worlds. Clearly none of the great players in the Court were going to put in an appearance: no Dukes, no Crown Prince, certainly no High King, and none of his great advisors or officers. Not a single noble of the rank of Baron or higher had yet appeared. Oh, but their wives certainly had, along with minor lords and lordlings of every stripe, merchants and moneylenders, courtiers and clerks. Elisa, Baroness of Karsiris was there, as was the Baroness of Loria, the Baroness of Chesterton, the Lady Sigalla, the Lady Ilona, and the Lady Gallas; *the gossip queens of the Court*, he thought, all of them there to see this fresh scandal visited upon his family, and cast their venomous, envious gazes upon the beauty of his sister. However Baroness Siglette of Djarfort and her daughter Lady Silga, whom his father had presumably hoped would marry him, were notably absent from that contingent, dashing whatever slim hope he might have clung to that something there was still possible.

And on top of that Annwyn was clearly, violently ill, and had been all week. She had been bed-ridden with fever, tossing and turning, moaning insensibly, ever since the night of Harvald's death. Her handmaidens had done their best, but after two days he had finally summoned a physiker to come and consult as to her condition. The physiker had been of no use, and each day Arduin had summoned a different healer, and each day her condition had not changed. He had been grateful for Malia that week; he did not normally like the Danian woman, having preferred that his sister's handmaidens be of proper Aurian bloodlines, but his sister had always been fond of her, and she had proven herself a capable helpmate that week and the household had run smoothly despite his sister's illness.

That morning he had been surprised when his sister had arisen from her bed at last. He had been thinking that the silver lining to her illness would have been that she could have skipped Harvald's funeral, and indeed if he could have thought of some excuse to leave her behind and be spared this humiliation, he would have. He had even suggested to her that perhaps staying home would have been the best course for her, given her condition; but in a weak and halting voice, she had insisted on coming, and he had known that her absence would have been just as remarked upon as her presence. But at least then she would not have had to directly endure their insincere condolences, their condemning glances, their whispers and snide giggles. The Duke had been right; all it had taken was the whiff of some fresh disgrace, and the decade-old scandal of his sister had been revived right along with it as though it had happened yesterday. *Harvald, you've ruined us*, he thought.

He had hoped for some word from Duke Pergwyn during the week, some note of condolence and confirmation that he would be summoned for the summer campaign against the Rebel Earl, but the Duke had been silent. *So that is likely how it will be, then*, he thought. *What chance of a marriage now? What opportunity to prove our worth to the High King? We will be known as a cursed house of fornicators and occultists. Scandal, ignominy, decline, and inevitably an end to our line. That will be our fate.*

And now, as if to add a final insult to injury, the crowd at the funeral had definitely taken on a rather low-rent quality. At first it had just been a few friends of Harvald's from his days at the University and members of the Chancery congregating off to one side of the plaza, respectable enough men from the lettered class of the city who had studied or worked with his brother. But Arduin had watched with increasing unhappiness as their ranks had been swollen by the arrival of a decidedly unsavory and increasingly peculiar cast of characters, most of whom seemed to be content to just mingle amongst themselves. He knew, of course, that Harvald had been connected to some sordid parts of the city ever since the street fighting around the University the year before scandal befell their family. He had often wondered if the fires of that tense autumn had been the precursor to all the troubles that befell them.

But quite another thing to have them all show up to his funeral.

He was barely listening to the prattling yet seemingly sincere moron in front of him, his eyes drawn increasingly to the ruffians and ne'er-do-wells that mixed and mingled with the University crowd. He could definitely tell that some amongst the city gentry had also noticed the divide, and their scandalized glances were now split between his sister and the rest of the crowd. A small comfort, he supposed, that at least they were no longer focused solely on Annwyn's shame and condition.

He wondered if anyone else had noticed, and glanced quickly about. To his right, several paces away, stood Rodrick Urgoar, the High Priest of the Public Temple; he, at least, seemed happy and blissfully unaware, noted Arduin ruefully. The Urgoars were not highborn, but they had risen to power and position over many years of service in the Inquisition and the priestly hierarchies of the Sun Court and the temples of the Divine King. Rodrick Urgoar had been less than pleased with his posting to be High Priest of the Public Temple, something that he had made abundantly and publicly clear, much to the chagrin of many of his parishioners. Rodrick might normally be expected to officiate at the funeral or wedding of at best a wealthy merchant, or perhaps some member of the city's lettered class, perhaps an Under-Magister at the University; all of which he considered beneath him. But despite the scandal surrounding Harvald's death and his family, the Orwains of Araswell were vassals of the High King. So Rodrick Urgoar was having a banner day.

Several paces to his left by the bier swayed his sister, Annwyn, barely able to stand. Malia and Ilona stood on each side of her, partly holding her by her elbows, and around them was another protective layer of a half dozen handmaidens, acting as a shield and cushion against the intrusions of well-wishers. She seemed insensible, barely cognizant of her surroundings. He thought about sending her back to her coach.

". . . and if my actions that day played some small part in Harvald's death, I humbly beseech your forgiveness," the man in front of him was saying. Arduin frowned and focused on him again. The man—some sort of clerk?—seemed genuinely broken up about something. "I cannot say he took me into his private confidences, for I know much of his work was confidential to the Court, but I believe ours was a friendship based on mutual respect. And nothing in his behavior that day would have led me to suspect that something was amiss." The man dabbed at his eyes. "He and I were supposed to have drinks this past week, you know. It shall forever weigh on my mind that we didn't get a chance to share a last pint of bitters." The man leaned in a little closer than made Arduin comfortable, and added in conspiratorial airs, "He was going to tell me what he could about the work he'd been doing for . . . you know who."

Arduin's face was a complete blank.

"You know . . . *Lord Rohan*," the man said, almost in a whisper.

Lord Rohan Brigadim? thought Arduin. *What on earth would my brother have had to do with Lord Rohan? Is that what people are saying now? That he worked for the king's spymaster?* He sighed inwardly. Arduin stared at the man a moment, realizing that he should be offering some sort of response, and then found himself saying, "Yes, well, I'm sure that Harvald would be grateful for your discretion in matters related to his work and the Court, whatever they might have been. And I'm also sure that he would be grateful for your presence and prayers here today, as I am."

"It is an honor to be here to help him finish his final journey," said the man with heartfelt conviction. "Should you ever need my help, you need

198

but ask in his name." He gave a great bow, and backed away, continuing to bow, until he disappeared into the crowd.

Arduin stared after him a moment, his mouth hanging open and a frown on his face, before finally shaking himself. He glanced about. Thankfully the line of well-wishers had gotten bottled up behind three old dowagers speaking to the High Priest, and he had a moment's respite. Sir Helgi handed him a flask of water, and he nodded his thanks as he took a sip.

"Who in the Six Hells are this lot?" asked Sir Helgi, indicating the growing crowd of well-dressed ruffians on the other side of the plaza.

"Since that is almost certainly where they are all going, I'm not sure their names really matter," Arduin said drily. "Perhaps the Public Temple gives away free food after a funeral."

"I wouldn't mind knowing the name of that one," said Sir Helgi, indicating a young exotic-looking foreign woman, dressed rather scandalously for a funeral. Whoever she was, Arduin was actually somewhat glad she was there, as her dress was proving a small distraction from his sister amongst the gossip queens.

"And who are that tall couple the rest of them keep bowing to?" asked Sir Holgar.

Arduin squinted and shrugged. "I don't recognize them. Perhaps someone of importance from one of the Merchant Courts?" he ventured. "They're not nobles." He scanned the sundry crowd, spotting the young clerk from the High King's Court that had been so helpful the other day there, and then a few others he knew by name. "I don't know the names of many of Harvald's old University friends. There's a few of them over there. That one, I remember. The Athairi. Stjepan, I think. His mother was some sort of witch, got burned at the stake. They call him the Black Heart or some sort of ridiculous thing."

At the mention of those two words, *black* and *heart*, Annwyn's mind woke up. She took a deep breath of air, a long gasping intake as though she had been underwater. She struggled for a moment, trying to focus, pulling herself from the supporting grips of her handmaidens and trying to stand on her own.

"My Lady, are you sure you are all right?" whispered Malia at her side.

Annwyn didn't respond. She swayed slightly, like a reed in the wind, and tried to take a step forward. Her body felt awkward, alien, as though it had not been used for months and the muscles had atrophied. Thirst and hunger struck her to her core. *When did I last eat?* she wondered, then shook her head. *That doesn't matter. That name. I know that name. Why do I know that name?*

That name is why I am here.

"Right, I've heard of him," said Sir Helgi, frowning. "He's the one that supposedly killed six men during all that fighting up at the University a few years ago, yes, but was never charged? Doesn't look too dangerous to me."

Stjepan's gaze scanned the mourning crowd, took in the high hill of the city with its halls and towers, swept out to sea and eyed ships tacking in the bay or resting at anchorage. Gulls, terns, pelicans and cormorants floated and circled in the air above, keeping a respectful distance from a single vulture high above them. He listened to the wind, heard the distant rattle of the city rising up behind them, the call of sea birds, the crash of wave and surf. He sniffed the air, smelt perfume and incense and the salty brine of the bay, and somewhere near the hint of something dead and rotting. He felt inconsolably sad.

". . . Rumors are flying everywhere about how he died," Gilgwyr was saying. "It's probably why there are so many people here; their curiosity has overcome their fear."

Coogan and Cynyr glanced at each other. "So," said Coogan after a moment. "How *did* he die?"

"Map had a curse on it, apparently," said Stjepan with a shrug, and then he grimaced. "Harvald wound up burning a copy of *De Malifır Magicis* of Ymaire. Presumably he was trying to use it to remove the curse. Fucking book was priceless. He was supposedly trying to use a Middle Tongue translation of it as well, perhaps without realizing that the translation was flawed."

"Did the map survive?" asked Cynyr, his mad-dog eyes glinting.

"Nope," said Stjepan, shaking his head. "Burned to ash, along with whatever notes or copies he was trying to make." They all stared at the ground for a moment.

"Shame, that," said Coogan with a sigh. He frowned. "*De Malifır Magicis*? Isn't that book forbidden? How'd he get a copy of it?"

"Somehow he broke into the Forbidden Rooms of the Library," Jonas said quietly.

Coogan's frown grew deeper and Cynyr whistled. "How many times did we try that when we were students?" Cynyr asked. "And he managed it by himself? How the fuck did he do that?"

"They're not sure," replied Jonas. "He had a particularly strong talisman upon his person, an unusual source of great occult power; it was undamaged, and the Magisters have locked it away for safekeeping, but the thought is that it might have aided him in overcoming the wards."

"What the fuck? Where'd he get it from?" asked Coogan.

"No one knows. Official word is going to be that he died in a . . . research accident, attempting to decipher a particularly venomous curse," Jonas said quietly. "But there's all sorts of questions that have drawn unwanted attention. Where he got the talisman, how he got into the Forbidden Rooms and found the book he was looking for; what the curse was on, since the map was destroyed; what spell he was casting when the curse killed him. And why he was trying to do it at all, since it clearly wasn't Court business and he lied his way into the Rare Books hall, claiming to be on a mission from Lord Rohan."

"That takes some balls," laughed Coogan. "Well, unless it was true." He seemed to think that possibility even more amusing.

"Do you suppose anyone knows what we were up to?" Erim asked Stjepan furtively. "They asked so many questions . . ."

"I'm not sure. I don't think all of the Magisters were entirely convinced of our ignorance of Harvald's actions and intentions, some of them know our lot too well," said Stjepan. He shrugged. "But it doesn't matter anymore. There's nothing left of the map, and we don't even know if it was real to begin with . . ." he trailed off slowly, and frowned, as he saw that Harvald's sister had turned toward him and seemed to be looking in his direction.

"Islik's balls, it'll haunt my dreams the rest of my life," groaned Gilgwyr. "That we might've had in our grasp a map to the Barrow of Azharad, a map to *Gladringer*. And instead . . . our hands close on empty air. I can't believe that bastard burned the fucking map."

"And by doing so likely saved us from the curse that claimed him. Are you so ungrateful?" Erim asked, glancing at him with narrowed eyes.

Alas, poor Erim, you have no idea the depth of my ingratitude, thought Gilgwyr sourly.

Annwyn's gaze fell upon a man on the other side of the plaza. Athairi, tall, lean, weathered, dark-haired, dark-eyed. A dark humor seemed to be upon him, as though his core was filled with sadness and hate. *That's him*, she said to herself. *Who else could it be? Black-Heart.*

Her head swam, and her eyes fluttered, and she teetered for a moment as she tried hard to focus. She blinked her eyes open, and just like that he was looking at her from across the plaza. Their eyes locked, and suddenly she felt clear-headed for a moment, as a spark of fear leapt like lightning up her spine. There was an intense sternness in his expression, a sharpness to his gaze, that filled her with trepidation. But at the same time she thought she saw something else there. Curiosity? Compassion? Did she imagine it?

She stepped forward with difficulty, her body unresponsive to her commands. She took one hesitating step, then another, and slowly started to make her way across the plaza, her eyes still locked with his.

"My Lady?" asked Malia, as she started to follow the mistress of her house across the plaza. "What are you doing?" Ilona and Henriette quickly joined her in flanking Annwyn, fluttering about her, but she ignored them and kept her stumbling steps forward. Her other handmaidens trailed behind them, confused. Malia looked over her shoulder for the lord of the house, but three elderly women were besieging Arduin and his two closest knights, busily and loudly explaining that they had been the midwives at Harvald's birth. She tried to signal Arduin with short waves of her hand, but he didn't see her.

"Frallas!" she hissed at a matronly blonde handmaiden. "Get the Lord. Quickly!"

Stjepan frowned as Harvald's sister started walking toward him, trailed by her worried entourage. There was something wrong with her; she almost looked like she was ill, or drunk, she was moving slowly and carefully, almost as if every step took a conscious effort and placed her in danger of toppling over. There was no question now that she was looking straight at him through her veil, her clear blue eyes locked to his. He stepped forward almost involuntarily, wondering what she was doing.

Erim noticed Stjepan move forward and followed his gaze. She blinked when she saw the woman moving toward them. Even with her features partly obscured under a lace mourning veil, it was obvious that she was one of the most beautiful women that Erim had ever seen. "Who is *that*?" she asked Stjepan. She had seen the woman with the tall, protective Aurian lord by the bier. "Is that Harvald's sister and her husband?"

"The man's their older brother Arduin. The Lady Annwyn is unmarried . . ." Stjepan trailed off. He took another step forward as she continued her odd approach.

"A beauty like that, daughter to a landed Baron, unmarried?" Erim asked, but Stjepan ignored her.

Gilgwyr, hearing her question, chimed in. "Ah. The Lady Annwyn was once a fixture of the Court, a beauty of great renown . . . But a scandal has all but guaranteed she will die a spinster. She fell in love with a gallant young knight of Tilfort . . ." He trailed off, joining Stjepan and Erim in staring at Annwyn; everyone in their immediate circle had their eyes on her now. There was no question she was intent on approaching them, approaching Stjepan in particular, in her peculiar stumbling gait.

She was mumbling and moaning to herself as she moved toward them. Her handmaidens moved up around and behind her, uncertainty and distress in their expressions as they tried alternately to help her and stop her, but she ignored them utterly, pushing through their offered arms, intent upon reaching Stjepan. Quiet spread through the nearby crowd of mourners as more and more turned to watch the strange proceeding. Closer, closer, step by excruciating step she struggled, until she was standing before him.

They stood for a moment, looking into each other's eyes.

"My Lady?" he asked in a low voice, standing very still as though afraid to move and hence startle her to flight.

She stared at him for a long moment, her lips slightly parted.

"Save me, Black-Heart," she finally whispered.

And then suddenly Annwyn collapsed into his surprised arms and began thrashing about as if in a seizure.

"My Lady!" shrieked several of her handmaidens, and they leapt forward to pull Annwyn out of Stjepan's gentle grasp, helping her to slump to the paved stone of the plaza at his feet. He didn't move as they clustered about her. She slowly writhed amongst them, her eyes rolling back into her head.

Malia looked askance at Stjepan, wondering who on earth he could be, but he was just staring at Annwyn with a frown, seemingly as perplexed as she was, and did not seem aware of her or anyone else at all. She turned swiftly and looked toward the bier. She could see Frallas leading Arduin toward them through the gathering crowd. "My Lord!" she cried loudly, waving her arm high in the air. "Please hurry!" Ilona let out a little cry and Malia looked down.

Her eyes widened in shock as she saw that Annwyn was suddenly struggling to shed her clothes, tearing at her bodice and its laces. "My Lady! What are you doing?" she asked in alarm. Malia knelt, joining the other handmaidens in trying to stop Annwyn from disrobing, a dark fear and confusion creeping into her. The crowd was pressing in around them, trying to see what was happening, and she was starting to feel as though she was packed into a small box.

Arduin had trouble pushing his way through the throng, but finally arrived and almost jumped back with a start, alarm on his face as he saw his sister clawing at her own clothes. He began pushing and shoving away some of the men that surrounded them, even as they pressed in to take a look. He turned and looked over his shoulder, spotting Sir Helgi and Sir Colin pressing toward him.

"Knights, squires, to me!" he called out. His voice was battle-trained and it rang out like a clarion call. Immediately all of his knights and squires started toward him through the crowd with haste, but his cry also had the unintended side effect of alerting anyone as yet still unaware that something was amiss. He turned back to Malia and the other handmaidens. "Your mistress is unwell. Get her to her coach!" he said as the attention of the entire plaza settled upon the scene.

Stjepan stared at Annwyn intently, trying to figure out what she was doing. He caught a flash of neck and collarbone and then something else and his eyes went wide. "Let her be. Don't you see it?" he said, suddenly pushing past her handmaidens, kneeling down and reaching in to help Annwyn open her bodice.

Arduin's eyes flashed wide with anger and incredulity, livid upon seeing a strange man's hands upon his sister. "What the . . . you go too far, sir!" Arduin said with great offense. "Knights. Squires!" Arduin pushed swiftly through the onlookers crowding about his sister toward Stjepan, intent on pulling him off of Annwyn even as she struggled with her own handmaidens on the paved stones of the plaza.

Arduin managed to get a hand on Stjepan's shoulder and yanked him partially to his feet, but as he did so Coogan and Cynyr casually crowded in on both sides of him, leaning into the knight to hem in his movements while craning their necks to get a glimpse of his sister. Erim pressed in from behind him, her hand snaking unnoticed around his hip to surreptitiously grasp the hilt of his sword should he try to unsheathe it.

And so Arduin found himself effectively and casually surrounded and immobilized in the press about his sister, seemingly as if by accident. He struggled in confusion, uncertain about what was happening.

"She's trying to show us something!" Stjepan hissed angrily, struggling to free his long coat from Arduin's strong grip. A scrum was forming as curious, wide-eyed onlookers continued to press in to take a look and Arduin and his knights struggled with the men around them. Annwyn was struggling with her handmaidens, and winning despite their best efforts, and her torso flashed bare beneath them. Arduin caught a glimpse of pale skin exposed in the struggle at his feet, and looked away instinctively, trying to redouble his efforts to clear the crowd. He was about to go for his sword—where he would have discovered Erim's grip on his sword's hilt—when suddenly Malia screamed.

Her handmaidens let go of Annwyn and pulled back as she stretched and writhed on the pavement, displaying herself for all to see. Arduin looked down and blanched with horror as everyone pressing into the tight circle around his sister froze, looking down at her with a mixture of lust, horror, and surprise. At first all that registered was her pale alabaster skin, and her perfect breasts, and her nipples, and she almost took his breath away.

And then he saw the end of his line written in her skin.

"King of Heaven help me . . ." Arduin managed to gasp.

Sliding over Annwyn's naked torso, fading in and out and moving over her shapely form, were signs, images, words and symbols in a strange and cruel calligraphy.

Stjepan followed some of the text that slid over her skin. "*Tereska malles malifiri tir garas, umess de beyir Azharad . . .*" he whispered as he read the words. Awe and wonder dawned on his face.

"Goddess above and below . . . it's the map to the barrow," he said under his breath.

A set of cryptic letters scrolled over her breasts as she writhed under

206

their shocked gaze, speaking in tongues. Her handmaidens, her brother, his knights and squires, Stjepan, Erim, Gilgwyr, Jonas, Coogan, Cynyr, dozens of courtiers, Marked Men, independents, clerks, and gossip queens in the tightly packed circle pressed in around her stood frozen and just stared, open-mouthed, at what they saw. Hundreds of others would later claim that they'd seen the marks upon her skin, but in truth it was only a small fraction of the mourners present. The only movement in her immediate vicinity was Rodrick Urgoar, the High Priest of the Public Temple, pushing his way through the ring of slack-jawed onlookers until he was close enough to get a good look at Annwyn.

And he was shocked and frightened by what he saw.

"Witchcraft. Witchcraft! Seize her! Seize the witch!" the High Priest called out in a high-pitched voice filled with hatred and terror, clearly audible across the whole of the plaza.

In an instant, the world seemed to slow to a crawl for Stjepan. He looked up slowly, seeing the shock and horror in the faces of the crowd. He could hear the gulls laughing in the air above them, the mocking roar of Heth in the surf. He could smell the stink and sweat of their fear, their hate, their lust and desire. His eyes narrowed and his lips skinned back from his teeth in a snarl.

Stjepan turned with sudden speed, twisting about despite Arduin's strong grip on his doublet, and struck Rodrick Urgoar right in the face, the top two knuckles of his fist flattening the High Priest's nose into the shape of a crushed bulb of cauliflower. Rodrick's head snapped back, blood spurting into the air in a high arc from his smashed and broken nose, and he fell backwards into the crowd, his body instantly going limp.

And the funerary plaza dissolved into bedlam and chaos.

Gilgwyr walked through the screaming, scattering, pell-mell crowd as though lost deep in thought, untouched by the riot around him. Most of the mourners were fleeing off the funerary plaza back toward the Public Temple of the Divine King and the docks and streets of the Public Quarter, even as Divine King priests and temple assistants tried to push through them to get to the bier and their fallen High Priest. Marked Men and independent crews lashed out to escort the two Princes of their Guild to safety, fighting with the escorts of high ladies from the Court, and Gilgwyr didn't even notice as a cassocked priest was lifted high into the air and tossed bodily off the plaza and into the urn-filled waters of the bay by Petterwin Grim's men. Arduin and his knights formed a protective cordon around his sister's handmaidens, as they bodily dragged her from the plaza and the clutches of Divine Kings priests who screamed for them to surrender her. Bottles and fists were flying in the general commotion, and something hard struck Stjepan in the back of the head, on purpose or by accident, and he went down, only to be hoisted up onto the shoulders of Erim and Jonas and Coogan and hustled into the crowds fighting to get off the plaza.

That is why my dreams are still so beautiful, Gilgwyr thought. *The gods have smiled upon us. We are truly blessed. We still have the map.* He looked up and realized he was walking toward Harvald's body and bier, now lying abandoned and forgotten in the chaos. He took up a torch off the marble pavement and lit it at one of the smoking braziers. He stepped beside the bier, looking down at the gauze-wrapped body. He took a last swig from his small bottle and then emptied the rest of it onto the body, smiling warmly.

"Thank you, old friend. Today is a great day, a blessed day, and soon, very soon, will come the best day of all. A great change is coming!" he said in a fierce whisper. "Forgive me for doubting you!"

The veiled woman dressed in white was the only person seemingly unmoved by the chaotic scene of the plaza; she still stood nearby, singing her dirge. Gilgwyr wondered for a moment if she was in fact the actual White Lady, the harbinger of death from Aurian legend, and he shuddered. He lowered the torch and walked in a slow circle about the bier, setting light to the corded stacks of firewood and tinder until they burned bright and the body was aflame, and soon the ashes of Harvald Orwain, son of Leonas, Baron of Araswell, were gusting out over the waters of the bay, floating on a song of mourning.

CHAPTER TEN
ABOVE SAYLES & GRIM, PRINTERS & ENGRAVERS

Stjepan was walking up a leaf-strewn forest path, broad high trees of birch and purple-leaf oak, maple and elm, cherry and white ash, cedar and pine stretching out for leagues in all directions. The trunks of the trees and the debris of the forest floor were coated with old layers of lichens and moss, and a rust-red under-brush complemented the ancient patina of grays and dull greens. The leaves were turning burnt red and orange-yellow, into fire and gold, all the brilliant shades of autumn, and so he began to suspect it was a dream. He turned and looked to his right through a break in the trees, and caught a glimpse of a far sloping range of forested evergreen hills, backdropped by a horizon of desolate high mountains. Down to the east a great stone castle sat on a rise over a small riverside city, and he knew that across that river would be the Plain of Stones. *An-Athair. The great Erid Wold. The woods of my birth*. A dream, then, but still it was pleasant, and so he kept walking the ancient forest path, drinking in its beauty.

A handful of starlings swooped past him and settled on the lower branches of a great elm as he approached it. *You are too late, too late*, they called to him.

"Too late for what, little lords?" he asked.

You'll see, you'll see, they called, and then they took to wing.

He followed the path and the flight of the disappearing starlings until they had passed beyond his sight. The woods fell silent. No animal scurried in the underbrush, no bird sang in the branches above. He could smell wet earth and leaf and needle, moss and sun-lit stone, and from nearby the smell of something burning.

He approached a high clearing in the woods. Massive, ancient trees surrounded the clearing, their lower branches filled with dangling amulets and chimes, small sculptures and offerings placed around their trunks. A pyre had been built in the center of the clearing, and a single post erected within it. A woman was tied to the post, her long silk dress slightly torn and soiled with dirt. She was beautiful, wild, her long wavy black hair framing a face of wisdom and power. His mother, Argante. A crowd of their neighbors watched with fear and excitement behind several circles of men dressed in black robes and brown hoods as some of those men stepped forward and lowered torches. The pyre began to catch.

A young boy stood stock still to the side, watching with wide eyes. Stjepan recognized his younger brother, Justin, and his heart broke. Two hooded men, with deer antlers attached to their masks, held a struggling young woman on her knees, forcing her to watch as the flames of the pyre grew stronger and higher. He couldn't see her face but her long curly hair was unmistakable, a deep, dark brown that was almost black, the color of burnt earth. His sister, Artesia.

He walked slowly toward the pyre, coming to stand behind his sister and the men restraining her. He could hear his sister whispering to herself: *"That won't be me. That won't be me. That won't be me."* His mother looked down at him and smiled, as she always did in his dreams. Smoke and flames were rising up around her. Her skin was blackening from the heat, but she seemed serene.

"Stjepan. Blood brother," said a familiar voice behind him.

Stjepan turned, and saw Harvald standing behind him, smiling apologetically. Behind Harvald looking toward him were Gilgwyr, Jonas the Grey, Coogan, Cynyr, and Duram, dressed in their street-worn finery, swords and daggers in braces at their hips. They nodded to him in turn. Beyond them, he could see a group of men with their backs to him: Austin, Fionne the Fingers, Timm Bellane, Myles the Younger, and Darant. *So Austin is dead, then*, he thought sadly.

"I'm so sorry, Black-Heart," said Harvald softly. "The Path of the Dead calls for us all eventually."

Stjepan looked at him for a moment. "Yeah. I suppose it does," he replied.

He turned back to stare as the flames consumed his mother.

From the window Erim could see smoke rising in the distance over the southern and eastern skyline of Therapoli, more smoke than was usual from the chimneys of its many fireplaces, kilns, and ovens. Bells were ringing in several parts of the city. She guessed that there was a fire down in the Public Quarter. The scene around the Public Temple had been a rough one, and it appeared as though some of the Marked or perhaps someone from one of the independents might have used the chaos and confusion as an excuse to do a bit of damage. Riots and near-riots were scary things, in her experience, as they had a life of their own; someone might start one for their own purposes, but there was nothing like running down a once familiar street with screams and the smell of smoke and panic in the air to escalate excitement into madness, and then who knew what could happen. The bells of the Public Temple had been ringing an alarm ever since the High Priest had gone down, and they'd seen horsemen from the City Watch marshaling on the streets as they'd carried Stjepan's unconscious body out of the quarter.

The smoke to the east she'd guess was somewhere in the High Quarter; not a conflagration yet, probably bonfires on the cobblestones, and likely outside the city house of Araswell, where she was certain the Lord and Lady had retreated from the funeral, and where Gilgwyr, Jonas, Coogan, and Cynyr had all headed after depositing Stjepan safely in his rented rooms in the small attic lofts above the print shops of Grim & Sayles, a few blocks up from the Forum where Tinker Street met Aqueduct Way. The Grim in Grim & Sayles was in fact Petterwin Grim, Marked Man of the Guild; she was pretty sure he couldn't read, but he had been persuaded by Stjepan and Harvald to back the purchase of a printing press to be run by the bookbinder Garrett Sayles, and as far as she could tell he had no reason to complain to date, as the press was minting new books and broadsides and pamphlets virtually at all hours, bringing letters to the commoners of the city. Stjepan had found it amusing that the functionally illiterate Grim was using a print shop as the cover for his activities and operations as a Marked Man. Grim had thought it funny, too.

As she watched the smoke rising from the High Quarter, she wondered a bit about the beautiful Aurian woman, and if she really was a witch. She'd seen the strange letters and symbols moving about the woman's skin, as though they were fish swimming in a murky bowl of water that she could only see when they were pressed against the glass, trying to get out. She wondered how they'd gotten into her, and if it hurt at all. The woman had that classic Aurian beauty—blonde hair like spun gold, pale skin like ivory, and full, shapely breasts that would be soft handfuls to the touch, a different kind of beauty than the Palatian Ariadesma, with her copper skin and lithe, tight, athletic dancer's body. She wondered what the blonde Lady would look like completely naked.

Erim was interrupted from her daydreaming by a grunt from the bed. She looked back. Bed was a generous term; Stjepan slept on a mattress lain over the top of several crates, surrounded by stacks of more crates. The print shop stored some of its old equipment up in the lofts, and so there were strange metal contraptions scattered amongst the crates and chests along the walls and corners. Stjepan was slowly sitting up, reaching for a flask of water that she had placed by his bedside. It had been hard to find a place to put it, as every available inch of flat surface in the loft was covered with stacks of paper, books, inkpots, and boxes of quills. She watched as he drank some of the water, then poured the rest of the flask over his head and shook his wet hair, heedless of where the dripping water was scattered. He grunted again, cleared his throat, and looked over at her. In one smooth motion, she hefted and then tossed his leather-wrapped brace of sword and daggers to him, and he caught the bundle casually in mid-air with one hand.

"Gilgwyr says city law be damned," she said softly, touching the rapier and dagger that she had slung to her side, retrieved from her own rooms while Stjepan slept. Anticipating a fast exit from the city, she'd also paid Master Cort a month in advance to hold her rooms in case they had to leave quickly. "You'd better hurry. We're missing the show, and it's starting to get ugly."

She indicated the window. Stjepan lifted his head, listening to the distant sounds of temple bells for a moment, and then nodded, his mouth and jaw set grimly.

212

CHAPTER ELEVEN

AT THE CİTY HOUSE OF THE BARON OF ARASWELL

Stjepan and Erim moved quickly up the cobble-stoned alley, their faces masked by black neck scarves pulled up over nose and mouth, Stjepan with his hat pulled low over his face. They carried their sheathed swords and daggers in leather-strapped bundles, in case they had to discard them quickly, and Stjepan had a leather satchel slung across his body. They had crossed the Public Quarter from the print shops of Grim & Sayles through back alleys and side streets, avoiding the main thoroughfares; on occasion, startled residents had ducked out of their way, the sight of masked and armed men adding to the air of danger created by the temple bells tolling their alarm in the distance. The King's Road that separated the Public Quarter from the High Quarter was the trickiest part of the journey, as even with the strange air that was settling over the city it was quite busy. But they had dashed across it so quickly that no one had time to notice.

Noble families and wealthy merchants lived in the High Quarter, and as they often brought centuries of their rivalries and internecine wars into the city, their houses were usually built as strong tower keeps, with either no or only small windows on the ground floors. Windows grew larger as the floors grew higher, but were usually built with strong wooden window shutters in case arrows and bolts started to fly from building to building. By law no tower could be built higher than the lowest stone of the High King's Hall, but as the Hall was built on a hilltop rise, that left plenty of room for some of the Quarter's towers to reach considerable height. The alley that Stjepan and Erim followed led them up to the Street of Orfeydda, named after the first Aurian King of Therapoli, and most of the tower houses there belonged to old pedigreed families of Aurian lineage.

At the top of the alley, Gilgwyr, Jonas, Coogan, and Cynyr leaned non-chalantly against stone walls and iron railings in the shadows, along with several members of Jonas' crew; Little Lucius and Horne held the rear, watching Stjepan and Erim approach, while the brothers Cole and Ruvos Till held point, standing nonchalantly a couple of yards in front of the alley. Their swords and daggers were hid from view behind their bodies or cloaks. They were watching the backs of a large crowd of jeering onlookers gathering in the wide street before them; somewhere in the crowd were a couple more of Jonas' men, Tall Myles and Little Myles (who, unlike Little Lucius, actually was little), slipping through the press to see what was happening up close. Across from their vantage point and up a few broad stone steps were the great doors of the city house of Araswell, now shut fast against the surly crowd and showing stains where fruits and vegetables had been hurled against it. Several bonfires had been lit, one directly in front of the building, and two at each end of the street, and their smoke wafted through the streets and alleys of the High Quarter and into the sky. Divine King priests filled the front ranks of the crowd, along with some armored Templars. The crowd had already swelled to over a thousand men, women, and occasional children; it seemed a mix of devout commoners, probably marched up from the Public Quarter; pilgrims, caught up in the specter of a witch hunt; curious servants and groomsmen from nearby noble houses; and some element of pure street rabble, scum that didn't even rate as amongst the independent crews, but skulked in the shadows on the leavings of their betters.

"The witch. Give us the witch!" the priests would cry and chant on occasion, and the crowd would take up the cry for a while until it died down again.

Gilgwyr snorted in frustrated amusement. Little Lucius gave a low whistle and Jonas, Coogan, and Cynyr turned and looked as Stjepan and Erim came up behind them. Nods and quick handshakes went around.

"Did you see who hit you?" asked Coogan with a wry grin.

"Could'a been anybody, right?" joked Horne.

Stjepan rolled his eyes. "Yeah, I suppose so. Never saw it coming," he said, touching the back of his head with a slight wince.

"I'm betting it was Naeras Braewode," said Jonas. "I spotted him in the crowd, despite his best efforts to stay hid. He's had it in for you ever since you fucked up that little scheme he had going on the Street of Smiths."

"He's still holding a grudge about that?" asked Stjepan. "That was six years ago."

"Wizards don't forget," shrugged Jonas.

"Wizard my ass," Stjepan grunted to general laughter, then moved up right behind Gilgwyr and joined him in observing the proceedings.

"Rodrick Urgoar is still unconscious," Gilgwyr said by way of greetings. "If news begins to spread of his unfortunate demise, some in this city will no doubt celebrate, given how unpopular he was; but these are the faithful, and this crowd will get really ugly."

"I didn't hit him that hard," protested Stjepan.

"Ah, but it's all in how you hit him, isn't it?" said Gilgwyr. "Besides, you needn't be the one to worry, as apparently the rumor is that Lord Arduin did the deed. Some of those present and many who weren't swear that he struck the High Priest to prevent him from revealing that his sister was a witch."

"If you had anything to do with those rumors starting, I shall not be appreciative," Stjepan said coldly. "I have no issue with standing for my actions, and Lord Arduin was wholly innocent in the matter."

"Wasn't me," Gilgwyr said, raising his hands defensively. "It seems to have been the genuine confusion of the crowd. Lucky you, off the hook. But regardless of the cause, this mess is going to make getting access to the Lady a bit harder. I've sent word for Leigh, but he might have left the city after Harvald died. That old bugger can be hard to find when he wants to be."

Erim slipped up next to Stjepan and craned her neck. Someone in the crowd threw some ripe piece of fruit against the doors of the tower house, and that prompted a small shower of imitators. *All that food going to waste*, she thought, shaking her head. She studied the facades of the houses of the various nobles who shared this street. "There'll be stables in the back, yeah?" she asked Stjepan. "The servant's entrances."

Stjepan grinned. "Aye," he said. "The priests will never think to go there."

They all stepped back a bit into the alleyway, leaving the Tills on watch.

"What are you thinking?" asked Gilgwyr.

"Nothing like the direct approach," Stjepan said with a shrug. "Let's go knock and say hello." He turned to the others. "Jonas, can you stay here, keep an eye on the crowd? Send one of your crew to alert us if things start to look dire?" Jonas nodded. "Coogan, Cynyr, I am beginning to suspect that a fast exit from this city might be required. You're not part of this, but can you pave our way, let's say at the Gate of Eldyr, and the West Gate?"

"Cutting across the whole city, that's crazy," said Cynyr. "But I get it, you're thinking Pierham?" Stjepan nodded. Cynyr and Coogan looked at each other and grinned. "Sure, we can do that. Six Hells, we'll even help you get a boat. Nothing like a bit of fun before we head back north to the Grand Duke, eh?"

Sir Holgar raised his head and his hand. There was definitely someone tapping at the rear gate. He glanced at Sir Theodore and the squire Wilhem Price, frozen in mid gesture as they paused in sharpening their swords. Holgar stood and gazed at the gates through the open arch of the stable's smithy. The double gates were solid oak, bound in iron, and set into one gate was an iron sally port with a spy hole set in its center. The tapping came again.

He slipped his sallet on his head and stepped out into the rear court-yard, shifting his frame and muscles to let his harness settle. Both he and Sir Theodore were now armored in three-quarter plate harnesses, and squire Wilhem wore a mail hauberk under his quilted gambeson. Holgar could smell smoke and ashes from the bonfires in front of the great house, and could hear the muffled shouts and cries of the crowd gathered in the street;

216

a small part of him was as excited as he was scared. But the rear of the house had so far been quiet. There was a small bell set in the wall by the rear gate with which visitors could announce themselves, but whoever was there was ignoring it and tapping on the iron sally port. *Perhaps trying not to attract too much attention?* He strode softly to the gate, his sword firm in his right hand, hearing the others rouse behind him. He slipped the visor of his sallet down, and then carefully opened up the spy hole in the sally port.

He saw three men waiting outside, standing politely and nonchalantly as if they were there to deliver milk and eggs, despite the swords and daggers they bore. He recognized the man in the lead from the funeral. *Black-Heart.* They locked eyes for a moment, and Holgar stared at him through narrow slits.

Holgar finally grunted and slid the spy hole closed.

From the window of his second floor chambers, Arduin could clearly see the entire street in front of the city house of his father, the Baron of Araswell. *Islik's balls, we're fucked*, he thought as he contemplated the end of his father's house and possibly his life. He was grimly cataloging the available defenses for the house in his head: *Eight knights, including myself; five squires; fourteen men of the household fit enough to fight, including six experienced bowmen; twenty women in sufficient condition to give assistance, with Tomas in the kitchens already directing the preparation of hot oil, bandages and stacks of arrows and bolts.* Even against a rabble numbering in the hundreds if not thousands by now, he was sure they could hold the front doors, possibly even for days— *as long as no one brought a battering ram; as long as Templars or the City Watch don't show up, and it stays this street rabble. But if men that know what they're doing show up, then we're done for.*

Given how angry he was, it was actually surprising that Arduin could hold a coherent thought in his head. But his livid anger had cooled enough for a kind of acceptance to ease into him. He had known all week that

Harvald's death under such mysterious and scandalous circumstances had almost certainly doomed his family to an ignominious fate; and now, with his sister accused of witchcraft by the High Priest of the Public Temple, and his brother's funeral dissolved into a riot to top it all off . . . well, the end would certainly come sooner rather than later. It was almost a relief. *Better that we all die and just get it all over with*, he thought. *Better a quick death than the slow death we've been dying for the last ten years.*

Two of the household's squires, Elbray and Enan, were finishing buckling him into his armor, a heavy three-quarter plate harness in the Sun Court style, slipped tight over his pourpoint arming doublet. Rolled edges, etching, and gold gilding marked it as an expensive harness, but in truth it was also slightly out of date; it had been made for him at the height of the family's power by the armorer Leon Lis Wain of the House of the Double Lion, back when Arduin was a Tourney Champion, and that was indeed a decade gone by. The current preference in Therapoli was for a sloped cuirass that came to a low point, while his was decidedly full and rounded; for high shoulder pieces, particularly on the left pauldron, to help protect the neck, but his had none; for large, sweeping couters at the elbow, while his were more medium-sized, if elaborately chased and etched. Still, the harness wasn't terribly less effective than the current fashions, and the armorer's mark upon it was a considerable point of pride. His plate gauntlets, bevor, and sallet rested on a tabletop nearby, awaiting the moment when the house was truly in danger.

"Do you really think they'll attack the house, my Lord?" asked Elbray as he wrapped the King's sword belt around Arduin's waist. Arduin glanced down; Elbray was about fourteen years of age, still young, with several more years of squiring to go before he could attempt a knighthood. Enan was even younger, twelve years of age. They both looked nervous. *Perhaps we can send them out the back, with some of the women*, he wondered.

"No, of course not," he said, with as reassuring a smile as he could muster. "But we'll be ready for them if they are stupid enough to try."

He could hear a small commotion outside his chambers, and Sir Helgi walked into the room. "My Lord, visitors at the back gate. Sir Holgar thought you'd want to see them," he said. Arduin nodded and gestured for Helgi to bring them in before turning back to the window. He eyed the crowd, idly speculating about which one of them he would shoot first with a crossbow. *Probably one of the priests; cut off the head, and this rabble won't know what to do.*

He could hear men filtering into his chamber so he turned; Elbray and Enan expertly turned with him to complete their last remaining buckles and adjustments. Sirs Helgi, Holgar, Clodin, and Colin were escorting three men into his presence. One of them he recognized instantly, and he contemplated the man coldly for a moment.

"You are Stjepan, son of Byron of An-Athair, yes, and a cartographer at the High King's Court?" Arduin finally asked. "We spoke briefly this morning on more than one occasion," he added with a slight hint of irony.

Stjepan nodded. "I am, Lord Arduin," he said. "Let me again offer my condolences. My companions are Erim, once of the city of Berrina, and Master Gilgwyr Liadaine. As you may recall, Gilgwyr and I knew your brother from our days at the University . . ."

"Your days at the University?" Arduin snorted. "You almost burned the city down. Rabble rousers and street brawlers, you were, the lot of you. You earned my brother a black mark against his name and life as a petty clerk at Court. Hardly fitting for a scion of our lineage." He waved in the general direction of the windows, indicating the commotion outside. "And trouble seems to follow you both, even to his very funeral. Even to the doors of this, my father's house." That last was almost a shout.

"Yes, my Lord," said Stjepan with a wince. "I do regret the manner in which his funeral ended, and the part I played in it."

Arduin contemplated him for a long moment, calming himself. "Is it true, what Harvald said about you?" he finally asked. "That you are a witch's get. I mean, everyone always says that about the Athairi, that you're all witch-born and *fae*-born, but Harvald, he said in your case it was actually true, that your mother was . . . what was it? Argante, called the Witch of An-Athair, who was burned at the stake some years ago . . ."

Stjepan set his chin higher, his mouth tight. "My mother was indeed

Argante, daughter of Yirgane, of the line of Arfane, and Urfante, and Morfane," he said, though he was not sure that Arduin knew what that meant.

Arduin nodded, satisfied, and started to walk out of the room, signaling for him to follow.

Arduin and then Stjepan entered a dark, austere chamber, followed discreetly by Sir Colin and the squire Elbray, and paused. The chamber's window shutters were drawn shut, and looked out over the rear courtyard, so the cries of the street rabble were distant and muffled but still audible. There was a gauze curtain around a divan, with figures behind it. They began approaching the curtain, and soon Stjepan could see a semi-conscious Annwyn tossing and mumbling to herself in the arms of a fearful but defiant Malia, who stared up at them wide-eyed.

Arduin stopped, and Stjepan stopped right behind him, but then Arduin glanced back at him and with a slight inclination of his head indicated that Stjepan could approach more closely. Stjepan nodded and walked past him toward the curtained area. Annwyn was still in her mourning dress and in obvious distress, her eyes unfocused, a faint gleam of sweat upon her face and neck, now unveiled. Her golden hair was tightly wound behind her head, though a few strands had come undone and were plastered by sweat across her forehead and face.

Stjepan crouched before her, and cocked his head, listening.

"The images on her body were bad enough," said Arduin quietly in the dark behind him. "But then the . . . words started. At first I thought they were just mad ravings . . ."

"No, it is an old tongue she speaks; has your sister ever studied Old Éduinan or its dialects?" Stjepan asked. Éduinan was the original language of the Danians, Daradjans, and Maelites—the *language of the mountains*, literally, for the peoples that lived upon the Éduins mountains or within their shadow.

"My sister has been brought up with the education befitting a Lady," said Arduin coldly. Stjepan grunted noncommittally as Arduin paused. "So . . . where do these words come from, then? Is this indeed some sort of witchcraft, then, as the High Priest said?"

Stjepan took a deep breath. "Your sister is in the grips of a Sending, an enchantment of the mind and body sent by your brother as his dying act, and I believe with a clear purpose. The images upon her skin are part of a map, sent for us to follow."

Arduin gaped at him. "My brother? Are you mad? My brother, the *clerk*, placed an enchantment upon my sister? He was no magician!"

"Perhaps you did not know your brother as well as you thought you did, my Lord," said Stjepan quietly. "A rudimentary understanding of the hermetic arts is taught to almost all students at the University."

"My brother . . ." Arduin began, then stopped. He thought on the questions of the Inquisition and the City Watch and the Magisters that he'd heard all week: *Did Harvald consort with wizards and sorcerers? Where might he have learned the arts of higher magic? Have you ever seen Harvald with magical amulets or talismans?* He thought about the glimpse of the body he had, before the priests and undertakers began their work on it. "My brother . . ." he started again, struggling. "My brother . . . my brother died from a curse and was unrecognizable to me even as we put him on the pyre. What is this a map to? What is so important that Harvald would risk death for it and endanger our sister?"

Stjepan looked at Annwyn for a long moment.

"It's a map to the Barrow of Azharad," he said.

Malia withdrew reflexively from her mistress with a loud gasp as the whole room seemed to freeze. Sir Colin began to whisper a prayer.

Arduin's face contorted—with fear, fascination, possibility. He drew back a bit, so his face was partially in shadows.

"The Sorcerer King of the Bale Mole?" Arduin asked quietly. "That is a cursed name. If this is true then why didn't Harvald turn the map over to the King's Court, or the University Magisters?"

Stjepan glanced back at him. He couldn't quite make out Arduin's expression in the darkness of the room. "Because we aimed to find the barrow ourselves. You've heard the rumors and stories, yes? That he had the sword *Gladringer* in his possession when he was buried?" Stjepan asked.

Arduin waved his hand dismissively, but his mind was already racing. "Campfire tales sung by bards," he said, even more softly.

Stjepan gave a little shrug. "Maybe. But Harvald believed the stories to be true. He'd found records in the archives of the Court, long forgotten letters and journals from men who'd been traveling with the King of Dania after the Black Day Battle; they gave report of the sword falling into ill hands and tracked it north. And then accounts from the campaign against Azharad a century later, from the wardens of the Lord of Gyrdiff, from the knights of An-Dama Logh and the so-called Erl of the Tiria Wold. All of them reporting seeing Azharad with *Gladringer* in the war in the woods."

King of Heaven, could it be true? Arduin wondered.

"What we needed was a map. This map. And we finally found it, thanks to the archives and a bit of luck. We thought if we could find the sword . . . well, recover the lost sword of the High Kings and you could command almost any reward for such a service to the crown . . . even restore the fortunes of your historic name, as Harvald wished," Stjepan said. He studied Arduin. "Even with this latest disaster courting your family, if you were to sponsor our expedition, and but grant me an audience with the Lady . . ." he trailed off, not needing to say it: *this could be enough to save you.*

Arduin closed his eyes and this mind spun and raced, making calculations, weighing his options, all of them terrible.

King of Heaven, the sword of the High Kings; let this be true, he thought to himself.

"Don't make me regret this," said Arduin. He walked past Stjepan and pulled the curtains open. He looked down at Annwyn. "Rouse your mistress," he said harshly to Malia. The handmaiden paused, looking at the two men as though they were crazy, and then slowly she started to shake Annwyn, whispering to her softly.

Annwyn's eyes fluttered open and slowly she focused on the people around her.

"Well, sister," said Arduin coldly. "You were eager enough to show yourself to this man before. Here he is." Her eyes fluttered again and closed, and her head sank back.

Arduin turned and stalked out of the room, followed by Sir Colin and his squire.

After a long moment in silence, Stjepan stepped forward, pulling the curtains further back. Malia held her Lady in her arms, cradling her torso, wiping her brow with a soft cloth.

"Lady Annwyn," Stjepan said softly, kneeling down before them.

Annwyn gave no reply, and Stjepan looked up at the distraught Malia. The handmaiden studied him with large eyes, clearly unsure of what to do; but finally Annwyn stirred, shaking her head, her eyes slowly coming to focus on his face. She stared at him for a long moment.

"Stjepan, man of An-Athair. My brother called you Black-Heart. Are you here to kill me?" she asked quietly, her voice barely audible above the faint din from outside the tower house.

Stjepan paused, looking into her eyes. "I was your brother's friend," he said. "I am a clerk at the High King's Court, as was Harvald . . . In fact, I'm a cartographer. I make maps. At your brother's funeral, you showed a map to me, a map sent by Harvald. And you asked me to save you."

"Did I?" Annwyn asked with a small laugh. She stirred again, as if trying to gather her strength. "And yet how do we know these actions were truly mine? I see myself doing those things but perhaps I only dreamed or imagined it. How do I know if it was me or the map, seeking you, map reader?"

She indicated with her hand; Stjepan followed her gesture and spotted a chair. He went to the chair and brought it over beside the divan, and took a seat. He set down his satchels and began to unpack a few items: a notebook bound in leather and closed with a leather tie; a wooden box with a sliding lid, in which were hidden small glass bottles filled with ink, sticks of charcoal, and brushes; and several sheaves of heavy vellum paper. Annwyn looked over his tools with the beginnings of curiosity.

"You say this . . . map, it was sent by Harvald?" asked Annwyn.

"Yes, my Lady, I believe so," said Stjepan. "I believe he used what magicians would call a Sending to cause the map to appear upon you."

"Why would he do that?" asked Malia.

Stjepan glanced at the handmaiden; her concern for her mistress was readily visible on her face. "I don't know, Mistress," said Stjepan. He looked at Annwyn again. "Your brother was in desperate straits when he did this thing; perhaps he thought that the map would be safe here with you. Or perhaps you were simply the foremost thing on his mind as he faced his impending death."

"Ah, a brother's love," she said flatly, the faces of the two women blank and unreadable to Stjepan. A small alarm bell sounded in his head, and he frowned, but could not place a finger on what was wrong. "Do you know what it is like, to feel as though your body and your mind are no longer your own? To feel like you are struggling to remain yourself? I can scarcely bear to look at myself . . . and yet here you are, so eager to study that which disfigures me," she said to him.

"My Lady," Stjepan said apologetically. "I know this is a most unusual circumstance, but your brother Arduin granted his permission for this audience . . ."

"*His* permission?" Annwyn said with a bitter laugh. "Arduin, like all my brothers, believes he knows what is best for me, he always has. And perhaps Harvald believed he too knew what was best for me, if as you say he passed this burden to me in death. And you, I expect you know what's best for me, don't you?"

Stjepan smiled wryly. "If we copy the map, then I hope Harvald's enchantment will end. Please trust me. The longer it remains upon you, the greater the danger, for this map possesses secrets that many might desire," Stjepan said, quietly but earnestly. "And you are already in grave danger, my Lady. I do not mean to frighten you, but your father's house is

224

under virtual siege, with the priests claiming that you are a witch. Should the map still be upon you when the Inquisition arrives . . ."

Annwyn smiled shyly. "You grow impatient with me. Very well, I will delay you no further. I have spent most of the day in a swoon, and when I have been myself no one has wanted to tell me what is happening outside; but the crowd's chants have been unmistakable and I do have some inkling of how dire the situation is."

She began to undo her clothing and Malia moved to help her. Stjepan turned away. They unbuttoned the high collar of her black velvet brocaded bodice, and then the front of the bodice itself. Malia slipped the bodice off her mistress, and next lifted Annwyn's black silk blouse over her head. She helped Annwyn arrange her bodice and shirt over her chest, so that her front was still covered. Annwyn shifted on the divan until she had turned away from Stjepan and her naked back was exposed to him; she was hunched over, as though trying to crawl inside herself. Malia fretted nervously, trying her best to preserve her mistress' modesty; tears limned her eyes. "Master Stjepan?" Malia finally said, holding back a sob.

He turned. Stjepan's gaze drew sharp and he took a sharp inhale. There were map images and letters fading in and out and moving on the exposed skin of her long, curved back, and for a moment he marveled in wonder.

"Will . . . will this be enough?" Annwyn said quietly over her shoulder to him.

"I will do my best, my Lady, with whatever you show me," Stjepan said. "I cannot imagine how difficult this is for you, and I wish there were another way, but time is pressing . . ."

"Difficult? Yes. I have only allowed one other man this kind of intimacy, to my great ruin and that of my father's house," Annwyn said quietly.

Stjepan froze, looking at the two women, studying Annwyn's downcast profile, the searching gaze of Malia. He was surprised at how directly she had acknowledged her scandal.

"Your story is known to me, my Lady, and I will not condemn you for having once taken a lover," Stjepan said carefully. "I am from An-Athair, and our traditions and mores are . . . different than in the rest of the Middle Kingdoms."

"My story. Of course," she sighed. "You say you know my story. Then you know that I have been alone a long time, just me, my family, my household, my books, sequestered here in this house. To show my body to a stranger . . ."

"You read, my Lady?" Stjepan asked cordially. "Your brother misrepresented you, then, I think. If you read, my Lady, then think of yourself like a book that someone else has written, and I must read." He glanced down across her naked back. "A book like no other. Please trust me that we shall all do our best to lift this enchantment from you."

Annwyn turned, and studied his face for a moment. He found her gaze inscrutable and uncomfortable, but he met her eyes with his own, and did not flinch or turn away.

"Then begin your work," she said finally.

Stjepan begins to write in his notebook as Malia drew close to her mistress; the two women clasped hands and smiled nervously at each other, but Malia's face betrayed her fear and she turned away a bit. Annwyn saw this and studied her handmaiden closely.

"What troubles you, Malia?" she asked.

"I . . . I should not say, for fear of frightening you," the handmaiden replied.

Annwyn stared at her a bit longer, then, keeping her eyes on Malia, she inclined her head toward Stjepan to address him.

"You speak of the secrets of this map, Athairi," she said. "Where does this map lead?"

Stjepan paused, studying her profile for a moment, then returned to his work, his eyes following the words and images moving upon and under her skin and noting each new apparition in his notebook. He started to speak quietly as the crowds outside chanted.

"Magic is everywhere in the world, if oft forbidden by those who deem it a threat. And magic swords are common enough, I suppose; quite a few of the knights at the High King's Court bear rune-swords of one provenance or another. But there are a few enchanted swords in our history that are the stuff of legend. One such is *Gladringer*, the sword forged by the Daradjan blacksmith Gobelin, of the Bodmall clan, in the last dark days of the Winter Century, when the last of the Dragon Kings sought to hunt down and exterminate the Worm Kings. This was in the days when it was discovered that Githwaine, last of the Worm Kings, wielded *Ghavaurer*, the sword forged by Nymarga the Devil."

"He used that cursed sword to kill the Dragon King Erlwulf," said Malia. "I remember hearing the bards telling tales from *The Last of the Dragon Kings,* once upon a time . . ."

"Ah. *De Denoumis Wyrmis Basillus*, one of the great epics in Danian literature," Stjepan said with a nod. "Then you know that for a time it looked as though evil would triumph, with the last Dragon King dead and Githwaine ruling openly over the lands of the western Mael. But good men sought a counter to his evil weapon, and one such was the blacksmith Gobelin. By legend it was one of my own ancestors, the Athairi witch Urfante, who led Gobelin to the ruins of the Green Temple of An-Athair. There he forged and enchanted the sword *Gladringer* out of star-iron, quenching it in the pools of the Spring Queen's blood that can still be found there. Gobelin made a gift of it to the Aurian hero Fortias the Brave, and with it Fortias slew Githwaine, and put an end to the cursed presence of the Worm Kings upon the earth. Fortias became the High King of the Middle Kingdoms; and Awain, our current High King, is his descendant."

"May the King of Heaven watch over and protect His greatest vassal," whispered Malia, seemingly out of reflex, and Annwyn echoed her a beat behind.

"*Gladringer* was held by the High Kings of the Middle Kingdoms as a great relic and holy weapon," said Stjepan. "Well, at least until it was dropped and lost in the Black Day Battle against the Empire by the High King Darwain Urfortias, ever after known as the Fumbler. And it became lost to history. But a story spread, repeated by bards in every tavern in the Middle Kingdoms: that *Gladringer* had been found on the battlefield where the Fumbler had dropped it, found by foul corpse-eaters, who spirited it away into the hands of the Nameless Cults who await the Devil's return. That it came into the possession of Azharad, the evil Sorcerer King of the Bale Mole, who ruled those hills and brought terror to the western Danias for a time. In the telling, Azharad sought some way to destroy *Gladringer* as a favor to his patron, Nymarga the Devil, but could not do it, so powerful were the magics of the artifact. And so he left orders to have it buried with him in secret when he died, so that the questing knights of the High King's Court could not recover it. Ever since, treasure-hunters have sought maps to where Azharad was buried, in the hopes that they might find *Gladringer*. But the location of his barrow, and with it the sword, was a secret held dear by the Nameless Cults."

"A secret no longer, apparently," said Annwyn faintly. "Pried from their fingers by you and Harvald." She had turned away so that he couldn't see her face to read her expression. "So I bear upon my body a cursed map made by the Nameless Cults to the hidden tomb of an evil wizard and the sword of the High Kings. The very map whose curse killed my brother."

"Yes, my Lady," said Stjepan. "I'm afraid so."

Malia was weeping softly.

"Give us the witch, give us the witch!" chanted the distant crowd.

Erim watched Arduin pacing impatiently back and forth in the middle of the fire-lit chamber while everyone else sat about the room looking at the inner doorway. She understood his frustration; things had been dragging on for a few hours now, long enough for the sun to set and the Dusk Maiden and a waning Spring Moon to have appeared in the sky, and the word they were getting from the street from the members of Jonas' crew was increasingly dire. First had come word that the crowds had swollen to perhaps three thousand in number, and there was no question to Erim that they'd gotten louder; then that armed and armored Templars had been spotted on the edges of the crowd, and then that a company of Templar horsemen had been spotted marshaling on the King's Road by the North Gate. The City Watch was out in force in the Public Quarter, having finally quelled the disturbances there, but Jonas sent word that they were letting the priests run the show in front of the house of Araswell, which was even more disturbing. With every passing hour the knights and squires and other members of the household that came and went looked more and more nervous, increasingly sweaty and pale as the tension mounted. Only Gilgwyr seemed to be absolutely, serenely calm as he watched the doorway to the Lady's inner chambers. Erim had an increasingly bad feeling in her stomach, a growing conviction that she was somehow in the absolute worst place to be in the whole city at that moment, trapped in a building about to receive the full attentions of an angry mob. *Hurry up, Black-Heart,* she thought.

Finally, Stjepan emerged, his notebook in one hand, frustration on his face as well. Arduin took the notebook from him and quickly scanned it. "There's no more of this map than before. This grows more scandalous by the hour!" he said in exasperation, thrusting the notebook back at Stjepan angrily.

"Forgive me, my Lord; I assure you the Lady does her best to preserve her modesty, but this is simply all that's appearing. The map will not reveal itself in full, only bits and pieces. I am at a loss," Stjepan said, running his ink-stained hand ruefully through his hair.

"You'll have to follow the map," came Leigh's voice.

They all turned, surprised, and sure enough Leigh was sitting amongst them. *He wasn't there a moment before,* Erim thought. Several of the knights and squires drew their weapons as they sprang away from him.

Arduin stared at the grizzled enchanter, calmly sitting in his house as though he'd been there all along. "Who in the Six Hells is this?" he finally asked.

"Ah. This is Leigh Myradim, my Lord; he was once a Magister at the University. Harvald, Gilgwyr, and I were his pupils for a time," Stjepan said apologetically.

"Aye, I remember now," Arduin said, staring at the man as though he were a bug. "Yes, Harvald told me about you. Banished from the University for improper conduct. Quite an entrance." He turned angrily to Stjepan. "I am not going to invite every hedge witch and back-alley warlock in the city to gawk at my sister!"

"I do not think I need to see the young lady to help diagnose her condition," Leigh said in a deep, calming voice. "The map will not reveal itself in full, you say? Only bits and pieces? A start, and an end, perhaps?"

"Yes," said Stjepan, glancing at the notes he'd made in his book. "There is no doubting its authenticity. The words are in Maerberos, an ancient dialect often used in the Nameless Cults as a secret tongue. A difficult cipher is used as well, but I've seen it before, it was popular amongst mapmakers of the 12th century. And it's given us enough to get started and lay out our prize, but . . ." He suddenly nodded with realization, and Leigh smiled. "Ah, I see. *She* is our map."

"Yes," said Leigh proudly. "You were always fast on the uptake, and always so good with map ciphers. Did you ever read the *Book of the Gate of Heaven* by Gammond of Wael?"

"No, Magister, that book is . . . forbidden," said Stjepan.

"Mmm? Oh, yes, of course it is," said Leigh with a tired, dismissive wave of his hand. "Gammond wrote that book while in exile himself, you know. I never met him, that was before my time at the University, but I studied under his pupil, Aéd Amav, and naturally he had a secret copy squirreled away. It describes just this very kind of spell; it's an old conjurer's trick, to curse someone so that they are compelled to the chosen task. We cannot risk trying to dispel the Sending. This map has power and danger of its own accord, as Harvald's gruesome death so helpfully illustrates. No, the map will reveal itself as you journey. And when you are done, she will be free of the enchantment . . ."

"As we journey?" Arduin said, incredulous. He spoke slowly, as though explaining himself to children, or the mentally disabled. "Are you daft? You want to take my sister on a quest for a wizard's barrow? Nonsense. We are safe here in my father's house. He is the Baron of Araswell and a Lord of the High Court, and not even the priests can violate this house without the High King's consent."

230

As if on cue, Sir Helgi appeared at a doorway with a harried-looking Little Myles in tow. Arduin frowned, his mouth hanging open. "Oh, and now who is *this?*" he barked.

Little Myles did a quick bow. "Forgive me, my Lords, but Jonas sends word; the jig is up!" he said, slightly out of breath. "No one outside knows it yet but Rodrick Urgoar has gone to meet the King of Heaven. The Watch has secretly issued arrest warrants for Lady Annwyn for witchcraft and Lord Arduin for the murder of the High Priest, with the seal of the High King's Court, and they are on their way. The Inquisition will be tasked by the Watch with the custody of the Lady, and their Templars are already about. You don't have much time before all Six Hells break loose!"

Arduin practically sputtered for several moments. "An arrest warrant? For me? For *murder?*" he finally got out. He turned to Stjepan and roared. "I didn't murder High Priest Rodrick, you did!"

"As a matter of jurisprudence the term 'murder' would imply pre-meditation, my Lord, and of that we are both innocent," Stjepan replied. "I would be more than happy to testify that I was the one that struck the unfortunate official and caused his wrongful death, but I fear that will rapidly be beside the point. Our primary concern must be the safety and wellbeing of your sister, my Lord, and please believe me that you do not want her in the hands of the Inquisition, or for that matter the mob. Above all you must spare her that fate. Indeed, there is the ch—"

He broke off and listened as a great roar of anger and rage swelled up from the crowd outside. Everyone paused as the nerve-wracking sound of several thousand throats howling for blood washed up and over the room.

"What was that?" asked someone quietly.

"*That* was the mob finally hearing that Urgoar is dead," said Stjepan, nodding to himself.

A sudden metallic banging started to reverberate through the house. The room froze, then unfroze as several knights and squires rushed to the windows in alarm.

"A battering ram, my Lord," shouted Sir Helgi. "And the Watch is with them."

"Well, it's official, then, my Lord Arduin," said Stjepan. "And the mob sounds angry enough that they might not even allow the Watch the chance to actually arrest anyone." Stjepan stepped beside Arduin, his voice low. "Harvald guides us still, from the Heavens, with this trick. He intends her to be our map. Let us make haste and take to flight while we still can."

"This is insane," Arduin gasped. "I can't possibly . . ." He closed his eyes and tried to think, listening to the battering ram at the doors.

Erim held her breath.

Finally Arduin's eyes flew open. "Prepare our escape. Hurry!"

Everyone in the chamber immediately nodded and bowed to Arduin, Leigh with a grand exaggerated flourish, and most of them exited in haste; Stjepan disappeared into Annwyn's chambers and then returned, quickly dropping the tools of his trade into his satchels. Sir Helgi had lingered, waiting to escort him from the room, and as they left, he turned to Stjepan and started speaking rapidly. "We might have a little time, we've spent the last several hours barricading the front doors, so it won't be easy for them to break through . . ."

As their voices receded, Arduin stared after them, alone and deep in thought, until finally he turned and walked through the doorway to his sister's inner chambers.

There was a low brazier set, sending flickers of light throughout the dark room, and a fire in the fireplace burned low. Annwyn was stretched out on the divan, her body covered up by an embroidered tapestry cloth. Arduin turned to Malia. "Summon the rest of my sister's handmaidens and prepare such of her things as you can very quickly. We will be leaving shortly," he said.

Malia looked very frightened, but she curtsied and left.

Arduin sat down on the edge of the divan, and slowly turned to his prone sister. He reached out, and slowly uncovered her body as she turned away from him onto her side. He looked at her naked back, watching the words and symbols of the map flicker in and out, as the battering ram banged loudly against the iron doors of his father's house.

A bustle of quiet but intense activity filled the stables and rear courtyard behind the house of Araswell. Dim lanterns lit a knot of knights with bill-hook poleaxes clustered at the rear gate, watching the rear alley and letting Jonas' crew slip in and out the sally port, while the loyal remnants of the once great Aurian family hurriedly prepared coaches and wagons and loaded them with what provisions and property they could easily carry. The squires and stable hands were saddling and armoring the best horses in their barding, and tying other horses to the rear of the wagons. Cole and Ruvos Till had taken up positions inside the house behind the boarded first floor windows directly above the ground floor main doors, and the brothers were busy heckling the crowd from above so as to provide the illusion that the doors were to be defended; they'd volunteered to be the last out.

Jonas and Horne slipped through the sally port and quickly spotted Stjepan and Erim beside one of the wagons, conferring with the rest of the knights and squires and the half dozen able men who were to teamster the coaches and wagons. They hurried over and joined them. "Just like old times, eh?" Jonas said with a grin to Stjepan, then quickly turned to the others. "Our friends have been busy. We've got a safe route all laid out for you. Once you're in the alley, head north to the Street of Loria and then head west. Cross the King's Road as fast as you can into Baker Street, and then follow it to the aqueducts. Follow the Aqueduct Way around and up to the High Promenade, and then it's a straight run through the Gates of Eldyr and the West Gate, and then you're out the city and on your way to Pierham."

"Pierham?" asked Sir Helgi, suddenly looking nervous. "You mean us to take the river?"

"Heth's curse only strikes when you are on the open seas, Sir Knight," said Jonas. "The rivers do not bend to his word."

"Oh, sure, some of us have taken the river before, but it ain't that fucking simple," said one tough-looking wagon-driver. "You want us to drive these wagons clear across the city while avoiding the crowd and the Watch? It's impossible!" Some of the others muttered nervously as well.

"The hard part will be the King's Road, if you get caught up in the Templar horse, but we've got some folks working on that," said Jonas. "The City Watch threw a lot of men into the Public Quarter today, and that means that the rest of the city is a bit light. Lots of folks looking to take advantage of that right now. The whole city's in chaos. The route we've laid out for you, you shouldn't see a single Watchman once you're past the King's Road. And I believe our enchanter is off trying to keep the crowd from the north side of the High Quarter." Erim looked around; Leigh was indeed nowhere in sight.

"Watch your pace," warned Stjepan. "Worst thing will be an accident with a wagon or coach, or a horse coming up lame, so go fast but stay in control. If you get stuck or lose a wheel, leave the wagon behind and leg it out of the city or to a friend you can trust as fast you can. Make for Araswell in the coming days if you get separated."

Arduin, now with gauntlets and sallet strapped on, stood nearby, half listening; he was mostly intent on watching as the household's hand-maidens helped a cloaked Annwyn into the back of the first coach. He looked at the back of the tower-house, his gaze scanning up the stone walls toward its top. *I wonder if there'll be anything left by morning*, he thought glumly. He started to worry about what his father might say, and then suddenly stopped. *No, you've lost the right to judge me on this, Father; you should have been here to see the end of our line.*

Suddenly Sir Theodras turned at the rear gates and shouted out. "They're coming. They're coming!" Some of the mob had finally figured out there was a back way in.

The rear courtyard burst into frenzied activity as panic set in. Stjepan tossed his extra gear into the back of a wagon and turned to Erim, Jonas, and Sir Helgi. "You've got to hold them off until we can get everyone out!" he said, fierce and quiet. Erim and Helgi glanced at each other, and she nodded and pulled her rapier and dagger.

Sir Helgi hefted a great sword and turned toward Sir Clodin and Sir Holgar and the two young squires, Elbray and Enan. "Stay with your liege!" he barked. "Lead the way out!" They nodded and started to mount their horses, big black-coated war-trained Aurian warmblood destriers for the knights and slightly smaller palfreys for the squires.

Sir Helgi, Jonas, and Erim started moving, gathering men as they hit the rear gates: the knights Lars and Colin Urwed, Theodras, and Theodore, all in three-quarter plate harness; the older squires Herefort, Wilhem, and Brayden Vogelwain, nephew to Sir Helgi; Horne, Little Lucius, and Tall Myles; four sturdy Aurian men from the household with bill-hook poleaxes; and three huntsmen with stout yew bows. They gathered for a moment right inside the rear gate, looking at each other, then Helgi was throwing the crossbars up on the gates and they were pulling them open.

Erim walked quickly toward the middle of the alleyway, rapier and dagger bared in the dim light. The narrow street was flanked on each side by tall stone walls and the backsides of tall stone buildings, for all the world a narrow man-made canyon. To her right, coming up from the south, she could see a large crowd rounding the corner and filling the alley, headed toward the rear gate entrance with malicious purpose. Some in the crowd bore torches, and so she could see priests in their vestments in the mix, a few armored Templars with their white surcoats marked with embroidered gold suns and holding swords of war, and a random assortment of the street rabble that had filled the streets before the house. The rabble bore clubs and pitch-forks and here and there she spotted spears or short hanger swords.

The rest of the group took up a line on each side of her, the knights and squires in the front rank and the rest backing them up, and they advanced toward the oncoming crowd enough to give those leaving the gates easy access to the alley behind them. She took a quick read; nine across, not quite shoulder-to-shoulder, and eight behind—enough to look like a solid wall across the narrow alley, decked in armor and bristling with swords and poleaxes. But that was a large crowd coming toward them.

Upon seeing the line, the Templars and priests slowed their advance to a crawl and readied their own weapons while the rabble began to show some confusion. One of the Templars stepped forward into the lead and in a gruff, commanding voice he shouted out to them as they approached. "In the name of the King of Heaven, and by order of the Patriarch Exemplar

Oslac the Fourth and the High King's Court, put down your weapons and surrender to us the witch!"

In the courtyard, Stjepan and Gilgwyr were maneuvering a large cart filled with hay, aided by several porters and stable hands. Arduin was seated astride his favorite destrier, Ironbound, caparisoned in a barding that matched his own armor, and he wheeled and approached, the high-spirited horse practically prancing. It could smell fire and fear in the air, and it was getting excited. Arduin looked down at them.

"My Lord, head west," said Stjepan. "Ride hard, ride down anyone that gets in your way, and follow the path that our man has laid out for us. Don't stop for anything, and we'll be right behind you."

Arduin looked angry at getting what sounded suspiciously like an order from Stjepan but he turned Ironbound around and went to the front of their slapdash caravan.

"Follow my lead!" he cried out, and put spur to Ironbound's flanks. The warhorse leapt forward, followed and flanked by Sir Clodin and Sir Holgar, both bearing long ten-foot lances, and then the two squires. The teamsters cried out and cracked whips and the coaches and wagons, piled high with provisions and with frightened members of the household, began to lurch forward, one after the other following the horsemen in the lead. Porters bearing torches and armed men from the household ran on foot on each side of the coaches and wagons, and Jonas ran beside the coach bearing the Lady Annwyn.

Erim heard rather than saw Arduin's horse come flying out from the gates behind them, then turn away north, and she instinctively glanced over her shoulder to catch a glimpse of massive figures in steel flowing into the narrow alley. The street felt like it was shaking under the hooves of the lead trio of heavily-barded warhorses, and then horses and coaches and wagons and men on foot started to pour out. *Gods save anyone in front of that lot*, she thought.

The Templar in the lead—she assumed some sort of captain—started to wave his men forward, seeing the column emerging from the rear gates behind the intervening line. "Stop! I order you to—"

"Now!" roared Sir Helgi Vogelwain. Three bows twanged behind her, and she felt something whistle past her right cheek. Screams came from the rabble as the arrows found their marks. "For Araswell!" Sir Helgi cried, and their entire front line charged forward, their weapons raised, Erim amongst them. This seemed to catch some of the rabble in front of them by surprise, and she saw anger and hate rapidly change to shock and alarm as they closed the distance with unlooked-for speed.

"For Orwain!" the knights cried right as they slammed into the first of the Templars and rabble-rousers with a ferocity born from fear and desperation, heavy blades and poleaxes rising and falling to chop and maim or being used, point-first, to pinion men and push them bodily back. Erim couldn't contribute that kind of brute force, so she ran her rapier and dagger straight in front of her and into whatever soft target she could find, which turned out to be the backside of some poor commoner who'd turned to try to run away, only to discover there was no place to run and got her dagger for his efforts; and then, reaching past him, she drove her rapier directly into the throat of a surprised Templar who hadn't seemed to realize yet that people were going to die in this fight.

In truth, Arduin's knights were hardly veteran warriors; they were more like elite sportsmen, their experience of combat and fighting the result of dozens of tournaments and only a handful of actual minor battles. They'd fought by Arduin's side when he'd had to hunt down bandits from the Manon Mole who had raided their tenant farms, conducted a punitive raid against the Lord of Goldwall on a land dispute, and some had once ridden with the Grand Duke against a recalcitrant Baron Avant of

An-Ogruth back when he'd been unhappy about a new tax that the High King had levied. But that already gave them at least two advantages over their opponents: they'd been in combat before, together; and most of them had killed men before.

The Divine King faithful, the pilgrims and the street scum that had joined the fight, caught up in the day's riotous energies and expecting to be seizing a witch and avenging their fallen High Priest and not fighting fully armored knights in a back alley, were quickly overmatched despite the crush of their superior numbers; even the Templars were surprised by the knights' stiff resistance and their willingness to kill. Sir Helgi relished the melee, bellowing with abandon as he hacked men down left and right with his greatsword, exhorting his men to fight, laying about him like a man with nothing to lose, and in a sense he didn't, none of them did; they'd already lost everything, and knew it, and all that was left was to take out their anger and fear on the poor fools that had come to collect their liege lord and his sister. As blood splattered everywhere, Erim almost felt sorry for the rabble.

Almost.

"Hurry, hurry!" Gilgwyr cried as he and Stjepan and several strong men finished loading a dozen small barrels onto the back of the large two-wheeled cart.

"That's it, that's all we have!" shouted one of the porters. With a torch, Stjepan touched flame to the hay while another man split the wood of several of the casks with an axe, spilling oil everywhere. As the hay ignited, they all grabbed either the sides of the cart or its pull-shafts and they pushed it toward the entrance, and then out into the street. It took them a frustrating moment to turn it, and then they were pushing the flaming mass toward the melee. "Ho. Beware, behind you. Out of the way!" the porters cried as they covered the last ground, and then bodies and dark shapes were leaping out of the way. The alley suddenly got bumpy as they ran the wheels of the cart, themselves almost five feet high, over the bodies and body parts of men dying or dead upon the alley cobblestones. The rabble, already breaking under the ferocious assault of Arduin's knights, broke completely upon seeing the flaming cart hurtling toward them, and fled en masse. One of the wheels jammed in a torso and suddenly it was overturning and spinning out of their hands, flaming hay and barrels of oil flying and smashing into the ground, and a great *whoosh* went up as flames filled the alleyway.

Erim looked up from where she had sprawled after jumping out of the way of the wagon, and then toward the roaring flames. The spilled and burning cart had effectively cut the alley in half, throwing up a barrier of fire across the narrow street between them and the retreating rabble. *Couldn't have planned it better*, she thought to herself, until she glanced to her right and realized that the man on the ground next to her, also looking back dazedly at the burning cart, was an armored Templar. They looked at each other in shock for a moment, and then she started stabbing him in the side of the face with her punch dagger as he screamed. The first couple of stabs got her into his cheek and an eye and some teeth and tongue, and the man was screaming and scrambling trying to roll and crawl away from her, and she had to pin him down until she could get the dagger into his throat.

When she was done killing him she staggered to her feet. Several of the knights were finishing off a few other stragglers caught on their side of the fire, while Jonas' men and some of the porters and huntsmen were hauling off two of their own wounded, one of their archers with a ruined leg and then one of the young squires. She winced as they passed; the squire looked pale and wan, blood pouring from a head wound. *He's not going to make it*, she knew at a glance.

Gilgwyr stood in the middle of the alleyway, bent at the waist with his hands on his knees, sucking air into his lungs to catch his breath. He finally straightened and walked up to join Stjepan where he stood glaring at the fire and the rabble beyond; Erim joined them a moment later, and the three of them contemplated the fiery scene, out of breath. Behind them the rear guard was gathering in front of the gates, mounting their horses or clustering around the last horse-drawn cart, into which they were loading their wounded compatriots. Several of the porters were bearing torches and preparing to run alongside the horses and wagon. Cole and Ruvos Till popped out the gates, having finally abandoned their posts inside the house, and looked askance at the carnage in the alleyway before joining Horne and Little Lucius and Tall Myles beside the wagon.

"We are *leaving!*" cried out Sir Helgi, and the rearguard lurched into motion.

Gilgwyr glanced over his shoulder, and then turned back and grinned at the burning wreckage, gasping for breath and laughing at the same time. "You keep trying to burn this city down, Black-Heart. One of these days, you'll get it right!" he said, clapping Stjepan on the shoulder. "Fuck, I haven't had this much fun in ages. I have to get out more!" He turned and started up the alley. Erim turned and hesitated. Stjepan still hadn't moved.

"Black-Heart," she said. "We have to go."

A voice came calling out to them, then, out of the dark from beyond the flaming wreckage. A deep voice filled with malice and fear and pregnant with power. "You are cursed. Cursed in the name of the Sun Court and the King of Heaven! All those who aid the witch, hear me and weep!" cried the voice.

Stjepan turned and walked away, fury on his face.

The trio started moving up the alley at a run, leaving the street on fire behind them.

CHAPTER TWELVE
·OUT ·OF THE CİTY

E rim was tense and nervous as they hit the Street of Loria and turned west, following the rearguard; her blood was still boiling hot and she kept expecting for them to run into a wave of street rabble or a company of Templar horse. But all they saw was smoke in the streets, a layer of thick, still smoke like a fog that made her feel frightened and nauseous. *Leigh's work, no doubt,* she thought with a shudder. Occasionally someone would come wandering toward them through the smoke, and upon encountering a group of fast-moving armored horsemen guarding a wagon, would immediately shrink back from their path. *Too far to go, far too far if we're aiming for the West Gate, we're having to run the entire city*, she thought, panic in her belly. They passed quickly over the King's Road, leaving the High Quarter behind, and the smoke started to dissipate a bit, and then they were on Baker Street. She could hear whistles and strange barking sounds coming from rooftops and alleyways as they rode down Baker Street, and she frowned, uncertain what to make of it, but the streets were eerily deserted.

When they hit the corner with Aqueduct Way, she saw a couple of bonfires being manned by a dozen of the Bastards of Baker Street standing armed and masked in the street; for a moment she thought they were about to have a fight but the Bastards waved them through, and the sneering leather-clad bravos made exaggerated bows as they ran past. Aqueduct Way ran along the south side of the ancient aqueducts, and they followed it until the Way hit the corner with Tinker Street and turned north. There she was shocked and mightily gladdened to see Petterwin Grim and his crew, masked and armed and out in force in front of the print shop, waiting with torches and lanterns and a trio of saddled horses; mightily gladdened indeed as she was about out of breath from running. The rearguard kept riding and running past the waiting men, turning up Aqueduct Way. Sir Clodin paused on his horse, looking at the three of them coming up behind them, but Stjepan waved him on.

One of the Grimsmen was holding the reins of Cúlain-mer and Erim practically flung herself into the saddle, barely breaking her stride, and for some reason she felt enormous relief that she managed to make the vault. *That could have been embarrassing*, was all she could think as she gathered up the reins from the Grimsman and brought the startled courser under control. One of the Grimsmen offered her a torch, and she lifted it high. Gilgwyr looked worse than she felt, and in fact he immediately slumped into the arms of several Grimsmen the moment he reached them, much to their general amusement, and they poured water into his mouth and over his head before pushing him to his feet. Gilgwyr shook his head, flinging water from his hair like a dog after a walk in the rain, and then let out a loud "Fuck *me!*" as he moved to mount the second waiting horse.

Stjepan had slowed to a walk and went right up to Petterwin Grim, who was holding the bridle of Cúlain-mal to keep the high-spirited courser still. The two men stood for a moment and shook hands and nodded to each other, and then Stjepan was pulling himself up into the saddle.

"Good to see you as always, Black-Heart," Petterwin said, grinning behind his scars.

"Good to see you too, Grim," Stjepan said with a smile, bringing his fingers up to lightly tap his forehead, and then they were off up Aqueduct Way at a brisk gallop. Erim looked over her shoulder and saw that the thirty-odd Grimsmen behind Petterwin had raised their swords silently into the air in a farewell salute.

They caught up with the rearguard halfway up the northbound stretch of the Way, falling in with Sirs Clodin and Colin at the back of the group. She was surprised to see some of the porters still running alongside the horse cart, holding torches high, along with Horne; she'd been right winded by the time they'd hit Grim & Sayles and these men were still going strong. But a few of the others, including Tall Myles and Little Lucius and the Tills, had jumped up into the now crowded wagon, and were watching the streets with loaded and cocked crossbows. It occurred to her suddenly that she'd forgotten to eat anything since the morning. *No wonder I'm so beat*, she thought. As they passed up the street, they ran a gauntlet of Red Rob Asprin's men, calling out in encouragement to Jonas' men in the wagon, and Red Rob nonchalantly gave a little wave to Stjepan and Gilgwyr. She suddenly realized they were being passed from the territory of one crew to another, and a shiver went up and down her spine.

By the gods, she thought. *They've got the whole fucking city in on this*. She laughed wildly.

Where Aqueduct Way hit the High Promenade they found their first sign of trouble. One of the wagons in the first group must have hit the corner too fast, despite Stjepan's admonitions, and the wagon had flipped on its side. Some of Bad Mowbray's men were there, milling about an injured and screaming horse that lay crumpled and thrashing on the road and trying to free the other from its yoke to the wagon's draught pole, along with a large group of what appeared to be street urchins combing through the wreckage and abandoned provisions. Most of the rearguard started to slow as they approached the wagon but Sir Helgi, in the lead, looked over his shoulder and shouted, "Don't stop. Move. Move!"

So the rearguard kept going, but Stjepan and Erim and Gilgwyr slowed down, as did Sir Clodin. Stjepan practically leapt from his saddle and drew his falchion as he walked up to the maimed and injured draft horse. The men clustered around it were just standing there confused, and they drew back as he approached. He crouched behind the thrashing horse, and held its head in his arm, and Erim could hear him whispering something to it. The horse grew still and then Stjepan cut its throat, and he held it as it bled out.

One of Mowbray's men, a tall Danian street captain that Erim recognized by the name of Peer Lance, stepped forward as Stjepan stood up. "You should find the ones from the wagon hoofing it on foot toward the Gate of Eldyr," he said. "Two are in a bad way, one's a woman with a broken leg." Stjepan nodded and he got back on Cúlain-mal and then they were racing to catch up to the rearguard.

And indeed the rearguard started to overtake the stragglers from the lost wagon as they moved down the High Promenade. The first was a knot of men and women from the household helping to carry one of the kitchen maids, who had indeed broken her leg when the wagon flipped. This time Sir Helgi did signal the rearguard to stop, and the women were quickly loaded into the horse-drawn wagon alongside the wounded, with all of the able-bodied men now moving to run on foot, flanking or following the wagon. Erim caught a glimpse of the woman's leg, and saw blood and exposed white bone in the torchlight, and she swallowed hard. They picked up other members of the household as they moved toward the Gate of Eldyr, including one man with a badly dislocated shoulder; but Erim heard some of their talk and apparently a few of them had panicked and run off into the night after the wagon flipped, and now no one knew where they were.

When they hit the Gate of Eldyr, in the Inner Wall that divided the Old City from the newer part of the city, she wasn't sure what to expect. The gate was rarely closed but there were usually some men from the City Watch there, and she grew apprehensive as they neared it and saw lights. As they passed through it, all that were waiting for them were more of Bad Mowbray's men, who stood casually in the gatehouse as though they were always on duty there, and a man on horseback dressed in dark leathers and wearing a black scarf tied over his mouth and nose, who turned out to be Cynyr. Stjepan slowed as he went through the gate. "We're the last, officially, but there's some lost little ducklings wandering the streets," he called out to a swarthy man that Erim didn't recognize.

"We'll keep open another spell, see what comes through," the man replied with a nod and a shrug.

"Give the Prince my regards," Stjepan said, and then they were off again, Cynyr falling in behind them.

Once past the Gate of Eldyr it was some of Jon Galbroke's men that provided a silent, running escort until they neared the Market Plaza and Jon Dhee's domain, where they peeled off into the dark. The rearguard caravan, now numbering eleven horsemen, almost two dozen on foot, and fifteen or so piled high into the wagon, sped along the High Promenade past the empty market stalls until they were on the approach to the West Gate and its welcoming committee. Erim spotted men from the City Watch on the ramparts of the tower and wall and there were men on the street and in the gate, and her heart went to her throat again, but then up ahead she could see Jonas on one side waving them through the open gates, and indeed Sir Helgi and the other knights and the members of Arduin's household didn't stop but kept right on going through.

Jonas' crew, running on foot, finally slowed to a stop by their captain, winded and laughing in relief. Gilgwyr and Stjepan slowed to a stop, and Erim did so as well, totally confused. There was no doubt that there were real Watch wardens glancing down at them as the fugitives of the Orwain clan rode loudly out the gates. But there was Jonas, and Little Myles was with him, she also spotted a half dozen heavily-armed enforcers from Jon Dhee's crew, big nasty brutes with shaved heads and scarred cheeks, and then there was Jon Dhee himself stepping out of the barbican onto the gatehouse landing above them with Sir Owen Lirewed, several other knights wearing the surcoat of the Watch guard, and then Coogan behind them. Dhee had a cool, calculating smile twisting across his scrunched, cruel visage under his long stringy hair, and Coogan was pulling up a black neck scarf to cover his mouth and nose as he grabbed the landing stairs and then vaulted onto a waiting horse.

Dumbfounded, she took in the scene and shook her head; there were handshakes and quick farewells all around, and she found her hand being firmly pressed by Horne and Little Lucius and Tall Myles, reaching up to her from on foot; they'd all seen her fight and she felt a bit of pride that they were all eager to wish her luck.

"There's going to be a few Hells to pay for this one, Black-Heart, particularly since you *are* on the blacklist," called down Jon Dhee in his raspy, frightening voice. "But it'll be our little secret, the Red Wyrm needn't know, nor the Painted Prince nor Prince Cutter either, and this small thing is the least we can do for the man who killed Rodrick Urgoar, may he rot in the Six Hells."

"I have no idea what you're talking about, Master Jon," said Stjepan drily. "No idea at all. But no doubt you're right that I'll have to pay for this, one way or the other."

"The city will miss you, Black-Heart," called down Sir Owen with a laugh, as he leaned casually on the landing's wooden guardrail. "It's always a lot more interesting when you're here."

"You're a liar, Sir Owen," said Stjepan with a rueful grin. "I'm sure it won't notice that I'm gone at all."

"Come, come, no time for banter, I think your patron is waiting just down the way," said Jonas, and he started jogging alongside them as they wheeled their horses about and through the gates. The rest of his crew stayed at the gatehouse, and Erim looked back to see them silhouetted in the archway along with some of the gate guards, with Jon Dhee and Sir Owen and the other knights watching from up top the landing.

Arduin sat high in his saddle, the visor of his sallet up, looking back across the expanse of the city visible from the road. Sir Helgi waited by his side, guzzling water from a leather bottle. Street lanterns and fire-lit windows twinkled across the city skyline, reflected off the sides of the highest and best-lit buildings. He could see the lights of the high spires of the High King's Hall and the Great Temple of the Divine King on their distant rise; normally it would have been a stirring sight, but he felt nothing, just a hollow ache in his belly. He could see a bright fire of some sort in the High Quarter; he vaguely wondered if the mob had put the city house of his father to the torch. The alarm bells of the temples and the Watch still rang faintly and furiously; he'd gotten so used to them that they barely registered in his thoughts. Behind him the rest of the caravan had started to make its way down the road to Pierham, ten miles they'd have to cover as fast and as carefully as possible in the dark.

Stjepan, Erim, and Gilgwyr rode up, with a man that Arduin didn't recognize at first jogging by their side, until he remembered seeing him briefly in the rear courtyard of the house as they prepared to flee, and then two other men in dark leathers and partially masked faces riding horses. He sighed. *I'm not even going to ask*, he thought wearily.

The group came to a halt around Arduin and Helgi, milling their horses about. Erim turned her horse and, like Arduin, stared back at the city skyline. She started to laugh lightly to herself, the relief and exhaustion palpable in her bones, and finally she let out a wild *whoop*. Gilgwyr, out of breath, his face sweaty and pale, looked over at her, at first askance, and then, as she stared at him and laughed and laughed, he started to laugh as well.

Stjepan dismounted and walked over to Jonas, his arms casually outstretched. The two men embraced, saying quiet words to each other, and then Stjepan was swinging back up onto his horse. "My Lords. May the Fates smile upon you 'til next we meet!" cried out Jonas with a wave, as he started to walk backwards toward the gate.

Erim could barely stop laughing to get the words out. "We crossed three-quarters of the fucking city, and *the City Watch held the gates open for us on the way out!*" she gasped out. "Who the fuck *are* you guys?" Coogan and Cynyr chuckled under their scarves, and Gilgwyr started laughing so hard he almost pissed himself.

Good question, that, thought Arduin.

"Why, we're the Lords of Book and Street, my dear Erim, at your service," shouted out Jonas with a shit-eating grin and a short bow. "Hasn't anyone told you that yet?" And with that, he turned and started walking briskly back to the waiting gates.

"By the gods, I've always hated that name," Gilgwyr barely managed to get out. Tears were rolling down his face. "I've forgotten which one of us fucking came up with it . . ."

"Fionne," Coogan and Cynyr said together with exasperated shrugs. "May the gods keep him," Coogan added. And with that their horses leapt into motion, surging down the road after the caravan. Erim and Gilgwyr turned to follow, as did Sir Helgi, and soon it was just Arduin and Stjepan sitting mounted and looking back at Therapoli Magni, capital of the Middle Kingdoms.

Stjepan looked out over the city toward the High King's Hall, sweeping his gaze down across rooftops and towers, to the black of the bay and the bobbing lights of the ships of thirty different cities near and far. He looked up at the cloudless night sky, saw the waning Spring Moon and the Star Child dancing the last of her days before the coming of the Serpent. He closed his eyes and listened to the wind, to the ringing of distant bells, to what sounded like someone weeping alone in the dark. He sniffed the air, smelt fire and ash, the sharpness of honest clean steel and the lather of horse sweat, and an undercurrent of desperate and abject fear. His gaze fluttered open and grew hard and grim, and he turned his horse away from the city.

"So," said Arduin, looking at Stjepan carefully. "Any reward, you say? I mean, I know, it's *Gladringer* . . . but can any sword really be so valuable?"

Stjepan returned his gaze for a moment, measuring him.

"It's fucking priceless," Stjepan said. He gave a sharp whistle, and Cúlain-mal sprang forward and onto the road.

Arduin looked bitterly, wistfully back at the city and the fires in the distance, and then he wheeled Ironbound and put his horse to spurs.

PART TWO

ON THE ROAD OF SWEAT AND TEARS

CHAPTER THIRTEEN

FAREWELLS AT PIERHAM
THE 18TH OF EMPERIUM, 1471iA

The road to Pierham was decently maintained, being part of the royal lands around the capital city, but the New Moon was almost upon them and the night sky did not provide much light. The torches and lanterns helped, but with two coaches and two wagons piled high with people and provisions the going was slower than they might have hoped, and so Coogan, Cynyr, and Stjepan picked up their pace and rode on ahead to begin making arrangements for the crossing of the river. By the time the Dawn Maiden rose, the main caravan was finally arriving—tired, frightened, and sleep-deprived—in the town of Pierham on the north shore of the Estuary of the Abenbrae. There was a low wall and towers and what seemed to be a keep at one end of the town, but the guards at the town gate greeted them cheerfully and the keep did not appear to be particularly active; Erim guessed its lord, whoever that was, was absent with most of his household. *Our luck is holding*, she thought.

They found Stjepan awaiting them down on one of the docks, alongside two river captains and their spritsail-rigged *hoys*, large shallow-draught coasters designed to maneuver the estuary and river of the Abenbrae and the coastal tides that swept in from the Bay of Guirant. Erim scowled a bit on seeing the vessels; they would barely be considered sea-worthy, and shouldn't be sailed out of sight of land, but she conceded that plenty of their type plied the port of her home city and they'd certainly do the job. Her bones aching, she dismounted gingerly and stood on the dock, sniffing the air and scanning across the estuary mouth toward the port city of Abenton, which anchored the southern side of the river as it opened into the Bay.

The Abenbrae was perhaps the greatest river in the Middle Kingdoms, almost three hundred and fifty miles in length, though almost half of that was in the Highlands of Daradja, where it started as a trickle from the base of the Dess Urharat, one of the great peaks of the Harath Éduins. It collected the cold waters of most of the Daradjan plateau, and brought them down out of the mountains into the lowlands, where the river served as the boundary between the Plain of Stones and the Plain of Horns. Once out of the mountains the river was a mile or two wide until it expanded to almost five miles wide in the Estuary (which was, in fact, a slight misnomer, as the actual tidal estuary pushed up the river all the way to the city of Collwyn; but the name "Estuary" itself was only used for the lowest part of the river where it fed into the Bay of Guirant). The river had once been the easternmost boundary of the great Erid Wold, the wood of An-Athair, before the coming of the Aurians.

A half dozen rival clans of merchant shippers and traders, all of them mixed Danian and Athairi in lineage, controlled the river traffic up and down the Abenbrae and its offshoots; the river folk called themselves Abenbrayers. The Danias to the west also had their Volbrayers and Eridbrayers, clannish river folk who plied their great rivers and who were of similar mixed roots; but the principal rivers to the east in Auria, the Dusabrae and the Fasabrae, were seemingly bereft of the modern descendants of their ancient river populations. Two families dominated the town docks in Pierham: the Lyrians, the largest of the Abenbrayer clans and tenants of the Baroness of Abenton; and the Herlas, a smaller clan that called Pierham itself their home. The two captains that Stjepan had found were from the Herla family, though Erim wasn't sure if he'd picked them because of some kind of local river politics, or just because they happened to have the two largest vessels in port at the moment.

The two river captains certainly looked to be related. They both had the same sunbaked skin, bald spots in the midst of their dark hair, thick black mustaches, and the lean, muscular physiques of men who worked for a living; but the senior of the two looked to have been putting on some weight in his later years. When he spoke, there was the hint of a slow drawl and an accent that Erim found familiar. "It's thirty miles of water 'tween here and Vesslos. The wind'n'll be in our favor, the fortuneteller promised me that this morn. So if'n we time the tide right, we can sail right up the Vessbrae to the city, if'n you want," said Master Wynram, the captain of the grandiosely named *River King's Crown*. "It'll mean we have to sail soon, though, to catch the tide pushing in. Otherwise'n you'll have to hire on a tow team at Badford to haul us up the last leg, or'n we could head to the bridge-docks at Tauria, *or'n* just wait another half day for the high tides to come again if'n you really want Vesslos. No matter'n to me," he concluded with a shrug.

"We'll have to sell the wagons; it will take too long to load them, and would require at least a third riverboat anyway," counseled Stjepan. "The captain here can purchase them from us on behalf of the Herlas."

"Aye, that'n I can," said Wynram with a nod.

"We can buy new wagons in Vesslos, my Lord," said Master Tomas. "But they might not have a coach suitable for your sister. Perhaps the markets at Abenton might have more choices . . ."

"Abenton's too close," said Stjepan, nodding out across the waters of the Estuary to where the city of Abenton was visible on the far away opposite bank.

"Agreed. We must to Vesslos, and the sooner we're on the ground there and moving again the better, so sell the wagons and we'll just make do with what we can find once we're there," Arduin said wearily, waving his hand. He was exhausted and barely able to stand on his two feet without swaying slightly, and the prospect of having to take the river was making him queasy, though he'd done it before. "King of Heaven, get us on the boats and off our feet before we all keel over from lack of sleep."

And so the captains nodded and the docks came alive with the cries of rivermen and stevedores as they started to load the horses and their provisions, such as the household had managed to secure in the final panic-strewn minutes at the city house of Araswell, up broad ramps and onto the decks or into the holds of both hoys. The men around them didn't seem particularly nonplussed by an entire armed household suddenly appearing on their docks, and Erim supposed they'd probably seen stranger things; but then that could also be why Stjepan had chosen the Herlas. Some of the household were having to be convinced to get into the *hoys*; she realized that the more superstitious amongst them had never set foot on a boat before, even one of the riverboats. She spotted a cluster of handmaidens and a couple of Arduin's knights escorting a cloaked and hooded figure, presumably Annwyn, onto the *River King's Crown*, and then was surprised to see Leigh already standing on the deck of the ship, peering about as though he wasn't sure where he was. She shook her head with a slight shiver. *Creepy, creeping, creeped*, she thought to herself.

Other groups of the household were clustered around their injured comrades. The man with the dislocated shoulder was doing okay, but the kitchen maid with the broken leg was clearly in agonizing pain despite the ministrations of her fellows. The wounded squire, Herefort Hrum, was unconscious, pale, and totally unresponsive; she didn't think he'd last much longer. The two youngest squires, Elbray and Enan, looked scared out of their minds. She shook her head, and turned away, not wanting to look if she didn't have to; there was nothing she could do, after all.

Coogan and Cynyr reappeared down the dock, their faces still half covered by their scarves; none of the dock workers gave them a second glance, and that confirmed in her mind that they'd had dealings with the Herlas before. She walked over to join them as they approached Lord Arduin and Sir Helgi talking to Stjepan.

"... if they can put us ashore at Vesslos, that'll put us close to home! Less than twenty miles," Sir Helgi was saying somewhat eagerly.

"Perhaps ... perhaps we can go to Araswell, and join my brother there," said Arduin. "That will give us time to figure out what to do with Annwyn, and this cursed map ..."

"Returning home won't save your sister, my Lord," said Stjepan quietly. "The enchantment upon her won't leave her until we've found the barrow, on that I agree with Magister Leigh. If you prefer another opinion, we can try to find one for you, but we'd likely have to summon Magisters from the University of Truse, and that will take valuable time you do not have.

All that will do is allow your opponents to maneuver while you sit in one place, waiting for news that will not help you."

"Perhaps we can just go to Truse ourselves," said Arduin, rubbing his temples.

"We should avoid the major roads and cities where possible, my Lord," said Stjepan. "That is where word of the arrest warrant and news of the events of yesterday will travel fastest. Our best chance of safety is to make our way west by the less-beaten path, even if in the end we lose some time. Send the bulk of your household back to Araswell, my Lord, and have your brother summon his knights and raise the levy. They should be safe there under your brother's protection and the stout walls of the castle, at least until they send the Grand Duke. And then we should—"

"The Grand Duke?" said Sir Helgi, a troubled expression on his face as he cut Stjepan off. "You can't be serious."

"He'll come, but not at first. I have no doubt that a force is already upon the road in our pursuit," said Stjepan. "The night's confusion will have disappeared in the cold light of day, and they will know that we have escaped the city. There will be an argument over jurisdiction, but ultimately the responsibility will fall to the Royal Guard; the lands we have passed through are the High King's Demesne, and only his knights and vassals have power here. We've maybe until mid-morning before they're here."

"I'm guessing it'll be Lord Constable Garin Highwain, who serves as the King's Sheriff in the Demesne," said Coogan. "Maybe Duke Pergwyn, if someone's really angry."

Arduin brought his hand to his head and rubbed his fingers into his temples again. He could feel a headache building. *Please don't let it be the Duke*, he thought. *Anyone but him, that would just be too humiliating.*

"Aye, probably with elements of the City Watch, and the Templars will insist on their company of horse," said Cynyr. "The forces of the Inquisition in the city are mostly for show, they're not the hard core like the temple knights out of An-Ydain or Dainphalia, but they're well harnessed and the city company is a hundred strong, and they'll be out for blood." Arduin and Sir Helgi gave him puzzled looks.

"We met them in open and fair battle as knights," said Sir Helgi. "We stood our ground and fought, as was our right by both law and custom."

"Rodrick Urgoar, High Priest of the Public Temple, was the son of Oswin Urgoar, High Priest of the Inquisition in the city of Therapoli," Stjepan said quietly.

Arduin groaned. Urgoar was a common enough name that he hadn't thought there might be a connection. *Fortune has turned against us so thoroughly*, he thought.

"But they'll only pursue you to here," Cynyr said. "This is the limit of the Lord Constable's writ. If you'd gone by land toward the bridge at Grawton they might have chosen to pursue you anyway past the limit of his reach, like a dog with the fox's scent running past the fence . . ."

"Particularly the Templars," said Stjepan.

"Aye," grunted Cynyr. "But the river works as well for men as for dogs; once you're in the river that'll bring them up short, and they'll have to figure out what to do next. And that will buy you some useful time."

"Two things will run in your favor then," said Stjepan. "One is that they'll have to summon the Grand Duke back to the city. They'll think you're headed for Araswell, it'll be the first place they look, and to contemplate dispatching a force against the home of one of the High King's vassals takes more than one of the Sheriffs; that's an act of war that will require the Grand Duke as Earl Marshall to lead. Besides, everyone knows Araswell is a well-built hold and he's got the most experience at that sort of thing."

"Even riding at top speed that's probably two days, one day for the heralds to reach him, and a day to return, but he's not likely to move that fast, so figure three or four days at the earliest before he's even back in Therapoli," said Coogan.

"Second, your father will have to be brought into it," continued Stjepan. "It's his hold, he's the High King's vassal, and you and your sister are ultimately his responsibility. Since you're on his lands, he can argue that he should be in charge of hunting you down. All that back and forth between nobles should allow people to calm down, and let cooler heads start to prevail."

256

"My father is at a weak point in his power," said Arduin with a heavy heart. "And he was too afraid to return to the city for Harvald's funeral. I can't imagine he'll want to return now . . ."

"Your father will be summoned back, he won't have a choice, and unless he's completely blind he'll realize that this is the future of his line that's at stake. Remember what word our friend brought us last night; arrest warrants, yes, but signed and sealed in the name of the High King's *Court*, not the High King himself," said Stjepan in as reassuring a tone as he could muster. "That's a key detail and an enormous difference. In other words, it was some other official that put his name and seal on the warrant, probably Lord Chancellor Reiner or his second, Lord Baldwin of the Keys, if you're lucky. They do that often for minor matters, or when the High King needs some wiggle room. So someone's trying to keep the doors open here. If the High King's personal seal had been on the arrest warrant, then you'd be fucked, if you'll pardon my language, my Lord. That'd be a sign they were willing to take your whole family down."

Arduin paced back and forth, his gaze sweeping over the activity buzzing the docks and riverboats. "Small things to be thankful for, is that it?" he asked bitterly.

"Despite the scandal and decline of your family, my Lord, you still have power, and friends, and a honored name, enough to give them pause," said Stjepan. "Your father's patrons nowadays are the Crown Prince and King Colin of Dainphalia, yes?" Arduin nodded, and Stjepan grimaced. "Unfortunately they're part of the traditionalist wing of the Aurian nobility, so chances are your sister's fate is probably sealed. His sons can carry on the family line, but no matter how much he might love her, a scandal-ridden daughter is, at this point, a liability, and she'll be sacrificed to save the rest of you."

"My father would never allow my sister to come to harm," said Arduin vehemently, but he did not believe the words even as he spoke them.

"The only thing that can save your sister now is for the enchantment to be lifted from her before she is in the hands of the Inquisition," said Stjepan. "If they have her in custody, and that map is still appearing upon

her, it will be all the proof they need that she is a witch and consorts with
the Devil. The priests of the city temples hate witches and anything that
smacks of the Old Religion, and she'll be more important to them than
you will, even with Urgoar dead. Rodrick Urgoar himself had been leading
the hunt to find someone to try for witchcraft; there haven't been any trials
or burnings since 1462, when the High King felt the Templars had over-
reached and were threatening to destabilize the general peace."

"The Court didn't care when it was witch burnings in the Danias, but
when they started in on Atallica, oh, they didn't much like that, when it
was Aurian nobles starting to complain," said Cynyr with a grimace.

"And the Earl of An-Athair was close to war, then," said Coogan.
"That would've made the fight against the Earl of Blackstone look like a
walk in the park."

"Aye, but memories are short when hate and religion are concerned,"
said Stjepan. "The Inquisition doesn't care if we slide into civil war; they
know only their holy mission, which is the persecution of idolatry and
heresy and all the forbidden things that the Divine King does not tol-
erate, and they will be most eager to bring an accused witch to trial. But
there will be enough reasons for the High King and the Court to find *some*
accommodation with your father. If I know how the Court works, they'll
bargain hard with him, but in the end he'll be allowed to accompany the
Grand Duke to Araswell. He will plead with your brother to surrender
the keep and the members of the city household under his protection,
upon promise of their safety. Your brother will do it. There will be some
hard questioning, but once they realize that you and your sister and your
knights have fled onward, your household will be safe, and allowed to
testify as to the actions that you took that night. The Grand Duke won't
pursue further, he's not going to be interested in a simple manhunt, shit
like that bores him to tears and he's got a summer campaign against the
Rebel Earl to plan, but the warrant will be allowed to stand until such
time as you have presented yourself for trial. The High King's heralds will
spread word of the warrant, and seek your arrest by local powers if they
should discover you."

"And you know all this how, exactly?" asked Arduin icily. "Are you an enchanter like your former Magister, here to divine the future?"

"We are clerks and cartographers at the High King's Court, my Lord," said Stjepan, indicating Coogan and Cynyr with a nod of his head. "We see the inner workings of the royal household on a daily basis. We write its warrants and record its every thought, word, and deed. And as a cartographer I have been thrice assigned to the company of the Grand Duke when on campaign, serving under his Quartermaster, Lord Alefric."

"You've served with the Grand Duke?" asked Sir Helgi, a look of surprise on his face.

"Aye," said Stjepan with a casual nod. "I was with him in Huelt in '65 when he was putting down the peasant rebellions there, in Angowrie in '68 enforcing the High King's peace between King Euwen and King Derrek, and this past summer in the Manon Mole hunting the Rebel Earl. We give him his maps, scout the land, and help him make sense of what is before him; where to move men and supplies, how to get his army to where he wants it. I can't claim to know with absolute surety what they will do, but let's call this my best educated guess."

Arduin and Sir Helgi eyed each other for a moment.

"Let's say you're right," said Arduin finally. "The High King and my father come to some sort of understanding, the Grand Duke accepts the surrender of my brother and Araswell, and does not directly pursue us further. What would you have us do?"

"Cut south and west along the edge of the Manon Mole," said Stjepan. "There are old paths there that can take us all the way to Reinvale. Our ultimate goal is the barrow, and it will be somewhere in the Bale Mole, so we'll have to be find a way across the Danias; but if we can keep off the West King's Road, we'll avoid the most likely initial route of the High King's heralds. The heralds and the news they bring tend to move due west first, straight to Truse, to Westmark and the Erid King, to Newgate, and then to Aprenna and the Dain King, and finally on to Warwark and King Derrek."

"The Bale Mole," said Sir Helgi quietly. "Islik's *balls*."

Stjepan studied Arduin and Helgi for a breath, before speaking in a low

259

voice. "If we come back with her freed of the map, and bearing *Gladringer* as a gift for the High King, then you'll be able to ask for anything you want, including her safety from the Inquisition and yours from blame in the death of Rodrick Urgoar," said Stjepan. "I'll testify that I struck the blow, and will accept the blood-price, even exile if they impose it. I'll even write out a sworn confession, to be witnessed by my companions here, that you can carry upon you in case I die."

Arduin looked at him for several moments. "Write it out, then," he said. "I'll follow your plan for now." He turned and walked off down the dock, Sir Helgi in tow.

And so Stjepan pulled out a sheet of parchment from one of his satchels, and wrote out a long paragraph taking full responsibility for the wrongful death of the High Priest Rodrick Urgoar and exonerating Lord Arduin of any role in the act, and signed it *Stjepan of An-Athair, son of Byron and Argante, and Servant to the High King.* And then Coogan and Cynyr signed it as witnesses. He offered to let Erim witness it, but she couldn't read or make her mark, so she shook her head and declined. He gave the parchment to Lord Arduin, who seemed satisfied, and Arduin rolled it up and slipped it inside his cuirass, between the metal of the armor and the quilted padding beneath it. Coogan and Cynyr said goodbye to them, then, embracing Stjepan and Gilgwyr as old friends, and her as a newer one. "Keep close to our Stjepan," Coogan said to her with a twinkle in his eye. "Don't let him out of your sight. But keep away from that one, or you might find yourself being pimped out to a boatload of horny rivermen eager to try the ass of a young city lad," he said, indicating Gilgwyr. "Rivermen are just like sailors, they'll fuck anything that moves, and Gilgwyr won't hesitate to make some pennies off your hard work."

"I am shocked at your low estimate of me, brother," Gilgwyr said, stricken. "I'm sure I can get six shillings a go for Erim's tight little ass, at the least."

"Aye, I think I can do that," she responded, blushing a bit and trying to look horrified. "Stick to Stjepan, that is."

"We always knew Stjepan had picked you right. If you make it back alive, we'll make you an honorary member of the Lords," Cynyr said with a laugh. "There's even a whole ceremony and everything." She wasn't sure she liked the way he said *ceremony*. They bowed to her, and she to them, and off they went, putting spurs to horses and heading north.

The riverboats were soon ready, money changed hands with the stevedores and a bored duty officer who finally wandered over to see what they were doing, and then they cast off from the docks. They'd barely put a mile between them and the docks when Erim spotted the glint of sun on steel on the low hills behind the town. She whistled to get Stjepan's attention, and they watched as a stream of horsemen came pouring over the hill from the east, banners snapping in the air. Stjepan reached into his satchel and pulled out his spyglass, a small side benefit of being a cartographer at the Court. He trained it on the incoming banners.

"The Lord Constable's banner, the banner of Lord Captain Conrad of the Inquisition, Captain Clodias of the City Watch . . . but not the Duke," said Stjepan under his breath. "Well, that's something, at least."

He handed the spyglass to Erim and she brought it to her eye, checking off the banners in view. "Nope, no Duke," she said.

"Just'n time, eh, Black-Heart?" came the captain's voice behind them. She glanced over her shoulder to see Wynram behind them, looking at the same scene.

"Aye, Master Wynram," said Stjepan, more loudly. "Our thanks that your crew loaded us so quickly."

"Tweren't a thing," said Wynram, with a satisfied *hrum* deep in his throat.

Behind them they heard a commotion; the squire Herefort had finally died. Weeping and fearful resignation swept through the members of the household that were on the *River King's Crown*, and even the veteran knights seemed to lose heart at the news. Erim suspected that this was the first time that most of them probably understood what kind of trouble they were in; there'd been fear and danger in the night, but they'd been running hot and scared and angry then, and now one of them had actually died, and in the cold light of day. The household quietly debated what to do; landing at Vesslos with a youth dead from wounds would undoubtedly attract attention of a sort they didn't want, and so Arduin made the decision that his body should be slipped into the river. Not the funeral pyre that should have been proper, but a close second for an Aurian, so that it might eventually find its way to their ancestor, Heth. The knights led the household in a round of prayers to the Divine King while his body was wrapped in clean white linens found in one of the hastily packed trunks.

Erim could hear the Abenbrayer crew near her whispering their own prayers for the young man even though they didn't know him; Erim guessed that a death on board their ship was not something they would let pass unobserved, but they were careful not to let the folk of Araswell hear them. Their prayers were a variation she'd heard before:

> *Geniché, Earth Mother, First Mother,*
> *one of your sons lies dead.*
> *Set Djara's daughters as his Guide,*
> *let Seedré light his path in the Great Dark*
> *as he approaches the Throne of Judgment.*
> *Let his ancestors know he is coming,*
> *that they may defend him against his accusers.*
> *The sacred river brings him to you.*
> *Yhera Abenbraea, guide him by the hand,*
> *and take him to Heth's Halls in the Deep.*
> *Let him not be lost in the journey.*

Followers of the Old Religion, then, she thought, which made sense given their Athairi blood and river work. *They'll believe the ship's been polluted by death, now; not a thing they're frightened by, but they'll perform rites to purify it the moment it gets to port and has been emptied of its Divine King passengers.*

And then the body of Herefort Hrum was ceremoniously slipped over the side and into the water.

262

Stjepan and Erim watched his body float for a bit and then disappear beneath the choppy surface of the river. Arduin stood at the railings at a distance from everyone else, looking out onto the water for a while by himself; and then he turned and went down into the hold where his sister had been hidden with most of her handmaidens.

"That was a pretty story you told Arduin back on the docks," Erim said quietly after watching Arduin disappear below. Fatigue was weighing heavily on her eyelids, and she decided to go find a place to take a quick nap soon, but she still felt she had to say something to Stjepan. "Dark and gloomy, but with just enough hope that he doesn't just jump in the river and drown himself."

"A story I very much hope comes true," said Stjepan, casually studying the morning sun on the water.

"A man like Arduin's never been on the wrong side of the Inquisition," said Erim. "He doesn't really know how they operate. He thinks he knows, but he doesn't. What they'll do to Annwyn if they find her. What they'll do to his household."

"No. No, he doesn't have a clue," said Stjepan, looking at her with a bleak expression full of anger. "But remember why we're here. We're here to follow a map." He looked back out over the water. "So one thing at a time. Getting out of the city was the easy part. The hard part's about to start."

I think I'm figuring out why everyone calls you Black-Heart, she thought.

CHAPTER FOURTEEN

SO · CLOSE · TO · HOME

Annwyn roused herself from slumber, and wondered where she was. The light was dim; there was a low lantern gently swaying overhead, and sunlight streaming in somewhere nearby. She stared at the lantern and its movements, could feel the room swaying as well, and she smelt water and brine. *This is different; the hold of a ship, then.* She couldn't remember if she had ever been on a ship before. She thought she had, but why and where? Being Aurian, her family always took the road over the bridge at Tauria when traveling to and from their ancestral halls and the capital, and at the bridge they would visit with its Lord, Garin Liefring, or his seneschal. Or had they taken a riverboat once when there was some sort of trouble with the bridge? She couldn't remember.

She looked around her; she was in a slightly separated part of the hold below decks, not quite a room exactly, but there was a partial wall and some wooden pillars that obscured the rest of the hold from where she lay. Odds and ends hung from the walls and ceiling, and tilted with the tossing and turning of the ship. She'd been placed on top of a small mound of cloth and burlap sacks and covered with a fox fur blanket; whatever was in the sacks was reasonably soft. Around her she saw a few of her handmaidens, sleeping fitfully on whatever soft place they could find. There were the two youngest and newest handmaidens in their household, Henriette and Ilona, both the daughters of respected tenants. Helga and Elisa slept nearby as well along with their children: Helga's youngest, her three-year old son Odwen, and Elisa's one-year old daughter Elisabeta. Several of the kitchen maids and other women from the household slept nearby with their young children. She did not see Frallas or Silbeta, or Malia at first, until she realized that Malia was sleeping on the floor of the hold right below her perch.

She looked down at her chief handmaiden's profile, studying it. Malia looked exhausted and disheveled; they all did. She wondered a bit at the ties that bound them all together, and at the fact that once again she had managed to plummet the household of her father and family into scandal and tragedy. She was too exhausted to feel anything but a kind of detached introspection, incapable even of feeling sad for herself or angry or piteous.

Malia stirred, perhaps sensing the gaze of her mistress upon her. Her eyes opened, and blinked in confusion until they found Annwyn's blue eyes looking down at her. Malia roused herself quickly.

"My Lady, are you all right?" she asked quietly, trying not to wake the others.

Annwyn gave her a nod. "Are we at sea?" she whispered hoarsely.

"No, my Lady," said Malia, shaking her head as she settled on her haunches by Annwyn's makeshift bed. "Else we'd probably all be drowned by now and in the grasp of Heth. We are on the Abenbrae, where the Sea God's curse against your kin does not reach, sailing upriver to Vesslos. Are you thirsty or hungry?"

Annwyn was about to wave her off, when she suddenly realized that she was both. In fact, she was starving. She couldn't remember when she last ate. "Yes, please, some food and drink," she whispered with a small smile.

"Wait here, my Lady, I'll see what I can find," Malia said, and she stood wearily and warily, testing her balance in the gently rocking hold. She wandered off and disappeared into the rest of the ship.

Annwyn closed her eyes and concentrated on breathing for a while, trying to calm her fluttering stomach and nerves. She felt a slight twinge of nausea at the root of her stomach and in the back of her throat, but she couldn't tell if it was seasickness from the rocking of the riverboat *hoy*, or if it was simply her body telling her that it was desperately in need of nourishment. She was not sure if it was appropriate yet to have an opinion on sailing and ships, but she was decidedly leaning toward being against such journeys in the future.

Malia returned, bearing a small basket and a glass. A handsome youth was with her, all black leather and disheveled, bed-headed swagger, carrying a large, heavy jug of water, which the youth poured into the glass

266

held by Malia. As Annwyn contemplated the newcomer, she decided that handsome was not so much the correct word as *pretty*.

"I do not think I know you, sir," she said. "Are you part of the crew of this ship?"

"No, my Lady," the youth said in a low, husky voice. "My name is Erim, I am a companion to Stjepan Black-Heart."

"Ah," said Annwyn. Her eyes fell on a brace of hilts at the youth's side. *A street-fighting ruffian and duelist, then, by the looks of it.* She took a sip from the proffered glass of water, and the water tasted sweet and wonderful to her parched lips and throat. She eyed Erim as she drank, and the youth seemed to grow uncomfortable.

"Please forgive the intrusion, my Lady, but your handmaiden appeared to need some help with the water jug, and the rest of your household is asleep at the moment," Erim said, and turned to go with a short bow.

"Wait," said Annwyn. She took another sip of water. "How long will we be on this ship?" She tried to remember the last time she'd talked to a man that wasn't a member of her father's household, or one of their regular suppliers or tenants.

"Shouldn't be more than another hour, maybe two," said Erim. "I only just awoke myself after a short nap, and I, uh, spoke to a few of the crew. We've got a strong tailwind and the tide is with us, so we've been moving pretty fast. We'll be in Vesslos before you know it."

"And we'll be headed to Araswell after that, then," Annwyn said. "To my father's castle."

Erim stared at her for a moment, as though the youth didn't know what to say. Both Malia and Annwyn looked at Erim, puzzled.

"Ah," said Erim finally. "Perhaps . . . perhaps you should speak to your Lord brother when he awakens."

"Why?" asked Annwyn, her eyes wide. "What do you mean?"

"It is not my place to say, but . . ." Erim started then paused. "But . . . I believe the general agreement was that you would not be safe there, my Lady. You'll really have to speak to either your Lord brother or to Black-Hea— to Master Stjepan."

"Of course," Annwyn said with a dry smile. "Thank you, Master Erim." Relieved, Erim bowed again and slipped back out of the secluded shelter.

Annwyn sighed when Erim was gone. "I'm sure my brother knows what's best for me," she said sourly.

Malia said nothing, but rummaged through the basket and produced some pastries left over from the day before, grabbed hastily from the kitchens in their flight from the city house—puff pastries rolled with egg and cilantro and basil and cheese and then baked. *I used to love these*, she thought as she took a bite of one of them. She frowned. *No, Harvald used to love these.* As she ate the pastry, she realized she was famished, and she ate another after she was done, and then another. Malia looked at her with surprise, but said nothing, glad that her mistress had finally regained her appetite.

Annwyn leaned back, finally, having had her fill for the moment.

"Where are Frallas and Silbeta?" she thought to ask. "Are they still with us?"

"Yes, my Lady, they are with their husbands," said Malia. "Do you wish me to summon them?"

"No," she said. "Let them find some peace for a time." Frallas had recently married Sir Clodin, and Silbeta had been married to Sir Theodras for only a year. Helga and Elisa were married to knights in the direct service of her father; they'd been married for some years and now had their own children to care for.

Annwyn and Malia sat there quietly for a time, and Malia reached out and took her mistresses' hand in hers. The ship rocked gently, and they could occasionally hear the accented cries of the rivermen up top, the crack and roar of wind in the sails, and the neighs and whinnies of stalled horses somewhere else in the hold.

Elisa's baby finally stirred, and she started to squall loudly. Elisa and Helga woke up, young mothers trained to the sound, and then Ilona as well; but Henriette and Helga's three-year old kept sleeping. Malia quietly shared the pastries and some dried spiced sausages and fruits with those awake, while Elisa opened up her bodice to breast-feed little Elisabeta.

268

"How much longer?" whispered Ilona, looking wearily about the cabin; her eyes were shadowed and puffy, and she looked like she had been crying recently, though Annwyn did not remember seeing or hearing her weep. She also looked a little pallid, they all did, from the tossing of the ship.

"An hour or two, we're told, and then we'll be in Vesslos," Malia said. She turned to Annwyn. "Where . . . where do you think we are going if not to Araswell, my Lady?" asked Malia. "Do they mean for us to take refuge in Vesslos?"

The other handmaidens stirred a bit at this news, looking at each other with worry. "We're not going to Araswell?" whispered Helga fiercely. "Why in the king's name not? The walls are high and strong, and your brother Albrecht awaits us there with his knights!" Annwyn thought for a bit as she watched Elisabeta suckling; the baby, at least, seemed content.

"My brother apparently does not think it is safe there," said Annwyn. "Perhaps there are not enough knights. Baron Conor of Vesslos has always been of cordial relations with our father and is of the line of Thorodür, another shield-thane to King Orfewain, but I do not think he is so great a friend that my brother would expect a strong welcome there. And we did not receive many invitations from the Lodyrs who hold the baronies of the Plain of Horns, nor from Baron Galreuth of Collwyn, even before our fall from favor." *And we have received none since*, she thought.

"Your father has never approved of Aurian families that have intermarried with Danians," Malia said quietly.

"No, he has not, and almost all of our immediate neighbors have Danian blood in their lineages; it is one of the reasons he so preferred to be in the capital, and stand with his equals at the Court," Annwyn said to her handmaiden. "The Cürwells of Abenton and the Liefrings of Misal Ruth have pure Aurian lineages; and of the great western families of Atallica, the Liefrings have been the most cordial since . . . our name became tarnished. Though that could always just be because we pass through their lands so often, on our way to and from the city. If we were to seek refuge somewhere, I would have thought perhaps it would be with Baron Wallis the Young at Misal Ruth . . ."

"Pure of blood they may be, but they follow the Old Religion in secret, and hold to old Athairi rites, my Lady!" said Helga. "Your father has never approved of them! It won't do for you to be seen taking refuge with those already tainted by such whispers!"

"Whispers indeed, Helga," said Annwyn with a slight frown. "I would hope all of you know better than to merely repeat the gossip and innuendo that so often poisons the Court; the Baron and his family have never extended us anything but the most proper courtesy." The handmaidens looked down and nodded, chagrined. "But if we were going to seek refuge with Baron Wallis, we would not be headed to Vesslos. We'd be sailing to the bridge at Tauria and his uncle, Lord Garin Liefring. I do not know my brother's mind in this . . ."

"Perhaps he means us to hide in the Hada Wold?" asked Malia.

"That's . . . that's preposterous," said Annwyn. *Would he do that? Would he take our entire household into the woods to find refuge from those that pursue us?* She frowned. "Out of the question." *Is our situation really so dire?* She looked at Malia. "Isn't it?"

She felt a sudden cramp in her stomach and winced. The sudden intake of solid food seemed to be triggering something potentially unpleasant. Annwyn looked around, suddenly worried. *And where do you suppose they keep the privies on a ship like this?* she wondered.

The bustling riverside docks in Vesslos, built of stone under its walls, were not as large as those in the seaports of Therapoli or her home of Berrina, or in the river port of Abenton, for that matter; but they were certainly larger than those in Pierham, where they'd entered the river. The *River King's Crown* and the *Pelican Diver* had been towed in amongst a half dozen boats of similar tonnage to be offloaded. There were at least two other docks that Erim could see with a crowd of smaller riverboats. She jumped down off the wide gangway onto the stone of the dock, happy to be on land again despite having reasonable sea legs. Most of the Aurian household of Orwain and Araswell had very little experience on the water, and this journey on the Abenbrae Estuary was the closest they had ever come to being on the sea; a few had paid for it with sea sickness and looked like they were at death's door. If she was glad to be back on land, then they were ecstatic in a way she thought almost comical. If they had ever lapsed in their devotions to the Divine King, they were making up for lost time now.

She looked up at the stout walls and dock gates of the baronial city; Vesslos sat on the eastern bank of the Vessbrae, one of the larger cities in the region, about the equal to Soros or Truse, though of course small in comparison to the capital. She thought back to the last time—was it really less than two weeks ago?—that she had been in Vesslos. Dwelling briefly on the parting words of Tall Duram, she was not sure this would be a city eager to see her and Stjepan again; but then it was a large city and there'd be no reason for them to be in the Free Quarter on this trip. *Better to wait a few months, or even a year or two, before stopping in to say hello*, she thought. *Assuming we're still alive then.*

Captain Wynram and the other Herla man, Captain Lolfyr, were already down at the end of the docks negotiating with the dock officers on the unloading fees. She looked behind her. Gilgwyr was groggily stumbling over the gangway, trying to shake the five hours or so of sleep that he'd managed to catch on the *River King's Crown*. He spotted her standing still amongst the stevedores and rivermen working the docks, and grunted with a wave and a nod. He pulled a plain dark coat around his clothes, and made his way down the stone docks to where she waited.

"Ah, young Erim," he said with a smile that couldn't help but look halfway to a leer. "A bright good afternoon to you. Did you get any sleep? I had the most marvelous dreams on our river voyage, must be the fresh river air."

"I am sufficiently rested, Master Gilgwyr," she said with a curt smile.

"Excellent," said Gilgwyr, rubbing his hands together with zest. "It's been some time since I was in Vesslos but I gather you were just here with Stjepan. Are you ready for our appointed mission?"

"Aye," she said, then started repeating from memory: "'Two wagons and a coach for the wounded and injured, for those on their way to Araswell; one coach capable of overland travel, for the Lady on our own trip, all to be held until the horses are disembarked and delivered. Provisions for two weeks journey off the roads, including water and wine, and plain clothing suitable for a well-off merchant's wife to help disguise the Lady and her handmaiden. And plain surcoats to disguise the knights, and make them look like mercenaries.'" Stjepan had been most clear on that last point; Arduin's men all bore the sigil of the Orwain family on their doublets, surcoats, and pourpoints. She looked at Gilgwyr. "You got the coin?"

He hefted a big fat leather coin purse that hung from his belt under his cloak. The bag was so packed with coin there wasn't even a jingle as he lightly shook it. "Your Treasurer is at your service, Lord Quartermaster," he said. "Let us proceed to the markets!"

They turned and started making their way toward the dock gate into the city. A couple of the rivermen from the *River King's Crown* blew her a kiss as she and Gilgwyr walked past them on their way off the docks. She blushed and hoped Gilgwyr didn't notice.

"And you're sure it's the Bale Mole?" Arduin asked again. He stood on the deck of the small forecastle, leaning his elbow against the foremast, and peering past it to survey the battlements of the city of Vesslos. He still had on his cuisses and half-greaves, but had shed his upper armor in favor of a thick, quilted arming doublet. He had barely slept on the journey upriver, and not just because of fear of the river itself, but because every time he had closed his eyes he had seen the dead face of the squire Herefort. *The White Lady walks amongst us now, and has ever since Harvald's funeral*, he thought. *She has come to claim her fill, and I fear she is ravenous.*

"Yes," said Stjepan, standing behind Arduin with Sir Helgi. "All the legends say he was buried somewhere in the dark hills of his sorcerous kingdom, and what has appeared of the map would seem to confirm it." From inside his coat he produced his notebook and undid the twine that kept it closed. He flipped through the pages. "It was hard to piece it together, but I believe the words I've translated so far are meant to say: *'To the Barrow of our Fallen Lord, Azharad, King of Kings, first west upon the High Road from Garner Lais, into his Kingdom's Heart.'* There are symbols for Garner Lais, which was always represented on their old maps as a tower with a sword through it, and for Lost Tir'gaile: a crowned silver eagle."

"These names mean nothing to me," Arduin said dully, trying to clear the fog in his head.

"Garner Lais is one of the citadels of the Uthed Wold, the dark forest that was once the eastern reaches of the Kingdom of Azharad," said Stjepan. "It's a dark ruin, as are all the citadels of that wood, but assuming the map was intended for someone amongst the Azharites or their hidden cult brethren in the east, then it makes sense the mapmaker would think they were starting through the Wold and Garner Lais. The Azharites still use those ruins today, by most accounts. There's an old road, hardly better than a hunter's path, that runs out of the wood and up into the Bale Mole, to the ancient hill town of Tir'gaile, which was blighted when the curse of the Sun Court fell upon Lost Uthedmael."

"So we have to go through the Uthed Wold?" Arduin asked, rubbing his face with both hands. *That* name he knew, though his rational mind refused to believe the stories he'd heard about the wood.

"No," said Stjepan, shaking his head. "It's possible to also get to Tir'gaile from the Wall, from the Watchtower of Mizer. We should head there. It'll be safer and easier for us. That's not a path that would be open to most Azharites or Nameless Cultists. But it's open for us."

"A small relief, then," Arduin grimaced. He looked out at the city walls. *If only we could make a stand somewhere; here, or at Araswell, with high walls to defend us . . . but a stand against whom, and to what end? The Grand Duke? The Inquisition? The High King himself?* He had seen the Grand Duke's companies at work when he rode with them once; they were efficient in battle and ruthless in sieges, and unafraid of killing the High King's own subjects in his name.

He looked down. Wagons had started to arrive in front of the two ships, and stevedores and his householders were starting to load them with their meager possessions. *If I'm going to change my mind, I should do it now.* He had brooded long and hard in the river-tossed hold, and he knew he had precious few options.

"Helgi, send Sir Clodin on our fastest horse to my brother," he said, finally. "Have Clodin appraise Albrecht of the situation, and let him know to expect the arrival of our household. Tell him to raise the levy at once. If Albrecht can send knights and sergeants in force to help escort the household home, all the better."

"Forgive me, my Lord, but . . . well, me and the others have discussed it, and our place is by your side, and your sister's," said Sir Helgi. "Send the two young squires, Elbray and Enan. They're both good riders, and the road between here and Araswell is safe enough. They're too young for the path we are about to take, anyway. Wilhem and my nephew Brayden are older, they're ready for this."

Arduin turned and studied the knight for a moment. "Are you disobeying my command, Sir Helgi?" he asked. A small smile played on his lips, but his eyes were cold.

"Merely suggesting an alternative, my Lord," said Sir Helgi with a straight face and a slight bow. Arduin stared at him a moment longer.

"Thank you, Sir Helgi," he said curtly. "Send the two squires, then, with my personal banner. Tell them I'm proud of them, and that they bear the honor of my family and line, in case I do not have a chance to do so myself." Helgi nodded and departed. Arduin turned and looked back at the city walls.

"I must inform my sister of our intentions, if we are not going to Araswell," he said finally, and turned away.

"The King's Fortune favor you, my Lord," said Stjepan with a bow, and he followed Arduin off the forecastle.

"This is your last chance to say your farewells," Arduin said stiffly. He supposed that she was taking the news better than he would have expected. He had expected . . . what? Tears, he supposed. Crying, weeping, pleading. Something. But after he had told her that to rid her of the map that they would have to travel deep into the dangerous, dark and cursed west, she had simply sat in the hold, a numb and blank expression on her face. "One of your handmaidens can come with us to provide what comforts that she can," he said. "But we will be trying to move quickly and lightly, so everyone else in the household will be sent on to Araswell. They will carry my banner there, so that anyone watching thinks that we have indeed taken refuge there, while we ride by different roads into the west. Choose who you wish to bring with us, and then say your farewells to the rest."

She took a deep breath and stood up. Arduin had ordered her hand-maidens out of the rear hold, where she had remained as the expedition had reorganized itself on the docks for the last several hours. She stepped over to the partition and looked beyond it, to where her handmaidens waited. "Malia, can you come here?" she asked quietly.

Malia Morwin stepped in to the rear hold, her face expressionless. Arduin nodded, and stepped out, leaving the two women alone. Malia looked at the floor.

"Master Stjepan's young squire was correct," Annwyn said in a low voice that was not quite a whisper. "The rest of the household is to head to Araswell and take refuge with my brother Albrecht, but Arduin intends to take me far into the west, where he and Master Stjepan believe the enchantment upon me can be lifted."

"How far into the west?" Malia asked after a long moment of silence.

"We are to cross the Wall of Fortias and enter the Bale Mole," Annwyn said. Malia said nothing. "Would you accompany me there as my lady-in-waiting?"

Malia lifted her gaze until they were looking into each other's eyes.

Annwyn could see the hints of tears lining Malia's lashes. Malia blinked once, then twice, and took a deep breath in, her reserve cracking with a look that flickered between fear and a peculiar joy, and the handmaiden had to look away.

"Of course, my Lady," she finally said, when she had composed herself and was able to look at Annwyn again.

I can do this, Annwyn thought. *I am a daughter of Leonas, the Baron of Araswell, and a direct descendant of Wain Far-Strider, shield-thane of King Orfeydda. Ours is a storied lineage, and my ancestors watch over me with pride from the Heavens. I have known the servants of our household since I was born, and they have known me. I have spent almost every waking hour with them for a decade, in a web partially of my own making. They will know what I mean to say, even if I cannot find the words.*

Several of her handmaidens wept openly as she left the rear hold of the ship and joined them in the main hold. She spoke quietly to each of them in turn, whispering a farewell, patting the baby Elisabeta and young Odwen on their tousled, blond heads. Henriette, Silbeta, and Ilona knelt and kissed her hands, though several of the older women—Frallas, and Helga, and Elisa—held back a bit; she had been touched by a curse, after all, and they'd all seen the map on her skin. She could not begrudge them for that, given how loyal they'd been to her and her family for so long. She could only imagine what they thought of what was happening to her.

Malia placed a great cloak over Annwyn, and she drew the hood up around her mistress' head to hide her face. Annwyn ascended to the main deck of the ship, followed by her handmaidens, and slowly crossed the gangway off the boat and onto the dock through a protective gauntlet of the rest of the household. Many of them wept as well, with some of them stepping forward to kiss her hand as she passed them, or kneeling or bowing deeply, doffing their hats if they were wearing them. She said nothing; she was afraid to speak, afraid she might say the wrong thing or forget someone's

276

name, afraid that her voice might crack and betray the fear that gnawed at her stomach and heart, and so she simply smiled and nodded as she could when they were willing to look her in the eyes. The rivermen of the two Helga ships and the stevedores and wharf rats of the docks slowly stopped what they were doing and fell silent, watching the strange proceedings, and some of them found themselves doffing their hats and caps by instinct, though they were not sure why.

She walked down the dock through the seven dismounted knights of her brother's entourage, holding their destriers and coursers still. Some wore new plain surcoats or tabards, others wore their traditional livery but with the badges of her family's arms hidden or removed, in some cases ripped away with seeming roughness to leave holes and stray thread. They bowed to her in turn. At the end of the dock, an enclosed four-poster coach of dark lacquered wood with strap and chain suspension awaited her; two pairs of their horses were tied to the yoke, and two pairs of pack horses and spares laden with saddle bags and supplies were tied to its rear. Large sacks and chests were fastened to the top of the coach. The squire Brayden sat up on the driver's seat, holding the reins, next to a Danian man that looked vaguely familiar. He wore an extravagant doublet beneath his plain coat, and his air immediately struck her as that of a city dandy; he watched her with a keen, overly familiar interest that she found unwholesome and did not appreciate. Her brother was mounted on his favorite horse, and even though he wore only a partial harness and covered it beneath a long sweeping cloak, his bearing would not be mistaken as anything other than that of an Aurian knight. Stjepan and Erim were also mounted, watching her progress—Stjepan with brooding apprehension, and Erim with curiosity. The squire Wilhem Price held the door of the coach open for her. A wild-eyed, wild-haired Danian man dressed in dark blue robes sat behind the coach box in one of two rumble seats. He also looked vaguely familiar, and terribly unhappy, and seemed to be talking to himself, and she puzzled at where she might have seen him before. Was it back in their city house? But then Wilhem was helping her ascend into the coach, and Malia was following after her.

PART TWO: ON THE ROAD OF SWEAT AND TEARS

The interior of the coach was covered in a padded cloth, a deep orange color that was not entirely unpleasant. There were baskets and sacks filled with provisions on the seats, and she carefully sat down on one seat amongst the gear there, and Malia sat across from her. The door closed, and the two women looked at each other, and then around the small cabin.

"Well, my Lady," said Malia finally. "I guess this shall be our home for the coming days. Pleasant enough, I suppose. They were lucky to find so excellently made a travel coach."

"Yes, pleasant enough," said Annwyn. "But a prison cell is still a prison cell."

"I can see why she was once the talk of the Court," said Erim to Stjepan in a low voice as Arduin's knights started to mount their horses. "Even after all that's happened to her, she still walks like bloody fucking royalty."

"She has borne the approbation of the Court for many years, and borne their whispers and their envenomed glances upright with her head held high, despite it all," said Stjepan. He squinted up at the sky. There was a dark cast to the clouds coming in from the southeast, and ravens circling in the air with the river terns. "But too much weight and even the strongest back will bend, and then break."

He urged his horse forward, and Erim followed, and they took the lead off the docks and through the dock gates. The carriage finally started moving, and the knightly escort fell in before and after it. From the dock gates a street ran between the high inner city wall and the outer river wall to the gatehouse that led into the city itself and the barbican that opened onto the bridge that would take them west. Stjepan reached the barbican and leaned low on his horse to talk to the gate guards there, slipping them a small bag of coins as the column of knights and coach rode past into the through passage. And then they were out on the bridge, crossing the Vessbrae and driving west toward the setting sun.

CHAPTER FİFTEEN
SKİRTİNG THE
MANON MOLE

The coach and its escorts first headed due west from Vesslos, as though they were headed toward Araswell. They waited until they had passed beyond the sight of anyone watching from the walls and towers of the city and they were fast approaching the lands of the Lord of Kielwell before they turned southwest along dirt roads that wound through the farming lands on the west bank of the Vessbrae. Stjepan led them around the river village of Mallis, held by a vassal of Baron Conor of Vesslos, and then west-southwest along the southern edge of the lands held by Arduin's father from his baronial seat at Araswell and his vassals. They skirted the lands of his father's tenants, Lord Bjorne Urwed of Riverguard, father to Sirs Lars and Colin, and Lord Swen Clowain of Araslawn. If the knights in Arduin's service occasionally let their gaze wander off their path, to seek a familiar silhouette against the darkening sky, he did not blame them; but as for Arduin, he kept his eyes focused on their scouts, Stjepan and Erim, riding in the fore and tracking the way ahead. These side roads made for a good initial test of the coach, as Arduin and his knights were reasonably well familiar with them, and Arduin checked several times with his squires and with Malia about how well the coach was handling the road until he was satisfied that the choice of carriage had been well made.

Eventually it became too dangerous to continue on in the dark, even with torches and lanterns, and they pulled in for the night at a small stone-walled, thatch-roofed hunting lodge that the men of Araswell used on occasion. It took a short while to make it presentable as it hadn't been used since the previous fall, but at least they were able to spend the first night of their journey with some small amount of comfort, and in familiar surroundings for many of them. They set a fire in the hearth, and hung some sheets and blankets as curtains for Annwyn and Malia. They ate some of the food that Erim and Gilgwyr had secured in Vesslos: several varieties of bread with olive oil, dried figs and dates and plums, the last of the winter pears and apples in the market brought up from cold storage, sliced pork liver pâté from a terrine, and eggs that they cooked in a skillet with some strong cheese and slices of dried pork sausage.

"Do you think they've reached Araswell by now?" asked Sir Clodin as they sat about the hearth.

"They won't be moving as fast as us, but yes, I would expect that they've reached the castle," Sir Helgi said with a gruff smile. "Don't worry, your lady Frallas is ensconced behind stout walls by now, and under Lord Albrecht's protection. He'll be summoning up the levy of sergeants overnight, and by morning the castle will be sealed up pretty tight."

Until the Grand Duke arrives, thought Erim; that part was left unsaid, but still Sir Helgi's words seemed to satisfy the knights and squires, and soon they were busy setting the watch rotation for the night.

Before the two women retired behind their makeshift screens, Stjepan caught Arduin's attention and spoke to the three of them.

"I do not want to impose myself more than is necessary, but obviously we need to know when new parts of the map might choose to reveal themselves," he said in a low voice. "Lady Annwyn, Mistress Malia, do you think you could familiarize yourself with the images that are currently appearing? If you could perhaps inspect the images each evening, as you prepare for sleep, and see if there is anything appearing that seems new and different, then you can alert Lord Arduin and myself that the map is changing and we can arrange another . . . viewing."

Annwyn and Malia exchanged a glance, and Malia nodded to Stjepan. "We will let you know the moment that anything new appears, Master Stjepan," the handmaiden said. The two women curtsied to the two men, and then drew their curtains closed.

When the Dawn Maiden arose the morning of the 19th of Emperium, they gathered themselves and set off at as fast a pace as the coach could manage west-southwest along old, seldom-used paths at the very limits of the domain of the Barony of Araswell, paralleling the Vessbrae as it rose into the foothills of the Manon Mole. By the time the sun had fully risen, they had already covered several miles, which Erim thought was a pretty good pace all things considered. Erim had been curious to note that only a handful of the knights—the Urwed brothers, and Sir Clodin—and the two squires, Brayden and Wilhem, joined together to say some quick quiet prayers to the Dawn Maiden in the morning dark, and then again to greet Islik the Divine King when the sun arose. The other men were all business and no piety, at least until Arduin called for a mid-day prayer for young Herefort on the Path of the Dead. "The household will hold the vigil for him at Araswell for his Seven Days, but we should offer our prayers to guide him on his way," Arduin said. "We are the ones that knew him best." And that prayer they all joined in on.

The local lord, Sir Percy Perwain of Ferham, distantly related to the main Orwain lineage and father to Sir Clodin in Arduin's entourage, was in charge of making sure the paths were tended and cleared, and Arduin was thankful to note that they appeared to have been well kept during the winter. They would occasionally see well-built stone farmhouses scattered on nearby rises or in the river valley, but the land here was not terribly hospitable and people were generally scarce. Lord Percy's hold was a stone tower on a crest to their north at the end of a better road that ran twenty miles back to Araswell, but they passed far enough to the south that they never even saw his keep. "Surely we can stop there," said Sir Clodin.

"Your father has likely ridden out to answer the levy call from Araswell," noted Stjepan. "And the fewer people that know where we went, the better." Arduin had nodded at that, and so on they had went, though Sir Clodin favored Stjepan with dark looks from then on.

Across the Vessbrae they could occasionally glimpse the start of the Hada Wold, and the low peaks of the Manon Mole were becoming visible in the distance to the south, and scattered around their path they were beginning to see the peculiar, trademarks stones that gave the Plain of Stones its name.

As they began to cross into the Plain of Stones itself, Arduin urged his horse forward until he was riding side-by-side with Stjepan. "We have reached the limits of my personal experience," he said, taking a swig of weak wine from a skin. "I have crossed the Plain of Stones many times, but always on the West King's Road, and have traveled my father's lands extensively. But I have never taken the high paths that skirt the Manon Mole."

"And normally I would never suggest that we take this route," said Stjepan. "It'll be hard on the coach, and there's some risk from the bandit knights of the hills. But those risks can be managed more easily than the risks we would have had on the West King's Road."

"I've fought the bandit knights before, but never on their own ground," admitted Arduin. "We chased a band of their raiders off several years ago, but called off the pursuit right back there," he said, indicating a spot they had passed several hundred yards back. "We'd already killed a dozen of them in some tough fighting, and it had seemed folly to chase them further."

"A wise choice, my Lord," said Stjepan with a nod of his head. "You should never enter the Manon Mole unless you absolutely have to."

"I . . . I had been offered a commission to ride with Duke Pergwyn this coming summer in the campaign against the Rebel Earl," Arduin said, brooding. "I suppose that is unlikely to happen now, unless we return with *Gladringer* in hand."

Stjepan looked at him carefully. "That would have been a great honor for you, my Lord Arduin," he said. "Perhaps it may still happen. If it does, then we may well be riding together again, as I am expecting to be summoned again to the campaign when the Grand Duke commences it in earnest this summer. Assuming I am not exiled or in jail, of course." He paused and pointed up the trail they were following. "The old roads and paths ahead were deemed insufficient for large bodies of troops, but we used them all the time last year to run messages down toward Truse or Therapoli."

"Yes, I remember our Lords of Ferham and Riverguard reporting that men bearing the seal of the High King and the Grand Duke were passing through their lands," said Arduin. "And then we received an order from the Court to provide fast boats at a small riverside dock where the Hada Wold ends, so that men could head downstream with ease. Do you mean to say you were one of those men?"

"Yes, my Lord, I have traveled your father's lands before, and enjoyed his hospitality, though I never had reason to personally meet him, or you for that matter," said Stjepan with a nod.

Arduin shook his head and snorted under his breath at the weave of the Fates in the world. "I don't remember the Grand Duke's main companies coming through our lands, though," he said.

"No, my Lord, they marched the West King's Road to the Danias," Stjepan said. "The launch point for most of the army was Reinvale or Stonham, coming from the western side of the Mole, but then most of the lords summoned by the Grand Duke to last year's campaign were Danian or from the Watchtowers anyway, and most of the fighting was in the western half of the Mole and down into the Neris Wold. But I know the roads ahead of us sufficiently well."

"Shall the bandit knights cause us trouble, then?" Arduin asked.

"I do not know, my Lord," Stjepan said with a frown. "I would hope we do not see another living soul until we reach the outskirts of the Earldom of Erid More. But if we see the knights of the hills, there may be alternatives to bloodshed."

"Oh?" said Arduin skeptically.

"Like most men, they can be bought," said Stjepan with a simple shrug.

They ate on the move, stopping only to rest and water the horses along a stream that fed down to the Vessbrae behind them, or to find some favorable spot to squat and undo their breeches and codpieces; Erim was always careful to find a spot well away from the others if she had to piss or shit. The landscape had shifted to a bleak semi-wasteland. Very little seemed to grow in the earth here besides short small shrubs and fuzzy lichens; the primary feature of the Plain of Stones as it overlapped the rolling foothills of the Manon Mole were the stones themselves, thousands of wide flat roughhewn slabs like paving stones scattered over the earth as far as the eye could see, at least until up in the hills where the ground was free of them. Their shape and placement seemed too regular to have been mere accident, and they bore some hint of the touch of man. Erim felt a vaguely creepy feeling beginning to tug at her spine and the hairs on the back of her head, and she noticed the Aurian knights starting to shoot nervous looks about them as they went. *Cursed by your own birthrights wherever you go*, she thought to herself, with very little sympathy.

With so little high growth around them, the paths through the stones were relatively flat and clear, and the coach was able to pass through at a relatively good pace. Several times they had to slow to be careful about one obstacle or another, but by the end of the day Erim guessed they'd made close to thirty-five miles. As the sun began to set behind clouds in the west, they made camp, setting a picket line for the horses; the women stayed in their coach, and the men set up several tents being carried on the carriage. Erim had noted earlier that the horses seemed content with munching on the short shrubs that grew around the flat stone slabs, and that was a bit of luck, as they could save their supply of feed grain for spots where there was nothing for the horses to eat.

They set two campfires that night, one where the knights and squires clustered, and then one where Stjepan, Erim, Gilgwyr, and Leigh gathered. It was as though once out in the open air, with the space to spread out a bit, that the natural social division of the group automatically reasserted itself by unspoken agreement. No one seemed to have an issue with that. As the others set tents and fires, Leigh began marking a perimeter around them, a wide circle of small stones and chalk dust that he poured from a leather bag. He found and marked a rock at one of the cardinal points of the circle with a rune. *"Ward this place against magic! Ward this place against ghosts and spirits! Ward this place against the Wild Hunt and the Black Hunter! They are not welcome here, where we make our mark upon the World!"* he whispered, and moved on to repeat himself at each of the cardinal points around the circle that he had inscribed around them.

The Black Hunter was only loosed from the Underworld once a year, with certainty, on the Night of the Wild Hunt before the first day of winter, and that night every mortal would find themselves behind walls or campfires ringed with protections such as the one that Leigh had just set or risk becoming the hunted. But the Wild Hunt occasionally slipped from its chains in the Underworld on other nights of the year, and just in case the wise and the prudent and the paranoid protected themselves after dark when in the wilderness. And Leigh was perhaps all three.

When all was finally settled and they had settled to eating their evening meal, Gilgwyr stretched out his legs by the fire. "By the gods," he groaned. "The next time I suggest that it's a good idea that I leave the comforts of city and home, just stab me in the fucking balls."

"Not enjoying yourself?" asked Stjepan with what could only be described as a smirk.

"What's not to like?" Gilgwyr asked. "I'm in desperate need of a bath, as is everyone around me; my ass hurts from riding that coach as though I'd been beaten and flayed by the Inquisition's best; and that young fellow Brayden has to be one of the most boring sods I have had the misfortune to encounter. How a young man can have no interest in any of the finer things in life is beyond me. He doesn't laugh at any of my jokes, and he just says 'Please, sir, mind your manners!' if I try to talk about anything remotely interesting, so I've had virtually no civilized conversation for the entire day. It's enough to drive a man mad."

"A man mad? A madman? Are you talking about me?" asked Leigh, peering at Gilgwyr with suspicion.

"Um; no, Magister," said Gilgwyr slowly, a bit puzzled. "I was just saying that I can't get the young squire driving the coach to listen to my stories."

"Then stop telling him stories about your cock," said Leigh with a snort. "Tell him stories about *his* cock. He'll probably find that much more interesting. Probably."

"Well, we'll have to cross a bit of the Trubrae tomorrow," said Stjepan. "We can all take a moment to bathe then. That'll solve one problem, at least. Perhaps you and Leigh can sit in the rumble seats of the coach together, and let the squires sit up top?"

"Aye, I think I make the other lad nervous," said Leigh. "Can't figure out why for the life of me."

None of them said anything, munching at their bread and dried figs in silence, until Leigh started to giggle under his breath. Then soon the four were laughing loud and hard into the night.

After their meal and a bit of wine, they settled into two small tents around the dying campfire as they prepared for sleep, Erim and Stjepan in one, and Leigh and Gilgwyr in the other. Gilgwyr had the flap of his tent open so that he could peer up at the night sky. The great constellation of *Shebetae*, the Star-Child, was ending the days of its rule and passing out of the First House of the Heavens and into the Second, and *Adaral*, the inter-twined Serpent, was rising from the position of the Twelfth House to take its place in the First House, to rule the next cycle of the Heavens.

"Ack, I can't believe it!" he suddenly moaned as he stared up at the stars.

"What? What's the matter?" asked Leigh.

"Tonight's the Festival of the Serpent! And therefore also the wake at the Sleight of Hand for Guizo the Fat, that fucking bastard," said Gilgwyr. "Back in Therapoli, my young Ariadesma is right about now getting the shit fucked out of her in front of the assembled Princes of the Guild. And *I'm fucking missing it!*"

"You shouldn't speak ill of the dead," said Leigh sleepily. "Unless you are also pissing on their graves, that is, in which case you can say whatever you want, as that tends to confuse and distract them."

"I told Sequintus and Siovan to think of something truly spectacular to put young Ariadesma through," Gilgwyr said with wistful excitement. "I wonder what they came up with. I can't believe I'm fucking missing it!"

"Well, don't let it get to you," said Leigh, his eyes already closed. "Just remember that if all goes well you will soon be able to command whatever entertainments you desire to your heart's content."

"Aye," said Gilgwyr, his voice practically a whisper as he stared up at the sky, the image of Ariadesma's delicious body spinning in the air above him. "Today is a great day, a blessed day, and soon, very soon, will come the best day of all. A great change is coming!"

"Careful now. How does that saying go? Don't count your chickens before they hatch," mumbled Leigh. "Don't count your cocks before they crow."

"*Don't count your cocks before they cum,*" whispered Gilgwyr, laughing to himself as he slowly and luxuriously masturbated, visions dancing in his head.

The next morning the new seating arrangements were taken with little objection, the two squires apparently having proposed a similar change to Sir Helgi during their evening meal. The weather seemed to be holding reasonably well for them, occasional clouds and brisk winds now that they were further up into the foothills, but the path also seemed to get a bit more difficult and the coach had to move a bit more slowly. They reached the Trubrae by late morning, and after getting the coach through the ford they stopped for their prayers for young Herefort, and then took the opportunity to refresh themselves in the waters there. This high up the tributary was not so much a river as perhaps a winding creek, perhaps forty or so feet at its widest and up to a man's thigh at its deepest. The shrubs here were larger than the ones they'd been seeing, some of them along the riverbank having grown almost into genuine brush. They tasted the water and refilled their canteens and jugs first. Then water was brought in a basin up to the coach so that Annwyn and Malia could have some element of privacy there; but the men just began stripping and wading into the waters in turns.

Erim wandered a bit upstream, where the creek wound sufficiently that she could find a bit of privacy out of view of the others around a bend. Still wary of one of them stumbling upon her, she didn't bother to take off her breeches or shirt, but waded into the water partially clothed. She washed her armpits under her shirt with soap, then squatted until her ass and haunches were under the water, and pulled her breeches down so she could soap and wash her loins and rear. It was a practiced move, having been in the country before, but she still thought about how odd it might look if someone were to see her. *Better they think me odd than see me naked*, she thought, and as she did so she looked up to see three horsemen watching her from a nearby hill.

She froze.

They were just sitting there: three horsemen in archaic, hodgepodge armor, partial plate over brigandines and bits of mail with hounskull bascinets upon their heads, visors raised. Two had long spears, one with a small grey and green pennant flying from it. They were several hundred yards away, with rocks and rough terrain and the creek between; as Erim didn't see any bows or crossbows, she realized that she was not in any immediate danger. If spurred to action, those horses could cross that distance quickly; but they didn't have a clear straight line to get to her. And they weren't necessarily presenting as hostile anyway.

They were just sitting there, watching her.

Her fear dimmed enough that she was able to move again. She slowly pulled her breeches up over her ass under the water, and then stood, being careful not to move too suddenly. Without turning her back to them, she walked backwards to the shore where her gear was, and as calmly as she could she dried herself a bit with a towel, and slipped her boots and doublet back on. She reached down and collected her brace of weapons, one eye on the three horsemen to gauge their reaction; but they didn't move.

Slowly she walked almost backwards down the creek bed back to the bend, keeping herself turned mostly to the riders, until she knew she stood in a place where the main group could see her. Without moving her gaze from the horsemen, she called out over her shoulder: "Black-Heart! Get over here! We've got company!"

She held her breath as she watched the three silent horsemen; behind her she could hear the shouts and commotion of her companions preparing themselves. She grew nervous, and the dampness on her brow was no longer just water from the creek; it was taking far longer than she would have liked. But eventually she heard splashing in the creek coming up behind her and then Stjepan was next to her on Cúlain-mal, with Cúlain-mer in tow, along with Sir Helgi and Sir Theodras, who were at least in their full three-quarter harness and mounted on their warhorses.

"Islik's balls, bandit knights!" swore Sir Helgi as Erim swung herself into the saddle of her horse with relief.

"There's only three of them," said Sir Theodras. "A few more of us and we can take them, easy."

"Be calm, don't do anything yet," said Stjepan. "There's always more of them than what you see. Well, maybe not always, but often enough. Don't pull anyone else away from the coach; protecting the Lady is all that matters. Erim, with me; gentlemen, please wait here."

Stjepan raised a hand in greeting, empty palm held to the sky. The knight without a spear raised his hand, palm open and up, in response. Stjepan whistled, and Cúlain-mal sprang forward, splashing up the creek bed and then onto the far bank and up toward the three horsemen. Erim followed, scanning the hills and rises around them and the brush along the creek, but she couldn't see anyone else. She followed Stjepan partway up the hill until they were maybe twenty yards from the horsemen, where he pulled reins and came to a stop.

On closer look Erim was uncertain she would agree with Theodras' bold claim. The three bandit knights had a wild and feral appearance, overall. Their armor was eclectically pieced together to be sure, dented from hard use and tarnished, but it also seemed to her to all be of fine make; many

289

pieces of their harnesses bore etchwork or embossing or barbaric-looking spikes. Their brigandines were either rich brown leather or dark velvet, with stamping and gold embroidery and dark metal studs. Their horses, sturdy but non-descript light chargers, were caparisoned in patchworks of dark velvet cloth, checkerboarded with barbaric emblems and animal symbols. The men had dark, curly beards twisted into points jutting out from their chins, and they shared the same flat look in their eyes. *They have killed men before, and probably women as well*, she thought. *They are unafraid of death and what awaits them in the Underworld.*

"Fates and Fortune be with you, strangers," Stjepan called out. "*La benedicia della deas Yhera sura toi.*"

"And with you, stranger," said the first knight. "Though if I heard your companion correct, you are not a stranger at all, but Black-Heart, who is known to us. Greetings in the name of the Queen."

"*Saluda en nomas della deas Reina*," the other two knights echoed behind him, nodding their heads.

"I am called Black-Heart by some; I am Stjepan of An-Athair, son of Argante of the lineage of Morfane, and therefore perhaps your ancient enemy," said Stjepan. "And this is Erim of Berrina." Erim nodded in greeting. "You are far from your lands."

"Not too far, and perhaps not your enemy," said the first knight. "I am Ulbraece, son of Dyfed of the lineage of Gawer, Hero-Knight of Mageva, and I serve the King of Therin More."

"An honored line, Sir Ulbraece, and my ancestors are beholden to yours, a debt I happily carry," said Stjepan with a slight bow. "I was amongst those that treated with King Ulwyn last summer, when the flag of parley was raised at Cael Maras. A fierce warlord and worthy adversary. But despite all that, this land is nonetheless claimed by the High King," he said, indicating the Plain of Stones around them.

"An Athairi of your line of all should know better, that the Plain of Stones belongs to no one man," said Ulbraece. "You have served the High King too long, to now guide the *árbotuerras* through the Plain. Your ancestors may find reason to complain."

"I said he claimed it," said Stjepan with a slight smile and narrowed eyes. "I did not say that it belonged to him."

Ulbraece showed a fleeting smile, then, and nodded. Eyeing Stjepan, he seemed to make a decision. "The Manon Mole has been busy these last few weeks. Someone stirred a hornet's nest, and the cursed Nameless have thrown off their usual caution and emerged from their holes to travel about in both day and night," the knight said. Erim's ears pricked up at that news. "We have been hunting one amongst them, lone survivor of a group wending its way west. The rest have gone to their places in the Six Hells, to fates deserved. Have you seen a man traveling alone, on foot?"

"No, Sir Ulbraece, we have seen no one, and we have been traveling from the east along the high paths for over a day," Stjepan said, shaking his head. "We hate the Nameless as you do, and will render judgment upon him should he cross our path, in the name of the blood of Gable and Gawer."

"This is meet," said Sir Ulbraece with a nod, and started to wheel his horse about. "We will take our leave of you, then. Receive the blessings of the Queen and the King both, Black-Heart of the line of Morfane." He paused, and smiled again. "Will you be visiting our beloved lands again this summer, then?"

"Only the Fates know that for sure, Sir Ulbraece," said Stjepan, his face a blank. The knight nodded, and the three men of Manon turned south and started over the hill. Stjepan and Erim watched them go until they had disappeared over the next rise.

"*Fuuuuck*," Erim said quietly. She felt like she'd been holding her breath, and her shoulders suddenly slumped and relaxed after the knights disappeared; she hadn't realized how tightly she'd been coiled. "What he said about the Nameless, is that because of us?"

"Could be," said Stjepan, his gaze troubled. "We raided one of their temples and took something that had been hidden there. Someone was bound to be unhappy about that, and come looking to reclaim it."

Erim shook herself in her seat, still trying to relax. "All things considered, that seemed pretty civil," she said. "When I first saw them I thought for sure I was dead."

Stjepan shrugged, wheeling his horse about. "Most people like to talk, if you give them the chance," he said, signaling to Sirs Helgi and Theodras with a wave that everything was okay. They started down the hill back toward the creek and the waiting knights. "But it also helps that we were outside their domain, if we'd been further into the Mole they'd have demanded a toll at the least, or if things had been hot like last summer then they'd have sought our deaths as invaders and interlopers. Luckily, this is the Plain of Stones, and the Manon knights are sticklers for what belongs to whom. So as an Athairi, I have more of a claim to these lands than they do. That's why they left first, rather than waiting for us to go."

"I thought all the bandit knights were descended of the Wyvern King and his lords, and hated the Athairi," said Erim, thinking about the old bards' tales she would hear in the taverns or the docks.

"Most do, even after all these centuries, and the feeling is often mutual," Stjepan said. "But Gawer and Gable were a brother and sister from the Maelite city of Mageva, who served the Wyvern King as knight and magician, and then turned against him. So his ancestors rejected the Wyvern King and helped the Spring Queen Ymaire to capture and bind him."

"Over a thousand years have passed and that still matters?" Erim asked, thinking about what he'd said to them. "You actually think you owe him for that?"

"To some it might as well have been yesterday," Stjepan said with a shrug.

They rejoined the waiting knights and made their way down the creek back to the rest of the caravan, where the other knights and squires were ringed in a formation around the coach. Gilgwyr and Leigh were barely visible, hunched down in the rumble seats. The waiting knights relaxed when the foursome appeared around the bend, and Arduin cried out to them. "Who was it?"

"Bandit knights from the hills," said Sir Helgi as he came abreast of Arduin. "But Master Stjepan spoke with them and they rode off."

"What did they want?" said Arduin with a frown as his knights murmured.

292

"They're hunting one of the Nameless," said Stjepan. "They destroyed a party of them heading to the west, but one escaped. We should be careful of anyone we meet along the trail, and keep our swords sharp." Gilgwyr shot a glance at Erim and Stjepan then, and Erim guessed at his meaning: *something to do with us?*

"I thought most of the bandit knights were themselves amongst the cursed Nameless," said Sir Clodin. "Eating human flesh, and fornicating their own mothers."

"Some might be, but most are simply of the Old Religion and its many gods and goddesses," said Stjepan.

"Same thing," said Sir Clodin with a nasty grin.

"As you say, sir knight," said Stjepan quietly. But it was Sir Clodin who turned away from the look in Stjepan's eyes.

They traveled the rest of the day through the foothills of the Manon Mole with little incident, through rolling hills dotted with the broad, flat stones of the Plain of Stones; but also with little conversation. Erim's hackles still raised, depending on which way the wind shifted, and from what she could see the Aurian knights and squires were even more spooked than she was. She took a long lead to run point, trying to put as much distance between her and the others as possible, and perhaps it was but a trick of the mind, but she felt better when she wasn't near the rest of the group. It was as though the land itself didn't mind her so much as it did the Aurians she traveled with. Stjepan seemed his usual self, if perhaps a bit sadder and grimmer, if that were possible; he was riding wide arcs around the coach and its escorts, scouring the ground for signs of a single man on foot.

Erim heard the encampment ahead of her before she saw it, the sounds of a drum marking out a beat, and *liras* and perhaps an *oud* and a *mandore*. At first she thought she must be imagining things, or hearing some *fae* accompaniment drifting in from the Otherworld to greet the Dusk

Maiden, who was visible now in the western sky to accompany the setting sun; but then the encampment came into sight and she brought her horse to a halt. She could see large reddish-brown box wagons, a horse picket line, and people mingling about several campfires.

Arduin and Sir Helgi rode up behind her and joined her in staring at the camp. They looked at her quizzically, and she shrugged.

Stjepan rode up and passed them, drawing in a bit further ahead to call over his shoulder. "It's an Athairi camp," Stjepan shouted back to them. "My people. With any luck, they'll share bread and wine with us."

He gave a whistle, and Cúlain-mal surged ahead.

The Athairi, at least, did not seem to mind visitors, even if their unexpected guests were armed and armored men with no livery, though Erim suspected that it was Stjepan that paved the way for their smooth reception. Arduin's knights and squires set up their tents at one end of the Athairi encampment, including a large pavilion for Annwyn and Malia; it was the only pavilion-style tent that she and Gilgwyr had been able to find on the market in Vesslos, with a single mast and guy ropes to hold up the canvas walls. Having finished their work the Aurians were now, albeit a bit warily, mingling with Athairi singers and dancers by the campfires.

Erim had seen copper-skinned Athairi in the streets of Therapoli before, and of course she'd known Stjepan for a couple of years now, but she realized that the Athairi she had seen had perhaps chosen their clothes quite deliberately to blend in a bit with the more conservative mode of dress in the capital. Fifty or so men and women made up this caravan, spread out amongst four finely-wrought box wagons and several dozen riding horses. They all seemed to favor dark colors: dark earthy reds and browns, deep indigos and blacks, with the occasional shimmer of embroidered cloth-of-gold. For the most part the men wore calf boots and loose, billowing pants that cinched tight around the waist, though a few of the younger men wore tight breeches like Stjepan's. Some wore long-sleeved shirts under vests or waist jackets, but the younger and more muscular men weren't wearing shirts under their vests and jackets. Erim could see the occasional flash of metal at nipples, ears, and noses amongst the men, and most wore metal or leather bracelets, arm bracers, or torques around the upper arm or the neck. Some of them wore neck scarves, or had their scarves wound up over their heads or hair, while others wore broad-brimmed hats whose brims curled up on the side, like Stjepan's, but with silver broaches and black feathers. Most of the men were clean-shaven, or had thick moustaches, but none wore beards; their dark hair tended to be long, swept back from the face and falling to the neck or tied back into a ponytail. Most wore leather belts chased in bronze or silver buckles, and every one of them bore at least one dagger. Swords and long curved sabers in their sheaths were scattered about the camp in easy reach of most of the men, along with unstrung bows and quivers of black-feathered arrows.

The Athairi women wore clothes that in Therapoli would have been quite risqué. Long brocade skirts or pantaloons cinched at knee or ankle that hung very, very low on the hips seemed universal. For tops they tended either toward a bolero jacket worn over a short bodice, or to a short vest or a short bodice alone, leaving at a minimum a long stretch of the midriff and belly and hips exposed. Some of the women went barefoot, while others wore dark leather sandals and a few wore calf boots similar to those worn by the men. Layers of copper, bronze, and silver jewelry were abundant: bracelets piled around wrists; torques around elbows, upper arms, and necks; shimmering waist belts made of interlinked coins and broaches; anklets, toe rings, finger rings, earrings, nose rings; necklaces and bejeweled collars made of leather. Long dark hair either flowed down backs almost to their rears, or was piled up on the head in complex braids or woven into headdresses made of coins and metal links and beads. The women favored heavily lined eyes and many had tattoos on their arms or bellies or lower backs.

Erim had not seen that much publicly exposed skin since the insides of the Sleight of Hand, and she guessed that the knights in Arduin's household had likely never seen the like outside a brothel (or in their marriage beds, but perhaps not even there). A half dozen of the Athairi men were set up around one of the campfires drumming, seemingly nonstop, in a kind of semi-improvised fashion, with a trio of female *lira* fiddlers jumping in every now and then to provide a melody. As she'd guessed on first hearing the camp, there were two *oud* players, and a *mandore* player as well, all three of them men, and they would step forward every now and then to perform a specific song at someone's shouted request, or to accompany a singer who started up. The rest of the camp went about its business, with most either preparing the evening meal or already drinking and dancing, and Arduin's knights and squires soon found themselves wandering through the light evening revelry in bemused shock, staring at women's belly buttons.

As did Erim. She wandered about the camp, noting the small delights of the traveling troupe, and finally found Stjepan speaking with several of the wagon masters. ". . . you have not seen a man alone, traveling through these parts? Perhaps has someone joined the caravan in the last day or two?" Stjepan was asking.

"No, *Serpente Linga*," said a handsome older man with salt-and-pepper hair that Stjepan had introduced to Erim as Elfyr, son of Dyrk and Gallas, of the lineage of Terwaine. Elfyr shook his head. "You are the first men we have seen in several days. There are few Kingsmen who walk the old paths of the Sleeping Wood, they stay on the King's Road, and the last we saw were of the Folk."

"True enough that a man alone in the Plain of Stones is a rare thing," said Stjepan. "But this man is a Nameless, fleeing the huntsmen knights of Therin More in the Manon Mole." The Athairi men stirred at that, looking darkly at each other.

"This is ill news, scion of Morfane," said Bragas, a strapping youth with a muscular chest that Erim found quite delightful. "We shall set the watch-wards tonight, and be vigilant in our travels in the coming days. If one of the Nameless comes upon us, he will find our doors closed to him, though normally they be open to all."

"All save the Nameless," said several of the men quietly in unison, and they spat to the side and made signs against the Evil Eye.

296

"He will be greeted with sword and light," said Elfyr with quiet pride. *"Yhera Anath, Yhera Invictus, la benedicia della deas Yhera sura tou'nou."*

"Sword and light," all of the men said in unison, including Stjepan.

"By Yhera Anath and Yhera Invictus, let the damned be brought before Seedré for their judgment, so that Hathhalla may consume them in the Underworld," Stjepan finished firmly. Elfyr gave a slight approving bow at that. The small group broke up then, and the Athairi men spread throughout the camp to bring warnings to their fellows. Erim noticed Stjepan watching them with narrowed eyes.

"You don't believe them?" asked Erim in a whisper, surprised at his suspicion.

"I believe them because I want to believe them," said Stjepan to Erim, stepping closer and whispering in her ear. "But there are Nameless even amongst the Athairi. I don't sense anything wrong here, but don't let your guard down too much."

Erim looked around and shook her head, feeling annoyed that Stjepan had come close to spoiling her happy mood. She wanted very much to believe that the free and open people she saw about her were just what they seemed to be. She eyed Stjepan. *Does he never let his guard down?* she wondered. *Not even here, amongst his own people? What a sad and lonely life. Black-Heart indeed.*

Gilgwyr had settled in at one of the campfires, sharing some of the food that the Athairi passed to him, and Erim and Stjepan walked over and settled in around the same fire, introducing themselves to their hosts. Leigh was happily eating nearby, but by himself; even the Athairi gave him a wide berth, though if he noticed or minded he made no sign, instead humming to himself and tapping his foot to the drumming.

Two of the Athairi women around their fire were clearly sisters, with the same high cheekbones and pointed chins and delicate ears. Erim thought for a moment they might be twins, but it turned out they were a year apart, with the elder named Leda and the younger Lestra; the daughters of Elfyr and his mate Anara, of the lineages of Terwaine and Iala, if Erim heard right, though she felt sure there were a few other names mentioned that she missed. *Much easier if they just have a single family name*, she thought.

"The Serpent has risen to the House of the White Queen, scion of Morfane," said Leda to Stjepan, a playful set to her lips. Leda wore a shimmering halter-top bodice of copper coins and copper links with seemingly nothing beneath; her black hair was swept up under a black cloth headdress embroidered with gold thread and pinned with worked copper ornaments and broaches. A chain hung from one earring to her nose ring. "Will you dance the Serpent with us tonight, and celebrate the end of the Celestial Year?"

"It would be a pleasure," said Stjepan with an easy smile.

"We will hold you to that, scion of Morfane," said Lestra, as the sisters stood up. She had gold-painted lips, and gold lines painted on her cheeks under her dark eyes, and a gold circle in the center of her forehead. The two sisters walked off, glancing over their shoulders at Stjepan, smiles playing on their lips and their chins held high.

Gilgwyr caught Erim's eye and shook his head, rolling his eyes. Erim shrugged and sighed. *That's Black-Heart for you*, she thought. "So who was this Morfane, then?" she asked. "Some ancestress of yours? That even seemed to impress that Manon knight, Sir Ulbraece, sure enough."

"Morfane was one of the Spring Queens of ancient An-Athair, at the height of the Golden Realm," said Stjepan.

"What, you're some kind of Athairi royalty, then?" asked Erim, startled.

Stjepan laughed. "No, no, my father was a yeoman tenant of the Earl of An-Athair. A farmer and woodsman, from a long line of farmers and woodsmen. The Spring Queens were but priestesses of the Green Temple. That was just what they were called, in those ancient days." He smiled at her, seeing her frown. "If the Spring Queens ruled the ancient Golden Realm it was through love and wisdom, not through title or bloodline or any formal right, and none ever wore a crown, unless it was of laurels and flowers. Any woman could become a Spring Queen, and many women did, not just from amongst the Athairi, though admittedly Morfane is pretty famous amongst them. The same was also true for the Golden Knights of

An-Athair, who drew their fabled ranks from Danians and Daradjans and Maelites, and even from amongst the Aurians, not just the Athairi."

"There were Aurians amongst the knights of An-Athair?" Erim asked, confused. She'd always thought of the Aurians and the Athairi as implacable enemies then, and even now.

"Aye," said Stjepan. "Any place that allied itself with the Golden Realm took the prefix *an-* to their name. Hence, An-Andria, An-Ogruth, An-Athark up in the Highlands . . ."

Erim frowned. "What, even An-Ydain, way to the east?"

"Yes, even An-Ydain; though that was the furthest east that An-Athair's allies stretched," said Stjepan. "Many of the old place names have been renamed, covered over by something new that erases its connection to the Golden Realm. The city of Truse was once An-Truwyn, Misal Ruth was once An-Daruthaine, Bessiter was once An-Bess. Any man could become a knight of An-Athair; some were originally farmers or woodsmen, crafters or tinkers. Amongst the Aurians, it was mostly their nobles who heeded the call; the Aurian lords Odyr and Helggar became Golden Knights first, then later in the east it was Günner and Giselher. Their descendants include the Lodyrs who rule in An-Andria and An-Ogruth; the Lohengrins, who rule in Dyn Cail and Whitebridge and Bainwell; the Liefrings who rule in Misal Ruth; the Günnersons who rule in An-Ydain; and the Goselhings, who rule in Bessiter."

"Some great and wealthy baronies on that list, then," said Erim. "But if memory serves of what you and Harvald used to tell me about the Court's politics, those families are also mostly out of favor of late, save the Günnersons? One of them's married to the Grand Duke . . ."

"Aye, the Duchess Ilyana is a Günnerson," said Stjepan. "The Aurians have never really gotten over the schism between those that went native and allied themselves with the local power of An-Athair, and those that sought to destroy An-Athair and impose Aurian rule over the whole of the Danias. And it's gotten worse in recent years, with the Crown Prince being the prick that he is, and listening to the bile coming out of King Colin of Dainphalia about the sanctity of Aurian bloodlines and their purity."

299

Erim studied Arduin's profile across the camp, and looked at his knights. "Let me guess, the Orwains of Araswell . . . I'm gonna guess that none of them became Golden Knights."

"No, Arduin's ancestors were amongst those that destroyed An-Athair, and tore down the Green Temple, and raped and killed the Spring Queens," said Stjepan quietly. He smiled playfully. "But blood and lineage do not bring guilt with them, do they?"

"Tell that to Heth, and the legions of the drowned," Erim said with a snort. "The God of the Sea condemns them, to this very day."

"That he does," Stjepan said with low satisfaction, his smile twisting into a feral grin as he watched Arduin a couple of campfires over. "That he does."

Stjepan noticed two cloaked figures approaching the campfire that Arduin and some of the other knights of his household had set, and he surmised it was Annwyn and Malia. They sat down discreetly at the fire, and Arduin glanced their way, but did not say anything; it was the first time they had mingled at the campfires since the start of their journey. Annwyn had her hood up, hiding her face, but Malia's face could be seen in the firelight, and she locked eyes with Stjepan. She signaled for his attention, beckoning him with her hand.

"Excuse me, but it would appear I am summoned," Stjepan said to Erim, and he stood, taking his plate with him as he started walking over toward Malia and Annwyn.

Erim watched him go, and took a deep breath, shaking her head.

Gilgwyr shifted so that he was next to her. "Don't let Stjepan fool you with his talk of his father being a farmer," he said with a conspiratorial air, leaning in close. "The Athairi trace lineage through both father and mother, and either can be a line of power and inheritance. His ancestors may not have been actual queens, but the women of his mother's lineage make every Athairi sit up and take notice. Morfane, a Spring Queen and the greatest Magician of the Golden Realm; her great-granddaughter, Urfante, the Winter Century Witch that aided the hunters of the Last Worm King and led Gobelin to the ruins of the Green Temple so that he could forge *Gladringer*; their descendant, Arfane, called the Queen of

Ghosts, who dwelt in the Witch's Cairns and could summon the very stars to her doorstep. Arfane was so powerful that some thought she might be the Throne Thief." Gilgwyr looked over at Stjepan and grew quiet. "And then there was his mother herself."

"Argante was her name, yes?" said Erim. "I've never asked him about her, but I know what happened to her."

They sat for a bit in silence.

"All these people with lineages steeped in ancient history," she said with a morbid tinge of sadness, watching Arduin and his knights and the Athairi about the campfires. She felt alone, and insignificant. "And what of your people, Gilgwyr?"

"No great story for me, I'm afraid," said Gilgwyr lightly. "My grandfather could remember his grandfather, and told us his stories about the Liadaine line, of which there are not many worth repeating. Danians, we are, of no particular note. As far as I know we've never been amongst the great land lords, never fought in any historic battles. And we have been worshippers of the Divine King for as long as anyone could remember, so all of our ancestors are safely ensconced in Heaven's vaults."

"No one to come visit you on the Day of the Dead, then?" asked Erim.

"Thankfully, no," said Gilgwyr, with a bit of a shudder. "The best thing about sending a soul to Heaven is that it stays there." He contemplated her for a moment. "And what of your people, Erim?"

"I wish I knew," she said with a shrug.

"No one knocks on your door on the Day of the Dead?" Gilgwyr asked. Erim shook her head. "Well, nothing to worry about, they're all up in Heaven, then."

Or locked up in Hell, she thought glumly.

Stjepan sat down next to Annwyn in a spot indicated by Malia. Arduin saw this and frowned, but he did not interfere.

"My Lady; Mistress Malia," he said in greeting. "Is there some new development with the map to report?"

"No, Master Stjepan," said Malia, shaking her head. "The images that are appearing seem to be the same as before."

Stjepan nodded. Annwyn cleared her throat, and Stjepan frowned. He wasn't sure if she had actually said something. He had to lean forward a bit so that he could see under Annwyn's hood; she looked pale and drawn, but focused, and she surveyed the scene around them with interest.

"It has been a long time since I traveled," said Annwyn finally, hesitating a bit as she spoke. "We used to travel the West King's Road every now and then, to follow the Great Tournaments and watch my brothers in the lists. I went almost every year once I was of age. But my debut was the Tournament of Gavant in 1459."

"She was the Tourney Queen there, and again at the Grand Tourney," said Malia proudly.

"I remember my fellow students at the University being very eager for a glimpse of you at Court after the Grand Tourney that year," said Stjepan with a nod.

Annwyn waved them both away. "That was a different age, a long time ago, and I feel like I have been cooped up for a long time. There is no point in dwelling on the past," she said. She looked the camp over. "If I am not mistaken, your kinsmen are far from their native woods."

"Yes and no. For many of the Athairi, the past is as much a part of the present as anything else," said Stjepan. He gestured out to the rolling hills and plains around them, black shapes beyond the campfires. "This was once part of the Erid Wold, the great wood of An-Athair. The Wold once stretched from where the Great Wall of Fortias is today, all the way east to the Abenbrae and what is now Abenton, the greatest wood of the lands of the *Mera Argenta*. The Hada Wold, the Haras Wold, the Neris Wold, the Uthed Wold, the Tiria Wold, the Gra Wold . . . most of the woods of the Middle Kingdoms were once part of the Erid Wold, until the fall of the Golden Realm; only the Sare Wold in the east and the Dav Wold in the far west were not part of the Erid Wold."

"What happened?" Annwyn asked, and immediately regretted it, as she already knew the answer.

"Your ancestors happened, my Lady," Stjepan said, evenly and without reproach. "In ancient days the Golden Knights of An-Athair drew power from the magic trees of the wood, and so their enemies learned to chop down the trees, and place an enchanted stone upon the stump, so that nothing would grow back." He pointed to the large flat stones that were spread out on the earth around them. "Buried under each of those stones is a dead tree stump. And the underside of each of those stones is marked with a rune, that curses the tree and earth beneath it."

Annwyn's eyes grew wide. "But . . . we've been skirting through the Plain of Stones for two days already . . . we've passed thousands of these stones . . ." she gasped.

"Yes," said Stjepan. He winced ruefully. "No one likes to talk about it but it is, I suppose, one of the greatest magical undertakings in our history, rivaled perhaps only by the cursing of Uthedmael by the Sun Court, and the Oracle Queen's call of doom upon the Imperial capital of Millene, and maybe the Wall of Fortias. It took years of labor, and whole cadres of Aurian shamans and magicians, to destroy so large a swath of the Wold. The slate came from the hill quarries near Har Misal; miners literally took apart entire hilltops to provide the stones for the effort. And so the forest was made smaller, and the Knights of An-Athair grew weaker, and the Golden Realm was lost." Stjepan shrugged. "And then over time man and nature have finished the rest, so that now the once-great Erid Wold is broken up into little pieces, and is now but a pale echo of what it was once before." He indicated the Athairi around the campfires. "My kinsmen still wander the old boundaries of the wood as an obligation to the *Fae* Courts, singing to dead trees the promise of the Spring Queen's return."

"The *Fae* Courts?" asked Malia, making a quick sign against the Evil Eye.

"Aye, for what transpires in the Known World has effect in the Otherworld, as well," said Stjepan. "When the old wood was broken up into pieces, and dismembered, so too were the *Fae* Courts; so where there was once a single great Court of the *Fae*, now there are Seven, and many of my people feel we owe them a great debt, having lost the battle to preserve the Wold and the Golden Realm."

"I suppose each of us bears the history of our blood in different ways," Annwyn said. She frowned. "Why not just remove the cursed stones, then?"

"It's been tried, but the stone's effect seems permanent unless the magic of each rune itself can be undone, and no one has ever been able to identify the rune that is carved in the stones. The mark was taught to the Aurian magicians by a mysterious man that most believe to have been either the Horned Man or the Corn King in disguise; a manifestation of the Devil, in other words," Stjepan said quietly. He leaned forward, and drew a mark into the earth. It looked like a complicated version of the letter *R* in the Middle Tongue, but with crossed lines that formed jagged forks. "Most think it is a corruption of the Mark of Binding of Bragea, the old smith-god. But it has never been encountered before, or since."

Annwyn and Malia both shuddered, looking at the mark in the earth; it was just a scribble in the dirt, but there still seemed to be some malevolent and malignant spirit that was attached to it. Stjepan wiped it away with his boot.

"Almost every Athairi magician for a millennia has tried to undo those runes, and failed," said Stjepan. "Most believe that until the Green Temple is restored, and the Spring Queens return, that any effort to undo this curse magic will be fruitless. And so my people travel the old paths, and sing songs to the trees, and ask them to be patient."

Annwyn felt a great sadness like a weight, as though one of those cursed stones was pressing down upon her body, crushing it to the earth.

"Ah, the great haunted Erid Wold of An-Athair . . ." she murmured at last, her eyes far away. "Was it really so large, once upon a time, that it reached to our home at Araswell? I would like to visit the Wold one day; I have passed it by, but never entered it." Her eyes came to rest on Stjepan. "Though I gather that for you it would not be a happy homecoming."

Stjepan froze, and then looked into her eyes. He didn't speak for a long moment, measuring her with his hard gaze; but she didn't look away. "My mother's ashes coat its leaves," he finally said in a flat, quiet voice. "My father wandered mad into its thickets, cursed with her dying breath; my sister ran away to hide in its boughs, and has not been seen since. What son of An-Athair would not yearn to see its depths again? I still have family there. But we will not pass through it on our way to the wizard's barrow." He looked at her carefully. "Perhaps when this journey is over your brother will let you find refuge there."

Annwyn broke his gaze, shyly smiling with sympathy, and with sadness.

"My brother . . . will not let me find refuge anywhere," she said quietly. She seemed to withdraw into herself a bit.

Stjepan started to say something when he sensed someone at his side. He looked up to find the Athairi woman Leda looking down at him with raised eyebrows. "Time for that dance, scion of Morfane," the Athairi woman said with a smile, and she grabbed him by the hand, pulling him up and away. He glanced over his shoulder apologetically back at Annwyn, and then he was being dragged into the dancing circle where Lestra awaited them. Each sister took an arm, and they started to move with Stjepan in tandem, taking several stutter steps to one side and then a kick, and then several stutter steps in the other direction.

Annwyn thought the three dancers looked like they were in a playful tug-of-war. And then the trio was spinning out in a circle, joining in with about thirty other revelers who were dancing in two circles around two campfires, occasionally switching from one circle to the other. The dancers were mostly their Athairi hosts, but she could see Stjepan's young squire Erim dancing, and Master Gilgwyr as well, along with a couple of Arduin's knights—Sir Holgar, and Sir Theodore, and there was the squire Brayden, looking very scared but excited as a pretty young Athairi showed him the basic sideways stutter steps of the dance.

She watched Stjepan dancing with the two Athairi sisters, and felt an ache of longing and jealousy that surprised her. Not about Stjepan, or at least she didn't think so; it was the Athairi women that she watched with startled, envious eyes. They had a freedom and surety of movement that she had never seen in a woman dancing before, a confidence about their bodies, their sexuality, their identity that she found dizzying and discomforting. The shake of their bare hips and bellies, the way they used their bracelets and anklets and shimmering belts as instruments to accompany the drummers, the sheer joy on their faces, the perspiration that made their sun-kissed copper skin glisten in the firelight, the way they improvised their dancing to the music. She'd been considered an excellent dancer when she was younger, but that was in the mannered, measured style of the courtly dancing of the High King's Court, all rigid steps and control. She had never danced like these women; she'd never had the chance to. But she could remember when she had wanted to dance like that, a long time ago, when she was young, when she . . . She stifled a sudden sob, caught it in her throat, and willed it to die.

The tempo of the drumming increased a notch, and the tenor of the dance changed; it became wilder, more barbaric, and suddenly long curved swords with watered steel blades were being passed about. She could sense Arduin and the other knights shift in confusion and nervousness. The swords were being handed to the Athairi women, and they lifted them over their heads and gave a great cry and a *whoop*, and suddenly they started weaving the curved swords in and out of the spaces between and around them and their dancing partners. She marveled at their skill, watching the bared blades flashing in the firelight, the bodies jumping and dancing through the whirling danger. *Athairi sword-dancing*, she thought suddenly. *I've read about this*. The two Athairi sisters effectively had Stjepan trapped as they danced, their swords flashing about on each side of him as the three of them spun about the fires.

And then the Athairi women started to sing as they sword-danced, and she felt like her heart had been pierced through and through.

Arduin frowned disapprovingly, one eye on his transfixed sister, and the other on the dancers circling the campfires. He almost opened his mouth to order Malia to take his sister back to her tent; but he stopped himself, and said nothing, and just let himself fume.

That night, Annwyn dreamt of a beautiful golden-haired youth with strong shoulders and arms, a gentle soul, piercing blue eyes, and a smile that could make any maiden's heart beat faster but was meant only for her. She had not dared dream of him in years; the pain and heartache it brought had simply become too much, and he had been banished away. And yet that night she dreamt of him, and in her dream they danced, and she danced with him as an Athairi woman might dance with a man. She danced with a freedom and a joy she'd never been able to feel before, letting her body move wildly and with abandon, a long curved sword in her hand. And then suddenly in her dream she wasn't dancing with him anymore, but instead with a tall dark Athairi man with a gaze of danger and death.

When she awoke she was surprised to find that she was breathing heavily, her pulse racing, a sheen of sweat on her forehead, her hands clawing into the bedroll, her nipples filled to bursting, her knees opened wide, and that a part of her that had long been dry was surprisingly very wet.

CHAPTER SIXTEEN

ACROSS THE ERIDBRAE

Gilgwyr awoke with a splitting headache that he could only partially attribute to the prodigious amount of wine he had consumed the night before. No weak sauce, that wine, like the watered-down bottles that they had picked up in Vesslos, but some serious red Erid vintages from the wineries near Orliac. Great report and celebration had been made in Therapoli that the vineyards had been thankfully untouched by the fighting during the Earl's rebellion the year before, and he had strongly suspected that the safety of the region's vines and casks and bottles had been more important to most of the city's citizens than the fact that one of Erid Dania's most powerful Earls was at full-fledged war with his King and High King. *Vines and grapes are hardy things, and man makes himself to be more important than he is in their life and death; but the royal edifice of power and allegiance, that's an illusion all too easily brought down and almost always solely at the behest of men and their actions,* he had thought to himself that tense summer. *What glorious fucking fun!*

Not so fun now, with his head feeling like a spike had been pounded through it.

But the pain in his head was not merely wine-driven; he'd drunk enough wine in his time to know that. The dreams he'd had during the night had been like his dreams of the past weeks: filled with beauty and promise, of stars aligning and the hint of great things to come. But underneath them he'd felt tremors of ache and panic and fear, an undercurrent to his dreams that seemed to have neither cause nor root, but built and built until culminating in stabbing, searing pain—first in his chest, then in his belly, and in his back, then in his loins, again and again and again in his loins, and then in between his eyes. He awoke choking on a scream, unaware of where he was for a few moments, lost in the pain and panic, already losing the details of his dreams but left with the unnerving conviction that someone was trying to tell him something, something of grave importance.

He disentangled himself from the sleeping bodies in the tent without bothering to discover who they were, and struggled to his feet and then out into the brisk morning wind. The Dawn Maiden had risen in the east to announce the beginning of the 21st day of Emperium, and the Plain of Stones stretched out blue and gray beyond their camp. He groggily shook his head, trying to clear it of cobwebs and rust and wool and all the other detritus of too much alcohol so that he could focus on his dreams and try to remember why he'd felt that nagging fear and sudden pain, but all he could think about was how terrible his mouth tasted and how thirsty he was. He stumbled over to a doused campfire and found a canteen and lifted it to his lips, taking large gulps of cold water until his thirst was parched. That cleared his head a bit, but by then the dreams had faded into their usual place in hazy half-memory. His eyes came to focus on a small sparrow perched on a flat stone, watching him with its head tilted quizzically. He cursed and threw the canteen at it, and it flew off with a mocking chirp.

Erim squatted one campfire over, cooking several eggs in olive oil in a skillet, eyeing him with a raised eyebrow. Gilgwyr finally looked over and saw her.

"Where's Stjepan?" he asked, voice scratchy and hoarse. He coughed. "I must needs get to a city!"

Erim shrugged. "Haven't seen him yet this morning."

Gilgwyr turned, exasperated, looking at the dozen or so tents, Athairi and Aurian, spread out around the camp amongst the wagons and picket lines for the horses. He was just about resolved to start poking into the tents at random, *Stjepan could be in any one of them, after all*, he thought, when he heard Erim call out behind him: "Gilgwyr!"

"Yes?" he snapped, foggily trying to decide which tent to start with.

"Your pants."

What's wrong with my pants? he wondered, and then he looked down. It took him several moments to realize he was looking at his penis.

"Right, thanks," he said. He looked at the tents around him for a moment in confusion, before turning back to Erim. She pointed at one of the Athairi tents to his left. "Right. Thanks," he said, and then plunged back into the tent.

"We can't take the risk of passing through a major city," Stjepan had argued with him, standing on a small rise well out of earshot of their fellow travelers and Athairi hosts, busy preparing the morning meal or praying in both the old way and the new to the Dawn Maiden. "Even assuming that the Court did not order the use of a magical Sending to send out warning, or that the priests of the city temples have not sent spirit messengers to alert their brethren, we know that heralds bearing news of the events in Therapoli will have reached Truse yesterday, and be in Westmark today, and in Newgate the day after. They will be traveling twice our speed on the best road in the Kingdoms." Gilgwyr had made exasperated noises in protest, but Stjepan had stifled them with a raised hand. "And if you separate from us, how are we supposed to meet later? We could set a meeting date and time, but if you were to miss the appointed hour, we'd have to leave without you. What's so important that you would risk missing the culmination of our journey?"

"I don't know!" Gilgwyr had cried, his face contorted with fear and confusion. "Don't you see? *That's the whole fucking point! I don't know!*"

He knew of course that Stjepan was correct; but still he had paced and raged and fumed at the pain in his head and the vague, fading sensations of the night's dreams, until at last the pain had lessened a bit and the fit of pique and anger had passed. They had stood together amongst the flat, chiseled stones, Stjepan staring down at the cursed stones with a melancholy anger, and Gilgwyr staring off at the horizon to the south, not saying anything to each other. Until Gilgwyr finally sighed and said wearily, "Right, let's go."

His unhappy mien stayed with him all throughout the day's travels, and into the night when they set camp. His dreams that night were just as beautiful as they had been of late, and again they had that undercurrent of fear and dread and pain, though the sharp pain that had driven him to the brink did not recur, and the fear had a duller quality to it, as though it was just the mind's echo of past terror, and not some present danger.

The next day their journey became rougher, which did little to improve Gilgwyr's mood; after consulting with Arduin, Stjepan decided to lead them across the northern edge of the Manon Mole in order to descend down into the Reinvale on the southern side of that valley, so that they could perhaps claim to be coming up from visiting the Watchtowers on the southern coast when they tried to cross the Eridbrae at the bridge at Erid More. Several times on the hill roads they passed small nameless hard-scrabble homesteads or villages or beneath half-ruined keeps, the eyes of suspicious locals in dark leathers and homespun cloth watching with curiosity or with calculation. But most of those calculations came up in their favor; a glance from Stjepan or from one of Arduin's increasingly grizzled-looking knights and the Wheel of Fortune spun aright for them, and they passed down out of the hills and down into the valley without incident, following the shallow northern edge of the Neris Wold.

Long years had passed since Gilgwyr had seen any of the great western woods, and even the simple sight of the Neris Wold and its tall trees and gloomy, *fae*-haunted interior was enough to make him wish like he'd never left the Sleight of Hand. The Wold was marked by a preponderance of purple leaf plums and copper and purple beech trees, giving the canopy a dark reddish-purple cast that it shared only with the Tiria Wold to the northwest. Beside him on the rumble seats Leigh had drawn himself into a tight ball, and he held a small horn-shaped amulet made from black jet. Gilgwyr looked at him quizzically. "A spirit bane," Leigh had whispered. "Can never be too careful."

Gilgwyr nodded sagely back at him. *You're a crazy old fucker*, he thought.

Leigh swiveled around to look forward at their progress, and saw a hooded face peering out of the coach from the open shutter of its side door's window. He reacted in alarm.

"My Lady!" cried Leigh. "Do not let the spirits see your face! Else they will follow you to take your beauty for themselves!" Annwyn looked startled; those were the first words that the enchanter had spoken to her during the whole of their journey so far, and she quickly withdrew back into the interior of her coach, and the shutters slammed shut.

Leigh turned back with a sigh of relief. "By the gods, that was close." He realized that Gilgwyr was staring at him, eyebrows raised. "Ha!" laughed Leigh. "You'll see! Mark my words: the Neris Wold is the haunt of the Brazen Court of the *Fae*. They love nothing more than to dally with mortals, which is all fine and good and a right pleasure until they try to steal your face or your cock right off your body." He made clawing, snatching motions with the gnarled fingers of one hand.

Gilgwyr stared at him for a moment longer. "You're a crazy old fucker," he said slowly with a smile. "And you're fucking making my head hurt."

As the Dusk Maiden rose and night fell, they turned down some shepherd's paths and set camp in rolling green hills dotted with brush and tree stands, just out of sight of both the Neris Wold to their south and the walled town of Stonham, whose lights were visible from the top of the next rise to their west. Stjepan intended them to slip around the southern side of Stonham in the morning and make their way in a broad arc down the valley so that they came up on Erid More and its bridges from a southern route; Erim and Sir Theodore were chosen to head into Stonham early in the morning and buy some fresh bread and other supplies, as they were starting to run low of what they had bought in Vesslos and traded for with the Athairi.

"Do you want to go with them in the morning?" Stjepan asked while they were about the campfires.

Gilgwyr's heart leapt eager for a moment, but then he thought about it. "Stonham? Under . . . Sir Ishal Garbras, currently a vassal of Caewyd, Earl of Erid More, right?" he asked. Stjepan nodded. Gilgwyr groaned and sighed, waving him off. "Oh, why bother? It's too small a town . . ."

Stjepan shrugged.

Gilgwyr's sleep that night was fitful, his beautiful dreams coming and going, sometimes with an echo of the distress and pain of the previous night, the pleasure teasing and tantalizing him but refusing to stay. He tossed and turned until suddenly he awoke in the grips of a hold and the sensation of weight bearing down upon his body; Leigh was on top of him, one hand pressed firmly over Gilgwyr's mouth, the other bringing his finger to his lips to shush Gilgwyr into silence. Gilgwyr struggled half-heartedly for a moment and then froze. The tent flaps were open slightly, as was Gilgwyr's wont at night so that he fell asleep seeing the stars and sky, and Leigh was staring off intently through the opening out into the dark of the camp.

A fear gripped Gilgwyr's spine then, and he struggled to turn himself over so he could look properly out the tent flaps, but Leigh held him firm. He was surprised at the enchanter's strength. Leigh rummaged about in his robes with his free hand, and then brought his hand over Gilgwyr's face. He worked his pinched fingers for a second and a fine powder fell into Gilgwyr's startled eyes. Gilgwyr struggled in earnest then, his eyes stinging and watering, his hands clawing at Leigh's face and the hand clamped over his mouth, and he almost screamed out in terror. Then the pain receded and the interior of the tent seemed suddenly to glow in a silvery blue light.

Oh thank the gods, it was just the White Elixir, he thought, the relief flooding his body as his eyes adjusted to the Second Sight. Leigh brought his free finger back to his lips for a second in silent admonition and then pointed out the tent flaps as he slowly released his grip on Gilgwyr's mouth and shifted his weight. Gilgwyr turned over until he was on his belly, holding his breath until he could see out the tent flaps.

The New Moon hung like a black portal in the Heavens, but with the Sight the camp was twilight bright and glowed silver under the vault of stars in the night. He noted that the campfires had all gone out, which was unusual; the watch should have kept them kindled until morning. But he could see the sleeping shape of two armored knights just beyond the next tent.

A tall silvery form stepped gracefully through the camp, delicately and deliberately placing one foot after the other in an exaggerated tiptoe, as if it were engaged in some slow dramatic dance. Its skin (or clothes, Gilgwyr was not sure) shimmered and sparkled, and a cloud of small white lights danced about it like fireflies. Gilgwyr could not readily identify a gender for the *fae* creature, its body was long and lean and willowy and it moved with a preternatural grace. Its hair spiked up above its head like the thickly entwined limbs of some magical white tree, and it wore a half-mask of some sort—or at least Gilgwyr very much hoped that what he saw was a mask. Its mouth was exposed beneath the half-mask, with sensuous full lips on display. Despite the sense of danger, Gilgwyr could feel himself grow hard at the sight of it. He wondered what he would see if the Elixir had not given him the Sight; nothing at all? A bird or a wolf stepping through their camp?

The walking creature was followed and flanked by two companions that appeared very much the same, but which crept gracefully along on hands and feet as though they were pantomimes imitating spiders or dogs. Their arm and leg movements were exaggerated in large sweeps up and down, as they played the faithful hounds to their upright master. They appeared to be following a scent or a trail, but not along the ground as a bloodhound might; they would creep forward, and then raise their heads up and slowly flick their tongues out as though tasting the air, and then creep forward a step or two again.

Gilgwyr didn't budge, but he began to calculate the reach to his weapons, as useless as they might have been against the *fae*. His rune-marked rapier was sheathed to his right, but Leigh's body lay heavily atop him to that side as the enchanter peered with him out the tent flaps. He had tucked a sharp dagger down on his right side, which was now (having turned over) on his left, and he slowly, inch by agonizing inch, started to snake his left hand down toward the hilt. He felt Leigh's grip on his shoulder tighten in silent warning, and his hand froze.

The *fae* passed on the other side of the doused campfire in front of their own small tent and began to approach the pavilion tent that had been set up for Annwyn and Malia. Gilgwyr immediately wondered at the enchanter's warning from earlier in the day; *are the* fae *aiming for that tent because they are looking for Annwyn, or just because it's the fanciest-looking tent?* he wondered. They stalked and crept closer and closer, and Gilgwyr held his breath, trying to will his heart into calm and praying that Leigh had some sort of magical charm to drive them away, as otherwise he was afraid that a confrontation with the *fae* would be very one-sided.

Just as Gilgwyr was sure he wasn't going to be able to take it a moment more and that his lungs would burst, Stjepan stepped into view and casually placed himself between Annwyn's tent and the three *fae*. He appeared to have perhaps just woken up, though he had breeches and boots on, along with an untucked and unruly looking shirt. An amulet of some sort glowed and dangled from a chain around his neck. His sheathed falchion was in his right hand, held slightly behind his body away from the *fae*.

Leigh breathed quickly into Gilgwyr's ear, and once more Gilgwyr reacted in surprise and confusion until his ear popped and suddenly the world changed again. He shook his head and suddenly he could hear a distant roar overhead, a chorus of stars and angels in the wind coming from the Heavens, and the tinkle of bells and chimes in the air, and the whisper of voices floating in from the nearby woods. And when he heard Stjepan speak, he knew it was not in any language that he would normally understand.

"*You are barred here, my prince,*" said Stjepan. "*There is no one here for you.*"

"*The beautiful one, she is here for us,*" the standing *fae* said. "*Her skin is pale as bone and ivory, her hair glimmers like liquid fire, and she bears upon her a great enchantment and the mark and veil of secrets upon secrets. Why else would she be here except that she is for us?*"

"*She is here at my request, and is under my protection,*" said Stjepan.

"*And who are you, then, mortal?*" asked the *fae*, its voice dripping with derision.

"*I am the son of Argante, daughter of Branwyn, of the line of Morfane, and Urfante, and Arfane,*" said Stjepan, and as he spoke each name the *fae* flinched as though physically struck, and they drew back a step.

"*Hex names, names of power,*" cooed the *Fae* Prince, with a lascivious smile and a trick of the tongue. "*And I know you now, Black-Heart, Ash-*

Knight, Huntsman-Grim. Djara Luna holds sway tonight as the first New Moon of Spring, and the doors between the worlds are open. Come with us to the Court of the Brazen Wood for the Festival of the Spring Moon, and bring the beautiful one with you. You will not regret it."

"*Another time and I would be eager and honored,*" Stjepan said, inclining his head. "*But we are called to a great and pressing duty that will brook no distractions.*"

"*You decline an invitation from a Prince of the First World?*" snarled the *Fae* Prince. It seemed to Gilgwyr as though the creature drew itself up to its full height, and became like a giant, towering over them, but somehow he knew it was but some glamour or projection, for he could also plainly see the *Fae* Prince still standing before Stjepan unchanged.

"*On this day, yes, I must with deepest regrets, my prince,*" said Stjepan, slowly and clearly, and he bowed quite low at the waist, his left knee slightly bent, his left hand to his heart and his right hand coming up straight behind him, the sheathed falchion held firmly in his upraised grip. The pose was courteous and proper, but also invited an attack, placing his head and the back of his neck forward as if on a chopping block; and yet at the same time, the upraised weapon behind him made it clear that he was already prepared for a fight.

The *Fae* Prince contemplated Stjepan's pose for a moment, tempted; and then it stepped back, and its two companions did so as well, coming upright. "*Then I bind you to return to take up my invitation, a year from now on the night of the Festival of the Spring Moon, upon penalty of a great Hex should you refuse or fail,*" the *Fae* Prince said with great satisfaction.

"*Your binding is accepted, my prince,*" said Stjepan, drawing himself upright.

"*Go in the grace of the Queens of Heaven and of Earth, then, Black-Heart, until the year has passed and I come to claim you for the Brazen Court,*" the *Fae* Prince said, and then he and his companions slowly walked backwards in the same odd, graceful way in which they had entered the camp. Stjepan didn't move, but just stood there, watching through narrowed eyes as they backed away into the night.

Once the *fae* were well out of sight, Leigh let go of Gilgwyr's shoulder and scrambled out of the tent. Gilgwyr gasped out loud, sucking in a huge breath of air as he grabbed up his rapier and then he was out of the tent and coming to his feet. He reeled for a moment, his eyes still opened by the Second Sight, his ears still in tune to the sounds beneath the surface of the world. He joined Leigh and Stjepan in standing in front of the women's tent, their gazes off on the distant tree line of the Neris Wold silhouetted against the night sky.

"You see!" cackled Leigh. "I told you, but you didn't believe me! They saw her, and would have taken her, and who knows when they would have given her back! Tomorrow? The next New Moon? In a year and a day? And fucked inside out and then back again!" He turned to Stjepan. "Well done! The sword, is it enchanted against the *fae*, then, some hidden rune to mark it as a bane to their kith and kin?"

"No, it's good ordinary steel," said Stjepan with a shrug. "Would've been useless against them." They gaped at him for a moment.

"You bluffed a Prince of the Brazen Wood?" Leigh asked with a laugh. "A student after mine own heart!"

"The names of my line have some small use in this world, even if they mean nothing in the High King's Court. But it's only a temporary victory, Magister," said Stjepan ruefully. "After all, assuming I am still alive next year, here I will stand, awaiting my summons." He grinned. "Though there are worse fates I can think of."

Stjepan stepped over to the doused campfire, stirring the embers with the toe of his boot, and glanced about the camp with a frown. "Looks like the Urwed brothers are asleep, enspelled by the *fae*," he said. "Magister, can you rouse them from the enchantment, while we make sure that nothing ill has befallen the rest of our camp and all are present and accounted for?"

"I will see what I can do," said Leigh, rubbing his hands together gleefully as he walked over to the sleeping knights.

"Oh, but best not to tell them that we were visited by the *fae*," said Stjepan. "Let's not give Arduin yet another reason to second-guess the wisdom of this trip."

"Two mildly embarrassed knights coming right up," said Leigh, waving at them over his shoulder.

Gilgwyr shook his head, staring up at the stars in the night sky, at the little firefly lights that seemed to now be floating around Stjepan's head, at the flickering silver-white glow that played over the surface of all things. He listened to the distant roar of a celestial choir, intoxicated by the music of the Heavens playing out in the wind above him.

By the gods, it's almost as beautiful as in my dreams, he thought with a smile.

The next day, Erim and Sir Theodore caught up with them about halfway down to Erid More, with a pack mule fully loaded with sacks of supplies bought in Stonham.

"There didn't seem to be any word of what happened in Therapoli yet," she told Stjepan, walking her horse well behind the coach with Stjepan and Gilgwyr also afoot. The country road they were on was lined by high stone walls, and the eyes of a stone tower house watched them as their small column passed through. "People were talking about the mild spring weather, about the Rebel Earl up in the hills and whether the Erid King is going to go get him, about bandit knights visiting outlying farms to bring gifts, about the engagement of the Erid Princess Fiona to the King of Angowrie . . . oh, and a baby was born in town yesterday, which they thought propitious since it was the Festival of the Spring Moon. But jack shit about the murder of a High Priest of the Divine King in Therapoli and the flight of his murderer and a suspected witch out of the city."

"The heralds would've likely been in Westmark two days ago, so the question just becomes whether King Eolred would have felt it important enough to send out riders immediately," mused Stjepan.

"And I'm going to guess *no*," said Gilgwyr. "Everyone probably thinks we have absconded into the Manon Mole, to hide amongst the bandit knights or perhaps even join up with the Rebel Earl. That's what almost every outlaw within spitting distance of the Manon Mole is doing, so they're not expecting us to be trying to cross the Danias . . ."

"Then we might be reasonably safe anywhere off the West King's Road and the primary path of the heralds," Stjepan said. "They should be reaching Aprenna today, to apprise the Dain King's Court."

"So we still cross the Eridbrae at Erid More, then?" asked Erim.

"Aye, then back roads to the north to cut across the West King's Road, and then across the North Road and the Plain of Flowers toward Hartford, I think," said Stjepan. "Mount up. Let's see if we can get across the Eridbrae before nightfall," he said, then glanced skyward at darkening clouds. "Or before the rain gets to us."

The rain started before they reached Erid More, spring showers that seemed to come and go in waves and cycles, the clouds alternating dark and light, with the occasional distant spot of sun breaking through to light the green flanks of the valley. A few of them were fortunate enough to have tabards or cloaks coated with linseed oil, but the rest made do with blankets wrapped around them or over their heads to protect against the rain and the damp.

Erim shivered as she and Stjepan eyed the small town of Erid More. Stjepan wore his usual hat, the brim curled up on the sides, the rain drizzling off it onto his dark brown tabard. Erim had drawn the hood of her cloak up over her head, and she felt like she could barely see anything.

The keep and town of Erid More sat at the corner of two rivers, the Reinbrae, whose broad valley they had followed to reach the town, and the Eridbrae, the shorter of the two great rivers of the western Middle Kingdoms, the other being the much longer Volbrae still further west. The Eridbrae was also shorter than the Abenbrae in the east, being only about two hundred miles in length, but like the Abenbrae it started in the Daradjan Highlands and wended its way through the Djar Éduins and down into the Middle Kingdoms, crossing the Erid Wold and An-Athair until it wound its way down to the Bay of Tears and the *Mera Argenta*. There were two bridges in and out of Erid More; they would have to cross from the south bank of the Reinbrae across one bridge into the walled town, and then turn west to cross the bridge over the Eridbrae. Erim was reasonably impressed with the size and quality of the pair of fortified bridges, and perhaps the great stone keep that towered between them, but the town itself looked, at least from a distance, to be small and compact.

"Is that really the seat of the Earls of Erid More?" she asked. "I mean, the keep looks fairly strong, but I would have thought the town would be larger."

"The strength of Erid More, like Orliac, is in its vineyards and its soil. So the land between here and Reinvale and then all the way down to Nop in Blackstone country is dotted with strong manors and villas and vineyards like the ones we've seen today. Fewer people in the town holds, more people in the villas," Stjepan said.

Erim had definitely noticed the prevalence of strong stone walls even in the vineyards they had passed, and as she thought about it the manors she had seen had definitely been built strong and high, with a utilitarian nature unlike the more comfortable country houses of the Aurian east. They reminded her of the stone houses and keeps along the Watchtower Coast, and she said so.

"Aye," said Stjepan. "I suppose it's like the old Maelite tower tradition, which is sparked by fear of the raider from the sea; though around here the enemy has always been the hill people of the Manon Mole. The country manors and villas in this area tend to be built as full keeps and strong watchtowers, and Reinvale has a castle that's actually bigger than the one we're looking at. The Athairi and Danian tradition was wood, back when the trees were plentiful—the wooden palisade, and wooden great hall. The Düréans left behind their great palace culture and their cities of concrete brick and stone. The Maelites and Daradjans always preferred the stone citadel. And the Aurians brought their long hall traditions as well. And now the Middle Kingdoms are pretty well blended at this point."

Erim glanced up the valley, tracing through the veil of rain and fog the routes of walls and keeps up into the distance. She could see patches of bright green high up the valley where the sun had cast its light. "The sun's come out again over there," she said. "Is the weather always like this over here in the Danias?"

"Oh, that's right, you've never been this far west," Stjepan said. "Well, pretty much so. My mother would have said it's because the old gods and goddesses of the earth and the sky are still welcome here. It rains a lot in the spring and early summer, but not necessarily huge downpours, so yeah, this is typical: some rain, some sun, some wind, sometimes even a little snow, repeat the next day. That's why it's so much greener over here than in Atallica and Auria, we just get a lot more rain over here."

He turned as Arduin rode up at the head of his household troop, the coach bringing up the rear. "Ah, this is Erid More, then?" asked Arduin, peering out from beneath his hood. His cloak was fringed with gold embroidery but was waterproofed against the rain, an expensive travel accessory. Stjepan noted with a wince that the embroidery included the heraldry of Arduin's family, the shield and auroch horns that marked him as of the line of Wain Far-Strider, shield-thane of King Orfewain. He was tempted to ask Arduin to exchange the cloak for another, but he suspected the knight's pride would overrule his good sense; an hour of argument had been required to get Arduin's knights to remove their sigils back on the docks of Vesslos. *The clothes make the man, and without their badges of honor they feel like they are nothing*, he thought. At least the heraldic emblems were only one small part of the design, and could easily escape notice except perhaps from a sharp-eyed herald trained to know a sigil at a glance.

"Yes, my Lord," said Stjepan. "There will be two tolls, one for each bridge. Erim and I will handle the payments, and if anyone asks we'll say that we are the servants of Master Owen Urwed of the merchant house of the Three Rings of Therapoli, newly ensconced in Orliac to do business with its new Earl, escorting his daughter to Westmark with armed guard." They'd been stopped and questioned by knights or yeoman archers at several points along the valley road, but Stjepan had always been quick enough with ready answers to allow them passage, the details changing a bit as they went along, first claiming Nop and points further south as their origin point when they were higher up the valley, and then finally saying Orliac as they reached far enough west for that to make sense.

"And if they've actually met Master Urwed or his daughter?" asked Arduin.

"No such persons, my Lord, so that won't be possible," said Stjepan. "And the Three Rings is large enough that there *could* be someone named Master Owen Urwed amongst its many traders and merchants, but it's unlikely that the gate guards at Erid More will know definitively. Just let our coins and calm demeanor do the rest."

Arduin grimaced. He wondered at men for whom lying and deceit came so easily; Stjepan and his brother Harvald were so very similar, almost like stage actors or entertainers for whom artifice and illusion were their stock-in-trade. Arduin thought of himself as a man of action, and as a man of action, *you are what you do. If you run from a battle or shirk from a fight, then you're a coward. If you stand upright and true, then you are a man of honor.* But Stjepan and Harvald were, or had been in the case of his brother, men of words, and like actors and diplomats, poets and bards, they could conjure things that sounded like truths out of thin air. Having spent so long at Court he had grown up surrounded by men of words; but at the Court there was, he thought, an expectation of truth and honor amongst its clerks and courtiers, a sense of propriety and an understanding of their place in the grand order of things that he found sorely missing in Stjepan, or Master Erim, or Master Gilgwyr and the disgraced enchanter. This was the first time he'd had to place his own safety in the hands of a man of words, and it was giving him a close-up view of how men with the right gift could work their illusions upon the world when they wished to.

And he definitely didn't like it.

"Certainly," said Arduin with a tight-lipped smile. "Let us hope we can pass through without incident."

"Business with the new Earl, then, for your Master?" the guard said to Stjepan, as he eyed the armed and armored men escorting the coach off the Reinbrae bridge and in through the barbican. A clerk was casually counting horses and wheels to total their entry costs into the walled town. Arduin's knights and squires were looking decidedly grungy after several days of hard travel on the road, and the rain didn't help matters any. Almost all of them sported grizzled growth on chin and cheek, with dirt and mud splattered on horses and boots, their armor tarnished where it was visible at all under cloaks and tabards. Dark circles under their eyes and a slight look of hunger and wariness completed their appearance, leaving them looking to all the world as proper mercenary knights would look. Except perhaps Arduin, who comported himself with a back so straight and a spine so rigid that he could pass for a statue; luckily the arched ceiling of the barbican entryway was quite high, else Stjepan might have feared for Arduin's safety. But given the hard times even a noble-born knight might find himself a free lance, jousting and fighting for coin.

"Aye," said Stjepan. "With Porloss now in the hills and Sir Kyrick elevated to the seat of Orliac, the commerce houses and merchants in Therapoli are all eager at the prospect of new business arrangements." The guard raised his eyebrow at the use of the honorific *Sir* for Kyrick, rather than Earl; technically accurate, as Kyrick Ross had been a knight sworn to the Lord of Nop before being chosen as the new Earl of Orliac, but it could be read several ways. What Stjepan said was indeed true on the face of it; with Porloss and his household and many of his chief retainers (including the aforementioned Lord of Nop) now fled into the hills, merchant princes from far and wide had been sending representatives to Orliac in the hopes of persuading the new Earl and his new men to grant new contracts on trade and transport, while those who did business with the old Earl were busy trying to convince him to keep the old contracts in place.

Stjepan gambled and gave a shrug, as if to say, *what're you gonna do?* The guard chuckled. "Yeah, with a Ross now the Earl of Orliac, and a Ross now the Lord of Nop, I guess that makes for a family on the rise," the guard said drily. "We seen a lot of new faces coming through here, and up at Reinvale, all eager to meet the new chief."

"Aye, we came down through Reinvale," Stjepan said with a nod. "Master Owen hired us on in Westmark to act as guides and scouts."

"You lot up there got your own problems with the Erid King, eh?" the guard asked.

Stjepan shrugged. "Him and the City Council don't see eye-to-eye on all things, particularly in regard to how much tax is owed him," said Stjepan. "Not too different, really, than the complaints of Earl Porloss. It's been ten years since the last time the Erid King laid siege to the city to get it to pay a tax, so we're probably overdue for another any time soon."

"Yeah, well, best of luck with that," the guard said as he noticed the clerk signaling that he had a total ready. "So how much?"

"Sixteen people, eighteen horses, and four wheels," said the clerk. "So twenty-nine shillings and eight pennies for the men of the Three Rings commerce house."

"Let's just call that thirty shillings, to make the additions easy for you," the guard said with a grin.

"Ain't my money," Stjepan said with a shrug; the bureaucrat in him was a bit annoyed at the casual extortion of a handful of pennies, but such small bits of corruption ultimately made his life easier and were simply part of the cost of doing business. The guard was meant to think that he meant the money belonged to the fictitious Master Owen Urwed, but of course technically it was Gilgwyr's money he was spending, as Gilgwyr was acting as the underwriter for their expedition at the moment. He counted over a gold crown and ten shillings and tapped his hat to the guard and clerk before heading over to where Erim waited with their horses.

"Close to thirty shillings, so it should be the same at the Eridbrae Bridge," he said. Erim grunted and shook her head as they led their horses through the barbican and out into the neck, a walled road that meandered around the main keep and town wall, essentially a shooting gallery where attackers trying to force the road could be fired down upon by defenders on both the outer and inner walls. The neck followed the tight curve of the western wall of the town directly to the barbican for the Eridbrae Bridge. Stjepan had never been in Erid More before; ignoring the light rain, he ran a practiced eye up the walls to the keep and towers that hulked high above them and was suitably impressed by the sheer bulk of the castle. Midway between the two barbicans there was a large gatehouse built into the inner town wall that would take them into Erid More proper, and there the group ahead of them had stopped. Stjepan frowned.

"Why have you stopped?" he asked Arduin as he and Erim approached.

"It's late afternoon already, and everyone is tired of travel on the open road," said Arduin from his perch atop his destrier. "Can we not stay within Erid More proper this night, perhaps at an inn?"

"We should at least cross the Eridbrae while we still have the light, Lord Arduin," Stjepan said, careful of who was within earshot to hear the name and title. "There should be an inn on the other side, as well, though perhaps of simpler fare than we might find here."

There was some grumbling amongst the nearby knights at that. "But your man Gilgwyr has already headed into the town itself," Arduin protested. Stjepan's frown grew deeper and he craned his neck; sure enough, the coach's rumble seat was half-empty, with a sheepish-looking Leigh giving Stjepan a little wave. Stjepan's mind was filled with black thoughts, and Arduin actually pulled his horse back a step or two at the expression on Stjepan's face.

"Then even more reason to get across the river as fast as possible," Stjepan said quietly. He turned to Erim, handing her a full purse. "Pay for the bridge crossing, yeah? And then let our Lord Arduin pick whatever inn he wants on the other side, preferably to the north." He handed her the reins of his horse and stalked off into the city.

For a clerk, that man can look exceedingly well versed in murder, thought Arduin, shaking his head with a snort. But then he remembered the rumors that had attached themselves to Stjepan during the troubles at the University years ago, and the fate of Rodrick Urgoar to which he had himself been a witness, and he stifled his laugh, and simply watched Stjepan's back recede into the darkness of the gatehouse.

"I'm so glad I found you, as I fear this is my only chance," said Gilgwyr.

He was in a dark antechamber on the first floor of a house within the town proper of Erid More, above a cheese shop. The antechamber did not belong to the cheese shop below it on the ground floor, but rather to an alchemist and enchanter who had taken the first, second, and third floors of the building as his shop and home, and hung a discreet sign in front of the first floor window, that of a crudely drawn *vas hermeticum*, an egg-shaped vessel sometimes used in alchemy. Gilgwyr sat at a round ebony-wood table across from the alchemist in question, a short Danian man by the name of Sayle Lyradim, dressed in deep, dark indigo robes with gold embroidery at the sleeves and hems. The top of the man's head was bald, quite not on purpose, and he had grown a long and full salt-and-pepper beard to compensate. The hair of his eyebrows had practically disappeared, and his eyes appeared plaintive and unprotected as a result.

"Only chance at what?" asked the alchemist, studying Gilgwyr intently.

"My only chance to send a message, of course," said Gilgwyr. "I . . . I had a terrible dream the other night. A veritable nightmare. It has made me . . . concerned about my loved ones back in Therapoli. I am traveling quickly to the west and do not know when I will next be in proper civilization, to send or receive a message by mundane means, and so it is to the high and hermetic arts that I must turn."

"Ah, a Sending, then, or a Reading?" asked Sayle.

"A Sending, I think," said Gilgwyr.

"Then you have come to the right place, as I am familiar with the Incantation of Sending and the rituals which can make it effective," said the alchemist. "For ease of purposes, I use a variety of trained messenger pigeons; I trust that will be satisfactory, or would you prefer to commission the summoning of a spirit, or a dream-vision?"

"I am afraid my time in your lovely town is short, so I guess we'll have to go with the pigeon," said Gilgwyr.

"Excellent," said Sayle, and he excused himself. Gilgwyr could hear him walk up the wooden stairwell to the top floor of the house, and then slowly return, bearing in his hand a birdcage. Within it was a gray and blue pigeon, selected for this most important task for its speed and intelligence. Sayle set the cage down at the edge of the table. "Now, to whom are we sending the Sending?"

"Sequintus Eridaine, enchanter of the Sleight of Hand, a gentleman's house of leisure on Flint's Lane, off of the Wall Street in Therapoli," said Gilgwyr.

"Well, that makes this more difficult, as the High King's city is quite far from here. That will make the Sending more expensive, as well . . . ?" Sayle trailed off, his missing eyebrows raised.

"Money is no object," Gilgwyr said with a smile.

"Excellent. Do you perhaps know his mother's name?" asked Sayle, making notes in a small grimoire.

"Sadha Tilas," said Gilgwyr.

"Excellent," said Sayle, writing again. "This is perhaps too much to hope for, but do you perhaps have some token of his?"

"I do, by chance," said Gilgwyr, and from a small pocket inside his coin purse he produced a small lock of white hair.

The alchemist had been expecting the answer to that question to be *no*, so he froze in surprise, hovering over his grimoire, his mouth partially open as though he were about to speak, staring at the lock of hair for a moment. He looked up at Gilgwyr, and Gilgwyr smiled at him. Sayle blinked once, then twice.

"Ah, excellent. Well done," said Sayle finally, putting his writing quill down and gingerly taking the lock of hair into his hand. "Always good to be prepared." He set it down in the center of the table, and retrieved a candle in a silver candleholder from a sideboard. The casement windows were made of leaded glass, a sign of some wealth, and ignoring the light rain outside he opened the nearest set before returning to the table and placing the candleholder next to the lock of hair.

"Is your message prepared?" Sayle asked as he reseated himself across from Gilgwyr.

"Yes," said Gilgwyr. "Ready when you are."

Sayle removed the pigeon from its cage and held it gently but firmly in his left hand. He drew himself up straight-backed, closed his eyes, and slowed his breathing. He mumbled at first, over and over, then as the minutes dragged to ten his voice grew louder: *"Nos nuntias est, velocitasa et intento a la prevista. Entruventa si destina inven et vera parlare le oratora que se enchargano a consenga. Heraldo, estes velocit et vera!* Sweet herald! Swift wings and steady aim be your gifts and watchwords! Three hundred miles due east, to Sequintus Eridaine, of the blood and son of Sadha Tilas, at the Sleight of Hand, on Flint's Lane, off of the Wall Street in Therapoli Magni, speed straight and true!"

When his voice was practically a shout he opened his eyes and held up the lock of white hair to the flame of the candle, and singed the hair until it was a small mass of embers. He held the pigeon near the burning hair so that it could inhale the acrid fumes.

"Quickly!" said Sayle. "Tell our chosen herald the message you wish to send!"

Gilgwyr leaned over and whispered into the pigeon's ear: "Sequintus, old friend and mentor, greetings from your apt pupil! My dreams have been troubled by pain and fear, and I am filled with worry! Send word to me that all our Friends are safe, so that my mind may rest at ease!"

"Go! Fly! Fly!" Sayle cried, and he flung the pigeon up into the air toward the windows. The pigeon took to wing in time to sail through the open panes. Sayle and Gilgwyr both rushed to the window to see the bird fly gracefully up into the rain-filled skies above the town and then straight to the east, moving swift and sure. "Morning Star, Sun's Herald, watch over your littlest messenger!" Sayle said solemnly as he watched the bird disappear.

"Well done, Master Sayle," said Gilgwyr, patting the alchemist on the shoulder. He glanced down into the street and saw Stjepan's familiar hat and tabard outside; he was speaking to two rough-looking men in front of the tavern across the street. Gilgwyr drew back from the window, and slowly pushed the casement panes shut, drawing the curtain over the view.

He turned to the alchemist. "Now, why don't we settle our bill?" he said with a smile.

"Stjepan, old boy, come looking for me?" Gilgwyr asked casually as he stepped up behind Stjepan, adjusting his cloak and hat against the rain.

Stjepan glanced over his shoulder at Gilgwyr, then turned back to the two men with whom he had been talking. "Well. Speak of the Devil, and here he is," he said to them, and they nodded at him and they all shook hands.

"Well met, *Coura Negra*," said the shorter and uglier of the two.

"Fortune follow you," said the taller and prettier.

"Good fortune and good hunting, gentlemen," said Stjepan, tapping the brim of his hat, and the two men stepped back into the tavern.

Stjepan turned and contemplated Gilgwyr with a flat stare and a slight smile. Gilgwyr grinned back at him. "I suppose we should be going; don't want to keep everyone waiting, eh?" Gilgwyr said.

"No, I suppose not. Erim's leading Arduin and the rest across the Erid bridge to find an inn on the other side," Stjepan said, and then he led the way out through winding streets to the gatehouse and the great barbican.

They were about halfway across the bridge over the Eridbrae when they heard fire bells ringing out from the town behind them. They stopped and looked back. Smoke was rising from something burning in the town center, the heavy wisps and tendrils struggling to rise against the rain.

"Huh. What do you know? A fire, somewhere in the town," said Stjepan flatly. He looked at Gilgwyr.

"Lucky for them it's raining?" offered Gilgwyr with a shrug. Then he turned and kept walking.

Stjepan looked back at the smoke, mixed black and white, curling through the light rain and the gray-white sky. He closed his eyes and listened to the wind, to the raindrops striking on earth and stone and rushing water, to the ringing of distant bells, to the sound of metal scraping sharply over bone. He sniffed the air, smelt fresh rain and wet earth and the familiar ancient river, smelt fire and ash and from somewhere near the hint of something dead and rotting. He took a deep breath to stifle the anger and hate that brewed up within him. His gaze fluttered open as he gazed back at the town of Erid More, and he sighed before turning away and following his companion over the bridge.

CHAPTER SEVENTEEN
WOAT'S INN

Arduin was livid, even apoplectic, barely able to formulate a coherent sentence thanks to rage and exhaustion. He stared at Stjepan incredulously, not believing what he had heard the man say. His lips and mouth moved, and his throat made a groaning, muttering sound, but no words came out. He struggled, and then finally sputtered: "W . . . w . . . what do you mean, we have to keep going?"

They stood in front of an inn with the sign of a ram's head and curled horns. It was a clean and friendly-looking compound, with a high stone wall about the main building and several outbuildings. The inn was one of several in a sprawling stone hamlet called Acyrage on the western bank of the Eridbrae right by the bridge, held by a knight in the service of the Earl of Erid More. Green farmland and rolling hills rose along this side of the river, along with a towpath running north along the riverbank. Sirs Helgi, Holgar, and Theodras stood off to one side, trying very hard not to be noticed by their Lord in his fury. Arduin turned and looked in desperate longing at the inn; despite the light drizzle that fell upon his hood (or indeed perhaps because of it), the inn was the most inviting thing he'd seen since their night in one of his family's hunting lodges. "You said we could stop right across the river," he said through clenched teeth.

"I'm afraid there's been an . . . incident in Erid More," said Stjepan, rubbing the back of his head wearily as he adjusted his dripping hat. "It might be best if we put some miles between us and the town."

Arduin's gaze swung back over the hamlet rooftops toward the bridge and town. He frowned. *Is that smoke?* he wondered. *Is that what those bells are all about?*

"One of the guards approached me in the market and was asking too many questions about you and your knights, my Lord Arduin," said

Gilgwyr smoothly. "He didn't quite believe the story we'd told him. I'm afraid I was very . . . curt in answering his questions."

Arduin looked back and forth between Gilgwyr, smiling nonchalantly, and Stjepan, grimly silent. "King of Heaven!" Arduin swore. "The Six Hells will be too good for the likes of you two." He looked up at the sky, letting the rain falling on his face. He tried to find the energy to argue with them, but he knew for safety's sake that their only recourse was to movement. He sighed, feeling defeated. "Fine, what do you suggest?"

"We should head up the river a bit as if we're headed to Westmark and then cut cross-country to Woat's Inn on the West King's Road," said Stjepan. "There should be a country road that cuts up through Dagger Vale."

"Woat's Inn? That is a vile place," said Arduin with a frown. "I've been there before, back when we used to make the journey to the Tournament of Flowers each annum."

"Vile it may be, but it might be the only safe place for us to stop anywhere along the West King's Road. The Woats generally don't care who you are or what you've done, so long as you have coin to spend. It'll have plenty of fresh food and water, and fodder for the horses. We can use the baths there, resupply for the run to the Wall, even change out our horses if necessary," said Stjepan.

"True, no argument on the provisioning there," said Arduin. He just wanted to go to sleep on a soft bed of down somewhere, and not wake up for a day or two, and at least he could do that at Woat's Inn.

"I have some contacts there, as well, my Lord," said Gilgwyr. "I should be able to find us a crew for the last leg of the journey, to aid in our travels."

"Why would we need more men? We've been doing fine so far," Arduin asked, his frown deepening.

"Aye, but when you're after a wizard's barrow in the Bale Mole, you either go in quick and quiet by yourself, or you go in with a small army. Right now, particularly with that coach, we're too many to slip in all quiet-like, but not enough not to get mistaken as easy prey," said Stjepan. "The hills are not as bad as the Wastes of Lost Uthedmael, but it takes a special kind of insanity to risk the danger. Gilgwyr'll find us a crew at Woat's mad or desperate enough to help guide us, or word of where we can hire one on our way up to Mizer."

"Oh? And have you ever been into the Wastes, or the Bale Mole, then?" asked Arduin, and he regretted asking the question before the words had left his mouth.

"I have, my Lord," said Stjepan. "I was attached to King Derrek of Warwark's household in '67 when he rode into the Lost Dav Wold and then up into the Bale Mole, and again in '69 when he routed a Thessid Imperial regiment encamped at Lost Av Lúin, and chased some of their Djar Maelite allies almost back into the Bora Éduins."

Arduin's knights traded appraising glances. Arduin sighed. *I have to learn not to ask questions to which I do not already know the answers*, he thought dryly. *For all I know he's just making all of this up.*

"Right," Arduin said with a stiff smile. "Find us a way to Woat's Inn, then."

From Acyrage they traveled north-north-east for a few miles along the roads and towpaths that ran up the Eridbrae toward Westmark, the capital city of Erid Dania, passing through or near clusters of thatched-roof stone houses and walls. They passed fields of winter wheat and new potatoes, leeks and rhubarb and spinach, and Danian Forest sheep and brown-and-white Danian cattle grazing at pasture. Stjepan then turned them northwesterly onto country farming roads, heading higher up into the hills and away from the river. As night fell the rain worsened, and they passed out of cultivated farmlands and into the wilds of a broken hill range, following a well-worn shepherd's path by fizzling torch and lantern light. The path led them through wooded copses and past small ruins, then down into the Dagger Vale and across the Daverbrae at an easy ford. Coming up the other side they split off the main path to follow a lesser path due north until they saw the lights of Woat's Inn up ahead.

Stjepan would have preferred that they swing to the west and onto the West King's Road, so that they could approach the inn as though they were coming from the west and the castle of Burnwall; arriving at close to midnight at this particular Inn was hardly unusual, but coming up out of the Dagger Vale might draw some attention. But they needed their lanterns and torches in the rainy dark, without the stars to guide them, and so would likely be seen anyway should there be a lookout at work, and the wet and cold and long day's march had everyone close to falling out of their saddles from exhaustion. So he led them directly to the Inn, deciding not to care if anyone noticed that they were coming up out of the Dagger Vale.

To describe Woat's Roadside Inn as an inn did not, perhaps, do it justice; better to say instead that it was a version of the caravanserai that could be found crisscrossing the wastes and deserts of the Great Midlands to the west or the deserts of the Thessid-Golan Empire in the south, a massive complex of buildings and walls that could potentially house men and animals by the hundreds, if not thousands. Though unlike the caravanserai of other parts of the Known World, Woat's was made mostly of wood with a bit of stone and, having grown piecemeal over the many years, was laid out somewhat haphazardly rather than by plan. The wall that surrounded its perimeter was mostly stone, but in some places the stones had fallen away and been replaced by wooden walls and fences of dubious construction, so its defensive value was nominal at best. Several large wooden gates led into the interior at seemingly almost random points along the wall.

The central feature was a long and ancient great hall, part stone and part wattle-and-daub framed with timber and much patched throughout. It was surrounded by stables, kitchens and smokehouses, smithies and farriers, a stone bathhouse, storehouses, a common sleeping hall (which during the heights of Tournament Season was for women only) and a long two-story wood boarding house with smaller rooms for rent, and then the "King's Hall," the fanciest looking building on the lot, with an ornamented gabled roof and leaded glass windows. Despite its name kings almost certainly did not stay there. One might have stayed there once, perhaps by accident, as royalty and high nobility could expect far better accommodations at the castle of Burnwall to the west, where they would be hosted by Prince Hektor, son of King Eolred, or in the capital city of Westmark to the east. But some amongst the more adventurous earls and barons of the Middle Kingdoms had been known to take the house for the night.

As they rode in through the wide-open gates, they could see horses, wagons, and coaches packed into its yards and sheds and stables. Drums and the muted roar of voices raised in song and argument came from the great hall. Dozens of drunken revelers were stumbling about through the rain, mixing with twice as many leather-clad stable hands and porters. All of them ignored the newcomers.

"King of Heaven, I think it looks even shoddier than the last time I was here," mumbled Arduin. He and Stjepan peered through the rain at some of the stable hands lounging, unconcerned, under dry awnings. They all looked more or less the same, but Stjepan finally focused in on one of them who seemed a bit older than his companions.

"Oi, you there! Woat!" barked Stjepan.

The stable hand peered over his shoulder and waved his hand. "Oi, whatcha want?" he cried.

"Is the King's Hall taken?" Stjepan asked loudly.

"No, it's free tonight!" the young man shouted back, suddenly a bit more interested. He started walking toward them, pulling his hood up over his head as he stepped out into the rain. He had long straggly black hair, and a patchy growth along his chin and mouth, as well as the curled lip and the surly, shifty, slightly crossed set to the eyes that seemed the mark of the Woat clan. He wore a jacket of patched, undyed leather under his hood and short chaperon cape, torn hose, and mismatched short ankle boots, and had a sheathed dagger tucked into his belt.

"We'll take it, then!" Stjepan said. "Private baths for two ladies in the King's Hall, oat bags and stabling for the horses, and food and drink now and in the morning for our whole party."

"Kitchens are still going, the baths are still hot, and the pussy's still warm, too," the Woat grinned.

"That part's to every man's individual discretion," Stjepan said with a sour grimace. "So tell your girls to ask for coin up front, Captain, it's not going on the general tab."

"Right, your call," the Woat said with a nod, and whistled. A half dozen of his brothers and cousins sprang into action, dashing out into the rain to help the dismounting knights lead their horses toward a set of stables right by the King's Hall, while a few ran off to deliver news and instructions to other parts of the compound. The coach was directed to swing in front of the King's Hall, and Gilgwyr and Leigh clambered off the rumble seats in the back as the knights and squires formed a cordon for the Lady and her handmaiden into the building. A few of the younger Woats looked on in not-so-idle curiosity until a long hard stare from Sir Helgi Vogelwain made them slink away, laughing into the rain and the night like a pack of wild dogs.

And wild dogs they were, for the Woat clan was marked by notoriety and infamy. Their line traced to the Wyvern King of the Manon Mole, from some bastard child of his that fled the hills and his father's cruel reign to find refuge in the hold of Davers and discovered some skill at procreation. For centuries the now-sprawling clan of murderers and thieves had been tied to every crime imaginable in the central hills between Newgate and Westmark, and despite the strenuous efforts of kings and earls and sheriffs and their god-fearing neighbors to stamp them out, the clan had not only survived but prospered and eventually settled into the role of innkeepers along the West King's Road. Many argued that the Inn was little more than a civilized form of highway robbery, given the prices they sometimes charged, and despite the thin veneer of respectability the establishment granted to the clan, rumor still associated them with every dastardly deed and foul doing within twenty miles of Dagger Vale.

"Stay armed the whole time you're here, though inside the Inn it's not the Woats you have to be worried about," Stjepan said under his breath to Erim as they pulled saddles and bags off their steeds. "And we'll arrange a private bath for you, if you want," he added. She nodded absently as she scanned the yards and the great hall from the dry refuge of the stables.

"It's after midnight. Is it normally so busy?" asked Erim, finding that she was warming to the place. "I'd expect this in Therapoli, but not out here in the middle of nowhere."

"This isn't really busy for Woat's, I'd guess it's just the first traders of spring hitting the roads," said Stjepan. "Just wait a couple of months until there are thousands of travelers on the roads to and from the Tournament of Flowers, and this place will be packed to the rafters and the late and unlucky will be camping outside the walls. They slaughter an entire herd of cattle during that month just to feed everyone coming through," he added with a hint of disapproval.

A small crowd of Woat serving girls and porters ran past them to prepare the King's Hall and the baths. "The privies and a bath, I think, in that order; and then it's off to see what there is to see," said Stjepan, and Erim nodded in agreement.

Annwyn stood in the dark, listening to the rain on the rooftop and the murmur of quiet voices from down the hall, silently watching Malia sleep. For days, she had been trapped either in the back of the coach when they were on the road, or in her pavilion when they were in camp. Arduin had allowed her to walk and stretch her legs once in a while, or to relieve herself should the necessities of her body demand it, but she had been under constant guard and discreet observation when she was outside. When she wasn't drifting in and out of consciousness or sleep, that is, as the events of the last weeks, the constant travel, and the enchantment that appeared to be upon her left her exhausted and at times delirious, sometimes forgetting who or where she was.

In some ways, she supposed, very little had changed in her life except for the opportunity to travel once again, as she had spent the last ten years . . . perhaps longer, perhaps even all of her life, if she thought about it . . . under constant guard and supervision. Her father, her brothers, her household; they were as much her jailers as anything else, keeping her locked away in a prison. They might have tried to line that prison with flowers and velvet and silk and finery, but sweet smells and fine textiles could not cover the stench of her own rot and decay and the walls that surrounded and kept her. And so she had slowly removed all of the gilded refinements from her life and her chambers until only the stark truth remained: that she was a prisoner, in black mourning clothes staring at blank walls. They all were. Her father; her brothers; Arduin, in particular, the golden boy heir to the family title now staring at a life without a future; Harvald, the brightest and smartest and most obscenely cruel of them, but born the youngest, and therefore of such limited prospects in society even from the start.

And now Harvald was dead. She had to remind herself of that. *We burned his body and he is now ash in the wind and water. Am I not now freed from what was once Harvald?*

But something *had* changed. She could feel it inside her, the presence of what for lack of a better word she simply thought of as *the map* like a living thing. She wondered if that was what it felt like to be pregnant; a rite of passage for most women that she had resigned herself to never experiencing. Except rather than just being concentrated in her belly, she could feel the tingle and pressure of the enchantment almost everywhere, playing over and under her skin, in her arms and shoulders, coiling about her heart and lungs, tightening around her spine. She could hear the map like a voice in her head, whispering to her in incomprehensible words, as though it were the wisp of a thought in search of form, poised forever on the tip of her tongue.

She had thought of telling Malia what she was feeling, what was happening to her, but could not figure out how to put it into words without scaring or even simply confusing her most loyal handmaiden and companion. They had prepared for bed almost wordlessly, helping each other bathe in the Aurian style and then inspecting her skin for new signs and images, but nothing new was moving upon her body yet. As she watched Malia sleep, she felt an overwhelming surge of gratitude that someone so steadfast was in her life: the sister she had never had.

She slid her black dress back on over her shift, and drew a dark cloak tightly about her before pulling the hood over her head. As quietly as she could, she opened the door to their room, and eyed the antechamber beyond; finding it empty, she slipped out the door and slowly closed it behind her. Through the door on her right she knew she would find the larger main hall that they had entered in through, and undoubtedly several of her brother's knights and squires talking softly as they drifted off; or perhaps they were already asleep, exhausted from their long journey. The door opposite was another private room, to be held by her brother when he was done with his late-night meal. But it was the small door on her left that held her interest.

She opened it, and peered through. It appeared to be a short servant's hall, with a small cloakroom or garderobe on one side, and a barred door at the other. She slipped to that door, lifted the bar, and stepped outside onto a small covered porch.

Annwyn stood for a while listening to the patter of the rain, and feeling the light wind on her face. She couldn't remember the last time she had stood outdoors alone, except perhaps a few stolen moments in the courtyards of her father's houses and holds.

From the rear porch she could see the shape and shadows of stacks of barrels and crates, hay bales, and wagons. Large braziers and lanterns hanging suspended from chains lit several nearby buildings in the compound, including what she took to be the bathhouse and another hall of some sort, both of which seemed to be alight with some signs of activity. She saw the doors to the bathhouse open and Gilgwyr stepped out, calling out something to someone still inside. She froze in the darkness of the rear porch, momentarily afraid that Gilgwyr might head toward her. But instead he slipped a tricorn hat onto his head and started out into the rain in the general direction of the great hall. She slowly stepped down off the porch so that she could follow his progress as he nonchalantly crossed the yards toward his destination. A large side door in the main building swung open, a block of orange-red light in the night with his silhouette within it, accompanied by a sudden rush of noise and music, and then the door was shut and the sound became muted again.

She stared at the great hall for a long time, uncertain of her next course. She knew *what* she wanted to do, she wanted to follow Gilgwyr inside; though *why* was perhaps a bit less clear, and she was also sure that some risk accompanied this desire. She wasn't sure how long she stood there, but eventually she began whispering to herself quietly. She gathered up her courage and hurried across the yards toward the great hall before she could change her mind.

In the back of a nearby wagon, Leigh sat unmoving, as still as a statue, his elbow propped on a crate and his top two fingers resting on his forehead above his eye. From beneath his hood and through narrowed eyelids he watched her cross the yard and then enter the great hall.

He smiled, and in his mind's eye he imagined her seated upon a fire-blackened throne of brass set over a jumbled field of polished bone, with a spiked crown made of brass upon her brow, and he thought to himself that she made quite a vision.

Upon entering the great hall of Woat's Roadside Inn, Annwyn came to a full and stunned stop as though the sights and sounds of the room were a physical wall that she had just run into. The main hall was a great timbered vault, and from the rafters hung soot-stained banners from every corner of the Middle Kingdoms, gifts left behind by previous travelers to mark their stay. The plastered stone walls at each end of the hall held a great fireplace, each so large several men could walk into it standing upright, and the walls themselves were festooned with antlers and horns from a dozen different kinds of beast, a veritable history of slaughter. Arcaded aisles ran along the sides of the main hall, disappearing into distant chambers at each end, and galleries ran above them. Two sets of long tables ran end-to-end the length of the hall, and around them sat or milled a sprawling, drunken crowd of travelers, traders, tinkers, robbers, thieves, brigands, landless knights, sell-swords, and slumming country lordlings. They clustered in the galleries and aisles of the hall, fell out of their chairs, mock-wrestled each other, fought for real until someone broke them up. They were watched over and served by scantily clad women and burly, leather-clad thugs, all of them at first glance seemingly related. A bawdy song was being roared at the top of a hundred lungs, and a loud, discordant drumming and piping was coming from somewhere, perhaps the gallery right above her. Naked dark-haired, pale-skinned women shimmied and shook on the tabletops, strutting and preening the length of the room for the crowds that caroused beneath them. Annwyn could smell roasting meat, unwashed bodies and vomit, and the sharp tang of freshly spilled beer.

She reeled, momentarily and completely disoriented.

There was almost nothing in her experience to remotely prepare her for a place such as this, not even the easy, joyous revelry of the Athairi camp. The Athairi were, despite their hedonism and loose morals, a refined, graceful, and courteous people; but the rough men and women that filled the hall at Woat's Inn were the kind that every part of her social world was designed to keep as far away from her as possible. Most of her time was spent within her own family and household, and outside the walls of her father's houses and estates, her encounters were generally with other members of the ruling class of the Middle Kingdoms and its High Court. The tradesmen and crafters, farmers and laborers that supplied her household and made its functioning possible only ever met her under the auspices of her authority, as a full Lady of a landed Aurian family with a baron's title before their name; and most of them were well versed in the behavior expected of them in an encounter with their social betters. But here the social niceties of the courtly culture of the Middle Kingdoms was replaced by the more mercenary give-and-take of want and fulfillment, supply and demand, a *need* and a *price*.

And she'd never seen anything quite like it.

A woman bearing a tray of wooden mugs filled with ale almost knocked her over, and that shook Annwyn out of her shocked reverie. She drew her cloak and hood tightly about her, so that her face was completely in shadow, and pressed herself tightly to a wooden arcade column, trying to make herself as small as possible. Thankfully the crowds near her were so besotted with wine and ale and the proximity of naked women that she went entirely unnoticed, a dark shape blended into a dark shape. And so, left to her own devices, she slowly got her bearings, and her shock began to turn into something like curiosity.

She had found the dancing of the Athairi women she'd seen a few short days ago to be sensual, and erotic, with a core of grace and beauty even as it invited the viewer to unchaste thoughts and acts. The dancing here was cruder, more animal, more primal, almost ugly, as though the art had been stripped away to reveal the dance at its most salacious core. It was certainly less practiced; some of the women moved quite clumsily, as though inhibited by drink or weight or age. As she looked more closely, she thought the women here looked tired and worn-down, even the ones that at first glance had seemed like they might be beautiful, which admittedly was not many; most of the women here were clearly Woatlings, with the same curled, sneering lips and slightly cross-eyed look as the men-folk from the clan. Unlike the Athairi dancers, who had moved according to an inner fire and heat, swept up in a passion for music and rhythm and sex, most of the women in this hall seemed duller fare, with faces that were either too hard or too soft, and eyes that were either predatory or simply vacant, as though their very spirits were being drained away.

But the drunken and desperate men here didn't seem to care very much, as far as she could tell. They happily tossed coins onto the tabletops under the feet of the dancing women, or into the air to fall haphazardly wherever they might land. Occasionally a dancer would reward a man that threw enough coins by taking him by the hand and leading him off somewhere behind the antlered walls, as his companions cheered his presumably good fortune.

As she surveyed the room and calmed her mind and racing heart, she came to realize that Gilgwyr was nowhere to be seen, unless he was in some dark corner hidden away somewhere. Slowly and carefully she wended her way through the crowds of men in the side aisles of the hall and, upon finding an ornamented staircase at the rear of one of those aisles, went up to the upper galleries looking out over the raucous hall. She passed men drunk and sober, gamblers playing at dice and ignoring the nudity hovering nearby, traders arguing over the fair price of a dozen Highlands half-bred chargers, partisans arguing over whether Prince Hektor should step aside as next in line to the Erid crown in favor of his younger and more dashing brother Prince Colin, and thieves plotting to rob a wealthy jeweler traveling next week from Newgate to Westmark, but she did not see Gilgwyr amongst any of them.

Annwyn frowned, looking down upon the main hall from the relative safety of one of the upper galleries, taking her time to scan the men milling amongst the two rows of long tables below. She looked long enough to be convinced that Gilgwyr was not there. Confusion was about to set in on her when she spied a naked dancer stumbling out of the back areas behind the stone wall at the far end of the hall, where the dancers were taking their trysts, and she realized it was the one place she hadn't looked.

She worked her way back downstairs and down one of the long aisles, then slipped into the back of the great hall. The chamber beyond was darker than the main hall and built into a warren of stalls. She could hear moans from men and women, gasps and shouts, from somewhere a kind of rhythmic slapping, and her heart started racing and her throat suddenly went dry. The stalls had no doors, and as she wandered light-headed down the tight passageway that wound its way through them, she glimpsed men and women in varying degrees of undress and in different poses. A heady mix of fear and a strange, inchoate desire welled up within her; she tried not to look, tried not to stare, tried to only see the faces of the men, to find the familiar face of her quarry amongst them, but it didn't always work. She gasped and stared into a stall as a Woatling pulled her mouth off an erect penis, a strand of saliva still connecting her tongue to the bulging tip, the act barely registering in her mind before she was hurrying on. She blushed and faltered at the sight of a man's pale, fat, hairy buttocks quivering and shaking as he thrust and thrust into a woman lying beneath him, her dainty but dirty feet waving in the air above his back. Annwyn felt flush, her body overheated, as though she might faint at any moment.

PART TWO: ON THE ROAD OF SWEAT AND TEARS

She stumbled through past the last of the stalls, and staggered against a dilapidated wooden wall, trying to catch her breath and calm her racing heart. She stood there, breathing heavily, until she realized that through the wall she could hear men cheering and shouting. There were a number of gaps and holes in the panels of the wall. She stared at a hole about eye-level for a moment, biting her lip. Then slowly, very deliberately, she stepped forward and she pressed her eye to the hole, and peered through it into a dark and dingy room.

A lurid scene was laid out before her. A grim-looking lot of six surly men in soiled leathers stood toward the center of the room, lit by lanterns. They weren't Woats, but might as well have been. Most of them had dark, dirty, straggly hair and unkempt beards or mustaches, though one of them had a shaved head and another had golden-red hair and a great bushy beard and very pale skin. Some of them had mugs of ale in their hands; others held and stroked cocks of varying degrees of hardness. They were loudly and profanely cheering on as a man and a woman had sex in front of them.

The woman was on all fours on an impromptu platform made of a hay bale covered by a dark red velvet cloak, her athletic, curvaceous body shaking and her arms and hands outstretched before her to tightly grip the cloak and bale for dear life as she was vigorously pounded from behind by a muscular beast of a man. She wore riding boots and had a jeweled half-mask over her eyes and nose, leaving her panting and gasping mouth exposed, and the mask bound up her dark hair in an elaborate jeweled black lace head-band. The man behind her was broad-shouldered and barrel-chested, with muscular arms and legs and hips, with wiry thick hair on his chest thinning down toward his loins, matted with sweat. He had a cruel, bestial look about his face, with a strong nose and thick brows and a stubble-covered chin that looked carved from stone, and his hair was growing long, hanging in front of his eyes and down past his ears. He held her hips in his big hands and pulled her ass back into his every forward thrust, hammering into her upraised pelvis, the round globes of her ass shaking from his efforts. They both glistened with sweat in the golden lamp light, droplets dripping and flying from their hair and bodies with every thrust and parry.

344

Annwyn gaped in shock and amazement. Part of her wanted to scream and tear herself away from her peephole, but she couldn't move a muscle. It took several moments for it to register upon her addled brain that there were several other figures in the room. One was a knight that she almost mistook for a statue; he stood motionless, fully clad from head-to-toe in russeted plate harness, a dark red cloak hanging over one of his spiked pauldrons, the visor of his broad sallet helm down, his gauntleted right hand on the hilt of an unsheathed greatsword. Next to him stood what was clearly one of the Woats, but an older and (if such a thing were possible) more distinguished specimen of the clan, wearing black leathers and slashed velvet, bearded and mustachioed with salt-and-pepper hair in a ponytail. And next to him stood Gilgwyr, eyeing the fornicating couple and casually saying something to the Woat that made the man laugh.

She had barely started to try getting her mind to start working again when a hand closed on her shoulder. She whirled around with a gasp, her face flushed beet red, and found herself face to face with Stjepan, his piercing gaze pinning her feet to the floor and her flustered tongue to the roof of her mouth.

She couldn't break his gaze, but she was vaguely aware that Erim and Sir Theodras stood behind him, looking at her and then scanning their surroundings with wary glances.

"My Lady Annwyn," said Stjepan in a quiet voice. "What are you doing?"

It took Annwyn several moments to answer, her breath catching in her throat. "I . . . I . . . I have never been in a place like this before," she finally gasped out.

"This is no place for a Lady," he said. "For your own safety, you should leave at once."

Annwyn seemed like she was about to say something, but his sternness was like a wall and she faltered at it. She nodded and drew her cloak and hood tightly around her. Erim took the lead to escort Annwyn back through the warren of stalls, with Sir Theodras tight behind her, one hand on his sword hilt.

Stjepan stood still and watched them leave, his eyes narrowing. *And that wasn't really an answer, my Lady Annwyn*, he thought. He waited until they had disappeared from sight.

Then he sighed and walked into the back room.

Gilgwyr and the venerable Woat nodded to him as he entered, and Stjepan leaned casually against the wall by the door and crossed his arms.

The man fucking the woman glanced toward Stjepan, and a flash of recognition snaked across his face. He grinned malevolently in greeting, and paused in his brutal thrusting, holding himself deep within the woman and grinding his hips into her pelvis. She gasped and moaned as he moved, then she made a sharp cry of displeasure as he slid out of her completely. His long, thickly veined erection bobbed in the air, shining with their juices, as he placed one hand in between her shoulder blades and forced the masked woman's face and chest down onto the cloak-covered bale, making her arch her upraised ass high into the air. Not breaking eye contact with Stjepan, he slowly stroked the length of his cock once, then twice with his free hand. He shifted himself above the woman's arched body, still pinning her down with one hand, and holding his long tool by the base he wetly slapped it against the woman's exposed pubes several times before he slid his length back into her to the hilt.

The big man started to fuck her in earnest. Soon he was grunting loudly with the effort, his face red and contorted, his veins popping and muscles straining, his hips almost a blur. He looked like he was trying to break her. The sounds of their wet flesh smacking together almost drowned out the masked woman's cries and moans of pleasure. She clawed at the velvet cloak for purchase as she thrust back against him, and there was a slight undercurrent of fear in her passion.

Stjepan glanced at the knight; he remained frozen, his expression unreadable behind the lowered visor, but Stjepan didn't see any noticeable tension in the way the knight held himself. Stjepan turned back to watch the scene impassively.

There was no question the big brute was a sure cocksman, if unsubtle. Stjepan idly wondered what it would be like to be on the receiving end of that particular member, so forcefully delivered, and guessed that it would not be to every body's liking. But the woman in question was enjoying herself, her body shivering in climax after climax as the big brute worked his rage and wonder on her. *She's a rare breed*, thought Stjepan. They were both clearly relishing having an audience, moving their bodies to most display themselves to their rapt onlookers, their poses and cries exaggerated for effect.

Soon the man and woman were finishing their act loudly and lustily, the big man's thrusts growing slower and more haphazard and then he was holding himself against her and moaning and grimacing. The watching men cheered as they decoupled, with a several of the men who had their cocks out stroking themselves to a finish, their seed jetting out to spill on the straw and rushes scattered about the floor. The masked woman rolled over onto her back and luxuriated on the cloak-covered bale, her legs rubbing together as she traced her fingers over her shuddering flesh. The big man walked a circle of triumph around her prone body, joking and joshing with his mates, his still-swollen cock swaying in front of him, dripping their combined juices.

After a few moments the woman slowly stood and stretched her long limbs. Stjepan stopped leaning against the wall and straightened, dropping his arms nonchalantly to his sides as the knight tossed a bag of coins to the big man, who caught it with a grin. The masked woman lifted her red velvet cloak from the hay bale, shook it, and slid it imperiously over her shoulders and around her body to cover her glistening bare skin. She drew the hood over her head and mask as she and the knight started to leave.

"Black-Heart," she said in greeting as she passed him, but she did not appear to look at him.

"Countess," he said, as he gave a short bow, and the Countess and her knight disappeared out the door. If the knight looked at Stjepan or was even aware of his presence, he gave no outward sign from beneath his lowered visor, and Stjepan studiously ignored him in favor of turning his narrowed gaze on the big naked man standing in the center of a celebratory gang of miscreants.

"Black-Heart! You piece of shit!" cried out the man in question. He had a nasty grin on his face, but his words carried no real element of humor in them. He was counting out some coins into the elder Woat's hand.

Stjepan turned to Gilgwyr. "Godewyn Red-Hand and his band of butchers are the best you can do?" he asked.

The men in the room giggled and cackled as Gilgwyr shrugged apologetically. "Considering where we're going, our options are quite limited, perhaps as limited here as back in Therapoli," said Gilgwyr.

"If you're really headed into the Bale Mole, your best bet would be to crew up with some of the Tirian lords or the huntsmen out of the Gyrdiff temple, or some Watchtower knights looking for scalps," said the elder Woat. Stjepan knew the Woat to be Gelber, one of the clan's chief patriarchs. "But they don't crew for money or swag, only for cause. This is the best crew in the house right now, Black-Heart, and maybe the best crew west of the Eridbrae. Except our own lads, that is, but we ain't stupid enough to tread into Azharad's old realm," he added with a wolfish smile. A few of the other men in the room started to grumble at that, suddenly realizing that he was, in fact, insulting them.

"No, I wouldn't imagine you would be, Gelber Woat," said Stjepan with a deferential nod to the elder Woat. "But Moran Gower's got a better crew than this, as does Dürace Lambadras, as does Gause Three-Penny. No offense, gentlemen," he added to hard looks and too-casual shrugs from the other men in the room, who seemingly did not appreciate the general drift of the conversation.

"Aye, but Moran's been run out of the Barrens into the Uthed Wold to hide with his brother Sayle. Sir Talley Ghent and Sir Cole Orenge came up out of Fort Schallis and Earl Geller came out of Hartford, and they almost had him at Dunnerden, but he managed to slip across the river," said Gelber Woat. "The Lamb would do it just for the lark, but he and his crew wintered up in the Highlands the last I heard, and they're not likely back before the Festival of Ascensium at the earliest. And we just got word that Three-Penny went into the Devil's Tower with his crew a couple of weeks ago and hasn't been seen since."

"We can't wait for the Lamb to come back. This is the best we can do, Stjepan," said Gilgwyr patiently.

Stjepan frowned at that last bit of news from the elder Woat. *Gause has always been a practical and smart man. He must have had his reasons to enter the Devil's Tower, though I can't imagine what they would have been*, thought Stjepan. "And what about Red Tomm Hardee and his men?" Stjepan asked.

"He's sworn to the straight and narrow and staying on his farm at Holbrass," said Gelber Woat. "Lord Duram and Earl Geller put it to him that if he didn't mend his ways they'd all do to him what they did to Moran Gower, and drive him into the woods with *his* brother, and hunt them both down."

"Is Black Jack still alive and playing the outlaw, then?" asked Stjepan with surprise.

"Aye, *fae*-kissed Black Jack Hardee is still hiding up in the Kestle March, and has been there the longest of them," said the Woat. "He's practically one of the Tirian lords by now, and he's the best of the lot, but it could take you days just to find him."

And that would put us in close amongst the Azharites and their fellows, and with only the smallest of errors we'd be handing them the map, thought Stjepan.

"Stjepan," said Gilgwyr. "This is the best we can do."

Godewyn Red-Hand, as indeed the big man was called, had still not bothered to put any clothes on, but had stood there naked, his flanks heaving as though he'd run a few miles, his cock slowly deflating to swing long and limp between his muscular thighs as he had listened to the others talk. "Damn straight that we're the best you can do," he finally interjected with a low growl and a sneer. "Fuck the Gowers, fuck the Lamb, and fuck even the Hardees. My crew's as good as theirs, and better than any you'd try to get out of Newgate, and we ain't on the run, we're walking the West King's Road with our heads held high. And maybe *some* might not think it a smart play, but we got the balls to walk out into the Bale Mole." He gave himself a slow shake for emphasis, grinning at Stjepan with daggers in his eyes. "Absolutely fucking right, if the price is right, even if the company ain't. Past differences aside, I say, when there's money to be made. Business before pleasure, and all that."

"There's no pleasure here for you, Red-Hand," said Stjepan coldly.

"We'll see, we'll see, pleasure is where you fucking find it," Godewyn said. "Good to see you, too, Athairi. Now, let's talk about this little trip of yours, and about our pay and our shares." He tossed the bag of coins into the air and caught it with a hearty, self-satisfied laugh as his cock dripped onto the floor.

Stjepan pursed his lips in a half-smile, half-grimace. *This trip is about to get interesting*, he thought.

The Dawn Maiden came and went her way, announcing the coming of the 24th day of Emperium and taking the rain clouds with her, and the sun was high in the sky before any of the guests staying in the King's Hall stirred. Long days of rough travel, nights of fitful sleep on hard ground under tents and stars, and the shock and trauma of their sudden departure from Therapoli had culminated in bone-weary exhaustion for many of them, and soft pillows and full bellies of food and wine had offered an irresistible invitation to long, deep sleep.

Leigh might have been the only one of them to resist that call; but then, he never even entered the King's Hall, but instead remained overnight in the back of a wagon surrounded by hay bales, silently observing the comings and goings of the Inn's yards from beneath his hooded cowl. The Inn had grown quietest in the darkest hour right before the dawn, but even then he could hear a handful of drunken voices still raised in song from within the great hall, and the sounds of vigorous sex coming from an open window somewhere to his left. He wasn't really listening to anything outside his own head, however; he registered and catalogued the sounds and sights around him, but his attention was focused intently on a scratching and wriggling that seemed to be coming from right inside his own left ear, as though something very small, perhaps an insect or a spirit, was pressed up against his ear drum and trying to scratch its way through so that it could write its message directly into his brain. *Yes, yes,* he thought. *I know, I know: drown them all, they do not love me, they hate me, they deserve death, they deserve death.*

By mid-morning many groggy travelers had finally appeared from their lodgings to resume the road, and several wagon trains had already come and gone. Woats flittered in and out of the King's Hall, bearing food and water and other sundries, and then eventually Sir Helgi and Sir Holgar were the first to emerge from amongst its guests, blinking in surprise at the bright spring sun. They eventually wandered off into the great hall, and then reemerged after a time with Stjepan and Gilgwyr and a few Woats. The group toured some of the stable yards, and there was some pointing and negotiating and some coin changing hands, and slowly a lot more Woats were summoned and set to new tasks. The coach was brought out and swung around in front of the King's Hall, and two wagons were brought up behind it. Bales of hay, bags of oat, barrels of water and wine, crates and jugs, bed rolls, blankets, furs, tents, coils of rope, shovels and picks and all manner of tools were added to the wagons, even spare wheels and wooden planks and poles. Draft horses and burros were selected and either yoked to pull the wagons or tied to their rears to follow.

As the activity in the yard in front of the King's Hall increased, so did the number of their party that emerged to observe and wonder at the growing size of their caravan. The two women were the last to appear, the hoods of their cloaks hiding their faces. Flanked by the Urweds and the squires, they were carefully helped into the coach. Leigh finally stirred then, and slipped his Book of Dooms out of his vestments, his fingers stroking the cards. He closed his eyes, and cut the cards twice, then tapped once on the top of the deck. He flipped the top card, held it up in front of his face, and opened his eyes. It showed the profile of a man in barbaric and mismatched armor, holding a sword upright in one hand and a bared dagger held behind his back in the other. *The Knave of Swords,* he thought. *The calling card of cutthroats and assassins.* He lowered the card in time to see Stjepan and Gilgwyr walk out of the great hall. Godewyn and his pack of ruffians were right behind them, festooned with weapons and carrying packs slung over their shoulders.

Godewyn had a smug smirk on his face. Stjepan simply looked peeved. And Gilgwyr looked like he hadn't slept a wink either.

Leigh started to laugh quietly under his breath. "Ah," he said out loud to himself. "I think we're finally all here . . ."

With Sirs Helgi and Holgar in tow, Arduin walked up to the men approaching the caravan and, ignoring Gilgwyr and Godewyn, he addressed Stjepan angrily. "Sir Helgi informed me that you had made arrangements for additional help. Am I to understand it correctly that *these* are the men that you have hired to help us on our journey?"

"They are, Lord Arduin," said Stjepan. "This is —"

"Godewyn Red-Hand, at your service," interrupted Godewyn, and he gave an exaggerated and ill-formed bow, as did several of his men.

Arduin ignored the big man and fixed angry eyes on Stjepan. "These men are common bandits," he fumed.

Stjepan paused, a confused look on his face. "We're headed into the Bale Mole, my Lord, to dig into a dead man's barrow and rob it. Whom did you expect to help us?" he finally asked. Several of Godewyn's gang snickered at that.

Arduin looked as though he was about to strike Stjepan, and at the last second seemed to reconsider. He drew himself up and contemplated Stjepan coldly. "If any of them so much as sneezes in my sister's direction, I'll cut him in half," he finally declared.

Arduin turned and walked back to the rest of his knights and the coach.

Godewyn looked at Stjepan and Gilgwyr and raised an eyebrow. "We haven't even started this little expedition and already I'm tired of you lot talking about me and my crew in front of us as though we ain't even fucking here," he said. "And I think there's a part of this story that you lads neglected to spin when we were talking last night."

Stjepan and Gilgwyr looked at each other. Stjepan cleared his throat, and indicated Arduin with a nod. "He and his sister are our patrons, and they're coming along to . . . protect their investment," said Stjepan. Gilgwyr maintained a bland, blank look on his face.

Godewyn turned to watch Arduin mount his destrier, a toothy grin starting to spread across his face. "I've seen him fight in the tourneys, he and his brothers. That was years ago, but you don't forget quality. So you're taking a full-fledged champion knight of the High King's Court on a barrow run? And his sister?" Godewyn laughed heartily. "Oh, Black-Heart! And you told me there was no pleasure to be found on this trip!" He shook his head, chortling. "Fine with me. Some of the king's steel will be handy to have around, less bleeding for the rest of us to do. A treasure hunt like this takes a price in blood and flesh, and better theirs than ours." He leaned in and stage-whispered to them. "And I'm sure we'll find a use for the Lady, too . . ."

Godewyn sauntered off laughing at the sky as his crew started loading their goods onto the wagons, while an exasperated Stjepan watched.

Leigh appeared at his elbow. "So we're . . . ready . . . now?" he asked, barely able to contain his laughter.

Before he could answer, Stjepan's attention was drawn to the coach; Malia had opened the window shutter on the door and she beckoned to him once he saw her. He nodded and walked over.

Stjepan looked in through a dark curtain. In the shadows of the coach, Annwyn sat with the hood of her cloak still settled over her head. She locked eyes with him, appearing fatigued and testy, but more bemused than angry.

"You spoke last night of my safety. So I will be *safe* on the road and into the hills, protected by this lot, protected by you, map reader?" she asked him softly.

"With that map upon you, my Lady, your life is in danger no matter where you are," said Stjepan. "At least this way you will be rid of the map, once its purpose is fulfilled and Harvald's enchantment has no reason to linger."

Annwyn looked at him for a long moment, her dead eyes unreadable.

"And what is the purpose of a map to the barrow of an evil wizard?" she finally asked.

Stjepan looked at her blankly for a few moments. He withdrew from the window, and reached in to close the curtain.

CHAPTER EIGHTEEN
THE PLAIN OF FLOWERS

Azhararad. *Gladringer*. Those were not names that Godewyn had expected to hear when Gilgwyr and Black-Heart had gotten down to brass tacks. When he'd heard Gelber Woat calling out to him over the noise that the Countess was making that Gilgwyr of the Sleight of Hand in Therapoli was there looking for hard men for a trip into the Bale Mole, he hadn't figured it would be a barrow run. He'd figured that, like some he'd worked for, they needed protection while aiming for a secret meeting with strange folk from the mountains or the wild, wild west, as fit what he knew about Gilgwyr as a dealer in secrets and whispers; that would've been fine by him. Sometimes it was the eggs of the great Black Vultures up by Vulture Lake that a man might be after, prized by alchemists; for some, a chance to hunt for wyverns or wyrms and make their mark as hero-huntsmen; for others, a chance to sit on the great carved seat of what everyone called Geniché's Throne, looking out over the Vale of Barrows for a glimpse of the dead and the future.

But arguably those were for folks with a bit of imagination or ambition. For the average treasure hunter, it was a box of coin or some trinket rumored lost or buried up in the damned hills or the Wastes or the Vale, and of those artifacts there were countless options: the Horn of Palé Meffiré, that could summon ghostly knights from their graves; the three magic rings of Taran, ancient King of the Vale, that bound three of the four elements; the great black dragon-scale shield of Dyfyr, buried with him somewhere in the Vale, which no blade made by man could pierce or shatter. For other dreamers, it'd be one of the weapons of legend associated with the rough Danian west: the sword *Mhorismal*, the so-called Red Talon of the Wyvern King, a dark and barbarous blade that was said to drip poison, last seen in the Black Tower of Azharad; *Glimmerdras*, the sword of the Dragon King Petraeus of the Danias, last held by the traitor lord Brandeslas of Angharad and supposedly buried with him; *Bonebreaker*, the warhammer of King Cynan of Finleth, commander of the Daradjan forces that aided the Middle Kingdoms against Akkalion and the Empire at the Black Day Battle, lost in the Vale of Barrows by Rorik of Finleth in 1232. And on and on, up until the two at the top of the legend pile: *Gladringer*, the sword of the High Kings, forged by Gobelin to kill the Last Worm King; and *Ghavaurer*, the sword forged by Nymarga, the Devil Himself, and wielded by the Last Worm King until his last undying breath—the most cursed and evil thing made in the history of the Known World.

All of them were wild goose chases, as far as Godewyn was concerned, but smiling he took the coin and promises of the men who sought them, and smiling he led them up into the hills, and smiling he all too often picked their bodies clean when they ended up dead or dying through no fault of his own and despite all his best advice and efforts. *A fool gets what's coming to him*, Godewyn figured, and a lot of men were fools of one sort or another, particularly when they announced they knew some secret that had somehow escaped countless smarter men over the last thousand years. He'd been around, had Godewyn, not just into the bad places of the Bale Mole and the Wastes but up into the wild Highlands and the length and breadth of the Middle Kingdoms at least once or twice, and if he thought he knew anything it was how to know a man was a fool.

Godewyn had many ways to divide the world in his mind—*sharp* and *dull*; *eager cunt* and *closed cunt*; *strong* and *weak*; *lord* and *servant* and *free*; *dangerous* and *ignorable*—but above all else he'd always placed knowing who was a fool and who wasn't. Fools weren't usually dangerous on purpose; they tended to be dangerous by accident, all inadvertent-like. When he was young, he remembered being in a fortuneteller's shop with his mother, who had wanted a Reading for some reason or another. He remembered vividly the cards of the Book of Dooms that had been laid out on the table, and the image on the unnumbered Fool card had caught his eye and imagination in particular. The card had been decorated with gold leaf, with a band of writing in its ornamental borders that he could not read. But the image had stuck with him: a handsome young man wearing a jaunty coat and with a bag tied to the end of a stick and slung over his shoulder, the very picture of the casual, effortless world traveler, gazing up in joy at the bright sky . . . even as he was about to walk off a cliff. To be so intent on your destination and your dreams that you don't see the danger right in front of you; the idea had filled the young Godewyn with a kind of existential dread, and in the years since, he had seen its echo all too often in the mad and desperate faces that filled his end of the world.

He didn't care if a fool wanted to hire him; indeed, they were often easier to part from their coin than most. He just liked to identify the fools so he could minimize their danger to him and his crew. Godewyn liked to think he was a quick study, able to size up a man (or woman) in a glance or two. He liked to think it was what had kept him alive through some tough and hairy spots. Sitting in the back of a wagonload of supplies as their little caravan worked its way through faint trails north of the West King's Road and through the Scented Hills gave him plenty of time to observe his new companions. The knights were the easiest to read: brash, overconfident, born rulers and killers, masters of everything within arms' reach, typical of the Aurian specimens that he had encountered before in the east. The one called Helgi was the lead knight, and the ones named Holgar and Clodin both carried themselves like they'd one day take his place. The two brothers and the Theos and the squires were followers and crow fodder, as far as he was concerned. Godewyn hadn't lied when he said he remembered Lord Arduin from the Tournaments, even though it was a decade or more in the past; the future Baron of Araswell was born with a gift for swordplay, that was for sure, and now all that was left to figure out was whether he'd lost a step since Godewyn had last seen him fighting in the melee. A dark cloud hovered over him, but it occurred to Godewyn that a man like Arduin might not notice.

The two women piqued his interest, of course, but they were locked up nice and safe in the fancy coach and getting past all those knights was a high hurdle. That neither bothered nor offended Godewyn too much, he figured that on a trip like this there was plenty of time to figure out if they were the eager sort or the closed sort; indeed, he was already fig-uring closed, and unlike some men he didn't see much point in chasing after a closed cunt or trying to make it something it wasn't, so he was happy to save his energy and spend it elsewhere until opportunity to revisit availed itself. He still wasn't sure what the magician's name was, no one seemed to like to talk about or even to him; but the magician was obvi-ously insane and obviously dangerous, so he went pretty quickly to the top of Godewyn's *Do Not Trust and Kill As Soon As Possible* list and, having been so quickly and safely defined, was promptly forgotten.

That left Gilgwyr, Black-Heart, and the young Erim for him to figure out.

Being a new (at least, to Godewyn) companion to the other two known individuals, Erim was the most interesting to him; the youth was cagey and guarded, a wall around him to prevent anyone from getting too close. He seemed confident on his horse and wore his weapons with practiced ease: a pair of point daggers and a cut-and-thrust rapier. A duelist and city fighter, then, and probably quick; he moved with an easy physical grace and seemed to watch everyone and everything with sharp, wary eyes under a furrowed brow. *Hard to surprise, unless you're on the inside of the wall*, Godewyn thought. *But then aren't we all.* Godewyn knew how to handle city fighters, they were always surprised at how fast he could move for a man of his size, but there was something about Erim he couldn't quite put a finger on, something that made him a bit uneasy that pushed Erim toward the top of the danger list. Maybe it was simply his proximity to Gilgwyr and Black-Heart, who were most definitely in the dangerous cat-egory. He hadn't figured either Gilgwyr, who he'd thought a sharp canny-too-canny operator in their previous dealings, or Black-Heart, who still made Godewyn nervous precisely because he *couldn't* figure out what his real game really was, as fools.

But here they were, saying they were going after the Barrow of Azharad and the sword *Gladringer*. So fools, then, the both of them, and dangerous fools at that.

But he had to admit he'd been wrong before on rare occasion.

"Whatcha think, chief?" came a voice to one side. He glanced over at "Handsome" Pallas Quinn, a lean, wiry dark-haired man with a hand-some scar running down across his face. Handsome must've spotted him sizing up their employers and companions, and was looking at him with an expectant grin. Godewyn glanced over the rest of his crew. Caider Ross was driving the wagon that Godewyn rode in, glancing back over his shoulder to hear his response. Caider was from Westmark, and once upon a time had been a city fighter, discreetly fleeing a murder writ; now he was a veteran jack-of-all-trades, who'd been practically everywhere and could kill with practically anything. In addition to Handsome, golden-red-haired and -bearded Giordus Roame sprawled his big-boned frame out in this wagon, as did Garrett Akin, a short man from down near Volmore that they all called Too Tall on account of him being so fucking short. Too Tall was sharpening a long wicked dirk with a whetstone. Isham Wall with his shaved head drove the other wagon behind them, the newest addition to their hearty company, with Cole Thimber, a dumb brute of a man that Godewyn knew he could trust to follow any order, sitting next to him. Gilgwyr and the magician had settled into the back of the wagon that Isham was driving, apparently feeling it more suitable than continuing to ride the rumble seats of the Lady's coach.

He looked his crew over and felt pride, knowing them for what they were: one of the hardest lots in the Danias, roustabouts and cutthroats, rogues and rutterkins, wag-halters and thugs all, no deed too low, no crime too ugly to contemplate, every single one of them loyal and dependable to the bitter dark end that they all knew was coming for them.

He grinned back at Handsome. He knew exactly what they wanted to hear.

"No worries, boys, we got this lot covered," he said easily.

Those that heard him laughed quietly and nodded to each other as he turned back to stare at Black-Heart and Erim in the lead, his eyes narrowing.

Stjepan aimed to get them across the Scented Hills and into the trackless Plain of Flowers so that they could stay off both the West King's Road and the Road of the Mark, which ran up and around the Plain of Flowers and marked the onetime limit of the wood of An-Athair. As they followed the shepherd's paths through the gently rolling hills, Erim could occasionally feel the eyes of the newcomers tracking her as they passed each other. No more or less than she expected or was used to, particularly the faintly curious stare of their crew captain, Godewyn. She knew that stare well, the one that asked *and what, pray tell, are you?*

She measured them the same way they were measuring her, though she felt she managed it a bit more discreetly. She catalogued the weapons they wore, the weapons they hid, their scars, their missing teeth, their haphazard but effective-looking gear. She pinpointed the one who looked like he'd fight left-handed (the one named Garrett); the one with a bum knee and every-so-slightly limping gait (the one they called Too Tall); the street duelist (Caider Ross); the one she shouldn't find herself alone with (the big scary one with the dead eyes they called Thimber, who just smelled wrong). She found herself intrigued a bit by Godewyn; under the greasy, unwashed hair and rough-hewn stubble he was handsome enough in a brutish sort of way, all peasant muscles and a cock-sure swagger that called some part of her to attention.

But she was surprised that the primary response Godewyn invoked in her was a kind of sadness, as he and his crew seemed little more than uncouth, country cousins to the late departed Guilford and *his* crew. And Guilford and his men had themselves been in turn little more than down-market versions of the great city crews of Therapoli. She had no doubt that Godewyn and his crew were a dangerous lot, destined for the same Hells as most of the men to whom Stjepan had introduced her, but there was also no doubt in her mind that they utterly lacked the glorious delinquency that marked the Gilded Lady or Bad Mowbray, Petterwin Grim or Mina the Dagger, Jon Deering or Red Rob Asprin. *Give me true city folk any day, and not these pale country echoes*, she thought glumly.

That sadness was compounded by the sneaking suspicion that the fate of Godewyn and his crew would be the same as Guilford and his; she was beginning to suspect, in fact, that being a friend and traveling companion to Stjepan Black-Heart was a fast way to an early and unfortunate end.

This somewhat morose thought was forgotten when she crested a final rise as lead scout and saw the beginnings of the Plain of Flowers ahead of them.

In the hills they had been riding and rolling through a landscape of shrubs and brush and tall grasses, with the occasional copse or a lone tree silhouetted against the sky, a gentler, greener version of the hills of the Manon Mole. Signs of spring were everywhere, with trees and flowers budding or blooming. But ahead of them, the green hills sloped down and leveled off into a vast rising plain that filled the western horizon with myriad shades of white, mostly white with dots of yellow, orange, pink, and red—flowers, flowering shrubs, even occasionally flowering trees, as far as the eye could see. She reined in her horse and stood in the saddle, staring at the sight. Stjepan rode up next to her and stopped. They said nothing for a while. From their spot on the hill, she could see hilltop castles to their north and their south, each about three or four miles from where they had emerged from the hills. She thought she could make out what would be the West King's Road leading to the castle to their south, and there was a pair of roads, one minor and one major, that cut cross across the vista in front of them. The minor road led up to the castle to their north, and also seemed to mark more or less the starting point of the flowering fields. The major road was a dark line that ran through the field across the horizon, north to south.

"The Plain of Flowers," she said, when she finally found her voice. "I always thought it was . . . I don't know, just an expression, you know? An old bard's tale, the 'fields that never lose their color' . . ."

"No, I'm afraid the name is a sad testament to the lack of imagination in our modern language," said Stjepan drily. "In Athairi this is the *Caewyr drum Genichallach*, the Bed of the Earth Goddess; in old Maelite it was *Mathene d'am'avargas Dessine*, which is more or less the Place of Drowning Dreams; in old Éduinan the *palaza rememorigas de Paradiso*, the Memory-

Place of Paradise. But nowadays in the Middle Tongue, we call it the Plain of Flowers. Since, after all, that is what it is. Over thirty miles of them, at its widest point."

Erim shook her head. "And they're always in bloom, like in the tales?"

"Yes, even in the dead of winter, though their colors tend to run more toward white and pale pinks when it's cold," said Stjepan. "Snow never seems to stick on the Plain. You can be struggling through a blizzard and then suddenly find yourself up to your waist in flowers, with a warm breeze like a kiss upon your face, and you know you've stumbled into the Plain."

"But . . . how?" Erim asked. "Why?"

Stjepan shrugged. "The Athairi believe that there are still many places where the earth remembers its departed Queen and Goddess, where Geniché's touch still lingers. In the case of the Plain of Flowers, at its center is a circle of *menhirs*, standing stones; a place of great power in both our world and the Otherworld." He reached into one of his satchels and pulled out his spyglass, which he handed to Erim. She brought it to her eye and gazed at the distant fields.

"It's beautiful," Erim whispered.

"Aye," said Stjepan. "But it's an old place, touched by the divine, and man is ultimately not welcome where we're about to go. Nothing grows but the flowers; if you try planting crops, the flowers just choke them out. Farmers have tried the plough, fire, even poisoning and salting the earth, and nothing works for long; the flowers always come back. A trail disappears, even as you're making it. It took years of work by laborers and magicians alike to get the North Road to stick, and to build the site of the Tournament of Flowers. Mind you, that's great for someone who wants to get lost, and that should be useful for us should someone decide to come ask us questions." He pointed to the castle to the south, and then to the one to the north. "That castle astride the West King's Road on our left is Burnwall, held by Crown Prince Hektor of Erid Dania. And the other one on our right is Hagenwall, held by Prince Fionne, the youngest of the sons of Eolred. If any of their watchmen are paying attention, they'll be able to see us coming out of the hills and making our way out into the Plain, and some overeager captain might decide to take an interest in why a small caravan chose to cross the hills rather than take the roads."

"We won't be able to move that fast, not with the wagons, and not through all that brush," said Erim. "A troop of horse will have no trouble catching up with us."

"The way through the Plain of Flowers is easier than you might think, and we'll have a head start, and as long as we get deep into the thickets before the sun sets we should be okay. There's many a bandit that's used it to throw off the sheriff; but there's also many a man that's wandered in circles in there and then just disappeared. It's worse than the *fae* woods; and it gets worse the further in you go." He reached into one of his satchels and removed a dry mariner's compass, a small brasswork wonder that cost quite a pretty penny. She'd never seen him use it if they had roads to follow.

"How far in are we going?"

"We'll start heading due west, but to get where we're going, we're going to eventually cut right across the middle."

Erim grimaced and nodded. "Of course we are," she said with a sigh.

Arduin fought it, but the pang of nostalgia and regret came hard and sudden into his heart and throat as they rode down into the Plain of Flowers. If he had his bearings correct, they would be passing just north of the site where the Tournament of Flowers was held each year. It was the first of the five Great Tournaments of the tourney season (the others being the Tournaments of Stone, Horns, and Gavant, followed last by the Grand Tourney hosted by the High King on the fields north of the capital, Therapoli Magni), and though it was still almost two months away Arduin was sure that there would already be groundskeepers and laborers beginning to prepare the site.

Over a decade had passed since his great glory, the pinnacle achievement of his life to date, his crowning as Champion of the Tournament of Flowers in 1459. Those had been heady days. He'd been doing better and better in each passing tourney, first learning the ropes as squire and then as a young knight testing himself against a great generation's champions. Old-time tourney watchers liked to claim that the early '50s had been the peak of knighthood in the Middle Kingdoms in living memory, and Arduin was inclined to believe it. He'd squired for Sir Bueves, who became champion for King Colin of Dainphalia, at the Tournament of Gavant in 1454, and for Arbier, Baron of Karsiris, in 1455 when Arbier won the Grand Tourney. Up close he'd seen some of the greatest jousters and swordsmen of the day: Sir Penwyn son of Penwyn; Sir Naeras Orenge of Tamatra; Sir Clodin Torgis, of Duke Tenreuth's vassals; Sir Lars Urgoar; Lord Gier Merislas, brother to King Fionne of Umis; Sir Mowbray, Lord of Gil-More; Sir Hec, Lord of Valenwall; Sir Gerard, Lord of the Sare; Wallis the Elder, Baron of Misal Ruth; the young Porloss, Earl of Orliac; Orphin the Bull, Earl of An-Athair; and the Lis Red brothers: the Grand Duke Owen and his brother Austin, Lord Sunhawk. He'd even lost to a few of them. Champions all, of one Tournament or another, building rivalries and striving to outdo each other, leading up to the Grand Tourney of 1456, when for the first time that anyone could remember they were all present in the lists. There were even rumors afterwards that Uthella of Uthmark had competed in that Tourney in disguise. And it was Derrek, Watchtower King of Warwark, who walked away the clear victor and with the best claim to be the greatest knight of his generation.

That had been Arduin's first experience competing in the Grand Tourney. He'd lost in the first round of the jousts, against Sir Naeras Orenge, an honorable loss. In the melee he'd gotten to the third round, finally losing against Lord Austin Lis Red. He could still remember the heady rush, the roar of the crowds, the power of the assembled Court, the pride of his father and younger brothers. He'd sworn to himself that he'd win the Grand Tourney eventually. The next two years were off years for aficionados of the tournament circuit, as they were marred by scandal (Uthella's victory at the Tournament of Flowers and subsequent banishment), disaster (the death of Elgias, Crown Prince of Angowrie at the

Tournament of Stones, and a huge fire at the Grand Tourney), and a passing of the torch, as many in that generation of great competitors decided to step back after Derrek's resounding victory. Into that lull stepped Arduin and hundreds of other eager young knights, and he won the melee twice, once at the Tournament of Stones and once at the Tournament of Horns, but then he'd always been better with the sword than the lance and his jousting kept him from being crowned Champion. Finally it had come, in 1459 only miles to the south from where they were now, when he'd won both melee and joust and been crowned the Champion of Flowers.

He'd been so sure it was going to be his year, the year that his sister also happened to come of age and be eligible for selection as a Tourney Queen. His father had chosen to debut her at the Tournament of Gavant, where she'd handily won against all the assembled flowers of eastern Auria, and so she'd gone into the Grand Tourney as one of the four Queens of the Tournaments. Everyone knew she would win Queen of the Grand Tourney; she'd outshone her three rivals the way the sun outshines a campfire. *How perfect, how fun*, Arduin had thought. *My sister the Queen of the Grand Tourney, and I shall be her Champion.* And he'd won the melee, twelve rounds against some of the best swordsmen he'd ever faced, including Sir Bueves, Wallis the Elder, *and* Wallis the Young. But the Wheel of Fortune turned against him, and he'd lost in the seventh round of the jousts to Sir Shale Harlowe, a Dain Danian knight in the service of the Lord of Hingriff and the Earl of Tamatra. He shouldn't have been ashamed; Sir Shale lasted to the eleventh round, and over the next few years he would be a Champion at both the Tournament of Flowers and of Stone, proving himself to be one of the best knights in all the Danias and going on to win great renown in the feuds between Tamatra and Hartford and on campaign with King Derrek.

But at the time it had felt like a crushing blow, and the next year Arduin had been unfocused and off his game. And then the year after that had come the scandal at the Tournament of Gavant, and their fall from grace, and he had not been to a Tournament since the Grand Tourney that year; his last time in the lists, with a lance in his hand. *Blood everywhere, dying blue eyes staring up at him, the silent shock of the crowd, and somewhere someone was laughing . . .*

He had been riding, as had been his practice when the roads and fields allowed it, on the left side of his sister's carriage, so that she might speak to him should the fancy strike her, though as far as he could tell she'd spent most of their journey in fitful silence, sliding in and out of dreams and reveries. Ironbound's hooves picked their way through a sea of white clover flower, red poppies, white and pink peonies, and white lily-of-the-valleys as the carriage and its team laid a less discriminate trail, treading roughshod over the brush.

"Brother," came her voice from the carriage. Startled out of his remembrances, he turned and saw her face in the carriage window. The sight of her brought him crashing back to earth. "This is one of the most beautiful places in the Known World, and should bring back happy memories for you, and yet you seem burdened with nothing but sadness," she said. He could not read her tone and he searched her face for a moment, but it remained curiously blank.

"Beauty has filled many a man with sadness, dear sister," he finally said with a tight smile. And then he spurred his horse forward.

The afternoon wore on, and they'd put about eight miles between them and the Scented Hills and were crossing the North Road and up the rise of the plain when Stjepan and Erim heard a sharp whistle from the rear of the caravan. They wheeled their horses about and rode back past the coach and Arduin's knights to find Godewyn and his men sitting up alert in the two rear wagons, slowly unlimbering crossbows as the wagons rolled forward.

Stjepan pulled in and paced Cúlain-mal with Godewyn's wagon while Erim rode past to the rear. Stjepan and Godewyn exchanged glances, and Godewyn nodded back toward the hills. "We're being followed," Godewyn said, a grin on his face.

Stjepan grunted and pivoted his horse around to join Erim in surveying the land behind them. As he pulled up beside her, she was already pointing at what appeared to be a group of dark specks crossing across the Old Wood Road at the limits of their vision, following the exact same track they had used coming down out of the hills. He pulled out his spyglass and trained it on the dark specks for a moment in silence. The late afternoon sun was behind them to the west, and the distant hillsides to the east were bathed in light. A light wind buffeted their ears. Bees flew around them in small numbers, and one would occasionally come to investigate them.

"Horsemen?" Erim finally asked, uncertainty in her voice as she shooed a bee away. "Kind of hard to tell from this distance, though thankfully they stand out against the hills and the flowers of the plains."

"Yes. I'd say a small company, maybe twenty or thirty or so. Maybe someone that picked up our trail at Woat's Inn?" Stjepan said, lowering the spyglass. "Could be a patrol of knights from Hagenwall or Burnwall, but I'd have expected them to be coming from the castles directly, not be following our trail out of the hills . . ." He trailed off, squinting at the distant castle of Hagenwall, which could still be seen as a small silhouette against the sky to their east, north of where the horsemen were emerging from the hills. He raised the spyglass to his eye again. "Fuck," he said after a moment.

"What?" she asked, squinting toward Hagenwall.

"Movement."

He handed her the spyglass and she stared at Hagenwall until she saw it as well. A line of horsemen streaming down the road from the castle. "Shit," she said. "A second patrol, riding out to join the first?"

They stared at the two small lines of dark specks coming down out of the hills.

"They won't be able to catch up with us before the sun is down, and if we're lucky and the clear sky holds, we'll be able to move for a while in the evening without lighting torches, using the stars to light our way," Stjepan said, glancing up at the skies. "Well, I suppose we should tell everyone to speed up a bit. Take rear guard, and keep an eye on those columns if you can." He wheeled Cúlain-mal and rode off, leaving Erim staring gloomily at their distant pursuers.

PART TWO: ON THE ROAD OF SWEAT AND TEARS

"Fantastic," she muttered to herself, then brought the spyglass to her eye again.

Moving through the flowering fields and brush of the plain was easier than Erim had hoped it might be, and some sort of luck seemed to hold for them and the coaches and wagons did not get stuck or snagged. Beneath the flowers and brush the earth seemed smooth and largely unbroken, with rough spots well telegraphed. There was an unnatural quality to the Plain, and from more than just the flowers themselves; it was as though some great magic or perhaps the gods themselves had some design in mind in making it the way it was. As the Dusk Maiden rose and Helios set in the west, the skies remained clear and by star- and partial moonlight they wound their way through a dark blue landscape. The Spring Moon had passed and the Axe Moon had risen, but it was only showing a small sliver of itself, not yet even a quarter full, and Erim kept wishing they could light torches and lanterns. She was afraid Cúlain-mer would trip and stumble in the bramble, but her horse seemed content to pick its way in the evening dark as though it knew where it was going.

Stjepan had consulted his compass and turned them more northwesterly once the sun went down and they were no longer visible to their pursuers, in the hopes that the change of direction might throw off those behind them. They were moving inexorably upward at a slight but noticeable incline, as though the plain were actually a hill and it was slowly leading them up to some final destination. She lost track of the number of hours they'd been moving in the dark, but at least the Midnight Star had not yet risen when there was a muted hue and cry from up ahead. A low ridge presented itself as the plain's slope began to crest, and she urged her horse up and over the first genuine obstacle that they'd encountered. The coach and wagons had found a small break in the ridge for an entry path to ease their way over to the top but she was able to ride up the ridge side without too much of a worry. But a shiver went down her spine when she crested the ridge and saw the *menhirs* silhouetted up ahead of them against the night sky. *My horse knew exactly where it was going*, she thought.

The caravan slowed and circled around in a large, pleasant meadow set halfway between the standing stones at the top of the rise and the eastern edge of the small ridge that she had just crossed. From that crest of the plain's summit they would have a relatively unobstructed view of the lands back to their east. The squires and Godewyn and his crew began laying out the camp, putting the Ladies' coach in the center. The two wagons formed walls to the south and east, and the picket line of horses on the north-western side of the camp between the coach and the stone circle formed the third leg of the triangle around the coach. They weren't bothering to break out the tents; the sense that they were being followed was too keen upon them. She found Stjepan and Arduin standing in the middle of the fields and arguing.

". . . you've led us right to the standing stones," Arduin was saying angrily. "This is a place of the Forbidden Gods."

"The Old Gods, perhaps, but not the Forbidden," Stjepan said.

"There is little difference to a true devotee of the Divine King," Arduin said sharply.

"This is Hallorenge, my Lord, and it is a sacred place to the Old Religion, and though the Nameless might scheme to corrupt and taint it, they have ever met with failure in trying," Stjepan replied calmly. "I hope our pursuers would not think that we would take refuge near a place of power, and even if they discover us here that they would think twice about attacking us if that is their intent."

"But . . . but we will be in danger here from the stones themselves!" Arduin said.

"No, my Lord," said Stjepan. "The *menhirs* may be rune-marked, and full of ancient wisdom, but the stones can do us no harm unless they were to topple over on top of us, and I would suggest that is highly unlikely. They were standing here, already old, when the first Danians and Daradjans came to this land, and have stood unchanged for over two thousand years.

We will not enter the stone circle itself except as a last resort and if we do we will enter within it with reverence and respect, and so should have no reason to fear."

Arduin looked skeptically at the Athairi. "What is this place for?" asked Arduin.

"Depends on who you are, I suppose. Magicians often come here to tap the magical power in the site and perform rituals here. The *fae* and followers of the Old Religion come here to make offerings to Geniché, the Queen of the Earth and the Dead, and to Yhera, the Queen of Heaven. It's one of at least four stone circles that are thought to be somehow interconnected, there's Hallorenge here, and then the labyrinth and standing stones at Cullrenge by the Temple of the Hunt, and then a labyrinth and standing stones at Taraden in the Tiria Wold, and supposedly another labyrinth that might have some standing stones at Falrenge, an isle in the murk of the Tirris Mire," Stjepan said, waving over his shoulder over to their north and west. "No one knows what they're for, really, but folks tales say there's something special to them if you do all the labyrinths in the right order and know the right rituals."

Erim could feel Arduin's frustration, but in the end he just sighed and shook his head in fatigue. "Peasant superstitions," he said under his breath. "Fine. We shall make our camp here. At least we're on a hilltop."

Stjepan nodded and turned. "No fires!" he called out to Godewyn and the squires. "At least not yet."

"We're not fucking morons, Black-Heart," came Godewyn's snarled reply. He and his men were already laying down quivers of bolts and arrows, and propping up long spears and long-hafted bills and poleaxes beside the wagons. Erim could see Caider and Giordus setting up firepots and oil-soaked torches; once they were discovered some quick firelight would come in handy. Several of Arduin's knights were taking up positions within the circled wagons, marking their chosen defensive posts, and the Urweds stood guard over Annwyn's coach, though their narrowed eyes were mostly on Godewyn's band.

Stjepan waved idly, which seemed to make Godewyn even angrier, and then he and Erim and Arduin, joined by Sir Helgi and Gilgwyr, walked to the crest line. The five of them crouched, looking out over the eastern Plain of Flowers.

"We've put in some good miles today after the late start," Stjepan said.

"Almost thirty. The Plain of Flowers is almost as smooth as a good road," grunted Sir Helgi, his hands brushing into the flowers and petals around them. "It's like the flowers are a bed, waiting for you to lie down on them."

"The Bed of the Earth Goddess," Erim said quietly.

Stjepan grinned at her in the dark. "Aye, but don't fall asleep directly on the flowers. Folk tales say they sometimes strangle people in their sleep, and pull them into the earth."

Arduin shook his head. "*Peasant superstitions,*" he repeated through gritted teeth. "Though I admit that we have few options, I will nonetheless reiterate my objections that this hardly seems a safe place for us to stop, on top of a place of *fae* power."

Gilgwyr and Stjepan glanced at each other in the evening gloom. "We shouldn't have to worry about the *fae* here, my Lord Arduin," said Stjepan. "What we have to worry about is whoever's following us out of the east." And he pointed off the rise down across the dark plain.

"I don't see any torches," Gilgwyr commented lightly. "Or campfires. I suspect that doesn't bode well."

"No," said Stjepan. "Two columns of horsemen, neither of which wants us to see them, apparently. They were a few hours behind us, but on this plain and without heavy wagons to slow them, they could well close the gap and be on us soon if they're pursuing us in the dark. Our main hope will lie in what cover the night gave us, to disguise the direction we were headed. If we're lucky, since we didn't turn toward Hallorenge until after the sun set they will pass to our south looking for us, thinking we were making for Hingriff, or perhaps turning off to the south toward Rosemont. We should post lookouts to all four points of the compass, but look mostly to the south-east, from whence we came, and the south."

And so Erim found herself with Stjepan and Gilgwyr, lying on a soft bed of flowers with a vantage point of the approaching dark plains, bows strung, and quivers set beside their swords. Erim set Stjepan's spyglass next to her bow but in the dark it was of little use. Three of Godewyn's men had been dispatched to three other lookout spots, and the rest of their caravan was waiting within the wagon circle, Arduin leading the heavily armored last line of defense around the Ladies' coach.

The three of them lay there silently, just watching and listening. The wind had picked up a bit, occasionally buffeting them on the exposed ridge. They could occasionally hear the tinkle of metal on metal from within the camp, or the muted whinny of one of the horses on the picket line. She hoped the sounds weren't carrying far, but it appeared as though they were on the highest point of the plain and she winced every time there was a noise from behind them. But for all the tension she felt, it was a beautiful night; the Celestial Path, the Star Road of heroes through the sky, was bright and clearly visible. She was about to ask Stjepan to point out the Star Signs on the Wheel of the Heavens, when he raised a hand. "There," he whispered. "Did you hear that?"

She shook her head, then froze when she heard a distant yell brought their way by the wind from out of the dark plains in front of them. She strained to listen. For a long moment there was nothing else and she began to wonder if she'd imagined it.

Then came the sharp ring of metal on metal, then again, and someone screamed, and a low hunting horn gave an ominous blast.

The sounds grew and built on each other; horses neighing and men screaming and yelling, clattering thuds and sharp rings, orders being barked, fading in and out as the wind ebbed and flowed and changed direction. But in the dark there was nothing to see. A phantom battle was occurring somewhere below them on the plain, its sounds floating up to their vantage spot on the ridge.

And for some reason that made it even more terrifying to Erim than if she could plainly see it.

"What the fuck is going on?" she finally hissed at Stjepan when she couldn't take it any longer. She felt him shrug next to her.

"How should I know? I'm guessing they're about a mile or two from us, whoever they are," he whispered back. "Some of the Erid King's men, for sure, as we saw them coming down from Prince Fionne's hold at Hagenwall; but then who the others might be . . ."

"Perhaps they're squabbling over the bounty," offered Gilgwyr with a snicker. "Surely the Court will have offered a reward?"

"The High Priest of the Public Temple in Therapoli is dead," whispered Stjepan. "Whoever has the honor of catching us will have a thousand priests praying for their safe entry into Heaven when they die. But if that is not reward enough for the faithful, I don't doubt that they threw in some gold crowns, as well."

They mulled that over in silence, listening to the sounds of the battle. The rings and cries slowly became less frequent, and then faded entirely into the wind. Several long minutes passed as they waited. Erim could feel tightness in her chest from holding her breath for so long and she realized she was gripping the hilt of her rapier so hard her knuckles and fingers were visibly white in the starlit blue-black darkness. She forced herself to relax, to breath normally, and for a time that was all she concentrated on.

There was a long, low call from the horn. Then silence again. Then after several minutes the horn sounded again.

"It's a rally signal, the knights of Erid Dania use that call," Stjepan whispered. "The Erid Prince is gathering his forces; they're the victors, presumably, though the Goddess only knows who they were fighting."

"I wonder if that is good for us or bad for us," said Gilgwyr.

"Little we can do about it, other than watch and wait," Stjepan replied, shrugging again.

Long minutes passed, and then Erim saw a small light appear, a torch sputtering to life some distance away. Two miles away? Maybe three miles, or even four? She found it hard to gauge distance in the dark of night. Other torches were lit, a growing group of small lights out on the darkened plain. Some of the lights were in constant motion, circling and milling about, so it was difficult to count them, but Erim guessed there were at least thirty of them. Her breathing slowed and became more measured. She slid an arrow out and nocked it.

"That's what, twenty, thirty horsemen?" she asked.

"If they are the Prince's men, as I suspect, then they'll be in groups of three and one man will be holding a torch for two others," Stjepan said quietly.

"Bad for us," said Gilgwyr glumly.

"No, I rather think good for us," said Stjepan. "If they knew where we were and were going to come at us, they'd have done so without lights in the dark, as they did with whoever they fought first. They don't care if anyone sees them now."

The lights seemed to spread out for a bit, in ever-widening circles, for long minutes. *They're searching for something; the enemy they fought? Or our tracks?* she thought. Finally the horn sounded again, and the lights came back into a tighter group, and then started moving off back toward the east.

They all let out a sigh of relief. "Good for us," said Gilgwyr, with a sense of surprised finality, and they all started to get up.

"Aye, but don't let anyone light any fires," said Stjepan. "You can see how visible they are from a distance out here on the Plain. Tell Godewyn to cut his watch in half, but keep a man at each of the cardinal points all night." He hefted a bow and slid the strap for a quiver of arrows over his head and shoulder so it could hang across his back.

"So where the fuck are you going?" asked Erim.

"I'm going to go see who lost that fight," Stjepan said. He grinned and she could see his white teeth reflecting starlight. "I'll be back in a few hours. Don't wait up." And with that he slid over the side of the ridgeline and disappeared out into the dark of the plain.

Stjepan moved through the fields of flowers swiftly, the night landscape illuminated in his eyes in shades of silver and blue and black thanks to an

Incantation of Seeing. He used the bearing of *Nisanu*, the sign of the Ram currently in the Twelfth House of the Celestial Wheel, and a cluster of ancient Düréan heroine-stars that lingered to the sign's south as markers to keep him on line with where they'd seen the torches out on the plain. But not so swiftly, being wary of observation and ambush, and he was briefly distracted by a great swarm of fireflies that danced in the night, so it took perhaps a half hour for him to reach the general area and find the first corpse. The dead man was stretched out in the flowers, his chest rent by a great piercing blow. *Lance*, thought Stjepan.

It took him twenty minutes of searching to the west to find the next bodies, a group of four spread out over a hundred yards or so. *Lance, sword or axe, sword, and lance*, he thought. *All run down from behind, two of them finished when they were on the ground.* It took him forty minutes to find what were most certainly the rest of them, as they weren't where he expected them to be and he had to widen his search circle; it looked like the defenders had tried to swing back toward the east and head back for the Scented Hills, only to get caught between two sets of attackers. He found fourteen dead men and three dead horses, most of them clustered before a stand of flowering trees but a few scattered inside the copse and a couple that had made it past the trees before they fell. There was a tight cluster of six bodies, almost back to back, just before the trees. *The last stand of the main group*, Stjepan speculated. *Or prisoners who had surrendered and then were summarily slaughtered.* The horses looked like they'd been lanced, either on purpose or by accident; only one hit had been instantly fatal, the other two horses had been put out of their misery afterwards.

He turned each man over so he could look at their faces, a dagger in one hand in case any of them were faking it. Some of them wore hoods or masks and he had to peel them away to see who they were. In life they would have looked tough, surly, mean, intimidating. In death they looked startled, scared, anguished, pained. Most of them had a familiar, familial set to the lips and eyes. Their weapons were largely left wherever they fell: a mix of broadswords and hangers and hunting swords, falchions and axes, perhaps a spear or two that would have passed for a lance for this motley crew. A few crossbows were scattered here and there, probably of minimal use in a horseback battle by starlight. The bodies appeared to be unlooted. They were mostly dressed in dark leathers and roughhewn, patched clothing, with brigandine jacks, plate cuirasses, or mail hauberks slipped over or under the leather clothes. *Definitely points to Danian knights and sergeants out of Hagenwall under Prince Fionne as the attackers; Fionne's men never loot the dead unless they are enemy knights, he considers it beneath them. But they took the horses that survived.*

He turned one man over, and underneath the man's hood, sopping with blood, Stjepan saw long straggly black hair, and a patchy growth along his chin and mouth, and the same curled lip and a slightly crossed set to the eyes as so many of the others, now frozen in death. A mail hauberk had been slipped over his jacket of patched, undyed leather. He'd taken a blow to the back of the head, and another to his gut that appeared to have ruptured skin and organs even though the mail had held.

I remember you, Stjepan thought grimly.

Godewyn had fallen asleep in the back of one of the two wagons on a pile of boxes and chests, a cloak pulled over him and his head nestled against a folded tent. He slept fitfully, his dreams filled with odd visions of beautiful women walking amongst fields of white flowers and standing stones, laughing at him. He awoke suddenly, sensing a presence nearby, and his fingers closed over the hilt of his dagger as his eyes widened and darted about. He could see the dark, bundled shapes of Caider Ross and Giordus Roame still sleeping on the other side of the wagon, and then his eyes settled on Stjepan casually sitting next to him to his right, leaning against the wagon's sideboard and looking off into the distance. Godewyn blinked once or twice, the grip on his dagger hilt tightening, and then he forced himself to relax.

"Nineteen dead Woats out there in the flowers," said Stjepan.

"You don't say," said Godewyn groggily. He rubbed his eyes and sat up to prop himself against the sideboard, squinting a bit to look at Stjepan.

"Now I suppose one or two might have gotten away, but by all appearances Prince Fionne Thurias had led almost ninety of his household knights and sergeants out into the field, having spotted the Woats riding into the no-man's land of the Plain of Flowers and in the bright of day. They don't get many chances to kill Woats outright these days, normally the elders are far too clever about hiding their business. But I don't think Gelber had much choice, we were moving too fast and they didn't know where we were going, he had to act hastily and move in the open. Prince Fionne is a young man, sharp, and eager for more experience of war and battle, and a passel of Woats out on a raid would've got his blood going. So I think they bottled them up pretty tight. Leaving nineteen dead Woats," said Stjepan. He studied the stars for a moment. "*Nineteen.* What does that number say to you?"

"I don't follow," said Godewyn, flat and quiet.

"Nineteen Woats," said Stjepan. "I mean, don't get me wrong, the Woats are a fearsome brood, murderers and rapists and cutthroats for a thousand years, with the blood of the Wyvern King running in their veins. But I don't believe for a second that Gelber Woat would have been stupid enough to send only nineteen of his kinsmen against a Tourney Champion, seven knights in full kit, two squires, an enchanter, Gilgwyr of the Sleight of Hand, myself, Erim, and Godewyn Red-Hand and his band of butchers. There's twenty-one of us. We actually outnumbered them."

He leaned in closer, fixing his gaze on Godewyn's narrowed eyes. "Unless maybe Gelber Woat was expecting the odds to be different when his kinsmen actually caught up with us," said Stjepan, almost in a whisper. "Unless he was thinking the odds would be more like twenty-six to fourteen in his favor, with the bonus of an inside job giving his lot the element of surprise and a lot of us dead before we knew what was happening."

A slow grin spread over Godewyn's face. "I'm sure I don't know what you mean, Black-Heart," he said.

"Keep it that way, Red-Hand," said Stjepan. "Do your job. Get paid. Go home alive. Yeah?"

"Oh, Black-Heart, really, must we do this?" Godewyn said, and opened his mouth to say something else when he heard a whisper even closer, right in his left ear.

"Do your job. Get paid. Go home alive," whispered Gilgwyr, pressed up behind him from the other side of the wagon sideboard and nestling his cheek against Godewyn's. Godewyn froze, his bowels suddenly clenching. He could feel the light touch of cold hard steel against his throat. He and Stjepan stared at each other for several heartbeats as he felt Gilgwyr breathe against his neck. He could see his death in Stjepan's eyes, feel it in the press of Gilgwyr's cheek and dagger.

"Yeah," said Godewyn, calm and easy. "Yeah, of course. Do our job. Get paid. Go home alive. Nice and simple, yeah?"

He felt the pressure against his left cheek and ear lift and disappear, and then Stjepan was slipping over the side of the wagon and off into the darkness.

Godewyn didn't move for close to a minute, then he let out a long breath and slumped against the sideboard. "Fuck me," he said with a groan.

"Everything all right, chief?" said Caider in the dark. Caider sat up, rubbing his eyes.

"Yeah, everything's fine," said Godewyn. He coughed and leaned his head over the sideboard to spit the bad taste out of his mouth. "But it looks like we might have to go with the back-up plan."

"What, actually do the job?" asked Caider, surprise in his voice.

"Yeah," said Godewyn with a sigh. "The Bale Mole on a fool's errand, here we come." He shook his head in the dark.

Fucking Woats.

CHAPTER NINETEEN
THE MIZER ROAD

Sleep came fitfully for most of them during the night. Perhaps in part due to the tensions of the long, mysterious pursuit the day before, in part due to the hurried cold dinner and lack of a hearth fire, in part due to the nearby presence of the circle of ancient *menhirs* that loomed beside them and marked the close proximity of the Otherworld and things of ancient ken and power. They kindled fires for breakfast, and that seemed to warm their spirits a touch, but only Stjepan and Leigh took the time to wander in and around the circle of standing stones in the light of day. Everyone else eyed the rune-carved stones with suspicion and dread, and were eager to be on their way across the Plain.

By mid-day on the 25th of Emperium, they were able to come down out of the Plain of Flowers without attracting too much attention from the castles and keeps that dotted the north side of the Holbrae, a creek that ran down out of the Plain into the great Volbrae River. At the juncture of the Holbrae and the Volbrae stood the city of Hartford once An-Damagraile, the hold of the Earl of Hartford. They passed through the towns on the south side of the creek and entered the Tiria Road, and crossed the bridge over the Holbrae into Hartford.

As they paid out the entry tolls into the city, Stjepan turned casually to one of the guards at the gatehouse. "Say, any word on where I might find a fellow named Gause Three-Penny?" Stjepan asked. "He's from around here, I'm told."

"He a friend of yours?" asked the guard. He looked at Stjepan a bit suspiciously.

"Acquaintance is more like it," Stjepan said with an easy grin. "The man owes me money from an evening of dice down in Aprenna." Which was, in fact, true.

"Good luck collecting, then," said another guard. "That scoundrel hasn't been seen in many a day. We heard he'd gone off into the Devil's Tower, the dumb bastard. You're too late by a few weeks."

"So much for that," Stjepan said with a shrug and a shake of his head as the guards laughed very much at him, rather than with him.

Their caravan rolled into the streets of the city, before coming to a stop by some wells and water troughs on the north side of several large public squares and markets. The north side of the Holbrae was heavily settled, a sprawling patchwork of houses and town centers and farms so close in together that it was hard to tell where the city stopped and the next town started. The Tiria Road ran north toward Gyrdiff, and to their west they could see the road splitting toward the bridge over the Volbrae.

As the squires started leading the horses in teams to water, most of the rest of them gathered by the coach. "Today is the last day of Herefort's journey on the Path of the Dead," said Arduin to Stjepan. "I assume there is a temple to the Divine King here in this city, and we would like very much to say our final prayers there and employ a priest and mourners."

"Of course, my Lord Arduin," said Stjepan. He pointed to the southwest across the shingled rooftops of the small city. "The temple should likely be down by the Volbrae, by the main castle. If I might suggest, my Lord, this is the last major market we're going to see from here on out. We should load up on as many supplies as we can, anything we didn't get at Woat's Inn. Could you perhaps detail a knight or two to accompany Malia to the market, so that she might acquire whatever she and the Lady might need? They have had no amenities or comforts on their journey, for the most part, and perhaps now that we have the additional wagon space we can be a bit more accommodating to making their lives more pleasant for the next leg of our journey."

"I shall go with them to make payments as needed," Gilgwyr said with a bow.

"I'll leave half my men to watch the wagons, and bring the other half to do the heavy lifting for the Lady's handmaiden," said Godewyn.

"Agreed, then," said Arduin. "We shall meet back here in, say, two hours?"

They all nodded their assent, and slowly the group sorted itself into its different missions. The Urwed brothers stayed with the coach, with Annwyn inside, as Malia went off with the Theos, Gilgwyr, Godewyn, and some muscle to go look at what was available in the markets. Arduin and the rest of his knights rode off to find the Divine King temple.

Erim found herself with Stjepan, standing by the wagons. He was looking off to the north. "It's only twelve miles from here to Gyrdiff and the Temple of the Hunt," mused Stjepan. "No one's going to give a shit about Gause Three-Penny gone missing, except maybe the Lamb, and he told me once that he always stops at the Temple upon his return from the Highlands. I could move at speed and be catching up with you by Aberdelan up the Mizer Road."

"I think that leaving Godewyn Red-Hand and his crew without clear adult supervision is a terrible idea," Erim said matter-of-factly. "Gilgwyr's just as like to egg them on if they start up trouble, and you know for damn sure they won't be listening to me. Someone'll be dead faster than you can say *Islik's huge throbbing cock*."

"Yeah, you're probably right," said Stjepan, his eyes narrowed and brooding. His gaze swept the street. "Then I'll have to trust to the Fates and Fortune." He looked up at the sky and whispered. "*Yhera, Queen of Heaven; Yhera Fortuna, lend me luck! Adjia, Great Huntress, who stalks the hills and woodland trails! I hunt a huntsman, bearing the badge of your temple, a swift messenger for one of your captains! An offering at your altar within the month, I swear it, if you favor me!*"

And with that he started down the busy streets, slipping in and out of the occasional taverns and watering holes that popped up, with Erim trailing close behind and watching him work. A nod here, a word there; she wondered if he'd have to resort to coin, but it seemed that Stjepan had an eye for choosing the right folks to approach. And the right folks seemed in this particular case to be weathered, rough-dressed men and women who looked like they spent a lot of time outdoors. "Check the King's Cup, there's some men down from Gyrdiff and they're as like to be there as anywhere else," a grizzled man in dirty leathers but bearing clean knives told them in the Flying Duck. Down a winding stone-walled alley they found the King's Cup, and there an old barmaid with only two teeth in her head told them, "Aye, some Gyrdiff men were here, but they's gone to the market. Looking for some rutabaga." At a rutabaga stall in the north market square, a stout farmer's wife directed them to the Wayfarer's Inn, saying, "Best hurry, they're not in town much longer." And so they found themselves arriving at the Wayfarer's Inn on the north side of town, just in time to see several men in faded brown and black leathers and faces burned by sun and wind preparing to mount sturdy roans, packed with full saddle bags, hunting swords, and long bows.

"Oi, there!" Stjepan called out as they approached. "Are you men from Gyrdiff, by chance?"

"Aye, that we are," said the eldest of them, a Danian with a wiry, grizzled salt-and-pepper beard and a head of close-cropped white hair. His creased and lined face was friendly but there was caution in his eyes, and Erim could see dagger and sword hilts in casual easy reach of all three of the men. She also saw that all three bore a brass sigil on the breasts of their leather coats, a crown of laurels circling a fox head. "Who wants to know?"

"My name is Stjepan, son of Byron, a yeoman to Earl Orphin of An-Athair," Stjepan said. "I seek to send word to a friend who travels through Gyrdiff regularly, and makes offering at the Temple of the Hunt and is known to the priestesses there. I can offer recompense for this service."

"Well, that might depend on who the friend is," said the older man.

"Dürace Lambadras, knight-errant of the Court of the Silver Wood," said Stjepan.

Erim's ears pricked up at Stjepan's phrasing, and the three woodsmen glanced at each other. *A knight sworn to one of the* Fae *Courts?* she wondered.

"Aye, might be we can take that message," said the eldest. "What would you want us to tell him?"

"Tell him that Stjepan Black-Heart sends word that Gause Three-Penny has gone into the Devil's Tower for reasons not yet known and has not returned, and that should the Lamb wish a chance to do right by an old friend, I will try to pass back through Aberdelan in the next few weeks if I am able and shall seek word at the inn there of his coming and going," Stjepan said.

The three men glanced at each other again.

"Stjepan Black-Heart," the eldest said, as much statement as question. Stjepan nodded. "Aye, we can take that message," the old man said. He extended a gnarled hand to Stjepan. "Emeril Tarlan, Chief Warden to Lord Naeras of Gyrdiff." As they shook hands, he indicated his two younger companions. "Pyle Garthing and Corwin Bregaine, both Wardens of Gyrdiff," he said.

"And this is Erim of Berrina," Stjepan said, and Erim found herself nodding solemnly and shaking hands with the three gruff men. "Well met, and my thanks. I have heard your name before, counted amongst those that brave the Uthed Wold to fight the Azharites. Can I offer coin for your troubles?"

"Not for ours," said Emeril with a shake of his head. "The Lamb is well known to us, and he has spoken highly of you, and your service to the King of Warwark, whom all good men in the west count as a friend and ally."

"The blessings of Heaven on King Derrek," Corwin said softly.

"*La benedicia delles deas Yhera Invictus an'Adjia sura regnus Derrek*," said Stjepan with a nod. That seemed to satisfy something in the three men, and Erim noticed their shoulders relax almost imperceptibly.

"Gause Three-Penny in the Devil's Tower, eh? I haven't seen him in a bit, he had a falling out with the last Lord of Gyrdiff and don't come round our neck of the woods no more, even though we got a new Lord of Gyrdiff. But I know he's still friends with the Lamb, and no man should remain in the Tower for long," old Emeril said, and then he cocked his head and raised an eyebrow. "You said passing *back* through Aberdelan? So you're headed into trouble, then?"

"Aye, good guess. It's up the Mizer Road and past the Wall for us," Stjepan said. Erim tried to look tough and nonchalant when he said that.

"Then we will make offerings in the temple for your safe return," Pyle said, a concerned look on his face. "The Kestle March is treacherous enough, but anywhere north or west of the Wall will be a place of great danger."

"No simpler truth is there, and so I would thank you for your offerings and prayers," Stjepan said. "Perhaps then I could ask you also to make offerings for me to Yhera Fortuna and Adjia the Huntress, who led me to you?" He held out some coins; Erim caught a glimpse of gold and silver. "I vowed an offering within the month upon my word, but the outcome of our journey is still in question."

Old Emeril took the proffered coins, counted them, and dropped them in a pocket. "Aye, we can do that for you as well," he said. "We will also ask the priestesses to offer prayers in your name and for your safe return."

"If their prayers are successful then I shall pass through Gyrdiff and make offering at the Temple of the Hunt myself, and pay my respects to you and yours," Stjepan said.

"That would be most welcome," old Emeril said with a satisfied nod.

"*La benedicia della deas Yhera sura tou'nou,*" the four men said in unison, shaking each other's hands and embracing briefly. They smiled and shook Erim's hand as well, but she felt for a moment like a bit of a fraud; there was a quick and clear mutual communion, a shared bond of Goddess and woodland culture, that she saw between Stjepan and the men of Gyrdiff that she simply did not share.

As the Gyrdiff men mounted their horses, she and Stjepan started back down the street, and she wondered a bit at his ability to find comrades and allies seemingly anywhere he went. She'd seen it in Therapoli before, that recognition that came with the mention of the name *Black-Heart;* but here they were almost to the Wall of Fortias and still that name and hint of Athairi lore was opening doors and easing their way. And there she was by his side, plain simple Erim, of no name and no family to speak of, with no epithet to call her own. The Divine King had no use for her, and the gods of Hell awaited her, that she had been told and that she knew, but still she could not bring herself to think of actually making offerings to the Forbidden. They would be her punishment, not her patrons. Nor could she imagine following in Stjepan's path; the Old Religion had never been part of her life and upbringing, and she still found it foreign and strange, even if it was simply ancient, the first religion followed by men and women.

All of which left her quite alone in the world.

They crossed to the west side of the Volbrae after regrouping a few hours later and started up the Mizer Road, entering what the locals called the Hinterlands. The hills and lands to the west of the river were widely and officially known as Ravera's Barrens; once upon a time they had been lush and green, like the rest of the Danian countryside that the caravan had been passing through, but the land had been spoiled in a great catastrophe hundreds of years ago. Far to the west stood the Great Wall of Fortias, built to hold back the enemies of the Middle Kingdoms and the great curse that the Sun Court had called down upon them at the end of the war against the Last Worm. That curse had turned Uthedmael into a land of desolation, where nothing could live, and the Wall was meant to mark the spot where the curse ended. But by legend a young woman named Ravera had opened the gates of the Watchtower of Pallanwyn one night, thinking that her lover was on the other side. What had awaited her was a foul wind bearing the Curse of Lost Uthedmael with it, and the wind had swept out over the upper reaches of the Watchtower lands and Dain Dania, and killed trees and crops and people, leaving behind a barren landscape east of the Wall that stretched sixty miles to the Volbrae.

Not all of the land between the Wall and the Volbrae had been made barren, however, and in scattered spots the land still supported the livelihoods of man; the Hinterlands were one such region, where a lord and knights sworn to the Earl of Hartford held dusty hilltop keeps and their tenants eked out a living from the dry soil. The caravan passed irrigation canals that brought in water from the Volbrae and the Dunnbrae, and fields of barley and groves of orange, tangerine, and olives.

"This doesn't seem so barren," Erim said to Stjepan, a bit disappointed.

"No, not this part," he said. "The Hinterlands are quite habitable. In fact the wine from this area is very good, maybe as good as the vintages from near Orliac. But the terrain gets rougher the further west we go."

"So do you think Ravera was an actual person?" asked Erim. "Odd to think that you'd go down in history with a whole region named after you because of a fuck-up."

"We debated that back at the University," Stjepan said. "The histories of the time all say yes, that she was the daughter of Lewyr, Watchtower King of Pallanwyn, and some books even name the lover that she thought was at the gate. I can't remember his name. Düras or Dürace or something like that. Shit, it's close enough to the Lamb's name that I'll never get it." He shrugged. "Despite the records in the books, a lot of us suspected that it was just a legend and a name put on a terrible drought during a more superstitious time. But that was back before I'd actually climbed the Wall and seen the Wastes, I suppose."

"And now that you've seen the Wastes?" asked Erim.

"Yes," he said. "She was real. And she opened the gates. The Divine King priests from Aprenna blamed the Horned Man; they said the Devil came to the gate and called out to her in the voice of her lover. And having seen the Wastes, I'm guessing they're right."

They rode for a bit in silence.

"I meant to ask you this earlier," Erim said. "This friend of yours, the one you call the Lamb. Dürace Lambadras? You told Emeril that the Lamb was a knight-errant of the Court of the Silver Wood. That's one of the *Fae* Courts. I didn't realize a mortal could be sworn to a *Fae* Prince."

"Both Athairi and Danian history have a number of knights-errant that claimed to be sworn to the *Fae* Courts. Indeed some say that's where the Golden Knights of An-Athair got their start, that they were sworn to the Golden Court of the *Fae* back when it was the only *Fae* Court, in addition to being knights sworn to protect the Green Temple and the Spring Queens, and that they could pass from our world to the Otherworld with ease," said Stjepan. "But Dürace is a bit different, he's genuinely *fae*-born. His father was a Tirian knight from An-Maghram who was invited to spend some time amongst the *fae*, and later found Dürace on his doorstep to raise."

A mortal father and a fae *mother*, thought Erim with a pang of envy. *Everywhere I turn I hear about people more interesting than I am.*

And she fell quiet for the rest of the day.

They spent the night in a rather poor inn outside the castle of Lewsmaeve, though the locals were friendly enough and Erim conceded that the wine there was in fact excellent. She had a bit more than she should have, however, and awoke the next morning filled with regrets.

They started up into the hills of the Hinterlands, and the terrain became quickly harsher, filled with dry shrubs toward the peaks of the hills and woodland copses in the valleys, where water was more plentiful. By late morning of the 27th of Emperium they were paying the road tolls under the watchful eyes of the men-at-arms of Aberdelan, the last officially occupied keep on the Mizer Road, held by Pellas West, called the Hinter Lord, who held all the land from Aberdelan back to the Volbrae. In terms of total area, he controlled as much land as his liege lord, Earl Geller of Hartford, but as the land itself was quite poor the Dain King was unlikely to elevate him to the title of Earl.

Two miles further west and they reached a point in the Mizer Road from which they could actually see the Devil's Tower, though it was but a distant and forlorn speck on a barren, rough-looking crag, outlined against the gray sky to their south.

Erim and Stjepan stopped their horses by the side of the road to contemplate the tower. Erim took out Stjepan's spyglass—which he seemed to have given her—and trained it on the distant citadel.

"Legend says at night you can sometimes see lights and fires coming out of the tower," Stjepan mused. "But I've been up and down this road twice before, and have never seen anything unusual. Well, unusual for the Barrens, at least."

"Why do they call it the Devil's Tower?" she asked.

"Because a great demon took up occupancy there after Ravera made her Mistake," said Stjepan. "One of the *Rahabi*. A *Golodriel*, by all report."

"Oh." Erim squinted. "It's only . . . what, maybe ten miles from here?"

"Less, probably eight or so," said Stjepan, biting his lip. "So fucking close!"

"Do you want to make a run for it?" Erim asked. "I'm telling you, I still think it's a bad idea."

Stjepan took a deep breath, and looked over at the rest of the caravan as it wound its way past them. Godewyn waved from the back of a wagon.

"No, you're right," Stjepan said firmly, looking back toward the distant tower. "Gause Three-Penny is—or more likely *was*, at this point—a good man, whom I have known to always do the right thing, and that's a rare thing in this world; but we have a duty first and foremost to those that walk and ride beside us. If Gause's corpse has been sitting in that Tower for several weeks, then it can keep until we're on our way back; if he's still alive, then I only hope he can forgive me for not coming directly for him and his."

He whistled, and turned Cúlain-mal back onto the Mizer Road. Erim watched him go for a moment before looking back toward the Devil's Tower.

Maybe not such a Black-Heart after all, she thought.

CHAPTER TWENTY
THE GREAT WALL OF FORTIAS THE BRAVE

With every passing mile out of the Hinterlands, the landscape of the Barrens had grown bleaker. The Mizer Road wound west-northwest and upward through what had once been rolling lush hills, and was now just mile after mile of long abandoned farms and castles, either dried out or overgrown with hardy desert brush. The landscape was not *entirely* barren—on occasion they could see small herds of roan antelopes, wild goats, and musk deer, and they tracked the spoor and prints of foxes and what Stjepan suspected were Daradjan wild dogs, come down from the Highlands. A variety of small birds passed by them, or observed them from crumbling stone perches, and overhead they often saw Éduins harrier hawks scouting or griffon vultures circling.

Nor was it in truth entirely abandoned. They were moving through a ghost landscape, the empty earldoms that had belonged to the Orenges and the Lews and the Jaines, once-great Danian families now reduced to being landless knights serving the landed lords of the Volbrae that had taken them in after Ravera's Mistake. But every now and then they'd spot a hardscrabble herder or a hunter in the distance, almost certainly an outlaw or a madman who had found freedom and some semblance of peace out in the bleak countryside. Their camp on the night of the 27th of Emperium was in a place Stjepan named Ushannon, a deserted village with the shell of a keep that had once belonged to a lord sworn to the Orenges.

"Is this what it's like in Lost Uthedmael?" Erim asked Stjepan that night.

He shook his head. "It's worse in Lost Uthedmael," he said. "Nothing grows there. Nothing at all. The land is ash. Here there's still green life, even up in the Bale Mole. But in the Wastes the only things left alive are filled with poison."

"Do you think anyone will ever come back here?" she wondered.

"Land's still too barren to be worth the effort for anyone but the desperate," Stjepan said with a shrug. "Not enough return on the investment. But maybe someday. The Orenges send a group through every spring to test the ground, and have for centuries, waiting for the day they think it ripe enough to reclaim their ancestral keeps. But at this point the ritual is observed more for habit's sake than anything else, I expect. The only folks out here are madmen, hermits, and outlaws." He laughed. "Our kind of people."

The morning of the 28th of Emperium found them beginning the ascent into the foothills of the Bale Mole and the lands of the Watchtower Kings, following the Mizer Road on its last legs to the Watchtower of Mizer. After half a day of journeying, they spotted the Great Wall of Fortias to their west and then the Watchtower of Mizer to their north, and they were breathtaking sights; a thirty foot high wall, crenulated on both sides, with a small tower post about every mile or so that stretched along the tops of the western hill line, climbing up toward the massive keep of the Watchtower in the high distance, silhouetted against the high range of the Bale Mole and the blue sky. The post towers could only be entered from the wall walk, and served as temporary quarters and strong points for the patrols that marched the desolate demarcation line between the Middle Kingdoms and the Wastes of Lost Uthedmael. Every fifteen miles or so along toward the south and the city of Warwark would stand a great Watchtower, though from their vantage point on the Mizer Road they could not easily see the closest to their south, which would have been Derc Cynan, only Mizer to their north.

By late afternoon they were on their approach to that tower, a massive round citadel that anchored the north end of the Wall on a great rock outcropping with commanding views west over the Wastes and north into the Bale Mole. The hills of the Bale Mole ended in a great cliff, the *Greierkrag* or White Palisades, which ran from the rock base of Mizer toward the east, overlooking the Dunnbrae. It was effectively impassable for almost twenty miles until the palisades crumbled into hills above the Uthed Wold, and it served as a natural barrier for armies as effective as the Wall itself.

The road led up to a squat gatehouse at the base of the tower complex, and Stjepan and Erim rode up to the gates under the watchful eyes of dozens of well-armed men-at-arms. Mizer had seen more than its share of battles over the years, perhaps even more than any other tower in the Wall, and even though they were approaching from the safe side, a grim aura hung over the tower as they approached. The guards' armor tended to be in an older style than would be considered fashionable elsewhere in the Middle Kingdoms, particularly in Therapoli and the wealthy Aurian east, but was nonetheless serviceable: long brigandine coats or mail under a surcoat, plate bracers, cuisses and greaves, and simple *celata* helms. A grizzled Watchtower knight strode forward, slipping his Daradj-style *hounskull* bascinet off his head and cradling it in the crook of his arm, and revealing craggy cheeks and a bushy mustache.

"Oi, Black-Heart," he grunted. Erim's eyes rolled into the back of her head and she sighed. *Just once I'd like to go someplace where Stjepan doesn't know anybody*, she thought.

"Sir Orace Angeloss," Stjepan said with a grin. "I was wondering if you were still alive and kicking. It's been a couple of years, yeah?"

"That it has, that is has," Sir Orace said, reaching up to shake hands with Stjepan. "Who else was it that last time? There was a black-skinned Amoran, some other foreigner, and Harvald Orwain, and what was his name? The other Aurian with you."

"Austin Ulefric," Stjepan said as he dismounted. "The Amoran was Omar Valenti, and we had a companion from the Kessite Kingdoms with us, Mareesh Amaghan hag'Ghazi."

"Right. With names like that I should remember them. A fun lot they were when you were last here, how are they now?" asked Sir Orace, smiling fondly.

"Omar and Mareesh signed on for a merchant venture into the Empire, to trade for silk and spices in the ports of Galia, but Austin is feared lost in Uthedmael, I'm afraid," said Stjepan.

"Ah!" said Sir Orace, his smile disappearing. "Where'd Austin cross over into the Wastes? Not here."

"No, he was aiming somewhere south and used the gates at Warwark," Stjepan said. "He was supposed to be back two months ago, but not a word, and the divinations have been unclear."

"As they so often are when it comes to the Wastes. There is still some small hope, then. I shall make offerings in our shrine to the Divine King to watch over him, as the Divine King shepherded the Kings in Exile through the Sea of Sands," Sir Orace said.

"My thanks, Sir Orace," said Stjepan. He turned and indicated Erim up in her saddle. "This is Erim, a companion from Berrina."

"Well met, lad," said Sir Orace. "And I see you have a small wagon train following you this time." He eyed the approaching coach, with Arduin and his knights in the lead.

"Aye," said Stjepan. "We're acting as guides for an expedition that wishes to cross into the Bale Mole."

Sir Orace laughed. "Last time you were all headed to Geniché's Throne, yeah? That Harvald of yours wanted a glimpse of the future, as I recall. I don't remember him telling me if he saw something good when you came back through. So what's this lot want? Perhaps the Three Rings of old King Taran? We've had two crews passing through in the last few weeks to look for that haul, all secretive like, but I got it out of them. Someone must be selling maps back east."

"Not the Three Rings, but something like that," laughed Stjepan. He pulled out a bag of coin. "Our employers would prefer as much discretion as possible."

"Luckily for you King Lewin is down at Pallanwyn treating with his cousin King Türaine," said Sir Orace with a grin. "Makes it easy to skip the paperwork."

"Lucky, indeed," said Stjepan. And he began counting out coins into Sir Orace's waiting hand.

And so the guards and porters opened the gates wide, and Sir Orace led the way as the caravan passed underneath the gatehouse and through a series of steep-walled courtyards and further gates. The guards eyed the sigil-less knights and closed coach with calm intensity, but Erim supposed that none of the visitors to as remote an outpost as this were ever strictly speaking *normal*, and so despite their keen vigilance the guards seemed to take it all in as a day's well-paid work. A fine coating of dust or ash seemed to be everywhere, on the guards' armor and clothes, on the ground. She noted that the guards all had dark expressions, with a slightly haunted look to their eyes. At the sight of Godewyn in the second wagon, however, a ripple of good cheer went through their dour observers and a cry was raised. "Ho, Godewyn!" some of the guards shouted. "What have you brought us this time?"

"Sorry, boys," Godewyn called out with a showman's wave of his big meaty hand. "I find myself lacking in entertainment this visit, as I am just a hired hand. Perhaps a game of dice, though?"

There was some disappointed grumbling as the final two wagons disappeared through the gatehouse. Stjepan remounted and he and Erim followed the train in through the gates.

"What was that all about?" she asked him quietly, nodding ahead to Godewyn as they passed under the dark mass of the gatehouse.

"Once the lands behind the Wall were fertile, and the Watchtower Kings and their knights could have their families nearby working farms and herds. But after Ravera's Mistake, the lands became barren, and if they didn't scatter into the Danias the families from here moved south to Warwark, marking its transformation from sleepy seaside port into squalid, teeming city," began Stjepan.

"So?" she asked, ducking her head under a portcullis.

"So after Ravera's Mistake, women aren't allowed to live in the Watchtowers anymore, yeah? A pointless rule, really, but it's become a bit of a superstitious tradition. And so their families are far away. They have to spend days marching back down to their families in Warwark, and the men of Mizer have the furthest to march. The knights and soldiers here don't get to see women all that often, maybe a few times a year if they're lucky," Stjepan said. "Unless some enterprising procurer brings a passel of whores through."

"An enterprising procurer like, say, your old friend Godewyn," Erim said.

"Aye," Stjepan said. "Be careful here."

"As careful as I am everywhere," Erim replied.

Past the gatehouse, they entered a series of interconnected courtyards and gatehouses, each one successively higher and bringing them toward the Watchtower itself at the summit of the crag. It was slow going for the wagons, as the pathway was designed to be narrow and easy to defend. The courtyards opened variously onto smithies, stables, chicken coops, workshops and storehouses, all finishing up the day's activities. Finally they reached a courtyard directly beneath the great Watchtower of Mizer itself, a massive keep of hewn stone that loomed above them. They stopped in front of a gate that led directly underneath the great edifice. The gate was made of enchanted bronze, patterns and runes woven into its surface, each door of the gate emblazoned with the figure of a rearing, armless wyvern, the symbol of Fortias the Brave and his descendants.

This courtyard was a bit larger than the others, and here they were able to draw in the coaches and wagons, unlimber the horse teams and stable them. Fresh water drawn up from wells and pumps filled the watering troughs, and dried oats filled the feedbags. Gilgwyr had the squires and some of the knights and a few of Godewyn's men start brushing the horses down, and then he began negotiating with a portly quartermaster for supplies and some quick repairs. One of the wagon wheels was running a bit wobbly after hitting a large pothole on the Mizer road, and there were frayed ropes and leather straps to mend and replace, and the stable hands and wheelwrights of the Watchtower were eager for some extra coin.

If Sir Orace was surprised to find two women in their caravan, he did not allow his face to betray him, but merely gave a formal bow when they stepped out of their coach. Stjepan watched the reactions of the guardsmen carefully with the women now out in the open; more than a few of them stole glances toward Annwyn in particular, craning their necks for a peek under the hoods of the women's cloaks, only to be met with the interposed bodies and stern visages of Arduin's knights. The women had returned to dressing in their customary mourning black, and while it was a severe look and Annwyn wore a mourning veil, it did little to hide the way she carried herself.

Sir Orace led Stjepan, Arduin, and Sir Helgi through one of several low stone doorways and up a narrow set of stairs into the belly of the Watchtower. They did not have to go far before he ushered them into a small complex of galleries with several offset rooms.

"These are the guest halls of the Watchtower, as Black-Heart knows," he said. Stjepan nodded in affirmation. "The side chambers can provide privacy for those that require it, while the rest of your men can stay in the common chambers. We are not likely to receive other guests tonight and so the chambers are yours to allot as you see fit." He pointed at an iron-bound wood door at one end of one of the galleries. "Through there you may access the upper levels of the Watchtower. You are invited to dine with us in the main hall when the sun sets. But we will bar the door once the evening meal is done."

"You have a shrine to the Divine King here," asked Arduin, though it sounded more like a statement.

"Of course," said Sir Orace with a nod. "In through the doors and across the lower gallery. I will leave you to settle in." He excused himself and left.

Arduin stared around at the spare walls of the guest galleries. "Well, I guess this will have to do," he said with a sigh. "Let my sister pick a room for her and her handmaiden, and place two men on guard over it."

Sir Helgi nodded, and left with Stjepan.

Arduin took a deep breath, and unslung his travel cloak from about his shoulders. There was a small plain bench nearby and he let it drop there. He stretched his neck and shoulders for a moment, his back (and, in truth, his rear) sore from days of hard riding. *And still more to come, on roads and paths that will get ever worse,* he thought. It occurred to him that this was likely their last night in anything that resembled civilization.

He opened the ironbound door and stepped up into the halls of the lower gallery of the Watchtower. He wasn't entirely sure where he was going but the layout seemed relatively straight forward, and he tried to cut diagonally across the halls. He passed through a central chamber that was some sort of armory, with racks of gleaming, polished polearms and swords and axes, and large barrels filled with red-feathered arrows. On the other side, through a small gallery with banners and shields hung decoratively on the walls, he finally found the entrance to the tower's shrine. A small basin filled with water stood beside the door, and he gently washed his hands before stepping inside.

The room was quite plain, though it had very large stained glass windows in two of its walls. Like most shrines to the Divine King, its central feature was a small altar, a stand set up for offerings before a statue of Islik, the King of Earth and Heaven. The stand held dozens of candles, some of them long reduced to stumps, while others were still tall and lit, along with a scattering of small objects left as gifts to the god: small ceramic figurines, dried pieces of fruit, a gold ring, a woman's broach. Several open bottles of wine were set at the base of the offering stand. The statue depicted the god as a man of regal stature seated upon a throne made of dragons, with a sun circle behind His head. The god bore the divine symbols of His right to rule: an orb surmounted by a cross in one hand, a scepter in the other, and a crown upon His head. Those three objects, plus a throne, made up the regalia of His earthly vassals, the Seated Kings of the Sun Court, and only a king could by right bear all three objects and sit upon a throne. Arduin's father, as a baron, had borne a scepter when he sat upon his seat at Araswell; most barons chose the scepter as symbol, but some few amongst the barons and earls chose to bear an orb instead. The Watchtower Kings of the Wall and the coast were not really true kings, in that they were not Seated Kings of the Sun Court; they were petty kings and used the title out of ancient custom, but really they were little more than country barons at best in terms of power and prestige. But they did usually take a crown upon the throne, and were so allowed by the priests of the temples.

Two other offering stands were set up in this shrine, on opposite walls facing the central cult statue. One stand sat before a small statue of a god with the head of a bull and the body of a man: Illiki Helios, the Sun-Bull, father of Islik and the god of the Sun before Irré, the Black Goat, usurped His place. The other stand sat before three small statues of men with either helmets shaped like the heads of dragons, or what were meant to be actual dragon heads worn upon their heads; the figurines were either old or poorly made, and Arduin couldn't tell what was supposed to be on their heads. But he knew who they were supposed to represent: the Dragon Kings, the great heroes of the ancient world, descended of King Ceram, who was the first to learn the secret of how to kill a dragon and take its powers for yourself, and from whose ranks rose both Islik the Divine King and Dauban Hess, the conquering Emperor. And in this of all places their blessings would be sought, as it was the Dragon Kings who had led the last wars and hunts that ended the Worm Kings.

The next day would be the 1st of Ascensium, the month in which the temples of the Divine King celebrated His ascension from King of Illia and the Earth to become the King of Heaven, to retake the throne of the Sun from the usurper Irré. Normally it would find Arduin in the Great Temple of the Divine King, watching the High King and the priests of the city anoint the cult statues with sacred oils and libations of wine. He resolved to do the same tomorrow before they set out, his last offering before they stepped into godless lands.

A small offering plate was set next to a box of candles near the entrance to the shrine, and he fished out some coins from his purse and placed them in the plate before taking three candles from the box. He knelt and set one candle before the statue of Illiki Helios and used another candle to light it, and whispered a quick prayer. *"Illiki Helios, Divine Father of the Divine King, watch over my own father and brothers, give them the strength to last through the Dark Night, until the coming of the Dawn and your Divine Son."*

He knelt and set the next candle before the statue of the Dragon Kings, and lit it. *"Dragon Kings! Hero-ancestors! Who kills the Dragon, becomes the Dragon! We march to war in the west and the Wastes, where the last of you fell to the hated Enemy. Give us some of your strength! Watch over us, and guide our swords!"*

Finally he knelt and set a candle at the central altar, and lit it. *"Islik, Divine King of Earth and Heaven, a vassal of your great vassal beseeches your aid. Set me as a King amongst Kings! Bring me Victory! Set my sister as a Queen amongst Queens! Save her from Darkness! Reveal our Enemies to us, and let them perish in the light of your divine strength!"*

And for some reason, the face that popped into his head as he uttered the last line of that prayer was the image of his brother Harvald.

Stjepan leaned into the doorway of the chamber he and Erim were going to share.

"Come on," he said. "While there's still a bit of light out."

She stopped unpacking some fresh clothes and slipped her brace of sword and daggers back on before stepping out of the chamber and following him. He led her through a dark ironbound wood door, around a corner into a stone staircase that they took up into the Watchtower. Only a few twists, and then they stepped through a small antechamber and out a small wooden door onto a paved stone terrace.

Gilgwyr and Godewyn and Leigh were already there, but they barely registered on Erim. The terrace had a crenellated parapet around it, and over that wall she could see in the light of dusk the broad western vista that spread out before the Watchtower on its rocky summit. To the south ran the Wall of Fortias; the terrace they were on appeared to be directly above its topmost portion where it finally ended in the Watchtower of Mizer, and a variety of stone battlements were stepped below them to provide a series of gates and firing platforms along the wall walk as it approached the tower. Hard-bitten men-at-arms manned each gate. The Wall itself disappeared off into the distance, and she could see a series of small tower platforms in the Wall as it stretched off toward the next great Watchtower, the keep at Derc Cynan, fifteen miles to the south. She could already see watch fires springing up at several of the platforms to mark where patrols were settling in for the night. To the north and northwest rose the rough and desolate hills of the Bale Mole, sienna and burnt red in the setting sun, and into which they were intending to march. And to the west . . .

To the west and southwest stretched out before her the vast Wastes of Lost Uthedmael, a bleak and desolate land of ash and dust that filled the horizon as far as her eye could see under a sky of orange and red and purple.

She blinked once, then twice, trying to take it all in. Great churning clouds of ash filled the horizon—though she could still make out the sun setting like a great burning ball of fire in the western haze—and dust and flecks of ash wafted up onto the terrace to swirl around her head like snow-flakes in a storm. The rolling hills before them flattened out to the south-west into more even ground. The earth looked as though the color had been bleached out of it by wind and acid, leaving it gray and lifeless. She could see twisted, petrified trees sticking up in clumps from dead earth on nearby hilltops, or fallen to the ground as though ripped from their moor-ings. The wind that swept up out of the Wastes and buffeted the terrace was hot, as though bearing heat all the way from the Sea of Sands, but the heat didn't reach her bones; instead it was the fierce, unrelenting grip of *cold* that settled over her insides. And the wind howled and moaned like it was a living thing, and she instantly thought of the voice of the Devil, calling out to poor Ravera in the guise of her lover.

She didn't think she could see anything moving, other than clouds of ash. She didn't think she could see anything alive at all.

"By the gods," she whispered.

"Not exactly," said Gilgwyr. "By the Sun Court." He leaned almost casually against a crenellation of the wall with Leigh, the two of them looking out over the Wastes.

"Indeed. The great curse of the Sun Court of Illia, called down to punish the Mael lords that took sides with the last Worm King," said Leigh quietly. "Over a hundred and fifty miles of what was once Uthed Dania—once green lands, once home to a hundred thousand Maelites and Danians, once ancient site of the great cities of Liadaine, Na Caila, Sanas Sill, and Av Lúin—blasted into dead ash. A burning sickness falls on those that enter it unprotected, and pox and death come calling quickly after. Nothing can live there for long that is not itself filled with poison: snakes, and giant scorpions, and spiders, and wyverns. It is a land of ghosts and ghouls."

"I do not mean to contradict you, Magister. But I've seen Daradj wolves and hyenas and jackals from the Red Wastes and the Sea of Sands in Uthedmael," said Stjepan from behind her.

"As have I," said Godewyn. He was leaning against the wall by the door through which they'd exited onto the terrace. "And great mountain lions from the Bora Éduins, the mountains on the other sides of the Wastes."

"Passing through, perhaps, but they won't stay," said Leigh. "Even those rough beasts will eventually fall prey to the curse. Have you ever read *De Secretis Wormis* . . . the *Book of Secrets of the Worm*, supposedly written by the sorcerer-architect Pallan?"

"No, Magister," said Stjepan. "I'm afraid that book is forbidden."

"The small minds of the University at work again," sighed Leigh. "Hurias of Truse referenced it in his book, *On the Last Worm*, and I was able to dig up a copy. Literally. It is Pallan's journal of Fortias' fight against Githwaine, and of the planning and construction of the Wall, and secret expeditions into the transformed lands of Uthedmael to search for Githwaine's last resting place. He wrote that he saw the secret text of the Sun Court's curse, and that they cursed 'every living thing, down to the last blade of grass and the lowest insect.' Poisonous creatures, being creatures of Hell, are only spared from the curse by the magics of their patrons Geteema Hamat, Irré the Black Goat, and Malkheb."

Godewyn, Gilgwyr, and Stjepan all spit to the side. "Bad names to be so bold with this close to the Wastes, old man," said Godewyn.

Leigh made a *woooo* sound, shaking his hands in the air as though they were the branches of an insane tree caught in the wind, before his voice broke and dissolved into a mix of cackles and coughs.

"We're . . . not actually going into the Wastes, though, right?" asked Erim, frowning as she watched the Magister double over in a fit of spasms. "We're not actually going into *that*."

400

"No, with any luck the map will only lead us through the hills of the Bale Mole," said Stjepan, indicating the heights to the north. "But the curse from Uthedmael sometimes drifts up into the hills as if carried by the wind, and seizes upon the unwary and unprotected, so we will have to be careful."

Erim took a step back from the wall. "Are we safe here?" she asked, feeling the wind of the Wastes on her face.

"Yes, we should be," said Leigh, finally recovered. He pounded appreciatively on the nearest merlon, and breathed in the ashen and sickly air blowing from the west as though he was standing on Baker Street as the morning's wares were being freshly unveiled. "The Wall of Fortias was built and bound with magic, the stones mortared with a mixture that included powdered *angelica* leaves, and runes of protection are inscribed upon it. It is the greatest feat of engineering and magic performed in recent memory, planned by the hero-magician Pallan at the behest of Fortias the Brave: a wall that keeps at bay both our enemies from the west and the curse that was loosed upon Lost Uthedmael by the Sun Court! So long as the bronze gates in the Wall are sealed at each of the gateway Watchtowers, the curse is contained."

"Great job it's done," said Gilgwyr drily. "Indeed, we've just rolled through fifty miles of barren land that would seem to indicate otherwise."

"It's only failed once in eight hundred years," Leigh protested.

Erim looked about her doubtfully. "Once is all it takes, yeah?" she said.

"From a single mistake, a foolish woman's error!" Leigh scoffed. "And besides, the curse didn't have the chance to take root after Ravera's Mistake in quite the same way. Things still grow there; the earth's not totally dead. Same up in the hills. If her father King Lewyr Whitehair had not sealed the gates and restored the Wall, it'd be even worse!"

"I'm not sure it's just the one time, Magister; it's not like the Wall hasn't been breached," Stjepan pointed out. "The Maelite warlock Madog led his warriors over the Wall on more than one occasion, and reached as far as Ogsden and Mossmor before Marshal Cotwin Orenge defeated him at the Battle of Schallis. And that's less than a hundred years ago. And the brigands of the *Cyr Faira Mal* once rode its entire length to raid the city of Warwark, slaughtering Watchtower knights as they went."

"The *Cyr Faira Mal* are rumored to be immortal and ride with the Black Hunter when he comes calling, and are possessed of magics that would make most men piss their fucking pants," spat Leigh. "Besides, technically they did not *cross* the wall from one side to the other, they entered it from here at Mizer and used the wall-walk as a road."

"And Madog?" asked Gilgwyr, one eyebrow raised.

"All the available evidence suggests that Madog did not cross the Wall, but rather like Carghita and Illigdir before him, he cut through the Bale Mole into the Uthed Wold and turned south from there, and only cleverly made it *look* like he'd crossed the Wall. I shall not allow you to spoil my enjoyment of this Wonder of the Known World," Leigh said icily, eyeing them both from under bristling brows.

"Magister," Stjepan and Gilgwyr said respectfully in unison, and bowed.

"But don't think the curse of Lost Uthedmael is the only thing to be worried about up in the Bale Mole," said Leigh. "Those hills didn't need the curse to be dangerous; they were dark and haunted long before the return of Githwaine to Uthed Dania, having been the gateway to the Vale of Barrows since the Golden Age. Every king and queen of the ancient Danias and Daradja is buried up there in the Vale, whole necropolises of the dead that were brought up the ancient sacred roads for burial." He pointed just to their north, where a trail led off into the hills from the north front of the Watchtower. "In fact in those days the Mizer Road was one of the paths of the dead, along which corpses would be brought up to the Vale."

It did seem to Erim as though the hills were filled with a foreboding watchfulness that she did not remember from their experience in the Manon Mole. "So we've been walking a dead man's trail," said Erim, a shudder going down her spine.

"Aye," said Leigh. "A road carved to carry bodies to their graves."

"Our own little funeral procession," said Gilgwyr lightly, with a wicked grin. "Marvelous."

402

They all stood silently on the terrace, taking in the vista.

"Right!" Leigh said finally, rubbing his hands with enthusiasm. "Let's get something to eat! A last meal for the condemned, before we start the most difficult leg of our journey."

The evening meal was simple but hearty. As the lands nearby were difficult to farm, the Watchtower relied on supplies brought in by merchants under contract to its king, from greener lands either south near Warwark and the foothills of the Pavas Mole or east from the Hinterlands and the Volbrae river valley. Breads, a bean soup with onions and root vegetables from cold storage, dried sausages and hard cheeses, and roasted chickens from the coops. All with a strong touch of spices and herbs to make sure the palate wasn't bored, and perhaps to cover any staleness that had crept into the food.

But Erim could find no delight in the serviceable meal, her thoughts still filled with the image of the Wastes, and the dark hills of the Bale Mole that awaited them. Finally she turned to Stjepan. "I thought that burial was considered all proper in the Old Religion," said Erim. "So why are the hills and the Vale so dark, if everything was done according to ancient rite?"

"Death may be the First Law: that all born of Geniché's Earth must follow her into Death and the Underworld," Stjepan said. "But the rites of the dead are still infused with the sadness and grief of the living, and mourning leaves a permanent mark in the world, where so many of the dead are interred. Particularly when they have been forgotten. Some say that's what the dead hate more than anything. That's why they come and visit us on the Day of the Dead, to remind us that they are waiting to greet us at the Hall of Judgment when our turn comes to obey the First Law."

They come and visit you, she thought glumly. *But not me. Should I feel lucky?*

"I begin to understand why the Divine King brings his followers up into the Heavens," she said. "Going to the Underworld's too fucking gloomy."

"Fourteen centuries of religious quarrel explained in a nutshell," laughed Stjepan. "Who wants to stand in judgment before the dead in the shadows of the dark, if worshipping the King of Heaven will lift you to a great reward in the brightness of His palace in the stars?"

The main hall of the Watchtower could easily fit several hundred men, though with several patrols out along the wall and two shifts for the meal, there were only about seventy-five with them at the tables. The king's table at the head of the hall was empty in his absence, with Sir Orace and his other chief vassals taking the head of a table on their right. Stjepan was a bit relieved that they were allowed to find their own tables, and so they filled two tables down at the far end of the hall, one with Arduin and most of his household knights, and the other with Godewyn's crew. Gilgwyr and Leigh were at another table, mixing with some of the locals; the Watchtower employed several enchanters and alchemists to prepare magics and amulets for their patrols, which sometimes marched out into the Wastes, and Gilgwyr was intent on purchasing some for use in the hills.

After some discussion, Annwyn and Malia had taken their meal in their rooms, brought to them by the squires and watched over by the Urwed brothers. Stjepan was relieved that there had not been any strenuous objections. Despite the absence of their liege lord, discipline did not seem to be lacking amongst the Watchtower guards, and the Watchtowers were old-fashioned in their courtesies, so Stjepan hadn't necessarily expected there to be too much potential for trouble, despite his warning to Erim. Unless there'd been too much drinking going on.

But still, better safe than sorry.

After their meals were done, Arduin and his remaining knights left the hall for the guest chambers, and Stjepan finally relaxed a bit. He saw Sir Orace beckon to him and excused himself, leaving Erim to fend for herself with Godewyn and his men. He made his way over to the knight's table and took a seat as several of the men-at-arms there got up and left, leaving him with Sir Orace. The gaunt man poured out a bit of harsh apple brandy for Stjepan before downing his own glass of the stuff.

"Your employer is a man of rank," said Sir Orace. "Though I am confused as to why he has brought his wife along; the Bale Mole is no place for a woman. I am beginning to think I didn't charge you enough. They're clearly Aurian nobility."

"My employer very much desires to remain anonymous," Stjepan said with an apologetic smile. "Treasure-hunting is considered terribly passé amongst the Aurian nobility, they think it's something that only poor people do. He'd be quite the laughingstock, particularly if the expedition comes up empty-handed."

"Did they hire you in Therapoli?"

"Aye, they filled up their expedition back in Therapoli a couple of weeks ago," said Stjepan. "Cartographer, scout, quartermaster, enchanter. Then we added Godewyn and his crew at Woat's Inn a few days back for extra muscle."

"If you've been on the road then you missed the excitement," said Sir Orace, and Stjepan froze the instant he heard the word *excitement*, and a part of his mind became focused on the dagger on his hip. "A bit of news arrived two days ago, buried in the mix with the patrol dispatches. The High Priest of the Public Temple of the Divine King was murdered on the 17th of Emperium by an Aurian lord, the future Baron of Araswell, after the High Priest implicated his sister in the witchcraft that killed their brother." He fixed Stjepan with a flat, unblinking look. "Their brother, Harvald Orwain."

Stjepan held Sir Orace's gaze for a moment, a relaxed smile on his lips and a faint crinkle of amusement in his eyes. *Warwark is the last stop of the heralds on the West King's Road, and that's five days travel from Therapoli if the heralds hit their marks. Then the news would have slowly made its way up the Wall for several days, passed from patrol to patrol or by messenger, to likely arrive at the earliest . . . two days ago.* He nonchalantly broke eye contact with Sir Orace and glanced out over the dining hall. He scanned the Watchtower men looking for tension or preparation, and saw none. He turned back to Sir Orace.

"There's terrible news if it's true. I haven't seen Harvald for a while. I will have to offer a prayer for him later. As I recall, Araswell is just west of

Vesslos. A man from Araswell would most likely flee into the Hada Wold or the Manon Mole, don't you think?" he asked. "He'd be looking to join up with the Rebel Earl. Like most other outlaws in that region."

"Could be as you say," said Sir Orace with an easy smile. "Hard to think of why a man like that would come all the way over to our far corner of the Middle Kingdoms. But like I said, I'm beginning to think I didn't charge you enough. A large reward was mentioned in the dispatch for the apprehension of this murderer and his witch sister, but you know, by my way of thinking, rewards always have to be shared when you're part of a company. A share to your commanders, a share to your underlings, and pretty soon you haven't got much left. A bribe, on the other hand, particularly a secret one that no one else needs to know about, doesn't have to be shared, and so needn't be quite as large."

"I suppose that's true. Why don't we take a look at this dispatch, then, and at the reward that is offered within it for the murderer? Then you can name your price, Sir Orace, and I'll see what I can do," said Stjepan. "Assuming that no one else will appear with hand outstretched, that is?"

"Lucky for you I'm the only one that has read the dispatch," said Sir Orace.

"Lucky for me and my purse, you mean," said Stjepan, smiling, as they stood. "Lead the way, sir."

And they quietly stepped from the main hall, Stjepan's mind resting on the hilt of his dagger.

Early the next morning, the expedition slowly rolled its way out of an open gate underneath the north side of the Watchtower of Mizer. The gates on this side were twins to the ones on the southern side that opened onto the highest courtyard, and they were strictly managed so that if one set of gates was open, the other set would be closed, thus ensuring that the Watchtowers always presented an unbroken magical line of defense against the curse that had transformed the Wastes. A rough-looking path led up into haunted, forlorn hills. Several Watchtower guards held the gate open, waving them through, and a guard captain named Dylam Morbraece stood to the side with Stjepan. He was young for a captain of the Watchtowers, perhaps twenty-five summers. But he already had a grizzled look that would give experienced older veterans pause before questioning his orders.

"Well, say goodbye to Sir Orace for me whenever he wakes," Stjepan said casually. "With any luck we'll be passing back through in perhaps a week's time."

Dylam nodded. "We'll see you on your way back, then, with any luck," he said. "The King's Fortune be with you, treasure-hunter."

Stjepan smiled back, but his smile was cold and didn't reach his eyes. "The king's got no claim out here," he said quietly.

"No, this land belongs to no god or king, so I suppose he doesn't, does he, Black-Heart," chucked Dylam, and he gave a casual salute. "But there's a king watching over you still, whether you like it or not."

Stjepan returned his salute and started walking to join the caravan, which was getting itself in order on the hill path. Rather than the coach in the lead, they had put it in the middle, with one of the supply wagons ahead of it and other behind it. As Stjepan rejoined the expedition, Gilgwyr and Leigh were going from man to man, handing each of them an amulet that they were pulling from a pair of ironbound boxes and indicating that they should wear the amulet about their neck. Leigh handed one up to Arduin, sitting astride Ironbound in his full harness and looking every inch an Aurian knight.

"An amulet to wear, my Lord: a ruby enchanted against curses and hexes, set in silver with a Labiran Rune to ward against magic and curses and ghosts," he said, setting the box down. "The enchanters here do good work, and are long experienced in protecting the Watchtowers against cursed Uthedmael. I will tie one into your horse's hair, as well, my Lord, so that so fine a steed is also protected." Arduin glanced ahead of him, and saw that others were tying amulets into the hair of their horses.

Arduin nodded his assent, but still watched with a frown as the enchanter took several long strands of Ironbound's hair and wove them into the silver chain of a matching amulet, securing it in place against the destrier's neck.

Leigh silently offered one to Stjepan, but the Athairi shook his head. "I have my own, Magister," Stjepan said politely. "And my horse bears such a rune as a brand."

Leigh smiled. "Of course," he said. "Ever prepared, o bright pupil." He picked up the box and walked to the last wagon and its horses.

Arduin eyed the amulet in his hand doubtfully. "King of Heaven forgive me; that an enchanter's talisman would be necessary against the evils of these hills!" he finally said.

Stjepan glanced up at him. "The Bale Mole is bounded to the south by the Wastes of Lost Uthedmael, and the shifting winds can bring its curse to the hills. To the north is the Vale of Barrows, the ancient valley of the dead, from which strange things have crawled since the first Queen of Daradja was buried there. And to our east is the haunted Uthed Wold, ruled over by the cannibal Azharites and their warlock captains, where even my people, woodfolk that we are, will not go except under flag of war," he said. "Don't lose the amulet, my Lord."

Stjepan mounted his horse and rode to the front of the caravan, and then past the lead wagon, signaling for it to follow. Then he swung out onto the hill path and started to pick up his pace.

Arduin watched him for a moment, then sighed, and slid the amulet on its silver chain over his head, tucking it under his cuirass to rest against his chest.

CHAPTER TWENTY-ONE
THE RUINS OF
LOST TIR'GAILE

They only made fifteen miles into the hills their first day past Mizer, but by the time the Dusk Maiden had arisen and the sun was setting they had gone far enough to reach the ruin of what might have once been a small fortified town sitting on a barren hilltop. The road had been far worse than anything they'd encountered so far, worse even than the trails and shepherd's paths through the foothills of the Manon Mole, or Dagger Vale, or the Scented Hills, far worse than the surprisingly smooth run through the trackless Plain of Flowers. But then Erim mused that this path was probably almost never used except by mounted patrols out of Mizer and the occasional expedition of treasure-hunters, most of them smart enough not to bring heavy wagons. Of course, most of them didn't have a Lady from Aurian nobility with them, and were able to apply a different calculus when it came to gear and mobility.

"Lost Tir'gaile," Stjepan announced as they rode up to the ruins. She was almost startled when he spoke. They'd spent most of the day in silence, as an oppressive weight had settled over the entire caravan. She'd been too busy watching every rock, crevice, dead shrub or tree, and ridge line for . . . well, she wasn't sure what for, but after only a few miles of travel into the hills she had become absolutely convinced that they were being watched.

The stone foundations of the settlement were still visible, as though someone had laid them out in plan and then forgotten to finish it all, with an occasional partial wall or in one case even a stone doorway standing in silhouette against the sky. The hill-town sat where three roads met: the one they had climbed up from Mizer, another road that came up out of the east from the Uthed Wold, and a third road that then wound west through the heart of the Bale Mole. Dead brush and hardy weeds crept amongst the stones scattered and piled everywhere, but the only living thing she could see was a single crow that perched on the bare limb of a petrified tree and observed their progress.

A southerly wind buffeted the hilltop, a howling wind from the Wastes, fetid and hot and bringing that same cold grip to her insides that she had felt on the Wall. She could hear what sounded like whispers in the wind as the expedition began to settle in amongst the ruins, setting tents and campfires. The whispers were new and different. They had started earlier in the day, about the time they'd passed through a series of large, wind-blasted and unrecognizable marble statues that had flanked their path. She hadn't been able to tell if they'd been great heroes or kings or gods once; but she was sure that over time they'd become demons, and that they now marked the true gateway into the Bale Mole.

Stjepan dismounted and walked through the ruins, his eyes searching the ground, until he was satisfied that no one else had come through there in recent days. They chose as their campsite what seemed to have once been a broad central plaza, now just a field of short dry weeds that betrayed evidence of having been used in the past by other parties moving through, perhaps as recently as a week ago.

"Who do you think they were?" Erim asked as they eyed the remains of fire pits.

"Probably the treasure-hunters that Sir Orace mentioned," Stjepan ventured. "I don't think the Azharites would camp in the open if they were using this road in and out of the Uthed Wold. They'd have some hidden bolt hole." That prompted Erim to glance around in worry at the stone ruins around them as Stjepan poked his boot into the fire pit. "If this lot were looking for the Three Rings of Taran, they'd have to cross the whole of the Vale of Barrows to get the vale that bears his name, but they could be on their way back by now. We'll have to keep an eye out. Of course, most treasure-hunters don't come back out of the Vale. It tends to be a one-way trip."

410

Erim shuddered. "Fantastic," she said.

While the others were setting the camp, Leigh began marking a perimeter as he had on previous nights before, pouring a wide circle of small stones and chalk dust out of his leather bag again. *"Ward this place against magic! Ward this place against ghosts and spirits! Ward this place against the Wild Hunt and the Black Hunter! They are not welcome here, where we make our mark upon the World!"* he whispered with unusual urgency, and moved on to repeat the ritual at the next rock.

Stjepan looked up from securing the tent that he and Erim were sharing to see Arduin and Malia approaching. The Danian woman curtsied. "Pardon me, Master Stjepan, but . . . Lady Annwyn requests your presence," she said. "Something is different this time," she added in a whisper. Stjepan finished anchoring the last tent peg into the ground, and stood and nodded. He stepped over to a small pile of bags waiting to be placed in the tent and fished out one of his saddlebags, which he slung over his shoulder.

Erim and Godewyn stood nearby, by one of the campfires, watching as Caider Ross and Too Tall set several black iron pots onto iron trivets for the evening's stews and beans. They turned to look as Arduin escorted Stjepan and Malia back to the Ladies' Tent, which was guarded by the Urwed brothers in their full harness, exposed greatswords gleaming in the light of the campfires.

"I still haven't gotten a good look at her, the Lady Annwyn. I remember hearing songs about her beauty, back when she was still in society. Nice songs, all proper-like," said Godewyn. "And I remember hearing songs about her scandal, too. Not so proper-like. I rather liked those songs." Erim didn't say anything. After a long moment, Godewyn turned to her. "So what're they doing in there, eh?"

Erim smirked. "The Red Hand is jealous?"

Godewyn shrugged and looked back toward the Ladies' Tent. "The hills can be a cold place," he said. "Nice to have someplace warm and wet to rest your prick. But then what would you know about that, eh?"

Erim snorted and looked at him quickly. *So, has he figured it out then, or does he just think me young and inexperienced?* she wondered. She studied his face to see if there was some clue there, but Godewyn wasn't really laughing at her, or even paying her much attention. He was just staring at the Ladies' Tent. Finally she shrugged.

"More than you might think," Erim replied softly.

Arduin and Stjepan stood waiting inside the Ladies' Tent. It had been hastily decorated to make it as homey as possible, and was lit by several small braziers that cast everything in a warm yellow-orange hue. A thick, heavy damask carpet decorated with eagles and griffins had been rolled out over the ground to form a floor, and several sets of folding screens were ringed to create a room within the tent. Stjepan remembered Gilgwyr telling him about the purchases they'd made. They'd bought them all from the shops and markets in Hartford when he'd been searching for the men from Gyrdiff. It looked like they had made the most of the brief opportunity.

Malia stepped out from behind the screens, curtsied to them both, and indicated that Stjepan could step within the screens. He hesitated for a moment, nodded, and moved past her.

Within the screened area, on a mound of furs and fabrics, sat Annwyn, her back to Stjepan. She had a fur coat drawn about her. Her golden hair was up in jeweled combs and bindings. A small wooden x-chair had been set up for him. Stjepan sat down and opened up his saddlebags, removing several books and his map-making kit.

"I think I have something new to show you . . ." Annwyn said.

She hesitated for a moment, then turned her head until she was in profile and she was speaking over her shoulder to him ever so slightly. She did not look toward him, but instead looked toward the ground. "I have had many days to think on it. Back at the Inn, that night in the rain, on the West King's Road . . . is that how men expect women to display themselves? To act, when in their company?"

Stjepan studied her a moment, his stare intense, wondering at her question. "Not all men. Not all women," he said finally.

"I have been cloistered for my whole life, it seems. My family has been so . . . concerned over my wellbeing," she said. Then she raised her voice louder. "Thank you, dear brother."

Arduin, listening on the other side of the screen, grimaced to himself, while Malia studiously pretended to be someplace else.

"The courts of Therapoli and the Aurian Kingdoms are prim and proper places, filled with rules and decorum . . ." Annwyn said as she slowly turned toward Stjepan and began to slide her coat open, baring one shoulder and part of her flank. "But even in our capital a man can find his entertainments, yes? If he knows where to look?" She opened her coat a bit more, finally revealing images sliding over her naked hip and breast. She looked up and deliberately held his gaze with her own.

Stjepan could not look away. "Aye," he finally replied. "Indeed, in Therapoli a man with coin and desire need not look far at all to find a woman in want of one or the other. The city is not so decadent as Palatia, or the cities of the Déskédran Coast, or our wanton neighbors in the Highlands, but it has its moments."

"Ah, lands where temples still stand to Dieva, the Dusk Maiden, the Goddess of Pleasure, and her priestesses are still honored," Annwyn said.

On the other side of the screen Arduin frowned and fumed. "Her temple prostitutes, you mean! Speak not of such vile things, dear sister, I beg you!" he whispered fiercely, not wanting anyone outside the tent to hear him should he raise his voice.

Stjepan broke eye contact with Annwyn and shook his head in exasperation, shooting a glance at the screens. "The Goddess of Pleasure revels in just that: *pleasure*. No more, and certainly no less, which makes Her a universal goddess, as all men and women desire pleasure of some kind or another, even if it is the pleasure of monasticism. And yet there are some who are so twisted as to find revulsion in the pleasure that others give and receive, and choose to treat as vile the pleasures that others find sacred," he said in Arduin's direction, and looked back toward Annwyn. He found himself looking deeply into her dead, deep blue eyes, and thinking for a moment that he saw some spark of mischief there.

And it startled him.

"Heathen sacrilege!" growled Arduin. "She opens doors that should remain shut, and makes way for Perversion! And so the Sun Court rightly condemns her for her wantonness!"

"The Divine King demands for reasons of His own that women's bodies be kept a mystery," Stjepan said slowly, staring into Annwyn's gaze. "But men with wealth and power may always find a way around the strictures of their own gods. And in the Middle Kingdoms, where all is 'prim and proper,' what is hidden can gain power in its revelation. So it is that some men desire to look at women, and some women desire to be looked at, and perhaps find some small measure of power there, in the exchange . . ."

He trailed off as Annwyn opened her coat wide, revealing the curves of her body, not taking her eyes from his, staring at him intently. Stjepan kept eye contact with her until he thought he could no longer stand it, and then looked down at her body. One of the amulets from Mizer, no doubt given to her by Leigh, dangled around her neck and between her breasts. Images and words and letters moved over her smooth, pale skin, and he started studying the icons being revealed upon her.

"There," he said, leaning forward, his eyes narrowing, his lips parting in excitement and anticipation. "These symbols. And those. They are new. Yes. Leigh was right."

Arduin choked out a small bitter cry, and stormed out of the tent, leaving Malia to stand there by herself, staring at the designs in the carpet, her cheeks burning red.

Pale blue crept into the black sky in the east over the hills of the Bale Mole, and a single bright star appeared above the far horizon, heralding the coming of the sun. Their camp was already astir, almost everyone clustered around the campfires before the last shift of the night's watch had come to its end. Sleep did not come easy in the Bale Mole. Gilgwyr squatted in front of the tent he shared with Leigh, his hands rubbing into his cheeks and chin, tears welling in his eyes to dribble down his face.

Stjepan had barely slept, spending most of the night hunched over books and papers by lamplight, trying to translate the new letters and words in Maerberos that had appeared upon Annwyn's skin. He was fairly sure now that he knew the next intended step along the path to the barrow, and it filled him with foreboding. He glanced at Gilgwyr as he walked past. "Are you all right?" he asked.

"Tears of joy, brother, tears of joy," said Gilgwyr in a husky voice. "I have been having the most beautiful dreams." He barked a laugh.

Stjepan grunted noncommittally, and continued off to one side, finding the eastern edge of Leigh's perimeter. He spotted Sir Clodin, who had been in the last watch, off ahead to one side, kneeling to the east in prayer as was his wont each morning. He stopped short, giving Clodin a wide berth, and found a similar position. The prayer he was about to offer was probably worded almost the same as that being offered by the knight, but Stjepan considered their intents and interests in prayer to be quite different. He took a deep breath, and tried to clear his mind before speaking in a low voice.

> *Dawn Maiden, Day Bringer, open the gate!*
> *Helios rises from the Underworld,*
> *having passed through the Halls of Death.*
> *Greet the sun, and guide his return.*
> *The world awaits!*
>
> *Dawn Maiden, Day Bringer, coming swiftly!*
> *Wake my spirit, stir my limbs,*
> *help me shake off the terrors of the night.*
> *Let me see with clear eyes.*
> *Let me speak with a clear tongue.*
> *Let me wake to grace!*

415

Dawn Maiden, Day Bringer, softly stirring!
Greet Helios at the gate of brass,
bring the morning again.
Rouse the world,
announce the coming of bright Day,
and fill the sky with light!

And as if on cue, the sun broke over the hilltops to their east.

"The gods need our prayers to remind them of, and sustain them in, their duties," his mother had once told him. "A day will come when enough people in the world will have forgotten the gods, and our prayers will have dwindled to a whisper. And when that happens, the gods will forget their duties, and abandon their divine tasks, and on that day the sun will not rise, the dead will wander the earth unjudged, the stars will recommence the War in Heaven, the Devil will take seat upon a throne of brass and fire to rule the wretched Earth, and the world will end once again."

Thank you, Mother, he thought drily. *But at least I have done my duty for this day.*

He rose, brushing dust and ash off his jacket and pants as he turned back to the camp. Arduin ignored him as he passed him, calling out to Sir Clodin. "Clodin! We're breaking camp! Get something to eat while you still can."

Sir Clodin struggled to his feet, getting up sluggishly, and turned.

"Clodin?" asked Arduin. Stjepan hadn't really been paying attention, but he heard the worry in Arduin's voice and caught Sir Clodin's movements out of the corner of his eye and he stopped, his head swiveling around so that he could focus on the knight. *Arduin is right, something is definitely wrong*, he thought. Sir Clodin was trying to walk toward Arduin, slowly, stumbling; his face looked like it was covered in white powder, his mouth was open as though he was trying to talk, but all that was coming out were choking sounds and a long low *hhiiiisssssssss*.

Stjepan was at a run in an instant, crying out "Lord Arduin! Stop!" as Sir Clodin collapsed to his knees. Arduin started to rush toward the kneeling knight, but something—perhaps Stjepan's cry, perhaps some instinct about what he saw—made him stop and then jump back with a start. Sir Clodin's body shivered one last time and then became still. Stjepan reached Arduin and a few moments later there was the sound of pounding feet and jangling armor and Erim, Sir Helgi, Sir Holgar, and Sir Theodras were there as well, weapons drawn. They all stared at Sir Clodin, kneeling motionless a few paces away.

He was dead, his flesh an odd grayish-white color, his mouth gaping open, his eyes sunken like black holes into his head.

"King of Heaven, what happened to him?" Arduin gasped out.

Stjepan stepped forward until he was almost touching the knight's body, peering closely at it as he went into a crouch.

"Stjepan, don't," said Erim behind him, but he raised his hand.

"The amulet . . . Leigh's amulet, the ones he got from the enchanters at Mizer . . . I don't see it anywhere, he's not wearing it," Stjepan said.

"Aye, he said he didn't want to wear any heathen magic charm," said Arduin. "He said he preferred to rely on his faith in the King of Heaven, which had always stood him in good stead, Islik be praised."

"Then your King of Heaven is what happened to him," Stjepan said quietly, standing straight and relaxing a bit. "The Sun Court cursed Uthedmael in His name. Leigh said a couple of days ago that the curse on Uthedmael was to punish those that sided with Githwaine, the Last Worm, and aye, that's true. But the curse was also intended just as much to keep men from even entering into Uthedmael, though for what reason only the Sun Court knows. The curse doesn't care who it touches; devout Kingsman or heathen Yheran, foul Devil-worshipper or simple unbeliever, the wind from the Wastes drives some men mad, poisons the life out of others, and cares not a whit who you pray to or even if you pray at all. Don't lose your amulets. And if you do, tell Leigh right away so he can give you another."

He started to walk away back to camp, and Erim fell in behind him.

Arduin cried out angrily. "Here, we have to burn him! Send his ashes to the Heavens!"

Stjepan looked back over his shoulder at the Aurian lord. "He's ash already." And he turned and kept walking back toward the center of camp.

Arduin and his knights stared at Sir Clodin.

Arduin took several tentative steps forward until he was standing in front of the kneeling body. He reached out with his booted foot and gave Sir Clodin a push.

The body toppled over and the armor it was in cracked and shattered as though it were ancient, brittle, rusted iron, and the flesh encased in that armor broke into great clumps of ash that spilled out across the hard ground. Small flakes of ash started to float up into the harsh wind. Sir Helgi, Sir Holgar, and Sir Theodras stepped back, making signs to ward off Evil.

Arduin took a sharp breath. "King of . . ." He cut himself short. He stared at Sir Clodin's ashes floating in the breeze for a moment, and then turned away.

CHAPTER TWENTY-TWO

THE BALE MOLE

They discovered that three horses had also perished in the night, collapsing into ash and clumps of hard stone. It was hard to tell if the amulets that had been woven into their hair had simply fallen out, or if someone, perhaps Sir Clodin, had removed them; one of the horses that died was his destrier.

Their progress that day, the 2nd of Ascensium, was slow going. The old funerary road that they were following had long fallen into disuse and disrepair; horses or men on foot would have had a better time of it, but with wagons and a coach they were forced to stop several times to sort out difficult turns or a stuck wheel. The lead wagon became stuck once, requiring six men to get it moving again, and the coach became stuck about an hour later as the road followed the top of a deep ravine. Some delicate and nerve-wracking moments followed for all while Annwyn and Malia dismounted from the coach and were helped to safe ground, and then Godewyn and his men were able to free the wheel that had gotten stuck.

A few hours later and they were stopped again, spread out on the funerary road through a stretch of dead and petrified trees and gnarled, thorny brush. They had cleared the ravine and were now on the other side of the Bale Mole; to their south ran the great central ridge of the hills, while now to their north they could see down a broad valley leading into the great central plain of the Vale of Barrows. Stjepan and Erim were on point, dismounted at a crossroads. The funerary road split in three different directions in front of them. One possible path turned back toward the south, back up into the hills. The middle path followed the curves of the hill line that they were on. And the third path turned north and down into the valley, toward the flat river plateau and the barrows and pyramid mounds that were dotted across it. Erim peered off into the Vale with curiosity and dread; in the eastern

Middle Kingdoms, burial grounds and cemeteries were unusual, as most of the people were worshippers of the Divine King and were cremated in their last rites, and the idea that the great highland plateau that they now looked over was filled with the bodies of the dead was mesmerizing and frightening. Across the flat, desert-like terrain Erim could see a mountain line far to the north, the great snow-capped peaks of the Harath Éduins, and a part of her wanted to scream in delight that she had gotten so far into the wild world as to see such a sight. Another part of her wanted to flee in terror back down the road on which they'd came.

There was a marble statue of some kind at the crossroads, damaged and decayed enough over time as to be unrecognizable. She was pretty sure it was a woman, though, or perhaps even a goddess. In the Old Religion, the goddess of the Dark Moon, Djara Luna, was also said to be the goddess of crossroads, and she guessed that the statue was meant to represent her. Strange amulets and stick figures made of branches dangled from the petrified tree branches nearby, swaying in the breeze. She wondered who had left them there, and how long ago. She turned to ask Stjepan, saw that he was busy consulting his journal and a book of maps, a frown on his face, and she shrugged and bit her tongue.

Gilgwyr and Leigh were in the front wagon, along with Caider and red-haired Giordus, who were nervously eyeing the countryside around them. Gilgwyr glanced at Leigh; the enchanter had his eyes half closed, staring back at the rest of the caravan. Gilgwyr followed his gaze. Arduin and his knights were clustered around the Ladies' Coach, forming a protective phalanx around it on their armored destriers. The Aurian lord was fuming, a dark cloud upon his face, and a sober shroud had settled upon his shoulders and that of his men. Gilgwyr hadn't seen them look so grim and dour since the death of their squire back on the river. That seemed like ages ago when he thought about it. He couldn't even remember the young man's name.

"I think our patron would very happily see Stjepan hanging from the nearest tree," said Gilgwyr lightly to Leigh. "That's two of his that we've lost on this trip."

The enchanter snorted. "And no doubt more to come. But *our patron* would likely be happy to see all of us hanging from the nearest tree," said Leigh. "He may now hold a special hate for Black-Heart, but I do not think that any of the rest of us are exempt from his condescension. A man like that knows in his heart that he's better than everyone around him by birthright. Makes it hard to find friends."

It was Gilgwyr's turn to snort. *It's true, I suppose; thanks to us and to Harvald, that family's entire life has been turned upside down and likely ruined, with the end of their line in sight, unless we can find a magic sword buried in the middle of nowhere,* he thought. *And yet my own dreams promise me a great day is coming. Why am I the only one to see the possibility of such joy?*

He jumped down from the wagon, on the sudden impulse to stretch his legs. As he settled his tricorn on his head he decided to join Stjepan and Erim at the front of the caravan. He slung his scabbarded rapier over his shoulder and sauntered up the hard trail to join them at the crossroads.

"I am beginning to sense some growing disquiet in the ranks," he said jovially. "And this day was already off to a bad start."

"Apologies, Master Gilgwyr," said Stjepan gruffly. "We are at a cross-roads, as you can see, and I just want to make sure that we head in the right direction." He pointed to the northward path. "That path leads down into the Vale, and that is not where we are going. But of the two remaining paths . . . I'm pretty sure the one to the south eventually turns toward Lost Angharad. The one in the center follows the hills out to a spur that juts into the Plain, and upon which sits Geniché's Throne, the great carved seat of rock where legend says Geniché once sat in the days when this was still part of her great Garden, and to which she was said to return on occasion to watch over the dead of the Vale."

"You took that with Harvald once," Gilgwyr said.

"Aye," said Stjepan. "Two summers ago."

"Did you sit on the Throne?" Erim asked. "Is it true you can see the Future, and talk to the Dead there?"

"I chose not to sit on it," said Stjepan with a shrug. "Wasn't my time to do so, I don't think. But Harvald did. I never asked him what he saw. But he didn't talk for a day afterwards."

Gilgwyr laughed. "Now that's an act of real magic," he said. "So which road do we take?"

"Yeah, that's the problem," Stjepan said. "We're headed for someplace in between Angharad and Geniché's Throne, so I have to figure out from my other maps of the area which of these two roads has a side trail going where we need to go."

"Fantastic," said Gilgwyr with a smile. "Hurry the fuck up."

He turned and rather than returning directly to his perch, he decided instead to stroll toward the rear. He could hear one of the squires whispering the Prayer for the Dead for Sir Clodin as he approached the coach. He promptly doffed his hat and nodded gravely to Arduin and his knights and squires as he passed them, and they icily ignored him. He heard Leigh laughing quietly behind him, and he winced a bit at that. *No need to provoke them with laughter*, he thought. *I know you're laughing at me, but they don't.* As he slipped his hat back on he stole a glance into the coach, but despite the fact that the window was ajar it merely opened into darkness, and he caught no glimpse of Harvald's beautiful sister.

As he approached the last wagon, Godewyn was pacing by its side, throwing angry glances up the column toward Stjepan in the lead. His men were ringed around it on foot, their motley assortment of weapons ready at hand, but there was a certain boredom mixed in with their nervousness. "How much longer, do you think?" Godewyn said, walking up to Gilgwyr with big Cole Thimber and Too Tall right behind him. "What's the delay? Where in the Six Hells are we going? Are we lost?"

"We're not lost. Well, not exactly," said Gilgwyr. "There's a crossroads up ahead and Stjepan isn't sure which fork takes us to where we're going. He's just checking his maps, we'll be fine."

"Black-Heart knows the rules out here! Unless you know you're in a safe place, you don't stop moving unless you've got a magician's wards set around you!" Godewyn snarled. "And hanging out on the side of this hill most definitely is not—"

"Hey, new guy! Careful over there!" shouted Handsome Pallas.

Godewyn and Gilgwyr both turned to look at the shout, following

Pallas' line of sight. Isham Wall had wandered away a bit up the hill-side, apparently taking a break to relieve a bloated bladder. He'd found a slightly sheltered spot behind a large, twisted, and petrified tree a few dozen paces away, and had dropped his pants to urinate on the ground.

"What the fuck? Get back here!" shouted Godewyn, turning and starting to unlimber his broadsword.

Isham glanced over his shoulder at them and made a bored wave. "Be right there, chief!" he shouted.

"Islik's balls," Godewyn spat, already starting to move. "I said—"

And then Isham gave a scream as his legs were swept out from under him, and he pitched back and was dragged with stunning speed halfway into the earth under the tree. Suddenly he stopped, momentarily jammed in place.

Godewyn, Pallas, and Too Tall were at a run in a shot, Godewyn cursing loudly as they drew their weapons. Gilgwyr was so startled by the sight that he lost a step or two and was behind them, and big Cole Thimber who was naturally slow wound up bringing up their rear. Gilgwyr glanced back up the caravan and saw the knights turning their horses about in alarm, and found himself thankful that Sirs Theodras and Theodore had put spur to flank and had started riding back toward them.

By the time Godewyn reached him, Isham was being pulled slowly further and further into a small hole of earth and rock in the ground under the base of the petrified tree, still screaming at the top of his lungs. "Fuck! It's got me! It's got me! Fu*accckkk*!" he cried. Godewyn and the others immediately grabbed his arms and started pulling as he pleaded, but in an instant they knew it was a losing battle. Whatever had a hold of him was incredibly strong and even though the hole looked very, very small it was making some progress at pulling him inside. Their efforts held him suspended for a moment, and his scream became wordless as he was pulled in both directions. His upper thighs and hips had been what had jammed him up in the hole, his exposed manhood flopping uselessly about for a moment, still free and urinating from both need and fear, until he got pulled in another few inches and his member was crushed into the hole along with his hips with the sound of bone breaking. His scream went up an octave and blood and liquid spurted onto his abdomen. Gilgwyr arrived just in time to wince and look away.

Isham and Godewyn locked eyes for a moment. They both knew he was going to get pulled under the tree.

"Sorry, mate," said Godewyn quietly. And then he plunged a dagger into Isham's neck. As the blood arced out of his jugular, Isham gurgled and his eyes started to roll back into his head, and his body started to go limp as he bled out.

Godewyn's gang let go of him as he died, and Isham was pulled from their sight, disappearing under the tree with a sickening crunch of bone and flesh. They spun away, shouting and screaming in rage and fear, weapons pointed at the ready as they stared at the hole, waiting for something to emerge.

And then suddenly Leigh appeared amongst them, a blur of blue-black robes, and he threw a bottle etched with runes at the hole. It exploded in a *whoosh* of blue flame as all of them leapt back and the horses of the two knights right behind them reared and whinnied in shock and surprise, almost throwing Sir Theodras to the ground.

"Begone, things of the cursed dark! Begone, things of the cursed earth! I bar you from this portal!" he cried out.

No one moved for a long moment.

Leigh slowly straightened, surveying his handiwork with a self-satisfied air; the hole in the ground was filled with blue fire, and the petrified wood of the tree was being slowly enveloped in the crackling blue flames, black and white smoke curling up from its branches.

He nodded. "Sorry about your lad. You did the right thing," he said to Godewyn. Then he turned and walked away from the burning tree.

Godewyn stared at the hole in the ground. He breathed in heavily. "He knew the risks. We all do," he said quietly.

The group moved away from the burning tree, at first slowly and then with increasing speed, hurrying back to the rear wagon. Cole and Too Tall clambered back up into the driver's seat of the wagon, their eyes and weapons still pointed back up the hill toward the growing conflagration, but Godewyn and Pallas keep marching, past the knights shifting about on their horses, past the first wagon toward Stjepan and Erim at the front of the caravan. Gilgwyr and Leigh followed in tow, and Giordus jumped off the first wagon as well, and Arduin urged his horse forward to see what was going to happen.

Stjepan and Erim had come back about halfway to the first wagon from the crossroads on hearing the shouts and cries from the back of the caravan, and now they waited there wordlessly as Godewyn walked right up to Stjepan. He swung a big fist with startling speed right at Stjepan's head, but almost seemingly by accident Stjepan half stumbled, half ducked out of the way at the last second and Godewyn caught nothing but air with his punch.

And then Pallas and Gilgwyr and Giordus were holding the big man back as he tried to get at Stjepan again, but already his heart wasn't in it, and then Erim and Leigh were stepping in front of him with hands upraised, separating the two men.

"Get us moving, you fucking Athairi, before any more of us die!" Godewyn shouted angrily. He let himself be dragged away by his men as they said soothing words to him until finally he shook himself free and turned around and started walking back toward the rear of the caravan, cursing and waving his arms dismissively. Arduin moved his horse out of the way with pursed lips, a look of satisfaction on his face as he let Godewyn and his men pass him. He looked coldly at Stjepan, and then he turned Ironbound and walked the destrier back to the coach and his waiting knights.

Stjepan watched Godewyn's receding back with narrowed eyes. Leigh, Gilgwyr, and Erim stood around him, breathing heavily. The petrified tree continued to burn in the distance behind the idled caravan.

"Well, lucky you. Now they all hate you," Gilgwyr said lightly.

"Yeah," said Stjepan. "Perfect."

CHAPTER TWENTY-THREE

THE RUINS OF
THE BLACK TOWER

They spent the night in a hollow beneath a hilltop ringed with the trace of stone formations, unsure whether the stones were ancient *menhirs* or the ruins of an ancient fort or hill-town. Neither Leigh nor Stjepan could find any trace of enchantment or *fae* power in the piles of rocks they found. The camp was quiet, dejected, drained of energy and life, the only conversations conducted in hushed tones. Eyes filled with hurt and loss watched Stjepan disappear into the Ladies' Tent for several hours.

The next morning, the 3rd of Ascensium, opened hazy and gray, with darker storm clouds looming in the west that seemed to threaten lightning or rain. They traveled only with difficulty, the road now reduced to a rough trail, requiring frequent stops to clear hardy brush from their path or free stuck wagon wheels. They no longer left it to chance, and every time they stopped Leigh would walk a perimeter, pouring his chalk dust and pronouncing some variation on a protective ritual, until the enchanter began to complain that he was running low and might indeed run out of his supplies.

But no one died, and the threatened storms never materialized. The skies lightened into gray and white, and every now and then a patch of blue appeared. By the evening yellow and orange mixed with the gray, and they arrived to stand in waist-high weed grass and thorny bramble on a ridge top overlooking a deep vale shaped almost like a bowl and filled with a thicket of gnarled and stunted trees, a brownish briar patch that had grown over and around the ruin of a burnt-out black-walled fortress at its center. A single great turreted tower still projected up from the middle of the fortress, its surface covered by dark, thorny vines. Ravens and carrion birds circled over the once ornate, slate-covered steeped spire, now riddled with holes and partially collapsed, and they appeared to be using it as a rookery.

Stjepan, Erim, Arduin, Gilgwyr, Leigh, and Godewyn stood side by side on the eastern side of the bowl in the earth, surveying the dark and foreboding tower at its center. Sir Holgar and Caider Ross stood back a bit, Sir Holgar with a greatsword tucked in the crook of an arm and Caider with a loaded crossbow held casually in his.

"The Black Tower of Azharad," said Leigh. "Or what's left of it."

Stjepan, Erim, Gilgwyr, and Godewyn promptly spat to one side.

"Shit," said Erim to no one in particular. She raised her spyglass and trained it on the Black Tower, looking for movement.

"Stjepan, have you ever read *De Daemonologis?*" asked Leigh. "That at least can't be forbidden! It's the Inquisition's handbook on demonology and the Nameless Cults, for Heaven's sake."

"No, Magister, that book has not been banned, and yes, I have read it," Stjepan said.

"Well, that's something at least. Attributed to a namesake of yours, Stephans, Patriarch of Therapoli, as I recall," said Leigh.

"Actually my name comes from the Athairi, *stjeppen*, meaning steppe or plain," said Stjepan, squinting at the Black Tower.

"Child of the Steppes, then?" Gilgwyr asked with a laugh. "An odd name for someone born in the woods."

"My mother always said I was conceived on the Plain of Stones, when she went there with my father to sing to the earth," Stjepan said. He grimaced. "Strictly speaking, that was more information than I needed to know." He glanced over at Erim. "Anything?"

"Nothing," she said, lowering the spyglass. "Some ravens and crows, that's about it."

Stjepan nodded and hefted two long wooden poles over his shoulder and started to walk slowly westward along the southern edge of the bowl. The rest of the group started to follow him, with Sir Holgar and Caider Ross as their rearguard, their heads swiveling between the surrounding hillsides and the vine-choked Black Tower.

428

"*De Daemonologis* is an excellent place to begin the study of the war against Githwaine and then the later war against Azharad," said Leigh as they walked through the waist-high grasses and weeds. "It collects and codifies many of the histories of the time, at least those thought reputable by the Sun Court . . . not that they are necessarily the best and most unbiased source. Patriarch Stephans wrote that after Fortias the Brave killed Githwaine, and the Sun Court called its curse down on Uthedmael and rendered it *Lost*, some of Githwaine's followers either found refuge here in the Bale Mole or were up here already."

"What sort of people would live up here?" asked Arduin. "Uthedmael at least was once green and prosperous, yes? Before Githwaine arrived to lead it into error and darkness. But this land has always been bleak and harsh." As if to prove his point, or in response to the insult, his boot caught on a hidden root and he almost pitched forward onto his face.

Leigh ignored the slight clatter from Arduin. "The first peoples of the Bale Mole were from the Daradjans and the Mael, hardy folk who loved the independence of the wild; they built the citadels of Angharad and Liss Dyved and towns like Tir'gaile to watch over the roads of the dead in and out of the Vale of Barrows," he said. "By the time of Githwaine, the roads had fallen into disuse as worship of the Divine King took hold amongst the Danians, and the hills became plagued by necromancers and magicians seeking to tap the power of its burial sites and holy places. Githwaine had found several ready allies in the hills during his war against the Danians, including the twin necromancers Gallesdone and Heddis."

"They held Angharad then, yes?" asked Gilgwyr. "Over . . . well, that away." He waved off to the south in the direction that the lost tower in theory would be found. He was not sure he had his bearings correctly, and only remembered the names because of some delectable perversions they indulged in, but no one corrected him.

"Yes," said Leigh. "In those days it was briefly called the *Brig A'duos Magos*, the Tower of the Two Wizards."

"Another favorite of treasure-hunters," said Godewyn. "It still stands, though only fools would enter it." *Fools like you lot, no doubt*, he thought with a snort. But Leigh turned and fixed him with a smile that seemed to say *I know what you're thinking*, and Godewyn found himself brought up short.

"They were powerful enchanters, so at some point that would have been a trip worth making," said Leigh pleasantly, before turning back around to follow Stjepan. "But no doubt not now. While not touched directly by the Sun Court's curse on Lost Uthedmael, the Bale Mole became a difficult place to hide, as the Watchtower Kings of Maece and the Wall used the Bale Mole as traversing ground into the Vale of Barrows and points westwards to seek out their enemies in the Djar Éduins. The followers of Githwaine and Nymarga who lived here were forced to lurk in the dark and forgotten corners of the hills, abandoning their citadels to burrow deep into the earth and escape their enemies."

"I have always heard rumors of the hills being honeycombed with tunnels," said Godewyn, staring with thoughts of murder at the back of Leigh's head.

"Gammond of Wael said that the Nameless Cults claimed you could walk from one end of the Bale Mole to the other and never see the sun if you so chose," said Leigh, now huffing a bit as they walked. "But after Ravera's Mistake, which plunged the Watchtowers into confusion for a time, the followers of Githwaine and Nymarga eking out an existence in the Bale Mole were able to gain some respite from those that hunted them, and slowly reemerge into the light. Amongst them stood the warlock and enchanter named Azharad. He conjured up dark allies out of the tombs and barrows of the Vale, and attracted foul and evil mercenaries from brigand bands and Djar Mael clans. He built this Black Tower, and from it launched a war into the Tiria Wold, fighting against the Danian and Athairi lords of the woods, and came to control half the forest, capturing the citadels of Bronrood, Garner Lais, Uth Glydmoredd, Penngraile, and Porgraile. Stjepan, a moment!"

Stjepan nodded and they paused in their walk along the rim of the bowl so the enchanter could take a rest and swig from a water bottle. A few of the others drank from their flasks as well, and for a few minutes they just eyed the Black Tower, brooding and dark.

"Fuck," said Erim at last. Leigh laughed as Stjepan started walking again and they followed.

430

"The self-styled 'Kingdom of Azharad' flared for a while as a dangerous new neighbor, and knights from the Watchtowers, Dania, and Daradja plunged into the woods to halt his progress," Leigh continued his tale. "By all accounts it was a war of horrors; Azharad and his followers had developed a taste for human flesh, made dark sacrifices to the Forbidden Gods, and engaged in bizarre and unnatural rituals. They made for formidable foes, possessed of black magic and sorcery and enchanted weapons. Azharad never actually used *Gladringer*, though he had it in his possession; they considered it an object of hatred as it had killed their cult-hero Githwaine, but one of his lieutenants, the villainous Harigrina, supposedly wielded *Mhorismal*, the Red Talon of the Wyvern King, which is almost as famous a blade as *Gladringer*. King Coric of Dania finally led an army against Azharad, catching and killing him while he was traveling between the citadels of Garner Lais and Uth Glydmoredd in the year 1127. Azharad's body was spirited from the field of battle by some of his followers, and King Coric and his knights pursued them back here to the Black Tower and put it to the torch."

"King Coric was the last king of the united Danias," said Godewyn. "With both King Aramo of Dain Dania and King Eolred of Erid Dania as his descendants, carrying on the feud of his sons."

"May the King of Heaven and Earth watch over His vassals," said Arduin and Sir Holgar said together. "May they rule justly in his name."

"I'm sure they will," said Leigh. "There were rumors that the feud between Coric's sons, Iawn and Medrawn, was the result of a curse that fell upon them when they entered the Black Tower." He waved toward the ruin down below them.

"Shit. Then the Barrow of Azharad is down there somewhere, yeah?" Erim asked, surveying the vale with shivers coursing her spine.

"As a friend of ours once said, ignore the bright bauble," Stjepan said gently over his shoulder. "The ruins of the Black Tower have been searched through for the last three centuries by every tomb robber and questing knight looking for Azharad's burial place and *Gladringer*. Or for the body of Harigrina and *Mhorismal,* which is supposedly buried there as well.

431

Well, those that walked away from it alive, that is. It's a place of darkness and death. So maybe something's still in there."

He came to a halt. They had walked to the other side of the bowl, and now stood on the western ridge looking down into it.

"But not *Gladringer*, at least according to our map," said Stjepan. "The map says we go . . . *this way*." And he turned to the west, putting his back to the Black Tower, and started to walk toward the yellow light of the setting sun behind the light grey clouds.

With glances at each other that betrayed a mix of excitement, curiosity, and skepticism, the rest of the group fell in behind him, following him as he walked slowly up to the crest of the ridge, and turned to survey the view back to the tower below them and the vista to the east. He slipped the dry mariner's compass out of his satchel, and slowly maneuvered himself until he was finally satisfied with his orientation with the tower and the hills and mountains visible in the distant east. Then he turned around again and started heading due west.

Stjepan led them down a gentle, shallow valley and then up a slope toward the crest of another hill. Ahead of them and stretching to their north they could see a line of great boulder formations that protruded up from the grass and bramble, and as they reached the crest of the hill they could see that the great rocks were actually massive pieces of stone carved into the shape of animal and bird heads and set into the earth. The closest two that they were approaching appeared to be a pair of lion heads, carved of black rock that might have once been smooth and polished, but were now weatherworn and pockmarked. Stjepan frowned as he approached them. They were easily three times his height and faced to the east. Enough survived of their appearance to give them a fierce, predatory cast. "Hello, guardians of the dead," he said under his breath. "But not what I was expecting." He looked in both directions, studying the stone heads until he spotted two great vulture-head statues just to their north.

"Hmm, off a bit," Stjepan said to himself. *Unless someone has moved them*, he thought.

Stjepan walked over and stood between them. The massive vulture heads were in slightly better shape than the lion heads, and their feral look was even more pronounced. He checked his west and east bearings with the compass, and started to count out paces to the west as he walked.

He went three hundred paces and almost tripped over something. He stopped and slipped the compass back into his satchel, and then he unlimbered the poles he was carrying, handing one off to Erim. He used one end of the pole to push and prod at the bramble and grass and thorns in front of him, slowly pushing some of them aside to reveal what appeared to be the lip of a stone step, almost buried under the top growth of the hill. He started to walk forward, probing, revealing more covered steps. Slowly he worked his way another three hundred paces and stopped.

He had come to the side of a steep nondescript hill, albeit covered with ugly weeds, thorns, and briars. The others came up behind him and joined him in staring at the side of the hill.

"What? This is it?" Godewyn asked.

Leigh mumbled under his breath and waved his hand through the air as though testing it. "I detect no magic here," he said.

"According to the map he was buried in iron and plain earth, with only subtle wards. Strong magic would only draw spirits and the *Fae* Courts, and they'd just trade the secret of the location to mortals, or steal his magics for themselves," said Stjepan.

Leigh rolled his head from side to side for a moment, pondering it. "Aye. That's how I'd hide it, I suppose," he said finally.

Stjepan stepped forward, and began to slowly prod and poke into the hillside. He tested it in several places, slowly pressing up and forward a bit until suddenly his pole slid easily into the roots of the briars. He poked again, and earth and roots crumbled a bit to reveal a darkness in the earth.

"Here. We'll dig here," Stjepan said quietly.

"I'll get my crew," Godewyn said, and he turned and started jogging back to the rest of the expedition.

Two hours later, bramble and thorn and loose earth had been shoveled out of the way, and Stjepan and Godewyn were slowly pulling away the last roots and thorns to reveal a vertical, stone-framed open maw in the side of the briar hill, unmistakably the entrance to a manmade tunnel. Dusk was near and the sky overcast, making everything gray. With the clouds it was dark enough already that they had set lanterns alight and set them to hang from poles around their work site. Cole Thimber, Giordus, and Too Tall stood to one side behind them, dirty and sweaty from digging into the side of the hill with shovels. If they had disliked being the ones doing the bulk of the digging, they had not complained; they knew it was why they were hired, after all. Gilgwyr, Erim, Arduin, and Sir Helgi also stood nearby, watching in grim expectation.

"Fuck me," Gilgwyr finally said with wonder.

"This is it," Stjepan said. "If the map is right, this is it. This is where it has been leading us."

"Fuck," Erim said.

For a while they stood stock still, staring at the entrance into the earth.

Finally Arduin stirred and spoke. "I'm . . . I'm not sure I thought it would be real, in the end . . . the Barrow of Azharad. I think I stopped thinking that we were actually going someplace, a real place. The Barrow of a Sorcerer-King."

"We don't actually know it's his barrow yet, my Lord Arduin. Right now it's just a mystery hole in the ground," Stjepan said quietly.

"What, do we just walk into it?" asked Godewyn, peering into the dark maw.

Stjepan's initial instinct was to say *yes*, but he looked up at the skies, tracking some dark carrion birds flying in the distance, and thinking better of it, shook his head. "The sun's setting too quickly. We shouldn't try to enter with night almost upon us. The sun is our friend in this, gentlemen, the dark our enemy, may the Queen of Night forgive me for saying so."

No one offered an argument. With looks of relief they took up their lanterns and slowly backed away until they felt safe enough to turn around and head back to the camp, leaving the hole into the earth to call out silently behind them in the looming darkness.

CHAPTER TWENTY-FOUR
CAMPED BEFORE
THE BARROW

After some small debate, they had set up their camp between and around the two vulture-head stone statues, within sight of the hilltop and the entrance into the ground. Leigh could find no evidence of enchantment about the statues, and so Stjepan and Godewyn had both agreed that they should be used as walls and defensive obstacles. They detached one of the tail boards from one of the wagons and had a set of the horses drag it around behind them by the heavy chains of their harnesses to tramp down an increasingly large circle in the grass and weeds. Once they were satisfied with the basic shape of the camp, they moved in with shovels and scythes to finish prepping the ground. Their campfires had gone in the center, between the two statues, and then the various tents around them. The two wagons and the coach were brought up and arrayed on the eastern side of their camp, placed front to back to create a wall facing the east and the vale of the Black Tower. Behind them they ran the picket lines for the dozens of horses; the young squire Brayden and the Theos were brushing the horses down, and checking their feedbags. Some of the horses seemed quite content to nibble at the tall grasses that covered the rolling hills, and Brayden collected and piled some of the cut grasses for them to munch on.

Colin Urwed stood guard by the Ladies' Tent while his brother set up their own tent nearby. Sir Holgar worked on a weapons' rack of polearms and unstrung bows and crossbows, while Caider Ross and Pallas Quinn finished the last of the other tents around the central campfire, where Wilhem Price was already preparing a meal. Erim had been the first to return, and she sat brooding by the fire. Giordus Roame and Too Tall were the next to reach the camp, and after their labors digging into dirt and thicket they had little inclination left to do anything other than just stumble back to the fire next to Erim and start digging again, this time into several bread loaves and one of the barrels of wine. Cole Thimber was a bit slower but right behind them. Arduin, Sir Helgi, Gilgwyr, Godewyn, and Stjepan were the last to return.

Stjepan saw that Leigh was marking the edge of their camp where the grasses still stood upright, whispering his ritual over a wider perimeter than usual of stones and chalk dust poured from his bag. He broke off from the others and walked over to Leigh as the former Magister straightened from marking the last of the four cardinal rocks with a rune.

"I am almost out of my ward marker," Leigh said in greeting. "Perhaps enough for two or three more encampments, and then we will just have to trust to the campfires alone."

"We'll move faster on the way out, so hopefully we can reach Mizer quickly," said Stjepan. "And then afterwards, perhaps we can return by a more central route, and not spend so much time so far from civilization."

"Civilization," Leigh said, and then laughed. He turned and looked up at the hilltop, a black shape against the dark of the blue-gray evening sky. "You know, I have a great deal of experience being far away from civilization. And yet, so close to the Black Tower of Azharad, in a land as haunted as the Bale Mole, I can barely tell whether one place is more evil than the next . . ." he said softly. He paused, his eyes closed and his body swaying for a moment, and then opened his eyes again. "But my hackles do not like being here. I think it *is* the barrow we seek."

Stjepan squinted at Leigh. "We'll find out soon enough, I suppose," Stjepan said.

They returned to camp to see most of the others gathered about the fire. Malia appeared from the Ladies' Tent and approached Stjepan, smoothing her dress as she did. "Forgive me, Master Stjepan, but my Lady has something to tell you," she said. Leigh grunted and nodded nearby as he settled into a seat.

"Lead the way, Mistress Malia," said Stjepan.

They began walking through the other tents toward the Ladies' Tent and

436

Sir Colin and his greatsword. "Our patron has a message for you? Perhaps she has a message for me too, Black-Heart!" Godewyn called out after them.

Stjepan ignored him. Malia bit her lip, looking up at him with uncertainty as they walked, then began to speak in a quiet voice. "At first I was happy that we were out and about, no matter the reason; over the last few years she has gotten worse and worse, and I feared she might take her own life, so much did she despair in her isolation. I wish . . . I wish you had seen her long ago, when she was in her element at Court. When she was happy. But now I don't know what to think. She seems so strange of late, Master Stjepan . . ."

Stjepan stopped, and Malia stopped with him. "How so?" he asked quietly.

"I'm not sure when it started to happen," Malia said slowly. "The week after her brother's death she was feverish and ill, barely able to speak or stand. She got better once we were traveling. She spent a great deal of time in the coach drifting in and out of fits of sleep. I thought she was still recovering from her illness." Malia looked toward the tent, with a look that approached fear on her face. "But it was while we were traveling that I started to notice. Little things, small differences in tone or word choice, a small confusion here or there about some word or deed misremembered from the past. Sometimes my Lady catches herself, and pauses, confused, and then makes a correction. Other times she blithely carries on, not realizing her mistake. I have been ever at her side for most of my life. I'm not sure I know who she is anymore."

"She is not herself," Stjepan said drily. He glanced back toward the main campfire. "Would that I could say the same for all of us." He took her hand in his. "If Fortune looks kindly upon us, her ordeal will soon be over and she will be freed of the map, and you will have your mistress back, herself once more."

Malia looked at the ground and curtsied.

Sir Colin nodded to them both as they approached. Stjepan pushed through the tent flap into the brazier-lit interior, and then he held it open for Malia as she followed him in.

Stjepan noted that Malia had become quite good at arranging the simple luxuries that they carried with them. Indeed, it struck him that after their stop in Hartford that the insides of the tent were now more heavily decorated than what he had seen of Annwyn's chambers back in her father's city house in Therapoli. Malia curtsied and gestured to the set of screens set about the center, and Stjepan stepped within them.

Within the screens, on a mound of furs and fabrics, reclined Annwyn, her back to Stjepan. He paused for a moment in slight surprise. She wore nothing but some jewelry. Her hair was a wild tumult barely contained by jeweled combs and bindings. The bits and pieces of the map moved about on her skin, appearing and disappearing, fading in and out. There was a large mirror set to one side that he did not remember them setting up previously, in which Annwyn was studying her reflection. In the mirror he could see that the amulet from Mizer dangled around her neck and between her breasts. His map-making kit was already open and waiting on a small folding table, next to the folding x-chair that acted as his proper seat.

Annwyn did not look at him. Her eyes were fixed on her own image in the mirror. "You say we are here, you say we have reached our destination, but would you be surprised if I told you the map is still furious inside me?" she asked him. "There is yet more to come."

Stjepan said nothing for a moment, then finally stirred. "I had indeed hoped you would be rid of the map by now," he said.

Annwyn rolled before the mirror, tracking a new set of letters that slid over her skin; she moved without hesitation or shame, and a fear awoke somewhere in the back of Stjepan's mind. "It matters not," she said lightly. "I have grown to think of it as a part of me. In some ways, I now find it beautiful to watch, the shapes of the letters rising in my skin. And you? Have you . . . learned to enjoy your work?"

Stjepan moved to stand next to the mirror, and looked down upon her. His eyes narrowed as he tracked and followed the same word that she was watching in her reflection.

"Yes, there is more . . . that's new, there," he said, pointing with his chin to icons and lines that were sliding over her hip. "As are some of the words. There are some that I do not recognize from before."

Stjepan drew up a seat by the mirror. He drew his notebook out from his satchel, selected a quill from the small table, dipped it in ink, and then began making some notes. Annwyn watched in the mirror and tried to move her body so the new images and words were always facing toward Stjepan. She smiled, and almost giggled, as though it were a game.

"Have you ever been in love?" she suddenly asked.

Stjepan looked up at her face, a bit surprised. "An odd question, given the circumstances, my Lady," he said guardedly.

"Is it?" she asked, smiling softly. "For all our . . . *talks*, you keep yourself at arm's length. You are not entirely unknown to me, you know. Harvald had a habit, you see." She rolled over again, this time deliberately putting her back to him. "He and I had been each other's confidantes when we were younger, once upon a time. He was my younger brother, the youngest of the Orwains of Araswell, and so we had always acted as though we had a special bond. He could spend all day with me, sometimes, just watching and following me."

She said nothing for a while, as if remembering something.

"Later, after my . . . scandal, he would come to me, and he would still act as though we were young and little again, sharing secrets," she said softly. "But as we get older his stories grew darker, and were sometimes about filthy things, things that made me blush to hear them, things that he knew I could never dare tell anyone else."

She turned around and looked at him straight in the eye. "Some of those stories were about the two of you. The things you were off doing, the adventures you were having, the maps you were following, the treasures you were seeking, the women you seduced, the men you killed," she said, studying his reactions intently. He kept his face a blank. "He told me once about a woman that the two of you shared one night. A barmaid at some tavern in Truse. He was quite graphic in his details . . . the sights, the sounds, the pleasures the two of you could wring out of her. How it felt being so close to you. His memories of skin, and flesh, and sweat."

Stjepan's eyes narrowed. *Ninava, at the Flying Cat*, he thought with surprise.

"He said it was one of the most amazing experiences of his life," she said dreamily, looking at him with surprisingly wise eyes. A half-smile played on her face, and then she looked away. "I knew there were things he was leaving out, little secrets here and there that he wasn't sharing; I was no longer young and foolish enough to think that he told me everything. But I could never tell if he outright lied to me."

She looked at him. "Have you ever lied to me, Stjepan?" she asked.

He said nothing as she crawled closer. She reached down, seemingly for his lap, and Stjepan tensed, but her hand closed on the hilt of his dagger. She slid it from its sheath, holding it up before him.

"Have you ever had to kill a woman before?" she asked.

That broke his mask, and Stjepan looked at her face with surprise and suspicion. He studied her for a long moment before speaking gently. "My Lady? Do you not feel safe with me?" he asked.

"I am sure that if he were somehow looking on us from the after-life, Harvald would be pleased . . . by the restraint you have shown in the company of his sister," she said.

Stjepan waited a moment. "Restraint, my Lady?" he finally asked, with the slightest hint of a smile tugging at the corner of his mouth.

Annwyn smiled slightly, and Stjepan looked back down at her skin, and resumed writing and sketching into his notebook. Annwyn watched him work for a while, and then resumed staring at her reflection. She pointed at the new words on her skin with the tip of the dagger. "I knew there was more to the map! Do you think it knows we are close? Perhaps the map would show you a path through this place of death, a safe path only it knows . . ." she said.

"Perhaps, a safe path, yes. We shall see," said Stjepan.

"Then I am still of use to you," Annwyn said.

Stjepan reached out and his hand slowly closed on hers. Gently he took the dagger back from her, and slowly he stood up.

"You can be of much use still, my Lady," he said.

"I shall do my best, Master Stjepan," she said coyly.

Tucking his notebook back in his satchel, Stjepan excused himself with a bow.

Stjepan crouched inside his tent, a low lantern nearby, searching through a small pack crammed with small books, codexes, maps, and scrolls. He took out a single leather-bound book with arcane markings upon it and began flipping through it.

Stjepan was so engrossed in his book that he was unaware of a presence filling the tent behind him.

"Stjepan," came a voice from within the tent.

Stjepan jumped with a start, and then relaxed. He glanced over his shoulder.

"Erim! Yhera, Queen of Heaven, don't sneak up on me like that . . ." he said. *You're getting far too good at it*, he thought.

"Sorry, it's not my fault you're not paying attention to what's around you," Erim said with a shrug. "What are you reading?"

"It's a copy of the *De Secretis Libris* of Eldyr, son of King Myrad," he said. "It's . . . a book of secret magic. Written by a powerful, and very mad, enchanter, who was one of the Hundred Sons of Myrad the Mad."

Erim sat down opposite him and thumbed through a book from Stjepan's stash, pretending to read it. He frowned, for it seemed an odd pantomime for Erim. "She's changing. She's acting different," she said; it wasn't so much a question as a statement.

"Yes. Each day, it seems, by both Malia's report and my own observations," he said ruefully, running his hand through his hair and rubbing his mouth.

Erim was now looking at him intently. "What are you thinking?" she asked.

Stjepan hesitated. "I'm not entirely sure. But I'm starting to wonder if perhaps something else is acting upon her, or through her," he said, his voice so low it was almost a whisper. "Eldyr described how you could place an enchantment upon someone to make them pursue a goal not their own. I think she may be under some sort of compulsion . . . or possession."

"A spell of some kind? By Harvald?" Erim asked.

"I don't know . . . perhaps," Stjepan said with a frown. "I did not recognize the type of Sending that he was performing in the library before he died, so perhaps he placed some sort of command or compulsion upon her to ensure the map would be followed. But the map itself may have had powers to compel those who possess and read it, perhaps even the power to transform them . . ." He hesitated. "I am not entirely sure if burning the map freed it of its curse, or simply transformed the curse into something new."

He looked up at her and sighed. "Yet I still want to believe that the Lady is innocent. I can sense my own hesitation to judge her with a cold eye and see her for what she really is. So . . ." he said, and paused for a moment. His words began to slow as he stared at Erim. "I fear . . . I'm not looking hard enough . . . I'm not seeing something I should . . ."

They stared at each other. *Something is wrong*, Stjepan thought. *Something doesn't look right. Something doesn't smell right. Erim doesn't just look like a man. She* smells *like a man.*

Erim put the book back down, frowning back at Stjepan. "What's the matter, Stjepan?" she asked. "Are you okay?"

"What's the matter with me?" Stjepan said, frowning back at her. "What's the matter with you?"

Both of them could suddenly hear the sound of someone approaching one of the tent's entrances.

"Someone's coming," Erim said, rising up into a standing crouch and backing toward the far tent flap. Stjepan was confused by her behavior but her worry and concern were contagious and he turned to await the new arrival, his hand slipping to the hilt of a dagger.

Erim pulled open the tent flap and stepped inside, laughing. "Hey, Godewyn's trying to . . ." she said, then stopped short, looking at herself standing at the back of the tent. "Fuck."

442

For a moment the two Erims stared at each other, as Stjepan looked back and forth between them in confusion.

The Erim to whom Stjepan had been talking smiled a sneering grin as its body turned black and its face a ghostly white. And then the figure suddenly slipped out the far tent flap, leaving the mask of its false smiling face hanging in mid-air behind it, slowly dissipating like smoke from a candle.

The real Erim stood frozen, staring at the fading false face, but Stjepan threw himself out to the tent in pursuit of the fleeing figure with a curse, weapons coming bared.

He quickly turned in a circle, falchion in his right hand and point dagger in his left, but there was nothing to see. The figure from inside the tent had vanished in an instant. *Where'd he go? I was right behind him . . .* Under his breath he began to quickly whisper: *"Show me! Show me the World, show me that which is hidden . . ."*

He began to move about the camp. Everything seemed normal, though a wind was rising. His eyes scanned the ground, looking for tracks, but the ground was covered by broken grass and fresh overturned earth and where footprints were possible there were many of them, from a dozen different shoes and boots. There was a faint trail in the air, though, the faint firefly lights of powerful magic, and he started to follow them, cursing the wind. He ran into Too Tall and Caider Ross, drunk and laughing. With the Incantation of Seeing, magic in the world began to glow before him: a hidden rune here on Too Tall's dagger, the amulets that Leigh had given them glowing there under their shirts. But neither bore the signs of a recent glamour upon them. They paid him no mind as he passed them, glancing in tents and wagons.

The softly glowing firefly lights that danced in the wind seemed to be dissipating where he was, and he was about to turn toward the central campfire to see who was there when he heard horses softly whinnying and shifting on the picket line off to one side. He shifted course immediately, stalking swiftly and quietly.

He turned the corner of a tent and was surprised to see several lean, pale-skinned, almost cadaverous men in barbaric masks and partial armor a dozen paces away, sneaking up behind the next tent over. They were as surprised as he was, and they all froze for a moment, staring at each other.

The three men were dressed similarly to the Nameless Cultists that had come upon them under the ground in the hills of the Manon Mole, but of markedly superior gear. They wore black oval masks of leather and wood that covered their entire faces, with slanted eye holes to give them a feral appearance and curled or straight spiral horns from rams and gazelles sticking out from their foreheads; tall spikes of wild black hair stuck up from behind the masks. One of the three had animal teeth inlaid on the front of his mask. He could see that the masks were enchanted to make their wearers all the more fearsome and terrifying, and the enchantments were certainly working. They wore leather bracers and rags and furs dyed black, their pants tucked into leather and cloth wraps that snaked around their ankles and short boots. Two of the three had bare chests, and he could see the gleam and glow of runes of warding and protection and strength branded into their pale skin, while the third bore a great round shield with red runes painted onto it. He could also see glowing amulets dangling around their necks next to gleaming golden torques, torques around their upper arms, amulets wrapped in leather cords around their wrists under their bracers, and the gleam of runes on their blackened, barbed spears and poisoned, curved swords.

Azharites, he had time to think.

And then the men screamed and suddenly charged.

Before they could reach him, Sir Theodore and Sir Helgi crashed in wearing their full three-quarter plate harnesses, sending two of the Azharites sprawling while Theodore's sword ran the third one through the stomach. The two Azharites sprang swiftly back to their feet as Sir Theodore pulled his sword out of their companion. Sir Theodore commenced to bashing away at the Azharite holding a shield, who blocked his flurry of blows, while Sir Helgi rather expertly threw the other back on the ground and then stabbed downward into his gut with his greatsword. As the sword streaked down Stjepan saw the flash of a gleaming rune of victory on the blade, and it pierced through the Azharite's warded skin to pin him into the ground.

Freeing his sword, Sir Helgi bellowed at the top of his lungs: "To arms! To arms! We are attacked!"

A wave of Azharites came rushing in on foot out of the dark as a partially armored Sir Theodras ran in to back up Sir Helgi and Sir Theodore. They met in a clash of arms, blood flying as Azharites went down, but Sir Theodras' unarmored leg took a great blow to the knee from a heavy iron mace and he went down with a scream with two of the masked berserks on top of him, trying to stab him to death. Sir Theodore leapt to his rescue, killing one of the Azharites with a sharp blow that sheared mask and skull, but a black-clad berserk behind him drove a barbed spear into Theodore's right buttock and ripped downwards, opening up the back of his thigh where it was unprotected except by cloth, and blood gushed out in great spurts as the knight screamed and stumbled away from the prone Sir Theodras toward where Sir Helgi held off three of the foul attackers. The Azharite shield man used the opening to bring the edge of his shield down in a strike on Sir Theodras' screaming mouth, silencing him with a bloody crunch.

All this barely registered on Stjepan; the moment the fighting started he had resumed his search, intent on finding the intruder to his tent, and he saw a trail of firefly lights waft into the air nearby. He slipped through the tents, scanning left and right, following the lights like floating embers. He could see Azharites streaming in on foot through the tall grass, and leaping over the short gaps between the wagons, and he ducked out of the way as one of them ran past him, charging at and spearing Cole Thimber as he lumbered forward. Despite the spear in the gut, the big man waded into a group of the Azharites with a long-hafted iron-headed mace, and bellowing proceeded to start knocking them about. Arrows and darts came flying out of the dark to pepper into the sides of the tents; some of the arrow were on fire, and a couple of the tents looked like they were about to go up in flames.

Stjepan reached the Ladies' Tent, where Sirs Lars and Colin Urwed were beset by more of the Azharites. A masked berserk, larger and more muscular than his lean fellows, spun a long-hafted axe in both hands, knocked Sir Lars' sword aside, and swiftly brought the heavy head of his axe down on the knight, crushing his sallet helmet. The squire Brayden rushed the axe-wielding berserk, and was cleaved almost in two. Seeing the odds going so badly at Annwyn's tent almost diverted Stjepan from his mission, but an armed and partially armored Arduin, runes gleaming on his sword and breastplate, charged in and with two quick cuts of his war sword he had separated one of the berserk's arms at the shoulder, and then his head. Squire Wilhem Price leapt in, sword ready, to stand behind Sir Colin, who swung his greatsword around to fend off the rest of the Azharites, and Stjepan kept moving.

The trail of firefly lights was fading and growing thinner, his frustration growing. A few dozen weaving steps and he found himself almost back at his own tent, having made a rough circle through the camp. Stjepan had to step over Giordus Roame, who'd had an arm lopped off. Stjepan's heart leapt into his throat and he picked up speed, and he came upon Godewyn, Caider Ross, and Too Tall using poleaxes and bills to advance into a small group of the Azharites, trying to fight side-by-side with some practiced discipline but mostly succeeding in pushing the Azharites back through wild enthusiasm, while Erim was acrobatically fighting two Azharites left standing from a larger group of a half dozen. One of them had an extra long mask, almost shaped like a teardrop and coming to a point, with two great antelope horns jutting up from its top, and he wore a leather cuirass affixed with brass scales and glistening with enchantment. Erim ducked in and out between the two Azharites, stabbing the one with a normal-sized mask in the throat. The long-masked Azharite with the leather cuirass bore down on her, their blades clashing in a cut-and-parry back and forth; he cut her across her left arm and she cried out, but then she dropped low under his next swing and came up, driving her rapier through his stomach under his cuirass and up into his rib cage. He spat blood, then collapsed.

At the fall of the Azharite with the long mask, the remaining Azharites bolted and fled into the dark, chased by Godewyn and Caider and Too Tall, yelling curses at the top of their lungs.

Erim, wild-eyed and still in a bit of shock, turned and pointed her weapons as Stjepan approached. The rest of the camp had started to grow quiet, except for someone wounded shrieking into the night. That quickly and it was over.

"Is it you? Is it you?" she asked him, staring at him, her rapier pointing straight at his throat.

"It's me. Is it you?" he replied.

Her wounded left arm started to shake, and she dropped the point dagger that it held, and then her rapier, and fell to her knees. She felt her face with her good hand as Stjepan crouched beside her. "What in the Six Hells was that?" she whispered. Her face was hot to the touch, as though she had a fever coming on.

"A *glamour*—a magician's mask. Someone took your form, to get close to me and ask some questions. But in the confusion of the attack I lost him . . ." he said, inspecting her wound.

"A magician? Attacking us with these lunatics?" she asked, looking around her at the masked men scattered around on the ground. She was having trouble focusing. A great fatigue seemed to be welling up inside her.

Stjepan studied the man with the leather cuirass and long mask for a moment. "Perhaps. They're Azharites," he said. "Berserker warriors and warlocks dedicated to the Nameless Cults, the inheritors of Azharad's Kingdom, either coming upon us or set as guardians for the Black Tower and the barrow. Careful; the blade was poisoned. Their captains and champions like to use the venom of the Éduins asp viper."

"What? Poisoned?" Erim asked, and then she fell over in a faint, and started to shake and make choking sounds.

Stjepan quickly slipped into their tent, and fished through one of his satchels until he found what he was looking for: poultices of the *goldenrod* leaf, mashed into a paste and enchanted with a simple folk ritual. He slipped back out with the satchel, and pressed several of the poultices onto the gash in her arm, and wound out some clean linen gauze to wrap around the poultices and pin them in place. There was already a bit of foam flaking at the corners of her mouth, but within moments after the poultice was applied her body stopped shaking and her breathing returned to normal.

Godewyn walked back into the firelight, and watched Stjepan work. Arduin appeared, splattered in blood; Leigh followed warily behind him, looking about nervously and clutching a short sword. One of the wagons and several of the tents were on fire, and Stjepan could see some of Caider and Too Tall trying to douse the wagon with spare water. The shrieking suddenly stopped, and it grew quiet except for faint moans and muffled weeping, the neighing of startled horses and the crackle of things on fire that weren't supposed to be.

"King of Heaven," Arduin said, surveying the scene.

Somewhere in the camp, a woman's voice rose.

Stjepan stood, and he and Godewyn and Arduin and Leigh looked back over the camp.

"That's . . . that's Annwyn," said Arduin, perplexed. "My sister is . . . *singing.*" He stared off into the night. "What in Heaven's name is she singing?"

Stjepan eyes narrowed. "It's the *Chant Amora d'Afare y Argus.* The Love Song of Afare and Argus," Stjepan said. He looked up at the starless night sky, saw the last of the firefly lights mixing with embers from the fires and fading into darkness. He closed his eyes and listened to the wind, to the ringing of distant bells, to a tragic love song floating on the gasps of the dying. He sniffed the air, smelt fire and ash, blood and bowels, the sharpness of honest clean steel and the lather of horse sweat, an undercurrent of desperate and abject fear, from somewhere near the hint of something dead and rotting, and underlying it all the rotten stench of abject and absolute corruption.

His gaze fluttered open and grew hard and grim, and he glanced up the hill toward the hole in the earth that awaited them out there somewhere in the darkness.

"Yeah," he said finally. "We're definitely in the right place."

448

PART THREE

IN THE BARROW OF
THE DEAD AND DYING

CHAPTER TWENTY-FIVE
THE FIRST ATTEMPT

Stjepan was walking up a leaf-strewn forest path, broad high trees of birch and purple-leaf oak, maple and elm, cherry and white ash, cedar and pine stretching out for leagues in all directions. The trunks of the trees and the debris of the forest floor were coated with old layers of lichens and moss, and a rust-red under-brush complemented the ancient patina of grays and dull greens. The leaves were turning burnt red and orange-yellow, into fire and gold, all the brilliant shades of autumn, and so he began to suspect it was a dream. He turned and looked to his right through a break in the trees, and caught a glimpse of a far sloping range of forested evergreen hills, backdropped by a horizon of desolate high mountains. Down to the east a great stone castle sat on a rise over a small riverside city, and he knew that across that river would be the Plain of Stones. *Ah. Indeed. This dream, of An-Athair, and my mother, and death.* A dream, then, and one that would soon fill him with pain, but still it was pleasant for the moment, and so he kept walking the ancient forest path, drinking in its beauty.

A fox appeared from out of the underbrush to take a seat on a rock by the side of the road. *You are too late, too late*, the fox called to him.

"Too late for what, little lord?" he asked.

You'll see, you'll see, the fox called, and then it slipped off the rock to disappear back into the underbrush.

He followed the path and the woods fell silent except for the sound of a woman singing somewhere in the distance. If the fox was still nearby he could neither see nor hear it; no bird sang in the branches above. But the woman's voice seemed familiar, and grew clearer as he walked. He could smell wet earth and leaf and needle, moss and sun-lit stone, and from nearby the smell of something burning.

He approached a high clearing in the woods. Massive, ancient trees surrounded the clearing, their lower branches filled with dangling amulets and chimes, small sculptures and offerings placed around their trunks. A pyre had been built in the center of the clearing, and a single post erected within it. A woman was tied to the post, her long silk dress slightly torn and soiled with dirt. She was beautiful, wild, her long wavy black hair framing a face of wisdom and power. His mother, Argante. A crowd of their neighbors watched with fear and excitement behind several circles of men dressed in black robes and brown hoods as some of those men stepped forward and lowered torches. The pyre began to catch. The singing was coming from somewhere in the crowd; he could see a woman with golden blonde hair moving behind the watching ranks of his neighbors, but he lost sight of her.

His young brother, Justin, stood stock still to the side, watching with wide eyes, and Stjepan's heart broke. Two hooded men, with deer antlers attached to their masks, held his sister on her knees, forcing her to watch as the flames of the pyre grew stronger and higher. He couldn't see her face but her long curly hair was unmistakable, a deep, dark brown that was almost black, the color of burnt earth. *Artesia.*

He walked slowly toward the pyre, coming to stand behind his sister and the men restraining her. He could hear his sister whispering to herself: *"That won't be me. That won't be me. That won't be me."* His mother looked down at him, and smiled, as she always did in his dreams. Smoke and flames were rising up around her. Her skin was blackening from the heat, but she seemed serene.

Artesia could see that her mother was looking at someone behind her. She looked over her shoulder and her eyes met his. He could see anguish, and pain, and hate in her gaze, made all the more terrible because they shared the same dark gaze of judgment. Her struggle intensified, anger welling up in her, and she tore free of the two hooded men. She ran to Stjepan, tears pouring down a face contorted by rage, and she began striking him in the chest, again and again.

"Why weren't you here? Why weren't you here? You could have done something! You could've saved her!" she screamed at him.

Stjepan shook his head. "I . . . I was away, at University . . ." he said. "There was nothing I could . . ." She fell against him, sobbing, and he embraced her in his arms.

He stared as the flames consumed his mother.

He did not see or sense the dark figure standing almost right behind him.

Stjepan awoke and stared at the canvas ceiling of the tent, cast in the blue-gray light of morning. The canvas creaked and rustled in a light breeze. He did not move for a long moment, until he became aware of someone looking at him.

He turned his head, and found himself looking into Erim's eyes. She lay on her side, staring at him bleakly from the other side of the small tent.

"Are you all right?" he asked.

"I don't want to die here," she whispered.

He turned and looked at the ceiling of the tent.

"Neither do I," he said.

With the poison in Erim at least neutralized, Stjepan had slipped off into the night, bow and quiver and blades at the ready, to scout the path the Azharites had taken to their camp. He had been filled with fear that they had come from the Black Tower and that more of them might be hidden there. He had found the tracks of a dozen men fleeing back into the east, back along the tracks from which they'd came on a high foot path that paralleled the road they'd come in on; so he could only hope that they had come up from the Uthed Wold and would have to travel all the way back to their hidden citadels in those dark woods in order to garner reinforcements. *Two days, maybe three, and then they'll be back . . . if we're lucky.*

453

Stjepan had reported his findings to Arduin and Gilgwyr and Godewyn, and they had wound up agreeing that they had little choice but to suppose that they were not in any further immediate danger, despite the scant little evidence on which to rest such hopes. They had gathered the survivors and then spent part of the night gathering the bodies of the dead into two separate piles. With their own dead—Sir Lars Urwed, Sir Holgar Torgisbain (who had been found on the other side of one of the giant stone vulture heads, in the midst of a cluster of half a dozen Azharite bodies, his armor crushed in by great blows and his flesh rent by stab wounds), Sir Theodras Clowain, Sir Theodore Lis Cawain, the young squire Brayden Vogelwain, red-haired Giordus Roame, and big Cole Thimber—they had cleaned and washed the bodies as best they could, and wrapped them in white cloth and placed them in the back of a wagon, and offered prayers to the King of Heaven. Sir Helgi had wept openly as he prepared the body of his nephew.

They had piled the Azharites into a shallow pit some small distance from their camp, and then covered it with a shallow heaping of dirt. Twenty-two of the Devil-worshippers, black-masked, rune-covered, dripping in charms and enchantments and poisoned weapons.

"Half of us gone in an instant," Arduin had said thickly, as Sir Helgi had spat on the mound of dirt.

"We're lucky more of us aren't dead," Stjepan had said, setting a shovel down and wiping his hands clean of dirt and sweat. "A testament to your skill at arms, gentlemen. But there was nothing to indicate, either from the tracks or the possessions we have found amongst the dead, if these men were just some random patrol or raiding party that had stumbled over us simply because we are traversing lands that the Azharites claim as theirs, or if our attackers had sought us out as specific quarry. Though I am inclined to think the former."

"You think it was just random chance that we were attacked here, right after finding the entrance to the Barrow of Azharad?" Arduin had asked with a scoff.

"Nonsense. Someone warned them we were coming," had said Gilgwyr. "By magic or by messenger they knew we would be here." He had taken a

454

swig from a bottle of wine and passed it to Pallas Quinn, who had already appeared to be well into his cups at that point.

"That's just it," Stjepan had replied. "If you were one of the Azharite warlords of the Uthed Wold and someone had sent you word that a large party of explorers was on its way with a map leading to the burial place of your ancient Sorcerer-King, would you just send thirty men?"

They had all paused for a moment, staring down at the fresh mound of dirt.

"Maybe that's all they had?" Sir Helgi had ventured.

"Nah, Black-Heart's right," Godewyn had said, spitting to one side. "I had a talk with Jack Hardee a few years back when we were on a job into the ruins at Bronrood, he lives up in the Kettle March and knows the Azharites better than just about anybody. He said there's one of them they call the Horned King, and he's their master, and several rival Witch-Kings that serve under him as captains of their ruined citadels, and they've each got hundreds of these warrior savages in their companies. We saw a fair number of them in their caves and tunnels there. On something potentially this big, if it was me, I'd have sent every available sword I had." He glanced at Black-Heart. "This could get really bad if they figured out why we were here."

Some of them had turned away from the pile of dirt, then, to scan the land around them in the dark with worried eyes.

"Let's move fast in the morning, yeah?" Stjepan had said.

Annwyn's hand moved the flap of her tent open, giving her a view of the camp. Sir Colin Urwed stood only a pace of two away with his back to her, his hands resting on his bared greatsword. He didn't seem to be aware that she had come to the tent flap behind him, intent instead on watching a group moving west up the hill toward the entrance to the barrow as the sun rose in the east behind them. She could see the young squire Wilhem

Price and her handmaiden Malia were moving about the camp beyond Sir Colin, doing busy work around the now-doused campfires, cleaning up after the hasty morning meal.

She followed Sir Colin's gaze, and could see Stjepan, Arduin, Sir Helgi, Gilgwyr, four of the ruffians they'd hired on at the Inn—Godewyn, Pallas Quinn, Too Tall, and Caider Ross, though she did not know their names— Erim, and Leigh; they were moving quietly but swiftly up the stone steps they had uncovered yesterday, carrying weapons, tools, and other gear either in leather and canvas bags or slung over their shoulders.

My champions, she thought idly. Then she closed the tent flap.

Pallas Quinn, Caider Ross, and Too Tall were busy preparing lanterns. Erim tested her still-bandaged left arm. Arduin and Sir Helgi stood to the side grimly, both of them in their full armor: a complete field harness for Arduin, and a three-quarter harness for Sir Helgi. Their sallet helmets hung from their sword belts. Gilgwyr wiped at his sweating brow, looking very out of his element.

Arduin stared at the entrance into the hillside before them, and shuddered a bit. "Burying your dead in the earth . . . a barbaric practice," he muttered.

Stjepan glanced his way. He wasn't sure if Arduin had intended anyone else to hear him, but he spoke to him anyway. "Each practice has its purpose, my Lord: burial, for those of the Old Religion, to return them to the Earth that gave us birth . . ." he said, motioning to the north and the Vale of Barrows. Then his hand swept up, indicating the sky. ". . . And the funeral pyre for those who wish their ashes to guide their spirits to the heavenly halls of our Divine King."

"And should you die, Athairi, how should we treat your body?" asked Arduin.

"I shall be buried in the Earth when I die," Stjepan said, staring at the entrance; it seemed to be calling to him. *But that's all right, it's calling all of us*, he thought.

Erim wanted to ask why witches were burned at the stake, but thought better of it.

"This wizard, then; he was one of your lot, a follower of the Great Goddess Yhera?" asked Sir Helgi with a frown. "I thought you've been telling us that we shouldn't think the Old Religion and the Nameless Cults are the same, and yet here now you tell us that they treat the dead the same."

"Not *exactly* the same," said Stjepan, shaking his head. "The followers of the Nameless Cults used to secret their dead in the earth so they might later be animated by necromancers, to become guardians and corpse warriors. In ancient days they might also seek to revive them in foul and secret rituals. But by all report their cults lost the knowledge of how to bring one of their wizards back to life as a Worm King centuries ago. Githwaine was the last one. Strictly speaking, I suppose it wasn't really burial for them, not in the way that the Old Religion thinks of burial; it was more like . . . *storage*."

Leigh laughed. "A wonderful image, pupil of mine, the dead beneath the earth like apples and potatoes in the root cellar," the enchanter chortled. "Delightful."

They all looked at Leigh as though he was crazy; which he was.

Godewyn clapped Stjepan on the shoulder. "Well, then; lead on, smart boy," Godewyn said.

Stjepan glanced at Arduin, who smiled weakly and inclined his head in invitation to Stjepan to proceed.

Stjepan turned and contemplated the entrance to the barrow again. With a grunt, he stepped forward, nodding to Caider Ross, who fell in behind him with a lantern lit and ready.

They moved into the barrow.

Sunlight streamed into the corridor from the entrance; with the sun rising to the east, its light filtered directly into the barrow. Silhouettes emerged one by one from the light, first Stjepan and then Caider Ross, followed by the rest, with Pallas Quinn last, bearing another lantern. The corridor was made of large flat upright stones arranged as the walls and etched with the bas-reliefs of horned demons with barbed tails, capped with other large stones laid over the top. The corridor slanted slightly downward. They walked over a floor of colorful stone mosaics covered by a thin layer of dust and dirt, seemingly undisturbed for hundreds of years, following the long passage until it ended in a small chamber of rough piled stone walls.

Stjepan paused before one of the bas-reliefs and Caider held the lamp closer so that Stjepan could inspect it.

"We've seen these before, some of the barrows down in the Vale have them," said Caider. "Carving's a lot better than the ones I've seen."

Stjepan studied the bas-relief for a moment and nodded. "A depiction of one of the *Baalhazor*, guardian demons of the First Hell. Done in an early Iron Age style, so it's of more recent make than you would expect over in the Vale of Barrows. Most of the barrows there were built in the Golden Age and the Age of Legends, up until the coming of Dauban Hess and the cult of the Divine King. Some were still being built during the Bronze Age, but use of the Vale pretty much stops after the Curse of Lost Uthedmael. Look, all of the faces are in profile, except the horns, which are depicted as though you're looking at it head-on, that's typical of the years after the Black Day Battle," he said, pointing at the row of figures and then looking back toward Leigh. "Magister, what do you think?" he asked.

Leigh moved forward and studied them. "Aye," said Leigh. "Definitely meant to be the *Baalhazor*. A reminder to thieves and grave robbers of which Hell awaits them, I would think. So in and of itself not an indication yet of whose tomb we are approaching. The old Daradj and Danian tradition sometimes included a depiction of the *Baalhazor* as a warning, as we use gargoyles today."

Caider glanced around at the walls and floor. "The stone floor is a little odd, usually these places are just packed earth for floors," he said.

"Aye," said Godewyn. "The floor's unusual, normally it ain't like this that we've seen."

Stjepan continued on and came to a stop in a small antechamber before a large, flat oval iron plate inlaid with leering faces in copper and bronze, which acted as a door and seal over the next passage. There were some small trinkets and urns placed around the walls of the antechamber and in front of the iron plate. A few of the others crowded in behind him, but the chamber was not large and most of them were still behind them in the entrance passage.

"This might explain why the floor is paved with stone," said Stjepan. "It's almost like a shrine here, with offerings and tribute left behind."

"A place for a hero's cult," said Leigh quietly, and everyone glanced at each other with a bit of excitement.

Stjepan passed a hand a few inches over the iron plate's surface, tracing an inlaid carving, as though feeling for something. Leigh stepped forward and similarly ran an amulet over the stone.

"Reveal that which is hidden!" Leigh whispered, and he paused for a long moment before stepping back. "Nothing. No wards, or curses upon this door, that I can see."

Stjepan nodded in agreement. He and Godewyn, Caider Ross, and Too Tall took positions to one side of the iron plate with crowbars, arranging themselves haphazardly so as not to get in each other's way.

"Step back, old man," Godewyn said to Leigh. The enchanter looked askance at him but moved back out into the entrance passage. The four men remaining in the chamber grunted as they struggled to push the iron plate aside. Mortar crumbled from the edges. A slight puff of air exited the opening, and then as if in response suddenly a tremendous gust of air from the outside got sucked in as if in a long prolonged *moan*. The lanterns flickered; men coughed from the swirling dust.

And the iron plate fell heavily away, revealing a doorway.

As the dust settled, Stjepan took the lead and entered within. Erim, Caider Ross, and Too Tall, now bearing lanterns and shouldering shovels and picks and bags of gear, followed next. As Leigh, Gilgwyr, Sir Helgi, and Arduin moved inside, Godewyn turned to Pallas Quinn and held up a hand.

"You're still fucking drunk, Handsome," he said. "Stay here and keep an eye out. If the sun starts to go down and we ain't back, start shouting."

Pallas Quinn swayed and shrugged. "Aye . . . right, chief," he said, and then he paused a beat. "You really think you're going to be gone that long?"

Godewyn disappeared into the doorway, leaving Pallas Quinn standing there nervously, his eyes darting from the dark doorway into the inner barrow and back to the sun-lit exit. He set down his lantern and drew his broadsword and held it before his body.

No sunlight reached the next chamber from the outside. The oscillating lanterns of the party penetrated the dark as they entered, and revealed walls of large inlaid upright stones. Their lamplight fell on a large iron plate, inlaid once again with copper and bronze, straight ahead at the far end, and there were less imposing plain iron plates on their left and their right, all of them set into mortared stone arches like seals. Too Tall kicked over an urn, and licked his lips; there were grave goods—pots, urns, bronze implements—littered about, though nothing gleamed with gold or silver. Godewyn prepared a new lantern, and spiked it into a crack in the stone walls.

Stjepan moved down the chamber toward the big inlaid iron door at the end. There were letters on it, etched into the iron and then inlaid with copper.

He paused briefly, reading the letters, then turned back and walked over to the smaller door on their right.

"This one," he said at the smaller door. "If I understand the map correctly, it's this one we should go through, the first on the right."

Godewyn walked over and stood in front of the big iron plate, looking at the bronze and copper inlays. He frowned. "That little one, and not this big iron door with all the markings that says: *Attention, here lies the evil wizard?*" Godewyn asked.

460

"Actually, that says: *Enter here at your peril*," Stjepan said.

Godewyn stepped back, staring at the door a moment before shrugging. "Same thing," he said.

Arduin walked over to stand by Godewyn. He studied the large iron door for a moment, then turned to the rest of the group. "The map has led us right this far; let it lead us a little further," he said.

Everyone else either shrugged or nodded, and so Stjepan and Caider Ross took up their crowbars and moved aside the stone, revealing another doorway. They moved through it, into another chamber passage.

There was nothing but darkness until a doorway cracked open sharply. The light in the passageway outside spilled into the darkness, revealing a larger chamber. Stjepan entered and panned a lantern across the interior, illuminating four large, carved stone pillars that held up a vaulted roof. Three large doors, this time of carved stone, were mortared into corbelled archways on the west, north, and east walls of the chamber. The pillars and walls were carved with images of bird-headed demons framed in borders of intricate intertwining foliage and strange symbols. Grave goods, including vulture-headed masks, urns, chests, and piles of animal skulls, were scattered amongst the pillars.

Erim prepared another lantern, and spiked it by one of the stone doors, revealing the beautiful but barbaric patterns carved upon it. The others crowded in, setting down their bundles of gear.

Stjepan held a lantern up by the bas-relief of a bird-headed demon carved into one of the pillars. "A *Golodriel*, a servant of Geteema Hamat as Queen of the Second Hell," he said quietly. "Definitely *not* what you'd expect to find in a barrow made by followers of Yhera and her Court."

Godewyn walked around and looked at the three doors set in the walls. "This ain't usual, either," he said. "I've robbed plenty of barrows in my time, and no doubt have an appointment with Amaymon after I

461

die because of it. But most old passage graves have maybe a small side chamber on each side, and that's about it. Pillars, and doors, and more chambers beyond them? This is quite a lot of digging, somebody did, just to put a man under the earth." He spat to the side. "So which door?"

"This one," said Stjepan, and he and Leigh approached the western door. As before, Stjepan passed a hand a few inches over the carved surface of the stone, while Leigh ran an amulet over the stone.

"*Reveal that which is hidden!*" said Leigh.

Stjepan and Leigh stepped back as magical glyphs and patterns emerged in the carvings on the surface of the stone; the glyphs reached out to intertwine with the stones of the archway, as though anchoring the stone plate into the frame of the arch.

"The chamber beyond is warded against our entry," Leigh said in a hushed voice.

"Or exit, by man or spirit," said Stjepan, slightly puzzled.

The others exchanged excited glances behind them and crowded forward a bit.

"Well, this's gotta be it then, yeah?" asked Erim with a mix of excitement and trepidation. "Can . . . can you get rid of the ward?" She looked troubled, as though she wasn't sure what she wanted the answer to her question to be.

"The wards here are very strong, but I know an incantation that might work," said Stjepan a bit dubiously. "It would require the use of a potent of the *wormwood* plant, however, and probably a considerable amount of it . . ."

"Folk magic," Leigh said dismissively. "I am the expert here, Stjepan. Let me check my books of lore." He began ruffling his hands through the folds of his robes as though searching for something. A satchel of black velvet appeared from within the folds, and he reached inside it and pulled out an old grimoire from the bag and leafed through it.

"The *Lexica Pentaculum* . . . Stjepan, dear boy, have you ever read it?" Leigh asked as he flipped through the old parchment pages.

"That book is forbidden, Magister," said Stjepan.

"Of course, yes, of course it is," mused Leigh absentmindedly as he busied himself with the book. "Bronze Age text in Old Éduinan, almost certainly written sometime in the Winter Century, as it mentions Hathhalla the Sun Lion drawing Her Veil over the sun, and covering the world in shadow. It's mostly, as the title would suggest, about summoning and commanding spirits and elementals through the use of a magic circle. The incantations and rituals within it are mostly drawn from the Golan tradition of hermetic magic, rooted in the *Sefer Hermetica Daedacti*. Which shouldn't make it forbidden, really. Except that the anonymous author mixed in material from the Palatian hermetic tradition as well, specifically from the *Pagina Magica de Necris*, a book on summonings and black magic. Have you ever read that one, Stjepan?"

"No, Magister," Stjepan said. "Forbidden. Again."

"Of course," said Leigh. "Despite being somewhat off-topic, the *Lexica Pentaculum* has within it, however . . . assuming I can ever find it . . . an excellent incantation to rid a passage of protective wards . . ."

He drifted off into silence as he flipped through the pages.

Several minutes passed.

Godewyn picked at his ear. Too Tall and Caider Ross exchanged looks.

"Ah! No, that's not quite it," mumbled Leigh. "Mmmmm . . . Oh, here we are . . . I need blood. I need some blood." He looked up and around at the others, who all took a concerned step back, before his eyes came to rest on Godewyn. "You. Cut my hand."

Godewyn looked around at the rest of the group. Leigh held out his hand, palm up. "Go on! Cut my hand!" Leigh said, as though he were talking to a child.

Godewyn shrugged. He drew a sharp foot-long dagger and quickly cut Leigh across his open palm. Leigh grimaced, and then began spreading blood over the surface of the upright stone door, as if washing it. In the other hand he held the grimoire open, and he read a spell from the book.

"*Cellis darris, te mere osveret tapesh! Earten darris, hellis hagrass! Purify this door, lift the wards upon it!*" he said, at first in a whisper, then slowly louder with growing boldness. The glyphs began to glow as Leigh washed the door's surface with his blood. *"Cellis darris, te mere osveret tapesh! Earten darris, hellis hagrass! Free it from binding chains, that others may pass through safely!"*

Stjepan, Erim, Caider Ross and Too Tall were the first to tense as a low-pitched *hum* resonated throughout the chamber. Then soon they all were wincing and turning slightly away, as they could feel the pressure building in their ears.

"Cellis darris, te mere osveret tapesh! Earten darris, hellis hagrass! Purify this door, lift the wards upon it!" Leigh repeated these words in a ringing, commanding voice, as he continued to wash the stone surface with his own blood. The *hum* grew louder, until it seemed to the onlookers that the door and walls began to subtly shake and vibrate. Dust began falling from the ceiling. It seemed as though they were watching an invisible contest of wills, between Leigh and the magics that were bound into the glyphs and the stone of the door, a contest that grew darker and more intense . . . until suddenly the glyphs deteriorated and fragmented, and the pressure in their ears disappeared with a *pop*.

"Well done, Magister," said Stjepan quietly.

Godewyn smiled and waved his men to the stone as they congratulated Leigh, slapping him on the back.

"Thank you," said Leigh, a sheen of sweat on his forehead. "Thank you very much. And has anyone seen my impression of a duck?"

Stjepan, Godewyn, Caider Ross, and Too Tall took position by the stone door and began to pry at it with their crowbars. Arduin began to pace impatiently as they struggled at the travail, but the stone was much heavier than the iron plates that they had moved earlier in their explorations.

They struggled, and struggled, and then gave one last collective grunt. With a sharp *crack*, the doorway was unsealed, and a blast of fetid air rushed past, sounding like a *moan* followed by whispers, obscuring the pillared chamber with a cloud of foul dust. Every lantern in the room flared and threw sparks into the air.

The stone fell heavily to the ground with a great, crashing thud as the men closest to it leapt back, and something like a shadow seemed to pass through the room.

Pallas Quinn felt a shudder run through the earth and stone around him, and heard something rattling in the passageway leading into the inner barrow. He held up his broadsword point-first in front of him and looked into the darkness beyond the doorway, tilting his head to one side as if to listen, and instantly got hit by a blast of air. The moans and the whispers passed by and enveloped him. His choking figure was swallowed up by fetid dust.

Wilhem Price and Sir Colin Urwed were walking around the Ladies' Tent, marking a sentry circle, scanning the fields and hills around them, when they heard something like a whisper come from up the hill. They turned and looked up the hill just in time to see a plume of dust jet out from the entrance to the barrow some six hundred paces away up the stone steps. The two of them took a few steps toward the hill and stopped, then looked at each other.

Annwyn was sitting before her mirror, singing quietly to herself, when a sudden wind blew through her tent, bringing whispers with it. She stopped singing and turned, looking over her shoulder at the source of the sound.

"My Lady?" asked Malia, standing and frowning. "What was that?"

After a moment, Annwyn turned back and resumed her singing, looking at her reflection with a slight smile.

"What in the Six Hells was that?" asked Wilhem.

"Nothing good," said Sir Colin. He unshouldered his greatsword and hefted it, about to start heading up the steps to the entrance, when a figure stumbled out of the stone-framed doorway in the hillside, coughing and sweeping dust from his clothes. The figure coughed some more and doubled over, retching a bit before straightening up and putting his hands on his hips and shouting something that sounded like a curse.

"Is that . . . that's one of the Danians we hired on at the Inn, yeah?" asked Sir Colin, squinting up the hill.

"Looks like it," said Wilhem with a shrug.

The distant figure saw them looking, waved, and turned around and went back into the earth of the hillside.

Malia poked her head out of the tent. "What was that?" she asked.

Sir Colin looked back at her over his shoulder. "No idea," he said with a shrug.

Muffled coughing and hacking echoed through the chamber as the dust began to clear. Everyone was staring at the unsealed doorway, either waving their hands at the air to clear the dust, covering their mouths and noses with whatever they could, or pointing weapons nervously at the yawning black arch. The lanterns flared and guttered and dimmed, leaving the chamber in partial darkness.

"Was that supposed to happen?" Erim finally whispered, crouched behind a pillar with one hand over her face.

"How am I supposed to know?" Stjepan whispered back, and shrugged. "Could've been a pocket of *damp*: trapped, fouled air . . . miners have different names for it, depending on what the air does: *firedamp*, *blackdamp*, *helldamp*."

"I done some mining, Black-Heart, down in the Pavas Mole," said Too Tall in a low muffled voice. "And that didn't sound or act like no *damp* I ever seen."

"Fucking fantastic. On your guard, everyone!" snarled Godewyn.

As the air began to clear they removed whatever was covering their faces and braved a few breaths of air, weapons ready and pointing. The open door stood before them. The dust cloud settled.

Erim gave Stjepan an unsure look as he prepared a new lantern. As soon as it was lit, he lifted it in his left hand and hefted his falchion in his right, and slipped forward at a crouch to one side of the archway. He peered inside, lifting the lantern high, trying to see into the chamber beyond.

"What do you see?" hissed Gilgwyr.

Stjepan didn't respond, but instead he rose up out of his crouch a bit and stepped through the archway into the dark beyond.

He found himself standing in the entrance of a large, circular room with a domed ceiling, holding his lantern high. From its light he could see that at their base the walls looked like they had been carved out of rough stone, as though the chamber had been hewn out of the very rock of the hill itself. The walls were covered with carved runes and warding symbols, and the stone arched up into a more finely detailed coffered stone ceiling. Each step-sided coffer in the ceiling bore a small bejeweled brass amulet set into its center panel. The floor was of hard packed earth.

And the room was completely empty.

The others began to file into the domed chamber after him, spreading out and setting lanterns about to better light the space.

"I don't understand . . ." said Arduin, looking around with his hands on his armored hips. "There's no exit from this chamber. Is this our destination?"

"What in the Six Hells is going on? This room's fucking empty!" said

Godewyn. "Shouldn't there be a stone bier with a body on it, or a stone casket? This ain't my first tomb robbing and that's how it's usually done, yeah?"

"This can't be right," said Stjepan mostly to himself. He set his lantern down and reached into his satchel for his notebook.

"Of course it's not right! Do you see a dead wizard? Do you see a sword for the taking? *This* is where that fucking map of yours leads?" spat Godewyn harshly.

As the others milled about in various states of anger and confusion, Stjepan, Leigh, and Erim stood in the center of the room, pouring over the notebook in Stjepan's hands. Gilgwyr stumbled off to the side, his head in his hands, and squatted with his back against the stone wall.

". . . this word, *arath*, should mean *north*, and *dain* would be *west* in any of the old languages of this region," Stjepan said, explaining his logic. "So it says: *take the first door to the north, and then the west door in the chamber of four pillars*. Look, there's even an image that seemed to point to the end goal being a circular chamber, just like this one."

"Well," said Leigh finally. "I don't know this alphabet, old Maerberos was always a bit of a mystery to me; you were always so good with languages and ciphers, far better than I ever was! It's your gift. But I cannot deny the logic of your thinking, at least not at first glance . . ."

"Great," laughed Godewyn. "So the magician-scholars are agreed: the treasure map leads across the Bale Mole to an empty room!"

Leigh shrugged. "Unless perhaps the order of the doors was reversed? And we should have gone west first?"

"The west door first?" asked Godewyn. He frowned, trying to figure out which door that would have been until it flashed in his mind. He turned to Caider and Too Tall. "Right! Back to the door we 'open at our peril!'"

"I don't think that's a good idea," Stjepan said, looking around the chamber with a frown.

But Godewyn stormed out of the room, cursing loudly, followed by Caider Ross and Too Tall. Arduin paused for a moment, gave a doubtful look to Stjepan, and then left with Sir Helgi right behind him. Erim shrugged and left next. Stjepan and Leigh eyed the room but then reluctantly turned and followed.

Gilgwyr was left alone with a single flickering lantern as their shouts faded into the distance. He stood up and walked to the center of the room, stretched out his arms, and made a slow turn.

By the time Stjepan and Leigh arrived back at the first major chamber of the inner barrow, Godewyn, Caider Ross, Too Tall, and Sir Helgi were already at the massive inlaid iron plate, and were pushing and prying at it eagerly with crowbars. Their bags of equipment and tools were haphazardly dropped behind them. Arduin stood nearby, hands on armored hips, as though he was supervising, and Erim stood behind him, watching the proceedings with her head cocked in curiosity.

"Wait! It may be warded!" shouted Leigh, his eyes going wide when he saw what they were doing.

But with a sudden *crack*, the iron plate came free of its mortar and rolled out of the way and there was another shock of air as the doorway was unsealed. Everyone froze. Godewyn's face was still but his eyes darted about the chamber as the dust passed by, but without any seeming effect.

"Fates and Fortune, hear my prayers! Right, follow me!" he said with a laugh. He took a lantern and moved confidently through the revealed archway into the passageway beyond. Caider and Too Tall seemed buoyed, and grabbed up their tools and lanterns and equipment bags and followed him through, with Sir Helgi and Arduin and Leigh close behind.

Erim took a step forward and hesitated, looking over her shoulder for a cue from Stjepan. He sighed and shrugged, nodding that she should follow.

Godewyn, Caider Ross, and Too Tall stood in an archway and held up their lanterns, illuminating a large, long chamber, flanked by a series of alcoves along each stone wall. Four great pillars held up a high, vaulted ceiling. Grave goods lay about at the foot of the walls, including many archaic implements of war: iron spears, and axes, and swords, and painted shields, their leather and wood and iron seemingly well preserved in the dry air of the sealed chamber. In the center of the room was a large bronze statue of ornate detail and great craftsmanship, depicting a demonic-looking four-armed winged creature, armored and armed with four curved swords and with the head and gaping beaked maw of a screaming eagle. In front of the statue on the earthen floor was set a large basin, specked with dark dried liquid and small bones. Human skulls of various sizes were piled around the basin; some were small enough to clearly be the skulls of children.

Godewyn stepped experimentally into the room, and started to thread his way through the urns and weapons. He came to a halt in front of one of the alcoves.

"Hello, beautiful," he said. His lantern revealed the contents of the alcove: the dried, desiccated remains of a man, presumably a warrior, propped upright in his archaic armor, his gauntleted hands folded over his chest. Caider Ross and Too Tall had not moved from the arched entryway, hesitant to follow Godewyn out of the passage and further into the chamber. As Godewyn walked by the alcoves he could see that each contained the standing corpse of a dead warrior, all armored and posed alike.

"Get moving, let us past . . ." Arduin said as he and Sir Helgi arrived and pushed past Caider Ross and Too Tall into the chamber, but his voice left him and he trailed off into silence as he saw what was in it.

Godewyn soon reached the far end of the chamber and came to stand in front of a large bronze oval plate, almost eight feet high and mortared into a stone archway, engraved with barbaric symbols and swirling, intertwined circular patterns. He scraped at the circular motifs inlaid with gold and smiled. "Hello, *beautiful*!" he said, a quiet smile on his face.

The rest of the group began to slowly and silently enter the room.

Every free hand held a bared weapon now. Leigh came to stand in front of the statue and inspected it.

"A shrine to Ishraha, the Rebel Angel," he said quietly, as almost everyone else in the chamber made a sign to ward off Evil. "The great *Rahabi* general who first dethroned Islik from the Sun Throne of the isle of Illia, and sent Him into exile to wander the world, where He would prove Himself fit to be the Divine King of both Heaven and of Earth with His Ten Great Victories. So I suppose, in a way, that all true Kingsmen actually owe Ishraha a debt of sorts, for if Ishraha had not cast him into exile, Islik would never have risen to become the great God that He is now."

"Careful, old man," said Arduin. "That sounds suspiciously like heresy. Ishraha is one of the Forbidden Gods and condemned to rule in Hell, guilty of the great crimes of treason and usurpation against his rightful lord, the Divine King. Always has been and always will be."

Leigh ignored the Aurian knight. "According to *De Malifir Magicia*, in the lore of the Nameless Cults, Ishraha is amongst other things charged with watching over their dead and being their patron in the Underworld. Stjepan, have you read it?"

"Forgive me, Magister, but . . ." Stjepan started, but Leigh waved his hand.

"Yes, yes. I know, I know," said Leigh with a sigh. "But the point is clear. Ishraha ruled as the King of Illia for a brief time during the War in Heaven, and so I suppose a shrine to him could have been built then for a seemingly legitimate purpose. But the armor here is not from the Age of Legends, is it?"

"No," said Stjepan, glancing at the remains of the warriors. "Late transitional armor. Iron cuirasses, mail hauberks, bits and pieces of plate here and there fixed to mail backing, bascinets with mail aventails . . . it's all from the start of our current Age of Iron and Fire, before the adoption of full plate." He looked back up at the statue of Ishraha. "I think it's settled, then; this barrow was definitely built by the Nameless, sometime in the years after the Black Day Battle, but before the 13th century. And that fits the timeframe of Azharad's death in 1127."

"Islik's balls, I don't like this . . . why would the map lead us to that other room, rather than here?" asked Erim.

"'Cause your boy got the map wrong," Godewyn said drily. He turned to his crew. "C'mon, time to bust this open."

"Gentlemen, some patience," said Stjepan, but Godewyn, Caider Ross, and Too Tall eagerly took up their crowbars and started working on the mortar that held the bronze plate in place. They managed to crack some small gaps and unhinge it a bit from the archway. They were struggling with the task, however, and Sir Helgi joined them, and the four men strained to move the weight of the great bronze plate. Erim set her lantern down and grabbed up a crowbar from a bag and moved forward to help, but Stjepan grabbed her good arm and shook his head. He indicated with his chin, drawing her attention to the fact that Leigh was finally moving forward and waving his arms, having stopped his inspection of the cult statue to Ishraha.

"Show us. Show us the World. Open our eyes, show us what is hidden," Leigh intoned.

The surface of the bronze plate suddenly swirled with dark designs, foul symbols and barbaric patterns in motion. Stjepan snarled as Leigh leapt back. "Beware! It's cursed!" yelled out Stjepan.

The four men working at the door started to leap back just as they succeeded in moving the huge bronze plate. It slipped out of the archway and fell to one side, revealing the entrance and unleashing a gust of stale, dusty air, and in the dust the symbols and patterns of the curse could be seen weaving around the four men like a swarm of butterflies.

Leigh waved his hands frantically in warding signs. The foul enchantment weaved, probed, shimmered . . . and then settled on Sir Helgi, Caider Ross, and Too Tall. In an instant their skin seemed to be blackening and peeling as though they were on fire, and the three men were screaming at the top of their lungs as they flailed about. Godewyn had fallen to the ground, somehow out of the curse's grasp, and was crawling and rolling to get away from the dust and the screaming men, and Erim blanched and leapt back, stricken, unsure what to do.

Leigh stepped forward and began shouting in old Éduinan. *"Mennas darris, los elissa! Giss more, cell darris, menn darris!"* he cried, and he flung a spray of white powder into the air over the three struggling men. Everywhere the white powder came into contact with the symbols and patterns of the enchantment there seemed to be a spark and fizzle as if a lit match were being submerged into water, and the air grew heavy with the wispy tendrils of white smoke.

Caider and Too Tall regained their footing and leapt back from the archway, gasping and breathing heavily. Their skin looked burned in some spots, while in other places the burns were slowly fading back to normal.

But Sir Helgi wasn't moving. He looked cooked in his armor.

Erim turned away from the grisly sight while Stjepan held a hand over his mouth. Arduin, his face ashen, stumbled to his knees next to Sir Helgi's body as Leigh came over to see if there was anything he could do; but there wasn't.

Leigh put his hand on the pauldron of Arduin's armor. "Sorry about your lad," he said in a grandfatherly tone.

Arduin stood and turned. The look on his face was enough to make Leigh remove his hand. He stepped forward, towering over the enchanter, and Leigh backed up several feet. It appeared to be all that Arduin could do not to just catch Leigh by the throat, lift the enchanter up off the ground and drive him bodily back against the wall.

"He was a knight of my household, had fought beside me and saved my life in battle, and had served my family well since the day he was old enough to swear the oath. He was a man of honor, something that you and the rest of this lot obviously know nothing about, and you would do well to never speak of him again in my presence," Arduin said through gritted teeth, his eyes ablaze with rage and fury.

And then a cold blankness fell over Arduin's features as he turned back to look down on the smoldering body of his knight, as though he was willing the anger and heat to leave him. "But he knew the risks. We all do," Arduin said quietly, his jaw set and his nostrils flaring.

Leigh gave a half-bow behind Arduin's back, but he sneered at the

Aurian lord through narrowed eyes. He looked like he was about to laugh, but luckily Arduin did not see his expression. Stjepan frowned at him.

"Aye," said Godewyn. "Well said, your Lordship. Right! Follow me, then!" Godewyn started into the dark hole revealed by the bronze plate door, followed a bit more slowly by Caider Ross and Too Tall, each bearing lanterns, and then slowly the others afterwards.

Stjepan was the last of them in the chamber and he rummaged through one of the equipment bags that had been set down and removed a woven blanket. He knelt by the body of Sir Helgi and reached in to close the man's open, lifeless eyes, one of which looked like it had been boiled into white puss, and Stjepan winced as he slid its lid shut. He placed the blanket over the body of Sir Helgi and stepped back.

Stjepan turned and looked back the way they came.

He frowned. "Gilgwyr?" he called out.

Gilgwyr was still standing in the middle of the empty, round, high-domed chamber, his arms still extended out to opposite walls, mumbling to himself. *I do not understand, o gods, I do not understand at all. My dreams have been so beautiful, and we have followed the signs you have laid before us, and we are here, and yet somehow nothing is right. It isn't beautiful, it isn't the way you have been showing me, it's all wrong. I have done something to offend you. I have failed you in some way. Please let me atone for my wrongs. Please let me right the insult that I have done you, so that everything may be as you have shown me in my beautiful dreams. Tell me what I should do. Tell me what offering I can make.*

He did not see the ghostly figure, hooded, horn-masked, standing behind him in the flickering shadows against the wall, watching him.

Erim reappeared from through the dark opening behind the great bronze plate, and grabbed Stjepan by the shoulder.

"Come on, they're already through to the next chamber!" she said to him.

Reluctantly Stjepan nodded and then followed her through the archway. They found themselves in a narrow passage like so many others that they had seen in the barrow. The walls were decorated with bas-relief carvings and mosaics inlaid in the stone, a series of scenes depicting the terrible wonders worked by a horn-masked magician. They could hear Godewyn and Caider and Too Tall cheering in the distance, and picked up their pace a bit.

Within moments they emerged into a long chamber of rough-hewn stone walls and a low, corbel-arched ceiling. Deep arched crevices were set in the sides of the chamber, and both the crevices and the perimeter of the packed earth floor of the chamber were lined with urns and chests filled with coins, artifacts, and small statues and figurines, all glistening in the lamplight with gold and silver and copper and sparkling gems; laughing, Godewyn, Caider Ross and Too Tall were sifting the treasure with their hands, picking up whole handfuls of coins to let them rain from their fingers. Leigh was slowly moving deeper into the chamber, his eyes darting this way and that, taking it all in.

"Now *this* is what I call grave-robbing!" Godewyn crowed.

"Here, Gilgwyr isn't with us . . ." Stjepan started to say, and then he trailed off as he saw what was in the middle of the room.

Arduin stood stock still at the foot of a long waist-high bier of rock and stone, staring down at the body that lay upon it. The body was dressed in a long, black robe, its dried and desiccated hands clasped over its chest as though in prayer; a long, pointed bronze mask, with a pair of gazelle horns spiraling up from its forehead lay upon the body's face and head. The mask's eyeholes had an evil, slanted cast to them, and opened onto blackness. Ornate circular patterns swirled and wove their way along the edges of the mask and were echoed in gold thread patterns embroidered into the body's robe. The robe had a collar of tufted horse hair, surrounding the

475

head like a black fan, and a chain of gold and bronze discs inlaid with silver symbols was slipped over the collar and around the body's neck, almost like a noble's chain of office.

And lying upon the body was a sword with bared blade, its hilt resting under the corpse's clasped hands.

It was a magnificent-looking weapon, gleaming in the lamplight as though freshly cleaned, a sword fit for kings. The sword was of an older Bronze Age style, almost certainly made when armor was first transitioning from mail and leather to plate, and it showed in the shape of the blade. The length of watered steel was double-edged and broad and while largely straight it tapered to a sharp point, a reflection of the shift from slashing with a blade against mail or unarmored opponents, and stabbing with the point. Its curved quillons were shorter than on most contemporary sword styles, and the hilt was short, suitable for use in one hand. The sword's quillons and large round wheel pommel were inlaid with swirling, intertwined designs in silver and gold, but the grip of the hilt was wrapped in a fine black leather that did not look as if it had aged a day from when it was placed in the barrow.

"We keep whatever we can carry out, right, and a partial share of the sword's price if it sold, as agreed, yeah?" Godewyn said to Stjepan. He laughed, staring at the wealth and treasure on display in the room. "Oh, Black-Heart, I take back every bad thing I've ever said or thought about your Athairi hide."

Ignoring Godewyn's good cheer, Arduin finally spoke softly. "*Gladringer*, sword of the High Kings! The sword that killed Githwaine, the last Worm King . . . King of Heaven, we make history, this day!" he said, his voice quivering with emotion. "One of the greatest heirlooms of the Middle Kingdoms, lost since the Black Day Battle, lies before us . . . oh, King of Heaven, our thanks!"

Erim moved up to stand by Arduin, eyeing the body on the bier. "He doesn't seem so frightening, lying here. He just seems . . . dead," she said.

"With a wizard of the Nameless Cults, telling the dead from the living could well be a problem," Leigh said quietly.

Hearing that, Caider Ross and Too Tall immediately stopped fussing with coins and treasure. Godewyn got up and turned to the body, considering it more carefully now with a frown. He dismissed it with a silent *bah*, but still stepped a bit closer to the bier.

Stjepan began to make a slow pass around the stone bier, his stern gaze taking in the body and its sword through narrowed eyes. "There's something wrong here," he said.

"What, like we're no longer poor?" said Godewyn, laughing.

Leigh began to mirror Stjepan as he walked around the bier, one of them on each side of the bier, circling it. Arduin took a deep breath, and drew himself up straight as Godewyn reached out to touch the sword.

"Wait! Don't touch it!" hissed Stjepan, raising his hand in warning.

"Indeed. Do not touch it," said Arduin in a voice of cold authority. "Such a sword as this should not be in base hands such as yours. I will take possession of it until we return to Therapoli."

Godewyn whirled toward Arduin, looking at him suspiciously. "I knew it. I knew you would try to exert a noble's privilege at some point. You mean to cheat us," he said through clenched teeth.

"Show us. Show us the World. Open our eyes, and let us see what is hidden," whispered Stjepan as he circled the bier.

"I have been crowned a Champion at tournament by the High King himself. You impugn my honor at your peril," Arduin said calmly. "Whatever deal you made with the Athairi about the treasure here will stand, I care nothing about the coins and trinkets in this wretched place. Keep what you want. But that sword will not be *sold* for mere profit, not by you nor by me."

"Brave of you to put your claim upon this sword without your remaining knight and squire to back you, here under the cold ground," Godewyn said with a malevolent grin.

Caider and Too Tall glanced at each other and then at Godewyn. Hands were going to hilts and weapons were being loosed in scabbards by everyone in the chamber save Stjepan and Leigh, who were solely focused on the body and sword. *"Show us. Show us the World. Open our eyes, and let us see what is hidden!"* said Stjepan and Leigh together, their voices louder.

The sword's surface shimmered as runes and symbols materialized upon it, including a pattern that almost looked like a twisting snake wrapping itself around the blade.

"That sword belongs to neither of us," Arduin said, chin held high. "I do not claim it for myself, but in the name of Awain Gauwes Urfortian, High King of the Middle Kingdoms, King of Atallica, Seated King of the Sun Court, to whom it belongs by right and whom my father serves as a sworn vassal. We have found the sword of the High Kings by the will of the King of Heaven, and He is present, here, in this chamber. Do you seriously think I am afraid of you, even should all of you stand against me?"

"No one said you were a smart man," Godewyn said, and his hand started to move on his hilt, only to find Stjepan's hand grabbing his arm and holding it in place.

"If he wants this sword, let him have it," Stjepan said. "It's a fake."

Everyone in the chamber turned in surprise to look at the sword lying on the body. Seeing the enchantments exposed upon the blade, Caider Ross and Too Tall drew back, while Erim and Godewyn stepped forward, frowning and craning their necks to see the runes and patterns.

"You lie!" exclaimed Arduin.

"To what possible purpose, my Lord?" Stjepan asked with disappointment and exasperation. "It's all very convincing, yes; this barrow, this body, this sword. But there is no enchantment upon this blade that I can see except a glamour overlaying a Curse." He wearily indicated the sword on the body. "I will not be the man to touch it, and suggest that no one else should either. But if you want it, my Lord, take it, and pray that Leigh's amulet protects you."

"But . . . but the rest of this looks real enough!" Godewyn said, looking nervously around at the grave goods scattered about the burial chamber.

"And so it is, I would think," Stjepan said, glancing around. "Great wealth there is here, indeed, so you are no longer a poor man, Godewyn Red-Hand. Congratulations. But all the coins and treasure in this room are but a fucking pittance compared to the worth of the real *Gladringer*."

Erim stood straight and scratched her head. "I . . . I don't understand," she said. "Then whose body is this? Is this Azharad? Is this the Sorcerer King of the Bale Mole?"

"I don't know," said Stjepan, running his hand through his hair before waving his hand to take in the whole of the chamber. "I mean, it's a corpse, like any other after centuries in a barrow. Despite the trappings, I'm not sure anything here says one way or the other . . ."

"Leigh, enchanter, Magister, what do you think about this?" Godewyn asked.

Leigh stood frozen, staring down at the body and the sword. "I'm afraid my student is correct," he said quietly.

"This can't be happening! Gilgwyr, you're not buying this, are you?" Godewyn said. He looked around, confused and frowning. "Where in the Six Hells is Gilgwyr?"

Stjepan stepped into the empty, round, high-domed chamber, followed by Godewyn and Erim. The single lantern that they had left behind still guttered in place, casting light and shadows across the rough-hewn walls and the crevices of the coffered dome ceiling. It was now truly empty once again; there was no sign of Gilgwyr. Only a few abandoned bags of tools and equipment.

"I don't understand," said Stjepan. "This is the last place I remember seeing him." He started walking the flat, packed earth, looking at the shoe and boot prints in the dirt.

"What? Did he just leave?" asked Erim.

Stjepan, Godewyn, and Erim emerged back into the outer entrance chamber. The sunlight filtering down into the entrance passage was no longer at a morning angle. Silhouetted up the exit shaft, Pallas Quinn sat against a wall. He almost looked like he was asleep. Godewyn started to walk up to him.

"Here, Handsome, has Gilgwyr come through here?" he asked as he put his hand on Handsome's shoulder, and Handsome Pallas Quinn's not-so-handsome head tipped back, revealing that his throat has been cut from ear to ear and that there was blood soaking the front of his clothes. Godewyn jumped back with a start. "Gah! King of Heaven!" he blurted as he stumbled back to the opposite wall and slumped down in a squat, his hands on his head, staring bleakly at Handsome's body. "King of Heaven, not another one!" he growled, growing angry. "That's Gilgwyr's signature cut! I've felt his dagger on my neck often enough to know. I'm gonna kill him. I'm gonna kill that bastard . . . what's he playing at?"

As Stjepan crouched by Pallas Quinn to inspect the cut and his body, Erim made a quick run up the passage toward the exit, scanning the ground for tracks. Godewyn, watching as Stjepan gingerly probed Handsome, grew still.

"Maybe I should be asking what *you're* playing at," Godewyn said.

Stjepan looked Godewyn in the eyes. "I did not take us into the tomb with the false sword," he said quietly. "You're the one who rushed head-long on, all eager to prove me wrong, leaving Gilgwyr behind. There's nothing here that says for sure this was Gilgwyr's doing, though I'll grant you it looks bad for him. Whatever his part in this, we really do have to find Gilgwyr now; he's either in danger, or is a danger to the rest of us."

Erim returned from the top of the passage, and crouched to look at Pallas Quinn's low boots. "Our tracks coming in, one set of tracks leading out and then back in, but judging by his boots I think that was Pallas. But what if . . . what if Gilgwyr was the Hidden Magician who was in our tent?" she said.

Godewyn's face was filled with fear and loathing. "Gilgwyr was a Hidden Magician? One of Nymarga's Cult is amongst us? The Lion of Vengeance aid me, a Red Veil upon the sun, do I grow tired of this!" he snarled and stood up, looming large in the entrance passage. "Too many secrets, Black-Heart, too many fucking secrets! You should have told us you'd had a visitor! I'm going to get the last of my crew and we're gonna tear this place apart, if I have to knock down every door in it! If he's in here, we'll find him!"

Stjepan stood and looked up at Godewyn. "We don't know that Gilgwyr was in our tent as a Hidden Magician. That could have been any of us, even you, any of us save Erim and myself, but of course you only have our word on that, just as we only have your word and reputation that you are not one of the Nameless yourself," he said. "That's always the problem with looking for the Nameless, and making assumptions about who is or is not one of the Nameless. Make such an assumption, and it's not long before the innocent are getting lynched while the Nameless stand right beside you laughing. Once you've rejoined your crew, stay together as a group! No man should ever be alone within the barrow! If you have to, travel in pairs or threes, but I would split up only as a last resort. Erim and I will search outside in case he covered his tracks . . ."

"If you find the bastard, he's mine," Godewyn drew his sword. "I don't care if he's one of the Nameless or not. I know he did Handsome, so I'm going to fucking kill him." He turned and clambered back down into the barrow proper.

Stjepan and Erim sprinted outside.

The body of Pallas Quinn slumped to the ground.

Erim exited the barrow, her rapier at the ready, followed swiftly by an armed Stjepan. She made a quick circle, surveying the hillside around them, but there was no immediate sign of Gilgwyr. She started back down the stairs set in the hill at a swift pace, and as she approached the camp she could see Arduin's young squire and his now last remaining knight standing watch around Annwyn's tent. She began waving her arms at them.

In a few moments she had reached their tents and lines, Stjepan right behind her. Sir Colin had half crossed the camp to greet them, and sensing trouble he had slipped his sallet onto his head and unshouldered his greatsword, and left Wilhem Price behind at the Ladies' Tent as a last line of defense. "What's the matter?" he asked with no small amount of suspicion. He held his greatsword at the ready. "What's going on?"

"Have you seen Gilgwyr? Has anyone left the barrow?" Erim asked.

"No, I haven't seen Master Gilgwyr," said Sir Colin, shaking his head. "The only person we saw leave the barrow looked like one of the Danians we hired on back at Woat's Inn. And he turned around and went right back inside. That was maybe an hour or two ago, there was a lot of dust coming out of the ground at the time. But we haven't exactly been watching up the hill every minute."

"A lot's happened since then," said Stjepan as Erim jogged off to the side to retrieve a composite horn bow and full quiver. "I regret to have to tell you that Sir Helgi is dead, he fell victim to a foul enchantment, a curse triggered within the barrow. So you are the last of his knights, Sir Colin." Colin looked grim and ash-faced, but just nodded. "And the man left as our rearguard, the one that you saw from Godewyn's crew, he has been murdered, his throat cut by parties unknown, though suspicion falls on Master Gilgwyr."

Sir Colin tightened the grip on his greatsword and took a subtle half-step back from the two of them, but not so subtle that they did not see it.

"Aye," Stjepan said, nodding his head to acknowledge the motion and what it implied. "Allow no one near the Ladies' Tent until Lord Arduin has returned, especially not Master Gilgwyr. Nor us. We'll circle the camp and the barrow and look to see if he might have slipped out while you weren't looking, but I fear our search will be fruitless and that he is still inside the barrow somewhere."

"Then go with the King of Heaven, Black-Heart," Sir Colin said, a slight challenge in his eyes as he backed away toward the tent.

"If you say so, Sir Colin," said Stjepan with a nod, and he and Erim turned back toward the barrow. "Well," he said to her with a sigh. "Where do you want to start?"

A stone door fell down with a thud, revealing yet another passage.

"Gilgwyr! Come out, come out, Gilgwyr!" Godewyn yelled as he moved swiftly through the archway, a heavy broadsword in his right hand. Caider Ross and Too Tall followed, their weapons glinting in their lamplight, followed by Arduin, his war sword held before him. Leigh trailed behind, looking out of sorts, distracted, confused. They practically ran down the stone passage until they reached an intersection. Stone passageways split off to their left and right through corbelled stone arches, and in front of them the passage became a steep stone stairwell that angled down into the depths of the earth.

They stopped, their lanterns casting light in each direction but providing no illumination. "Gilgwyr, you bastard, where are you?" Godewyn cried, mopping the sweat from his brow.

Caider frowned and stepped a couple of feet into the passageway on their left. He could see it dead-end and branch left to stairs leading down, and right to stairs leading up. "More stairs over here, chief," he said over his shoulder. "Up and down. This is starting to get tricky."

"This is pointless," hissed Arduin. "This is almost a maze, and we are in danger of becoming lost. If Master Gilgwyr is hiding himself somewhere, we will not find him simply running around like this."

Godewyn looked over his shoulder with murder in his eyes.

"Chief," said Caider quietly. "The man's got a point." Godewyn shifted his gaze to Caider, but Caider didn't flinch. "In my gut this is starting to feel like the time we lost Malcolme and Gause and Black Gawer in the ruins of Bronrood. Time to go, chief."

Godewyn looked at the three passages in front of them, frustration growing on his face. The rage built inside him until he could not contain it any longer.

"Gilgwyr! Gilgwyr, you miserable cur, where are you?" Godewyn bellowed at the top of his lungs. "I'll hang your miserable carcass, and curse you to Limbo! Gilgwyr! Gilgwyr! Hang all magicians! *Hang all magicians!*"

The sunlight in the entrance shaft was weaker and redder. Stjepan and Erim entered at a run and slowed to a walk when they saw that the passage was not empty. Caider Ross and Too Tall were watching over Godewyn, slumped to the floor and holding Handsome Pallas Quinn's body, mumbling to himself in a barely audible whisper. "Hang all magicians . . . hang all magicians . . ."

Leigh stood nearby, deep in thought. Arduin was by himself, his bared sword tucked into the crook of the left elbow couter of his plate harness, standing sentry and eyeing the entry to the inner parts of the barrow as he took a swig from a water bottle.

"There's no trace of him outside," said Stjepan.

"Nor down here," said Arduin over his shoulder. "It's just too large . . . we almost got lost. He could be hiding anywhere. There's more corpses in other burial chambers. And passages leading down and in all directions. Then there's . . ." He trailed off with a peculiar expression on his face.

"What?" asked Stjepan. "And then there's what?"

"A room. With a well," said Godewyn quietly. "Who puts a fucking well in a barrow?"

Alarmed, Stjepan looked from Godewyn back to Arduin. "Show me."

Godewyn entered a rough-hewn chamber, holding aloft a lantern. Stjepan, Erim, and Arduin followed him. The walls of the chamber looked earthen, like it had been carved or tunneled out of solid rock and earth, though there were what appeared to be false stone archways arranged into several of the walls, and carvings and crude, faded paintings on the walls. There were three biers of stone and rock, each with a body, though not as elaborate as the first body and bier that they had found, and slightly lower in height.

Grave goods were set in urns and small chests around the walls, though they did not appear as fine or sumptuous as the main haul they'd found. Stjepan stopped and briefly inspected the bodies—the corpses of three desiccated women in barbaric jewels and golden ornaments and slowly decaying silks.

Godewyn nudged Stjepan, indicating a large semi-circular opening on their left. Stjepan took the lantern from Godewyn and approached the opening warily, slipping his falchion out of its sheath, and then stepped through.

The chamber he entered was smaller in size than the previous, and appeared to be a natural cave in the rock. Parts of it looked like the chamber might have been expanded, as though to finish it someone had roughly hewn, almost scratched, more space out of stone and earth. Erim stepped through the opening and joined him in looking about the chamber, but the others held back. Stjepan and Erim saw a circular hole in the ground toward the back of the chamber that did indeed look like the low opening to a well. The pair slowly approached it until Stjepan could peer slightly over the sides.

He stared down into the hole; it looked like it had been tunneled into the earth. From the limited light from the lamp it appeared bottomless, though he supposed that was true about all deep holes in the ground. There was an ancient iron bar set into the stone near the hole. Stjepan glanced up and he could see screw-eye hooks and other rusty implements driven into the ceiling. Erim looked as white as a sheet, and wordlessly she tugged at Stjepan's jacket. Stjepan nodded, and they withdrew to where the others waited by the entrance, and begin whispering.

"So what's a well doing in a grave?" hissed Arduin.

"That's not a well. That's an entrance," said Stjepan. "If he did go that way, he's not coming back."

"What's down there?" asked Arduin.

Stjepan didn't answer. He took a deep breath.

"The sun's almost down," said Stjepan. "We have to collect our dead and seal this barrow and leave. Now."

They rolled the large, flat oval iron plate inlaid with leering faces in copper and bronze back into place, sealing the entrance to the inner barrow.

CHAPTER TWENTY-SIX
THE SHADOW IN THE NIGHT

Dark storm clouds roiled parts of the sky above them, though the growing orb of the Axe Moon, *Labra-luna*, now only a few days from being full, could be seen to the east against a field of stars. Two more bodies had been washed and wrapped in white cloth and placed in the back of the wagon. Several campfires were lit, though everyone was clustered in or near the central campfire after finishing their prayers over the dead, except Sir Colin Urwed, who still stood guard over the entrance to the Ladies' Tent, and the two women, who were inside it.

"What kind of name is Azharad, anyway?" asked Too Tall bitterly, finally breaking the silence.

"I've often wondered that," replied Stjepan absently, staring into the fire. He was seated on a low bench between Erim and Caider Ross and he paused in eating from a plate of food prepared by Wilhem Price and Malia. "There's no similar name in the old rolls of Danian and Mael lords and knights. It sounds a bit like the citadel named Angharad, of course, so I think the prevailing theory has always been that it's a variant of that old place name. I thought for a while that perhaps a Nameless wizard had taken the name because it sounded like Ahzazel, who was a great *Rahabi* general of Ishraha's and a prince amongst their kind, but that's just my own guess."

"It's not a bad guess," said Leigh, seated across the fire from him. "But it's the *De Malifir Magicia* to which we must turn again. You really should complain to the Magisters about how much your education has suffered from all the constant forbidding they do." Stjepan nodded in deference to the Magister.

"Githwaine, remember, was one of ours, a Danian lord who had gone south to serve the great Dauban Hess, the King of Illia who had risen up to throw down Nymarga the Tyrant, and in so doing Dauban Hess had become Emperor over the largest and greatest empire in history," Leigh said, his voice projecting out over the fire. "The priests of the Sun Court had cursed and cut up the body of the Devil and entombed the various pieces in salt. And Githwaine was entrusted with the knowledge of the secret locations of Nymarga's body parts, and told to guard them at all costs so that his followers could not find them and restore him."

Erim shuddered. "What, is he still alive?" she asked. "Even chopped up into pieces?"

"Who knows? How can you really kill the Devil?" Leigh asked with a grin that looked terrible in the firelight. "A great trust that was, to watch over his body, and it was betrayed after Dauban Hess sailed off into the east to find the Isles of the Dawn where the sun rises each day, and did not return. Either out of grief or greed, Githwaine listened to the voice of the Devil speaking to him from within its salt prison, and he found the secret location of *Ghavaurer*, the sword of the Devil, and he learned how to make himself into the first Worm King. And he spread this secret to the magicians and knights and nobles within the Empire and the Phoenix Court who were still loyal to Nymarga, their old master. And so the Worm Kings emerged to rule the Empire, first in secret and then in the open, and in time they plunged the world into dark and bloody war, until the Dragon Kings were finally victorious and swept the Worm Kings from the thrones of the Empire."

"And resolved to hunt down every last one of them," Arduin said with firm conviction.

"Aye, to their eventual mutual doom," said Leigh. "To flee the Dragon Kings as they hunted down his fellow Worm Kings during the Winter Century, Githwaine slid back to his homeland in the western Danias, and took up a mask, and pretended to be someone else. But he did not return alone. He had servants and followers from his time in the south with him, and amongst them were wizards from Sekeret, the Golan birthplace of ancient hermetic magic and a land well known for providing viziers to the Phoenix Court." Leigh made a face. "Even to this day, that land provides most of the viziers to the Dreaming Emperor and his Sultan."

"So Azharad was one of these wizards from the south, then?" asked Caider. "Kind of sounds like a southern name."

"*Az'harad*," Stjepan said suddenly, shaking his head with a rueful smile. "It's Sekereti, then."

"The name's origin is, yes, but it's unlikely that Azharad was one of Githwaine's original followers, that would have made him five hundred years old or so by the time he emerged to rule the Bale Mole, and while he was a powerful wizard I don't expect he was *that* powerful," said Leigh.

"The Emperor's been dreaming for four hundred years," said Erim with a frown. "Or so everyone says."

"Yes, seemingly trapped in a Curse of great power," said Leigh. "So it's not impossible that Azharad was one of the original wizards from Sekeret that came with Githwaine. But the tale told in *De Malifir Magicia* is that he was merely one of their descendants. They had taken refuge in secret holds in the Bale Mole after Githwaine was killed by Fortias and the sword *Gladringer*, and kept their worship of him alive in the dark, and passed their secret magics down across the generations, until one of them was strong enough to walk the earth and stake his claim."

No one said anything after that for a while. They just stared at the fire glumly, eating sparingly or drinking wine.

"That's all well and good," said Arduin finally as he turned to Stjepan. "But we are still left with the same questions as before: was that the body of the wizard Azharad, or not? And the sword? Is it *Gladringer*? Or some cursed, false blade?" he asked.

"A black curse is on that blade, and no other enchantment save a glamour to make it pleasing to the eye," said Stjepan. "So no, it's not *Gladringer*."

"What, we should just take the word of you and this crazed enchanter? Maybe the glamour deceives you both," said Godewyn, pacing nearby with a bottle of wine.

"Do you think I mean to keep us here?" Stjepan asked, incredulous. "If that were the sword, we'd have built a pyre for our dead and we'd be gone already. Every day, every hour we are in this cursed place brings us closer to disaster, and my life will be forfeit in the end the same as yours. It's only a matter of time before the Azharites return, in force, and then we'll all be in their cooking pots."

"Maybe you're in league with our missing friend," said Godewyn, stopping right behind Stjepan. "Maybe you mean to sneak back in there while we're all asleep and take it for yourself."

Stjepan stood and turned to face Godewyn. "Then you and I can sleep next to each other, each with one eye open," he said, a slight smile on his face. Godewyn snorted and continued his pacing as Stjepan sat back down.

"I don't want to die in this place," Erim said quietly, staring at the fire, her eyes wide and unfocused. "I think if you die in this place you are lost forever, trapped in Limbo or bound here as a ghost . . ."

Godewyn snarled and turned, walking a short distance away. "Don't say that! Don't even think it! Gah!" he cried over his shoulder.

"I don't want to die in this place," Erim said quietly to herself.

There was silence except for the roar and crackle of the campfire.

"Could someone have been here before us and taken what was here, the real sword?" Arduin asked.

"Could . . . this map be a false one? A false map to a false body and a false sword? A distraction from the real barrow, which is as yet undiscovered?" asked Erim. "Some sort of trap?"

Godewyn heard this and walked back to the campfire.

"I don't know," said Stjepan simply.

"Maybe you just translated it wrong," said Godewyn.

"My translation was right; the map leads here, for good or ill," Stjepan said.

"*Perhaps there is more to the map,*" Leigh said quietly, as if to himself.

Arduin turned. "Perhaps there is more to the map. Consult with my sister again, see if there is more to come, some detail to explain the empty room, the fake sword . . ." he said.

Godewyn looked at Arduin with confusion. "Wait, what does your sister have to do with the fucking map?" asked Godewyn, a perplexed frown on his face as Caider and Too Tall looked up, frozen in mid-chew.

Arduin and Stjepan looked at each other. Stjepan winced.

"Um . . . my sister . . ." started Arduin, but his mouth seemed to have trouble working.

"His sister was cursed by an enchantment in a book, and the map appears in her head," Stjepan stepped in smoothly. "As she remembers bits and pieces of the map, she describes it to me, and I write it down. It is dark magic, and why we had to bring her along with us."

Godewyn barked a laugh. "So that's what you've been doing, talking to her all the time in her tent," he said. "Everything finally makes some sense. Too many fucking secrets around here, Black-Heart. So she's got the map in her head, eh? And how do we know she don't know more than you say she does?" He paused for a second, his eyes narrowing. "How do we know she don't know more than *she* says she does?"

Stjepan set his plate down, slipped the strap of his satchel on over his shoulder and head and across his body, and stood up. He turned and matched Godewyn's stare. "I'm afraid you'll just have to trust me," Stjepan said. "If she has nothing new to tell me, there is nothing that I or anyone else can do."

He walked off to Annwyn's tent.

"Boy doesn't know how to deal with the likes of her, but I'll bet I could get the truth out of her," Godewyn said, his eyes following Stjepan's retreating back.

"Watch yourself," said Arduin grimly.

Stjepan entered the Ladies' Tent and stood for a moment, his eyes adjusting to the lamplight. Malia curtsied and exited the tent quickly without making eye contact with him. He took in the small details of the tent once more—folding chairs neatly piled with rich fabrics for comfort, chests open to reveal toiletries and bottles, knitting and embroidery work abandoned momentarily, dried herbs and flower petals scattered about the carpet to faintly scent the air. He took in the plain, sturdy weave of the canvas tent, the details of the eagles and griffins depicted in the damask carpet. He listened to the wind, to whispers and death cries, to the faint ringing of distant bells, to what sounded like someone weeping alone in the dark. He sniffed the air, smelt fire and ash, the sharpness of honest clean steel and the lather of horse sweat, the growing stench of the untimely dead, the raw pit of fear and hunger, and from nearby the faint scent of something moldy and rotten. His gaze grew hard and grim, and then he stepped past the screens set up around the center of the tent.

Annwyn was lying naked on her bed of furs and fabrics, bits and pieces of the map appearing and disappearing, ink swimming across her pale, ivory skin. She was looking at herself in the mirror.

"I tried to explain . . ." started Stjepan.

"Yes, I heard you. But they want more. Come," she said. She looked at him, and her hand smoothed down a spot of fur next to her on the make-shift bed.

Stjepan approached her slowly and sat on the furs next to her. She moved around beside him, languidly turning her body over, showing him different looks and angles.

"Do you see anything new?" she asked. A slight pout formed around her mouth. "Malia and I looked . . . everywhere, but it seems like it is all the same."

He studied her skin for a while. "No . . . no, I do not see anything new, either," he said finally.

"Perhaps you've seen all that you can see," she said. "Perhaps to learn more, you will need to use your hands instead of just your eyes."

She took his hand and placed it on her chest. For a moment Stjepan didn't move, feeling the heat of her body, and then his fingers slowly traveled down the length of her torso, following the letters and lines on her skin as they undulated and reacted to his touch, as though they were living things sensing a hovering danger.

"Is this truly your own desire or does it come from somewhere else?" he asked softly.

"Would that truly matter to you?" she asked. He didn't blink. "Have you not considered that perhaps there might be some further revelations waiting . . . inside me? Where you cannot see?"

She took his hand and gently guided it between her legs. But he simply cupped her mound and did not move, eyeing her with curiosity.

"Ah. Do you think me some poor untouched flower, that has been kept locked away under glass and key?" she asked. "You told me once that you knew my story. From rumor and the gossip of the Court, no doubt. But did Harvald ever tell you exactly how I was discovered with my lover?" She stared off into the distance, her mind elsewhere, else-when, and her voice dropped to a whisper. *"Galrode Tierwell.* I have not said his name aloud in years. I have not even allowed myself to think it. My father, you see, did not approve; he might have been a knight but his family was not sufficiently highborn for them to marry an Orwain. But he was beautiful to look upon, a bright star upon the field, and noble of heart and sweet in disposition when it came to me." She laughed bitterly. "A classic enough story, I suppose, told in every romance ever written. Do I seem foolish to you?"

"No, my Lady," he said. "Romances are written that way for a reason."

"Well, I *was* a fool, and deeply in love, and desperate to spend time with my beloved," she said, looking back into his eyes. "Harvald offered to abet our meetings. It was leading up to the Tournament of Gavant two years after I was the Queen there, when the entire Court heads up to the Plain for rest and sport and games. Harvald arranged a tent in a far meadow where my lover and I could meet in secret for our trysts. Harvald and I would excuse ourselves from our family's encampment and pretend to go on long country rides together, but instead he would take me to meet Galrode, who awaited me. Those were happy hours, happy days for me."

Her expression grew dark, and she looked away from Stjepan again. "Until one day the High King was afield with part of his Court on a country ride. My father and my brothers were with him, and they came upon the tent and recognized the markings and thought it placed there just for them. We were so enraptured of each other, so lost in bliss, that we never even heard them until they were walking into the tent."

She grew quiet, and said nothing for a time.

"If it were possible to die of shame alone, my life would have ended in that moment," she said. "I could see the disappointment in the High King's face. And as always his desire, unabated even as he saw me in the arms of a man that I loved. And of the look on my father's face I will say nothing, except to say that the hate born for me that day has never left him."

She looked at him, and a strange light seemed to come into her eyes.

"I have never told anyone else, but the worst of my ordeal that day was not the moment of our discovery," she said, leaning forward into him and whispering huskily. "For after the High King and my father had left without a word, the Crown Prince had stayed behind. He is a cruel man, Prince Edrick. He made Galrode and I finish what we had started while he and his sycophants watched and gave instruction."

There was wetness on his fingers as she said that, and Stjepan frowned.

He withdrew his hand from her skin and body and pulled back to sit up.

"A great wrong was done to you then, my Lady," he said. "And not just by the Crown Prince. For if I knew Harvald as well as I think I did, I do not believe the High King stumbled across your tent by accident."

She looked away from him, studying the design in the carpet. "I have often thought the same thing, for after that day I saw a cruel side to him emerge that I had never seen before," she said quietly. "I thought at first that he was disappointed in me, like all the others, and was merely expressing himself in anger. But over time I realized I was seeing for the first time some part of his true nature. He often dropped hints that he had betrayed me, but never said it outright. He was one for secrets, was our Harvald, always keeping some core of himself hidden away beneath mask after mask."

She looked up and fixed him with clear blue eyes. "And you are the same, Stjepan Black-Heart," she said. "Never letting anyone in past the hard, grim surface."

"I don't know what you mean," Stjepan ventured with a small smile, and Annwyn laughed at that. She rolled herself back onto her elbows, and brought one knee up to her chest.

"Ah, but you really do keep yourself at arm's length, Stjepan," Annwyn said, her face a cryptic, smiling mask. "You come to me, I bare myself before you, you use my body for your purposes, but what of me? What of what I want?"

He looked at her intently. "What *do* you want?" he asked.

She leaned toward him.

"Stjepan," she said softly. "Take me into the barrow."

Stjepan pushed her away and stood.

"What?" he asked, his eyes narrowing.

"If I told you it was pulling on me, that I feel it in my blood, that it wanted me to enter, would you believe me?" she said.

"You will not enter the barrow," he said firmly.

"Not even if it is the only way to see the whole of the map?" she asked.

Stjepan met her gaze for a moment, then turned and walked out.

Stjepan was walking up a leaf-strewn forest path, broad high trees of birch and purple-leaf oak, maple and elm, cherry and white ash, cedar and pine stretching out for leagues in all directions. The sky was dusky, a blend of blues and purples as the sun set and the stars appeared. The blue tone of the sky had settled over everything, slowly bleaching out the colors of the day, taking what should have been the russet browns and burnt oranges and deep yellows and ancient greens in the trunks of the trees and the debris of the forest floor, the old layers of lichens and moss, and turning them blue and gray and black. The leaves of the trees looked pale and white, as though they were made of spun silk and snow, and so he began to suspect it was a dream. He turned and looked to his right through a break in the trees, and caught a glimpse of a far sloping range of dark forested hills, backdropped by a horizon of desolate high mountains. Down to the east a great stone castle sat on a rise over a small riverside city, and he knew that across that river would be the Plain of Stones. *Ah. Indeed. This dream, of An-Athair, and my mother, and night and death.* A dream, then, and one that would soon fill him with pain, but still it was pleasant for the moment, and so he kept walking the ancient forest path in the dusk, drinking in its beauty.

A great stag appeared from beneath the trees to pace beside him on the road, its majestic antlers marking its age and power. *You are too late, too late*, the stag said to him.

"Too late for what, great lord?" he asked.

You'll see, you'll see, the stag called, and then it leapt over a fallen tree and sprang away into the underbrush.

He followed the path and the woods fell silent except for the sound of a woman singing somewhere in the distance. If the stag was still nearby he could neither see nor hear it; no bird sang in the branches above. But the woman's voice seemed familiar, and grew clearer as he walked. He could smell wet earth and leaf and needle, moss and stone, and from nearby the smell of something burning.

He approached a dark, high clearing in the woods. Massive, ancient trees surrounded the clearing, their lower branches filled with dangling amulets and chimes, small sculptures and offerings placed around their trunks. A pyre had been built in the center of the clearing, and a single post erected within it. A woman was tied to the post, her long silk dress slightly torn and soiled with dirt. She was beautiful, wild, her long wavy black hair framing a face of wisdom and power. His mother, Argante. A crowd of their neighbors watched with fear and excitement behind several circles of men dressed in black robes and brown hoods as some of those men stepped forward and lowered torches. The pyre began to catch. The singing was coming from somewhere in the crowd; he could see a woman with golden blonde hair moving behind the watching ranks of his neighbors, but then he lost sight of her.

His young brother, Justin, stood stock still to the side, watching with wide eyes, and Stjepan's heart broke. Two hooded men, with deer antlers attached to their masks, held his sister on her knees, forcing her to watch

496

as the flames of the pyre grew stronger and higher. He couldn't see her face but her long curly hair was unmistakable, a deep, dark brown that was almost black, the color of burnt earth. *Artesia.*

He walked slowly toward the pyre, coming to stand behind his sister and the men restraining her. He could hear his sister whispering to herself: *"That won't be me. That won't be me. That won't be me."* His mother looked down at him, and smiled, as she always did in his dreams. Smoke and flames were rising up around her. Her skin was blackening from the heat, but she seemed serene.

He felt a hand on his shoulder and turned. It was Annwyn, peering at him from under a hooded cloak with a secret smile. She took him by the hand and started to pull him away from the pyre. He looked back over his shoulder at his mother and sister, and then allowed himself to be pulled away.

He and Annwyn started to run through the woods of An-Athair. The forest grew darker and more dangerous, and then it was as though they were running through a mist. The underbrush became grass and weeds, and he could see the twisted shapes of dead, petrified trees silhouetted in the mist. And he knew they were no longer in An-Athair, but were instead in the Bale Mole.

They ran up a hill, and he could see and feel steps under his feet. Up ahead loomed the entrance to the barrow, a dark maw in the hillside. He started to slow, but Annwyn pulled him toward it. She was smiling at him as they plunged into darkness.

Stjepan could feel the passageway tight around him, see a pale blue light glowing ahead of him as he stepped over Annwyn's discarded cloak into a long chamber of rough-hewn stone walls and a low, corbel-arched ceiling. Deep arched crevices were set in the sides of the chamber, and both the crevices and the perimeter of the packed earth floor of the chamber were lined with urns and chests filled with coins, artifacts, and small statues and figurines, all glistening in the lamplight with gold and silver and copper and sparkling gems. In the center of the long chamber was a waist-high bier of rock and stone, but in his dream there was no body upon the bier, no false sword cursed and tempting.

Instead, Annwyn was there awaiting him, leaning against the now empty bier, casually wrapped in the golden finery of a noblewoman, her shoulders and legs tantalizingly bare. He approached her and they embraced passionately, and his lips found hers. As they kissed he thought he could hear a familiar voice chanting, calling out as if from far away: *Nathrak arass tedema urus! Nathrak arass urus!*

As they embraced, the symbols on her body were moving, and suddenly Stjepan flinched in pain as the symbols began to move onto and into his flesh wherever their bodies were touching. He could feel a pressure growing behind his ears. As he tried to pull away from her, she was holding him tight, refusing to let go. The map symbols were all over him now. His skin erupted in a maelstrom of signs and movement.

He pushed her away. But it was too late.

Annwyn's skin had turned bluish-white and was blackening rapidly. Stjepan's face blanched with horror and fear.

The surface of Annwyn's body suddenly erupted with maggots.

And then Stjepan heard a shout.

The shouting continued: "Alarm! Alarm! Murder! Murder!"

Stjepan opened his eyes, sitting upright quickly. Groggily he grabbed up his weapons and moved toward the tent flap as the shouts continued.

Stjepan hurtled out of his tent, falchion drawn, and stumbled a bit in the dark, for some reason all the campfires were out, but Caider Ross appeared with a lantern. They looked at each other and then moved together toward the cries of alarm coming from near Annwyn's tent. The lantern's light revealed Erim and Wilhem Price shouting desperately over the body of Sir Colin Urwed. His throat had been cut, his eyes staring blankly up at the night sky.

The tent flap opened, and out stepped an ashen-faced Arduin. "She's not here! There's no sign of my sister, or of her handmaiden . . ." he said, despair and anger contorting his features. "Is anyone else missing?"

Godewyn and Too Tall, still partially dressed, finally arrived with their own lantern. Godewyn gave everyone a skeptical look as Stjepan knelt by Sir Colin, examining the cut along his neck.

"Gilgwyr's handiwork again?" asked Erim.

Stjepan looked up, surveying the group. "Where's Leigh?" he asked.

Suddenly Wilhem Price pointed. "Look there!"

They all looked up the hill to where the squire was pointing, but they could see nothing except darkness beyond their lamplights.

"What?" hissed Caider.

"I . . . I could have sworn . . ." said Wilhem, frowning.

"Douse the lights!" said Stjepan, and in a moment they were plunged into darkness.

They stood there, breathing heavily in the dark, waiting for their eyes to adjust. Dark clouds loomed on the horizons of the night, but the moon shown down from the east a day closer to being full, only a few more days now, and the night stars were out in force and the Serpent looked down upon them.

"See, there!" cried Wilhem Price, pointing once again. And there were two cloaked shapes, faintly visible by the light of the moon and stars, moving up to the entrance to the barrow and about to enter it.

"Everyone, to arms! Now!" barked Stjepan.

And the camp burst into activity as Sir Colin Urwed's eyes stared blankly at the night sky.

Arduin, Stjepan, Erim, Godewyn, Caider Ross, Too Tall, and Wilhem Price sprinted up the hill, all partially armed and armored as best they could in a few short minutes, and with lanterns and torches raised to light their way.

They barely paused before they plunged into the entrance shaft, passing quickly down the decorated stone entrance shaft and reaching the main doorway into the inner barrow; the large, flat oval iron plate inlaid with leering faces in copper and bronze was laid flat on the ground, as if pushed over from the inside.

Arduin reached the archway first and skidded to a halt by its side. He pressed up against one lip of the arch and shouted through the doorway. "Annwyn? Annwyn?!"

"Was that fucking Leigh we saw?" hissed Godewyn, eyeing the iron plate face down on the stone mosaics of the entrance shaft. "Or Gilgwyr, come out of this hole?"

"We'll find out soon enough, I fear," replied Stjepan. "This barrow has secrets still. Everyone stay together!"

He plunged past Arduin into the doorway, falchion bared and a torch leading the way in his outstretched left hand.

They emerged into the first great inner chamber. Godewyn stopped to hang a lantern from a spike they'd set in the wall earlier. Several of them surged forward, the light from their lanterns and torches dancing chaotically on the walls, as if they were going to head to the shrine of Ishraha and then on to the burial chamber where they'd found the first body and the gleaming, enchanted sword, but Stjepan stopped short at the right-side doorway, the first one they'd taken during their initial entry. He scanned the ground quickly.

"No! Not that way! This way!" he cried, and then he plunged into the doorway, followed by the others.

They emerged into the pillared antechamber, slowing as they did. The archway to the empty high-domed chamber loomed darkly on their left. The light of their lamps and torches illuminated some of the scattered bundles and bags of tools they'd left behind. They were quiet, nervous, as they approached the open archway.

Slowly the light illuminated the round and empty high-domed chamber beyond. Stjepan and Arduin were first to enter, followed slowly by the others. A figure stood stock still in the center of the room, wearing a hooded, heavy damask cloak embroidered in gold thread; the figure appeared to be a woman, and she stood with her back to the entrance. Leigh stood a few paces in front of her, facing her, staring under her hood intently.

Stjepan put his sword arm up, and everyone halted in a cluster in the entrance, waiting behind him and Arduin and peering at the woman with Leigh.

"My Lady? Are you all right?" asked Stjepan, raising his torch to better light the figures before them.

"Step away from my sister, warlock. I owe you a death already," growled Arduin.

Leigh sighed. "I did not harm your knight. I came upon his body as I sought the Lady," he said patiently.

Annwyn's voice came from beneath the hood very faintly, as though from far away. "There was a visitor to our tent," she murmured. "A dark shape, foul and masked. It took Malia."

"You shouldn't be here, my Lady. It's not safe here," Stjepan said, taking a step forward.

"And where have I ever been safe?" Annwyn asked.

"She needs to be here," said Leigh. "I brought her here because she needs to be here. She needs to be here. So she can show you this." Leigh crossed the short steps to Annwyn, turned her roughly to face the entrance, and ripped down her cloak to let it pool around her legs.

She was naked beneath the cloak, but for pieces of elaborately wrought gold jewelry around wrists and ankles and the map's images and words, some parts still, others in motion. Her dead, blue eyes slowly looked up at Stjepan as his gaze fell on a single new word moving across the front of her torso.

"Do you know what this means?" she asked him.

No one said anything for a few moments. Everyone in the entrance to the chamber was frozen in shock, staring open-mouthed at the vision before them.

"*Islik's balls*," Godewyn managed to finally get out, and Arduin suddenly came to as if out of a terrible dream and he realized what they were all staring at.

"Out! Out! Get out!" Arduin cried, and he turned and stretched out his arms as if partly to block their view and partly to corral them all and begin moving them bodily back into the pillared antechamber, but Godewyn pushed back with his great strength and moved into the room, followed by Caider and Too Tall.

"I don't think so, my Lord," Godewyn said, almost giddily. Godewyn started to walk a broad circle around Annwyn and Leigh, followed by the two remaining members of his crew. He spoke toward Stjepan next, but his eyes never left the pale, ivory beauty that stood in the center of the chamber. "You been holding out on us, Stjepan Black-Heart. And you told me there was no pleasure to be found on this trip. All those nights alone in her tent . . . looking at this . . . *map*. What was it he was doing in there with your sister, my Lord? 'E was in there a lot, was our Black-Heart."

Too Tall grinned and tapped Godewyn on the shoulder as they circled, and indicated Arduin with a leer and a wave. "'E was in there a lot, too, chief," he said.

"Shut your mouth, street scum!" snarled Arduin.

The vehemence in his tone caught Godewyn's attention, and he tore his eyes away from Annwyn's naked form to look at her brother. He could see the emotions running across Arduin's face: anger, *shame*. Godewyn laughed as a particularly nasty thought occurred to him. "Oh, oh, oh, my Lord! Maybe more than lookin', eh?" he said with a laugh. *This is going to get good*, he thought.

Arduin began to stalk Godewyn and Caider and Too Tall around the room as Stjepan stepped closer to Annwyn, his head tilted and torch raised high, trying to decipher the new word. Leigh watched his former pupil placidly, but through narrowed eyes, while Annwyn looked upon him with great anticipation.

"A jousting accident, wasn't it, my Lord, when you killed her lover?" said Godewyn as they backed away in a circle from the approaching armored knight. "But everyone says you and your brothers drew lots to see who would do the deed, after their affair was discovered! Everyone thinks you didn't think him grand enough for her . . . but something more maybe? Wanted to take his place, did we? They say rank has its privileges but I do not think the Temple-Priests would approve!"

Erim and Wilhem Price looked at each other in confusion, still standing in the entrance, uncertain of what to do. So they raised their weapons.

Arduin hefted his war sword up, gleaming dangerous in the lamp and torchlight. "Shut your hole, peasant! I've put up with your insolence long enough!" he growled. He started to pick up speed, his pursuit of the three Danian men around the room now in earnest. They started to stumble backwards faster, laughing and cursing and shouting in fear and surprise, weapons raised, Godewyn's eyes flashing with the anticipation of the coming fight.

But Stjepan's voice cut through their cries high and sharp. "My Lord, the map!"

Everyone else in the chamber came to a halt and froze, staring at him and Annwyn, standing in the middle of the chamber, looking at each other under his upraised torch.

"The map, my Lord," said Stjepan. "It says . . . *dig*."

Everyone looked at Annwyn, then down at the floor, at the flat earthen ground on which she stood.

Annwyn smiled broadly at Stjepan, then, a look of triumph on her face.

CHAPTER TWENTY-SEVEN

DİGGİNG

Too Tall and Wilhem Price passed tools and bags of equipment from the pillared antechamber into the high-domed tomb to Caider Ross and Godewyn. Annwyn walked around the chamber, her cloak wrapped tight about her body and her modesty restored, and yet it kept slipping off her shoulders. Stjepan stood in the center of the room as Leigh marked off a circular area of the floor around him.

"So then we dig," called Godewyn over his shoulder as he set down a set of shovels and picks. "Even with Gilgwyr wandering around here still?"

"I'll stand guard," offered Arduin.

Godewyn snorted derisively and exchanged glances with Stjepan and Caider Ross as they began removing the heavier layers of their brigandine and leathers and clothing. "Aye, his Lordship will stand guard," Godewyn said under his breath.

Wilhem Price was about to follow suit and started to unbuckle his cuirass, but Arduin raised his hand to stop him. "No, no, Wilhem, my sister must be removed from this place. Take her back to the camp, and watch over her there," he said.

Leigh grunted and nodded. "I will be part of her escort. I brought her here; it is my duty to see her safe," the Magister said gruffly.

Godewyn frowned and looked around to Too Tall. "Here, Garrett, you go with them, too," he said, and Too Tall shrugged.

"But Garrett's a miner," objected Stjepan.

"Meaning I've had my fill of digging in the dirt," Too Tall said with a grin.

Stjepan and Godewyn exchanged a glance, and then Stjepan turned to Erim. "If things look safe in camp, you and Too Tall try making it back here," he said. "Everyone digs on this one, if we can afford them." Too Tall shrugged again, and Erim grunted and nodded grimly, joining those who were headed back to camp.

Wilhem Price, Leigh, Too Tall, Erim, and Annwyn slipped one by one from the chamber; Annwyn paused in the archway and took one last look back at them over her shoulder.

Stjepan caught her eye for a moment as he pulled on a pair of tight leather gloves. And then he turned, hefted up a pick, and swung it into the dirt.

Erim stepped back into the inner barrow's first chamber and surveyed the chamber and its exits, holding a lantern high in one hand and her rapier in the other as she cataloged the prints on the ground, the position of the urns and grave goods. She listened, and other than the breathing and light clatter of her comrades behind her, she could hear nothing. She stepped to the side, slipping the handle ring of her lantern over a spike that had been driven into the wall opposite to where Godewyn had earlier left his lantern.

Too Tall stepped in the chamber next and started working on lighting yet another extra lantern, followed by Leigh, Annwyn, and Wilhem Price, also bearing a lamplight.

Erim moved to lead them out through the exit passage but Annwyn's voice stopped her. "Please," said Annwyn. "Before we go, we must find Malia."

Erim felt a pang of guilt but shook her head. "My Lady, it's dangerous down here," she said. "We don't know where Gilgwyr is, and he may have killed two of us already . . . and it's also very easy to get lost."

"Please," said Annwyn, stepping closer. "She is like a sister to me. If she is in danger, we must at least try." Annwyn implored Erim with clear blue, dead eyes.

Erim blinked once, nervously, and glanced at Too Tall; Garrett shrugged in response. Erim debated silently with herself for a moment. Leigh watched quietly and patiently as she made up her mind.

"Very well, my Lady," Erim said. She indicated the archway that led to the shrine of Ishraha. "Let's try this way first." She turned to Too Tall. "Let's change the order. Can you take rear? We'll need something sharp at each end now."

The short man nodded. "Sure, no point in having Gilgwyr come up behind us."

Erim grunted her thanks and led the way out. Wilhem Price followed, holding a lantern up to light their way. Annwyn and Leigh followed, and Too Tall was last. He stopped for a moment, lifting his lantern to scan the room and listen to the sounds of the barrow, and heard nothing.

Stjepan, Godewyn, and Caider Ross were working in a rough circle by multiple lamplight, shoveling cold, hard dirt from the center of the high-domed chamber and trying to be careful not to hit each other or each other's shovels. After a few minutes of hesitant experimentation they'd found a decent rhythm. Many minutes later they'd managed to dig a couple of feet into the ground in the center of the chamber and were slowly expanding the hole. They were tossing the displaced earth away from the center as far as they could, but every now and then one of them would stop digging in the hole to shift a mound of dirt a bit further away.

Arduin stood by the entrance to the chamber, one eye on what they were doing, one eye on the pillared chamber beyond the archway, his war sword cradled in the crook of his couter. Caider stepped out of the hole, breathing heavily, and sopped his brow with his gloved hand and his shirt; grimacing, Arduin picked up a water skin from a satchel and handed it to him.

"Thanks, milord," said Caider with a grin that showed off a couple of teeth missing from brawls and fistfights, and he took a swig.

Arduin grimaced. "Don't mention it," he said sourly.

They stood within the treasure-filled burial chamber. Erim watched with a bit of confusion and curiosity as Annwyn walked around the bier, looking at the body and sword intently, attended by her brother's squire. Too Tall lounged in the entrance, watching and listening back into the entry passageway.

Leigh also studied the body as Annwyn did, but whereas her gaze held some element of fascination or curiosity, he could only look at the body and sword with an expression of sour, bitter disappointment.

"My Lady? Can we go now?" asked Erim gently.

Annwyn gave a small smile. "Forgive me," she said. "I've never seen anything quite like this. And you say you don't know if this is actually the great wizard Azharad?"

Erim shrugged and shook her head. "Book's still out on that one," she said.

Annwyn nodded, and looked around the chamber. "Well, Malia is clearly not here," she said. "Please lead on to wherever you think best to search next."

Too Tall grunted and headed out of the room.

Stjepan and Caider Ross were now about three feet under the dirt floor in the center of the chamber, the upper halves of their bodies visible above the uneven lip of the expanding hole. The speed of their digging had slowed the deeper they got and as they were forced to dig outward as well as downward to give themselves room to maneuver.

Arduin still stood sentry by the entrance archway. Godewyn rested on his haunches on the opposite side of the chamber, his back pressed against the wall, drinking from a canteen. His gaze wandered the corbelled ceiling, idly wondering how much the gems and gold inlays would be

508

worth if he could figure out a way to get up there and pry them loose; only the first tier of corbels was in easy reach. The frames of the corbels almost passed for square, recessed doors, and the thought suddenly occurred to him that perhaps one of them was just that.

"You sure it said dig, Black-Heart?" said Godewyn, his eyes narrowing as he stared at the ceiling.

Suddenly, there was a sharp metal *clang*.

Standing with surprise, Godewyn rose and came opposite of Arduin as he also walked over to look down into the hole. Stjepan and Caider Ross were half bent, staring at each other; Caider moved his shovel and it clanged again. Stjepan tested the same spot, with the same sound.

"Metal for sure," whispered Caider, and he dropped down to his knees and cleared a bit of dirt with his hands.

Black, rusted iron looked up at them.

Too Tall led them back into the inner barrow's first antechamber, and paused beside the southerly exit while the rest of the group filed in after him.

"What's down there?" Annwyn asked.

"You'll see," Too Tall said with a shrug.

He took lead as they entered the passage. Leigh and Annwyn and Wilhem Price followed, and then Erim.

She'd gotten maybe twenty paces down the passage when she thought she heard a faint sound behind her. A *scritch* or a *scratch*.

Erim stopped and turned around while the others continued to follow Too Tall down the passage, taking the noise they were making with them. As the passage grew quiet, the sound repeated itself, and Erim slowly slid one of her point daggers out into her left hand to join the rapier in her right, and silently she slipped back up the passage toward the antechamber.

Stjepan stood outside the expanding hole this time, his shirt drenched in sweat. He guzzled water from a canteen. Godewyn and Caider Ross were the ones down in the pit now. They were using picks and mattocks and the thinner shovels to break up the dirt and packed earth, and then switching to the wider shovels to fling the dirt out of the pit where Stjepan was then clearing it to the sides of the chamber. The pit was four, almost five feet deep, and they had exposed the top of what appeared to be a rounded casket made of black iron, buried upright in the ground. Strange swirling designs and markings in Maerberos similar to the ones on the map were etched into its surface, and one exposed side of it was etched with what appeared to be the start of an image of a man wearing a horned mask.

"Queen of Heaven help me," gasped Stjepan, after drinking his fill. He looked down at the two feet of casket that they had exposed. "If that's what we think it is, we'll have to dig . . . what, probably at least nine feet down to get it out. This could take the rest of the night still."

"Been a while since you had to do a real man's work, eh, cartographer?" called out Godewyn as he swung a pick into the earth.

Stjepan snorted and spat to the side. "And what would you know about a real man's work? You're a robber and a pimp," he said.

Godewyn paused in his digging and shrugged.

"That's a real man's work," he said.

Carefully and stealthily, Erim entered the antechamber of the inner barrow, blades at the ready. The lanterns she and Godewyn had left spiked to the walls still guttered and lit the chamber in flickering shadows. But there was no one else there.

She slid softly in a half-crouch from one end of the chamber to the other, studying the tracks on the ground and listening at each of the arched exits.

Nothing, she thought.

She straightened, shaking her head. She stood silently for a long minute, relaxed, her blades ready, just listening.

Fuck, still nothing, she thought.

She sheathed her point dagger and slid Godewyn's lantern off its spike on the wall. She turned and headed back into the southerly passage.

Twenty paces down the passage, Erim heard the sound behind her again, back from where she had just come. She turned, almost angry, setting the lantern down and slipping her dagger back into her left hand and lifting bared steel points at the ready again.

She slid forward a step or two back toward the antechamber and the lantern on the ground behind her suddenly guttered and almost plunged the passageway into darkness. Her instincts kicked in and she turned quickly, barely in time to parry a blow to her neck from someone behind her.

She fought the figure in the semi-dark, she wasn't sure what was happening to the lantern, it was as though a strong wind was catching the flame and making it flicker and gutter, threatening to douse it, but there was no wind in the tunnel, just a dark figure, cloaked in the shadows of the passageway and lurking behind a point of flickering steel. A rapier, wielded by a trained duelist, and Erim found herself desperately giving ground against an onslaught of cuts and lunges.

And yet, *I know this pattern*, she thought suddenly. A second or two later and she had just about seen enough to know how to run the dark shadow through, when suddenly a black shape flew out of the darkness at Erim and wrapped itself around her left thigh. She looked down. It was a giant millipede, glistening black in the flickering lamplight. She could feel its many legs start to dig into her flesh, even through her flared black breeches. As it began to crawl up her leg, she jumped up and back and whirled in a panic, kicking her leg and bringing the cutting edge of her rapier down to slash at the hideous creature.

But the millipede vanished under her blow as if it had never been there, and instead the cutting edge of her rapier sliced deep through her breeches and into her own leg.

The pain was enough to distract her. A hand appeared from behind her to cover her mouth and her eyes widened in shock as she watched a foot of bloodied steel spring from her guts, her mind briefly uncomprehending as to what her eyes were seeing.

Erim screamed into the hand as the pain and sensation and knowledge of being run through gripped her tight.

Annwyn stood before the three stone biers in the chamber and stared at the bodies of three desiccated women in barbaric jewels and cloth. She ignored the large tunneled opening in the wall to her left.

"We shouldn't be here, my Lady. It is not safe here, in this place," whispered Wilhem Price. He stood near her, his arming sword at the ready in one hand, a lantern in the other to provide his Lady with light.

"I am quite tired of being continually warned about my safety, when we stand in the middle of a wizard's barrow in the Bale Mole," chided Annwyn softly. "None of us are safe here."

Too Tall had taken a spot by the entrance archway into the chamber, and while he would occasionally look out into the hall he spent most of his time watching Annwyn. Leigh stood impassively holding up another lantern, and he too watched Annwyn with beady eyes. She approached the woman's body on the central cairn, and began to walk around it slowly, studying it.

"This woman was a queen, I think," said Annwyn.

"One of Azharad's brides, I would guess," said Leigh. "It was said by both his enemies and his allies that he loved to indulge in the flesh of beautiful young women. In more ways than one. But these women must either have pleased him greatly, then, or themselves been witches and priestesses amongst the Nameless, to avoid his cooking pots and instead receive the honor of being interred here in his barrow." Wilhem Price looked quite queasy at that.

"Look how women would dress in so dark an age," Annwyn said. She ran a hand over the sheer garments that were left upon the body. Thin, sheer silks with slits that exposed legs and thighs and hips, now rotting with age, tightly wound tops banded with thin rings of woven gold, high gem-set necklaces and bronze bracelets made to look like twining serpents. "So crude, so revealing. I have been cloistered for so long, but still I would sometimes hear my brothers or our knights and servants talking, and I have heard that the temple-courtesans of Dieva, Goddess of Pleasure, still wear such things . . . where her temples are allowed, that is . . ."

"Dieva and her sacred prostitutes, my ass. A whore's a whore," muttered Too Tall.

"Watch your tongue!" hissed Wilhem Price, his face blushing a deep red. "You are in the presence of a Lady!"

"I expect for you, we are all whores, isn't that right?" Annwyn asked. As she walked around the bier, she let her robe slide open a bit, showing a bit of pale ivory leg. Too Tall chuckled at his good fortune and turned to watch her more closely while Wilhem Price swallowed nervously. She indicated the body and its garb. "Perhaps you'd like to see me wearing such barbaric things . . . dressed the ancient Queen? Or the temple whore, if you prefer."

Too Tall grinned at that. "Queen, whore, makes no difference to me how a woman dresses," he said. Annwyn turned and looked at him, her robe now sliding off her body almost completely, revealing her pale shoulders and shapely breasts and hips and a flat, smooth belly. The pieces of the map appeared and disappeared in her skin, and seemed to be moving most around her nipples and down her belly, as though the words and images were touching her skin from within her. Wilhem Price gawked, totally confused at what was happening. "Only thing that matters is whether she's wet and willing when she undresses," Too Tall said. "And sometimes I guess even that don't matter all that much."

Annwyn smiled and stepped back a bit, showing off more of her body. Too Tall took a step forward, grinning as he started loosening his doublet. Wilhem Price was frozen, his eyes darting back and forth between them.

"Willing? Oh, aye," said Annwyn breathily.

There was a flash of steel from behind Too Tall and his head popped off and a geyser of blood shot up into the air and spattered over the ground, even reaching Wilhem Price, and the short Danian man was suddenly much shorter.

The squire turned, wide-eyed, finally freed to move by the sudden act of violence, and he swung himself protectively in front of the Lady Annwyn, lifting both his arming sword and his lantern and facing the entrance to the chamber as the twitching, headless body of Too Tall fell to the floor.

"I think indeed that I shall be willing to be the Queen of the Bale Mole," whispered Annwyn in Wilhem Price's ear, as she slid an arm around him and pressed herself against his back.

A cowled and hooded figure stepped over the body of Too Tall. Gilgwyr slid the hood back from his face, revealing himself to the lamplight as he dragged Erim's body into the chamber behind him by the collar of her doublet. His face was marked by a strange, almost regal madness. He gave a great flourish of a bow to Annwyn and Leigh, and giggled a bit.

Her words finally registered on him and Wilhem Price looked over his shoulder at Annwyn, and when he saw her smile the squire realized instantly that he was in danger, though he could not understand for the life of him why. He freed himself from her arm and backed away from her, trying to watch all of them at once. His only exit was out the tunneled opening into the next chamber.

"My Lady?" he asked. "I . . . I don't understand what is happening."

"Azharad will be glad that you have chosen to be his bride. So you shall replace Harvald, and now we are three again. Excellent," Leigh said, as he stepped forward and started to approach Wilhem. "The others do not worry me, except Black-Heart."

"Leave Stjepan to me," said Annwyn quietly, her eyes on the squire. "We have . . . unfinished business."

"My Lady? Please, what's happening?" Wilhem asked again.

Annwyn gave him a lurid and malevolent smile. Sword and lantern shaking, Wilhem Price whimpered and backed into the next chamber.

Gilgwyr followed him in, walking slowly, his bloodied cut-and-thrust rapier in his hand, followed by Leigh.

Annwyn was the last in the chamber. She looked up, and then she stepped past Leigh, staring up at the ceiling behind Wilhem Price, her face shifting through confusion and anger and sadness until finally becoming a cruel mask of cold, hard disdain.

The squire turned and followed her gaze.

Suspended upside-down above what looked like a well was the dead, naked body of Malia Morwin, blood trickling from a dozen small wounds in her torso to drip down into the hole in the ground.

Wilhem Price opened his mouth to scream, but Gilgwyr moved first and faster.

They attacked the earth with pick and shovel and mattock, hauling dirt out of the growing, deepening pit by bucket and sack. They sang Danian folk songs, and argued over whether Aurian or Danian or Athairi women were better in bed (a short argument, actually, as everyone wound up agreeing on Athairi women). They wolfed down stale bread and nuts and dried figs, guzzled water and wine. They abandoned sect and cult and prayed for strength and endurance from any god or hero they thought might help. They prayed to Islik, King of Heaven; to his father, Illiki Helios, the Sun Bull; to Great Yhera, the Queen of Heaven; to Geniché, Queen of the Earth into which they dug; to Hathhalla, the Lioness of the Sun. They prayed to the Dragon Kings for the secrets of a dragon's strength, they prayed to Agall the First Hero for the strength he used to break the gates of Agrapios, they prayed to Ammon Agdah, the Keeper and Lord of Animals, for the strength he used to tame bulls and horses, they prayed to Yhera Fortuna and the Fates to bring them a treasure hunter's luck. And they sang some more, old songs of field and furrow, of men and sweat and labor, songs that had a touch of magic in them.

They lost track of time. And down they dug, until the bottom of the pit was almost nine feet down and the rough walls of the pit angled up almost like a funnel into the earth, almost twenty feet wide at the top. The displaced earth was piled about the walls of the circular room and formed a piled lip around the hole in the earth. And at the base of the funneled pit was an upright black iron casket, sticking up out of the earth like a pillar, now exposed to the air for the first time in almost four centuries. They had concentrated on clearing the earth from in front of the casket, so there was a bit more room on one side than on the other.

Stjepan was at the base of the pit, shoveling away a last bit of earth in front of the casket, while Godewyn and Caider worked above him on the slopes of the pit to haul up the last buckets of earth and unceremoniously dump them out on the lip. All three had stripped down to breeches and boots, their torsos and arms glistening in the flickering lamplight with sweat. Magical amulets dangled from chains and cords about their necks. Godewyn and Caider had exchanged a glance over Stjepan's nipple rings when they spotted them, but had said nothing. All three were very winded and slowing down while Arduin stood over them watching.

"Quite impressive, I think, that you have accomplished what you have," Arduin said, quietly. "In fact, it almost seems impossible." He surveyed the excavation from above, standing with one steel-shod foot on the raised lip of the pit and with his war sword in the crook of his couter.

"Perhaps a bit of old folk magic for you, my Lord," said Stjepan, straightening from his last labors and trying to catch his breath as he looked up at the Aurian knight. "Maybe not as flashy as what you get from the University Magisters . . . but there's a reason farmers sing the old songs as they work in the field, and miners below the earth." He turned back to look at the iron casket. "I . . . think we can get it open now," breathed Stjepan. He turned and looked up at Arduin. "My Lord Arduin . . . the hammers please?"

Arduin looked annoyed but he glanced around him and spotted an open leather satchel filled with hammers and mallets and chisels and punches. He gathered up the satchel and passed it down to Caider, who brought it down to the base of the pit.

As Caider started to sort some of the tools, Godewyn refilled a pair of lanterns and set them halfway down each side of the pit to better illuminate the object of their attention. Stjepan performed a familiar ritual, though he was breathing heavily. He started to walk slowly around the upright casket. "Show us. Show us the . . ." He was so winded, he had to stop and start over. *"Show us. Show us the World. Open our eyes, and let us see what is hidden . . ."*

They all eyed the casket warily. The exposed casket lid had revealed the etched image of a man in robes and wearing a horned mask, his hands clasped before his chest, similar to the body they had found in the treasure-filled burial chamber. The arcane patterns and symbols from the language of Macrberos that were etched around the central image into its black, rusted surface seemed to come alive and move about, like a basket full of glistening snakes. *Or like the images and letters on Annwyn's skin*, thought Stjepan.

"I don't like the looks of that," muttered Godewyn.

"No, it's . . . they won't harm us," said Stjepan, squinting hard at the letters. "They're wards . . . wards against detection, so no magic could reveal the whereabouts of the casket. There are no curses here that I can see . . ."

"No curses?" Godewyn asked. He grimaced, and considered the shimmering enchantments for a moment. "All right. If you're wrong . . ."

"Then we'll know very, very quickly," Stjepan said with a shrug.

The two sides of the casket were held in place by bolts driven through matching nuts that protruded from the sides of the front and back. Godewyn and Stjepan each took up a hammer and steel punch and set themselves at each side of the casket. They readied themselves and set their punches behind the bolts that held the front of the casket in place, looked at each other, and then started hammering. The *clanging* sound of metal on metal started to echo through the room.

All was dark and there was a constant dull roar, like a distant crowd of thousands cheering or a deep waterfall around the river bend. But then came the faint, distorted echo of something sharp and rhythmic to cut through the roar: clang, clang, clang, clang.

Erim's eyes fluttered open. She couldn't figure out what she was looking at, perhaps a rough wall of earth and exposed stone, flickering yellow and orange in lamplight? Her head felt wrapped in wool, she was groggy like she was drunk or hung over and she couldn't remember where she was or how she got there. But she could definitely hear the faint *clang, clang, clang* of metal striking metal. Something was terribly wrong, and she couldn't figure out what it was. Her body felt strange and far away, almost weightless.

Her vision shifted, and she couldn't figure out what she was seeing. She could barely keep her eyes open. She saw dust-covered brown leather, registered its texture and the rough wear and tear on what she realized was a sleeve. *What am I looking at?* She closed her eyes.

She felt the world and her body shift, and she forced her eyes to open again, and she found herself looking into the dead, staring eyes of Malia, and she came to her full senses with a start.

She was hanging upside down over the strange well they'd found, swaying gently back and forth between the naked, ruined body of the handmaiden and a headless body that she did not recognize at first. Her head swam and her body suddenly screamed in pain, and she bit her lip to stop herself from crying out. Adrenalin shot through her as memory returned. *I fought him. Magic. I was stabbed.*

Fucking Gilgwyr.

She looked around, trying to calm her suddenly racing heart, trying to get her bearings. She was upside down, a rope tied around her ankles running up to a makeshift pulley driven into the stone ceiling of the chamber. Similar pulleys and ropes held up Malia and the other body, and were tied off on the iron bar set into the rock next to the well. The three of them had been positioned so that the blood that dripped from their various wounds would drip down into the well. She brushed up against Malia's body, and craned her neck briefly to take in the violence that had been visited upon the handmaiden. Her naked body bore bruises and marks and she had been stabbed repeatedly. *A point dagger, similar to my own, something with a sharp tip and thin blade. I'm sorry you came to a terrible end. You shouldn't have been here with us.* She looked with sadness and revulsion at Malia's staring, lifeless eyes and realized with a start that the woman's eyelids had been cut away.

She closed her own eyes, and the world went safely dark for a bit.

When her eyes opened again, she had swung around enough to see the other body next to her without too much difficulty. She worried for a moment that it might be Stjepan, but after studying the clothes she knew it was one of Godewyn's crew, Too Tall, from the cut of his leather jerkin and the bronze studs set in its sleeves. Decapitated with a clean blow, by the looks of it.

She let her head hang loose, listening. She could hear low voices from nearby, and someone whimpering. It was hard to move, her body felt wooden and unresponsive, but eventually she was able to swing around to stare at the rest of the chamber. A couple of lanterns lit the dark space, and she could see the squire Wilhem Price lying several yards away from the well, stripped down to shirt and knee breeches and bound at hands and feet. He was crying softly.

Her hands had not been tied, only her feet, so her arms dangled beneath her. She had to move slowly at first, moving her shoulders and spine, trying to get her blood to flow and her hands and arms to work again. She craned her neck and looked up her body, at her blood-drenched shirt, and then for her brace of rapier and daggers, but they were missing. She groaned inwardly but immediately looked across Too Tall's body.

A sheathed dagger was still tucked by his left hip.

She took several deep breaths, steeling herself, then reached up with her left hand to grasp the front of Too Tall's jerkin. She tried to swing her right hand up and over to grab for the dagger, but that required her to twist her hanging body up and over to the left, and the moment she twisted pain shot out of her belly and fresh blood soaked her shirt. She gasped and let herself hang, staring down into the blackness of the deep well.

One chance to do this or I'll likely bleed to death soon, she forced herself to think regardless of if it was true or not, and with a grunt she launched herself back up and over, pulling hard with her left hand on Too Tall's jerkin. Despite the crippling pain in her stomach and bowels, she managed to swing her right hand up and over and her fingers slid around the handle of the dagger and suddenly she was collapsing back to hang upside down, staring at the blade she had ripped from its sheath. It was a nice dagger, a foot of steel, sharply pointed and sharp on both sides, with a rondel hilt, and it made her feel safer to hold it in her hands.

She studied the three ropes that held their bodies to the ceiling, and slipped the dagger between her teeth. By moving her arms and hips she started swinging closer to the ropes. It took a few swings for her to reach them, and she reached out and grabbed the rope that held Too Tall up and pulled herself close to it. She slid her left arm around it a couple of times and then gripped it tight with her left hand, anchoring the rope against her shoulder so that her body was safely anchored over solid ground and not the yawning chasm of the well. She took the dagger from her mouth and then reached through space to cut at the rope that held her aloft.

The effort was making her grow tired, and she could feel fresh blood seeping into her shirt, down her chest, and onto her neck. She sawed the blade of the rondel dagger back and forth into the rope with increasing desperation. Blood and sweat were starting to bead into her eyes and she blinked to be able to see.

And then the rope gave way and her body was suddenly free-falling. She half bounced off the ground and her feet and shins smacked into the lip of the well, and her left arm screamed in pain as the rope wrapped around it anchored her in place and almost wrenched it from its socket with a sudden jolt, and she blacked out.

Master Erim . . . please, wake up.

She opened her eyes.

"Master Erim . . ." whimpered Wilhem Price nearby. "Please, wake up."

She looked around and was elated to discover that she'd kept a death grip on the dagger; the squire was looking at her now from several paces

520

away, his eyes desperate. She groaned and untangled her left arm from the rope and fell onto her back, which sent a sharp pain through her body. She reached down to her belly, and cried out as her hand came back glistening in her own blood. She writhed on the ground until she could bend her body a bit, she tried to get her legs to work but between her time spent suspended upside-down and the wound to her back and stomach, they were being terribly uncooperative. She pulled her knees toward her with her left hand and then her legs, almost bending herself in half to bring her feet near enough that she could undo the rope that bound her legs. Luckily the knot was one familiar to her and she was free of it shortly, and it slid over the edge of the hole to fall soundlessly into the well. She started to crawl toward Wilhem.

And as she did she could see Gilgwyr step into the room.

No, not now, so close, so close! she thought in despair.

He smiled down at her with pursed lips as he stepped fully into the lamplight in his foppish best, his black crushed velvet doublet open and exposing a fine silk shirt.

"Ah, dearest Erim," he said conversationally. "Do forgive me, I quite thought I'd killed you." He eyed the dagger in her hand and gave her a wide berth as he walked toward the pit, and she took the moment to continue dragging herself with her hands and elbows toward Wilhem. Gilgwyr inspected the ropes and grunted. "Oh, well done, well done. Stjepan was quite right to pick you out from the street trash of Therapoli as a protégé, the little diamond in the rough."

Gilgwyr looked down into the well, and smiled. He turned back to look at her. She had reached Wilhem and was half crawling, half pulling herself along and up onto his body. Her legs seemed to be finally able to respond to her commands, and they kicked out against the ground behind her. "It's really been terribly amusing, you know, watching him groom you to be one of us, when you have no idea who any of us actually are," Gilgwyr said.

"I know who you are now, Nameless," she hissed back at him as she draped herself over Wilhem Price and started to cut at the knots tying the squire's hands behind his back.

"That's the spirit," said Gilgwyr with a laugh. "That's the spirit. But I'm the easy one to figure out. It's Stjepan you have to worry about," he said with a sigh. "This is actually for the best, you know. They do so hate to eat dead meat. They much prefer warm, living flesh with the blood still flowing. And now there's two of you to feed them, instead of just the one."

Wilhem Price's eyes went wide and his face went ashen, and in a hopeless panic he started weeping and babbling and began to struggle under Erim's efforts to cut his bonds. "Keep still!" she hissed as his babbling grew to a wail and she looked back over her shoulder and froze and Wilhem Price froze beneath her.

A hand and half a forearm had appeared from within the well behind a smiling Gilgwyr. An unnaturally pale, gnarled hand, barely skin and bones, with long, sharp, filthy-looking nails, sticking straight up out of the well, stock still.

Then the hand swayed a moment as though feeling the air in the chamber before it dropped to probe the lip of the well. As she watched with held breath, other hands started to emerge from within the hole to probe the edge.

Some part of her mind was screaming for her to begin moving, and she blinked, and she turned back and started working at the ropes that bound Wilhem's hands together. She tried to use the dagger to pry the knot open but this knot seemed harder to undo than her own had been. She cursed and pulled herself over the weeping squire and once she was on the other side of him she slid her dagger in between her teeth and started trying to pull him along the ground with her hands, but with her wounds it was difficult to pull him away. He did his best to work his way along the ground with his arms and legs bounds, but a cold chill was settling on her spine; she knew they weren't moving fast enough.

She could see back to the well now, and Gilgwyr standing silhouetted proud and handsome against the flickering lamplight. A creature started to hoist itself out of the well behind him. Its head appeared first, a head that bore some resemblance to a man, but with only a few straggly strands of white hair, and pale blue-white skin, and white eyes, and a missing gap where its nose used to be. Its thin lips skinned back to reveal a mouth of sharp teeth, and a black tongue flickered out to taste the air.

Then a second climbed out, and a third. Thin, pale things like walking cadavers, moving slowly and disjointedly in a half-crouch, climbing up out of the well, tasting the air. And more of them coming.

Hathaz-Ghúl, she thought. *Corpse-eaters.* And she wished that she was dead.

A couple of the *Ghúl* reached out and grasped hold of the body of Malia, pulling it toward them and away from being directly over the hole in the earth. They huddled around her suspended body, sniffing at her flesh and her blood, and began to chew on her arms and face. Several more of the *Ghúl* began sniffing at the hanging body of Too Tall, and at Gilgwyr as well, but Gilgwyr made a warding sign in the air and waved his hand toward Erim and Wilhem Price as though inviting the *Ghúl* to have their pick. The corpse-eaters sniffed and tasted the air, and several slowly clambered toward Wilhem Price with agonizing slowness as he and Erim struggled to get away from them. Cold, clawing hands finally reached out to take hold of his legs, and they started pulling him away from Erim. She screamed in anger and frustration around the dagger clenched in her teeth, for she could not match their uncanny strength and she felt him being pulled from her grasp.

One of the *Ghúl* opened its serrated teeth and bit down into the exposed calf of Wilhem's leg and began to chew. Wilhem Price screamed and thrashed about but the Ghúl had a strong grip on him and there were more of them now. A second one leaned in and began eating his foot. He looked toward Erim with desperate eyes. Suddenly her mind flashed on Isham Wall back at the tree, what seemed like ages ago but couldn't have been more than a few days, and her heart sank and she knew what to do.

She reached up, pulled the dagger from her teeth and plunged it into Wilhem's neck. His eyes went wide and glassy with surprise as blood jetted out from the puncture through-and-through.

Erim yanked the dagger out and the spray increased, and she turned and pulled herself out of the entrance hole, sobbing and cursing, as the sounds of feeding rose behind her and Gilgwyr laughed in delight.

The three-biered antechamber beyond the tunneled hole was lit by lanterns and torches. Annwyn's robe was on the floor. The nude woman herself crouched tightly over the body on the center bier in a lewd squat, whispering to herself. Leigh stood near her, admiring her naked form and the map images and words that played across her skin. She took a bracelet from the body on the bier and slid it on her wrist. "Oh, yes, you will make an excellent bride for Azharad," Leigh said.

Annwyn turned and looked at Erim with a strange smile on her face, watching as she crawled along the ground. "We have much in common, you and I. You yearn to be seen for who you are, to be yourself, and me, well I . . ." Annwyn said to her. "Well. I'm not myself, as our dear Stjepan likes to say." Annwyn paused again and contemplated Erim for a moment, as Erim, sobbing, kept crawling for the exit. "He sees you, doesn't he?" she asked with surprising earnestness. "But he doesn't see me. Not yet."

"They haven't eaten for a long time. They'll be very slow," Leigh called out to Erim. "You might even make it."

Annwyn and Leigh watched as Erim began clawing the dirt even harder, pulling herself into the passageway out of the chamber. Leigh started to laugh in delight at her predicament.

"King in Heaven! Sss . . . Stjepan . . . Stjepan . . . Help me . . . Stjepan . . ." Erim started to cry out, her voice rising into the corridor and becoming a scream. *"Help me!"*

The *clang* of hammers working steel punches against iron bolts rang through the room. Arduin stood perched at the lip of the hole, half turned to the entrance but looking down at the labor below him, where they had half the bolts freed. Suddenly he went tense and turned his head quickly, looking toward the entrance archway with a frown.

"Quiet!" he hissed.

Down in the pit, Stjepan, Godewyn, and Caider Ross stopped their hammering and froze in crouches, looking up at him in surprise, and the room fell into a long silence.

Finally Godewyn stirred. "What? What?" he hissed in a loud whisper.

"Did you hear something?" Arduin called down to them.

Stjepan and Godewyn glanced at their tools, then up at Arduin.

"You really think we can hear anything over all this hammering?" asked Godewyn, incredulous.

Arduin relaxed and turned back to them. "Sorry, I thought I heard something," he said with a shrug. And the men in the pit went back to work.

Erim pulled herself along, crawling through the dirt. Behind her there was silence. Ahead of her she could hear the rhythmic *clang* of metal-on-metal, clearer now than before. Her tears had dried up, there was nothing left in her to come out. There was virtually no light, but up ahead she could see the lantern that she had set down in the passageway before being attacked, and beyond it something glimmering on the ground. Soon she reached the lamp and she stopped, using the light to quickly check her wounds. The self-inflicted wound on her left leg was still bleeding and the leg was rapidly becoming numb, so she cut off a sleeve from her shirt and used it to tie around the wound. She grimaced, and slipped off the rest of her shirt, and tied it tight about her waist to try and cover the entrance and exit of the through-and-through stab wound into her belly.

Behind her, back from where she had come, she started to hear a faint scratching in the hallway that sounded like nails slowly moving along the floor or the wall. She ignored it, and turned and concentrated on the glimmers along the ground beyond the lamp, her rapier and dagger lying where she must have dropped them after being stabbed. She started crawling again, grabbing her rapier with her right hand as she passed it.

As she crawled across the threshold into the first chamber of the inner barrow, she could hear the clanging sound much more clearly coming from the archway to the north, where she would find Stjepan and Arduin and the rest of them.

She didn't hesitate. She turned to the east and started crawling up the mosaic stone passage leading to the entrance chamber to the barrow and the exit beyond.

Stjepan and Godewyn stepped back, tossing aside their hammers, as Caider Ross knocked out the final bolt. They circled the upright casket and Caider exchanged his hammer for a crowbar. He slid it into a slight space that had opened up between two of the protruding nuts. They all exchanged wary glances and then prepared to pull the casket lid forward and off.

They started to put some muscle into the effort, and there was a *crack* as the iron lid unsealed from the standing base of the casket. As they started to ease the lid forward, a wave of stench hit them from inside the iron casket and they began coughing and retching.

"King of Heaven!" Godewyn gasped, and he and Caider Ross leapt back, covering their mouths and noses with their hands; Stjepan struggled to hold the iron casket lid up by himself, but he couldn't, it was too heavy and the stench compelled him to stumble back, and as the lid spun and fell onto the side of the pit, front side up, a wall of dead maggots coated in black filth cascaded out of the open casket, filling the bottom of the pit and splashing up onto the men in the pit as they leapt back.

"Careful! What in the world—" Arduin started to ask, but he trailed off and grimaced as the smell reached him.

Inside the casket stood a headless corpse, dressed in decaying finery, its hands clasped as if in prayer. Long robe, fringed collar, jeweled chain of office around its neck; everything in the casket was coated in a lustrous black filth, like unrefined oil, and dead maggots were embedded in the muck.

Godewyn, Caider Ross, and Stjepan stood still, their boots ankle-deep in dead maggots, staring at the inside of the casket with fear and anticipation as the stench dissipated. They each held a shovel or a crowbar or a mattock now, snatched up from the ground and readied as though they were weapons.

"It's him, isn't it? It's him. It's Azharad," said Godewyn in a whisper.

"It's him," Stjepan replied grimly.

Godewyn grimaced. "Where's his fucking head?" he asked.

Arduin called down from the lip of the pit. "Where's the *sword*?"

The men in the pit moved forward, gingerly stepping on the dead worms beneath them, and looked closer.

There was no sword upon the body, or in the casket, that they could see.

"Shit," said Stjepan.

Erim pulled herself out of the passage to the inner barrow, pain and effort and determination on her face. She began pulling herself up the stone floor of the passageway out.

Stjepan warily inspected the insides of the casket, poking about with the adze edge of his mattock. Godewyn, and Caider Ross pressed in behind him and looked over his shoulders, craning their necks.

"It's . . . it's not here! It's just a headless body," Stjepan finally called out. "That's all that's in the casket."

Arduin gaped down at him, incredulous. "What? Is . . . is it really Azharad?" he asked.

"Yes. Yes, it must be," Stjepan said. He put a gloved hand to his head, staring at the insides of the casket.

"Of course it's him, you idiot!" shouted Godewyn. "But where's the fucking sword? What in the Six Hells are we doing here? We lost how many men for this? I do not fucking believe this horseshit!" Godewyn continued to rant and rave, pacing back and forth in the black muck at the base of the pit and filling the air with foul curses, his face turning beet red. Caider started to slowly back away from Godewyn.

"I don't understand. What's going on? Why is there no sword here?" Arduin called out, trying to be heard above Godewyn's shouting.

"I don't know . . . unless there's more to the map," Stjepan said. *Annwyn. She wanted to get in here. Why? Why did she have to be in here?* he wondered to himself. He looked up. "Lord Arduin, we must go back to camp and find your sister."

Stjepan stood and started to climb out of the pit, but behind him Godewyn's ranting had reached a fever pitch. ". . . and that's the last time I listen to some witch-born Athairi bastard!" Godewyn shouted. And he grabbed up his shovel and swung the flat of its blade into the back of Stjepan's head, and Stjepan spun around almost completely and went down with a thud, coming to a stop with his head against the lid of the casket where it rested on the sloped earth of the side of the pit.

Arduin stared impassively down at them.

Panting, Godewyn stood smugly behind Stjepan's unconscious body, while Caider Ross, his crowbar held like a weapon, looked up at Arduin.

"I really do think that's quite enough from you," said Arduin quietly.

Godewyn turned and looked up at Arduin, holding his shovel out like a pointer. "To the Six Hells with you. To the Six Hells with all of this. To the Six Hells with the fucking sword," he hissed. He tossed the shovel aside and spat. "There's a fortune in that other room, and we're gonna go get it. Then me and my boys are leaving, with or without the rest of you sorry lot." He turned to Caider Ross. "Here, go get me some of that rope."

Caider Ross climbed out of the pit on the opposite side from where Arduin stood and rummaged in some of the satchels and bags they had brought with them. He found a coiled-up rope and tossed it down to Godewyn in the pit, then shrugged a shirt on and started buckling his sword belt around his waist. Arduin watched with a tilted head and blank

528

expression as Godewyn turned the unconscious Stjepan over and started tying his hands behind his back.

When he was finished he flipped Stjepan onto his back again, and patted his face with mock affection. "Shit, Athairi, what'd you say about being buried when you were dead?" Godewyn said with a snicker. He climbed out of the pit, grabbing up his sword and daggers and his brigandine jack.

He looked down at Stjepan in the pit, and then at Arduin. "It's been a fucking disaster knowing you two," he said.

Godewyn and Caider Ross walked past Arduin and out the high-domed chamber.

Arduin silently watched them go and stared at the empty archway for a moment. He looked back down at Stjepan's prostrate form and gave an apologetic shrug.

"I really must go find my sister," he said.

He turned and walked out of the chamber.

CHAPTER TWENTY-EIGHT

DREAMS IN THE WITCH HOUSE

S tjepan awoke to find that he was lying upon a carved stone bench in a clearing on a wooded hilltop. The forest nearby was filled with broad high trees of birch and purple-leaf oak, maple and elm, cherry and white ash, cedar and pine stretching out for leagues in all directions, their trunks coated with old layers of lichens and moss. Leaves were falling to pile on the perimeter of the clearing, or floating past him, stirred in the light wind. Storm clouds roiled the skies above, but he heard no thunder and felt no rain. He felt sure that it was late autumn, but rather than the riot of fall colors, of burnt red and orange-yellow and fire and gold, instead the landscape around him was but shades of blue and grey and black, as though the world was caught in a moment of perpetual dusk. A dream, then. He stirred and sat up, and looked around. He was looking to the east, that he was certain; the desolate high mountains of the Djar Éduins were visible through the trees to his left. Below him he could see a great stone castle that sat on a rise over a small riverside city, and he knew that across that river would be the Plain of Stones.

No, this is not your home, this is not An-Athair. And no, you are not dead. This is not Limbo, either, came an ancient, gravelly voice from behind him.

Stjepan turned and looked over his shoulder. He could see a figure standing in the shadows of the trees, wearing a long, black robe with a collar of tufted horse hair, surrounding the head like a black fan, and a long, pointed bronze mask, with a pair of gazelle horns spiraling up from its forehead. The mask's eyeholes had an evil, slanted cast to them, and opened onto blackness. Ornate circular patterns swirled and wove their way along the edges of the mask and were echoed in gold thread patterns embroidered into the figure's robe. A chain of gold and bronze discs inlaid with silver symbols was slipped over the collar and around its neck, almost like a noble's chain of office.

'Tis but a dream, while you are in a place where men should not dream. Dreaming is for temples, not for graves. Not for my *grave,* the figure said.

Stjepan stood up, alarmed.

Arduin stepped into the first chamber of the inner barrow; he paused, uncertain. For a moment he looked toward the south passage, and then east out toward the exit. He swayed suddenly, and had to put a hand against the wall to steady himself. He almost retched onto the ground. *My family is ruined,* he thought. *Our line is ended. There shall be no redemption for us here. And I have lost every knight of my household on this useless quest. Unless . . . unless . . .*

He took a deep breath, and then he turned to his right, and west toward the shrine of Ishraha and the treasure chamber with the bier and body.

Stjepan stepped warily into the center of the clearing. He kept his body turned toward Azharad, who began circling the clearing, never entirely leaving the shadows of the trees. He tried not to let the ghostly figure out of his sight.

"What do you want with me?" asked Stjepan.

Azharad laughed with a hiss. *What do I want with you? My barrow has at long last been opened, and I smell it in the air: metal and blood, leather and rust, sweat and fear. I hear it on the wind: the clash of arms and iron, the murmur of rumor and riot.*

As he spoke, the trees began to fade away and the shadows turned to men roiling in armored combat. And they were no longer in a clearing in

An-Athair, instead they were standing in the midst of a dark and chaotic battlefield that moved about them in slow motion, as though the combatants were trapped in honey becoming amber. Stjepan looked but he could not see who was fighting; the armored warriors that whirled about them were hazy, indistinct, shadows and blurs.

Wolves are howling, ravens taking wing, spirits of death and fire stirring beyond the veil! War is coming, and oh, how I would love to be back in the world for this! Azharad said as he walked amongst the fighting men. *To feast on the bones and flesh of the dead! To sate myself on the bodies of those I have corrupted! Oh, to be free again to feed on the world!*

Stjepan's eyes were narrowing.

Oh, what I want with you is obvious, I think, said the ghost. *No, the question is: what do* you *want with* me?

The light of several lamps illumined the long chamber of rough-hewn stone walls and its low, corbel-arched ceiling and the deep arched crevices set in its sides. Godewyn and Caider Ross were quickly and quietly sorting through the urns and chests that lined the crevices and the perimeter of the floor, stuffing sacks with gold statues and figurines and anything that sparkled with gems, creating a pile of sacks by the door. Godewyn had slipped his brigandine back on, though he had not had the time to tie it properly and it hung open in the front, exposing the hair on his chest. They looked up as Arduin entered the chamber, his bared war sword still carried in the crook of his coulter, and both of them stood and drew their weapons, Godewyn with a broadsword in one hand and an axe in the other.

"This is all that's left of value and it's *ours* by our rightful contract, this is, not yours!" Godewyn snarled.

Arduin stared at him a moment, his face a blank, before he turned away. "Keep it," he finally said. "Keep it all. I care not for those trinkets." His gaze fell upon the long waist-high bier of rock and stone in the center of the chamber, and the beautiful sword clasped beneath the hands of the body that rested upon it.

Godewyn followed his eyes, and snorted. "Here to claim a cursed sword?" he asked.

"Who says it's cursed?" Arduin said with a shrug. "I mean, how do we really know? Master Stjepan has been wrong about so many other things, so why not this as well?"

Slowly Godewyn and Caider Ross turned and looked at the sword.

Azharad continued to circle Stjepan, creeping closer and closer as he walked. *What can I offer you? A chance to be a king, rather than a servant?* the ghost hissed and gloated. *I see the oaths that bind you!*

Azharad pointed and a ghostlike rune appeared on Stjepan's bare chest. Ghostly chains seemed to bind the rune to his heart. A dagger was suddenly in Stjepan's right hand.

You walk the world in shadows, steeped in secret murder and crimes of state, pollution marring your spirit so men who think themselves your betters can enter the Heavens, while you are condemned to suffer one day in Hell! the ghost of the ancient wizard said. Blood dripped from the dagger in Stjepan's hand onto the earth at his feet. *Why hide in the shadows? Why be a servant, when instead these could be your rewards: golden crowns and laurels upon your brow, legions at your beck and call, kings and queens at your feet, all the trophies of war and lust!*

Stjepan laughed drily. "A feeble offer from a ghost: the riches of the material world. Do you think me so easily bought?" he asked.

Oh, but I most certainly do, said Azharad. *Anger and hate consume you; love has been burnt from you, burnt away in the pyre that consumed your mother, by years of service to men you secretly hate and who do not deserve your loyalty.* The battle around them grew more and more vicious; the world grew darker, with fires raging on the horizon in every direction. Azharad seemed to be feeding off the chaos around him. *And a man without love is a man for the taking. A man's destiny is spun by the Wheels of Fate and written in the Book of Dooms, but I was a Magician-King in the service of Nameless Cults. I worshipped Nymarga the Devil and Githwaine his first and last Worm King, and I strived to read the future in all its possibilities. The Book of Dooms is not fixed; the Queen of Heaven gave men that gift, that they may write themselves a new page. You walk a servant's path, but I can offer a different one, the path of war and conquest, glowing bright with fire and slaughter. The Sword, held high in triumph! The Sphinx, the source of mystery! And the Riven Tower, earth-shaker, destroyer of the order of things!*

Azharad raised his hands up to the Heavens. *An Age is ending! And in the fires that are coming, someone will surely walk this path! It could be you, if you wanted it; you need but ask and this path is your path. Free me, and become my captain! Free me, and become my champion! Help me back into the world you hate so much, and I will help you break it!*

Stjepan eyed Azharad with a slight smile.

"I have only one thing to ask of you, dread Lord," he said quietly. "The sword *Gladringer* . . . where is it?"

Around the bier no one moved.

Arduin stood still staring at the sword, as did Godewyn and Caider Ross. The beautifully made sword glistened to them in the flickering lamplight.

Finally Godewyn and Caider glanced at each other, then at Arduin, and then back to the sword. Godewyn caught Caider Ross' eye, and gave an imperceptible nod at the sword.

Caider Ross grinned and nodded, and made a quick step forward as if to lunge for the sword lying on the body on the bier.

And Arduin swept his war sword from its place of rest in the crook of his couter and it flashed high in the air in a blur, and then he cut straight down through Caider Ross' shoulder and into his chest, cleaving the startled man open before he had a chance even to flinch.

Godewyn leapt back against a wall, almost tripping over an urn filled with coins, his eyes wide. "King of Heaven!" he spat.

He stared aghast as Arduin put an iron-shod foot against Caider's chest and pushed the body back onto the dirt floor of the chamber to free his sword from the man's ruined ribs and lungs. Arduin turned toward him, a murderous glint in his eyes. Godewyn licked his lips, starting to measure his chances against the Champion of the Tournament of Flowers standing before him in full harness and with bloodied sword raised in challenge.

Azharad paused and looked away from Stjepan.

"Where is Gladringer?" Stjepan repeated.

Azharad looked back at him and stretched out a hand to the Athairi. *Free me, bring me back into the World, and I will tell you!*

"Do you even know where it is?" Stjepan asked.

Free me, take the hero's path, and I will tell you where to find it, said the ghost.

Stjepan studied him a long moment. "I think not," he finally said. "If I help break the World, it'll be without you."

Azharad laughed bitterly. *Then you are a fool*, the ghost said. And he turned and faced Stjepan and raised his mask, revealing a face corrupted by disease and eaten by worms and maggots, his eyes missing, his teeth sharpened into fangs. He moved toward Stjepan, his hideous face opening in a frustrated and terrifying scream.

CHAPTER TWENTY-NINE
TWO · BY TWO ·

Stjepan sat up with a start to discover he had been lying against the lid of the iron casket as it rested on the sloping sides of the pit. He breathed deeply, and then winced at the pain of Godewyn's blow. He tried instinctively to bring his hand to the back of his head and when that didn't happen he realized that his hands were tied behind his back.

And then he froze as he became aware that above him someone was walking along the lip of the funneled pit, just as Azharad had been circling him in his dream.

"Azharad," said Stjepan with a tired sigh. "Even awake my answer is the same."

"No. Not Azharad," came Annwyn's voice.

Stjepan rolled a bit onto his side on the sloping wall of the pit and looked up and over his shoulder; it was indeed Annwyn, walking around the chamber above him. She wore golden serpent bracelets, ornate anklets and arm torques and a jeweled necklace, and little else except the moving, pulsing map. She trailed her damask robes behind her.

He frowned, staring at her, his mind still groggy and shaken.

"Where's Erim? The others?" he asked.

"I fear they've all gone and left us. But then, what's happening here no longer concerns them. It is just you and I, here, alone in the dark. The map, and the map reader," she said.

Stjepan turned away from her. "I think I dreamed this moment," he said quietly. He began to surreptitiously struggle against his bonds.

"A pleasant dream? The two of us giving rise to something new, here, in this place, beneath the earth," said Annwyn with a tone of hope.

"I don't think so," he said. His head hung low in resignation, but his voice was sharp and clear. "It is time for this charade to end, Annwyn.

The map has placed a compulsion upon you. You've become a pawn of the Nameless Cults, and I will aid you no further."

Arduin and Godewyn circled each other around the bier and the body and its sword, slowly and calmly. Godewyn looked down at Caider Ross' body as he stepped over it, and a dark cloud of anger passed over his face. His nostrils flared and his lips skinned back from his teeth in a vicious snarl as he hefted his broadsword in his left hand and his axe in his right. But some part of him raised a warning flag. *Careful, careful*, he thought. *This one's a born killer, trained from birth to take men apart with a sword, and he clearly hasn't lost a step since they named him a Champion of the Tourneys . . .*

"You know why they call me Red-Hand?" Godewyn asked Arduin suddenly with a grin. "I was given that name when I was but fourteen, when a local bard sang a song about the revenge I took on a man that had stolen from me. I was already well on a path steeped in other people's blood and misery, and I've never looked back. When I die, the men and women I've killed will be lined up at the Place of Judgment waiting for me, whole flocks of them, a full fucking chorus of the unhappy, untimely dead waiting to greet me with their moans and wails."

"I look forward to sending you to them, then," said Arduin with gritted teeth. "It's high time, I think, that you take your place in whatever Hell is waiting for you."

"Ah, it won't be that easy, my Lord. You're hardly the first to try, and I don't think you're gonna be the last. After I kill you, I'm gonna take that sword and I'm gonna find that cursed little shit Gilgwyr," said Godewyn. "I'll cut him limb from limb, slice his lying tongue out and feed it to him." His grin got wider and meaner. "Then I'm gonna find your sister and I'm gonna stick her with the sword in my pants, and make her scream like you never could."

Arduin shook with rage. "You . . . you . . . you . . . you . . ." he stammered, until words utterly failed him and all that was left was a blinding hunger for death.

They stopped circling and lunged for each other, blades crossing.

Annwyn laughed as Stjepan staggered unsteadily to his feet, his hands tied behind him, and turned to look up at her walking her circle around the lip of the pit.

"Is that what you think when you look at me? The others . . . when they looked at me . . . when they looked at *me*, they first saw this form," she said as she dropped the damask robe to the earth behind her, and let her hands run over her body, over her hips and sides and up her breasts. ". . . This flesh, this skin . . . And *then* they saw the map." She looked at him with curious eyes, and she began to walk down into the pit, taking a long circular spiral down its sloped, funneled walls, slowly getting closer and closer to him as she spoke. "But not you. When you look at me, you see the map first. In fact, it's all you see. You don't see my form, my flesh, my skin. You don't see me, you don't see what I am becoming."

Stjepan stood at the base of the pit, his boots in muck and dead maggots, and he looked into her clear blue eyes. "I see full well what you've become," he said.

"No, you don't," she said. "I want you to look at me. Not at the map, look at *me*."

"I see you better than you think, Annwyn, and you are not yourself," he said.

"I am more myself than I have ever been," she said with a smile. Stjepan said nothing, watching her warily as she got closer.

Annwyn reached the floor of the pit and walked around him and the casket, carefully stepping so that she did not enter the muck and dead maggots pooled at the pit's lowest point in front of the open casket. As she passed behind him, her hand reached out to touch him on his bare shoulder. Her finger trailed across his back, tracing a line on his skin from one shoulder to his spine to his other shoulder. "All these days and nights you've looked at me. It's only fair that you show me *your* form, *your* flesh, *your* skin," she whispered in his ear. "Let me see you. And then we can finish what we've started."

She turned him around. She looked down across his smooth chest, her eyes coming to rest on the rings in his nipples, then down across his flat, muscled abdomen. She could smell sweat and sun-burnt copper skin and the heat rising from his body.

"You and me and the map, alone under the earth," she said, looking up into his eyes with a knowing smile.

She started to undo the buttons on his breeches. She slid her hands under the waist of his breeches, separating it from his skin, sliding her hands behind him to glide her fingers over his firm buttocks. She crouched in front of him, and as she did so, she pulled her hands down and with them his breeches, and she smiled in delight at what she found rising to greet her.

Godewyn and Arduin threw themselves at each other in a fast, dizzying clash of arms, each surprising the other with their speed and skill. Holding his war sword with both hands in the Aurian longsword style, Arduin delivered three fast killing strokes to the head and body of a rapidly and desperately backpedaling Godewyn, only to have each either turned aside by broadsword parry or find empty air where the big man should have been, and then found himself ducking a blow from Godewyn's axe that would have taken his head off had he been a hair slower.

They separated, eyeing each other warily and perhaps a bit more respectfully. The next time they approached each other with quick feints and little jabs, tests to see speed and reflexes, dueling around the bier slowly at first, then with increasing vigor as they began to take each other's measure.

Arduin fought like a champion sportsman, confident in the protection of his full steel harness; Godewyn like a veteran street fighter using guile and speed and sheer bravado. Godewyn quickly realized that his broadsword and axe were ill-suited against Arduin's steel harness; without a sharp pointed tip to drive through a bit of mail or under a joint in the armor, his only chance lay either in a shot to Arduin's bare, blond head, or to batter the armor until he crushed it in on the flesh beneath it. But the axe head was too lightweight, and Arduin had been trained to wear and fight in a full harness since he was eight, and he used the armor like a shield to deflect and turn Godewyn's blades, never taking a blow flat to the surface, and managing to keep his opponent well away from his head and face.

Godewyn felt a rising frustration and sinking desperation as his blows caromed off the curves and planes of the hard armor shell. He sent a series of sharp, hard blows right at Arduin's head from both sword and axe, hoping the flurry would overcome Arduin's defenses, but the knight parried them deftly with his war sword and counterattacked, sending Godewyn spinning back to escape his onslaught. Godewyn managed to punch his broadsword out and across Arduin's stomach in a move that would have gutted an unarmored man, but all he did was ring the armor like a bell and the knight's cuirass didn't even dent.

Although they were well matched, Arduin was gaining the upper hand.

Stjepan lay on the iron casket lid, his hands still tied behind him, his boots braced in the black muck at the bottom of the pit. Annwyn's shapely ivory legs straddled him and the casket lid, her feet digging into the slopes of the funneled pit, and she ground her hips down onto his lap, one hand clutching the back of his bloodied head, the other braced against the casket lid above him.

Her head went back, wide-mouthed in pleasure as she gasped and moaned at the sensations of being filled. She laughed as she ground against him, running her hands over his skin then back to grasp his hair.

She leaned back and thrust down onto his lap, harder and harder.

The headless corpse leaned upright in the standing casket, a few feet behind her, a mute witness to their coupling.

Godewyn knew he was losing his duel with Arduin, he knew it in his bones, and grew angry at the unfairness of it all. In skill they were perhaps well matched, but the knight's superior harness was all the difference that he needed. It changed the way the knight fought, the way he could afford to take risks, and there was nothing Godewyn could do about it.

Arduin slammed his war sword across Godewyn's right arm, biting deep into the brigandine sleeve's leather and plates and sending a shock of pain up and down the arm, and Godewyn dropped his axe with a sharp cry. Godewyn backed away from him and almost toppled over several urns filled with grave goods into one of the arched crevices that ran the length of the sides of the room. He had to put out his right hand into the crevice to brace himself against the fall.

Triumphantly, Arduin grinned and leapt in for the kill, but Godewyn had put his hand on top of a small pile of coins, and his fingers closed around them and he hurled a handful of gold coins, glinting in the lamp-light, right into Arduin's face. It was just enough to distract the knight, and Godewyn's broadsword snaked out to slap Arduin's sword from his grasp, and it flew across the small chamber.

Arduin leapt back, unarmed.

And now it was Godewyn who wore a jackal's grin of triumph.

Arduin measured with his eye the distance to his war sword on the ground, and he knew in an instant that he couldn't get to it before Godewyn could get to him. Grimly he looked at Godewyn and raised his hands to beckon him forward in defiance: *come and get me if you dare.*

Annwyn leaned back further, arching her torso as she ground down against him, and Stjepan could see the whole of the map swirling on her skin. His body shuddered at the sensations of her tightness slipping wetly up and down upon his shaft, and he groaned and thrust his hips up at her, his eyes fluttering. And then suddenly his eyes were wide open with surprise; he frowned and stared, mouth open in confusion, but no, he was correct, there was a new set of letters and runes swirling on her skin, letters he had not seen before. He looked up at her; she was in the throes of passion, her head thrown back and her sweetly parted lips issuing wordless, insensible sounds, and he was uncertain if she was even aware of what was appearing on her writhing body.

Godewyn switched his broadsword to his right hand and lunged at Arduin, but the knight hurled himself across the bier, knocking the corpse that lay upon it off and onto the floor.

The masked head of the body bounced into a corner of the chamber, and came to a rest as if watching the proceedings.

Godewyn made to come around the bier, broadsword raised high in both hands for a quick chopping deathblow, but he skidded to a halt and froze.

Arduin slowly stood, holding the beautiful sword that had been on top of the body in his right hand, a look of cold disdain on his face as he contemplated his opponent.

"Ah, fuck me," Godewyn cursed.

Annwyn leaned forward until she was coiled about him and they were in an embrace. She stared down into his eyes, her golden hair falling about his face like a veil. She grabbed him by the hair, looking at him imploringly, and his final reserves crumbled and despite his hands tied behind his back he began thrusting up into her, faster and harder, pushing toward climax, and she thrust her hips and pelvis down against him.

She began to laugh as his pace increased, a laugh of joy, of pleasure and delight, of discovery and surprise. He thought it was one of the most incredible things he'd ever heard in his life.

And suddenly he went stiff against her, arching his back and hips off the casket lid to lift her bodily into the air, and she wrapped her legs around his and ground herself down onto him, riding his orgasm.

The masked head sat in its corner, its blackened, sightless eyeholes given a grand view of the final confrontation between Arduin and Godewyn. Breathing heavily, they contemplated each other with a mix of wary respect and condescension and hatred.

"Hardly seems right that a sword of legend, once wielded by the hands of kings and great heroes, would need to be used on the likes of you," said Arduin, raising the sword up in both hands and contemplating its gleaming length.

"No," Godewyn said with resignation. "No, it don't seem right at all."

Arduin leapt forward and slashed downward for Godewyn's head. Godewyn brought his broadsword up for a parry to sweep the blow aside, and when the two blades connected the sword from the bier shattered into pieces.

They stared at each other and at the broken blade for a split second in shock.

And then Godewyn was springing forward and jamming his own sword up through the gap in Arduin's armor under his left arm, using sheer strength to drive the dull, broad point past his arming doublet and the bit of mail there and then into muscle and tissue and bone and lung, and bodily carrying Arduin backwards in the rush. The broken blade went flying out of Arduin's grasp and blood spat from Arduin's mouth as he was driven right-shoulder-first into the wall, his empty hands clawing at Godewyn's face and neck as they grappled and Godewyn jammed the broadsword in further.

Stjepan lay back on the casket lid, Annwyn lying entwined upon him as her hands and legs stroked his flesh. He was still semi-hard inside her, and she humped her hips against him slowly, luxuriating in the feeling of their sweat-slickened bodies sliding against each other.

"Would that I had been born a woman in a land that loves them," she whispered softly as she nuzzled into his neck.

"I couldn't agree more," came a voice from above them.

Stjepan, exhausted, looked up in confusion.

Above them on the lip of the pit Leigh stood casually, looking down on them. Gilgwyr stood behind him and giggled. And several of the *Hathaz-Ghúl* could be seen peering in the archway into the chamber behind them both, tasting the air with their black tongues. Stjepan blanched, his eyes narrowing at the sight of the *Ghúl*.

"That really was *most* entertaining," Leigh said with a cruel smile.

Arduin, clutching his side, slumped to the ground as Godewyn wrenched his broadsword out from under the knight's armpit, blood splattering everywhere, pouring out from under Arduin's armor onto the ground. An exhausted Godewyn looked down at the dying knight with contempt and elation.

"And you were once crowned a Champion in one of the Great Tournaments?" Godewyn said with a sneer, and spat to the side. "Maybe I'll buy myself a title and a grand estate with the loot from this hole, and enter a tournament or two myself . . . *Lord Godewyn, Champi'n of the Tourney*, how do you like the sound of that, eh?"

He sheathed his broadsword and walked over to the pile of loot by the exit. He reached down and grabbed up a few heavy sacks of coins and hoisted them over his shoulder, and staggered out the entrance without nary a look back.

Arduin's body shook, and he coughed up blood, the viscous stuff flowing from his mouth; he was choking, having trouble breathing, and he knew that he was dying. His eyes rolled up to look at the ceiling as he tried to gasp for breath.

Forgive me, oh my father, I have failed you, he thought. *Forgive me, oh my king, for I have failed you. Do not forsake me, for I am your loyal vassal.*

The masked head of the body looked on impassively.

Godewyn took a couple of heavy, exhausted steps into the shrine of Ishraha, with its demonic statue and warrior bodies resting in alcoves, and he looked up from carrying his heavy burden, and froze.

Several *Hathaz-Ghúl* crouched in the semi-darkness of the guttering lamplight, waiting silently and staring at him.

"Oh, for fuck's sake," Godewyn whined.

The *Ghúl* stirred and moved forward.

And Godewyn screamed.

CHAPTER THIRTY
THE RETURN ⊙F AZHARAD

Annwyn pulled herself off of Stjepan's deflating erection and casually stepped off to the side, and he slid off the iron casket lid and crumpled to the ground, curling to protect himself. She stood imperiously and Gilgwyr licked his lips at the sight of her curvaceous body, her breasts lifted high on her chest as she raised her arms and ran her hands through her golden hair, her body gleaming with sweat in the lamplight.

And then he gasped when his eyes finally registered the headless body that stood in the upright casket behind her.

"The body of Azharad!" he cried. "So it *was* here! But . . . where's his head?"

"Ah, dismembering the body is an old tactic to foil divinations," Leigh said patiently. "It destroys the totality of the body, the physical self, and thereby makes it invisible to magic scrying and fortune-telling. Usually it is done as a curse on an enemy, but in this case, the *Nymargatia* in his service may have used it to hide his body from those that might have sought him out to destroy him utterly. I do not doubt that his head will be hidden somewhere in the barrow."

Annwyn laughed. "Did you really not recognize it, hidden in plain sight?" she asked. When the two men glanced at each other in confusion, she laughed again. "Do not worry. I know where it is."

She started walking up out the pit, and as she reached near the top Gilgwyr reached down and extended a courteous hand to help her out of the pit. She was humming to herself as she picked up her damask robes and casually wrapped them around her body. Stretching and shaking out her muscles, Annwyn made to leave the room, trailing the robe behind her on the ground, and Gilgwyr watched her go with a leer. The *Hathaz-Ghúl* parted for her, recoiling with respect and fear.

Leigh walked down into the pit, and stared haughtily down at Stjepan.

"Well, Magister," said Stjepan lightly, looking up at him with a crooked smile. "Who would've thought the crazed, evil magician would turn out to be . . . well, a crazed evil magician?"

Leigh kicked him in the stomach and Stjepan curled into a ball, coughing and hacking.

Erim came to, and felt broken grass against her face and hands and pressing against her front and right side. She blinked her eyes open and rolled onto her back. She could barely keep her eyes open, but she knew that she would be seeing stars and storm clouds and night sky if she could but focus properly. She realized slowly that she was lying head-down right next to the steps that led away from the barrow and back down the hillside toward their camp. She could feel the weakness in her body, a deadly fatigue threatening to pull her down into eternal sleep. *By the gods, I can't let that happen again*, she chided herself. *If it does, next time I won't wake up.*

Despite the numbness that seemed to envelop her body, she rolled back onto her stomach and started to crawl her way down the hill, grimacing as she went. She thought she could see the dark shape of their camp blurrily in the distance.

Suddenly a badly limping and bloodied Godewyn passed her, half walking, half stumbling down the steps, several large and heavy-looking sacks slung over his shoulders.

"Hey . . . Hey there . . . Godewyn," she croaked out, her throat parched and unresponsive. "Godewyn!"

Godewyn continued on, without a word or look to acknowledge he'd even heard her, disappearing down the steps toward the camp.

Erim kept crawling through the grass, but faster now.

Annwyn entered the false tomb, and her eyes roamed over the scattered evidence of looting and a fight. She frowned and grew tense when she saw that the body was no longer on the low rock-and-stone bier, but relaxed again when her eyes fell on the masked head of Azharad lying by itself in the far corner.

Her view of the other corner was blocked by several *Ghúl*, perched on the bier or crouching next to it. As she moved forward, she saw past them and stopped, frozen: the *Ghúl* were watching her dying brother with rapt fascination.

Arduin coughed blood, and struggled, his body shaking, his wide, wild eyes taking in his unnatural audience with fear and confusion. He weakly held up the handle and shard of a broken sword as a last line of defense against the *Ghúl*. And then Arduin saw her, and he opened his mouth, and blood spilt out to drip from his chin onto his breastplate.

Annwyn walked slowly to him, the *Ghúl* parting before her. Her mind was a blank for a moment, as it registered what she was seeing, and then her head started to fill with all the things she'd ever wanted to say to him: *I love you. I hate you. You should have truly loved me. You have no idea who I am. I was nothing to you. You should have stopped them. Why didn't you stop them? You killed him. You deserve this. You deserve worse.* Her face went through a variety of emotions: sorrow, disdain, delight, pity. Then she crouched down next to him, and cradled his head briefly before kissing him on his forehead.

Confused, Arduin looked up at her with tears in his eyes, and he tried to speak to his sister, but no sound came out of his throat but a last gurgle. His eyes went blank as he died and his body relaxed and slumped into its armor.

After a minute Annwyn stood, her face settling once again into a calm mask.

She walked to the other corner, and picked up the mask and head, and wrapping them in a fold of her damask robes she cradled them carefully in her arms.

She left the chamber, and the *Ghúl* moved forward and began eating.

The high-domed chamber now gleamed in orange light. Candles now ringed the perimeter of the chamber and the lip of the pit to join their light with the lanterns, and Gilgwyr was placing a ring of candles around the upright casket. Stjepan was still down in the hole, his hands tied behind his back, his pants mercifully back up. Leigh stood silently nearby, meditating.

Annwyn entered, bearing the masked head of Azharad in her arms. The *Ghûl* began trickling into the room behind her. She crouched by the lip of the pit and with two hands she held aloft Azharad's head before handing it down to Gilgwyr, who studied it reverently.

"Oh, my Lord, forgive me; that I spent all day within the earth, and did not recognize you," Gilgwyr said. He turned and walked down into the base of the pit, and he approached the open upright casket, and placed the masked head of Azharad back onto its body.

"And what did he promise you, old friend?" Stjepan asked, seemingly more out of curiosity than bitterness. "Azharad's voice, calling out from his prison here, what did he promise you?"

"Oh, Stjepan, my dreams have been so beautiful, I cannot begin to describe them to you. The moment Harvald said he had the map, the voices of a hundred corpses promised me that I could have anything I wanted, any treasure, any pleasure of my heart's desire, even live forever," Gilgwyr breathed triumphantly. Then he sighed. "I would have asked for your death first, just as a surprise present, but you were always the only one who could read it."

"How long were you and Harvald in the Nameless Cults?" Stjepan asked.

"We had made our first sacrifice to the Forbidden Gods even before we met you, Black-Heart," Gilgwyr said with a grin. He turned to look at Stjepan. "But we'd begun to suspect Harvald was no longer a true believer, and was looking for a way out: your influence, you heathen bastard. Your heart may be black, but you still have one. He'd started to grow a conscience again." Gilgwyr shrugged. "But alas, once you're in the Nameless Cults, there's no turning back. That's why the curse on the map killed him, you know, it knew he was a traitor."

Stjepan smiled to himself. "Good for you, Harvald," he said quietly. He turned to look up at Gilgwyr. "But you? You always were a pretty twisted fuck, Gilgwyr, even for our lot, even for Therapoli." He bared his teeth in a feral grin. "But still, did you think no one would notice? The things you knew, the games you were playing. You had grown too brazen, Gilgwyr. And too many people had started to ask who you really were, and how you knew the things you did. Do you think this is your moment of triumph?" Stjepan laughed. "You overplayed your hand, dear Gilgwyr. The Fat Prince isn't dead. You tipped your hand too far, after you let your pride get the better of you and you showed off just how much the Whisperers could tell you, and then in your anger and despair let a priestess of the cult of Ligrid walk openly at the Sleight of Hand. Too brazen by far, dear Gilgwyr. And so they set a trap to catch your beautiful priestess in the open again, and you fell for it. She's likely dead, as are all her coven, they had the best eyes amongst the Marked waiting to see where she'd lead them next, and a hundred swords waiting to purge the festering rot of your Nameless brethren from the city streets. You've nothing to return to. No more Sleight of Hand for you, old friend."

As Stjepan spoke, a look of growing fear and anger crept up Gilgwyr's face, distorting his features until he was almost unrecognizable. "You lie!" he finally hissed, and yet he thought back to his sudden odd dreams and unexplained fears during their journey and in his heart he knew that Stjepan was telling the truth. *"You lie!"* he screamed.

"Of course he's lying," said Leigh calmly, stirring from his meditations. "That's what Black-Heart does. He's the best liar I've ever met. He's merely trying to manipulate you into doing something stupid."

"Am I?" Stjepan asked casually.

Gilgwyr kicked Stjepan between the legs, screaming down at him in mindless rage.

Godewyn was wrapping a bandage around a gouge in his leg as Erim crawled into the campsite. He had stoked the campfires back up to a comfortable roar and had clearly been ransacking the tent she shared with Stjepan.

He turned and casually tossed a vial onto the ground in front of her.

"Have some of that. I found it in Black-Heart's bags, so it's something he brewed up, curse his heathen hide, but it'll help," he said.

Erim arrived at the vial. She took it in her hands, fumbling with the stopper for a moment, and then finally got it open and took a swig as Godewyn began to pack his meager belongings. She drank the vial down, not even stopping to ask herself what it was she was drinking. When she had drained it dry, she breathed and then looked at the small hand-written label. As she had never learned her letters, they were just squiggly lines. But she could feel a warm, restorative heat radiating from within her belly and spreading to her limbs.

Godewyn's voice floated to her. "Where's Too Tall?"

"What?" she asked, a little dizzy.

"Garrett. Garret Akins. The one we called Too Tall, where's he at?" he asked again.

"Oh, him," she said, her voice thick with sorrow. "Sorry. He didn't make it."

"Right," came Godewyn's voice, and he kept rummaging about.

She looked up at Godewyn, and she frowned suddenly.

"What . . . what are you doing?" she asked.

"What am I doing? I'm getting the Six Hells out of here, that's what I'm doing," said Godewyn.

Erim looked around the deserted camp. They were the only ones there, aside from the horses and burros. "Where's Stjepan?" she asked in alarm.

At that moment, Stjepan was still down in the bottom of the pit, kneeling in black muck and dead maggots with his back to the open upright casket, his hands tied behind his back, eyeing the many *Ghúl* that now clustered about the chamber above him. Gilgwyr was perched on the lip of the hole, whetting a long dagger, and angrily studying Stjepan. Annwyn walked around the lip of the pit, finishing lighting the circle of candles around it. The candles around the casket were all lit as well.

"So," said Stjepan. "I guess it's obvious you're not here for *Gladringer*, if it was ever even here to begin with. But even with his head returned, you won't be able to revive him . . . did you think it would be that simple? There's only one book I've ever heard of that describes *that* ritual . . ."

Leigh popped over to Stjepan and crouched in front of him. He felt within his robes for a moment absent-mindedly, as though he couldn't remember where he'd left something, before carefully pulling a fragile-looking book from within their mysterious blue-black folds like a stage magician pulling a rabbit from a hat, and reverently he held it up before Stjepan. The ancient parchment pages of the book were haphazardly bound between copper plates, with faint letters etched into the surface.

"The *Libra de Secretum Malifiri de Nymargae*. A translation of the *Khodex a'dan Quresh*, the Book of Secrets attributed to Nymarga the Devil himself. Written after he took the throne of the Empire, to prepare his devotees for the days when he would be gone," Leigh said. He laughed. "Luckily for me it's in the Éduinan alphabet. Have you ever read it?"

Stjepan looked at Leigh and the book with a peculiar light in his eye. "Oh, *that* book is most definitely forbidden, Magister," he said softly.

"Aye, that it is, dearest pupil, that it is," said Leigh in a conspiratorial tone. "I found this copy hidden deep in the University Library, a secret hidden so long that none lived that remembered to guard it, not even poor Clodarius, the fool, though he eventually guessed that something of great evil and import had been removed, and suspicion naturally fell on me. Me, of all people! As though somehow I was the only Magister with a black reputation. My revenge shall be sweet and it shall be long, for indeed the rumors were true, and the book contains within it a ritual to bring back a wizard from the dead, the first step on the path to becoming a true Worm King. And for bringing back Azharad, Sorcerer King of the Bale Mole, one of the greatest Devil-worshippers in our history, I'll be placed upon a throne of brass and fire, to watch my enemies suffer the greatest torments that I can dream of, and for that I can thank you, Stjepan, and your translation of the map that led us here."

Leigh spun away and began to mark out a magic circle.

"Now that his body is whole, three things are necessary to complete the ritual!" cried out Leigh in a magisterial voice. "First, a healthy body for him to eat, to sate his hunger!"

Leigh glanced back at Stjepan, and Stjepan started to struggle at his bonds, suddenly concerned that the open upright casket was right behind him. Gilgwyr dropped down into the pit behind Stjepan and slipped his dagger under Stjepan's chin.

"Not so fast, Stjepan old boy. Can't let our new Lord go hungry," Gilgwyr said into his ear.

"Second, a willing bride for him to fuck, to sate his lust!" Leigh cried out, and he gestured up at Annwyn as she circled the room. She looked down at Stjepan and met his sad gaze with an inscrutable look. "Fortunately she doesn't need to be a virgin," Leigh said as an aside before raising his voice again. "And finally, a stalwart spirit for him to corrupt!"

Turning to face the open casket, Leigh cried out in a thunderous voice. *"De lunda mundi illume! Open the World! Open the pathways! Open the door between the Worlds! Unlock the chains that bind this spirit, and free it to return! Unbind this spirit, that it may return to the flesh of this World!"*

A swirling wind seemed to be flitting about in the upper reaches of the chamber, causing the myriad candles and lamps to flicker.

As she circled the chamber above them, Annwyn listened to what Leigh was chanting, and slowly she added her voice to his.

"Open the World! Open the pathways! Open the door between the Worlds! Unlock the chains that bind this spirit, and free it to return! Unbind this spirit, that it may return to the flesh of this World!" they chanted together.

554

Godewyn had picked out a horse, a destrier that had belonged to Sir Helgi. It was a fine and expensive warhorse that would likely get him in a spot of trouble once he was back in civilization, as anyone who knew anything about horses would assume he had stolen it; which, he supposed, he was in fact in the middle of doing, strictly speaking. He was quickly loading the horse with supplies and weapons from the camp and the sacks of coin and treasure that he had managed to haul out of the barrow, and trying to ignore Erim as she spoke to him.

"We have to go back into the barrow . . . we have people in there. Please help me," she said. She had managed to rise to her knees, the healing effects of the vial slowly working on her.

"Help you do what? Get killed?" Godewyn asked. "No need to crawl back in there, if you're really so desperate to die then I can take care of that right now." He walked toward her, pulling a crossbow and a quarrel from the rack of weapons in the center of the camp as he passed it, swiftly yanking the bowstring taut to the nut and latching it, and slipping the quarrel into place. He stopped a few paces away and pointed the loaded crossbow at her. She was surprised that she could eye him steadily. "You and I ain't a we, and I ain't got nothing in there. Maybe you got people back there, but not me, not any more. All my people are gone from this earth, and if they're lucky they're on the Path of the Dead." He looked at her with a strange expression on his face. Like something was starting to dawn on him. She suddenly remembered that she had taken off her shirt and tied it around her waist to staunch her wounds, and that he was looking at her naked chest. He nodded. "But why the fuck do you want to go back in there anyway? You don't belong here any more than I do."

"I'm no fool," Erim said bitterly. "I know there's no place for me in this world. I've no king, no country that will claim the likes of me. All I've got is the people by my side. We rode and fought and bled together, side by side, you and me and Stjepan. Does all that mean nothing to you? Does revenge mean so little? For your dead men, your friends, your boys."

"Aye. Gilgwyr," said Godewyn, considering. "I do owe him at least one death. You know, the truth is, when you set out to rob a wizard's barrow, the greatest danger is always from the 'friends' you bring with you. Tell you what." He smoothly reversed the crossbow and handed it to her. "That little shit ever comes out for air, you shoot him for me. That mad fucker Leigh, too, if you want."

Godewyn turned around and limped back to his chosen horse and the sacks of loot it carried. He barely managed, bad leg and all, to get into the saddle.

Erim managed to haul herself up onto her feet and stood, swaying. "You coward," she spat.

"Sorry mate, I ain't that easy and life ain't that simple," he said. "If you've got something you think you gotta prove, you go right ahead. Me, I came out here cause I needed the money. I wasn't in this for nothin' else an' I never pretended to be. No, I got what I came for. See you around."

Godewyn turned the big horse and urged it to start walking. Erim stared after him as he moved through the camp, slowly working up toward a trot and starting to pass beyond the flickering light of the lamps and campfires.

"Fuck it," she said to herself.

She raised and fired the crossbow in one smooth motion.

There was a wet smacking sound and a scream as the quarrel hit home.

Leigh sat down in a meditative stance on the casket lid, facing Stjepan and Gilgwyr and the open casket behind them, the *Libra de Secretum Malifiri de Nymargae* open in his lap. As Annwyn kept repeating the base formula of the ritual, Leigh opened the book and began to vary his words on top of hers.

"*Azharad! King of the Bale Mole!*" Leigh cried out. "*I summon you! Azharad! King of the Uthed Wold, Master of the Vale of Barrows! I summon you!*

Azharad! Master of the Nameless Cults! I summon you! I summon you from your prison! I release you back into the World! The sacrifices are prepared for you, the way made safe!"

Stjepan looked down, his eyes widening, as the dead maggots piled in the black muck at the bottom of the pit began to wriggle and move, as though they were suddenly coming back to life. He struggled, repulsed and nauseated by the sight and sensation around his knees, but Gilgwyr laughed and tightened his grip and pressed the dagger against Stjepan's chin and neck with enough force to draw blood. The maggots began to wriggle through the mud, back toward the casket, initially to Stjepan's relief, but then to his greater alarm, as he twisted to look back over his shoulder. The maggots were wriggling up under Azharad's muck-covered robes, filling the hollowed out flesh of his body. Stjepan looked at the corpse's hands, pressed together as if in prayer, and watched in horror as the thin, dried, desiccated skin began to swell, the maggots filling out the flesh beneath, looking for all the world like a deflated sack slowly filling with air or water. The skin had become a thin membrane, almost like the thinnest of parchment paper, and he could clearly see the maggots wriggling and writhing and pressing against the surface.

As Annwyn and Leigh chanted, the body of Azharad twitched, though Stjepan could not tell if it was merely the echoing ripple of the multitude of maggots beneath the body's skin, or because of the return of some semblance of life. Gilgwyr started to stand up behind Stjepan, his dagger now at Stjepan's ear.

"You know, I'm not sure which I'm going to enjoy more, watching our Lord eat you, or watching him stuff his decaying flesh into that scrumptious bit of snatch," Gilgwyr said with a leer. "Today is a beautiful day, a great d—"

Suddenly the body of Azharad lurched forward, his maggot-infested arms embracing Gilgwyr, and the bottom half of his mask opened up to reveal a mangled mouth of sharpened teeth. The body of Azharad clamped its teeth down on the crook of Gilgwyr's neck and took a deep, ravenous bite as Gilgwyr screamed in pain and surprise.

And a dark spirit took shape and form near the peak of the corbelled ceiling of the chamber.

A whispering wind swirled through the passages and chambers of the other parts of the barrow. The wind brought a message for all that were left to hear: Our Lord and King has returned. Rejoice! *A dim light began to glow in the eye-sockets of the desiccated warriors standing silent guard in the alcoves of the shrine to Ishraha, the Rebel Angel, the Bright King. First a finger moved; then a neck began to turn. Dust fell from their armored limbs as they stirred, called to duty once more.*

Stjepan grimaced and ducked away, crawling and rolling through muck and dirt as the body of Azharad chewed and rent Gilgwyr's face and neck, eating his flesh and his features and drinking his blood. The repulsive, wretched thing dropped Gilgwyr's twitching body lifeless to the ground, and leaned its head back, reveling in the taste of human flesh after so long.

Leigh stood to one side of the casket lid, holding the ancient book open, and faced the swaying body of the Sorcerer King. "Azharad!" he cried. "Take the body of Annwyn, daughter of Leonas of Araswell, as your first bride upon your return! Indulge your lust! Taste the world again!" Above them, some of the *Ghúl* lowered themselves to their hands and knees and began linking themselves together, interlocking their legs and arms as though weaving themselves into a bed of backs. Annwyn slowly lowered herself back onto them, writhing now with a look of rapture as she whispered the words of the ritual.

The body of Azharad walked up out of the pit, moving slowly, as though unused to what passed for flesh and muscle upon its bones. The wind moved about the room with a low roar now, as though a hundred voices were whispering loudly all at once. The dark, unfathomable spirit shape began to lower itself down from the recesses of the corbelled ceiling, wispy smoke drifting with purpose through the air toward the body in motion.

Annwyn opened her legs wide, revealing her glistening slit, and her hands reached up to greet the body of Azharad as it reached the lip of the pit. The moving corpse opened its dark robes, revealing the peculiar quality of its flesh, the stretched-thin skin gray and white over the mass of maggots that now gave it bulk and form.

Annwyn's eyes fluttered as her lustful gaze took in the creature before her and then drifted down to what it offered her as it moved between her open legs. Its cock was erect and monstrous, twitching eagerly with both lust and the wriggling of the maggots that filled it to bursting. She smiled and looked up with hooded eyes at the creature's mask as it hovered above her. The body of Azharad reached out with its hands and stroked along her torso with sharp nails, settled itself at the juncture of her thighs and hips, lined up its cock, and thrust itself within her.

Her gasp interrupted her chanting, but then she resumed, her voice husky with unnatural lust and passion. The map was moving frenetically on her skin, like a hornet's nest stirred by a stick. She was now staring up past the brazen, horned mask to the dark spirit shape that hovered in the air above them. *"I open myself to you, Azharad, as the World opens itself to you! I am open to you, O King! I am the path, the door between the Worlds! Azharad! King of the Bale Mole! I am open to you! Azharad! King of the Uthed Wold, Master of the Vale of Barrows! I am open to you! Return to the World! Azharad! Master of the Nameless Cults! I am open to you! Return to the World!"*

Leigh was watching the coupling above him with rapt attention. The wind in the chamber was swirling in circles under the coffered dome above them. Behind him, Stjepan lay on his side, momentarily forgotten. He looked around and spotted Gilgwyr's dagger lying in the muck nearby, and as silently as he could manage he shifted around so that the hands tied behind his back could grasp the sharp blade. He rolled back on the dirt so that the dagger was out of sight behind and beneath him, and he started to work its sharp edges on the rope holding his hands.

As if he sensed something behind him deserved his attention, Leigh turned slowly and looked over his shoulder at Stjepan.

"Everyone thought you were insane long before you were exiled from the University," Stjepan said, shaking his head up at his former Magister. "How could you have gone so terribly wrong, Magister?"

Leigh walked over and crouched in front of Stjepan, peering into his face. Stjepan stopped moving the dagger, holding still.

"Insane? *Insane?*" Leigh laughed. "Since when has the pursuit of power and wealth been the province of the insane? Unless you think every merchant and noble, every priest and king, to be insane like me!"

Above them, Annwyn writhed passionately as the body of Azharad moved upon and in her, at first slowly and awkwardly, then with increasing surety as control over its functions and limbs returned. The dark spirit shape enveloped both of them, its wispy, smoky tendrils running over the flesh of both its body and hers, as though seeking to direct its body's actions and raise the flames of lust that wracked her skin and the riotous images of the map displayed upon her. Soon Annwyn was having difficulty repeating her chants, as every thrust of the hideous corpse-thing was now producing a sharp cry of passion.

"Most of them will not bring ruin to the world in their greed!" said Stjepan.

"They have already ruined it, with their petty pursuits and mindless sorrows!" cried Leigh, standing and towering over Stjepan. "Gone are the days of magic, when men and heroes of true power walked the world!"

"And is that how you see yourself?" asked Stjepan.

"Do you really think you have the right to judge me? You were a great student at the University, at least when you could put your mind to it, but you're just a hedge-witch, like your dead mother; no match for the likes of a true magician like me! You know not the game here, nor the stakes!" ranted Leigh as he backed into the center of the pit and began turning in circles, his arms wide. "We change the fate of the World today!"

Annwyn's eyes rolled back into her head, eyelids fluttering. The bed of *Ghûl* backs roiled beneath the sweating skin of her back and ass as the body of Azharad pressed down and into her, making her feel like she was caught in a great vise of flesh that pistoned its hardest part deep within her. Annwyn was no longer chanting, instead she was moaning and gasping and babbling like a mad woman, caught up in the frenzied motions of her lustful coupling with the body of Azharad, the roar of voices in the air, the ministrations of the dark spirit shape, the furies of the map within her body and upon her skin, and the thrusting of the unnatural cock within her—all of which was driving toward a climax.

"I am the servant of a Nameless Cult!" roared Leigh, triumphant and deranged. "Nymarga, the Devil, the Magician King, knows well my worth! I will usher Azharad back into the World, and after that we will raise the Worm Kings again, and they will rule the broken Earth from Thrones of Brass and Fire! I will be his Vizier, and Annwyn his first Bride, his first Queen . . ."

The dark spirit shape hovering in the air about the body of Azharad finally began to move onto the body, seep inside it, to try and *inhabit* it, to reach down through it and touch her insides through its plunging member. And at that Annwyn's eyes flew open. The appearance of rapture on her face changed in an instant. Her face hardened, became stern and purposeful. And she cried out in a different voice now. *"Sumes paradeska malathratta ir dures, dume lira malathratta! Malathratta ir dures! Malathratta ill dures!"*

Leigh stopped and stared down at Stjepan for a moment in confusion, then turned and looked up at Annwyn and the body of Azharad in outright alarm.

"Somehow I think Annwyn has other plans," said Stjepan with a grim grin playing on his face as the dagger started moving against his bindings again.

Above them, the spirit and body of Azharad realized something was wrong and tried to withdraw, but Annwyn wrapped her leg and arms tightly around the body and would not let it go. Wisps and tendrils of dark matter seemed to waver and lash out around the body of Azharad as his spirit, not yet fully connected to his body, was being slowly pulled away and down into Annwyn. But the dark shape seemed to be fighting back against Annwyn's spell, struggling to remain tethered to its flesh, clinging to its body like a man might cling to a rock to avoid the pull of the whirlpool, but the spirit was weak after centuries imprisoned, and it was losing the fight. Her blue eyes flashed as she cried out: *"Malathratta ir dures! Malathratta ill dures! I open myself to you, Azharad, as the World opens itself to you! I am the gate! I am the path, O King! And I close the gate, and I bind you! Azharad! King of the Bale Mole! I bind you! Azharad! King of the Uthed Wold, Master of the Vale of Barrows! I bind you! Azharad! Master of the Nameless Cults! I shut the door, and I bind you!"*

Leigh's eyes flew open as he realized what was happening. "No . . . no . . . no, no, no, my Lord!" he stammered as he tossed the ancient book aside and started to move up the slope of the pit.

Stjepan finally undid his bonds. He raised the dagger and in a flash hurled it straight up into the back of Azharad's head, then launched himself at Leigh, the rope used to tie his hands now held as a garrote. They went down in a heap against the side of the pit, the rope around Leigh's neck.

The dagger into his skull severed the last ties between Azharad's body and his spirit, and the dark spirit shape was now fully unmoored. Annwyn's body arched back and her arms and legs spread wide, opening herself to the winds in the chamber, and the foul spirit was being drawn out of the air and out of its own body and instead into hers. Her chant was lost in the roar of the wind and a great cry of terror and despair that seemed to rend the very air of the chamber.

With a face of grim determination, Stjepan slowly strangled Leigh with his makeshift garrote, his knee planted firmly in the middle of Leigh's back. The Magister clawed against the dirt, his eyes bulging. *This cannot be how it ends*, he thought desperately. *I was so close. All my plans. So many people to ruin. It's not fair. It's not fair.* And a voice, scratching at his left ear, barely audible beneath the roar of his heart and his lungs, answered back: *Of course it isn't fair. But it's not the end.*

With a final great cry, Annwyn consumed the spirit of Azharad. The brazen, horned mask shattered, and the body of Azharad fell away from hers, limp and useless, dead once more, as dead maggots poured out from the bag of its skin and bones onto the ground. The *Ghûl* slowly lowered Annwyn's shuddering body to the earth and gently clustered around her.

Leigh, red-faced, his mouth working soundlessly, started to convulse as his heart seized up, and then his bowels released in his death spasms.

When he was sure the Magister was dead, Stjepan let go of the rope around Leigh's neck and spun about, snatching up a discarded pickaxe from the earth, and turned and took a step as if about to run up the side of the pit, looked up, and froze.

The room was quiet and still.

The lip of the pit near the entrance was crowded with the revived corpses of the barrow's guardian warriors, armed and armored in their archaic finery and bearing large oval shields, pointing the rusted points of their spears and swords down at him. They formed an arc across part of the lip, and surrounded a group of the *Ghûl* that seemed to be clustered behind them. Stjepan could barely see Annwyn, he got the barest glimpse of her pale ivory body beneath the huddle of the cadaverous creatures. A part of him was afraid they were consuming her; a part of him was afraid they weren't.

"Annwyn! Annwyn? Can you hear me?" he shouted, almost laughing. "A witch! A sorceress! You're a witch . . . the Divine King's priests were *right* . . . I don't understand, but how?"

Annwyn spoke weakly from behind the arc of barrow warriors and *Ghûl*, her voice floating down to him as if from far away. "I asked you to look at me. But you didn't. No one did . . . no one knew my measure, no one thought me capable of anything but sorrow. Poor despondent Annwyn, cloistered away for so long that I scarce remembered I was alive, and yet all that time, I read, I read the books that I paid the old women to bring me, books with silly, pretty covers, and I learned and I practiced the arts of magic hidden within them."

"Annwyn, what have you done?" Stjepan asked. "What have you done with the spirit of Azharad?"

Her voice gained in strength and surety. "When Harvald cast his Sending, he thought I would be an easy vessel to compel . . . but he did not know what I was capable of. I fought his spell, and beheld the map and its purpose, to allow the Nameless Cults to one day return Azharad to this world! And so I dreamed this charade, a subterfuge of skin and body, to foil their plans; to escape the prison my father and my brothers had made for me at last; to remake my place in the World!"

"What have you done? Show yourself, Annwyn!" Stjepan cried out.

The *Ghûl* and the barrow warriors parted, and Annwyn appeared behind them, naked but for the glint of gold and gems at her wrists and ankles and neck, poised and imperious, looking down at Stjepan in the pit. Her skin was smooth and unblemished, without a trace of the map upon her, an image of perfection. She held out her arms to her sides, and the *Ghûl* began to slip her dark damask robes back upon her body. She tucked her arms into its sleeves, and allowed the robe to slip down off her bare shoulders. She did not bother to close it about her, leaving her breasts and belly and a finely turned leg exposed to the flickering lights of candle and lamp.

"Do you think me some fresh evil, with all the powers and knowledge of a wizard's bound spirit at my command?" she asked, with a voice rich with laughter and spite. "That is the self-serving thinking of the Sun Court that burned your mother at the stake: to divide always the World in two, a single bright light and a single malignant dark. You are too long from the woods of your birth, Athairi, that you forget the lessons of the Queen of Heaven and of Night! The World is not lit by a single bright light, but by a hundred hundred stars, both bright and dim, and the dark is not a single hue, but a hundred hundred shades of gray and black and blue. And between them, the Known World is a riot of color."

Stjepan looked up at her, and he breathed heavily, still trying to catch his breath. "I wish I could . . ." he started to say. "I truly wish I could . . . But I can't let you leave, not with Azharad's magics at your command . . ."

Annwyn studied him for a moment. "But then I was never to leave here alive, was I, Black-Heart?" she asked quietly.

Stjepan looked down at the earth, and gave a wry chuckle, and looked up at her with a small smile.

"I am no threat," she said softly. "I despise the world we came from, the petty doings of the High King's Court, but that does not mean I wish to see the World ended, for theirs is but a small and miserly part of it. I wanted to remake my place in the World, and I have done so: *my* world is different, *my* world has changed. I have become myself. No, you need not worry, for my role in the wars and chaos to come will be but a small one . . ." She studied him again for a moment, as if seeing something about him for the first time. "But if you have the courage, bear this message back to your masters: I will find my own way in the world, and they will disturb me at their peril."

Stjepan closed his eyes, and then he nodded. As Annwyn turned to leave the chamber, one of the *Ghúl* offered her the pieces of the horned mask of Azharad. The top part of it had survived in more or less one piece, the horns spiraling up out of the forehead plate, and she lifted it up out of the *Ghúl's* hands and contemplated it.

"Annwyn!" he cried, his eyes flying open.

She looked back down at him.

"How can I know you're really you?" he asked.

She smiled then, a secret kind of smile, and it seemed to him for a moment that she looked down at him with genuine affection. A look of affection that turned to sadness, to longing, to pity.

"You can't," she said.

She turned to the barrow warriors and gave voice to a command. "Ne tuattha tem." And then Annwyn turned and walked out of the high-domed chamber with barrow warriors for escorts and a trailing pack of the *Ghúl*.

"Annwyn! Annwyn!" Stjepan shouted desperately. He hefted the pickaxe in his hands.

A line of barrow warriors remained, looking down at him from behind their helms and shield and pointed spears and swords, silent and unmoving.

Annwyn and her grisly entourage moved through the barrow that had been built for her. She walked at a stately pace, holding her chin high with royal hauteur, bearing a horned half-mask tucked in the crook of her left arm, trailing a damask robe behind her as her train. The barrow warriors walked before and behind her, her royal guard, and the *Ghúl* trailed behind them. The corpses of her courtiers, awakened now to new purpose, emerged from dark chambers and passages as she walked past them, bearing with them the treasures and offerings of the barrow and joining in behind her, forming the beginnings of her new court.

Stjepan steeled himself, then charged up the side of the pit, but one of the waiting barrow warriors stepped forward with surprising speed and swung its shield up and into his face, catching him square in the jaw. He went flying into the air, blood arcing in a high arc from his mouth, and he fell back into the pit below him. He landed heavily in the muck in front of the open casket.

Annwyn and her growing entourage arrived in the chamber of the three biers, and there she found Azharad's brides awaiting her as her new handmaidens. They bowed to her, and fell in behind her amongst her courtiers. They all turned and entered into the chamber with the well, and some of the *Ghúl* and some of the barrow warriors immediately went ahead and began to descend into the dark hole.

The body of the young squire and the two bodies suspended over the hole had been made into a feast, and reduced to carcasses of bone and gristle and scraps of flesh. Ignoring the body of Too Tall, Annwyn looked up with sorrow at what had once been Malia Morwin. She reached out and gently stroked what was left of the ruined, unrecognizable face and hair of her handmaiden. Her expression was cryptic and inscrutable.

Then she looked down at the hole into the earth, a secret smile playing on her beautiful face.

"There's always another way out," she said quietly to herself.

Some of the *Ghûl* linked their bodies together to form a writhing throne for her to sit on. She took an offered hand and gracefully stepped up to sit upon the throne of bodies, leaning back in regal comfort. And then the entire mass of *Ghûl* lifted her up, and then slowly climbed down into the hole, with her seated upon them and gazing around to look at the chamber as though in final farewell.

The barrow warriors begin clambering down after her.

Stjepan struggled to remain conscious, staring up at the empty casket, looming like a dark and empty door into nowhere. And then mercifully the darkness took him.

CHAPTER THIRTY-ONE
THE LAST DAY

E rim came hobbling up the hillside to the barrow entrance beneath the starlit skies. Dirt and dried blood was smeared into her clothing, her skin. She had poultices bandaged upon her left thigh, and across her belly and back, and had pulled on a linen arming doublet that had belonged to one of the squires. She had her cut-and-thrust rapier and point daggers strapped to her waist, a loaded crossbow in her hands, a quiver of quarrels slung over her shoulder. Though she could walk, she was already breathing heavily from the strain. She stood at the top of the steps, undecided, uncertain.

"Fuck," she said.

The entrance of the barrow yawned black before her.

Beneath the earth everything was as black as pitch. Until the blackness was finally illuminated by the sparks from a white-blue torch that bloomed into full flame, revealing the half-eaten face of Gilgwyr staring up at nothing out of the muck.

Stjepan held up the torch, looking around groggily. He was bleeding from his mouth, and he winced as he gingerly tested his jaw and his skull. He rummaged around in the bags and equipment laying strewn about the dug pit, and found a water flask. He poured some water over his head, matting his hair, and then drank a huge swig of it, and then drank again, and again, eventually draining it dry. He looked around, studying the bodies in the pit with him. He spotted the ancient book that Leigh had revealed, and he tossed the empty flask aside as he walked over to it and picked it up. He placed it carefully beside his satchel.

He screwed the torch into the earth in the side of the pit so that it was upright and burning, and he grabbed up a shovel. He first went to Leigh's body, and used the shovel to push through the Magister's robes and clothes. But whatever he was looking for wasn't there, and he grunted. He turned toward the upright and empty casket.

He stared at it a moment, running over the images in his mind, the letters and symbols moving over Annwyn's skin while she had writhed above him in coitus, translating in his head the words he had seen.

"Dig . . . *and dig again*," he said to himself.

With great effort he pushed against the upright iron casket, knocking it over onto its back. And then he started digging into the ground on the spot where it once stood.

Stjepan walked out of the barrow into the light of the morning of the 5th of Ascensium. He had the ancient copper-bound book of Leigh clutched in his left hand, his satchels and his brace of sword and dagger slung over his shoulder, and an old, scabbarded sword covered in dirt in his right.

"Don't move," came a voice.

He stopped in mid-stride and froze.

"Turn around," came the voice. "Slowly."

He turned slowly and looked up. Erim sat perched on the hill slope right above the entrance of the barrow, pointing a loaded crossbow down at him.

"Where's Gilgwyr?" she asked.

"He's dead," Stjepan said. "He got . . . eaten."

"How about Leigh?" she asked.

"Him, I killed," Stjepan said.

Erim studied him for a moment. "Is there anyone else coming out?" she asked.

Stjepan thought about it for a moment, and then glanced down to look deep into the entrance of the barrow. He looked back up at her. "No. I think I'm it."

She looked at the dirt-covered sword and scabbard that he carried in his hand. "Is that the sword?" she asked.

"*Gladringer*. The sword of the High Kings, forged by the magician-smith Gobelin, of the Bodmall clan," he said quietly. He looked down at it, and then back at her. "Here, catch."

He softly tossed the sword high into the air to her, and the pommel caught the glint of the sun as it arced through the air. She caught the sword by the scabbarded blade in her left hand, still pointing the crossbow at him with her right.

She looked at Stjepan with a frown on her face, and then at the sword, and then back at him. "What . . . you're just giving it to me?" she asked.

Stjepan smiled. "Always distracted by the bright bauble. Things are never what they seem. Yes, it's yours, if you want it. It should be in the hands of a true swordmaster. And I got what I came for." He looked down at the book in his left hand.

"What, that book?" she asked, incredulous.

"The missing copy of the *Libra de Secretum Malifiri de Nymargae*, taken from the Library at the University," he said reverently. "It's one of the rarest books in the Known World. The Magisters always suspected that Leigh had stolen it after they discovered it was missing, but a true enchanter, as Leigh was, has any number of tricks to hide something away, and it was hard to flush it into the open."

Erim stared at him, her mouth hanging open. "All this for a fucking book? This is *Gladringer*, the lost sword of the High Kings!" she said. She deftly changed her hold on the sword to take it by the grip and she flicked her left wrist with a *snap* and the scabbard flew off the sword to land in the grass, revealing the length of the sword's blade to the morning light. It was a twin to the cursed and false blade that they'd first found: broad, double-edged watered steel that tapered to a sharp point, with curved quillons and a large round wheel pommel inlaid with swirling, intertwined designs in silver and gold. But she could feel that the leather on the grip of the hilt

571

had decayed over time, sealed beneath the cold earth, and the blade looked like it needed to be polished, and for a moment doubt entered into her.

"Aye. One of the greatest swords in history," said Stjepan, eyeing it with a proud smile. "That sword killed Githwaine, the Last Worm King. It pierced through his glamours, and his wards, and his armor, and into his dark, black heart, and ended him. Upon its blade are secretly etched the Riven Runes of *weapons*, and *motion*, and *death*, and *victory*, and *strength*. If you could see them, the enchantments on that blade would blind you with their glory and their power. And if you want, I'm sure that sword will lead you to whatever fate you think you seek."

Then he shrugged. "But a single enchanted weapon, even a great one, can't change the fate of the state, of the nation, of the world. We survived for centuries without it. The Thrones of the Middle Kingdoms are stolen and missing, the lines of the Dragon King scions of Islik are ended, and yet here we are. We endure. The Kingdoms endure. For the Middle Kingdoms are not threatened or saved by weapons, but by words, ideas, temptations, desires, magics; the words that inspire people to turn from one path to another, the words that fill them with faith, or take it away from them, that threaten their sense of who and what they are." He held up the copper-bound book. "Such as are contained in this book. A book written by the Devil Incarnate."

"Well, aren't you the philosopher," she snorted, and then laughed, her eyes narrowing. "A lot of maps in that book, eh?"

Stjepan laughed. "Yeah. A lot of maps," he said with a small smile.

She stared at him for a long moment.

"How do I know it's really you?" she asked wistfully.

"No glamours here, Erim," he said, shaking his head.

She picked herself up, and walked slowly down the hill around the entrance to the barrow, keeping the crossbow trained on him. She stopped a few yards away.

"How do I know it's you?" she asked again.

Stjepan opened his mouth, paused, then shrugged. "You don't."

Erim took a deep breath.

She walked toward him slowly, crossbow pointed at his chest.

She lowered it, and they embraced gingerly, each wincing from their wounds.

The late afternoon sun was starting its descent. The carriage and the two wagons had been pushed and partially disassembled and set in the middle of the campsite as the base for a great bonfire, and piled with the tents and just about anything that would burn and with the bodies of the dead: what was left of Malia Morwin, the squire Wilhem Price, Caider Ross, Garrett "Too Tall" Akins, "Handsome" Pallas Quinn, Giordus Roame, big Cole Thimber, Lord Arduin Orwain, Sir Lars Urwed, Sir Colin Urwed, Sir Helgi Vogelwain, Sir Holgar Torgisbain, Sir Theodras Clowain, Sir Theodore Lis Cawain, the squire Brayden Vogelwain, Leigh, and Gilgwyr, either their whole bodies wrapped in cloth, or bags of body parts where the *Ghúl* had not left enough in one piece.

Stjepan splashed lamp oil over the improvised pyre.

Erim held some horses ready for herself. She had Cúlain-mer and Ironbound and a spare packhorse; each was loaded with gear and grave goods packed into saddlebags and satchels. She wore the high-necked gorget and partial pauldrons from Arduin's garniture over a quilted arming doublet, and his cuisses and knee poleyns were strapped to her legs above her black boots. The rest of his armor had been packed onto the spare packhorse. Her sword brace now bore a different sword next to her daggers rather than her familiar cut-and-thrust rapier.

Cúlain-mal waited patiently for Stjepan, along with a small herd of horses and mules, over thirty of them: knight's destriers, spare riding mounts, draft horses, burros, all standing about in the tall grasses and weeds and occasionally grazing on them.

Stjepan stood back from the improvised pyre and tossed the bottle of lamp oil aside. He lit it. The fire started to crackle and pop, smoke slowly rising as the flames started to take hold of the wood.

"So who do you really work for? The Magisters at the University? The High Court? The High King himself?" asked Erim.

"Do you really want to know?" Stjepan asked her as he looked at the flames.

Erim studied his profile for a moment, then shook her head.

"What are you going to tell them when you get back?" she asked finally. "Whoever they are."

"Don't you mean when *we* get back?" he asked, turning to look at her.

"No. Time to start over again, I think, someplace different with new faces and new names. Someplace where this sword can be of service," she said, conscious of a peculiar weight on her hip. She paused. "Some place where *I* can be of service. Do you mind being sole survivor?"

"Nah," Stjepan said with a shrug. "Makes for a better story." He eyed her for a moment. "Stick with me to Aberdelan, at least, will you? If the Lamb is there and we decide to go into the Devil's Tower, we could use you and that sword."

"Yeah, why not," she said.

Stjepan smiled.

He turned back to the rising heat of the pyre and started to pray.

> *Dawn Maiden. Awaken!*
> *Bright Star. Awaken!*
> *Sun's Herald. Awaken!*
> *And announce . . .*

He stopped, mouth open, and stared up past the rising smoke, up the hill toward the barrow.

Ravens and vultures by the hundreds were taking wing and lifting up into the sky from the top of the hill above them. The great, dark swarm flew about the top of the hill in an expanding circle, until eventually they flew directly overhead and then off to the north and a line of distant mountains.

Stjepan watched them go until he couldn't see them anymore, and he surveyed the horizon with his sharp gaze for several long moments. He listened to the wind, to the faint jangle of unseen bells, to whispers and wails and the distant sound of brazen horns and howling wolves coming closer and closer. He sniffed the air, smelt dry earth and old stone, grass and rotting wood, acrid smoke and burning flesh, bile and blood, sun-burnt leather and rusted iron, horse sweat and horse shit and polished steel and the strong, clean scent of someone he loved and trusted.

His sharp, hard gaze returned to stare at the rising heat and the flames flickering up before him.

"Fuck it. You know the way," he said finally.

And then he turned and walked away from the burning pyre.

WOAT'S İNN

G elber Woat stood behind the long wooden bar at Woat's Roadside Inn and slid a flagon under the valve tapping one of the long line of casks arrayed on the back mantle. The old man poured a heavy amber ale into the flagon, turned and set it down on the bar before looking up to eye his customer.

"And you're the only survivor," he said with a raised eyebrow.

The customer on the other side of the bar lifted the flagon in a toast to himself and slowly drained it dry. He licked his lips and wiped them clean with the back of his sleeve. He wore a fine, dark brown doublet with a touch of red in it, and had bought new breeches and leather boots as well along the way, but despite the expensive quality of his new clothes there was nonetheless a familiar, ragged quality to his appearance. His damp, unkempt hair, the rough stubble on his chin and mouth, and the dirt under his fingernails gave him away. "Admit it, you're glad to see me," Godewyn said with a grin, setting the empty flagon back onto the bar.

Behind him at a nearby table sat the beginnings of his new crew: a young Danian man, Moris Quinn, not nearly as scarred nor as handsome as his older and now deceased brother Pallas, and a Mael lad, a deserter from the ranks of the Watchtowers named Dyver Bragoss. They surveyed the nearly empty great hall of the Inn with quick eyes that took in every detail, pretending a jaded look as they reveled in their new adventure. Sunshine trickled in through the shuttered windows and the holes in the patched walls. A few passed-out patrons were scattered about, and a few tired dancers either wandered aimlessly or clustered at their own table on the far side of the room.

Gelber Woat grinned slyly as he refilled the flagon, and indicated a bag on the bar in front of Godewyn, overflowing with barrow treasures. "Well.

I'm glad to see all that, at least," he said. He set the ale-filled flagon back on the bar.

"Look, I'll cut you a good deal on these pieces, it's the least I can do," said Godewyn. "I was sorry about your crew, but we never had a chance to weigh in on it. I mean, they never even got to us. Prince Fionne's men, was it?"

"Aye, and now their corpses help feed the flowers," said the Woat Elder quietly, his hands idly sorting through gold jewelry and small figurines and gem-encrusted cups. "Such is the way it's always been, that we are merely hunting sport for land lords and princes. Quick enough to come in and drink our ale and fuck our women when the mood strikes them, and just as quick to cut our throats because we got the wrong blood."

"Well, perhaps I can go a ways toward changing that," Godewyn said with a laugh. "Oh, I have such plans, you'll see! I'm a changed man, I am, I seen things no man should ever see, looked upon the body of Azharad in the dark beneath the earth, dueled a champion of the Tourneys over a sword with a curse on it, escaped corpse-eaters, the unquiet dead, and an arrow in the back to walk out of the Bale Mole, the last man standing! You don't go through all that and not be a changed man!" He raised the flagon in the air. "To Stjepan Black-Heart!" He took a huge gulp of ale and laughed. "To think it's all thanks to that dumb heathen bastard."

Gelber Woat's eyes narrowed a bit. "Shouldn't speak ill of the dead," he said.

Godewyn looked up, catching something in his tone. "Well, I don't know he's dead," he said defensively. He shrugged. "Sure, I left him tied up in a dead wizard's barrow with some lunatic magician and an army of walking corpses running around in it, but he could be alive." He turned and indicated the front door to the Inn with a broad, regal sweep of his arm. "He could walk through that door at any moment."

"Yeah, right," said Gelber Woat.

They started to laugh together, harder and harder, as Godewyn threw back his drink.

But the laughter didn't quite reach Gelber Woat's eyes.

THERAPOLİ MAGNİ

On the morning of the 18th day of Ascensium, the old man using the name Sequintus Eridaine rose in his small rented chambers on Murky Street in the eastern end of the Public Quarter, practically in the shadows of the great hill upon which the High King's Hall was raised. He used the chamber pot and unceremoniously dumped it out the window onto the street below, to a shout and curse from an unfortunate passer-by. The building he had found was too old to have the more modern attempts at plumbing installed within it that could be found in some parts of the city, and not old enough to have the pipes and waterworks common to cities built during the Great Palace period of Düréan expansion. But *beggars can't be choosers*, he thought to himself. And, he supposed, he should probably count himself lucky to be alive and able to rent rooms at all. Many of those who had been privy to the darker parts of Gilgwyr's affairs had met with much more permanent ends than the state of limbo in which he found himself.

After eating a light breakfast of fruits and stale, days-old pastries, he had dressed and prepared himself for his interview. He checked briefly on the condition of the various brewings and concoctions ongoing in his small workshop and allowed himself to leave only when he was satisfied that all was proceeding according to direction.

Given his age, Sequintus could at best manage a slow mosey through the city. The faces he passed on the street bore about them the downtrodden look shared by the poor and the desperate everywhere, and they took on an even more subdued and dour undertone as he slowly turned into the Plaza of Ergist. The six handmaidens of the notorious witch Annwyn Orwain had been burned at the stake only several days before in the center of the square. Justice had been swift; the Grand Duke, his personal household

knights, and a company of Templar knights and priests of the Inquisition
had returned to Therapoli from Araswell with the women in custody on the
4th of Ascensium, and in under two weeks they had been tortured, broken,
tried, convicted, sentenced to death, and executed. Their burnt cadavers,
still lashed to blackened stakes, were to be left on display for a month by
edict of the Inquisition as a warning and a reminder to the public at large
of the ever-present danger of the enemies of the Divine King. The women
had confessed to aiding and abetting the witch in her necromantic rituals,
placing curses upon the High King and his Court, casting spells to divine
the future, and engaging in sordid sexual practices with Lady Annwyn and
her brother Arduin in their worship of the Devil. They had confessed that
the beauty for which the Lady Annwyn had been famous had been an illusion, fabricated by the foulest black magic, and that the Lady was in reality
hideous and deformed.

Thankfully for all concerned, the witch's influence had not extended
beyond her handmaidens and her unfortunate and murderous brother, and
the Inquisition had proclaimed the Baron of Araswell and the rest of his
family and household above reproach, victims of the terrible monster that
had hidden itself in their midst. But Baron Leonas and his remaining sons
and knights remained in self-imposed exile at their country estates and had
not yet returned to the Court; their house in the High Quarter of Therapoli
remained a burnt shell. The arrest warrant for Lord Arduin for murder
remained standing, as did that for Lady Annwyn Orwain for witchcraft,
though as both were thought to have absconded into the Manon Mole
where they were expected to spend the rest of their days in hiding, it
was not considered likely that anyone would claim the rewards for their
capture and confinement anytime in the immediate future, until perhaps
the Grand Duke's highly anticipated campaign against the Rebel Earl that
coming summer.

And so the High King's Court had initially considered the matter
closed and sufficiently resolved.

On the streets of the city, however, a great deal of anger still festered,
and tensions between the city's ruling classes and its teeming urban masses

had slowly risen in the weeks since the death of Rodrick Urgoar and what had now come to be called—in the popular ballads that circulated the city's taverns—*Lord Arduin's Midnight Ride*. Almost five thousand people had turned out to watch the burnings of Lady Annwyn's confederates, and while many of them were the Divine King's faithful there to cheer the Inquisition on, a sizeable portion of the assembled crowds had watched in silent disapproval. The enthusiasm of some of the faithful had even dampened a bit when the women were brought out and unveiled, as two of them appeared to have been rendered insensible by the tortures and beatings inflicted upon them; three of the others had wept and cried in a most piteous manner, which seemed to confuse some in the crowd even as it excited others to louder cheers; and one went to her death with a serene calm that many remarked on as being uncanny. A witch hadn't actually been publicly burned in the city for over a hundred years, so the reality of it might have caught some of the assembled masses by surprise, despite their general familiarity with public executions and torture.

As he passed through the plaza that morning, Sequintus noticed that someone had left fresh flowers by the pyres of each woman overnight, in clear violation of the law and as yet unnoticed and untouched by the City Watch. Unrest had swept the Middle Kingdoms repeatedly in the last few years, even after the Inquisition had been brought to heel back in 1462 and its previous spate of witch burnings ended. The High King's imposition of special taxes in 1464, the poor harvest of 1467 leading to a three-fold rise in the price of bread, an increase in the poll tax in 1469; all had led to riots, unrest, and minor rebellions in one corner of the Kingdoms or another. And in the few days since the executions, the city had seemed be walking a razor's edge. In his slow walks across the city Sequintus had himself witnessed several men beating the priest Garin Urgoar, a distant cousin to the deceased Rodrick, almost to death; seen an irate mob pelting a squadron of Templar knights with eggs and stones, until the knights responded by killing several of their attackers; and stumbled across the City Watch investigating the murder of Colin Rowain, a wealthy merchant well-known for his piety and support of the Urgoar family, who was found in an alley with the words "Arduin's Revenge" scrawled on the wall nearby, leaving the constables bewildered and hard-pressed.

Once he was within the throngs on the Grand Promenade his pace slowed even more, and he found he was bumped, jostled, and cursed virtually the whole way down to the Forum. It seemed to him that the tension on the streets was approaching the level right before the bread riots of '67. And it was still just spring.

It's going to be a long, hot summer, he thought.

Once inside the Forum the general mood improved a bit, but even there it was obvious that there were fewer buyers about than would have been considered normal for a sunny Septtum morning. He slowly worked his way to one of the quiet corner meeting houses that had sprung up throughout the city in recent years offering addictive spiced drinks from Sabuta. And at the rear of the meetinghouse, past Danian and Amoran toughs who clearly did not care for the way he looked (or perhaps smelled), he found his appointment. Sequintus gave a short half-bow and then slowly eased himself into the seat across from Guizo the Fat as sparrows fluttered from perch to perch above them on the high walls.

"Ah, Master Sequintus!" Guizo breathed as he peeled an orange. A slight sheen of sweat shone on the black skin of his forehead. "I trust that the morning has treated you well."

"Ah. I think as well as can be expected in this city, my Prince," said Sequintus. "I fear that tempers are generally short."

"And I would agree," said Guizo. "Murders and strange deaths, witch burnings, brothel closings, the Grand Duke's preparations for war, the War Star and the Eye of Ishraha in the night sky, and now even rumors that an envoy of the Emperor is on his way to speak to the High King. It's enough to put everyone off their breakfast." He popped a slice of the orange into his mouth. "And you, Master Sequintus, how is your appetite these days?"

"Ah. Yes, well, I admit that I stand somewhat in suspense. I await your word, my Prince," said the old man. "I gather that I am the last of the household of the Sleight of Hand that has not been taken on by a new employer. Well, except those that are dead, of course. I do think my knowledge of aphrodisiacs alone would make me of use to any brothel house in the city. Have I been black-listed by the Guild?"

Guizo studied him in silence for a long moment, long enough that Sequintus was surprised to find he was growing uncomfortable. The old man shifted in his seat. "You were not simply an employee of the Sleight of Hand," Guizo said to him finally. "You were, as far as any of us can tell, Gilgwyr's confidante and closest aide. If the mark of Ligrid had been found upon you, you would have met the same fate as the others at the Sleight of Hand who were revealed to be amongst the coven. Indeed, if there had been the slightest suggestion from anyone else at the brothel that you had been a *Ligridist*, your fate would have been sealed." Guizo looked back down to continue with his orange. "But you have only received the kindest of words. What was it, that most of the women at the Sleight of Hand called you? *Little Grandfather.*"

"Ah," said Sequintus. "I do understand. Completely. How could a man serve one of the Nameless as closely as I have served Gilgwyr and yet not know that he is one of the Nameless? I have wracked my own thoughts and memories, faulty as they may be, and cannot offer an explanation, other than to say that I have reached an age where I think of little more than the task in front of me. If Gilgwyr said *make this potion*, I made the potion. If he said *send this message*, I sent the message, not thinking of what it might mean or to whom it was going. I think that is why he trusted me so much. While I was not privy to all of his doings and dealings, I do indeed have a considerable amount of knowledge about Gilgwyr's operations and plans, at least where he had deigned to include me. All that I know is at your disposal while my faculties remain."

Guizo popped another slice of orange into his mouth. "A most generous offer," he said. "We already know about most of his blackmail, which seems to have been pretty pedestrian stuff and well within the rules of the Guild. And we have learned a great deal about the coven of Ligrid to which he belonged, and the ways that they had sought to corrupt their targets at the Court and in the citizenry, which is without question Forbidden by Guild, Court, and Temple." He tilted his head. "But there are still a few things that we are uncertain of. For example, why did he choose now to leave the city and go with Black-Heart?"

"Ah. Well, that was *Gladringer*, of course. They had a map, you know," said Sequintus. "I believe he had wanted to come to you about that, but then the Guild had black-listed Black-Heart. Too much at stake on that one not to go himself." He allowed himself a look of sadness. "But the Readings have come black and dim; Gilgwyr will not be returning, neither with the lost sword nor without it."

If Guizo was surprised to learn of *Gladringer*, he did not show it. "A fine enough reason to leave the city, I suppose," he said with a shrug. "Here's another. One of the dancers at the Sleight of Hand told us that Gilgwyr had hinted at something *interesting* coming up. He had suggested that she would be richly rewarded, as much as she could earn in a year on her back."

Ah, the fine Palatian, Sequintus thought. He paused, weighing the options. "Ah. Yes. *That*. Tell me, my Prince, what do you know about the history of the Festival of Herrata?" asked Sequintus.

Guizo raised an eyebrow, his face a mask.

Well, the door has been opened, the trap laid, the old man using the name Sequintus Eridaine thought as he slowly walked out of the Forum. He did not know if the rest of the coven would approve of the risk he had just taken, as the Black College preached and taught patience above all else, and moved with such care as to almost not move at all. But to lose so many of his best and brightest pupils in such a short span had been such a heavy blow—first Harvald, then if the Readings were correct Leigh and Gilgwyr at the same time, so close to victory—and so perhaps he was feeling a tad desperate, a tad dangerous. *So close, so close. Closer than anyone has come in centuries. And we got that close by rolling the dice, not by playing it safe. Screw the College.*

He stood on the steps of the Forum, looking out at the sea of people sweeping to and fro in front of him. *We will get our chance again soon, and next time we will not fail. Next time we will bring the Middle Kingdoms to wrack and ruin*, he thought. *A great day is coming.*

And then he wandered off to get some meat pie.

It was rare, Guizo mused, to meet genuine, true evil. He had thought he had seen enough of it in Gilgwyr when he finally knew him for a Whisperer, a worshipper of Amaymon, the Prince of Intrigue and Secret Power who dealt in secrets and corruption. To discover that he was also a worshipper of Ligrid was hardly a surprise. But as he had listened to Sequintus calmly and quietly lay out Gilgwyr's involvement in the perverse plans of a cabal within the Inquisition, Guizo feared he had underestimated both the depths to which Gilgwyr would sink and also the nature of the man who sat before him.

He had strongly suspected that Sequintus was one of the Nameless, and his suspicions had grown stronger the closer he'd looked, for he could find no trace of the man or his name before he had come to the Sleight of Hand as an enchanter back when Gilgwyr had opened the brothel. And what he'd told Sequintus had been true; none from the brothel had a bad word to say about the old man, none save Ariadesma, who had given him his first warning. *He enjoys himself too much, and too secretly. It is in his eyes, and in his fingers*, she had said. And now he feared he had suddenly seen something much worse than even the Nameless in Sequintus: a man who through age or experience or disposition had passed beyond caring about what was right and wrong into a jadedness so thorough that nothing in the human imagination remained that could stir in him repulsion or regret. *Is there any atrocity dark enough and perverse enough to move that man to say: this cannot stand, this cannot be allowed?* Guizo wondered. He suspected the answer was very much a *no*.

His immediate instinct was to quietly arrange the old man's demise and safely lock away so sordid a Rumor about the Inquisition deep where he did not need to look at it, perhaps even ever again; for with Gilgwyr suddenly missing and the Sleight of Hand standing empty, it was unlikely they would be able to make alternative arrangements in time for the Festival, less than a week away, unless they were so desperate as to toss aside any discretion. Their patron might reemerge the next year or the year after with the same request, but by then Guizo would know what to look and listen for, and perhaps could catch them out.

And yet to simply keep this tucked away in his Rumor-hoard for a year seemed impossible. He was torn; corruption at such heights within the Inquisition, and the possibility that a Seated King might actually be involved, was hardly something that could be simply ignored, particularly by a man like Guizo. He loved knowing things. And at the same time, he knew that knowledge and secrets and the power they gave were the temptations that led to Amaymon, as it had for Gilgwyr; just as pleasure and lust were the temptations that led to Ligrid.

He recognized the temptation that had been laid before him, quite casually and quite on purpose by the old man, and chuckled as he sat at the table. *Replace Gilgwyr as the pimp, and you can gain the favor of the powerful in the Inquisition and learn the secrets that were about to be revealed to him, the kinds of secrets that men kill to learn or to protect. Could the Nameless cult of Ligrid, Queen of Perversion, have reached that deeply into the very body that was intended to root it out and destroy it and its fellow walkers-in-darkness? Were the Inquisitors so wrapped up in their own convictions, so beholden to the power they sought to please, that they could not see what had happened to them? Could a Seated King be so lost to corruption?*

He started toying with the idea; it would be simple enough. He knew Ariadesma to be both a true libertine and an adventuress of steely discipline—it was why he had sent her to Gilgwyr in the first place—and if he asked her to go through with this thing he knew she would say yes, with fear and delight. He could feel himself blushing at the thought, his breathing strained as he swallowed nervously at his own excitement. *I could borrow her back from the Gilded Lady, I could guarantee her safety, make sure that she was not harmed, and she would emerge with secrets for me that could bring about the downfall of a Seated King and—*

A sparrow landed on the table in front of him, and turned its head to contemplate him with one eye, and that stopped him in mid-thought.

He was surprised, even ashamed, to discover that he had even contemplated it. Rumors and secrets were his business.

But he didn't worship them.

He laughed aloud until his body shook.

"What's so funny?" asked Otalo Galluessi, a black-skinned Amoran like himself, dressed in a street bravo's black leather doublet and fine brocade breeches.

"I have just been reminded of the limits of myself," said Guizo. "And I am a happy man for it." He breathed a little easier. "Send word to the Council of Princes. A man from the Inquisition may be seeking a prostitute in the coming days. He is to be denied, by all amongst the Marked and by those that honor our decrees. The law forbidding prostitution on the day of the Festival of Herrata is to be strictly enforced this year."

Otalo nodded and left, followed by several others from Guizo's crew.

He held out his hand, and the small sparrow jumped up on to his fat pointer finger. "Thank you," he said. He raised it to his lips, and whispered in its ear: "To the King's Shadow speed. And bear this message: *A debt I owe you is about to be repaid. A Rumor that is a matter for the State, and for your ears alone. Visit when you can.*"

The sparrow chirped once, and then flew up and out an open window high in the recesses of the ceiling.

Guizo settled back and returned to his orange.

And now: what to do about Sequintus? he wondered.

A BRIEF GLOSSARY
OF DEITIES, PLACES, PEOPLE, *AND* EVENTS

ACHRE—rebellious daughter of *Bragea*, who refused to become an *Oracle Queen*. Instead she wounded her father, bound a great Dragon and, as the mother of *Archaia*, became ancestress of the Palatians (see *Palatia*).

ADJIA LUNA—the Moon Huntress, one of the three goddesses of the Moon, along with her sisters *Yhera* and *Djara*. She is the goddess of birth, growth, maturity, maternity, the hunt, and dreams. As the Archer she brings a swift death. Sometimes called *Adjiana*.

AGALL—demigod son of *Agdah Cosmopeiia*, famous for his considerable temper, strength and courage; he is worshipped as the first Hero. The Sacker of Cities, he fought alongside *Geteema's* children at the destruction of *Ürüne Düré*. One of the *Four Kings in Exile*, slain in the *Far West* but redeemed by *Islik* in the Underworld.

AGDAH COSMOPEIIA—the Year God and God of the Shining Sky, the god of the year-cycle: the growths of spring, the harvests of the fall, and the deprivations of the winter. He was slain by *Geteema* in defense of *Düréa*, but later restored by *Yhera* to Heaven. Also called *Agdah Helios* (the Cosmos Sun) and *Ammon Agdah* (the Household Protector and the Keeper of Animals).

AGE OF CREATION, the—period prior to the beginning of history proper, when *Yhera* and the other gods created the world in twenty-two great Acts, starting with Yhera's dream of overcoming a Great Dragon in the primordial Darkness, and ending with a great Crime committed by mortal man which causes *Geniché* to pass into the Underworld and pronounce the *First Law*.

AGE OF LEGENDS, the—second age of *Known World* history, beginning with *Islik's* ascension to the Sun Throne in Heaven and ending with the destruction of the Imperial capital of Millene some 498 years later.

AKKALION—the Lion Emperor of *Thessid-Gola*. The first prince of Thessid-Gola to claim the throne of *Dauban Hess* since the wars of the *Worm Kings*. He embarked on a series of conquests to restore the Empire to its former glory until he was overcome by the *Gray Dream* the night before the *Black Day Battle*. His mind has been trapped in the Gray Dream ever since, and he has sat dreaming on his throne in *Avella* for over four hundred years.

AKINE MOG—Sorcerer-King of Kathek, a city in *Setine*, who rose to power in the *Winter Century*. Started the Fire War with Sekeret in which cannon and bombards fueled by the *Black Elixir* were used for the first time (see *Grand Sekeret*).

AMAYMON—the Whisperer, the Prince of Intrigue and Secret Power, and the god of secret knowledge, bribery, corruption, and assassins, worshipped by those who want something for nothing. One of the *Forbidden Gods* and a Servant-Ruler in the Six Hells. He counseled *Irré* to overthrow *Illiki Helios* and *Ishraha* to begin his rebellion against *Islik* the Divine King, thus beginning the *War in Heaven*. One of the *Forbidden Gods*.

AMI—the Morning Star, the Dawn Maiden, twin sister of *Dieva*, and the goddess of love, fertility, and romance. As the Sun's Herald she holds a special place in *Divine King* cult practice.

AMORA—anciently a *Düréan* colony favored by *Illiki Helios*, now a realm balancing the worship of the old gods and more recent influence of the *Sun Court*. Once part of the *Thessid-Golan Empire*, Amora is now independent with the help of *Palatia*, and has annexed nearby *Meretia* as a buffer state with the Empire.

AN-ATHAIR—currently a castle and small city in the *Erid Wold*, but once the center of a great realm of the same name ruled by the *Spring Queens*. Home to the *Athairi*.

ANGOWRIE—one of the *Middle Kingdoms*, originally the hold of one of the *Watchtower Kings*. The current king is Euwen Jaraslas, betrothed to a daughter of the King of Erid *Dania*.

ARCHAIA—the daughter of *Achre*, student of *Ariahavé*, and the founder of the city of *Palatia* and builder of its Seven Gates. She bore three daughters, who founded the three most ancient Houses of Palatia. With her daughters, she sailed to war against *Geteema's* children, and was slain in defense of *Düréa*.

ARIAHAVÉ—the Civilizer, *Yhera's* brightest and most rebellious daughter. She is the protectress of cities and citadels and their citizens and defenders; she is the patroness of civilization and its heroes. After *Geniché* abandoned the Earth, she taught the lost peoples of the world the arts of society—agriculture, poetry, spinning, pottery, music, and mining. She is Yhera's general and the chief war goddess of the *Palatians*, her most dedicated adherents.

ASSASSIN CYCLES, the—hundred-year period in recent Palatian history of internecine, inter-House struggle for control over the thrones of *Palatia*, ending with the rise of the *Usurper*.

ATALLICA—primary kingdom of the eastern Middle Kingdoms, centered on the city of Therapoli. Ruled by Aurian kings and nobles (see *Auria*), and populated by both Aurians and Danians (see *Dania*).

ATHAIRI—the peoples of *An-Athair* and the *Erid Wold*. The Athairi mix the bloodlines of the peoples of *Dania*, *Düréa*, and *Daradja*, as well as the *Fae*, and have a reputation for folk magic and wisdom as a result.

AUDRA—the Voyager, legendary Queen of *Palatia* at the beginning of the *Bronze Age* largely responsible for that city's rise to current power. Last of the Black Arrow Queens and first of the Copper Queens.

AURIA—a principality of *Atallica* and the *Middle Kingdoms*, and ancient name for the lands settled by the Aurians, seagoing pillagers descended of *Heth*.

AWAIN—Awain Gauwes Urfortian, the current High King of *Therapoli* and the *Middle Kingdoms*; a descendant of *Fortias the Brave*.

AVELLA—the Immortal City, current Imperial Capital of the *Thessid-Golan Empire*. Once a minor city of *Thessidia*, it was chosen by *Akkalion* to be his capital while he was recuperating from wars against the *Isliklidae* and transformed into a city of great beauty. Home to the *Phoenix Court*.

AZHARAD—a Sorcerer and worshipper of the *Forbidden Gods* who rose to power in the *Bale Mole* and the Uthed Wold. A cannibal and hunter of men, allegedly buried with the sword *Gladringer*.

BALE MOLE—high, desolate hill range that separates *Lost Uthedmael* from the *Vale of Barrows*. A place of dark magic.

BLACK DAY BATTLE, the—battle fought on the shores of *Dania* between the forces of the *Middle Kingdoms* and *Daradja* and the invading *Thessid-Golan Empire* on a day when *Irré* the Black Sun rose in the sky instead of *Islik*. Because *Akkalion* was in the thrall of the *Gray Dream* and absent from the battle, the Empire was routed.

BLACK ELIXIR—one of the three magical elixirs produced by alchemy. A black powder that generates enormous heat and energy when properly harnessed.

BLACK HUNTER, the—favored son of *Geniché*, brother of Ammon *Agdah*, and leader of the Wild Hunt. At the beginning of winter and sometimes when he escapes the Underworld, he leads a host of ghosts, spirits, and demons across the Known World hunting those that stray from protected shelter.

BOOK OF DOOMS, the—book of 22 plates created by *Bragea* for his queen and their descendants to aid their oracles. Based upon the Celestial Book of *Yhera*. Briefly lost after the sack of *Khael*, but recovered by *Audra*.

BRAGEA—the first smith, the creator of the arts of metalworking; he is the fire-god of hearth, kiln, and foundry, creator of rune-systems and artifacts of great power. Bragea eloped with a Düréan Queen to the Isle of *Khael*, and their daughters became the *Oracle Queens*. Also called *Abrage* and *Braphagos*.

BRONZE AGE, the—third age of *Known World* history, dating from the *Catastrophe* and the *Winter Century* to the ascension of *Akkalion* to the throne of *Thessid-Gola* some 528 years later.

CATASTROPHE, the—the destruction of *Millene*, capital of the *Thessid-Golan Empire*, at the end of the *Age of Legends* by a volcanic maelstro; caused by a curse from the *Oracle Queens*. Begins the *Winter Century*.

CELESTIAL COURT, the—the ruling court of *Samarappa* during the *Golden Age*, which under *Surep* included the deities of Heaven in its ranks. During the *War in Heaven* the Court was ruled by *Nymarga*, until he was deposed by the return of *Jala*. The Court faded in power during the *Age of Legends*, was held by the *Isliklidae* for a dark time, and ended after the disappearance of its hero-savior, *Dauban Hess*.

CERAM—the Thunderer, a son of *Thula* and *Illiki* the Sun-Bull, ancestor-god of the nomads of the *Midlands*. Ceram hunted the *Four Kings in Exile* across the Midlands.

COROMAT—a son of *Geteema* and tragic hero of the ancient world. Banished from *Vanimoria* for withdrawing from his mother's war on *Düréa*, he became one of the *Four Kings in Exile* and went mad for many years before returning home to reconcile with his people and resume his throne. Deposed and slain by *Nymarga*.

DAEDEKAMANI—a son of *Yhera*; the first magician, creator of the magical arts and the first magical runes. Daedekamani is a wanderer, a patron of travelers, and sometimes a psychopomp.

DALL AND PULMA—twin daughters of *Thula* and chief amongst her children. They bound horses, fought by Thula's side in defense of *Düréa*, and now appear in the Heavens as the Twins constellation.

DANIA—lands of the Danians, now part of the *Middle Kingdoms*. Once comprised of Uthed Dania and Dania proper, until Uthed Dania was lost in the war against *Githwaine* (see *Lost Uthedmael*). Later Dania split into Dain Dania and Erid Dania.

DARA—first Queen of *Daradja*, from whom the land derives its name. Slain by *Thula*.

DARA DESS—called the greatest of the four ancient citadels of *Daradja* (Dara Dess, Heth Moll, An-Athark, and Finleth).

DARADJA—traditional name for the mountainous highlands of the *Middle Kingdoms*. Literally "Realm Of Dara" in *Old Éduinan*.

DAUBAN HESS—the Golden Emperor, the Conqueror King, greatest of the *Dragon Kings*. He was reputed to be a son of *Islik*, rose to power in *Hemispia*, defeated *Nymarga* with the sword Daybringer and drove the *Isliklidae* out of the *Celestial Court*, and came to rule the whole of the *Known World*. He set sail to find the *Dawn Isles* to greet his alleged father, and was never seen again.

DAWN ISLES, the—fabulous islands at the edge of the world, where every morning *Ami* throws open the Gates of the Dawn to let in the Sun.

DÉSKÉDRÉ—swath of coastal cities just north of the *Middle Kingdoms*. Déskédran cities are known for their licentiousness and devotion to the worship of *Dieva*.

DIEVA—the Evening Star, the Dusk Maiden, twin sister of *Ami*, and the goddess of sex and physical pleasures. She closes the Gates of the Dusk behind the Sun to usher in the night.

DIVINE KING, the CULT of the—cult of *Islik*, the King of Heaven and of Earth. Divine King cultists stand in opposition to the followers of the *Old Religion* and eschew sacrifice to the gods and eat unsacrificed meat regularly. The cult of the Divine King is split by a schism between the *Sun Court* and the *Phoenix Court*.

DJAR MAEL—land of the Maelites, a cursed people distantly related to the Daradjans and Danians, now servants of the *Isliklidae*.

DJARA LUNA—the Moon goddess of Death and Darkness, the queen of ghosts and dark magic, the giver of lunacy and nightmares, the keeper and revealer of secrets; goddess of crossroads, curse magic and divinations. Also called *Urgale* or *Morgale*.

DRAGON KINGS, the—ancient kings and heroes possessed of great might and powers of dominion. *Ceram* was the first, *Dauban Hess* was the greatest; descent from either indicated Dragon King blood and great latent power, but they were wiped out in wars exterminating their hated enemies, the *Worm Kings*, during the *Winter Century*. *Islik* was also a Dragon King.

DÜMÉGHAL—warlords and warriors of the *Isliklidae*, recruited from their subjects in the *Far West* and bound to their service by foul magics.

DÜRÉA—ancient queendom of the *Golden Age* and cradle and crucible of civilization. Lost to the armies of *Geteema* and sunk beneath the *Mera Argenta* at the end of the *Golden Age*. (See *Ürüne Düré*).

ÉDUINS—mountain range in the *Midlands*, forming a peninsula into the *Mera Argenta*; constituted by the Dain Éduins in the west, the Harath Éduins in the east, and the minor ranges of the Bora, Djar, and Tel Éduins as well as many smaller Moles.

EMIR—*Thessid-Golan Empire* term for an officer of high rank.

ERID WOLD, the—great wood in *Dania*, once ruled by the *Spring Queens* and now a haunted place, full of ghosts and spirits and reputed the refuge of witches fleeing the persecution of the *Sun Court*. The Erid Wold was once much larger, but is now a fraction of its ancient size.

ERLWULF—last of the known *Dragon Kings*, slain by *Githwaine*.

FAE, the—immortal earth spirits that dwell in the Otherworld and often interact with the mortal men of the *Known World*. The fae are organized into seven great courts that are connected to woods in the Known World: the Court of the Golden Wood (the *Erid Wold*), the Court of the Silver Wood (the Tiria Wold), the Court of the Brazen Wood (the Neris Wold), the Court of the Night Wood (the Haras Wold), the Court of the Stone Wood (the Hada Wold), the Court of the Sable Wood (the Grav Wold), and the Court of the Drowned Wood (the Uthed Wold).

FAR WEST, the—common name for any lands west of the *Midlands*.

FIRST LAW, the—mandate of *Geniché*, cursing the world with mortality: "All those born of my Earth must follow me into Death and the Underworld."

FORBIDDEN GODS—term first used by the Inquisition of the *Sun Court* to categorize the dark gods that rebelled against *Illiki* and *Islik* during the *War in Heaven* and reemerged as patrons of the *Worm Kings*. Includes *Amaymon*, the Corn King, *Geteema*, the Horned Man, *Irré*, *Ishraha*, *Ligrid*, Malkheb, and *Nymarga*.

FORTIAS THE BRAVE—Aurian hero-knight of the *Middle Kingdoms*, who slew *Githwaine* with the sword Gladringer to end the *Winter Century* and who later built the Great Wall that stands between the Middle Kingdoms and *Lost Uthedmael*. His descendants are the High Kings of the Middle Kingdoms.

FOUR KINGS IN EXILE, the—during the *War in Heaven*, four kings banished and in exile—*Islik*, *Agall*, *Coromat*, and *Jala*—joined together for adventures. They fought many battles, resisted the temptations of the Daradj Queen, were pursued by *Ceram* across the *Midlands*, and broke up their fellowship in the *Far West* after the death of *Agall* at the hands of a treacherous enemy called the Blooded (see *Isliklidae*).

GALIA—an emirate of the *Thessid-Golan Empire* just south of the *Middle Kingdoms*. Anciently the kingdom of *Agall*, now a realm of prosperous merchant-traders.

GENICHÉ—Queen of the Underworld and once Goddess and Queen of the Earth, the giver of life, and, with her sister *Geteema*, the mother of all within *Yhera's* creation. The Earth was once her garden, and she ruled it as a Paradise until, in a moment of grief and anger, she abandoned the world and fled into darkness. She created the Underworld and spoke the *First Law*.

GETEEMA—sister to *Geniché* and *Yhera*, monstrous Queen of the Dark Earth, the Dragon Mother and the Mother of the Giants; her children include *Irré* the Black Sun, *Amaymon* the Whisperer, *Vani* the Mountain King, *Heth* the Sea King, and many others. Out of jealousy she sent many of her children to destroy ancient *Ürüne Düré*, and she herself consumed the body of *Agdah Cosmopeiia*, after which *Yhera* imprisoned her in the Underworld.

GITHWAINE—last of the *Worm Kings*, discovered masquerading amongst the warlords of *Djar Mael* and Uthed Dania. He killed *Erlwulf*, the last known *Dragon King*, before being slain by *Fortias the Brave*; his death marked the end of the *Winter Century*.

GOLA, the—name for the lands of the south around the Leta river and home to some of the oldest cities in the *Known World*. Now organized as *Grand Sekeret* and *Setine*, key emirates of the *Thessid-Golan Empire*.

GOLDEN AGE, the—first age of *Known World* history after *Geniché* left the Earth for the Underworld. Generally dated from the founding of *Düréa* and considered to have lasted just over 1000 years, until the fall of *Ürüne Düré* and the *War in Heaven*.

GORGONAE, the—the Triple War Goddess, daughters of *Djara*, worshipped singly and as a trio. The Gorgonae are kept chained in the Underworld, and only *Yhera* Anath or her general, *Ariahavé*, may set them loose.

GRAND SEKERET—the city-states of the *Gola*, as they have come to be known, after their victory over *Akine Mog*; scene to some of the greatest fighting in the wars against the *Worm Kings* following the *Catastrophe*. The largest and oldest is Seker, followed by Camathune, both of which have some of the oldest *Great Schools*.

GRAY DREAM, the—cursed dream that befell *Akkalion* before the *Black Day Battle*, now the subject of intense speculation amongst mystery cults throughout the *Thessid-Golan Empire*, the *Hemapoline League*, and *Palatia*.

GREAT SCHOOLS—halls of learning originally founded and patroned by *Daedekamani* himself, found throughout the *Gola* and *Thessidia*.

HALÉ—the Goddess of Slaughter, goddess of (mindless) rage and berserker fury. One of the *Gorgonae*.

HANNATH HAMMERGREIA—greatest of the last Queens of Düréa, and considered by many its last True Queen and last of the *Rethet Thesa*. A virgin huntress and voracious warrior, she defeated the *Black Hunter* and died many deaths, until her final death at the fall of *Ürüne Düré*.

HATHAZ-GHÚL—*Old Éduinan* name for cursed once-men, things that should be dead but cling to life by feeding on the bodies of the living and recently deceased. They are often said to come from *Lost Uthedmael*.

HATHHALLA—the Devouring Fire of the Sun, worshipped as the lion-headed goddess of battle and vengeance, goddess of the Sun's righteous strength. At *Yhera's* behest she imprisoned her half brother *Irré* in the Underworld after he cast down her half brother *Illiki Helios*. She ruled the Heavens as the Sun's Veil during the *Winter Century,* and rules the Six Hells as their great guardian and keeper.

HEMAPOLI MAGNI—greatest city of *Hemispia*, and a rival to *Palatia* in all things mercantile and military.

HEMAPOLINE LEAGUE, the—patchwork of city-states and kingdoms in *Hemispia* and *Illia* dedicated primarily to trade, led by the rulers of the city of *Hemapoli Magni*. Stronghold of the followers of the *Sun Court*, but beset by republicanism.

HEMISPIA—lands east of the *Mera Argenta* now ruled by the *Hemapoline League*. Anciently the lands of the first *Dragon Kings*.

HETH—the Sea Bull, the Sea King, god of surface waves, sea storms, and the Deep. Ancestor-god of the Aurians, who cursed his descendants and turned his back upon them after they destroyed the Green Temple of *An-Athair*.

ILLIA—isle just north of *Hemispia*, favored by the gods of the Sun and location of the first Dragon Throne. Home to the *Sun Court*.

ILLIKI HELIOS—the Sun-Bull, a son of *Agdah Cosmopeiia* and *Ami* the Morning

Star, the father of *Islik* the Divine King. As the Spring Sun he bestows progeny and protects crops, an archetype of divine kingship, and as the Winter Sun, he is the dying god with knowledge of the Underworld, cast from the Heavens by his half brother *Irré* the Black Sun. He was later restored, either by *Yhera* or by his son *Islik*.

IRON AGE, the—fourth and current age of *Known World* history, beginning with *Akkalion's* assumption of the Imperial throne 446 years ago and leading to the current date: 1471 in the standard Imperial Avellan calendar used by the *Sun Court* and *Middle Kingdoms*, 2615 in the old *Düréan* calendar, 2431 in the Celestial calendar, or 1638 in the *Palatian* calendar.

IRRÉ—the Black Sun, bringer of unbearable heat, drought, and the blinding intensity of both darkness and light; the Bow Bearer, god of plague and fire; the Black Goat, god of war, struggle, disaster, disorder, the desert and the wilderness; the Last Defender, who guarded the gates of *Düréa* from the armies of *Geteema*. He overthrew *Illiki Helios* for abandoning *Düréa* before its fall, starting the *War in Heaven*. One of the *Forbidden Gods*.

ISHRAHA—the Rebel Angel, a son of *Ligrid* and a general to *Islik* when he was King of *Illia*. After *Irré* cast down *Illiki Helios* at the start of the *War in Heaven*, Ishraha led a rebellion against *Islik* for withholding the sacrifices due the gods and usurped his throne, casting *Islik* into exile. He was defeated when Islik returned and is imprisoned in the Underworld. One of the *Forbidden Gods*.

ISLIK—the Divine King, demigod son of *Illiki Helios*. He was the first of the Illian *Dragon Kings*, the founder of the *Sun Court*, and ruled as King of the Earth. After his father was cast down by *Irré*, Islik was usurped by *Ishraha*. After wandering the world for 21 years as one of the *Four Kings in Exile*, he achieved Ten Great Victories and returned to reclaim his throne, and after imprisoning Ishraha in the Underworld, Islik ascended to the Heavens and became King of both Heaven and Earth. His worshippers do not make sacrifices to the old gods and believe that rather than descending to *Geniché's* Underworld, they ascend to the Heavens to Islik's Palace after they die, but they have divided into two rival schisms, the *Sun Court* and the *Phoenix Court*.

ISLIKLIDAE, the—strange and evil Kings who arose in the *Far West* and conquered the lands of *Djar Mael* some two hundred years ago, dividing the land into three kingdoms: Morica, Ugeram, and Boradja. They claim descent from *Islik*, and are served by the *Düméghal* and Maelite warlords. Called the Isliklidae, Isliklids, Islikids, and the Pretenderai.

597

JALA—the Good Prince, son of *Surep*. One of the *Four Kings in Exile*, he returned to *Samarappa* to confront *Nymarga*, regain his father's throne, and restore the *Celestial Court*.

KHAEL—isle just east of *Palatia*, where the *Oracle Queens* live. Sacked by the *Worm King*s at the end of the *Age of Legends*, now protected by Palatian legions.

KNOWN WORLD, the—term used to describe the whole of the known, mapped world, to distinguish it from the unknown, unmapped world.

LIGRID—the Temptress, the Queen of Perversity, the breaker of taboos and the corruptor of flesh and spirit; a daughter of *Geteema*, she is described variously as a rival, tutor, or mask of *Dieva*. One of the *Forbidden Gods*.

LORD MOTT, the—vizier to the *Usurper* of *Palatia*, inventor of the first Indexes, and rumored to be the Philosopher-King-in-Waiting who will usher in the next age of history.

LOST UTHEDMAEL—name given to Maelite and Danian lands loyal to *Githwaine* and cursed by the *Sun Court* after his fall at the end of the *Winter Century* (see *Djar Mael* and *Dania*). Now a barren and ashen wasteland of inhospitable ruins.

MAECE—name of the realm taken by the Maelites Kings who stood against *Githwaine* (see *Djar Mael*). Their strength was wasted in wars against the *Isliklidae*, and they remain only as the *Watchtower Kings*.

MANON MOLE—high hills along the coast of the southern *Middle Kingdoms*, home to reclusive hill peoples and bandit knights descended from the *Wyvern King* who refuse to acknowledge the High King of *Therapoli*.

MÉDÜRE—the Cunning One, goddess of warlike skill and heroic valor. One of the *Gorgonae*.

MERA ARGENTA—inland sea framed by *Hemispia* in the east, the *Gola* in the south, the coast of the *Midlands* to the west, and *Déskédré* and the territories of *Palatia* in the north. Also called the Silver Scale Sea.

MERETIA—small realm next to the *Gola*, once part of the *Thessid-Golan Empire* and now annexed by *Amora*.

MIDLANDS, the—common name for the lands to the west of the *Silver Scale Sea*. Once the Paradise of *Geniché*, now mostly inhospitable desert and mountain.

MIDDLE KINGDOMS, the—common name for the Aurian and Danian kingdoms on a peninsula in the *Silver Scale Seas* (see *Auria*, *Dania*), all aligned with the *Sun Court* and ruled by the High King of *Therapoli*.

MILLENE—legendary capital of *Dauban Hess'* Golden Empire, destroyed by a volcanic maelstrom in the *Catastrophe*. All that is left are a few ruins at the center of a plain of volcanic ash.

MOGRAN—the Riot Goddess, goddess of terror, confusion, and dissension. One of the *Gorgonae*.

NAMELESS CULTS, the—common term for the cults surrounding the *Forbidden Gods*.

NYMARGA—the Magician, the Devil Incarnate, called by some the first and greatest evil of the *Known World*, who rose to power in the *Celestial Court*. He slew King *Surep* to usurp the throne of *Samarappa*, but *Jala* returned and threw him down. He next appeared in *Vanimoria*, where he killed *Coromat* to usurp the throne, conquered *Thessidia*, and ruled as the Worldly Tyrant until *Dauban Hess* slew him and dismembered his body, hiding and burying the pieces in salt. Some believe he also incarnated as the King of Brass, the Horned Man, the Corn King, and Maelfess at different points in ancient history and legend. One of the *Forbidden Gods*.

OLD ÉDUINAN—ancient language of *Dania*, *Daradja*, and the Maelites (see *Djar Mael*), similar to the language of ancient *Düréa*.

OLD RELIGION, the—common term for the worship of *Yhera* and other ancient gods and goddesses. Followers of the Old Religion believe that meat should only be consumed by mortals in the context of an animal sacrifice to a god or goddess.

ORACLE QUEENS, the—the descendants of *Bragea*, possessed of the greatest oracular visions in the *Known World*, and rulers of the Isle of *Khael*.

PALATIA—city-state of the northern *Mera Argenta,* founded by *Achre* and *Archaia*. A minor city in the *Golden Age*, but now the center of a vast and expanding empire, possessed of legions, fleets, and merchant networks rivaled only by the *Hemapoline League* and *Thessid-Golan Empire*, each of which it has defeated in recent wars. Now ruled by the *Usurper*.

PHOENIX COURT, the—Imperial Court of the Empire of *Thessid-Gola* located in *Avella*; also the highest *Divine King* authority in the West (see *Islik*). Opposed to the *Sun Court*, the Phoenix Court advocates a model of kingship based on appointment or election rather than inheritance, and so chooses or elects the officers of the Court and the emirates of the Empire. Briefly but disastrously corrupted by the *Worm Kings*.

RAHABI—great spirits of darkness and fire that sided with *Irré* during the *War in Heaven*. Their name comes from Rahab, the great monster-general that led the army of *Irré*. Their ranks included the Dhuréleal, the Bharab Dzerek, the Gamezhiel, the Ghazarab, the Golodriel, the Nephilim, and the Sharab Deceal. They now dwell mostly in the Underworld and the Six Hells.

RED ELIXIR—one of the three magical elixirs produced by alchemy. A red powder (or as the Alkahest, a red liquid) that can be used to turn base metals into gold, give oracular dreams or visions of the future, create a basilisk, or impart immortality.

RETHET THESA, the—name for the Carrion Queens of *Düréa* during the *Golden Age* when they were most active in the *Known World* as warriors, hunters, and conquerors, just prior to the fall of *Ürüne Düré*.

SAMARAPPA—fabled land of spices in the *Far West*, known for its literate and sensuous peoples.

SEATED KING—a King recognized by the *Sun Court*. Seated Kings were granted power once it was obvious there would be no more *Dragon Kings*.

SEEDRÉ—a son of *Geniché* who was the first to follow his mother to the Underworld and became the Judge of the Dead. Also called Osidred by cult of the *Divine King*.

SETINE—an emirate of the *Thessid-Golan Empire*, inland of the cities of *Grand Sekeret* in the *Gola*. Ruled by *Akine Mog* during and after the *Winter Century*, until his defeat by the armies of Sekeret.

SPRING QUEENS, the—priestesses of the Green Temple of *An-Athair* during the *Age of Legends*, who created a wondrous and magical land centered in the *Erid Wold*. They were protected by the order of the Golden Knights. Their realm was ended by the arrival of the Aurians (see *Auria)*.

SULTAN—title given an *Emir* elected by the *Phoenix Court* to speak in the name of *Akkalion*. The current Sultan is Agameen tep Marahet.

SUN COURT, the—highest religious authority in eastern lands devoted to *Islik*. Located on *Illia*, once the home of *Islik* himself, the Sun Court stands against the *Phoenix Court* and champions the tradition of hereditary kingship passed from father to son. Sun Court lands include the *Hemapoline League*, *Amora* and *Meretia*, and the *Middle Kingdoms*.

SUREP—son of *Yhera* and *Agdah Cosmopeiia*; a legendary and divine ruler of *Samarappa* during the *Golden Age*, slain by *Nymarga*.

THERAPOLI MAGNI—ancient capital of the *Middle Kingdoms*, built during the *Golden Age*.

THESSID-GOLAN EMPIRE, the—name for the vast empire first created by

Dauban Hess, then dismembered after his disappearance, first during civil wars between the *Sun Court* and rebel generals in the west, and then by the wars of the *Worm Kings*. At the height of its expansion under Dauban Hess in whole of the *Known World* only *Palatia* and *Khael* were outside the Empire and even they sent tribute. *Akkalion* began to reconstitute the Empire after the *Bronze Age*, but his efforts were halted by his lapse into the *Gray Dream*, and have only been recently been continued by the most recent *Sultan*. Currently includes *Vanimoria*, *Thessidia*, *Grand Sekeret*, *Setine*, *Galia*, and a host of minor emirates and principalities. Nominally allied to the *Isliklidae*, with whom the Empire fought the Long War of Night Horrors before reaching a truce.

THESSIDIA—principal emirate of the *Thessid-Golan Empire* just to the west of the *Gola*; home to the current Imperial Capital of *Avella* and site of the ruins of the old capital, *Millene*.

THRONE THIEF, WARS of the—fifty-year period of civil war and upheaval in the *Middle Kingdoms*, caused when a person or persons unknown proceeded over several years to steal the magical thrones of the kings of the Aurian and Danian Kingdoms. The thrones are still missing two centuries later.

THULA—a daughter of *Geniché*; the Forked Tongue, the Mother of Heroes, the Fire Queen who stole the secrets of magic and civilization from the *Düréans* and the Otherworld for her descendants, the *Thulamites*. She killed *Dara* in one of her many raids, and dueled *Achre* with both weapons and dance to a standoff; according to some stories she could change appearance and gender as easily as a snake sheds its skin, and performed magics that allowed her to bear a child by Achre. Thula sailed to defend *Ürüne Düré* against *Geteema's* children, though she had herself weakened its defenses. Mother of *Ceram* and *Dall and Pulma*.

THULAMITES—barbarians of the *Midlands*, horse-riding raiders who dwell in great stone citadels. Now allied to *Palatia*.

URGRAYNE—a daughter of *Djara* Luna; one of the Four Queens of the Compass, and called the Witch-Queen of the Harath *Éduins*. Active throughout the world since the days of *Ürüne Düré*, she has a reputation as a mysterious meddler. Some Daradjans are said to follow her instructions and are called members of the Witch's Host (see *Daradja*).

ÜRÜNE DÜRÉ—a great isle in the *Mera Argenta*, where *Ariahavé* led her favorites in the *Golden Age* to teach them the arts of civilization and found the realm of *Düréa*. Lost beneath the sea at the end of the Golden Age. Usually translated from the Düréan as "Mountain of Thrones."

USURPER, the—common name for Urech Aiths, the current Duke of *Palatia*, who took the Ducal Throne in a coup at the end of the *Assassin Cycles*.

UTHED WOLD—one of the seven great woods of the *Middle Kingdoms*, a place of darkness and death held by the Azharites, followers of *Azharad* and the *Nameless Cults*.

VALE OF BARROWS, the—ancient burial place of the queens and kings of *Daradja* and *Dania*. Largely unused for centuries, now considered cursed and home to necromancers, witches, ghosts, and ghouls.

VANI—a son of *Ammon Agdah* and *Geteema*, often depicted as having either an eagle or vulture head; the Mountain King who brings the Spring thaw. Ancestor god of the Vanimorians (see *Vanimoria*).

VANIMORIA—mountainous land to the west of the *Mera Argenta*; considered the southern edge of the *Midlands*, but during the *Golden Age* was the earthly realm of *Geteema*, and so was spared some of the desolation which has marked the rest of Geniché's Paradise. Inhabited by proud, martial mountain barbarians and considered a key component of the *Thessid-Golan Empire*.

WAR IN HEAVEN, the—a 21-year war at the end of the *Golden Age*. After the sinking of *Ürüne Düré* and while *Yhera* wandered in grief, *Irré* accused *Illiki* Helios of abandoning the defense of *Düréa* to become the Sun King after the death of *Agdah* Cosmopeiia, and organized a rebellion in the Heavens against him. Illiki Helios was cast into the Underworld and Irré assumed the mantle of the Sun King. On Earth, *Ishraha* usurped the Dragon Throne of *Illia* from *Islik* in a parallel rebellion. At the end of the war, Yhera returned from the Underworld and restored Agdah and Illiki to the Heavens, though neither could be Sun King. That position was taken by Islik himself, who returned from exile to claim both the Dragon Throne of Illia and the Sun Throne.

WATCHTOWER KINGS, the—Maelite and Danian kings and warlords who fought against *Githwaine* and were granted citadels in western *Dania* to keep watch over *Lost Uthedmael* and the *Thessid-Golan Empire* by *Fortias the Brave* (see *Djar Mael*). Once their domain was called *Maece*.

WHITE ELIXIR—one of the three magical elixirs produced by alchemy. A white liquid or powder that can be used to heal, create magic mirrors, turn base metals into silver, or impart the gift of languages or Second Sight.

WINTER CENTURY, the—period of over 100 years following the *Catastrophe*, during which the world saw a period of cold and darkness, and *Hathhalla* ruled as the Sun's Veil. The hunt for the *Worm Kings* is most intense during this period. Ends with the death of *Githwaine*.

WORM KINGS, the—common name for the kings and generals of the Imperial Court of the *Thessid-Gola Empire* who became twisted by foul magics after the disappearance of *Dauban Hess*. To retain their appointed thrones, they embraced bloodthirsty rituals that extended their lives at the price of their humanity and the corruption and decay of their bodies. The *Oracle Queens* cursed them in revenge for the sack of *Khael*, and after the *Catastrophe* befell them, they were hunted to extinction by the last of the *Dragon Kings*.

WYVERN KING, the—brutal ruler of the *Manon Mole* during the *Age of Legends*, avowed enemy of the *Spring Queens*. Defanged by the Spring Queen Ymaire.

YHERA—Queen of Heaven, Goddess of Night, Queen of the Waters, one of the goddesses of the Moon, and often worshipped as the Creatrix, the divine origin of all that is. She is the goddess of language, sovereignty, rulership, wealth, wisdom, love, fertility, protection, and war. Also known as Yhera Cosmopeiia, Yhera Luna, Yhera Chthonia, Yhera Anath, Yhera Fortuna, and Yhera Invictus, amongst other epithets.

ACKNOWLEDGMENTS

For some years I wrote and illustrated a fantasy comic called Artesia. With my various duties at the graphic novel publishing company (and now BOOM! Studios imprint) Archaia increasingly taking me away from my drawing tables, finding the time to actually finish what I had started became increasingly difficult. With comics, the drawing and painting is the time-consuming part (at least for me), so after a while I turned to the idea of writing (without the art) as a way to continue working with the world and characters of the Artesia graphic novels. Years ago I had worked on a "prequel" screenplay to Artesia with my brother, John, and our mutual friend Hidetoshi Oneda, and that screenplay served as the basis for this book. To them I owe a great deal of thanks and no small portion of credit.

Familiarity with Artesia is not required, I hope, to enjoy *The Barrow*. Over the years a lot of people have contributed their support, enthusiasm, critiques, and comments to the Artesia comics and graphic novels or the Artesia roleplaying game, and to all of them I extend once more my thanks and gratitude, as well as my hope that they find this a worthy iteration of the characters and world with which they may already be familiar.

For either their general advice or specific comments on this manuscript, my thanks to Thomas Harlan, John Fultz, Mike Lee, and Myke Cole (and my apologies where I have occasionally ignored what I've been told). And many, many thanks to my editor, Lou Anders; to the fine folks at Pyr and Prometheus Books, including Catherine Roberts-Abel, Nicole Sommer-Lecht, Bruce Carle, Gabrielle Harbowy, Jade Zora Scibilia, Melissa Raé Shofner, Mary Read, Jill Maxick, and Lisa Michalski; and to Sam Weber and Gene Mollica.

ABOUT THE AUTHOR

Mark Smylie has worked as a writer, illustrator, editor, and publisher for over a decade. His epic military fantasy graphic novel series, Artesia, was first published by Sirius beginning in 1999. He was nominated for the Russ Manning Award for Best Newcomer that year, and for an Eisner Award for Talent Deserving of Wider Recognition in 2001. Over the years his illustrations have appeared in game books from Wizards of the Coast, White Wolf, and most recently Kobold Press, and in collectible card games from AEG. He designed and illustrated a role-playing game based on Artesia that won the Origins Award for Role-

Author photo by Monika Broz

Playing Game of 2006 and three Indie RPG Awards; the game was also nominated for six ENnies. Mark founded Archaia Studios Press (ASP) in 2002 as a self-publishing home for his graphic novels, and the company, now an imprint at BOOM! Studios, has expanded over the years to publish a wide variety of American and European graphic novels, including award-winning titles such as *Mouse Guard*, *The Killer*, *Return of the Dapper Men*, and *Jim Henson's Tale of Sand*. Mark still serves as the imprint's chief creative officer. He lives in New Jersey, which he actually enjoys a great deal. Author Site: www.swordandbarrow.com